D1094119

THE AMAZING MISS MARPLE

A MYSTERY GUILD LOST CLASSICS OMNIBUS

AGATHA CHRISTIE TITLES PUBLISHED BY PENGUIN PUTNAM INC.

Featuring Hercule Poirot:

The A.B.C. Murders • *After the Funeral* (also published as *Funerals Are Fatal*) • *Appointment With Death* • *The Big Four* • *Cards on the Table* • *Cat Among the Pigeons* • *The Clocks* • *Curtain* • *Dead Man's Folly* • *Death in the Clouds* (also published as *Death in the Air*) • *Death on the Nile* • *Dumb Witness* (also published as *Poirot Loses a Client*) • *Elephants Can Remember* • *Evil Under the Sun* • *Five Little Pigs* (also published as *Murder in Retrospect*) • *Halloween Party* • *The Harlequin Tea Set and Other Stories* • *Hercule Poirot's Christmas* (also published as *Murder for Christmas* and *A Holiday for Murder*) • *Hickory Dickory Dock* (also published as *Hickory Dickory Death*) • *The Hollow* (also published as *Murder After Hours*) • *The Labors of Hercules* • *Lord Edgware Dies* (also published as *Thirteen at Dinner*) • *Mrs. McGinty's Dead* • *Murder in Mesopotamia* • *Murder in the Mews* (also published as *Dead Man's Mirror*) • *The Murder of Roger Ackroyd* • *Murder on the Links* • *Murder on the Orient Express* (also published as *Murder in the Calais Coach*) • *The Mysterious Affair at Styles* • *The Mystery of the Blue Train* • *One, Two, Buckle My Shoe* (also published as *The Patriotic Murders*) • *Peril at End House* • *Poirot Investigates* • *The Regatta Mystery and Other Stories* • *Sad Cypress* • *Taken at the Flood* (also published as *There Is a Tide*) • *Third Girl* • *Three Act Tragedy* (also published as *Murder in Three Acts*) • *The Under Dog and Other Stories*

Featuring Miss Jane Marple:

At Bertram's Hotel • *The Body in the Library* • *A Caribbean Mystery* • *4:50 From Paddington* (also published as *What Mrs. McGillicuddy Saw!*) • *The Mirror Crack'd* (also published as *The Mirror Crack'd From Side to Side*) • *The Moving Finger* • *Murder at the Vicarage* • *A Murder Is Announced* • *Nemesis* • *A Pocket Full of Rye* • *Sleeping Murder* • *The Thirteen Problems* (also published as *The Tuesday Club Murders*) • *They Do It With Mirrors* (also published as *Murder With Mirrors*)

Featuring Tommy and Tuppence Beresford:

By the Pricking of My Thumbs • *N or M?* • *Partners in Crime* • *Postern of Fate* • *The Secret Adversary* *The Mousetrap and Other Plays*

THE AMAZING MISS MARPLE:

THE MOVING FINGER

A MURDER IS ANNOUNCED

4:50 FROM PADDINGTON

by

Agatha Christie

Mystery Guild
Garden City, New York

Contents

Agatha Christie

The Moving Finger

1

I have often recalled the morning when the first of the anonymous letters came.

It arrived at breakfast and I turned it over in the idle way one does when time goes slowly and every event must be spun out to its full extent. It was, I saw, a local letter with a typewritten address. I opened it before the two with London postmarks, since one of them was clearly a bill, and on the other I recognized the handwriting of one of my more tiresome cousins.

It seems odd, now, to remember that Joanna and I were more amused by the letter than anything else. We hadn't, then, the faintest inkling of what was to come—the trail of blood and violence and suspicion and fear.

One simply didn't associate that sort of thing with Lymstock.

I see that I have begun badly. I haven't explained Lymstock.

When I took a bad crash flying, I was afraid for a long time, in spite of soothing words from doctors and nurses, that I was going to be condemned to lie on my back all my life. Then at last they took me out of the plaster and I learned cautiously to use my limbs, and finally Marcus Kent, my doctor, clapped me on my back and told me that everything was going to be all right, but that I'd got to go and live in the country and lead the life of a vegetable for at least six months.

"Go to some part of the world where you haven't any friends. Get right away from things. Take an interest in local politics, get excited about village gossip, absorb all the local scandal. Small beer—that's the prescription for you. Absolute rest and quiet."

3

Rest and quiet! It seems funny to think of that now.

And so Lymstock—and Little Furze.

Lymstock had been a place of importance at the time of the Norman Conquest. In the twentieth century it was a place of no importance whatsoever. It was three miles from a main road—a little provincial market town with a sweep of moorland rising above it. Little Furze was situated on the road leading up to the moors. It was a prim, low, white house with a sloping Victorian veranda painted a faded green.

My sister Joanna, as soon as she saw it, decided that it was the ideal spot for a convalescent. Its owner matched the house, a charming little old lady, quite incredibly Victorian, who explained to Joanna that she would never have dreamed of letting her house if "things had not been so different nowadays—this terrible taxation."

So everything was settled, and the agreement signed, and in due course Joanna and I arrived and settled in, while Miss Emily Barton went into rooms in Lymstock kept by a former parlormaid ("my faithful Florence") and we were looked after by Miss Barton's present maid, Partridge, a grim but efficient personage who was assisted by a daily "girl."

As soon as we had been given a few days to settle down, Lymstock came solemnly to call. Everybody in Lymstock had a label—"rather like happy families" as Joanna said. There was Mr. Symmington the lawyer, thin and dry, with his querulous bridge-playing wife. Dr. Griffith—the dark, melancholy doctor—and his sister who was big and hearty. The vicar, a scholarly absent-minded elderly man and his erratic eager-faced wife. Rich dilettante Mr. Pye of Prior's End, and finally Miss Emily Barton herself, the perfect spinster of village tradition.

Joanna fingered the cards with something like awe. "I didn't know," she said in an awestruck voice, "that people really *called*—with *cards!*"

"That," I told her, "is because you know nothing about the country."

Joanna is very pretty and very gay, and she likes dancing and cocktails and love affairs and rushing about in high-powered cars. She is definitely and entirely urban.

"At any rate," said Joanna, "I look all right."

I studied her critically and was not able to agree.

Joanna was dressed (by Mirotin) for le sport. The effect was quite charming, but a bit startling for Lymstock.

"No," I said. "You're all wrong. You ought to be wearing an old faded tweed skirt with a nice cashmere jumper matching it and per-

4

haps a rather baggy cardigan coat, and you'd wear a felt hat and thick stockings and old well-worn brogues. Your face is all wrong, too," I added.

"What's wrong with that? I've got on my Country Tan Make-Up No. 2."

"Exactly," I said. "If you lived here, you would have just a little powder to take the shine off the nose and you would almost certainly be wearing all your eyebrows instead of only a quarter of them."

Joanna laughed, and said that coming to the country was a new experience and she was going to enjoy it.

"I'm afraid you'll be terribly bored," I said remorsefully.

"No, I shan't. I really was fed up with all my crowd, and though you won't be sympathetic I really was very cut up about Paul. It will take me a long time to get over it."

I was skeptical over this. Joanna's love affairs always run the same course. She has a mad infatuation for some completely spineless young man who is a misunderstood genius. She listens to his endless complaints and works to get him recognition. Then, when he is ungrateful, she is deeply wounded and says her heart is broken—until the next gloomy young man comes along, which is usually about three weeks later.

I did not take Joanna's broken heart very seriously, but I did see that living in the country was like a new game to my attractive sister. She entered with zest into the pastime of returning calls. We duly received invitations to tea and to bridge, which we accepted, and issued invitations in our turn.

To us, it was all novel and entertaining—a new game.

And, as I say, when the anonymous letter came, it struck me, at first, as amusing too.

For a minute or two after opening the letter, I stared at it uncomprehendingly. Printed words had been cut out and pasted on a sheet of paper.

The letter, using terms of the coarsest character, expressed the writer's opinion that Joanna and I were not brother and sister.

"Hullo," said Joanna. "What is it?"

"It's a particularly foul anonymous letter," I said.

I was still suffering from shock. Somehow one didn't expect that kind of thing in the placid backwater of Lymstock.

Joanna at once displayed lively interest. "*No? What does it say?*"

In novels, I have noticed, anonymous letters of a foul and disgusting character are never shown, if possible, to women. It is implied that women must at all cost be shielded from the shock it might give their delicate nervous systems.

I am sorry to say it never occurred to me not to show the letter to Joanna. I handed it to her at once.

She vindicated my belief in her toughness by displaying no emotion but that of amusement. "What an awful bit of dirt! I've always heard about anonymous letters, but I've never seen one before. Are they always like this?"

"I can't tell you," I said. "It's my first experience, too."

Joanna began to giggle. "You must have been right about my make-up, Jerry. I suppose they think I just *must* be an abandoned female!"

"That," I said, "coupled with the fact that our father was a tall, dark, lantern-jawed man and our mother a fair-haired blue-eyed little creature, and that I take after him and you take after her."

Joanna nodded thoughtfully. "Yes, we're not a bit alike. Nobody would take us for brother and sister."

"Somebody certainly hasn't," I said with feeling.

Joanna said she thought it was frightfully funny. She dangled the letter thoughtfully by one corner and asked what we were to do with it.

"The correct procedure, I believe," I said, "is to drop it into the fire with a sharp exclamation of disgust."

I suited the action to the word, and Joanna applauded. "You did that beautifully," she said. "You ought to have been on the stage. It's lucky we still have fires, isn't it?"

"The wastepaper basket would have been much less dramatic," I agreed. "I could, of course, have set light to it with a match and slowly watched it burn—or watched it slowly burn."

"Things never burn when you want them to," said Joanna. "They go out. You'd probably have had to strike match after match."

She got up and went toward the window. Then, standing there, she turned her head sharply. "I wonder," she said, "who wrote it?"

"We're never likely to know," I said.

"No—I suppose not." She was silent a moment, and then said: "I don't know when I come to think of it that it is so funny after all. You know, I thought they—they *liked* us down here."

"So they do," I said. "This is just some half-crazy brain on the borderline."

"I suppose so. Ugh—nasty!"

As she went out into the sunshine I thought to myself as I smoked my after-breakfast cigarette that she was quite right. It *was* nasty. Someone resented our coming here—someone resented Joanna's bright young sophisticated beauty—someone wanted to *hurt*. To take it with a laugh was perhaps the best way—but deep down it wasn't funny.

Dr. Griffith came that morning. I had fixed up for him to give me a weekly overhaul. I liked Owen Griffith. He was dark, ungainly, with awkward ways of moving and deftly very gentle hands. He had a jerky way of talking and was rather shy.

He reported progress to be encouraging. Then he added, "You're feeling all right, aren't you? Is it my fancy, or are you a bit under the weather this morning?"

"Not really," I said. "A particularly scurrilous anonymous letter arrived with the morning coffee, and it's left rather a nasty taste in the mouth."

He dropped his bag on the floor. His thin dark face was excited. "Do you mean to say that *you've* had one of them?"

I was interested. "They've been going about, then?"

"Yes. For some time."

"Oh," I said. "I see. I was under the impression that our presence as strangers was resented here."

"No, no, it's nothing to do with that. It's just—" He paused and then asked, "What did it say? At least"—he turned suddenly red and embarrassed—"perhaps I oughtn't to ask?"

"I'll tell you with pleasure," I said. "It just said that the fancy tart I'd brought down with me wasn't my sister—not 'alf! And that, I may say, is a shortened version."

His dark face flushed angrily. "How damnable! Your sister didn't—she's not upset, I hope?"

"Joanna," I said, "looks a little like the angel off the top of the Christmas tree, but she's eminently modern and quite tough. She found it highly entertaining. Such things haven't come her way before."

"I should hope not, indeed," said Griffith warmly.

"And anyway," I said firmly, "that's the best way to take it, I think. As something utterly ridiculous."

"Yes," said Owen Griffith, "only—"

He stopped, and I chimed in quickly. "Quite so," I said. "Only is the word!"

"The trouble is," he said, "that this sort of thing, once it starts, *grows.*"

"So I should imagine."

"It's pathological, of course."

I nodded. "Any idea who's behind it?" I asked.

"No, I wish I had. You see, the anonymous letter pest arises from one of two causes. Either it's *particular*—directed at one person or set of people, that is to say it's *motivated*, it's someone who's got a definite grudge (or thinks he has) and who chooses a particularly nasty and underhand way of working it off. It's mean and disgusting but it's not necessarily crazy, and it's usually fairly easy to trace the writer—a discharged servant, a jealous woman, and so on. But if it's *general*, and not particular, then it's more serious.

"The letters are sent indiscriminately and serve the purpose of working off some frustration in the writer's mind. As I say, it's definitely pathological. And the craze grows. In the end, of course, you track down the person in question—(it's often someone extremely unlikely) and that's that. There was a bad outburst of the kind over the other side of the county last year—turned out to be the head of the millinery department in a big draper's establishment. Quiet, refined woman—had been there for years.

"I remember something of the same kind in my last practice up north. But that turned out to be purely personal spite. Still, as I say, I've seen something of this kind of thing, and, quite frankly, it frightens me!"

"Has it been going on long?" I asked.

"I don't think so. Hard to say, of course, because people who get these letters don't go round advertising the fact. They put them in the fire."

He paused.

"I've had one myself. Symmington, the solicitor, he's had one. And one or two of my poorer patients have told me about them."

"All much the same sort of thing?"

"Oh, yes. A definite harping on the sex theme. That's always a feature." He grinned. "Symmington was accused of illicit relations with his lady clerk—poor old Miss Ginch, who's forty at least, with pince-nez and teeth like a rabbit. Symmington took it straight to the police. My letters accused me of violating professional decorum with my lady patients, stressing the details. They're all quite childish and absurd, but horribly venomous." His face changed, grew grave. "But all the same, I'm *afraid*. These things can be *dangerous*, you know."

"I suppose they can."

"You see," he said, "crude, childish spite though it is, sooner or later *one of these letters will hit the mark*. And then, God knows what may happen! I'm afraid, too, of the effect upon the slow, suspicious, uneducated mind. If they see a thing written, they believe it's true. All sorts of complications may arise."

"It was an illiterate sort of letter," I said thoughtfully, "written by somebody practically illiterate, I should say."

"Was it?" said Owen and went away.

Thinking it over afterward, I found that "Was it?" rather disturbing.

I am not going to pretend that the arrival of our anonymous letter did not leave a nasty taste in the mouth. It did. At the same time, it soon passed out of my mind. I did not, you see, at that point, take it seriously. I think I remember saying to myself that these things probably happen fairly often in out-of-the-way villages. Some hysterical woman with a taste for dramatizing herself was probably at the bottom of it. Anyway, if the letters were as childish and silly as the one we had got, they couldn't do much harm.

The next *incident*, if I may put it so, occurred about a week later, when Partridge, her lips set tightly together, informed me that Beatrice, the daily help, would not be coming today.

"I gather, sir," said Partridge, "that the girl has been upset."

I was not very sure what Partridge was implying, but I diagnosed (wrongly) some stomach trouble to which Partridge was too delicate to allude more directly. I said I was sorry and hoped she would soon be better.

"The girl is perfectly well, sir," said Partridge. "She is upset in her feelings."

"Oh," I said rather doubtfully.

"Owing," went on Partridge, "to a letter she has received. Making, I understand, insinuations."

The grimness of Partridge's eye made me apprehensive that the insinuations were concerned with me. Since I could hardly have recognized Beatrice by sight if I had met her in the town, so unaware of her had I been, I felt a not unnatural annoyance. An invalid hobbling about on two sticks is hardly cast for the role of deceiver of village girls.

I said irritably, "What nonsense!"

"My very words, sir, to the girl's mother," said Partridge. " 'Goings-on in this house,' I said to her, 'there never have been and never will be while I am in charge. As to Beatrice,' I said, 'girls are different nowadays, and as to goings-on elsewhere I can say nothing.' But the truth is, sir, that Beatrice's friend from the garage as she walks out with got one of them nasty letters, too, and he isn't acting reasonable at all."

"I have never heard anything so preposterous in my life," I said angrily.

"It's my opinion, sir," said Partridge, "that we're well rid of the girl. What I say is, she wouldn't take on so if there wasn't *something* she didn't want found out. No smoke without fire, that's what I say."

I had no idea how horribly tired I was going to get of that particular phrase.

That morning, by way of adventure, I was to walk down to the village. The sun was shining, the air was cool and crisp and with the sweetness of spring in it. I assembled my sticks and started off, firmly refusing to permit Joanna to accompany me.

It was arranged that she should pick me up with the car and drive me back up the hill in time for lunch.

"That ought to give you time to pass the time of day with everyone in Lymstock."

"I have no doubt," I said, "that I shall have seen anybody who is anybody by then."

For morning in the High Street was a kind of rendezvous for shoppers, when news was exchanged.

I did not, after all, walk down to the town unaccompanied. I had gone about two hundred yards, when I heard a bicycle bell behind me, then a scrunching of brakes, and then Megan Hunter more or less fell off her machine at my feet.

"Hullo," she said breathlessly as she rose and dusted herself off.

I rather liked Megan and always felt oddly sorry for her.

She was Symmington the lawyer's stepdaughter, Mrs. Symmington's daughter by a first marriage. Nobody talked much about Mr. (or Captain) Hunter, and I gathered that he was considered best forgotten. He was reported to have treated Mrs. Symmington very badly. She had divorced him a year or two after the marriage. She was a woman with means of her own and had settled down with her little daughter in Lymstock "to forget," and had eventually married the only eligible bachelor in the place, Richard Symmington.

There were two boys of the second marriage to whom their parents were devoted, and I fancied that Megan sometimes felt odd-man in the establishment. She certainly did not resemble her mother, who was a small anemic woman, fadedly pretty, who talked in a thin melancholy voice of servant difficulties and her health.

Megan was a tall awkward girl, and although she was actually twenty, she looked more like a school-girlish sixteen. She had a shock of untidy brown hair, hazel green eyes, a thin bony face, and an unexpectedly charming one-sided smile. Her clothes were drab and unattractive and she usually had on lisle-thread stockings with holes in them.

She looked, I decided this morning, much more like a horse than a human being. In fact, she would have been a very nice horse with a little grooming.

She spoke, as usual, in a kind of breathless rush:

"I've been up to the farm—you know, Lasher's—to see if they'd got any duck eggs. They've got an awfully nice lot of little pigs. Sweet! Do you like pigs? I do. I even like the smell."

"Well-kept pigs shouldn't smell," I said.

"Shouldn't they? They all do around here. Are you walking down to the town? I saw you were alone, so I thought I'd stop and walk with you, only I stopped rather suddenly."

"You've torn your stocking," I said.

Megan looked rather ruefully at her right leg. "So I have. But it's got two holes already, so it doesn't matter very much, does it?"

"Don't you ever mend your stockings, Megan?"

"Rather. When Mummie catches me. But she doesn't notice awfully what I do—so it's lucky in a way, isn't it?"

"You don't seem to realize you're grown up," I said.

"You mean I ought to be more like your sister? All dolled up?"

I rather resented this description of Joanna. "She looks clean and tidy and pleasing to the eye," I said.

"She's awfully pretty," said Megan. "She isn't a bit like you, is she? Why not?"

"Brothers and sisters aren't always alike."

"No. Of course I'm not very like Brian or Colin. And Brian and Colin aren't like each other." She paused and said, "It's very rum, isn't it?"

"What is?"

Megan replied briefly:

"Families."

I said thoughtfully, "I suppose they are."

I wondered just what was passing in her mind. We walked on in silence for a moment or two, then Megan said in a rather shy voice, "You fly, don't you?"

"Yes."

"That's how you got hurt?"

"Yes, I crashed."

Megan said, "Nobody down here flies."

"No," I said, "I suppose not. Would you like to fly, Megan?"

"Me?" Megan seemed surprised. "Goodness, no. I should be sick. I'm sick in a train even."

She paused and then asked with that directness which only a child usually displays: "Will you get all right and be able to fly again, or will you always be a bit of a crock?"

"My doctor says I shall be quite all right."

"Yes, but is he the kind of man who tells lies?"

"I don't think so," I replied. "In fact, I'm quite sure of it. I trust him."

"That's all right then. But a lot of people do tell lies."

I accepted this undeniable statement of fact in silence.

Megan said in a detached judicial kind of way, "I'm glad. I was afraid you looked bad-tempered because you were crocked up for life—but if it's just natural, it's different."

"I'm not bad-tempered," I said coldly.

"Well, irritable, then."

"I'm irritable because I'm in a hurry to get fit again—and these things can't be hurried."

"Then why fuss?"

I began to laugh. "My dear girl, aren't you ever in a hurry for things to happen?"

Megan considered the question. She said, "No. Why should I be? There's nothing to be in a hurry about. Nothing ever happens."

I was struck by something forlorn in the words. I said gently, "What do you do with yourself down here?"

She shrugged her shoulders. "What is there to do?"

"Haven't you any hobbies? Don't you play games? Haven't you got friends around about?"

"I'm stupid at games. There aren't many girls around here, and the ones there are I don't like. They think I'm awful."

"Nonsense. Why should they?"

Megan shook her head.

We were now entering the High Street. Megan said sharply:

"Here's Miss Griffith coming. Hateful woman. She's always at me to join her foul Guides. I hate Guides. Why dress up and go about in clumps and put badges on yourself for something you haven't really learned to do properly. I think it's all rot."

On the whole I rather agreed with Megan. But Miss Griffith had descended upon us before I could voice any assent.

The doctor's sister, who rejoiced in the singularly inappropriate name of Aimée, had all the positive assurance her brother lacked. She was a handsome woman in a masculine weather-beaten way, with a deep voice.

"Hullo, you two," she bayed at us. "Gorgeous morning, isn't it? Megan, you're just the person I want to see. I want some help. Addressing envelopes for the Conservative Association."

Megan muttered something elusive, propped up her bicycle against the curb and dived in a purposeful way into the International Stores.

"Extraordinary child," said Miss Griffith, looking after her. "Bone lazy. Spends her time mooning about. Must be a great trial to poor Mrs. Symmington. I know her mother's tried more than once to get her to take up something—shorthand-typing, you know, or cookery, or keeping Angora rabbits. She needs an *interest* in life."

I thought that was probably true, but felt that in Megan's place I should have withstood firmly any of Aimée Griffith's suggestions for the simple reason that her aggressive personality would have put my back up.

"I don't believe in idleness," went on Miss Griffith. "And certainly not for young people. It's not as though Megan was pretty or attractive or anything like that. Sometimes I think the girl's half-witted. A great disappointment to her mother. The father, you know," she lowered her voice slightly, "was definitely a wrong 'un. Afraid the child takes after him. Painful for her mother. Oh, well, it takes all sorts to make a world, that's what I say."

"Fortunately," I responded.

Aimée Griffith gave a "jolly" laugh.

"Yes, it wouldn't do if we were all made to one pattern. But I don't

13

like to see anyone not getting all he can out of life. I enjoy life myself and I want everyone to enjoy it too. People say to me you must be bored to death living down there in the country all the year around. Not a bit of it, I say. I'm always busy, always happy! There's always something going on in the country. My time's taken up, what with my Guides, and the Institute and various committees—to say nothing of looking after Owen."

At this minute, Miss Griffith saw an acquaintance on the other side of the street, and uttering a bay of recognition she leaped across the road, leaving me free to pursue my course to the bank.

I always found Miss Griffith rather overwhelming.

My business at the bank transacted satisfactorily. I went on to the offices of Messrs. Galbraith, Galbraith and Symmington. I don't know if there were any Galbraith's extant. I never saw any. I was shown into Richard Symmington's inner office which had the agreeable mustiness of a long-established legal firm.

Vast numbers of deed boxes labeled Lady Hope, Sir Everard Carr, William Yatesby-Hoares Esq., Deceased, etc., gave the required atmosphere of decorous county families and legitimate, long-established business.

Studying Mr. Symmington as he bent over the documents I had brought, it occurred to me that if Mrs. Symmington had encountered disaster in her first marriage, she had certainly played safe in her second. Richard Symmington was the acme of calm respectability, the sort of man who would never give his wife a moment's anxiety. A long neck with a pronounced Adam's apple, a slightly cadaverous face and a long thin nose. A kindly man, no doubt, a good husband and father, but not one to set the pulses madly racing.

Presently Mr. Symmington began to speak. He spoke clearly and slowly, delivering himself of much good sense and shrewd acumen. We settled the matter in hand and I rose to go, remarking as I did so, "I walked down the hill with your stepdaughter."

For a moment Mr. Symmington looked as though he did not know who his stepdaughter was, then he smiled.

"Oh, yes, of course—Megan. She—er—has been back from school some time. We're thinking about finding her something to do—yes, to do. But, of course, she's very young still. And backward for her age, so they say. Yes, so they tell me."

I went out. In the outer office was a very old man on a stool writing slowly and laboriously, a small, cheeky-looking boy and a middle-aged woman with frizzy hair and pince-nez who was typing with some speed and dash.

If this was Miss Ginch I agreed with Owen Griffith that tender passages between her and her employer were exceedingly unlikely.

I went into the baker's and said my piece about the currant loaf. It was received with the exclamations and incredulity proper to the occasion, and a new currant loaf was thrust upon me in replacement—"fresh from the oven, this minute"—as its indecent heat pressed against my chest proclaimed to be no less than truth.

I came out of the shop and looked up and down the street, hoping to see Joanna with the car. The walk had tired me a good deal and it was awkward getting along with my sticks and the currant loaf.

But there was no sign of Joanna as yet.

Suddenly my eyes were held in glad and incredulous surprise. Along the pavement toward me there came floating a goddess. There is really no other word for it. The perfect features, the crisply curling golden hair, the tall exquisitely shaped body. And she walked like a goddess, without effort, seeming to swim nearer and near. A glorious, an incredible, a breath-taking girl!

In my intense excitement something had to go. What went was the currant loaf. It slipped from my clutches. I made a dive after it and lost my stick, which clattered to the pavement, and I slipped and nearly fell myself.

It was the strong arm of the goddess that caught and held me.

I began to stammer: "Th-thanks awfully, I'm f-f-frightfully sorry."

She had retrieved the currant loaf and handed it to me together with the stick. And then she smiled kindly and said cheerfully, "Don't mention it. No trouble, I assure you," and the magic died completely before the flat, competent voice.

A nice, healthy-looking, well set-up girl; no more.

I fell to reflecting what would have happened if the gods had given Helen of Troy exactly those flat accents. How strange that a girl could trouble your inmost soul so long as she kept her mouth shut, and that the moment she spoke the glamour could vanish as though it had never been.

I had known the reverse happen, though. I had seen a little sad monkey-faced woman whom no one would turn to look at twice. Then she had opened her mouth and suddenly enchantment had lived and bloomed and Cleopatra had cast her spell anew.

Joanna had drawn up at the curb beside me without my noticing her arrival. She asked if there was anything the matter.

"Nothing," I said, pulling myself together. "I was reflecting on Helen of Troy and others."

"What a funny place to do it," said Joanna. "You looked *most* odd, standing there clasping currant bread to your breast with your mouth wide open."

"I've had a shock," I said. "I had been transplanted to Ilium and back again."

I added, indicating a retreating back that was swimming gracefully away, "Do you know who that is?"

Peering after the girl Joanna said that it was Elsie Holland, the Symmingtons' nursery governess.

"Is that what struck you all of a heap?" she asked. "She's good-looking, but a bit of a wet fish."

"I know," I said. "Just a nice kind girl. And I'd been thinking her Aphrodite."

Joanna opened the door of the car and I got in.

"It's funny, isn't it?" she said. "Some people have lots of looks and absolutely no S. A. That girl hasn't. It seems such a pity."

I said that if she was a nursery governess it was probably just as well.

That afternoon we went to tea with Mr. Pye.

Mr. Pye was an extremely ladylike plump little man, devoted to his *petit point* chairs, his Dresden shepherdesses and his collection of period furniture. He lived at Prior's Lodge in the grounds of which were the ruins of the old Priory dissolved at the Reformation.

It was hardly a man's house. The curtains and cushions were of pastel shades in the most expensive silks.

Mr. Pye's small plump hands quivered with excitement as he described and exhibited his treasures, and his voice rose to a falsetto squeak as he narrated the exciting circumstances in which he had brought his Italian bedstead home from Verona.

Joanna and I, both being fond of antiques, met with approval.

"It is really a pleasure, a great pleasure, to have such an acquisition to our little community. The dear good people down here, you know, so painfully bucolic—not to say *provincial*. Vandals—absolute vandals! And the insides of their houses—it would make you weep, dear lady, I assure you it would make you weep. Perhaps it has done so?"

Joanna said she hadn't gone quite as far as that.

"The house you have taken," went on Mr. Pye, "Miss Emily Barton's house. Now that is charming, and she has some quite nice pieces. Quite nice. One or two of them are really first-class. And she has taste, too—although I'm not quite so sure of that as I was. Sometimes, I am afraid, I think it's really sentiment. She likes to keep things as they were—but not for *le bon motif*—not because of the resultant harmony—but because it is the way her mother had them."

He transferred his attention to me, and his voice changed. It altered from that of the rapt artist to that of the born gossip:

"You didn't know the family at all? No, quite so—yes, through house agents. But, my dears, you *ought* to have known that family! When I came here the old mother was still alive. An incredible person—quite incredible! A *monster*, if you know what I mean. Positively a monster. The old-fashioned Victorian monster, devouring her young. Yes, that's what it amounted to. She was monumental, you know, must have weighed seventeen stone, and all the five daughters revolved around her. 'The girls!' That's how she always spoke of them. The girls! And the eldest was well over sixty then.

"'Those stupid girls!' she used to call them sometimes. Black slaves, that's all they were, fetching and carrying and agreeing with her. Ten o'clock they had to go to bed and they weren't allowed a fire in their bedroom, and as for asking their own friends to the house, that would have been unheard of. She despised them, you know, for not getting married, and yet so arranged their lives that it was practically impossible for them to meet anybody. I believe Emily, or perhaps it was Agnes, did have some kind of affair with a curate. But his family wasn't good enough and Mamma soon put a stop to *that*!"

"It sounds like a novel," said Joanna.

"Oh, my dear, it was. And then the dreadful old woman died, but of course, it was far too late *then*. They just went on living there and talking in hushed voices about what poor Mamma would have wished. Even repapering her bedroom they felt to be quite sacrilegious. Still they did enjoy themselves in the parish in a quiet way. . . . But none of them had much stamina, and they just died off one by one. Influenza took off Edith, and Minnie had an operation and didn't recover and poor Mable had a stroke—Emily looked after her in the most devoted manner. Really that poor woman has done nothing but nursing for the last ten years. A charming creature, don't you think? Like a piece of Dresden. So sad for her having financial anxieties—but of course, all investments have depreciated."

"We feel rather awful being in her house," said Joanna.

"No, no, my dear young lady. You mustn't feel that way. Her dear good Florence is devoted to her and she told me herself how happy she was to have got such nice tenants." Here Mr. Pye made a little bow. "She told me she thought she had been most fortunate."

"The house," I said, "has a very soothing atmosphere."

Mr. Pye darted a quick glance at me.

"Really? You feel that? Now, that's very interesting. I wondered, you know. Yes, I wondered."

"What do you mean, Mr. Pye?" asked Joanna.

Mr. Pye spread out his plump hands. "Nothing, nothing. One wondered, that is all. I do believe in atmosphere, you know. People's thoughts and feelings. They give their impression to the walls and the furniture."

I did not speak for a moment or two. I was looking around me and wondering how I would describe the atmosphere of Prior's Lodge. It seemed to me that the curious thing was that it hadn't any atmosphere! That was really very remarkable.

I reflected on this point so long that I heard nothing of the conversation going on between Joanna and her host. I was recalled to myself, however, by hearing Joanna uttering farewell preliminaries. I came out of my dream and added my quota.

We all went out into the hall. As we came toward the front door a letter came through the box and fell on the mat.

"Afternoon post," murmured Mr. Pye as he picked it up. "Now, my dear young people, you will come again, won't you? Such a pleasure to meet some broader minds, if you understand me, in this peaceful backwater where nothing ever happens."

Shaking hands with us twice over, he helped me with exaggerated care into the car. Joanna took the wheel, she negotiated with some care the circular sweep around a plot of unblemished grass, then with a straight drive ahead, she raised a hand to wave goodbye to our host where he stood on the steps of the house. I leaned forward to do the same.

But our gesture of farewell went unheeded. Mr. Pye had opened his mail. He was standing staring down at the open sheet in his hand.

Joanna had described him once as a plump pink cherub. He was still plump, but he was not looking like a cherub now. His face was a dark congested purple, contorted with rage and surprise. Yes, and fear, too.

And at that moment I realized that there had been something familiar about the look of that envelope. I had not realized it at the time—indeed, it had been one of those things that you note unconsciously without knowing that you do note them.

"Goodness," said Joanna, "what's bitten the poor pet?"

"I rather fancy," I said, "that it's the Hidden Hand again."

She turned an astonished face toward me and the car swerved.

"Careful, wench," I said.

Joanna refixed her attention on the road. She was frowning. "You mean a letter like the one you got."

"That's my guess."

"What is this place?" asked Joanna. "It looks the most innocent, sleepy harmless little bit of England you can imagine."

"Where, to quote Mr. Pye, nothing ever happens," I cut in. "He chose the wrong minute to say that. Something has happened."

"Jerry," said Joanna. "I—I don't think I like this." For the first time, there was a note of fear in her voice.

I did not answer, for I, too, did not like it. . . .

Such a peaceful smiling happy countryside—and down underneath something evil. . . .

It was as though at that moment I had a premonition of all that was to come. . . .

The days passed. We went and played bridge at the Symmingtons and Mrs. Symmington annoyed me a good deal by the way she referred to Megan.

"The poor child's so awkward. They are at that age, when they've left school and before they are properly grown up."

Joanna said sweetly, "But Megan's twenty, isn't she?"

"Oh, yes, yes. But of course, she's very young for her age. Quite a child still. It's so nice, I think, when girls don't grow up too quickly." She laughed. "I expect all mothers want their children to remain babies."

"I can't think why," said Joanna. "After all, it would be a bit awkward if one had a child who remained mentally six while his body grew up."

Mrs. Symmington looked annoyed and said Miss Burton mustn't take things so literally.

I was pleased with Joanna, and it occurred to me that I did not really much care for Mrs. Symmington. That anemic middle-aged prettiness concealed, I thought, a selfish, grasping nature.

Joanna asked maliciously if Mrs. Symmington were going to give a dance for Megan.

"A dance?" Mrs. Symmington seemed surprised and amused. "Oh, no, we don't do things like that down here."

"I see. Just tennis parties and things like that."

"Our tennis court has not been played on for years. Neither Richard nor I play. I suppose, later, when the boys grow up—oh, Megan will find plenty to do. She's quite happy just pottering about, you know. Let me see, did I deal? Two no trumps."

As we drove home, Joanna said with a vicious pressure on the accelerator pedal that made the car leap forward, "I feel awfully sorry for that girl."

"Megan?"

"Yes. Her mother doesn't like her."

"Oh, come now, Joanna, it's not as bad as that."

"Yes, it is. Lots of mothers don't like their children. Megan, I should imagine, is an awkward sort of creature to have about the house. She disturbs the pattern—the Symmington pattern. It's a complete unit without her—and that's a most unhappy feeling for a sensitive creature to have—and she *is* sensitive."

"Yes," I said, "I think she is."

I was silent for a moment.

Joanna suddenly laughed mischievously. "Bad luck for you about the governess."

"I don't know what you mean," I said with dignity.

"Nonsense. Masculine chagrin was written on your face every time you looked at her. I agree with you, it is a waste. And I don't see who else there is here for you. You'll have to fall back upon Aimée Griffith."

"God forbid," I said with a shudder. "And anyway," I added, "why all this concern about my love life? What about you, my girl? You'll need a little distraction down here, if I know you. No unappreciated genius, knocking about here. You'll have to fall back on Owen Griffith. He's the only unattached male in the place."

Joanna tossed her head. "Dr. Griffith doesn't like me."

"He's not seen much of you."

"He's seen enough apparently to make him cross over if he sees me coming along the High Street!"

"A most unusual reaction," I said sympathetically. "And one you're not used to."

Joanna drove in silence through the gate of Little Furze and around to the garage. Then she said, "There may be something in that idea of yours. I don't see why any man should deliberately cross the street to avoid me. It's rude apart from everything else."

"I see," I said. "You're going to hunt the man down in cold blood."

"Well, I don't like being avoided."

I got slowly and carefully out of the car and balanced my sticks. Then I offered my sister a piece of advice:

"Let me tell you this, girl. Owen Griffith isn't any of your tame, whining, artistic young men. Unless you're careful, you'll stir up a hornets' nest about your ears. That man could be dangerous."

"Oh, do you think so?" demanded Joanna with every symptom of pleasure at the prospect.

"Leave the poor devil alone," I said sternly.

"How dare he cross the street when he saw me coming?"

"All you women are alike. You harp on one theme. You'll have sister Aimée gunning for you, too, if I'm not mistaken."

"She dislikes me already," said Joanna. She spoke meditatively, but with a certain satisfaction.

"We have come down here," I said sternly, "for peace and quiet, and I mean to see we get it."

But peace and quiet were the last things we were to have.

2

It was about a week later that I came back to the house to find Megan sitting on the veranda steps, her chin resting on her knees.

She greeted me with her usual lack of ceremony. "Hullo," she said. "Do you think I could come to lunch?"

"Certainly," I said.

"If it's chops, or anything difficult like that and they won't go around, just tell me," shouted Megan as I went around to apprise Partridge of the fact that there would be three to lunch.

I fancy that Partridge sniffed. She certainly managed to convey without saying a word of any kind, that she didn't think much of that Miss Megan.

I went back to the veranda.

"Is it all right?" asked Megan anxiously.

"Quite all right," I said. "Irish stew."

"Oh, well, that's rather like dogs' dinner anyway, isn't it? I mean it's mostly potato and flavor."

"Quite," I said.

We were silent while I smoked my pipe. It was quite a companionable silence.

Megan broke it by saying suddenly and violently, "I suppose you think I'm awful like everyone else."

I was so startled that my pipe fell out of my mouth. It was a meerschaum, just coloring nicely, and it broke. I said angrily to Megan, "Now see what you've done."

That most unaccountable of children, instead of being upset, merely grinned broadly. "I do like you," she said.

It was a most warming remark. It is the remark that one fancies perhaps erroneously that one's dog would say if he could talk. It occurred to me that Megan, for all she looked like a horse had the disposition of a dog. She was certainly not quite human.

"What did you say before the catastrophe?" I asked, carefully picking up the fragments of my cherished pipe.

"I said I supposed you thought me awful," said Megan but not at all in the same tone she had said it before.

"Why should I?"

Megan said gravely, "Because I am."

I said sharply, "Don't be stupid."

Megan shook her head. "That's just it. I'm not really stupid. People think I am. They don't know that inside I know just what they're like, and that all the time I'm hating them."

"*Hating* them?"

"Yes," said Megan.

Her eyes, those melancholy, unchildlike eyes stared straight into mine, without blinking. It was a long, mournful gaze.

"You would hate people if you were like me," she said. "If you weren't wanted."

"Don't you think you're being rather morbid?" I asked.

"Yes," said Megan. "That's what people always say when you're saying the truth. And it is true. I'm not wanted and I can quite see why. Mummie doesn't like me a bit. I remind her, I think, of my father, who was cruel to her and pretty dreadful from all I can hear. Only mothers can't say they don't want their children and just go away. Or eat them. Cats eat the kittens they don't like. Awfully sensible, I think. No waste or mess. But human mothers have to keep their children, and look after them. It hasn't been so bad while I could be sent away to school—but you see what Mummie would really like is to be just herself and my stepfather and the boys."

I said slowly, "I still think you're morbid, Megan, but accepting some of what you say as true, why don't you go away and have a life of your own?"

She gave me an odd unchildlike smile. "You mean take up a career. Earn my living?"

"Yes."

"What at?"

"You could train for something, I suppose. Shorthand, typing, bookkeeping."

"I don't believe I could. I am stupid about doing things. And besides—"

"Well?"

She had turned her head away, now she turned it slowly back again. It was crimson and there were tears in her eyes. She spoke now with all the childishness back in her voice:

"Why should I go away? And be made to go away? They don't want me, but I'll *stay*. I'll stay and make everyone sorry. I'll make them all sorry. Hateful pigs! I hate everyone here in Lymstock. They all think I'm stupid and ugly. I'll show them! I'll show them! I'll—"

It was a childish, oddly pathetic rage.

I heard a step on the gravel around the corner of the house.

"Get up," I said savagely. "Go into the house through the drawing room. Go up to the bathroom. Wash your face. Quick."

She sprang awkwardly to her feet and darted through the window as Joanna came around the corner of the house.

I told her Megan had come to lunch.

"Good," said Joanna. "I like Megan, though I rather think she's a changeling. Something left on a doorstep by the fairies. But she's interesting."

I see that so far I have made little mention of the Reverend and Mrs. Calthrop.

And yet both the vicar and his wife were distinct personalities. Dane Calthrop himself was perhaps a being more remote from everyday life than anyone I have ever met. His existence was in his books and in his study. Mrs. Dane Calthrop, on the other hand, was quite terrifyingly on the spot. Though she seldom gave advice and never interfered, yet she represented to the uneasy consciences of the village the Deity personified.

She stopped me in the High Street the day after Megan had come to lunch. I had the usual feeling of surprise, because Mrs. Dane Calthrop's progress resembled coursing more than walking, thus according with her startling resemblance to a greyhound, and as her eyes were always fixed on the distant horizon you felt sure that her real objective was about a mile and a half away.

"Oh!" she said. "Mr. Burton!"

She said it rather triumphantly, as someone might who had solved a particularly clever puzzle. I admitted that I was Mr. Burton and Mrs. Dane Calthrop stopped focusing on the horizon and seemed to be trying to focus on me instead.

"Now what," she said, "did I want to see you about?"

I could not help her there. She stood frowning, deeply perplexed. "Something rather nasty," she said.

"I'm sorry about that," I said startled.

"Ah," cried Mrs. Dane Calthrop. "*Anonymous letters!* What's this story you've brought down here about anonymous letters?"

"I didn't bring it," I said, "it was here already."

"Nobody got any until you came, though," said Mrs. Dane Calthrop accusingly.

"But they did, Mrs. Dane Calthrop. The trouble had already started."

"Oh, dear," said Mrs. Dane Calthrop. "I don't like that."

She stood there, her eyes absent and far away again. She said:

"I can't help feeling it's all *wrong*. We're not like that here. Envy, of course, and malice, and all the mean spiteful little sins—but I didn't think there was anyone who would do that. No, I really didn't. And it distresses me, you see, because *I* ought to know."

Her fine eyes came back from the horizon and met mine. They were worried, and seemed to hold the honest bewilderment of a child's.

"Why ought you to know?" I said.

"I usually do. I've always felt that's my function. Caleb preaches good sound doctrine and administers the sacraments. That's a priest's duty, but if you admit marriage at all for a priest, then I think his wife's duty is to know what people are feeling and thinking, even if she can't do anything about it. And I haven't the least idea whose mind is—"

She broke off, adding absently, "They are such silly letters, too."

"Have you—er—had any yourself?"

I was a little diffident of asking, but Mrs. Dane Calthrop replied perfectly naturally, her eyes opening a little wider:

"Oh, yes, two—no, three. I forget exactly what they said. Something very silly about Caleb and the schoolmistress, I think. Quite absurd, because Caleb has absolutely no taste for flirtation. He never has had. So lucky being a clergyman."

"Quite," I said, "oh, quite."

"Caleb would have been a saint," said Mrs. Dane Calthrop, "if he hadn't been just a little too intellectual."

I did not feel qualified to answer this criticism, and anyway Mrs. Dane Calthrop went on, leaping back from her husband to the letters in rather a puzzling way.

"There are so many things the letters might say, but don't. That's what is so curious."

"I should hardly have thought they erred on the side of restraint," I said bitterly.

"But they don't seem to *know* anything. None of the real things."

"You mean?"

Those fine vague eyes met mine.

"Well, of course. There's plenty of wrongdoing here—any amount of shameful secrets. Why doesn't the writer use those?" She paused and then asked abruptly, "What did they say in your letter?"

"They suggested that my sister wasn't my sister."

"And she is?"

Mrs. Dane Calthrop asked the question with unembarrassed friendly interest.

"Certainly Joanna is my sister."

Mrs. Dane Calthrop nodded her head. "That just shows you what I mean. I daresay there are other things—"

Her clear uninterested eyes looked at me thoughtfully, and I suddenly understood why Lymstock was afraid of Mrs. Dane Calthrop.

In everybody's life there are hidden chapters which they hope may never be known. I felt that Mrs. Dane Calthrop knew them.

For once in my life, I was positively delighted when Aimée Griffith's hearty voice boomed out:

"Hullo, Maud. Glad I've just caught you. I want to suggest an alteration of date for the Sale of Work. Morning, Mr. Burton."

She went on:

"I must just pop into the grocer's and leave my order, then I'll come along to the Institute if that suits you?"

"Yes, yes, that will do quite well," said Mrs. Dane Calthrop.

Aimée Griffith went into the International Stores.

Mrs. Dane Calthrop said, "Poor thing."

I was puzzled. Surely she could not be pitying Aimée?

She went on, however: "You know, Mr. Burton, I'm rather afraid—"

"About this letter business?"

"Yes, you see it means—it must mean—" She paused, lost in thought, her eyes screwed up. Then she said slowly, as one who solves a problem, "Blind hatred . . . yes, blind hatred. But even a blind man

26

might stab to the heart by pure chance . . . And what would happen then, Mr. Burton?"

We were to know that before another day had passed.

Partridge, who enjoys calamity, came into Joanna's room at an early hour the following morning, and told her with considerable relish that Mrs. Symmington had committed suicide on the preceding afternoon.

Joanna, who had been lost in the mists of sleep, sat up in bed shocked wide awake.

"Oh, Partridge, how awful."

"Awful it is, Miss. It's wickedness taking your own life. Not but what she was drove to it, poor soul."

Joanna had an inkling of the truth then. She felt rather sick.

"Not—?" Her eyes questioned Partridge and Partridge nodded.

"That's right, Miss. One of them nasty letters."

"How beastly," said Joanna. "How absolutely beastly! All the same, I don't see why she should kill herself for a letter like that."

"Looks as though what was in the letter was true, Miss."

"What was in it?"

But that, Partridge couldn't or wouldn't say. Joanna came in to me, looking white and shocked. It seemed worse, somehow, that Mrs. Symmington was not the kind of person you associated with tragedy.

Joanna suggested that we might ask Megan to come to us for a day or two. Elsie Holland, she said, would be all right with the children, but was the kind of person who would, almost certainly, drive Megan half mad.

I agreed. I could imagine Elsie Holland uttering platitude after platitude and suggesting innumerable cups of tea. A kindly creature but not the right person for Megan.

We drove down to the Symmingtons' house after breakfast. We were both of us a little nervous. Our arrival might look like sheer ghoulish curiosity. Luckily we met Owen Griffith just coming out. He greeted me with some warmth, his worried face lighting up.

"Oh, hullo, Burton, I'm glad to see you. What I was afraid would happen sooner or later has happened. A damnable business!"

"Good morning, Dr. Griffith," said Joanna, using the voice she keeps for one of our deafer aunts.

Griffith started and flushed. "Oh—oh, good morning, Miss Burton."

"I thought perhaps," said Joanna, "that you didn't see me."

Owen Griffith got redder still. His shyness enveloped him like a mantle. "I'm—I'm so sorry—preoccupied—I didn't."

Joanna went on mercilessly.

"After all, I *am* life-size."

"Merely kit-kat," I said in a stern aside to her. Then I went on:

"My sister and I, Griffith, wondered whether it would be a good thing if the girl came and stopped with us for a day or two? What do you think? I don't want to butt in—but it must be rather grim for the poor child. What would Symmington feel about it, do you think?"

Griffith turned the idea over in his mind for a moment or two.

"I think it would be an excellent thing," he said at last. "She's a queer, nervous sort of girl, and it would be good for her to get away from the whole thing. Miss Holland is doing wonders—she's an excellent head on her shoulders, but she really has quite enough to do with the two children and Symmington himself. He's quite broken up—bewildered."

"It was"—I hesitated—"suicide?"

Griffith nodded.

"Oh, yes. No question of accident. She wrote, 'I can't go on,' on a scrap of paper. The letter must have come by yesterday afternoon's post. The envelope was down on the floor by her chair and the letter itself was screwed up into a ball and thrown into the fireplace."

"What did—"

I stopped, rather horrified at myself.

"I beg your pardon," I said.

Griffith gave a quick, unhappy smile.

"You needn't mind asking. That letter will have to be read at the inquest. No getting out of it, more's the pity. It was the usual kind of thing—couched in the same foul style. The specific accusation was that the second boy, Colin, was not Symmington's child."

"Do you think that was true?" I exclaimed incredulously.

Griffith shrugged his shoulders.

"I've no means of forming a judgment. I've only been here five years. As far as I've ever seen, the Symmingtons were a placid, happy couple devoted to each other and their children. It's true that the boy doesn't particularly resemble his parents—he's got bright red hair, for one thing—but a child often throws back in appearance to a grandfather or grandmother."

"That lack of resemblance might have been what prompted the particular accusation. A foul and quite uncalled-for blow at a venture."

"But it happened to hit the bull's-eye," said Joanna. "After all, she wouldn't have killed herself otherwise, would she?"

Griffith said doubtfully:

"I'm not quite sure. She's been ailing in health for sometime—neurotic, hysterical. I've been treating her for a nervous condition. It's possible, I think, that the shock of receiving such a letter, couched in those terms, may have induced such a state of panic and despondency that she may have decided to take her life. She may have worked herself up to feel that her husband might not believe her if she denied the story, and the general shame and disgust might have worked upon her so powerfully as to unbalance her judgment temporarily."

"Suicide while of unsound mind," said Joanna.

"Exactly. I shall be quite justified, I think, in putting forward that point of view at the inquest."

Joanna and I went on into the house.

The front door was open and it seemed easier than ringing the bell, especially as we heard Elsie Holland's voice inside.

She was talking to Mr. Symmington who, huddled in a chair, was looking completely dazed.

"No, but really, Mr. Symmington, you must take something. You haven't had any breakfast, not what I call a proper breakfast, and nothing to eat last night, and what with the shock and all, you'll be getting ill yourself, and you'll need all your strength. The doctor said so before he left."

Symmington said in a toneless voice, "You're very kind, Miss Holland, but—"

"A nice cup of hot tea," said Elsie Holland, thrusting the beverage on him firmly.

Personally I should have given the poor devil a stiff whisky-and-soda. He looked as though he needed it. However he accepted the tea, and looking up at Elsie Holland:

"I can't thank you for all you've done and are doing, Miss Holland. You've been perfectly splendid."

The girl flushed and looked pleased.

"It's nice of you to say that, Mr. Symmington. You must let me do all I can to help. Don't worry about the children—I'll see to them, and I've got the servants calmed down, and if there's anything I can do, letter-writing or telephoning, don't hesitate to ask me."

"You're very kind," Symmington said again.

Elsie Holland, turning, caught sight of us and came hurrying out into the hall.

"Isn't it terrible?" she said in a hushed whisper.

I thought, as I looked at her, that she was really a very nice girl. Kind, competent, practical in an emergency. Her magnificent blue eyes were just faintly rimmed with pink, showing that she had been soft-hearted enough to shed tears for her employer's death.

"Can we speak to you a minute?" asked Joanna. "We don't want to disturb Mr. Symmington."

Elsie Holland nodded comprehendingly and led the way into the dining room on the other side of the hall.

"It's been awful for him," she said. "Such a shock. Who ever would have thought a thing like this could happen? But of course, I do realize now that she had been queer for some time. Awfully nervous and weepy. I thought it was her health, though Dr. Griffith always said there was nothing really wrong with her. But she was snappy and irritable and some days you wouldn't know just how to take her."

"What we really came for," said Joanna, "was to know whether we could have Megan for a few days—that is, if she'd like to come."

Elsie Holland looked rather surprised.

"Megan?" she said doubtfully. "I don't know, I'm sure. I mean, it's ever so kind of you, but she's such a queer girl. One never knows what she's going to say or feel about things."

Joanna said rather vaguely, "We thought it might be a help, perhaps."

"Oh, well, as far as that goes, it would. I mean, I've got the boys to look after (they're with cook just now) and poor Mr. Symmington—he really needs looking after as much as anyone, and such a lot to do and see to. I really haven't had time to say much to Megan. I think she's upstairs in the old nursery at the top of the house. She seems to want to get away from everyone. I don't know if—"

Joanna gave me the faintest of looks. I slipped quickly out of the room and upstairs.

The old nursery was at the top of the house. I opened the door and went in. The room downstairs had given on to the garden behind and the blinds had not been down there. But in this room which faced the road they were decorously drawn down.

Through a dim gray gloom I saw Megan. She was crouching on a divan set against the far wall, and I was reminded at once of some terrified animal, hiding. She looked petrified with fear.

"Megan," I said.

I came forward, and unconsciously I adopted the tone one does adopt when you want to reassure a frightened animal. I'm really surprised I didn't hold out a carrot or a piece of sugar. I felt like that.

She stared at me, but she did not move, and her expression did not alter.

"Megan," I said again. "Joanna and I have come to ask you if you would like to come and stay with us for a little."

Her voice came hollowly out of the dim twilight:

"Stay with you? In your house?"

"Yes."

"You mean, you'll take me away from here?"

"Yes, my dear."

Suddenly she began to shake all over. It was frightening and very moving.

"Oh, do take me away! Please do. It's so awful, being here, and feeling so wicked."

I came over to her and her hands fastened on my coat sleeve.

"I'm an awful coward. I didn't know what a coward I was."

"It's all right, funnyface," I said. "These things are a bit shattering. Come along."

"Can we go at once Without waiting a minute?"

"Well, you'll have to put a few things together, I suppose."

"What sort of things? Why?"

"My dear girl," I said. "We can provide you with a bed and a bath and the rest of it, but I'm darned if I lend you my toothbrush."

She gave a very faint weak little laugh.

"I see. I think I'm stupid today. You mustn't mind. I'll go and pack some things. You—you won't go away? You'll wait for me?"

"I'll be on the mat."

"Thank you. Thank you so very much. I'm sorry I'm so stupid. But you see it's rather dreadful when your mother dies."

"I know," I said.

I gave her a friendly pat on the back and she flashed me a grateful look and disappeared into a bedroom. I went on downstairs.

"I found Megan," I said. "She's coming."

"Oh, now, that *is* a good thing," exclaimed Elsie Holland. "It will take her out of herself. She's rather a nervy girl, you know. Difficult. It will be a great relief to feel I haven't got her on my mind as well as everything else. It's very kind of you, Miss Burton. I hope she won't be a nuisance. Oh, dear, there's the telephone. I must go and answer it. Mr. Symmington isn't fit."

She hurried out of the room.

Joanna said, "Quite the ministering angel!"

"You said that rather nastily," I observed. "She's a nice, kind girl, and obviously most capable."

"Most. And she knows it."

"This is unworthy of you, Joanna," I said.

"Meaning why shouldn't the girl do her stuff?"

"Exactly."

"I never can stand seeing people pleased with themselves," said Joanna. "It arouses all my worst instincts. How did you find Megan?"

"Crouching in a darkened room looking rather like a stricken gazelle."

"Poor kid. She was quite willing to come?"

"She leaped at it."

A series of thuds out in the hall announced the descent of Megan and her suitcase. I went out and took it from her.

Joanna, behind me, said urgently, "Come on. I've already refused some nice hot tea twice."

We went out to the car. It annoyed me that Joanna had to sling the suitcase in. I could get along with one stick now, but I couldn't do any athletic feats.

"Get in," I said to Megan.

She got in, I followed her. Joanna started the car and we drove off.

We got to Little Furze and went into the drawing room.

Megan dropped into a chair and burst into tears She cried with the hearty fervor of a child—bawled, I think, is the right word. I left the room in search of a remedy. Joanna stood by feeling rather helpless, I think.

Presently I heard Megan say in a thick choked voice, "I'm sorry for doing this. It seems idiotic."

Joanna said kindly, "Not at all. Have another handkerchief."

I gather she supplied the necessary article. I reentered the room and handed Megan a brimming glass.

"What is it?"

"A cocktail," I said.

"Is it? Is it really?" Megan's tears were instantly dried. "I've never drunk a cocktail."

"Everything has to have a beginning," I said.

Megan sipped her drink gingerly, then a beaming smile spread over her face, she tilted her head back and gulped it down at a draught.

"It's lovely," she said. "Can I have another?"

"No," I said.

"Why not?"

"In about ten minutes you'll probably know."

"Oh!"

Megan transferred her attention to Joanna.

"I really am awfully sorry for having made such a nuisance of myself howling away like that. I can't think why. It seems awfully silly when I'm so glad to be here."

"That's all right," said Joanna. "We're very pleased to have you."

"You can't be really. It's just kindness on your part. But I am grateful."

"Please don't be grateful," said Joanna, "it will embarrass me. You're our friend and we're glad to have you here. That's all there is to it. . . ."

She took Megan upstairs to unpack.

Partridge came in, looking sour, and said she had made two cup custards for lunch and what should she do about it?

The inquest was held three days later.

The time of Mrs. Symmington's death was put at between three and four o'clock. She was alone in the house, Symmington was at his office, the maids were having their day out, Elsie Holland and the children were out walking and Megan had gone for a bicycle ride.

The letter must have come by the afternoon post, Mrs. Symmington must have taken it out of the box, read it—and then in a state of agitation she had gone to the potting shed, fetched some of the cyanide kept there for taking wasps' nests, dissolved it in water and drunk it after writing those last agitated words, "I can't go on. . . ."

Owen Griffith gave medical evidence and stressed the view he had outlined to us of Mrs. Symmington's nervous condition and poor stamina. The coroner was suave and discreet. He spoke with bitter condemnation of people who write those despicable things, anonymous letters. Whoever had written that wicked and lying letter was morally guilty of murder, he said. He hoped the police would soon discover the culprit and take action against him or her. Such a das-tardly and malicious piece of spite deserved to be punished with the utmost rigor of the law. Directed by him, the jury brought in the in-evitable verdict: Suicide while temporarily insane.

The coroner had done his best—Owen Griffith also, but after-ward, jammed in the crowd of eager village women, I heard the same hateful sibilant whisper I had begun to know so well: "No smoke without fire, that's what *I* say!" "Must 'a been something in it for cer-tain sure. She wouldn't never have done it otherwise. . . ."

Just for a moment I hated Lymstock and its narrow boundaries, and its gossiping whispering women.

Outside, Aimée Griffith said with a sigh:

"Well, that's over. Bad luck on Dick Symmington, its all having to come out. I wonder whether he'd ever had any suspicion."

I was startled.

"But surely you heard him say most emphatically that there wasn't a word of truth in that lying letter?"

"Of course he said so. Quite right. A man's got to stick up for his wife. Dick would." She paused and then explained: "You see, I've known Dick Symmington a long time."

"Really?" I said surprised. "I understood from your brother that he only bought this practice a few years ago."

"Yes, but Dick Symmington used to come and stay in our part of the world up north. I've known him for years."

I looked at Aimée curiously. She went on, still in that softened tone, "I know Dick very well . . . He's a proud man and very reserved. But he's the sort of man who could be very jealous."

"That would explain," I said deliberately, "why Mrs. Symmington was afraid to show him or tell him about the letter. She was afraid that, being a jealous man, he might not believe her denials."

Miss Griffith looked at me angrily and scornfully. "Good Lord," she said. "Do you think any woman would go and swallow a lot of cyanide of potassium for an accusation that wasn't true?"

"The coroner seemed to think it was possible. Your brother, too—"

Aimée interrupted me:

"Men are all alike. All for preserving the decencies. But you don't catch *me* believing that stuff. If an innocent woman gets some foul anonymous letter, she laughs and chucks it away. That's what I—" she paused suddenly, and then finished—"would do."

But I had noticed the pause. I was almost sure that what she had been about to say was "That's what I did."

I decided to take the war into the enemy's country.

"I see," I said pleasantly. "So you've had one, too?"

Aimée Griffith was the type of woman who scorns to lie. She paused a minute—flushed, then said, "Well, yes. But I didn't let it worry me!"

"Nasty?" I inquired sympathetically, as a fellow sufferer.

"Naturally. These things always are. The ravings of a lunatic! I read a few words of it, realized what it was and chucked it straight into the wastepaper basket."

"You didn't think of taking it to the police?"

"Not then. Least said soonest mended—that's what I felt."

An urge came over me to say solemnly, "No smoke without fire!" but I restrained myself.

I asked her if she had any idea how her mother's death would affect Megan financially. Would it be necessary for the girl to earn her own living?

"I believe she has a small income left her by her grandmother and of course Dick would always give her a home. But it would be much better for her to do something—not just slack about the way she does."

"I should have said Megan is at the age when a girl wants to enjoy herself—not to work."

Aimée flushed and said sharply, "You're like all men—you dislike the idea of women competing. It is incredible to you that women should want a career. It was incredible to my parents. I was anxious to study for a doctor. They would not hear of paying the fees. But they paid them readily for Owen. Yet I should have made a better doctor than my brother."

"I'm sorry about that," I said. "It was tough on you. If one wants to do a thing—"

She went on quickly.

"Oh, I've got over it now. I've plenty of will power. My life is busy and active. I'm one of the happiest people in Lymstock. Plenty to do. But I go up in arms against the silly old-fashioned prejudice that woman's place is always the home."

"I'm sorry if I offended you," I said. I had had no idea that Aimée Griffith could be so vehement.

3

I met Symmington in the town later in the day.

"Is it quite all right for Megan to stay on with us for a bit?" I asked. "It's company for Joanna—she's rather lonely sometimes with none of her own friends."

"Oh—er—Megan? Oh, yes, very good of you."

I took a dislike to Symmington then which I never quite overcame. He had so obviously forgotten all about Megan. I wouldn't have minded if he had actively disliked the girl—a man may sometimes be jealous of a first husband's child—but he didn't dislike her, he just hardly noticed her. He felt toward her much as a man who doesn't care much for dogs would feel about a dog in the house. You notice it when you fall over it and swear at it, and you give it a vague pat sometimes when it presents itself to be patted. Symmington's complete indifference to his step-daughter annoyed me very much.

I said, "What are you planning to do with her?"

"With Megan?" He seemed rather startled. "Well, she'll go on living at home. I mean, naturally, it is her home."

My grandmother, of whom I had been very fond, used to sing old-fashioned songs to her guitar. One of them, I remember, ended thus:

> *"Oh, maid most dear, I am not here,*
> *I have no place, no part,*
> *No dwelling more, by sea nor shore,*
> *But only in your heart."*

I went home humming it.

Emily Barton came just after tea had been cleared away.
She wanted to talk about the garden.
We talked garden for about half an hour. Then we turned back toward the house.

It was then that lowering her voice, she murmured, "I do hope that that child—that she hasn't been too much *upset* by all this dreadful business?"

"Her mother's death, you mean?"

"That, of course. But I really meant, the—the unpleasantness *behind* it."

I was curious. I wanted Miss Barton's reaction.

"What do you think about that? Was it true?"

"Oh, no, no, surely not. I'm quite sure that Mrs. Symmington never—that he wasn't—" little Emily Barton was pink and confused—"I mean it's quite untrue—although of course it may have been a judgment."

"A judgment?" I said, staring.

Emily Barton was very pink, very Dresden china shepherdess-like.

"I cannot help feeling that all these dreadful letters, all the sorrow and pain they have caused, may have been sent for a *purpose*."

"They were sent for a purpose, certainly," I said grimly.

"No, no, Mr. Burton, you misunderstand me. I'm not talking of the misguided creature who wrote them—someone quite abandoned that must be. I mean that they have been permitted—by Providence! To awaken us to a sense of our shortcomings."

"Surely," I said, "the Almighty could choose a less unsavory weapon."

Miss Emily murmured that God moved in a mysterious way.

"No," I said. "There's too much tendency to attribute to God the evils that man does of his own free will. I might concede you the Devil. God doesn't really need to punish us, Miss Barton. We're so very busy punishing ourselves."

"What I can't make out is *why* should anyone want to do such a thing?"

I shrugged my shoulders. "A warped mentality."

"It seems very sad."

"It doesn't seem to me sad. It seems to me just damnable. And I don't apologize for the word. I mean just that."

The pink had gone out of Miss Barton's cheeks. They were very white.

"But why, Mr. Burton, *why?* What pleasure can anyone get out of it?"

"Nothing you and I can understand, thank goodness."

Emily Barton lowered her voice; "Nothing of this kind has ever happened before—never in my memory. It has been such a happy little community. What would my dear mother have said? Well, one must be thankful that she has been spared."

I thought from all I heard that old Mrs. Barton had been sufficiently tough to have taken anything, and would probably have enjoyed this sensation.

Emily went on, "It distresses me deeply."

"You've not—er—had anything yourself?"

She flushed crimson. "Oh, no—oh, no, indeed. Oh! that would be dreadful."

I apologized hastily, but she went away looking rather upset.

I went into the house. Joanna was standing by the drawing-room fire which she had just lit, for the evenings were still chilly. She had an open letter in her hand.

She turned her head quickly as I entered.

"Jerry! I found this in the letter box—dropped in by hand. It begins: 'You painted trollop . . .'"

"What else does it say?"

Joanna gave a wide grimace. "Same old muck."

She dropped it on to the fire. With a quick gesture that hurt my back I jerked it off again just before it caught.

"Don't," I said. "We may need it."

"Need it?"

"For the police."

Superintendent Nash came to see me the following morning. From the first moment I saw him I took a great liking to him. He was the best type of C.I.D. County Superintendent. Tall, soldierly, with quiet, reflective eyes and a straightforward, unassuming manner.

"Good morning, Mr. Burton," he said. "I expect you can guess what I've come to see you about."

"Yes, I think so. This letter business."

He nodded.

"I understand you had one of them?"

"Yes, soon after we got here."

"What did it say exactly?"

I thought a minute, then conscientiously repeated the wording of the letter as closely as possible.

The superintendent listened with an immovable face, showing no signs of any kind of emotion.

When I had finished, he said, "I see. You didn't keep the letter, Mr. Burton?"

"I'm sorry. I didn't. You see, I thought it was just an isolated instance of spite against the newcomers to the place."

The superintendent inclined his head comprehendingly.

"A pity," he said briefly.

"However," I said, "my sister got one yesterday. I just stopped her putting it in the fire."

"Thank you, Mr. Burton, that was thoughtful of you."

I went across to my desk and unlocked the drawer in which I had put it. It was not, I thought, very suitable for Partridge's eyes. I gave it to Nash.

He read it through. Then he looked up and asked:

"Is this the same in appearance as the last one?"

"I think so—as far as I can remember."

"The same difference between the envelope and the text?"

"Yes," I said. "The envelope was typed. The letter itself had printed words pasted on to a sheet of paper."

Nash nodded and put it in his pocket. Then he said:

"I wonder, Mr. Burton, if you would mind coming down to the station with me? We could have a conference there and it would save a good deal of time and overlapping."

"Certainly," I said. "You would like me to come now?"

"If you don't mind."

There was a police car at the door. We drove down in it.

I said, "Do you think you'll be able to get to the bottom of this?"

Nash nodded with easy confidence. "Oh, yes, we'll get to the bottom of it all right. It's a question of time and routine. They're slow, these cases, but they're pretty sure. It's a matter of narrowing things down."

"Elimination?" I said.

"Yes. And general routine."

"Watching post boxes, examining typewriters, fingerprints, all that?"

He smiled. "As you say."

At the police station I found Symmington and Griffith were already there. I was introduced to a tall, lantern-jawed man in plain clothes, Inspector Graves.

"Inspector Graves," explained Nash, "has come down from London to help us. He's an expert on anonymous letter cases."

Inspector Graves smiled mournfully. I reflected that a life spent in the pursuit of anonymous letter writers must be singularly depressing. Inspector Graves, however, showed a kind of melancholy enthusiasm.

"They're all the same, these cases," he said in a deep lugubrious voice like a depressed bloodhound. "You'd be surprised. The wording of the letters and the things they say."

"We had a case just on two years ago," said Nash. "Inspector Graves helped us then."

Some of the letters, I saw, were spread out on the table in front of Graves. He had evidently been examining them.

"Difficulty is," said Nash, "to get hold of the letters. Either people put them in the fire, or they won't admit to having received anything of the kind. Stupid, you see, and afraid of being mixed up with the police. They're a backward lot here."

"Still we've got a fair amount to get on with," said Graves. Nash took the letter I had given him from his pocket and tossed it over to Graves.

The latter glanced through it, laid it with the others and observed approvingly, "Very nice—very nice indeed."

It was not the way I should have chosen to describe the epistle in question, but experts, I suppose, have their own point of view. I was glad that that screed of vituperative and obscene abuse gave *somebody* pleasure.

"We've got enough, I think, to go on with," said Inspector Graves, "and I'll ask all you gentlemen, if you should get any more, to bring them along at once. Also, if you hear of someone else getting one (you, in particular, doctor, among your patients) do your best to get them to come along here with them. I've got"—he sorted with deft fingers among his exhibits—"one to Mr. Symmington, received as far back as two months ago, one to Dr. Griffith, one to Miss Ginch, one written to Mrs. Mudge, the butcher's wife, one to Jennifer Clark, barmaid at the

Three Crowns, the one received by Mrs. Symmington, this one now to Miss Burton—oh, yes, and one to the bank manager."

"Quite a representative collection," I remarked.

"And not one I couldn't match from other cases! This one here is as near as nothing to one written by that milliner woman. This one is the dead spit of an outbreak we had up in Northumberland—written by a schoolgirl, they were. I can tell you, gentlemen, I'd like to see something *new* sometimes, instead of the same old treadmill."

"There is nothing new under the sun," I murmured.

"Quite so, sir. You'd know that if you were in our profession."

Nash sighed and said, "Yes, indeed."

Symmington asked, "Have you come to any definite opinion as to the writer?"

Graves cleared his throat and delivered a small lecture:

"There are certain similarities shared by all these letters. I shall enumerate them, gentlemen, in case they suggest anything to your minds. The text of the letters is composed of words made up from individual letters cut out of a printed book. It's an old book, printed, I should say, about the year 1830. This has obviously been done to avoid the risk of recognition through handwriting which is, as most people know nowadays, a fairly easy matter . . . the so-called disguising of a hand not amounting to much when faced with expert tests. There are no fingerprints on the letters and envelopes of a distinctive character. That is to say, they have been handled by the postal authorities, the recipient, and there are other stray fingerprints, but no set common to all, showing therefore that the person who put them together was careful to wear gloves.

"The envelopes are typewritten by a Windsor 7 machine, well worn, with the *a* and the *t* out of alignment. Most of them have been posted locally, or put in the box of a house by hand. It is therefore evident that they are of local provenance. They were written by a woman, and in my opinion a woman of middle age or over, and probably, though not certainly, unmarried."

We maintained a respectful silence for a minute or two. Then I said, "The typewriter's your best bet, isn't it? That oughtn't to be difficult in a little place like this."

Inspector Graves shook his head sadly and said, "That's where you're wrong, sir."

"The typewriter," said Superintendent Nash, "is unfortunately too easy. It is an old one from Mr. Symmington's office, given by him to the Women's Institute where, I may say, it's fairly easy of access. The ladies here all often go into the Institute."

"Can't you tell something definite from the—er—the touch, don't you call it?"

Again Graves nodded. "Yes, that can be done—but these envelopes have all been typed by someone using one finger."

"Someone, then, unused to the typewriter?"

"No, I wouldn't say that. Someone, perhaps, who can type but doesn't want us to know the fact."

"Whoever writes these things has been very cunning," I said slowly.

"She is, sir, she is," said Graves. "Up to every trick of the trade."

"I shouldn't have thought one of these bucolic women down here would have had the brains," I said.

Graves coughed. "I haven't made myself plain, I'm afraid. Those letters were written by an educated woman."

"What, by a lady?"

The word slipped out involuntarily. I hadn't used the term "lady" for years. But now it came automatically to my lips, re-echoed from days long ago, and my grandmother's faint unconsciously arrogant voice saying, "Of course, she isn't a *lady*, dear."

Nash understood at once. The word "lady" still meant something to him.

"Not necessarily a lady," he said. "But certainly not a village woman. They're mostly pretty illiterate down here, can't spell, and certainly can't express themselves with fluency."

I was silent, for I had had a shock. The community was so small. Unconsciously I had visualized the writer of the letters as a Mrs. Cleat or her like, some spiteful, cunning half-wit.

Symmington put my thoughts into words. He said sharply, "But that narrows it down to about half a dozen to a dozen people in the whole place! I can't believe it."

Then, with a slight effort, and looking straight in front of him as though the mere sound of his own words was distasteful, he said:

"You have heard what I stated at the inquest. In case you may have thought that that statement was actuated by a desire to protect my wife's memory, I should like to repeat now that I am firmly convinced that the subject matter of the letter my wife received was absolutely false. I *know* it was false. My wife was a very sensitive woman, and—er—well, you might call it *prudish* in some respects. Such a letter would have been a great shock to her, and she was in poor health."

Graves responded instantly:

"That's quite likely to be right, sir. None of these letters show any signs of intimate knowledge. They're just blind accusations. There's been no attempt to blackmail. And there doesn't seem to be any religious bias—such as we sometimes get. It's just sex and spite! And that's going to give us quite a good pointer toward the writer."

Symmington got up. Dry and unemotional as the man was, his lips were trembling.

"I hope you find the devil who writes these soon. She murdered my wife as surely as if she'd put a knife into her." He paused. "How does she feel now, I wonder?"

He went out, leaving that question unanswered.

"How does she feel, Griffith?" I asked. It seemed to me the answer was in his province.

"God knows. Remorseful, perhaps. On the other hand, it may be that she's enjoying her power. Mrs. Symmington's death may have fed her mania."

"I hope not," I said, with a slight shiver. "Because if so, she'll—"

I hesitated and Nash finished the sentence for me:

"She'll try it again? That, Mr. Burton, would be the best thing that could happen, for us. The pitcher goes to the well once too often, remember."

"She'd be mad to go on with it," I exclaimed.

"She'll go on," said Graves. "They always do. It's a vice, you know, they can't let it alone."

I shook my head with a shudder. I asked if they needed me any longer, I wanted to get out into the air. The atmosphere seemed tinged with evil.

"There's nothing more, Mr. Burton," said Nash. "Only keep your eyes open, and do as much propaganda as you can—that is to say, urge on everyone that they've got to report any letter they receive."

I nodded.

"I should think everyone in the place has had one of the foul things by now," I said.

"I wonder," said Graves. He put his sad head a little on one side and asked, "You don't know, definitely, of anyone who *hasn't* had a letter?"

"What an extraordinary question! The population at large isn't likely to take me into their confidence."

"No, no, Mr. Burton, I didn't mean that. I just wondered if you knew of any one person who quite definitely, to your certain knowledge, has not received an anonymous letter."

"Well, as a matter of fact," I hesitated, "I do, in a way."

And I repeated my conversation with Emily Barton and what she had said.

Graves received the information with a wooden face and said, "Well, that may come in useful. I'll note it down."

I went out into the afternoon sunshine with Owen Griffith. Once in the street, I swore aloud.

"What kind of place is this for a man to come to to lie in the sun and heal his wounds? It's full of festering poison, this place, and it looks as peaceful and as innocent as the Garden of Eden."

"Even there," said Owen dryly, "there was one serpent."

"Look here, Griffith, do they know anything? Have they got any idea?"

"I don't know. They've got a wonderful technique, the police. They're seemingly so frank, and they tell you nothing."

"Yes. Nash is a nice fellow."

"And a very capable one."

"If anyone's batty in this place, you ought to know it," I said accusingly.

Griffith shook his head. He looked discouraged. But he looked more than that—he looked worried. I wondered if he had an inkling of some kind.

We had been walking along the High Street. I stopped at the door of the house agents.

"I believe my second installment of rent is due—in advance. I've got a good mind to pay it and clear out with Joanna right away. Forfeit the rest of the tenancy."

"Don't go," said Owen.

"Why not?"

He didn't answer. He said slowly after a minute or two, "After all—I dare say you're right. Lymstock isn't healthy just now. It might—it might harm you or—or your sister."

"Nothing harms Joanna," I said. "She's tough. I'm the weakly one. Somehow this business makes me sick."

"It makes *me* sick," said Owen.

I pushed the door of the house agents' place half open.

"But I shan't go," I said. "Vulgar curiosity is stronger than pusillanimity. I want to know the solution."

I went in.

A woman who was typing got up and came toward me. She had frizzy hair and simpered, but I found her more intelligent than the spectacled youth who had previously held sway in the outer office.

A minute or two later something familiar about her penetrated through to my consciousness. It was Miss Ginch, lately Symmington's lady clerk.

I commented on the fact.

"You used to be with Galbraith, Galbraith and Symmington, weren't you?" I said.

"Yes. Yes, indeed. But I thought it was better to leave. This is quite a good post, though not quite so well paid. But there are things that are more valuable than money, don't you think so?"

"Undoubtedly," I said.

"Those awful letters," breathed Miss Ginch in a sibilant whisper. "I got a dreadful one. About me and Mr. Symmington—oh, terrible it was, saying the most *awful* things! I knew my duty and I took it to the police, though of course it wasn't exactly *pleasant* for me, was it?"

"No, no, most unpleasant."

"But they thanked me and said I had done quite right. But I felt that, after that, if people were talking—and evidently they *must* have been, or where did the writer get the idea from?—then I must avoid even the appearance of evil, though there has never been anything at all *wrong* between me and Mr. Symmington."

I felt rather embarrassed.

"No, no, of course not."

"But people have such evil minds. Yes, alas, such evil minds!"

Nervously trying to avoid it, I nevertheless met her eye, and I made a most unpleasant discovery.

Miss Ginch was thoroughly enjoying herself.

Already once today I had come across someone who reacted pleasurably to anonymous letters. Inspector Graves' enthusiasm was professional. Miss Ginch's enjoyment I found merely suggestive and disgusting.

An idea flashed across my startled mind.

Had Miss Ginch written these letters herself?

* * *

When I got home I found Mrs. Dane Calthrop sitting talking to Joanna. She looked, I thought, gray and ill.

"This has been a terrible shock to me, Mr. Burton," she said. "Poor thing, poor thing."

"Yes," I said. "It's awful to think of someone being driven to the stage of taking their own life."

"Oh, you mean Mrs. Symmington?"

"Didn't you?"

Mrs. Dane Calthrop shook her head. "Of course one is sorry for her, but it would have been bound to happen anyway, wouldn't it?"

"Would it?" said Joanna dryly.

Mrs. Dane Calthrop turned to her.

"Oh, I think so, dear. If suicide is your idea of escape from trouble then it doesn't very much matter what the trouble is. Whenever some very unpleasant shock had to be faced, she'd have done the same thing. What it really comes down to is that she was that kind of woman. Not that one would have guessed it. She always seemed to me a selfish rather stupid woman, with a good firm hold on life. Not the kind to panic, you would think—but I'm beginning to realize how little I really know about anyone."

"I'm still curious as to whom you meant when you said 'Poor thing,' " I remarked.

She stared at me. "The woman who wrote the letters, of course."

"I don't think," I said dryly, "I shall waste sympathy on her."

Mrs. Dane Calthrop leaned forward. She laid a hand on my knee.

"But don't you realize—can't you *feel*? Use your imagination. Think how desperately, violently unhappy anyone must be to sit down and write those things. How lonely, how cut off from human kind. Poisoned through and through, with a dark stream of poison that finds its outlet in this way. That's why I feel so self-reproachful. Somebody in this town has been racked with that terrible unhappiness, and I've had no idea of it. I should have had. You can't interfere with actions—I never do. But that black inward unhappiness—like a septic arm physically, all black and swollen. If you could cut it and let the poison out it would flow away harmlessly. Yes, poor soul, poor soul."

She got up to go.

I did not feel like agreeing with her. I had no sympathy for our anonymous letter writer whatsoever. But I did ask curiously:

"Have you any idea at all, Mrs. Calthrop, who this woman is?"

She turned her fine perplexed eyes on me. "Well, I can guess," she said. "But then I might be wrong, mightn't I?"

She went swiftly out through the door, popping her head back to ask: "Do tell me, why have you never married, Mr. Burton?"

In anyone else it would have been impertinence, but with Mrs. Dane Calthrop you felt that the idea had suddenly come into her head and she had really wanted to know.

"Shall we say," I said, rallying, "that I have never met the right woman?"

"We can say so," said Mrs. Dane Calthrop, "but it wouldn't be a very good answer, because so many men have obviously married the wrong woman."

This time she really departed.

Joanna said, "You know I really do think she's mad. But I like her. The people in the village here are afraid of her."

"So am I, a little."

"Because you never know what's coming next?"

"Yes. And there's a careless brilliancy about her guesses."

Joanna said slowly, "Do you really think whoever wrote these letters is very unhappy?"

"I don't know what the damned hag is thinking or feeling! And I don't care. It's her victims I'm sorry for."

It seems odd to me now that in our speculations about Poison Pen's frame of mind, we missed the most obvious one. Griffith had pictured her as possibly exultant. I had envisaged her as remorseful—appalled by the result of her handiwork. Mrs. Dane Calthrop had seen her as suffering.

Yet the obvious, the inevitable reaction we did not consider—or perhaps I should say, I did not consider. That reaction was Fear.

For with the death of Mrs. Symmington, the letters had passed out of one category into another. I don't know what the legal position was—Symmington knew, I suppose, but it was clear that with a death resulting, the position of the writer of the letters was much more serious. There could now be no question of passing it off as a joke if the identity of the writer was discovered. The police were active, a Scotland Yard expert was called in. It was vital now for the anonymous author to remain anonymous.

And granted that Fear was the principal reaction, other things followed. Those possibilities also I was blind to. Yet surely they should have been obvious.

* * *

Joanna and I came down rather late to breakfast the next morning. That is to say, late by the standards of Lymstock. It was nine-thirty, an hour at which, in London, Joanna was just unclosing an eyelid, and mine would probably be still tight shut.

However when Partridge had asked, "Breakfast at half past eight, or nine o'clock?" neither Joanna nor I had had the nerve to suggest a later hour.

To my annoyance, Aimée Griffith was standing on the doorstep talking to Megan.

She gave tongue with her usual heartiness at the sight of us: "Hullo, there, slackers! I've been up for hours."

That, of course, was her own business. A doctor, no doubt, has to have early breakfast, and a dutiful sister is there to pour out his tea or coffee. But it is no excuse for coming and butting in on one's more somnolent neighbors. Nine-thirty is not the time for a morning call.

Megan slipped back into the house and into the dining room, where I gathered she had been interrupted in her breakfast.

"I said I wouldn't come in," said Aimée Griffith—"though why it is more of a merit to force people to come and speak to you on the doorstep, than to talk to them inside the house I do not know. Just wanted to ask Miss Burton if she'd any vegetables to spare for our Red Cross stall on the main road. If so, I'd get Owen to call for them in the car."

"You're out and about very early," I said.

"The early bird catches the worm," said Aimée. "You have a better chance of finding people in this time of day. I'm off to Mr. Pye's next. Got to go over to Brenton this afternoon. Guides."

"Your energy makes me quite tired," I said, and at that moment the telephone rang and I retired to the back of the hall to answer it, leaving Joanna murmuring rather doubtfully something about rhubarb and French beans and exposing her ignorance of the vegetable garden.

"Yes?" I said into the telephone mouthpiece.

A confused noise of deep breathing came from the other end of the wire and a doubtful female voice said, "Oh!"

"Yes?" I said again encouragingly.

"Oh," said the voice again, and then it inquired adenoidally, "Is that—what I mean—is that Little Furze?"

"This is Little Furze."

"Oh!" This clearly a stock beginning to every sentence. The voice inquired cautiously: "Could I speak to Miss Partridge just a minute?"

"Certainly," I said. "Who shall I say?"

"Oh. Tell her it's Agnes, would you? Agnes Waddle."

"Agnes Waddle?"

"That's right."

Resisting the temptation to say "Donald Duck to you," I put down the telephone receiver and called up the stairs to where I could hear the sound of Partridge's activities overhead.

"Partridge! Partridge!"

Partridge appeared at the head of the stairs, a long mop in one hand, and a look of "What is it *now*?" clearly discernible behind her invariably respectful manner.

"Yes, sir?"

"Agnes Waddle wants to speak to you on the telephone."

"I beg your pardon, sir?"

I raised my voice: "Agnes Waddle."

I have spelled the name as it presented itself to my mind. But I will now spell it as it was actually written:

"Agnes Woddell—whatever can she want now?"

Very much put out of countenance Partridge relinquished her mop and rustled down the stairs, her print dress crackling with agitation.

I beat an unobtrusive retreat into the dining room where Megan was wolfing down kidneys and bacon. Megan, unlike Aimée Griffith, was displaying no "glorious morning face." In fact she replied very gruffly to my morning salutations and continued to eat in silence.

I opened the morning paper and a minute or two later Joanna entered looking somewhat shattered.

"Whew!" she said. "I'm so tired. And I think I've exposed my utter ignorance of what grows when. Aren't there runner beans this time of year?"

"August," said Megan.

"Well, one has them any time in London," said Joanna defensively.

"Tins, sweet fool," I said. "And cold storage on ships from the far-flung limits of Empire."

"Like ivory, apes and peacocks?" asked Joanna.

"Exactly."

"I'd rather have peacocks," said Joanna thoughtfully.

"I'd like a monkey of my own as a pet," said Megan.

Meditatively peeling an orange, Joanna said:

"I wonder what it would feel like to be Aimée Griffith, all bursting with health and vigor and enjoyment of life. Do you think she's ever tired, or depressed, or—or wistful?"

I said I was quite certain Aimée Griffith was never wistful, and followed Megan out of the open French window onto the veranda.

Standing there, filling my pipe, I heard Partridge enter the dining room from the hall and heard her voice say grimly, "Can I speak to you a minute, Miss?"

"Dear me," I thought. "I hope Partridge isn't going to give notice. Emily Barton would be very annoyed with us if so."

Partridge went on:

"I must apologize, Miss, for being rung up on the telephone. That is to say, the young person who did so should have known better. I have never been in the habit of using the telephone or of permitting my friends to ring me up on it, and I'm very sorry indeed that it should have occurred, and the master taking the call and everything."

"Why, that's quite all right, Partridge," said Joanna soothingly, "why shouldn't your friends use the phone if they want to speak to you?"

Partridge's face, I could feel, though I could not see it, was more dour than ever as she replied coldly:

"It is not the kind of thing that has ever been done in this house. Miss Emily would never permit it. As I say, I am sorry it occurred, but Agnes Woddell, the girl who did it, was upset and she's young too, and doesn't know what's fitting in a gentleman's house."

"That's one for you, Joanna," I thought gleefully.

"This Agnes who rung me up, Miss," went on Partridge, "she used to be in service here under me. Sixteen she was, then, and come straight from the orphanage. And you see, not having a home, or a mother or any relations to advise her, she's been in the habit of coming to me. I can tell her what's what, you see."

"Yes?" said Joanna and waited. Clearly there was more to follow.

"So I am taking the liberty of asking you, Miss, if you would allow Agnes to come here to tea this afternoon in the kitchen. It's her day out, you see, and she's got something on her mind she wants to consult me about. I wouldn't dream of suggesting such a thing in the usual way."

Joanna said bewildered, "But why shouldn't you have anyone to tea with you?"

Partridge drew herself up at this, so Joanna said afterward and really looked most formidable, as she replied:

"It has never been the custom of this house, Miss. Old Mrs. Barton never allowed visitors in the kitchen, excepting as it should be our own day out, in which case we were allowed to entertain friends here instead of going out, but otherwise, on ordinary days, no. And Miss Emily keeps to the old ways."

Joanna is very nice to servants and most of them like her but she has never cut any ice with Partridge.

"It's no good, my girl," I said when Partridge had gone and Joanna had joined me outside. "Your sympathy and leniency are not appreciated. The good old overbearing ways for Partridge and things done the way they should be done in a gentleman's house."

"I never heard of such tyranny as not allowing them to have their friends to see them," said Joanna. "It's all very well, Jerry, but they can't *like* being treated like black slaves."

"Evidently they do," I said. "At least the Partridges of this world do."

"I can't imagine why she doesn't like me. Most people do."

"She probably despises you as an inadequate housekeeper. You never draw your hand across a shelf and examine it for traces of dust. You don't look under the mats. You don't ask what happened to the remains of the chocolate soufflé, and you never order a nice bread pudding."

"Ugh!" said Joanna.

She went on sadly: "I'm a failure all around today. Despised by our Aimée for ignorance of the vegetable kingdom. Snubbed by Partridge for being a human being. I shall now go out into the garden and eat worms."

"Megan's there already," I said.

For Megan had wandered away a few minutes previously and was now standing aimlessly in the middle of a patch of lawn looking not unlike a meditative bird waiting for nourishment.

She came back however toward us and said abruptly, "I say, I must go home today."

"What?" I was dismayed.

She went on, flushing, but speaking with nervous determination: "It's been awfully good of you having me and I expect I've been a fearful nuisance, but I have enjoyed it awfully, only now I must go back, because after all, well, it's my home and one can't stay away for ever, so I think I'll go this morning."

Both Joanna and I tried to make her change her mind, but she was quite adamant, and finally Joanna got out the car and Megan went upstairs and came down a few minutes later with her belongings packed up again.

The only person pleased seemed to be Partridge, who had almost a smile on her grim face. She had never liked Megan much.

I was standing in the middle of the lawn when Joanna returned.

She asked me if I thought I was a sundial.

"Why?"

"Standing there like a garden ornament. Only one couldn't put on you the motto of only marking the sunny hours. You looked like thunder!"

"I'm out of humor. First Aimée Griffith—'Gracious!' murmured Joanna in parenthesis, 'I must speak about those vegetables!' and then Megan beetling off. I'd thought of taking her for a walk up to Legge Tor."

"With a collar and lead, I suppose," said Joanna.

"What?"

Joanna repeated loudly and clearly as she moved off around the corner of the house to the kitchen garden:

"I said 'With a collar and lead, I suppose?' Master's lost his dog, that's what's the matter with you!"

4

I was annoyed, I must confess, at the abrupt way in which Megan had left us. Perhaps she had suddenly got bored with us.

After all, it wasn't a very amusing life for a girl. At home she had the kids and Elsie Holland.

I heard Joanna returning and hastily moved in case she should make more rude remarks about sundials.

Owen Griffith called in his car just before lunch time, and the gardener was waiting for him with the necessary garden produce.

While Old Adams was stowing it in the car I brought Owen indoors for a drink. He wouldn't stay to lunch.

When I came in with the sherry I found Joanna had begun doing her stuff.

No signs of animosity now. She was curled up in the corner of the sofa and was positively purring, asking Owen questions about his work, if he liked being a G. P., if he wouldn't rather have specialized? She thought doctoring was one of the most fascinating things in the world.

Say what you will of her, Joanna is a lovely, a heaven-born listener. And after listening to so many would-be geniuses telling her how they had been unappreciated, listening to Owen Griffith was easy money. By the time we had got to the third glass of sherry, Griffith was telling her about some obscure reaction or lesion in such scientific terms that nobody could have understood a word of it except a fellow medico.

Joanna was looking intelligent and deeply interested.

I felt a moment's qualm. It was really too bad of Joanna. Griffith was too good a chap to be played fast and loose with. Women really were devils.

Then I caught a sideways view of Griffith, his long, purposeful chin and the grim set of his lips, and I was not so sure that Joanna was going to have it her own way after all. And anyway a man has no business to let himself be made a fool of by a woman. It's his own lookout if he does.

Then Joanna said:

"Do change your mind and stay to lunch with us, Dr. Griffith," and Griffith flushed a little and said he would, only his sister would be expecting him back—

"We'll ring her up and explain," said Joanna quickly and went out into the hall and did so.

I thought Griffith looked a little uneasy, and it crossed my mind that he was probably a little afraid of his sister.

Joanna came back smiling and said that that was all right.

And Owen Griffith stayed to lunch and seemed to enjoy himself. We talked about books and plays and world politics, and about music and painting and modern architecture.

We didn't talk about Lymstock at all, or about anonymous letters, or Mrs. Symmington's suicide.

We got right away from everything, and I think Owen Griffith was happy. His dark sad face lighted up, and he revealed an interesting mind.

When he had gone I said to Joanna, "That fellow's too good for your tricks."

"That's what *you* say!" Joanna said. "You men all stick together!"

"Why are you out after his hide, Joanna? Wounded vanity?"

"Perhaps," said my sister.

That afternoon we were to go to tea with Miss Emily Barton at her rooms in the village.

We strolled down there on foot, for I felt strong enough now to manage the hill back again.

We must actually have allowed too much time and got there early, for the door was opened to us by a tall, raw-boned, fierce-looking woman who told us that Miss Barton wasn't in yet.

"But she's expecting you, I know, so if you'll come up and wait, please."

This was evidently faithful Florence.

We followed her up the stairs and she threw open a door and showed us into what was quite a comfortable sitting room, though perhaps a little over-furnished. Some of the things, I suspected, had come from Little Furze.

The woman was clearly proud of her room.

"It's nice, isn't it?" she demanded.

"Very nice," said Joanna warmly.

"I make her as comfortable as I can. Not that I can do for her as I'd like to and in the way she ought to have. She ought to be in her own house, properly, not turned out into rooms."

Florence, who was clearly a dragon, looked from one to the other of us reproachfully. It was not, I felt, our lucky day. Joanna had been ticked off by Aimée Griffith and Partridge and now we were both being ticked off by the dragon Florence.

"Parlormaid I was for nine years there," she added.

Joanna, goaded by injustice, said, "Well, Miss Barton wanted to let the house. She put it down at the house agents."

"Forced to it," said Florence. "And she living so frugal and careful. But even then, the government can't leave her alone! Has to have its pound of flesh just the same."

I shook my head sadly.

"Plenty of money there was in the old lady's time," said Florence. "And then they all died off one after another, poor dears. Miss Emily nursing of them one after the other. Wore herself out she did, and always so patient and uncomplaining. But it told on her, and then to have worry about money on top of it all! Shares not bringing in what they used to, so she says, and why not, I should like to know? They ought to be ashamed of themselves. Doing down a lady like her who's got no head for figures and can't be up to their tricks."

"Practically everyone has been hit that way," I said, but Florence remained unsoftened.

"It's all right for some as can look after themselves, but not for *her*. She needs looking after, and as long as she's with me I'm going to see no one imposes on her or upsets her in any way. I'd do anything for Miss Emily."

And glaring at us for some moments in order to drive that point thoroughly home, the indomitable Florence left the room, carefully shutting the door behind her.

"Do you feel like a bloodsucker, Jerry?" inquired Joanna. "Because I do. What's the matter with us?"

"We don't seem to be going down very well," I said. "Megan gets tired of us. Partridge disapproves of you, faithful Florence disapproves of both of us."

Joanna murmured, "I wonder why Megan *did* leave?"

"She got bored."

"I don't think she did at all. I wonder—do you think, Jerry, it could have been something that Aimée Griffith said?"

"You mean this morning, when they were talking on the doorstep?"

"Yes. There wasn't much time, of course, but—"

I finished the sentence: "But that woman's got the tread of a cow elephant! She might have—"

The door opened and Miss Emily came in. She was pink and a little out of breath and seemed excited. Her eyes were very blue and shining.

She chirruped at us in quite a distracted manner:

"Oh, dear, I'm so sorry I'm late. Just doing a little shopping in the town, and the cakes at the Blue Rose didn't seem to me quite fresh, so I went on to Mrs. Lygon's. I always like to get my cakes the last thing, then one gets the newest batch just out of the oven, and one isn't put off with the day before's. But I am so distressed to have kept you waiting—really unpardonable—"

Joanna cut in:

"It's our fault, Miss Barton. We're early. We walked down and Jerry strides along so fast now that we arrive everywhere too soon."

"Never too soon, dear. Don't say that. One cannot have too much of a good thing, you know."

And the old lady petted Joanna affectionately on the shoulder.

Joanna brightened up. At last, so it seemed, she was being a success. Emily Barton extended her smile to include me, but with a slight timidity in it, rather as one might approach a man-eating tiger guaranteed for the moment harmless.

"It's very good of you to come to such a feminine meal as tea, Mr. Burton."

Emily Barton, I think, has a mental picture of men as interminably consuming whisky-and-sodas and smoking cigars, and in the intervals dropping out to do a few seductions of village maidens, or to conduct a liaison with a married woman.

When I said this to Joanna later, she replied that it was probably

56

wishful thinking, that Emily Barton would have liked to come across such a man, but alas, had never done so.

In the meantime, Miss Emily was fussing around the room, arranging Joanna and myself with little tables, and carefully providing ashtrays, and a minute later the door opened and Florence came in bearing a tray of tea with some fine Crown Derby cups on it, which I gathered Miss Emily had brought with her. The tea was China and delicious and there were plates of sandwiches and thin bread and butter, and a quantity of little cakes.

Florence was beaming now, and looked at Miss Emily with a kind of maternal pleasure, as at a favorite child enjoying a doll's tea party.

Joanna and I ate far more than we wanted to, our hostess pressed us so earnestly. The little lady was clearly enjoying her tea party and I perceived that to Emily Barton, Joanna and I were a big adventure, two people from the mysterious world of London and sophistication.

Naturally, our talk soon dropped into local channels. Miss Barton spoke warmly of Dr. Griffith, his kindness and his cleverness as a doctor. Mr. Symmington, too, was a very clever lawyer, and had helped Miss Barton to get some money back from the Income Tax which she would never have known about. He was so nice to his children, too, devoted to them and to his wife—she caught herself up. "Poor Mrs. Symmington, it's so dreadfully sad, with those young children left motherless. Never, perhaps, a very strong woman—and her health had been bad of late.

"A brain storm, that is what it must have been. I read about such a thing in the paper. People really do not know what they are doing under those circumstances. And she can't have known what she was doing or else she would have remembered Mr. Symmington and the children."

"That anonymous letter must have shaken her up very badly," said Joanna.

Miss Barton flushed. She said, with a tinge of reproof in her voice: "Not a very nice thing to discuss, do you think, dear? I know there have been—er—letters, but we won't talk about them. Nasty things. I think they are better just ignored."

Well, Miss Barton might be able to ignore them, but for some people it wasn't so easy. However I obediently changed the subject and we discussed Aimée Griffith.

"Wonderful, quite wonderful," said Emily Barton. "Her energy and her organizing powers are really splendid. She's so good with girls too. And she's so practical and up to date in every way. She really runs this place. And absolutely devoted to her brother. It's very nice to see such devotion between brother and sister."

"Doesn't he ever find her a little overwhelming?" asked Joanna.

Emily Barton stared at her in a startled fashion.

"She has sacrificed a great deal for his sake," she said with a touch of reproachful dignity.

I saw a touch of Oh, Yeah? in Joanna's eye and hastened to divert the conversation to Mr. Pye.

Emily Barton was a little dubious about Mr. Pye.

All she could say was, repeated rather doubtfully, that he was very kind—yes, very kind. Very well off, too, and most generous. He had very strange visitors sometimes, but then, of course, he had traveled a lot.

We agreed that travel not only broadened the mind, but occasionally resulted in the forming of strange acquaintances.

"I have often wished, myself, to go on a cruise," said Emily Barton wistfully. "One reads about them in the papers and they sound so attractive."

"Why don't you go?" asked Joanna.

This turning of a dream into a reality seemed to alarm Miss Emily.

"Oh, no, no, that would be *quite* impossible."

"But why? They're fairly cheap."

"Oh, it's not only the expense. But I shouldn't like to go alone. Traveling alone would look very peculiar, don't you think?"

"No," said Joanna.

Miss Emily looked at her doubtfully.

"And I don't know how I would manage about my luggage—and going ashore at foreign ports—and all the different currencies—"

Innumerable pitfalls seemed to rise up before the little lady's affrighted gaze, and Joanna hastened to calm her by a question about an approaching garden fete and sale of work. This led us quite naturally to Mrs. Dane Calthrop.

A faint spasm showed for a minute on Miss Barton's face. "You know, dear," she said, "she is really a very *odd* woman. The things she says sometimes."

I asked what things.

"Oh. I don't know. Such very *unexpected* things. And the way she looks at you, as though you weren't there but somebody else was—I'm expressing it badly but it is so hard to convey the impression I mean. And then she won't—well, *interfere* at all. There are so many cases where a vicar's wife could advise and—perhaps *admonish*. Pull people up, you know, and make them mend their ways. Because people would listen to her, I'm sure of that, they're all quite in awe of her. But she insists on being aloof and far away, and has such a curious habit of feeling sorry for the most unworthy people."

"That's interesting," I said, exchanging a quick glance with Joanna.

"Still, she is a very well-bred woman. She was a Miss Farroway of Bellpath, very good family, but these old families sometimes *are* a little peculiar, I believe. But she is devoted to her husband who is a man of very fine intellect—wasted, I am sometimes afraid, in this country circle. A good man, and most sincere, but I always find his habit of quoting Latin a little confusing."

"Hear, hear," I said fervently.

"Jerry had an expensive public school education, so he doesn't recognize Latin when he hears it," said Joanna.

This led Miss Barton to a new topic.

"The schoolmistress here is a most unpleasant young woman," she said. "Quite *Red*, I'm afraid." She lowered her voice over the word "Red."

Later, as we walked home up the hill, Joanna said to me:

"She's rather sweet."

At dinner that night Joanna said to Partridge that she hoped her tea party had been a success.

Partridge got rather red in the face and held herself even more stiffly. "Thank you, Miss, but Agnes never turned up after all."

"Oh, I'm sorry."

"It didn't matter to *me*," said Partridge.

She was so swelling with grievance that she condescended to pour it out to us:

"It wasn't me who thought of asking her! She rang up herself, said she'd something on her mind and could she come here, it being her day off. And I said, yes, subject to your permission which I obtained. And after that, not a sound or sign of her! And no word of apology either, though I should hope I'll get a postcard tomorrow morning. These girls nowadays—don't know their place—no idea of how to behave."

Joanna attempted to soothe Partridge's wounded feelings: "She mightn't have felt well. You didn't ring up to find out?" Partridge drew herself up again. "No, I did *not*, Miss! No, indeed. If Agnes likes to behave rudely that's her lookout, but I shall give her a piece of my mind when we meet."

Partridge went out of the room still stiff with indignation, and Joanna and I laughed.

"Probably a case of 'Advice from Aunt Nancy's Column,'" I said. "'*My boy is very cold in his manner to me, what shall I do about it?*' Failing Aunt Nancy, Partridge was to be applied to for advice, but instead there has been a reconciliation and I expect at this minute that Agnes and her boy are one of those speechless couples locked in each other's arms that you come upon suddenly standing by a dark hedge. They embarrass you horribly, but you don't embarrass them."

Joanna laughed and said she expected that was it.

We began talking of the anonymous letters and wondered how Nash and the melancholy Graves were getting on.

"It's a week today exactly," said Joanna, "since Mrs. Symmington's suicide. I should think they must have got on to something by now. Fingerprints, or handwriting, or *something*."

I answered her absently. Somewhere behind my conscious mind, a queer uneasiness was growing. It was connected in some way with the phrase that Joanna had used, "a week exactly."

I ought, I dare say, to have put two and two together earlier. Perhaps, unconsciously, my mind was already suspicious.

Anyway the leaven was working now. The uneasiness was growing—coming to a head.

Joanna noticed suddenly that I wasn't listening to her spirited account of a village encounter.

"What's the matter, Jerry?"

I did not answer because my mind was busy piecing things together.

Mrs. Symmington's suicide. . . . She was alone in the house that afternoon. . . . Alone in the house *because the maids were having their day out.* . . . A week ago exactly. . . .

"Jerry, what—"

I interrupted:

"Joanna, maids have days out once a week, don't they?"

"And alternate Sundays," said Joanna. "What on—"

"Never mind Sundays. They go out the same day every week?"

"Yes. That's the usual thing."

Joanna was staring at me curiously. Her mind had not taken the track mine had.

I crossed the room and rang the bell.

Partridge came.

"Tell me," I said, "this Agnes Woddell. She's in service?"

"Yes, sir. At Mrs. Symmington's. At Mr. Symmington's I should say now."

I drew a deep breath. I glanced at the clock. It was half past ten.

"Would she be back now, do you think?"

Partridge was looking disapproving. "Yes, sir. The maids have to be in by ten there. They're old-fashioned."

I said, "I'm going to ring up."

I went out to the hall. Joanna and Partridge followed me. Partridge was clearly furious. Joanna was puzzled. She said as I was trying to get the number, "What are you going to do, Jerry?"

"I'd like to be sure that the girl has come in all right."

Partridge sniffed. Just sniffed, nothing more. But I did not care twopence about Partridge's sniffs.

Elsie Holland answered the telephone from the other end.

"Sorry to ring you up," I said. "This is Jerry Burton speaking. Is— has—your maid Agnes come in?"

It was not until after I had said it that I suddenly felt a bit of a fool. For if the girl had come in and it was all right, how on earth was I going to explain my ringing up and asking. It would have been better if I had let Joanna ask the question, though even that would need a bit of explaining. I foresaw a new trail of gossip started in Lymstock, with myself and the unknown Agnes Woddell as its center.

Elsie Holland sounded, not unnaturally, very much surprised: "Agnes? Oh, she's sure to be in by now."

I felt a fool, but I went on with it: "Do you mind just seeing if she has come in, Miss Holland?"

There is one thing to be said for a nursery governess; she is used to doing things when told. Hers not to reason why! Elsie Holland put down the receiver and went off obediently.

Two minutes later I heard her voice:

"Are you there, Mr. Burton?"

"Yes."

"Agnes isn't in yet, as a matter of fact."

I knew then that my hunch had been right.

I heard a noise of voices vaguely from the other end, then Symington himself spoke:

"Hullo, Burton, what's the matter?"

"Your maid Agnes isn't back yet."

"No. Miss Holland has just been to see. What's the matter? There's not been an accident, has there?"

"Not an *accident*," I said.

"Do you mean you have reason to believe something has happened to the girl?"

I said grimly, "I shouldn't be surprised."

I slept badly that night.

I think that, even then, there were pieces of the puzzle floating about in my mind. I believe that if I had given my mind to it, I could have solved the whole thing then and there. Otherwise why did those fragments tag along so persistently?

How much do we know at any time? Much more, or so I believe, than we know we know! But we cannot break through to that subterranean knowledge. It is there, but we cannot reach it.

I lay on my bed, tossing uneasily, and only vague bits of the puzzle came to torture me.

There was a pattern, if only I could get hold of it. I ought to know who wrote those damned letters. There was a trail somewhere if only I could follow it. . . .

As I dropped off to sleep, words danced irritatingly through my drowsy mind:

"No smoke without fire. No fire without smoke. Smoke. . . . Smoke? Smoke screen. . . . No, that was the war—a war phrase. War. Scrap of paper. . . . Only a scrap of paper. Belgium—Germany. . . ."

I fell asleep. I dreamed that I was taking Mrs. Dane Calthrop, who had turned into a greyhound, for a walk with a collar and lead.

It was the ringing of the telephone that roused me. A persistent ringing.

I sat up in bed, glanced at my watch. It was half past seven. I had not yet been called. The telephone was ringing in the hall downstairs.

I jumped out of bed, pulled on a dressing gown, and raced down. I beat Partridge coming through the back door from the kitchen by a short head. I picked up the receiver.

"Hullo?"

"Oh—" It was a sob of relief. "It's *you!*" Megan's voice. Megan's voice indescribably forlorn and frightened. "Oh, please do come—*do* come. Oh, please do! Will you?"

"I'm coming at once," I said. "Do you hear? *At once.*"

I took the stairs two at a time and burst in on Joanna.

"Look here, Jo, I'm going off to the Symmingtons'."

Joanna lifted a curly blond head from the pillow and rubbed her eyes like a small child.

"Why—what's happened?"

"I don't know. It was the child—Megan. She sounded all in."

"What do you think it is?"

"The girl Agnes, unless I'm very much mistaken."

As I went out of the door, Joanna called after me, "Wait. I'll get up and drive you down."

"No need. I'll drive myself."

"You can't drive the car."

"Yes, I can."

I did, too. It hurt, but not too much. I'd washed, shaved, dressed, got the car out and driven to the Symmingtons' in half an hour. Not bad going.

Megan must have been watching for me. She came out of the house at a run and clutched me. Her poor little face was white and twitching.

"Oh, you've come—you've *come!*"

"Hold up, funnyface," I said. "Yes, I've come. Now what is it?"

She began to shake. I put my arm around her.

"I—I found her."

"You found Agnes? Where?"

The trembling grew.

"Under the stairs. There's a cupboard there. It has fishing rods and golf clubs and things. You know."

I nodded. It was the usual cupboard.

Megan went on:

"She was there—all huddled up—and—and *cold*—horribly cold. She was—she was *dead*, you know!"

I asked curiously, "What made you look there?"

"I—I don't know. You telephoned last night. And we all began wondering where Agnes was. We waited up some time, but she didn't come in, and at last we went to bed. I didn't sleep very well and I got up early. There was only Rose (the cook, you know) about. She was

63

very cross about Agnes not having come back. She said she'd been before somewhere when a girl did a flit like that. I had some milk and bread and butter in the kitchen—and then suddenly Rose came in looking queer and she said that Agnes' outdoor things were still in her room. Her best ones that she goes out in. And I began to wonder if—if she'd ever left the house, and I started looking around, and I opened the cupboard under the stairs and—and she was there . . ."

"Somebody's rung up the police, I suppose?"

"Yes, they're here now. My stepfather rang them up straightaway. And then I—I felt I couldn't bear it, and I rang *you* up. You don't mind?"

"No," I said. "I don't mind."

I looked at her curiously.

"Did anybody give you some brandy, or some coffee, or some tea after—after you found her?"

Megan shook her head.

I cursed the whole Symmington *ménage*. That stuffed shirt, Symmington, thought of nothing but the police. Neither Elsie Holland nor the cook seemed to have thought of the effect on the sensitive child who had made that gruesome discovery.

"Come on, slabface," I said. "We'll go to the kitchen."

We went around the house to the back door and into the kitchen. Rose, a plump pudding-faced woman of forty, was drinking strong tea by the kitchen fire. She greeted us with a flow of talk and her hand to her heart.

She'd come all over queer, she told me, awful the palpitations were! Just think of it, it might have been *her*, it might have been any of them, murdered in their beds they might have been.

"Dish out a good strong cup of that tea for Miss Megan," I said. "She's had a shock, you know. Remember it was she who found the body."

The mere mention of a body nearly sent Rose off again, but I quelled her with a stern eye and she poured out a cup of inky fluid.

"There you are, young woman," I said to Megan. "You drink that down. You haven't got any brandy, I suppose, Rose?"

Rose said rather doubtfully that there was a drop of cooking brandy left over from the Xmas puddings.

"That'll do," I said, and put a dollop of it into Megan's cup. I saw by Rose's eyes that she thought it a good idea.

I told Megan to stay with Rose.

"I can trust you to look after Miss Megan?" I said, and Rose replied in a gratified way, "Oh, yes, sir."

I went through into the house. If I knew Rose and her kind, she would soon find it necessary to keep her strength up with a little food, and that would be good for Megan too. Confound these people, why couldn't they look after the child?

Fuming inwardly I ran into Elsie Holland in the hall. She didn't seem surprised to see me. I suppose that the gruesome excitement of the discovery made one oblivious of who was coming and going. The constable, Bert Rundle, was by the front door.

Elsie Holland gasped out, "Oh, Mr. Burton, isn't it *awful*? Whoever can have done such a dreadful thing?"

"It was murder, then?"

"Oh, yes. She was struck on the back of the head. It's all blood and hair—oh! it's *awful*—and bundled into that cupboard. Who can have done such a wicked thing? And *why*? Poor Agnes, I'm sure she never did anyone any harm."

"No," I said. "Somebody saw to that pretty promptly."

She stared at me. Not, I thought, a quick-witted girl. But she had good nerves. Her color was as usual, slightly heightened by excitement, and I even fancied that in a macabre kind of way, and in spite of a naturally kind heart, she was enjoying the drama.

She said apologetically, "I must go up to the boys. Mr. Symmington is so anxious that they shouldn't get a shock. He wants me to keep them right away."

"Megan found the body, I hear," I said. "I hope somebody is looking after her."

I will say for Elsie Holland that she looked conscience-stricken.

"Oh, dear," she said. "I forgot all about her. I do hope she's all right. I've been so rushed, you know, and the police and everything—but it was remiss of me. Poor girl, she must be feeling bad. I'll go and look for her at once."

I relented.

"She's all right," I said. "Rose is looking after her. You get along to the kids."

She thanked me with a flash of white tombstone teeth and hurried upstairs. After all, the boys were her job, and not Megan—Megan was nobody's job. Elsie was paid to look after Symmington's blinking brats. One could hardly blame her for attending to it.

As she flashed around the corner of the stairs, I caught my breath. For a minute I caught a glimpse of a Winged Victory, deathless and incredibly beautiful, instead of a conscientious nursery governess.

Then a door opened and Superintendent Nash stepped out into the hall with Symmington behind him.

"Oh, Mr. Burton," he said, "I was just going to telephone you. I'm glad you are here."

He didn't ask me—then—why I was here.

He turned his head and said to Symmington, "I'll use this room if I may."

It was a small morning room with a window on the front of the house.

"Certainly, certainly."

Symmington's poise was pretty good, but he looked desperately tired. Superintendent Nash said gently:

"I should have some breakfast if I were you, Mr. Symmington. You and Miss Holland and Miss Megan will feel much better after coffee and eggs and bacon. Murder is a nasty business on an empty stomach."

He spoke in a comfortable family-doctor kind of way.

Symmington gave a faint attempt at a smile and said, "Thank you, Superintendent, I'll take your advice."

I followed Nash into the little morning room and he shut the door.

He said then, "You've got here very quickly? How did you hear?"

I told him that Megan had rung me up. I felt well-disposed toward Superintendent Nash. He, at any rate, had not forgotten that Megan, too, would be in need of breakfast.

"I hear that you telephoned last night, Mr. Burton, asking about this girl? Why was that?"

I suppose it did seem odd. I told him about Agnes' telephone call to Partridge and her nonappearance. He said, "Yes, I see. . . ."

He said it slowly and reflectively, rubbing his chin.

Then he sighed.

"Well," he said. "It's murder now, right enough. Direct physical action. The question is, what did the girl know? Did she say anything to this Partridge? Anything definite?"

"I don't think so. But you can ask her."

"Yes, I shall come up and see her when I've finished here."

"What happened exactly?" I asked. "Or don't you know yet?"

"Near enough. It was the maids' day out—"

"Both of them?"

"Yes, it seems that there used to be two sisters here who liked to go out together, so Mrs. Symmington arranged it that way. Then when these two came, she kept to the same arrangement. They used to have cold supper laid out in the dining room, and Miss Holland used to get tea."

"I see."

"It's pretty clear up to a point. The cook, Rose, comes from Nether Mickford, and in order to get there on her day out she has to catch the half-past-two bus. So Agnes has to finish clearing up lunch always. Rose used to wash up the supper things in the evenings to even things up.

"That's what happened today. Rose went off to catch the bus at two-twenty-five, Symmington left for his office at twenty-five to three. Elsie Holland and the children went out at a quarter to three. Megan Hunter went out on her bicycle about five minutes later. Agnes would then be alone in the house. As far as I can make out, she normally left the house between three o'clock and half past three."

"The house being then left empty?"

"Oh, they don't worry about that down here. There's not much locking up done in these parts. As I say, at ten minutes to three Agnes was alone in the house. That she never left it is clear, for she was in her cap and apron still when we found her body."

"I suppose you can tell roughly the time of death?"

"Doctor Griffith won't commit himself. Between two o'clock and four-thirty is his official medical verdict."

"How was she killed?"

"She was first stunned by a blow on the back of the head. Afterward an ordinary kitchen skewer, sharpened to a fine point, was thrust into the base of the skull, causing instantaneous death."

I lit a cigarette. It was not a nice picture.

"Pretty cold-blooded," I said.

"Oh, yes, yes, that was indicated."

I inhaled deeply.

"Who did it?" I said. "And why?"

"I don't suppose," said Nash slowly, "that we shall ever know exactly why. But we can guess."

"She knew something?"

"She knew something."

"She didn't give anyone here a hint?"

"As far as I can make out, no. She's been upset, so the cook says, ever since Mrs. Symmington's death, and according to this Rose, she's been getting more and more worried, and kept saying she didn't know what she ought to do."

He gave a short exasperated sigh.

"It's always the way. They won't come to us. They've got that deep-seated prejudice against 'being mixed up with the police.' If she'd come along and told us what was worrying her, she'd be alive today."

"Didn't she give the other women *any* hint?"

"No, or so Rose says, and I'm inclined to believe her. For if she had, Rose would have blurted it out at once with a good many fancy embellishments of her own."

"It's maddening," I said, "not to know."

"We can still guess, Mr. Burton. To begin with, it can't be anything very definite. It's got to be the sort of thing that you think over, and as you think it over, your uneasiness grows. You see what I mean?"

"Yes."

"Actually, I think I know what it was."

I looked at him with respect.

"That's good work, Superintendent."

"Well, you see, Mr. Burton, I know something that you don't. On the afternoon that Mrs. Symmington committed suicide both maids were supposed to be out. It was their day out. But actually Agnes came back to the house."

"You know that?"

"Yes. Agnes has a boy friend—young Rendell from the fish shop. Wednesday is early closing and he comes along to meet Agnes and they go for a walk, or to the pictures if it's wet. That Wednesday they had a row practically as soon as they met. Our letter writer had been active, suggesting that Agnes had other fish to fry, and young Fred Rendell was all worked up. They quarreled violently and Agnes bolted back home and said she wasn't coming out unless Fred said he was sorry."

"Well?"

"Well, Mr. Burton, the kitchen faces the back of the house, but the pantry looks out where we are looking now. There's only one entrance gate. You come through it and either up to the front door, or else along the path at the side of the house to the back door."

He paused.

"Now I'll tell you something: That letter that came to Mrs. Symmington that afternoon *didn't come by post.* It had a used stamp affixed to it, and the postmark faked quite convincingly in lamp black, so that it would seem to have been delivered by the postman with the afternoon letters. But actually *it had not been through the post.* You see what that means?"

"It means," I said slowly, "that it was left *by hand,* pushed through the letter box some time before the afternoon post was delivered, so that it should be among the other letters."

"Exactly. The afternoon post comes around about a quarter to four. My theory is this: The girl was in the pantry looking through the window (it's masked by shrubs but you can see through them quite well) watching out for her young man to turn up and apologize."

I said, *"And she saw whoever it was delivered that note?"*

"That's my guess, Mr. Burton. I may be wrong, of course."

"I don't think you are. . . . It's simple—and convincing—and it means that Agnes knew *who the anonymous letter writer was."*

5

"Yes," Nash said. "Agnes knew who wrote those letters."

"But then why didn't she—?" I paused, frowning.

Nash said quickly, "As I see it, the girl *didn't realize what she had seen.* Not at first. Somebody had left a letter at the house, yes—but that somebody was nobody she would dream of connecting with the anonymous letters. It was somebody, from that point of view, quite above suspicion.

"But the more she thought about it, the more uneasy she grew. Ought she, perhaps, to tell someone about it? In her perplexity she thinks of Miss Barton's Partridge who, I gather, is a somewhat dominant personality and whose judgment Agnes would accept unhesitatingly. She decides to ask Partridge what she ought to do."

"Yes," I said thoughtfully. "It fits well enough. And somehow or other, Poison Pen found out. How did she find out, Superintendent?"

"You're not used to living in the country, Mr. Burton. It's a kind of miracle how things get around. First of all there's the telephone call. Who overheard it on your end?"

I reflected.

"I took the call originally. I called up to Partridge."

"Mentioning the girl's name?"

"Yes—yes, I did."

"Anyone overhear you?"

"My sister or Miss Griffith might have done so."

"Ah, Miss Griffith. What was she doing up there?"

I explained.

70

"Was she going back to the village?"

"She was going to Mr. Pye first."

Superintendent Nash sighed. "That's two ways it could have gone all over the place."

I was incredulous. "Do you mean that either Miss Griffith or Mr. Pye would bother to repeat a meaningless little bit of information like that?"

"Anything's news in a place like this. You'd be surprised. If the dressmaker's mother has got a bad corn everybody hears about it! And then there is this end. Miss Holland, Rose—they could have heard what Agnes said. And there's Fred Rendell. It may have got around through him that Agnes went back to the house that afternoon."

I gave a slight shiver. I was looking out of the window. In front of me was a neat square of grass and a path and the low prim gate.

Someone had opened the gate, had walked very correctly and quietly up to the house, and had pushed a letter through the letter box. I saw, hazily, in my mind's eye, that vague woman's shape. The face was blank—but it must be a face that I knew . . .

Superintendent Nash was saying:

"All the same, this narrows things down. That's always the way we get 'em in the end. Steady, patient elimination. There aren't so very many people it could be now."

"You mean—?"

"It knocks out any women clerks who were at their work all the afternoon. It knocks out the schoolmistress. She was teaching. And the district nurse. I know where she was yesterday. Not that I ever thought it was any of *them*, but now we're *sure*. You see, Mr. Burton, we've got two definite times now on which to concentrate—yesterday afternoon, and the week before. On the day of Mrs. Symmington's death from, say, a quarter past three (the earliest possible time at which Agnes could have been back in the house after her quarrel) and four o'clock when the post must have come (but I can get that fixed more accurately with the postman). And yesterday from ten minutes to three (when Miss Megan Hunter left the house) until half past three or more probably a quarter past three as Agnes hadn't begun to change."

"What do you think happened yesterday?"

Nash made a grimace.

"What do I think? I think a certain lady walked up to the front door and rang the bell, quite calm and smiling, the afternoon caller. . . . Maybe she asked for Miss Holland, or for Miss Megan, or perhaps she had brought a parcel. Anyway Agnes turns around to get a salver for cards, or to take the parcel in, and our ladylike caller bats her on the back of her unsuspecting head."

"What with?"

Nash said, "The ladies around here usually carry large sizes in handbags. No saying what mightn't be inside it."

"And then stabs her through the back of the neck and bundles her into the cupboard? Wouldn't that be a hefty job for a woman?"

Superintendent Nash looked at me with rather a queer expression. "The woman we're after isn't normal—not by a long way—and that type of mental instability goes with surprising strength. Agnes wasn't a big girl!" He paused and then asked, "What made Miss Megan Hunter think of looking in that cupboard?"

"Sheer instinct," I said.

Then I asked, "Why drag her out of the way? What was the point?"

"The longer it was before the body was found, the more difficult it would be to fix the time of death accurately. If Miss Holland, for instance, fell over the body as soon as she came in, a doctor might be able to fix it within ten minutes or so—which might be awkward for our lady friend."

I said, frowning, "But if Agnes was suspicious of this person—"

Nash interrupted me: "She wasn't. Not to this pitch. She just thought it 'queer' shall we say? She was a slow-witted girl, I imagine, and she was only vaguely suspicious with a feeling that something was wrong. She certainly didn't suspect that she was up against a woman who would do murder."

"Did you suspect that?" I asked.

Nash shook his head. He said, with feeling:

"I ought to have known. That suicide business, you see, frightened Poison Pen. She got the wind up. Fear, Mr. Burton, is an incalculable thing."

Yes, fear. That was the thing we ought to have foreseen. Fear—in a lunatic brain. . . .

"You see," said Superintendent Nash, and somehow his words made the whole thing seem absolutely horrible. "We're up against someone who's respected and thought highly of—someone, in fact, of good social position!"

Presently Nash said that he was going to interview Rose once more. I asked him, rather diffidently, if I might come too. Rather to my surprise he assented cordially.

"I'm very glad of your co-operation, Mr. Burton, if I may say so."

"That sounds suspicious," I said. "In books when a detective welcomes someone's assistance, that someone is usually the murderer."

Nash laughed shortly. He said, "You're hardly the type to write anonymous letters, Mr. Burton." He added: "Frankly, you can be useful to us."

"I'm glad, but I don't see how."

"You're a stranger down here, that's why. You've got no preconceived ideas about the people here. But at the same time, you've got the opportunity of getting to know things in what I may call a social way."

"The murderer is a person of good social position," I murmured.

"Exactly."

"I'm to be the spy within the gates?"

"Have you any objection?"

I thought it over. "No," I said, "frankly I haven't. If there's a dangerous lunatic about, driving inoffensive women to suicide and hitting miserable little maidservants on the head, then I'm not averse to doing a bit of dirty work to put that lunatic under restraint."

"That's sensible of you, sir. And let me tell you, the person we're after is dangerous. She's about as dangerous as a rattlesnake and a cobra and a black mamba rolled into one."

I gave a slight shiver. I said, "In fact, we've got to make haste?"

"That's right. Don't think we're inactive in the force. We're not. We're working on several different lines."

He said it grimly.

I had a vision of a fine, far-flung spider's web . . .

Nash wanted to hear Rose's story again, so he explained to me, because she had already told him two different versions, and the more versions he got from her, the more likely it was that a few grains of truth might be incorporated.

We found Rose washing up breakfast, and she stopped at once and rolled her eyes and clutched her heart and explained again how she'd been coming over queer all the morning.

Nash was patient with her but firm. He'd been soothing the first time, so he told me, and peremptory the second, and he now employed a mixture of the two.

Rose enlarged pleasurably on the details of the past week, of how Agnes had gone about in deadly fear, and had shivered and said "Don't ask me" when Rose had urged her to say what was the matter. "It would be death if she told me, that's what she said," finished Rose, rolling her eyes happily.

"Had Agnes given no hint of what was troubling her?"

No, except that she went in fear of her life.

Superintendent Nash sighed and abandoned the theme, contenting himself with extracting an exact account of Rose's own activities the preceding afternoon.

This, put baldly, was that Rose had caught the 2:30 bus and had spent the afternoon and evening with her family, returning by the 8:40 bus from Nether Mickford. The recital was complicated by the extraordinary presentiments of evil that Rose had had all the afternoon and how her sister had commented on it and how she hadn't been able to touch a morsel of seed cake.

From the kitchen we went in search of Elsie Holland, who was superintending the children's lessons.

As always, Elsie Holland was competent and obliging. She rose and said, "Now, Colin, you and Brian will do these three sums and have the answers ready for me when I come back."

She then led us into the night nursery.

"Will this do? I thought it would be better not to talk before the children."

"Thank you, Miss Holland. Just tell me, once more, are you *quite* sure that Agnes never mentioned to you being worried over anything—since Mrs. Symmington's death, I mean?"

"No, she never said anything. She was a very quiet girl, you know, and didn't talk much."

"A change from the other one, then!"

"Yes, Rose talks much too much. I have to tell her not to be impertinent sometimes."

"Now, will you tell me exactly what happened yesterday afternoon? Everything you can remember."

"Well, we had lunch as usual. One o'clock, and we hurried just a little. I don't let the boys dawdle. Let me see. Mr. Symmington went back to the office, and I helped Agnes by laying the table for supper—the boys ran out in the garden till I was ready to take them."

"Where did you go?"

"Toward Combe Acre, by the field path—the boys wanted to fish. I forgot their bait and had to go back for it."

"What time was that?"

"Let me see, we started about twenty to three—or just after. Megan was coming but changed her mind. She was going out on her bicycle. She's got quite a craze for bicycling."

"I mean what time was it when you went back for the bait? Did you go into the house?"

"No. I'd left it in the conservatory at the back. I don't know what time it was then—about ten minutes to three, perhaps."

"Did you see Megan or Agnes?"

"Megan must have started, I think. No, I didn't see Agnes. I didn't see anyone."

"And after that you went fishing?"

"Yes, we went along by the stream. We didn't catch anything. We hardly ever do, but the boys enjoy it. Brian got rather wet. I had to change his things when we got in."

"You attend to tea on Wednesdays?"

"Yes. It's all ready in the drawing room for Mr. Symmington. I just make the tea when he comes in. The children and I have ours in the schoolroom—and Megan, of course. I have my own tea things and everything in the cupboard up there."

"What time did you get in?"

"At ten minutes to five. I took the boys up and started to lay tea. Then when Mr. Symmington came in at five I went down to make his but he said he would have it with us in the schoolroom. The boys were so pleased. We played Animal Grab afterward. It seems so awful to think of now—with that poor girl in the cupboard all the time."

"Would anybody go to that cupboard normally?"

"Oh, no, it's only used for keeping junk. The hats and coats hang in the little cloakroom to the right of the front door as you come in. No one might have gone to the other cupboard for months."

"I see. And you noticed nothing unusual, nothing abnormal at all when you came back?"

The blue eyes opened very wide. "Oh, no, Superintendent nothing at all. Everything was just the same as usual. That's what was so awful about it."

"And the week before?"

"You mean the day Mrs. Symmington—"

"Yes."

"Oh, that was terrible—terrible!"

"Yes, yes, I know. You were out all that afternoon also?"

"Oh, yes, I always take the boys out in the afternoon—if it's fine enough. We do lessons in the morning. We went up on the moor, I remember—quite a long way. I was afraid I was late back because as I turned in at the gate I saw Mr. Symmington coming from his office at the other end of the road, and I hadn't even put the kettle on, but it was just ten minutes to five."

"You didn't go up to Mrs. Symmington?"

"Oh, no. I never did. She always rested after lunch. She had attacks of neuralgia—and they used to come on after meals. Dr. Griffith had given her some powders to take. She used to lie down and try to sleep."

Nash said in a casual voice, "So no one would take her up the post?"

"The afternoon post? No, I'd look in the letter box and put the letters on the hall table when I came in. But very often Mrs. Symmington used to come down and get it herself. She didn't sleep all the afternoon. She was usually up again by four."

"You didn't think anything was wrong because she wasn't up that afternoon?"

"Oh, no, I never dreamed of such a thing. Mr. Symmington was hanging up his coat in the hall and I said, 'Tea's not quite ready, but the kettle's nearly boiling,' and he nodded and called out, 'Mona, Mona!'— and then as Mrs. Symmington didn't answer he went upstairs to her bedroom, and it must have been the most terrible shock to him. He called me and I came, and he said, 'Keep the children away,' and then he phoned Dr. Griffith and we forgot all about the kettle and it burned the bottom out! Oh, dear, it *was* dreadful, and she'd been so happy and cheerful at lunch."

Nash said abruptly, "What is your own opinion of that letter she received, Miss Holland?"

Elsie Holland said indignantly, "Oh, I think it was wicked— wicked!"

"Yes, yes, I don't mean that. Did you think it was true?"

Elsie Holland said firmly:

"No, indeed I don't. Mrs. Symmington was very sensitive—very sensitive indeed. She had to take all sorts of things for her nerves. And she was very—well, *particular*." Elsie flushed. "Anything of that sort—*nasty*, I mean—would have given her a great shock."

Nash was silent for a moment, then he asked: "Have you had any of these letters, Miss Holland?"

"No. No, I haven't had any."

"Are you sure? Please"—he lifted a hand—"don't answer in a

hurry. They're not pleasant things to get, I know. And sometimes people don't like to admit they've had them. But it's very important in this case that we should know. We're quite aware that the statements in them are just a tissue of lies, so you needn't feel embarrassed."

"But I haven't, Superintendent. Really I haven't. Not anything of the kind."

She was indignant, almost tearful, and her denials seemed genuine enough.

When she went back to the children, Nash stood looking out of the window.

"Well," he said, "that's that! She says she hasn't received any of these letters. And she sounds as though she's speaking the truth."

"She did certainly. I'm sure she was."

"H'm," said Nash. "Then what I want to know is, why the devil hasn't she?"

He went on rather impatiently, as I stared at him:

"She's a pretty girl, isn't she?"

"Rather more than pretty."

"Exactly. As a matter of fact, she's uncommonly good-looking. And she's young. In fact she's just the meat an anonymous letter writer would like. Then why has she been left out?"

I shook my head.

"It's interesting, you know. I must mention it to Graves. He asked if we could tell him definitely of anyone who hadn't had one."

"She's the second person," I said. "There's Emily Barton, remember."

Nash gave a faint chuckle. "You shouldn't believe everything you're told, Mr. Burton. Miss Barton had one all right—more than one."

"How do you know?"

"The devoted dragon she's lodging with told me—her late parlormaid or cook. Florence Elford. Very indignant she was about it. Would like to have the writer's blood."

"Why did Miss Emily say she hadn't had any?"

"Delicacy. Their language isn't nice. Little Miss Barton has spent her life avoiding the coarse and unrefined."

"What did the letter say?"

"The usual. Quite ludicrous in her case. And incidentally insinuated that she poisoned off her old mother and most of her sisters!"

I said incredulously, "Do you mean to say there's really this dangerous lunatic going about and we can't spot her right away?"

"We'll spot her," said Nash, and his voice was grim. "She'll write just one letter too many."

"But, my goodness, man, she won't go on writing these things—not now."

He looked at me.

"Oh, yes, she will. You see, *she can't stop now.* It's a morbid craving. The letters will go on, make no mistake about that."

I went and found Megan before leaving the house. She was in the garden and seemed almost back to her usual self. She greeted me quite cheerfully.

I suggested that she should come back to us again for a while, but after a momentary hesitation she shook her head.

"It's nice of you—but I think I'll stay here. After all, it is—well, I suppose it's my home. And I dare say I can help with the boys a bit."

"Well," I said, "it's as you like."

"Then I think I'll stay. I could—I could—"

"Yes" I prompted.

"If—if anything awful happened, I could ring you up, couldn't I, and you'd come."

I was touched. "Of course. But what awful thing do you think might happen?"

"Oh, I don't know." She looked vague. "Things seem rather like that just now, don't they?"

"Stop it!" I said. "And don't go nosing out any more bodies! It's not good for you."

She gave me a brief flash of a smile. "No, it isn't. It made me feel awfully sick."

I didn't much like leaving her there, but after all, as she had said, it was her home. And I fancied now that Elsie Holland would feel more responsible for her.

Nash and I went up together to Little Furze. While I gave Joanna an account of the morning's doings, Nash tackled Partridge. He rejoined us, looking discouraged.

"Not much help there. According to this woman, the girl only said she was worried about something and didn't know what to do and that she'd like Miss Partridge's advice."

"Did Partridge mention the fact to anyone?" asked Joanna.

Nash nodded, looking grim.

"Yes, she told Mrs. Emory—your daily woman—on the lines, as

far as I can gather, that there were *some* young women who were willing to take advice from their elders and didn't think they could settle
everything for themselves offhand! Agnes mightn't be very bright,
but she was a nice respectful girl and knew her manners."

"Partridge preening herself, in fact," murmured Joanna. "And
Mrs. Emory could have passed it around the town?"

"That's right, Miss Burton."

"There's one thing rather surprises me," I said. "Why were my
sister and I included? We were strangers down here—nobody could
have had a grudge against us."

"You're failing to allow for the mentality of a Poison Pen—all is
grist that comes to their mill. Their grudge, you might say, is against
humanity."

"I suppose," said Joanna thoughtfully, "that that is what Mrs.
Dane Calthrop meant."

Nash looked at her inquiringly, but she did not enlighten him.

The superintendent said:

"I don't know if you happened to look closely at the envelope of
the letter you got, Miss Burton. If so, you may have noticed that it was
actually addressed to Miss Barton, and the *a* altered to a *u* afterward."

That remark, properly interpreted, ought to have given us a clue
to the whole business. As it was, none of us saw any significance in it.

Nash went off, and I was left with Joanna. She actually said: "You
don't think that letter can really have been meant for Miss Emily, do
you?"

"It would hardly have begun 'You painted trollop,' " I pointed,
and Joanna agreed.

Then she suggested that I should go down to the town. "You ought
to hear what everyone is saying. It will be *the* topic this morning!"

I suggested that she should come too, but rather to my surprise
Joanna refused. She said she was going to mess about in the garden.

I paused in the doorway and said, lowering my voice, "I suppose
Partridge is all right."

"Partridge!"

The amazement in Joanna's voice made me feel ashamed of my
idea.

I said apologetically, "I just wondered. She's rather 'queer' in some
ways—a grim spinster—the sort of person who might have religious
mania."

"This isn't religious mania—or so you told me Graves said."

"Well, sex mania. They're very closely tied up together, I understand. She's repressed and respectable, and has been shut up here with a lot of elderly women for years."

"What put the idea into your head?"

"Well," I said slowly, "we've only her word for it, haven't we, as to what the girl Agnes said to her? Suppose Agnes asked Partridge to tell her why Partridge came and left a note that day—and Partridge said she'd call around that afternoon and explain."

"And then camouflaged it by coming to us and asking if the girl could come here?"

"Yes."

"But she never went out that afternoon."

"You don't know that. We were out ourselves, remember."

"Yes, that's true. It's possible, I suppose." Joanna turned it over in her mind. "But I don't think so, all the same. I don't think Partridge has the mentality to cover her tracks over the letters. To wipe off fingerprints, and all that. It isn't only cunning you want—it's knowledge. I don't think she's got that. I suppose—" Joanna hesitated, then said slowly, "they are sure it is a woman, aren't they?"

"You don't think it's a man?" I exclaimed incredulously.

"Not—not an ordinary man—but a certain kind of man. I'm thinking, really, of Mr. Pye."

"So Pye is your selection?"

"Don't you feel yourself that he's a possibility? He's the sort of person who might be lonely—and unhappy—and spiteful. Everyone, you see, rather laughs at him. Can't you see him secretly hating all the normal happy people, and taking a queer, perverse, artistic pleasure in what he was doing?"

"Graves said a middle-aged spinster."

"Mr. Pye," said Joanna, "*is* a middle-aged spinster."

"A misfit," I said slowly.

"Very much so. He's rich, but money doesn't help. And I do feel he might be unbalanced. He is, really, rather a *frightening* little man."

"He got a letter himself, remember."

"We don't know that," Joanna pointed out. "We only thought so. And anyway, he might have been putting on an act."

"For our benefit?"

"Yes. He's clever enough to think of that—and not to overdo it."

"He must be a first-class actor."

"But of course, Jerry, whoever is doing this *must* be a first-class actor. That's partly where the pleasure comes in."

"For heaven's sake, Joanna, don't speak so understandingly! You make me feel that you—that you understand the mentality."

"I think I do. I can—just—get into the mood. If I wasn't Joanna Burton, if I wasn't young and reasonably attractive and able to have a good time, if I was—how shall I put it?—behind bars, watching other people enjoy life, would a black, evil tide rise in me, making me want to hurt, to torture—even to destroy?"

"Joanna!" I took her by the shoulders and shook her. She gave a little sigh and shiver, and smiled at me.

"I frightened you, didn't I, Jerry? But I have a feeling that that's the right way to solve this problem. You've got to be the person, knowing how they feel and what makes them act, and then—and then perhaps you'll know what they're going to do next."

"Oh, gee!" I said. "And I came down here to be a vegetable and get interested in all the dear little local scandals. Dear little local scandals! Libel, vilification, obscene language and murder!"

Joanna was quite right. The High Street was full of interesting groups. I was determined to get everyone's reactions in turn.

I met Griffith first. He looked terribly ill and tired. So much so that I wondered. Murder is not, certainly, all in the day's work to a doctor, but his profession does equip him to face most things including suffering, the ugly side of human nature, and the fact of death.

"You look all in," I said.

"Do I?" He was vague. "Oh! I've had some worrying cases lately."

"Including our lunatic at large?"

"That, certainly." He looked away from me across the street. I saw a fine nerve twitching in his eyelid.

"You've no suspicions as to—*who*?"

"No. No. I wish I had."

He asked abruptly after Joanna and said, hesitatingly, that he had some photographs she'd wanted to see.

I offered to take them to her.

"Oh, it doesn't matter. I shall be passing that way actually later in the morning."

I began to be afraid that Griffith had got it badly. Curse Joanna! Griffith was too good a man to be dangled as a scalp.

I let him go, for I saw his sister coming and I wanted, for once, to talk to her.

Aimée Griffith began, as it were, in the middle of conversation. "Absolutely shocking!" she boomed. "I hear you were there—quite early?"

There was a question in the words, and her eyes glinted as she stressed the word "early." I wasn't going to tell her that Megan had rung me up. I said instead, "You see, I was a bit uneasy last night. The girl was due to tea at our house and didn't turn up."

"And so you feared the worst? Very smart of you!"

"Yes," I said. "I'm quite the human bloodhound."

"It's the first murder we've ever had in Lymstock. Excitement is terrific. Hope the police can handle it all right."

"I shouldn't worry," I said. "They're an efficient body of men."

"Can't even remember what the girl looked like, although I suppose she's opened the door to me dozens of times. Quiet, insignificant little thing. Knocked on the head and then stabbed through the back of the neck, so Owen tells me. Looks like a boy friend to me. What do you think?"

"That's your solution?"

"Seems the most likely one. Had a quarrel, I expect. They're very inbred around here—bad heredity, a lot of them." She paused, and then went on: "I hear Megan Hunter found the body? Must have given her a bit of a shock."

I said shortly, "It did."

"Not too good for her, I should imagine. In my opinion she's not too strong in the head—and a thing like this might send her completely off her onion."

I took a sudden resolution. I had to know something.

"Tell me, Miss Griffith, was it you who persuaded Megan to return home yesterday?"

"Well, I wouldn't say exactly persuaded."

I stuck to my guns. "But you did say something to her?"

Aimée Griffith planted her feet firmly and stared me in the eyes. She was, just slightly, on the defensive. She said:

"It's no good—that young woman shirking her responsibility. She's young and she doesn't know how tongues wag, so I felt it my duty to give her a hint."

"Tongues—?" I broke off because I was too angry to go on.

Aimée Griffith continued with that maddeningly complacent confidence in herself which was her chief characteristic:

"Oh, I dare say you don't hear all the gossip that goes around. I do! I know what people are saying. Mind you, I don't for a minute think there's anything in it—not for a minute! But you know what people are—if they can say something ill-natured, they do! And it's rather hard lines on the girl when she's got her living to earn."

"Her living to earn?" I said, puzzled.

Aimée went on:

"It's a difficult position for her, naturally. And I think she did the right thing. I mean, she couldn't go off at a moment's notice and leave the children with no one to look after them. She's been splendid—absolutely splendid. I say so to everybody! But there it is, it's an invidious position, and people will talk."

"Who are you talking about?" I asked.

"Elsie Holland, of course," said Aimée Griffith impatiently. "In my opinion, she's a thoroughly nice girl and has only been doing her duty."

"And what are people saying?"

Aimée Griffith laughed. It was, I thought, rather an unpleasant laugh.

"They're saying that she's already considering the possibility of becoming Mrs. Symmington No. 2—that she's all out to console the widower and make herself indispensable."

"But," I said, shocked, "Mrs. Symmington's only been dead a week!"

Aimée Griffith shrugged her shoulders.

"Of course. It's absurd! But you know what people are! The Holland girl is young and she's good-looking—that's enough. And mind you, being a nursery governess isn't much of a prospect for a girl. I wouldn't blame her if she wanted a settled home and a husband and was playing her cards accordingly.

"Of course," she went on. "Poor Dick Symmington hasn't the least idea of all this! He's still completely knocked out by Mona Symmington's death. But you know what men are! If the girl is always there, making him comfortable, looking after him, being obviously devoted to the children—well, he gets to be dependent on her."

I said quietly, "So you do think that Elsie Holland is a designing hussy?"

Aimée Griffith flushed.

"Not at all. I'm sorry for the girl—with people saying nasty things! That's why I more or less told Megan that she ought to go home. It looks better than having Dick Symmington and the girl alone in the house."

I began to understand things.

Aimée Griffith gave her jolly laugh. "You're shocked, Mr. Burton, at hearing what our gossiping little town thinks. I can tell you this— they always think the worst!"

She laughed and nodded and strode away.

I came upon Mr. Pye by the church. He was talking to Emily Barton, who looked pink and excited.

Mr. Pye greeted me with every evidence of delight:

"Ah, Burton, good morning, good morning! How is your charming sister?"

I told him that Joanna was well.

"But not joining our village Parliament? We are all agog over the news. Murder! Real Sunday newspaper murder in our midst! Not the most interesting of crimes, I fear. Somewhat sordid. The brutal murder of a little serving maid. No finer points about the crime, but still undeniably news."

Miss Barton said tremulously, "It is shocking—quite shocking."

Mr. Pye turned on her: "But you enjoy it, dear lady, you enjoy it. Confess it now. You disapprove, you deplore, but there *is* the thrill. I insist, there *is* the thrill!"

"Such a nice girl," said Emily Barton. "She came to me from St. Clotilde's Home. Quite a raw girl. But most teachable. She turned into such a nice little maid. Partridge was very pleased with her."

I said quickly, "She was coming to tea with Partridge yesterday afternoon." I turned to Pye: "I expect Aimée Griffith told you."

My tone was quite casual. Pye responded apparently quite unsuspiciously:

"She did mention it, yes. She said, I remember, that it was something quite new for servants to ring up on their employers' telephones."

"Partridge would never dream of doing such a thing," said Miss Emily, "and I am really surprised at Agnes doing so."

"You are behind the times, dear lady," said Mr. Pye. "My two terrors use the telephone constantly and smoked all over the house until I objected. But one daren't say too much. Prescott is a divine cook, though temperamental, and Mrs. Prescott is an admirable house-parlor maid."

"Yes, indeed, we all think you're very lucky."

I intervened, since I did not want the conversation to become purely domestic.

"The news of the murder has got around very quickly," I said.

"Of course, of course," said Mr. Pye. "The butcher, the baker, the candlestick maker. Enter Rumor, painted full of tongues! Lymstock, alas! is going to the dogs. Anonymous letters, murders, any amount of criminal tendencies."

Emily Barton said nervously, "They don't think—there's no idea—that—that the two are connected."

Mr. Pye pounced on the idea. "An interesting speculation. The girl knew something, therefore she was murdered. Yes, yes, most promising. How clever of you to think of it."

"I—I can't bear it."

Emily Barton spoke abruptly and turned away, walking very fast. Pye looked after her. His cherubic face was pursed up quizzically. He turned back to me and shook his head gently.

"A sensitive soul. A charming creature, don't you think? Absolutely a period piece. She's not, you know, of her own generation, she's of the generation before that. The mother must have been a woman of very strong character. She kept the family time ticking at about 1870, I should say. The whole family preserved under a glass case. I do like to come across that sort of thing."

I did not want to talk about period pieces.

"What do you really think about all this business?" I asked.

"Meaning by that?"

"Anonymous letters, murder . . ."

"Our local crime wave? What do you?"

"I asked you first," I said pleasantly.

Mr. Pye said gently:

"I'm a student, you know, of abnormalities. They interest me. Such apparently unlikely people do the most fantastic things. Take the case of Lizzie Borden. There's not really a reasonable explanation of that. In this case, my advice to the police would be—study *character*. Leave your fingerprints and your measuring of handwriting and your microscopes. Notice instead what people do with their hands, and their little tricks of manner, and the way they eat their food, and if they laugh sometimes for no apparent reason."

I raised my eyebrows.

"Mad?" I said.

"Quite, quite mad," said Mr. Pye, and added, "but you'd never know it!"

"Who?"

His eyes met mine. He smiled.

"No, no, Burton, that would be slander. We can't add slander to all the rest of it."

He fairly skipped off down the street.

6

As I stood staring after Mr. Pye the church door opened and the Rev. Caleb Dane Calthrop came out.

He smiled vaguely at me. "Good—good morning, Mr.—er—er—"

I helped him. "Burton."

"Of course, of course, you mustn't think I don't remember you. Your name had just slipped my memory for the moment. A beautiful day."

"Yes," I said rather shortly.

He peered at me.

"But something—something, ah, yes, that poor unfortunate child who was in service at the Symmingtons'. I find it hard to believe, I must confess, that we have a murderer in our midst, Mr.—er—Burton."

"It does seem a bit fantastic," I said.

"Something else has just reached my ears." He leaned toward me. "I learn that there have been anonymous letters going about. Have you heard any rumor of such things?"

"I have heard," I said.

"Cowardly and dastardly things." He paused and quoted an enormous stream of Latin. "Those words of Horace are very applicable, don't you think?" he said.

"Absolutely," I said.

There didn't seem anyone more I could profitably talk to, so I went home, dropping in for some tobacco and for a bottle of sherry, so as to get some of the humbler opinions on the crime.

"A narsty tramp," seemed to be the verdict.

"Come to the door, they do, and whine and ask for money, and then if it's a girl alone in the house, they turn nasty. My sister Dora, over to Combe Acre, she had a narsty experience one day—drunk, he was, and selling those little printed poems. . . ."

The story went on, ending with the intrepid Dora courageously banging the door in the man's face and taking refuge and barricading herself in some vague retreat, which I gathered from the delicacy in mentioning it, must be the lavatory. "And there she stayed till her lady came home!"

I reached Little Furze just a few minutes before lunch time. Joanna was standing in the drawing-room window doing nothing at all and looking as though her thoughts were miles away.

"What have you been doing with yourself?" I asked.

"Oh, I don't know. Nothing particular."

I went out on the veranda. Two chairs were drawn up to an iron table and there were two empty sherry glasses. On another chair was an object at which I looked with bewilderment for some time.

"What on earth is this?"

"Oh," said Joanna, "I think it's a photograph of a diseased spleen or something. Dr. Griffith seemed to think I'd be interested to see it."

I looked at the photograph with some interest. Every man has his own ways of courting the female sex. I should not, myself, choose to do it with photographs of spleens, diseased or otherwise. Still no doubt Joanna had asked for it!

"It looks most unpleasant," I said.

Joanna said it did, rather.

"How was Griffith?" I asked.

"He looked tired and very unhappy. I think he's got something on his mind."

"A spleen that won't yield to treatment?"

"Don't be silly. I mean something real."

"I should say the man's got *you* on his mind. I wish you'd lay off him, Joanna."

"Oh, do shut up. I haven't done anything."

"Women always say that."

Joanna whirled angrily out of the room.

The diseased spleen was beginning to curl up in the sun. I took it by one corner and brought it in to the drawing room. I had no affection for it myself, but I presumed it was one of Griffith's treasures.

I stooped down and pulled out a heavy book from the bottom shelf of the bookcase in order to press the photograph flat between its leaves. It was a ponderous volume of somebody's sermons.

The book came open in my hand in rather a surprising way. In another minute I saw why. *From the middle of it a number of pages had been neatly cut out.*

I stood staring at it. I looked at the title page. It had been published in 1840.

There could be no doubt at all. I was looking at the book from the pages of which the anonymous letters had been put together. Who had cut them out?

Well, to begin with, it could be Emily Barton herself. She was, perhaps, the obvious person to think of. Or it could have been Partridge.

But there were other possibilities. The pages could have been cut out by anyone who had been alone in this room, any visitor, for instance, who had sat there waiting for Miss Emily. Or even anyone who called on business.

No, that wasn't so likely. I had noticed that when, one day, a clerk from the bank had come to see me, Partridge had shown him into the little study at the back of the house. That was clearly the house routine.

A visitor, then? Someone "of good social position." Mr. Pye? Aimée Griffith? Mrs. Dane Calthrop?

The gong sounded and I went in to lunch. Afterward, in the drawing room I showed Joanna my find.

We discussed it from every aspect. Then I took it down to the police station.

They were elated at the find, and I was patted on the back for what was, after all, the sheerest piece of luck.

Graves was not there, but Nash was, and rang up the other man. They would test the book for fingerprints, though Nash was not hopeful of finding anything. I may say that he did not. There were mine, Partridge's and nobody else's, merely showing that Partridge dusted conscientiously.

Nash walked back with me up the hill. I asked how he was getting on.

"We're narrowing it down, Mr. Burton. We've eliminated the people it couldn't be."

"Ah," I said. "And who remains?"

"Miss Ginch. She was to meet a client at a house yesterday afternoon by appointment. That house was situated not far along the Combe Acre road—that's the road that goes past the Symmingtons'. She would have to pass the house both going and coming . . . the week before, the day the anonymous letter was delivered and Mrs. Symmington committed suicide, was her last day at Symmington's office.

"Mr. Symmington thought at first she had not left the office at all that afternoon. He had Sir Henry Lushington with him all the afternoon and rang several times for Miss Ginch. I find, however, that she did leave the office between three and four. She went out to get some high denomination of stamp of which they had run short. The office boy could have gone, but Miss Ginch elected to go, saying she had a headache and would like the air. She was not gone long."

"But long enough?"

"Yes, long enough to hurry along to the other end of the village, slip the letter in the box and hurry back. I must say, however, that I cannot find anybody who saw her near the Symmingtons' house."

"Would they notice?"

"They might and they might not."

"Who else is in your bag?"

Nash looked very straight ahead of him. "You'll understand that we can't exclude anybody—anybody at all."

"No," I said. "I see that."

He said gravely, "Miss Griffith went to Brenton for a meeting of Girl Guides yesterday. She arrived rather late."

"You don't think—"

"No, I don't think. But I don't *know*. Miss Griffith seems an eminently sane, healthy-minded woman—but I say, I don't *know*."

"What about the previous week? Could she have slipped the letter in the box?"

"It's possible. She was shopping in the town that afternoon." He paused. "The same applies to Miss Emily Barton. She was out shopping early yesterday afternoon and she went for a walk to see some friends on the road past the Symmingtons' house the week before."

I shook my head unbelievingly. Finding the cut book in Little Furze was bound, I knew, to direct attention to the owner of that house, but when I remembered Miss Emily coming in yesterday so bright and happy and excited . . .

90

Damn it all—excited. . . . Yes, excited—pink cheeks—shining eyes—surely not because—not because—

I said thickly, "This business is bad for one! One sees things—one imagines things—"

Nash nodded sympathetically. "Yes, it isn't very pleasant to look upon the fellow creatures one meets as possible criminal lunatics."

He paused for a moment, then went on, "And there's Mr. Pye—"

I said sharply, "So you have considered him?"

Nash smiled. "Oh, yes, we've considered him all right. A very curious character—not, I should say, a very nice character. He has no alibi. He was in his garden, alone, on both occasions."

"So you're not only suspecting women?"

"I don't think a man wrote the letters—in fact, I'm sure of it—and so is Graves—always excepting our Mr. Pye, that is to say, who's got an abnormally female streak in his character. But we've checked up on *everybody* for yesterday afternoon. That's a murder case, you see. *You're* all right," he grinned, "and so's your sister, and Mr. Symmington didn't leave his office after he got there and Dr. Griffith was on a round in the other direction, and I've checked up on his visits."

He paused, smiled again, and said, "You see, we *are* thorough."

I said slowly: "So your case is eliminated down to those three? Mr. Pye, Miss Griffith, little Miss Barton?"

"Oh, no, no, we've got a couple more—besides the vicar's lady."

"You've thought of *her?*"

"We've thought of *everybody*, but Mrs. Dane Calthrop is a little too openly mad, if you know what I mean. Still she *could* have done it. She was in a wood watching birds yesterday afternoon—and the birds can't speak for her."

He turned sharply as Owen Griffith came into the police station.

"Hullo, Nash. I heard you were around asking for me this morning. Anything important?"

"Inquest on Friday, if that suits you, Dr. Griffith."

"Right. Moresby and I are doing the P.M. tonight."

Nash said, "There's just one other thing, Dr. Griffith. Mrs. Symmington was taking some powders or something, that you prescribed for her—"

He paused.

Owen Griffith said interrogatively, "Yes?"

"Would an overdose of those powders have been fatal?"

"Certainly not," Griffith said dryly. "Not unless she'd taken about twenty-five of them!"

"But you once warned her about exceeding the dose, so Miss Holland tells me."

"Oh, that, yes. Mrs. Symmington was the sort of woman who would go and overdo anything she was given—fancy that to take twice as much would do her twice as much good, and you don't want anyone to overdo even phenacetin or aspirin—bad for the heart. And anyway there's absolutely no doubt about the cause of death. It was cyanide."

"Oh, I know that—you don't get my meaning. I only thought that when committing suicide you'd prefer to take an overdose of a soporific rather than to feed yourself prussic acid."

"Oh, quite. On the other hand, prussic acid is more dramatic and is pretty certain to do the trick. With barbiturates, for instance, you can bring the victim around if only a short time has elapsed."

"I see; thank you, Dr. Griffith."

Griffith departed, and I said goodbye to Nash. I went slowly up the hill home. Joanna was out—at least there was no sign of her, and there was an enigmatical memorandum scribbled on the telephone block presumably for the guidance of either Partridge or myself:

"If Dr. Griffith rings up, I can't go on Tuesday, but could manage Wednesday or Thursday."

I raised my eyebrows and went into the drawing room. I sat down in the most comfortable armchair—(none of them were very comfortable, they tended to have straight backs and were reminiscent of the late Mrs. Barton)—stretched out my legs and tried to think the whole thing out.

With sudden annoyance I remembered that Owen's arrival had interrupted my conversation with the superintendent, and that he had mentioned two other people as being possibilities.

I wondered who they were.

Partridge, perhaps, for one? After all, the cut book had been found in this house. And Agnes could have been struck down quite unsuspectingly by her guide and mentor. No, you couldn't eliminate Partridge.

But who was the other?

Somebody, perhaps, that I didn't know? Mrs. Cleat? The original local suspect?

I closed my eyes. I considered the four people, these strangely unlikely people, in turn: Gentle, frail little Emily Barton? What points were there actually against her? A starved life? Dominated and repressed from early childhood? Too many sacrifices asked of her? Her curious horror of discussing anything "not quite nice"? Was that actually a sign of inner preoccupation with just these themes? Was I getting too horribly Freudian? I remembered a doctor once telling me that the mutterings of gentle maiden ladies when going off under an anesthetic were a revelation. "You wouldn't think they knew such words!"

Aimée Griffith?

Surely nothing repressed or "inhibited" about her. Cheery, mannish, successful. A full, busy life. Yet Mrs. Dane Calthrop had said, "Poor thing!"

And there was something—something—some remembrance . . . Ah! I'd got it. Owen Griffith saying something like, "We had an outbreak of anonymous letters up north where I had a practice."

Had that been Aimée Griffith's work, too? Surely rather a coincidence. Two outbreaks of the same thing.

Stop a minute, they'd tracked down the author of those. Griffith had said so. A schoolgirl.

Cold it was suddenly—must be a draft, from the window. I turned uncomfortably in my chair. Why did I suddenly feel so queer and upset?

Go on thinking . . . Aimée Griffith? Perhaps it was Aimée Griffith, *not* that other girl? And Aimée had come down here and started her tricks again. And that was why Owen Griffith was looking so unhappy and hag-ridden. He suspected. Yes, he suspected. . . .

Mr. Pye? Not, somehow, a very nice little man. I could imagine him staging the whole business, laughing . . .

That telephone message on the telephone pad in the hall—why did I keep thinking of it? Griffith and Joanna—he was falling for her. No, that wasn't why the message worried me. It was something else. . . .

My senses were swimming, sleep was very near. I repeated idiotically to myself: "No smoke without fire. No smoke without fire. . . . That's it . . . it all links up together. . . ."

And then I was walking down the street with Megan, and Elsie Holland passed. She was dressed as a bride, and people were murmuring, "She's going to marry Dr. Griffith at last. Of course, they've been engaged secretly for years . . ."

There we were, in the church, and Dane Calthrop was reading the service in Latin.

And in the middle of it Mrs. Dane Calthrop jumped up and cried energetically, "It's got to be stopped, I tell you. It's got to be stopped!" For a minute or two I didn't know whether I was asleep or awake. Then my brain cleared, and I realized I was in the drawing room of Little Furze and that Mrs. Dane Calthrop had just come through the window and was standing in front of me saying with nervous violence:

"It has got to be *stopped*, I tell you."

I jumped up. "I beg your pardon," I said. "I'm afraid I was asleep. What did you say?"

Mrs. Dane Calthrop beat one fist fiercely on the palm of her other hand. "It's got to be stopped. These letters! Murder! You can't go on having poor innocent children like Agnes Woddell *killed*!"

"You're quite right," I said. "But how do you propose to set about it?"

Mrs. Dane Calthrop said, "We've got to do something!"

I smiled, perhaps in rather a superior fashion. "And what do you suggest that we should do?"

"Get the whole thing cleared up! I said this wasn't a wicked place. I was wrong. It is."

I felt annoyed. "Yes, my dear woman," I said, not too politely, "but what are you going to *do*?"

Mrs. Dane Calthrop said, "Put a stop to it all, of course."

"The police are doing their best."

"If Agnes could be killed yesterday, their best isn't good enough."

"So you know better than they do?"

"Not at all. *I* don't know anything at all. That's why I'm going to call in an expert."

I shook my head. "You can't do that. Scotland Yard will only take over on a demand from the chief constable of the county. Actually they *have* sent Graves."

"I don't mean *that* kind of an expert. I don't mean someone who knows about anonymous letters or even about murder. I mean someone who knows *people*. Don't you see? We want someone who knows a great deal about *wickedness*!"

It was a queer point of view. But it was, somehow, stimulating.

Before I could say anything more, Mrs. Dane Calthrop nodded her head at me and said in a quick, confident tone:

"I'm going to see about it right away."

And she went out of the window again.

* * *

The next week, I think, was one of the queerest times I have ever passed through. It had an odd dream quality. Nothing seemed real.

The inquest on Agnes Woddell was held and the curious of Lymstock attended *en masse*. No new facts came to light and the only possible verdict was returned: "Murder by person or persons unknown."

So poor little Agnes Woddell, having had her hour of limelight, was duly buried in the quiet old churchyard and life in Lymstock went on as before.

No, that last statement is untrue. Not as before. . . .

There was a half-scared, half-avid gleam in almost everybody's eye. Neighbor looked at neighbor. One thing had been brought out clearly at the inquest—it was most unlikely that any stranger had killed Agnes Woddell. No tramps or unknown men had been noticed or reported in the district. Somewhere, then, in Lymstock, walking down the High Street, shopping, passing the time of day, was a person who had cracked a defenseless girl's skull and driven a sharp skewer home to her brain.

And no one knew who that person was.

As I say, the days went on in a kind of dream. I looked at everyone I met in a new light, the light of a possible murderer. It was not an agreeable sensation!

And in the evenings, with the curtain drawn, Joanna and I sat talking, talking, arguing, going over in turn all the various possibilities that still seemed so fantastic and incredible.

Joanna held firm to her theory of Mr. Pye. I, after wavering a little, had gone back to my original suspect, Miss Ginch. But we went over the possible names again and again:

Mr. Pye?
Miss Ginch?
Mrs. Dane Calthrop?
Aimée Griffith?
Emily Barton?
Partridge?

And all the time, nervously, apprehensively, we waited for something to happen.

But nothing did happen. Nobody, so far as we knew, received any more letters. Nash made periodic appearances in the town but what he was doing and what traps the police were setting, I had no idea. Graves had gone again.

Emily Barton came to tea. Megan came to lunch. Owen Griffith went about his practice. We went and drank sherry with Mr. Pye. And we went to tea at the vicarage.

I was glad to find that Mrs. Dane Calthrop displayed none of the militant ferocity she had shown on the occasion of our last meeting. I think she had forgotten all about it.

She seemed now principally concerned with the destruction of white butterflies so as to preserve cauliflower and cabbage plants.

Our afternoon at the vicarage was really one of the most peaceful we had spent. It was an attractive old house and had a big, shabby, comfortable drawing room with a faded rose cretonne. The Dane Calthrops had a guest staying with them, an amiable, elderly lady who was knitting something with white, fleecy wool. We had very good hot scones for tea, the vicar came in, and beamed placidly on us while he pursued his gentle erudite conversation. It was very pleasant.

I don't mean that we got away from the topic of the murder, because we didn't.

Miss Marple, the guest, was naturally thrilled by the subject. As she said apologetically:

"We have so little to talk about in the country!" She had made up her mind that the dead girl must have been just like her Edith.

"Such a nice little maid, and so willing, but sometimes just a *little* slow to take in things."

Miss Marple also had a cousin whose niece's sister-in-law had had a great deal of annoyance and trouble over some anonymous letters, so that, too, was very interesting to the charming old lady.

"But tell me, dear," she said to Mrs. Dane Calthrop, "what do the village people—I mean the townspeople—say? What do *they* think?"

"Mrs. Cleat still, I suppose," said Joanna.

"Oh, no," said Mrs. Dane Calthrop. "Not *now*."

Miss Marple asked who Mrs. Cleat was.

Joanna said she was the village witch.

"That's right, isn't it, Mrs. Dane Calthrop?"

The vicar murmured a long Latin quotation about, I think, the evil power of witches, to which we all listened in respectful and uncomprehending silence.

"She's a very silly woman," said his wife. "Likes to show off. Goes out to gather herbs and things at the full of the moon and takes care that everybody in the place knows about it."

"And silly girls go and consult her, I suppose?" said Miss Marple.

I saw the vicar getting ready to unload more Latin on us and I asked hastily, "But why shouldn't people suspect her of the murder now? They thought the letters were her doing."

Miss Marple said finally:

"Oh! But the girl was killed with a *skewer*, so I hear. Very unpleasant! Well, naturally, that takes *all* suspicion away from this Mrs. Cleat. Because, you see, she could ill-wish her, so that the girl would waste away and die from natural causes."

"Strange how those old beliefs linger," said the vicar. "In early Christian times, local superstitions were wisely incorporated with Christian doctrines and their most unpleasant attributes gradually eliminated."

"It isn't superstition we've got to deal with here," said Mrs. Dane Calthrop, "but *facts*."

"And very unpleasant facts," I said.

"As you say, Mr. Burton," said Miss Marple. "Now *you*—excuse me if I am being too personal—are a stranger here, and have a knowledge of the world and of various aspects of life. It seems to me that you ought to be able to find a solution to this distasteful problem."

I smiled.

"The best solution I have had was a dream. In my dream it all fitted in and panned out beautifully. Unfortunately when I woke up the whole thing was nonsense!"

"How interesting, though. Do tell me how the nonsense went."

"Oh, it all started with the silly phrase 'No smoke without fire.' People have been saying that *ad nauseam*. And then I got it mixed up with war terms. Smoke screen, scrap of paper, telephone messages—no, that was another dream."

"And what was that dream?"

The old lady was so eager about it, that I felt sure she was a secret reader of Napoleon's Book of Dreams, which had been the great stand-by of my old nurse.

"Oh! Only Elsie Holland—the Symmingtons' nursery governess, you know, was getting married to Dr. Griffith and the vicar here was reading the service in Latin—('Very appropriate, dear,' murmured Mrs. Dane Calthrop to her spouse) and then Mrs. Dane Calthrop got up and forbade the banns and said it had got to be stopped!

"But that part," I added with a smile, "was true. I woke up and found you standing over me saying it."

"And I was quite right," said Mrs. Dane Calthrop—but quite mildly, I was glad to note.

"But where did a telephone message come in?" asked Miss Marple, crinkling her brows.

"I'm afraid I'm being rather stupid. That wasn't in the dream. It was just before it. I came through the hall and noticed Joanna had written down a message to be given to someone if they rang up."

Miss Marple leaned forward. There was a pink spot in each cheek. "Will you think me *very* inquisitive and *very* rude if I ask just what that message was?" She cast a glance at Joanna. "I *do* apologize, my dear."

Joanna, however, was highly entertained.

"Oh, I don't mind," she assured the old lady. "I can't remember anything about it myself, but perhaps Jerry can. It must have been something quite trivial."

Solemnly I repeated the message as best I could remember, enormously tickled at the old lady's rapt attention.

I was afraid the actual words were going to disappoint her, but perhaps she had some sentimental idea of a romance, for she nodded her head and smiled and seemed pleased.

"I see," she said. "I thought it might be something like that."

Mrs. Dane Calthrop said sharply, "Like what, Jane?"

"Something quite ordinary," said Miss Marple.

She looked at me thoughtfully for a moment or two, then she said unexpectedly, "I can see you are a very clever young man—but with not quite enough confidence in yourself. You ought to have!"

Joanna gave a loud hoot. "For goodness' sake don't encourage him to feel like that. He thinks quite enough of himself as it is."

"Be quiet, Joanna," I said. "Miss Marple understands me."

Miss Marple had resumed her fleecy knitting. "You know," she observed pensively, "to commit a successful murder must be very much like bringing off a conjuring trick."

"The quickness of the hand deceives the eye?"

"Not only that. You've got to make people look at the wrong thing and in the wrong place—misdirection, they call it, I believe."

"Well," I remarked, "so far everybody seems to have looked in the wrong place for our lunatic at large."

"I should be inclined, myself," said Miss Marple, "to look for somebody very sane."

"Yes," I said thoughtfully, "that's what Nash said. I remember he stressed respectability, too."

"Yes," agreed Miss Marple. "That's *very* important."

Well, we all seemed agreed.

I addressed Mrs. Calthrop. "Nash thinks," I said, "that there will be more anonymous letters. What do you think?"

"There may be," she said slowly, "I suppose."

"If the police think that, there will have to be, no doubt," said Miss Marple.

I went on doggedly to Mrs. Dane Calthrop: "Are you still sorry for the writer?"

She flushed. "Why not?"

"I don't think I agree with you, dear," said Miss Marple. "Not in this case."

I said hotly, "They've driven one woman to suicide, and caused untold misery and heartburnings!"

"Have you had one, Miss Burton?" asked Miss Marple of Joanna.

Joanna gurgled: "Oh, yes! It said the most frightful things."

"I'm afraid," said Miss Marple, "that the people who are young and pretty are apt to be singled out by the writer."

"That's why I certainly think it's odd that Elsie Holland hasn't had any," I said.

"Let me see," said Miss Marple. "Is that the Symmingtons' nursery governess—the one you dreamed about, Mr. Burton?"

"Yes."

"She's probably had one and won't say so," said Joanna.

"No," I said, "I believe her. So does Nash."

"Dear me," said Miss Marple. "Now that's *very* interesting. That's the most interesting thing I've heard yet."

As we were going home Joanna told me that I ought not to have repeated what Nash said about more letters coming.

"Why not?"

"Because Mrs. Dane Calthrop might be It."

"You don't really believe that!"

"I'm not sure. She's a queer woman."

We began our discussion of probables all over again.

It was two nights later that I was coming back in the car from Exhampton. I had had dinner there and then started back and it was already dark before I got into Lymstock.

Something was wrong with the car lights, and after slowing up and switching on and off, I finally got out to see what I could do. I was some time fiddling, but I managed to fix them up finally.

The road was quite deserted. Nobody in Lymstock is about after dark. The first few houses were just ahead, among them the ugly gabled building of the Women's Institute. It loomed up in the dim starlight and something impelled me to go and have a look at it. I don't know whether I had caught a faint glimpse of a stealthy figure flitting through the gate—if so, it must have been so indeterminate that it did not register in my conscious mind, but I did suddenly feel a kind of overweening curiosity about the place.

The gate was slightly ajar, and I pushed it open and walked in. A short path and four steps led up to the door.

I stood there a moment hesitating. What was I really doing there? I didn't know, and then, suddenly, just near at hand, I caught the sound of a rustle. It sounded like a woman's dress.

I took a sharp turn and went around the corner of the building toward where the sound had come from.

I couldn't see anybody. I went on and again turned a corner. I was at the back of the house now and suddenly I saw, only two feet away from me, an open window.

I crept up to it and listened. I could hear nothing, but somehow or other I felt convinced that there was someone inside.

My back wasn't too good for acrobatics as yet, but I managed to hoist myself up and drop over the sill inside. I made rather a noise unfortunately.

I stood just inside the window listening. Then I walked forward, my hands outstretched. I heard then the faintest sound ahead of me to my right.

I had a torch in my pocket and I switched it on.

Immediately a low, sharp voice said, "Put that out."

I obeyed instantly, for in that brief second I had recognized Superintendent Nash.

I felt him take my arm and propel me through a door and into a passage. Here, where there was no window to betray our presence to anyone outside, he switched on a lamp and looked at me more in sorrow than in anger.

"You *would* have to butt in just that minute, Mr. Burton."

"Sorry," I apologized. "But I got a hunch that I was on to something."

"And so you were probably. Did you see anyone?"

I hesitated.

"I'm not sure," I said slowly. "I've got a vague feeling I saw someone sneak in through the front gate but I didn't really see anyone. Then I heard a rustle around the side of the house."

Nash nodded. "That's right. Somebody came around the house before you. He—or she—hesitated by the window, then went on quickly—heard *you*, I expect."

I apologized again. "What's the big idea?" I asked.

Nash said:

"I'm banking on the fact that an anonymous letter writer can't stop writing letters. She may know it's dangerous, but she'll have to do it. It's like a craving for drink or drugs."

I nodded.

"Now you see, Mr. Burton, I fancy whoever it is will want to keep the letters looking the same as much as possible. She's got the cutout pages of that book, and can go on using letters and words cut out of them. But the envelopes present a difficulty. She'll want to type them on the same machine. She can't risk using another typewriter or her own handwriting."

"Do you really think she'll go on with the game?" I asked incredulously.

"Yes, I do. And I'll bet you anything you like she's full of confidence. They're always vain as hell, these people! Well, then, I figured out that whoever it was would come to the Institute after dark so as to get at the typewriter."

"Miss Ginch," I said.

"Maybe."

"You don't know yet?"

"I don't *know*."

"But you suspect?"

"Yes. But somebody's very cunning, Mr. Burton. Somebody knows all the tricks of the game."

I could imagine some of the network that Nash had spread abroad. I had no doubt that every letter written by a suspect and posted or left by hand was immediately inspected. Sooner or later the criminal would slip up, would grow careless.

For the third time I apologized for my zealous and unwanted presence.

"Oh, well," said Nash philosophically, "it can't be helped. Better luck next time."

I went out into the night. A dim figure was standing beside my car. To my astonishment I recognized Megan.

"Hullo!" she said. "I thought this was your car. What have you been doing?"

"What are you doing is much more to the point?" I said.

"I'm out for a walk. I like walking at night. Nobody stops you and says silly things, and I like the stars, and things smell better, and every-day things look all mysterious."

"All of that I grant you freely," I said. "But only cats and witches walk in the dark. They'll wonder about you at home."

"No, they won't. They never wonder where I am or what *I'm* doing."

"How are you getting on?" I asked.

"All right, I suppose."

"Miss Holland look after you and all that?"

"Elsie's all right. She can't help being a perfect fool."

"Unkind—but probably true," I said. "Hop in and I'll drive you home."

It was not quite true that Megan was never missed.

Symmington was standing on the doorstep as we drove up.

He peered toward us.

"Hullo, is Megan there?"

"Yes," I said. "I've brought her home."

Symmington said sharply, "You mustn't go off like this without telling us, Megan. Miss Holland has been quite worried about you."

Megan muttered something and went past him into the house.

Symmington sighed. "A grown-up girl is a great responsibility with no mother to look after her. She's too old for school, I suppose."

He looked toward me rather suspiciously.

"I suppose you took her for a drive?" I thought it best to leave it like that.

7

On the following day I went mad. Looking back on it, that is really the only explanation I can find.

I was due for my monthly visit to Marcus Kent. . . . I went up by train. To my intense surprise Joanna elected to stay behind. As a rule she was eager to come and we usually stayed up for a couple of days.

This time, however, I proposed to return the same day by the evening train, but even so I was astonished at Joanna. She merely said enigmatically that she'd got plenty to do, and why spend hours in a nasty stuffy train when it was a lovely day in the country?

That, of course, was undeniable, but sounded very unlike Joanna.

She said she didn't want the car, so I was to drive it to the station and leave it parked there against my return.

The station of Lymstock is situated, for some obscure reason known to railway companies only, quite half a mile from Lymstock itself. Halfway along the road I overtook Megan shuffling along in an aimless manner. I pulled up.

"Hullo, what are you doing?"

"Just out for a walk."

"But not what is called a good brisk walk, I gather. You were crawling along like a dispirited crab."

"Well, I wasn't going anywhere particular."

"Then you'd better come and see me off at the station." I opened the door of the car and Megan jumped in.

"Where are you going?" she asked.

"London. To see my doctor."

"Your back's not worse, is it?"

"No, it's practically all right again. I'm expecting him to be very pleased about it."

Megan nodded.

We drew up at the station. I parked the car and went in and bought my ticket at the booking office. There were very few people on the platform and nobody I knew.

"You wouldn't like to lend me a penny, would you?" said Megan. "Then I'd get a bit of chocolate out of the slot machine."

"Here you are, baby," I said, handing her the coin in question. "Sure you wouldn't like some clear gums or some throat pastilles as well?"

"I like chocolate best," said Megan without suspecting sarcasm.

She went off to the chocolate machine, and I looked after her with a feeling of mounting irritation.

She was wearing trodden-over shoes, and coarse unattractive stockings and a particularly shapeless jumper and skirt. I don't know why all this should have infuriated me, but it did.

I said angrily as she came back, "Why do you wear those disgusting stockings?"

Megan looked down at them, surprised. "What's the matter with them?"

"Everything's the matter with them. They're loathsome. And why wear a pullover like a decayed cabbage?"

"It's all right, isn't it? I've had it for years."

"So I should imagine. And why do you—"

At this minute the train came in and interrupted my angry lecture.

I got into an empty first-class carriage, let down the window and leaned out to continue the conversation.

Megan stood below me, her face upturned. She asked me why I was so cross.

"I'm not cross," I said untruly. "It just infuriates me to see you so slack, and not caring how you look."

"I couldn't look nice, anyway, so what does it matter?"

"Cut it!" I said. "I'd like to see you turned out properly. I'd like to take you to London and outfit you from tip to toe."

"I wish you could," said Megan.

The train began to move. I looked down into Megan's upturned, wistful face.

And then as I have said, madness came upon me.

I opened the door, grabbed Megan with one arm and fairly hauled her into the carriage.

There was an outraged shout from a porter, but all he could do was dexterously to bang shut the door again. I pulled Megan up from the floor where my impetuous action had landed her.

"What on earth did you do that for?" she demanded, rubbing one knee.

"Shut up," I said. "You're coming to London with me and when I've done with you you won't know yourself. I'll show you what you can look like if you try. I'm tired of seeing you mouch about down at heel and all anyhow."

"Oh!" said Megan in an ecstatic whisper.

The ticket collector came along and I bought Megan a return ticket. She sat in her corner looking at me in a kind of awed respect.

"I say," she said when the man had gone. "You are sudden, aren't you?"

"Very," I said. "It runs in our family."

How explain to Megan the impulse that had come over me?—She had looked like a wistful dog being left behind. She now had on her face the incredulous pleasure of the dog who has been taken on the walk after all.

"I suppose you don't know London very well?" I said to Megan.

"Yes, I do," said Megan. "I always went through it to school. And I've been to the dentist there and to a pantomime."

"This," I said darkly, "will be a different London."

We arrived with half an hour to spare before my appointment in Harley Street.

I took a taxi and we drove straight to Mirotin, Joanna's dressmaker. Mirotin is, in the flesh, an unconventional and breezy woman of forty-five, Mary Grey. She is a clever woman and very good company. I have always liked her.

I said to Megan, "You're my cousin."

"Why?"

"Don't argue," I said.

Mary Grey was being firm with a stout woman who was enamored of a skin-tight powder-blue evening dress. I detached her and took her aside.

"Listen," I said. "I've brought a little cousin of mine along. Joanna was coming up but was prevented. But she said I could leave it all to you. You see what the girl looks like now?"

"I most certainly do!" said Mary Grey with feeling.

"Well, I want her turned out right in every particular from head to foot. Carte blanche. Stockings, shoes, undies, everything! By the way, the man who does Joanna's hair is close around here, isn't he?"

"Antoine? Around the corner. I'll see to that too."

"You're a woman in a thousand."

"Oh, I shall enjoy it—apart from the money—and that's not to be sneezed at in these days—half my damned brutes of women never pay their bills. But as I say, I shall enjoy it." She shot a quick professional glance at Megan standing a little way off. "She's got a lovely figure."

"You must have X-ray eyes," I said. "She looks completely shapeless to me."

Mary Grey laughed.

"It's these schools," she said. "They seem to take a pride in turning out girls who preen themselves on looking like nothing on earth. They call it being sweet and unsophisticated. Sometimes it takes a whole season before a girl can pull herself together and look human. Don't worry, leave it all to me."

"Right," I said. "I'll come back and fetch her about six."

Marcus Kent was pleased with me. He told me that I surpassed his wildest expectations.

"You must have the constitution of an elephant," he said, "to make a comeback like this. Oh, well, wonderful what country air and no late hours or excitement will do for a man if he can only stick it."

"I grant you your first two," I said. "But don't think that the country is free from excitement. We've had a good deal in my part."

"What sort of excitement?"

"Murder," I said.

Marcus Kent pursed up his mouth and whistled. "Some bucolic love tragedy? Farm lad kills his lass?"

"Not at all. A crafty, determined lunatic killer."

"I haven't read anything about it? When did they lay him by the heels?"

"They haven't, and it's a she!"

"Whew! I'm not sure that Lymstock's quite the right place for you, old boy."

I said firmly, "Yes, it is. And you're not going to get me out of it."

Marcus Kent has a low mind. He said at once, "So that's it! Found a blonde?"

"Not at all," I said, with a guilty thought of Elsie Holland. "It's merely that the psychology of crime interests me a good deal."

"Oh, all right. It certainly hasn't done you any harm so far, but just make sure that your lunatic killer doesn't obliterate *you*."

"No fear of that," I said.

"What about dining with me this evening? You can tell me all about your revolting murder."

"Sorry. I'm booked."

"Date with a lady—eh? Yes, you're definitely on the mend."

"I suppose you could call it that," I said, rather tickled at the idea of Megan in the role.

I was at Mirotin's at six o'clock when the establishment was officially closing. Mary Grey came to meet me at the top of the stairs outside the showroom. She had a finger to her lips.

"You're going to have a shock! If I say it myself, I've put in a good bit of work."

I went on into the big showroom. Megan was standing looking at herself in a long mirror. I give you my word I hardly recognized her! For the minute it took my breath away. Tall and slim as a willow with delicate ankles and feet shown off by sheer silk stockings and well-cut shoes. Yes, lovely feet and hands, small bones—quality and distinction in every line of her. Her hair had been trimmed and shaped to her head and it was glowing like a glossy chestnut. They'd had the sense to leave her face alone. She was not made up, or if she was it was so slight and delicate that it did not show. Her mouth needed no lipstick.

Moreover there was about her something that I had never seen before, a new innocent pride in the arch of her neck. She looked at me gravely with a small, shy smile.

"I do look—rather nice, don't I?" said Megan.

"Nice?" I said. "Nice isn't the word! Come on out to dinner and if every second man doesn't turn around to look at you I'll be surprised. You'll knock all the other girls into a cocked hat."

Megan was not beautiful, but she was unusual and striking-looking. She had personality. She walked into the restaurant ahead of me and as the head waiter hurried toward us, I felt the thrill of idiotic pride that a man feels when he has got something out of the ordinary with him.

We had cocktails first and lingered over them. Then we dined. And later we danced. Megan was keen to dance and I didn't want to disappoint her, but for some reason or other I hadn't thought she would dance well. But she did. She was light as a feather in my arms, and her body and feet followed the rhythm perfectly.

"Gosh!" I said. "You can dance!"

She seemed a little surprised.

"Well, of course I can. We had dancing class every week at school."

"It takes more than dancing class to make a dancer," I said.

We went back to our table.

"Isn't this food lovely?" said Megan. "And everything!"

She heaved a delighted sigh.

"Exactly my sentiments," I said.

It was a delirious evening. I was still mad. Megan brought me down to earth when she said doubtfully, "Oughtn't we to be going home?"

My jaw dropped. Yes, definitely I was mad. I had forgotten everything! I was in a world divorced from reality, existing in it with the creature I had created.

"Good Lord!" I said.

I realized that the last train had gone.

"Stay there," I said. "I'm going to telephone."

I rang up the Llewellyn Hire people and ordered their biggest and fastest car to come around as soon as possible.

I came back to Megan.

"The last train has gone," I said. "So we're going home by car."

"Are we? What fun!"

What a nice child she was, I thought. So pleased with everything, so unquestioning, accepting all my suggestions without fuss or bother.

The car came, and it was large and fast, but all the same it was very late when we came into Lymstock.

Suddenly conscience-stricken, I said, "They'll have been sending out search parties for you!"

But Megan seemed in an equable mood. "Oh, I don't think so," she said vaguely. "I often go out and don't come home for lunch."

"Yes, my dear child, but you've been out for tea and dinner too."

However, Megan's lucky star was in the ascendant. The house was dark and silent. On Megan's advice, we went around to the back and threw stones at Rose's window.

In due course Rose looked out and with many suppressed exclamations and palpitations came down to let us in.

"Well now, and I saying you were asleep in your bed. The master and Miss Holland—" (slight sniff after Miss Holland's name) "had early supper and went for a drive. I said I'd keep an eye to the boys. I thought I heard you come in when I was up in the nursery trying to quiet Colin, who was playing up, but you weren't about when I came down so I thought you'd gone to bed. And that's what I said when the master came in and asked for you."

I cut short the conversation by remarking that that was where Megan had better go now.

"Good night," said Megan, "and thank you *awfully*. It's been the loveliest day I've ever had."

I drove home slightly lightheaded still, and tipped the chauffeur handsomely, offering him a bed if he liked. But he preferred to drive back through the night.

The hall door had opened during our colloquy and as he drove away it was flung wide open and Joanna said, "So it's you at last, is it?"

"Were you worried about me?" I asked, coming in and shutting the door.

Joanna went into the drawing room and I followed her. There was a coffee-pot on the trivet and Joanna made herself coffee while I helped myself to a whisky-and-soda.

"Worried about you? No, of course not. I thought you'd decided to stay in town and have a binge."

"I've had a binge—of a kind."

I grinned and then began to laugh.

Joanna asked what I was laughing at and I told her.

"But, Jerry, you must have been mad—quite mad!"

"I suppose I was."

"But, my dear boy, you can't do things like that—not in a place like this. It will be all around Lymstock tomorrow."

"I suppose it will. But, after all, Megan's only a child."

"She isn't. She's twenty. You can't take a girl of twenty to London and buy her clothes without a most frightful scandal. Good gracious, Jerry, you'll probably have to marry the girl."

Joanna was half serious, half laughing.

It was at that moment that I made a very important discovery.

"Damn it all," I said. "I don't mind if I do. In fact—I should like it."

A very funny expression came over Joanna's face. She got up and said dryly, as she went toward the door, "Yes, I've known that for some time . . ."

She left me standing, glass in hand, aghast at my new discovery.

* * *

I don't know what the usual reactions are of a man who goes to propose marriage.

In fiction his throat is dry and his collar feels too tight and he is in a pitiable state of nervousness.

I didn't feel at all like that. Having thought of a good idea I just wanted to get it all settled as soon as possible. I didn't see any particular need for embarrassment.

I went along to the Symmingtons' house about eleven o'clock. I rang the bell and when Rose came, I asked for Miss Megan.

It was the knowing look that Rose gave me that first made me feel slightly shy.

She put me in the little morning room and while waiting there I hoped uneasily that they hadn't been upsetting Megan.

When the door opened and I wheeled around, I was instantly relieved. Megan was not looking shy or upset at all. Her head was still like a glossy chestnut, and she wore that air of pride and self-respect that she had acquired yesterday. She was in her old clothes again but she had managed to make them look different. It's wonderful what knowledge of her own attractiveness will do for a girl. Megan, I realized suddenly, had grown up.

I suppose I must really have been rather nervous, otherwise I should not have opened the conversation by saying affectionately: "Hullo, catfish!" It was hardly, in the circumstances, a loverlike greeting.

It seemed to suit Megan. She grinned and said, "Hullo!"

"Look here," I said. "You didn't get into a row about yesterday, I hope?"

Megan said with assurance, "Oh, *no*," and then blinked, and said vaguely, "Yes, I believe I did. I mean, they said a lot of things and seemed to think it had been very odd—but then you know what people are and what fusses they make all about nothing."

I was relieved to see that shocked disapproval had slipped off Megan like water off a duck's back.

"I came around this morning," I said, "because I've a suggestion to make. You see I like you a lot, and I think you like me—"

"Frightfully," said Megan with rather disquieting enthusiasm.

"And we get on awfully well together, so I think it would be a good idea if we got married."

"Oh," said Megan.

110

She looked surprised. Just that. Not startled. Not shocked. Just mildly surprised.

"You mean you really want to marry me?" she asked with the air of one getting a thing perfectly clear.

"More than anything in the world," I said—and I meant it.

"You mean, you're in love with me?"

"I'm in love with you."

Her eyes were steady and grave. She said, "I think you're the nicest person in the world—but I'm not in love with you."

"I'll make you love me."

"That wouldn't do. I don't want to be *made*." She paused and then said gravely, "I'm not the sort of wife for you. I'm better at hating than at loving."

She said it with a queer intensity.

I said, "Hate doesn't last. Love does."

"Is that true?"

"It's what I believe."

Again there was a silence. Then I said, "So it's 'No,' is it?"

"Yes, it's 'No.'"

"And you don't encourage me to hope?"

"What would be the good of that?"

"None whatever," I agreed. "Quite redundant in fact—because I'm going to hope whether you tell me to or not."

Well, that was that.

I walked away from the house feeling slightly dazed but irritatingly conscious of Rose's passionately interested gaze following me.

Rose had had a good deal to say before I could escape.

That she'd never felt the same since that awful day! That she wouldn't have stayed except for the children and being sorry for poor Mr. Symmington. That she wasn't going to stay unless they got another maid quick—and they wouldn't be likely to do that when there had been a murder in the house! That it was all very well for that Miss Holland to say she'd do the housework in the meantime.

Very sweet and obliging she was—oh, yes, but it was mistress of the house that she was fancying herself going to be one fine day! Mr. Symmington, poor man, never saw anything—but one knew what a widower was, a poor helpless creature made to be the prey of a designing woman. And that it wouldn't be for want of trying if Miss Holland didn't step into the dead mistress's shoes!

I assented mechanically to everything, yearning to get away and unable to do so because Rose was holding firmly on to my hat while she indulged in her flood of spite.

I wondered if there was any truth in what she said. Had Elsie Holland envisaged the possibility of becoming the second Mrs. Symmington? Or was she just a decent kindhearted girl doing her best to look after a bereaved household?

The result would quite likely be the same in either case. And why not? Symmington's young children needed a mother—Elsie was a decent soul—besides being quite indecently beautiful—a point which a man might appreciate—even such a stuffed fish as Symmington!

I thought all this, I know, because I was trying to put off thinking about Megan.

You may say that I had gone to ask Megan to marry me in an absurdly complacent frame of mind and that I deserved what I got—but it was not really like that. It was because I felt so assured, so certain, that Megan belonged to me—that she was my business, that to look after her and make her happy and keep her from harm was the only natural right way of life for me, that I had expected her to feel, too—that she and I—belonged to each other.

But I was not giving up. Oh, no! Megan was my woman and I was going to have her.

After a moment's thought, I went to Symmington's office. Megan might pay no attention to strictures on her conduct, but I would like to get things straight.

Mr. Symmington was disengaged, I was told, and I was shown into the room.

By a pinching of the lips, and an additional stiffness of manner, I gathered that I was not exactly popular at the moment.

"Good morning," I said. "I'm afraid this isn't a professional call, but a personal one. I'll put it plainly. I dare say you'll have realized that I'm in love with Megan. I've asked her to marry me and she has refused. But I'm not taking that as final."

I saw Symmington's expression change, and I read his mind with ludicrous ease. Megan was a disharmonious element in his house. He was, I felt sure, a just and kindly man, and he would never have dreamed of not providing a home for his dead wife's daughter. But her marriage to me would certainly be a relief. The frozen halibut thawed. He gave me a pale, cautious smile.

"Frankly, do you know, Burton, I had no idea of such a thing. I know you've taken a lot of notice of her, but we've always regarded her as such a child."

"She's not a child," I said shortly.

"No, no, not in years."

"She can be her age any time she's allowed to be," I said, still slightly angry. "She's not of age, I know, but she will be in a month or two. I'll let you have all the information about myself you want. I'm well off and have led quite a decent life. I'll look after her and do all I can to make her happy."

"Quite—quite. Still, it's up to Megan herself."

"She'll come round in time," I said. "But I just thought I'd like to get straight with you about it."

He said he appreciated that, and we parted amicably.

I ran into Miss Emily Barton outside. She had a shopping basket on her arm.

"Good morning, Mr. Burton, I hear you went to London yesterday."

Yes, she had heard all right. Her eyes were, I thought, kindly, but full of curiosity, too.

"I went to see my doctor," I said.

Miss Emily smiled.

That smile made little of Marcus Kent. She murmured, "I hear Megan nearly missed the train. She jumped in when it was going."

"Helped by me," I said. "I hauled her in."

"How very lucky you were there. Otherwise there might have been an accident."

It is extraordinary how much of a fool one gentle, inquisitive, old maiden lady can make a man feel!

I was saved further suffering by the onslaught of Mrs. Dane Calthrop. She had her own tame elderly maiden lady in tow, but she herself was full of direct speech.

"Good morning," she said. "I hear you've made Megan buy herself some decent clothes? Very sensible of you. It takes a man to think of something really practical like that. I've been worried about that girl for a long time. Girls with brains are so liable to turn into morons, aren't they?"

With which remarkable statement, she shot into the fish shop.

Miss Marple, left standing by me, twinkled a little and said, "Mrs. Dane Calthrop is a very remarkable woman, you know. She's nearly always right."

"It makes her rather alarming," I said.

"Sincerity has that effect," said Miss Marple.

Mrs. Dane Calthrop shot out of the fish shop again and rejoined us. She was holding a large red lobster.

"Have you ever seen anything so unlike Mr. Pye?" she said. "Very virile and handsome, isn't it?"

I was a little nervous of meeting Joanna but I found when I got home that I needn't have worried. She was out and she did not return for lunch. This aggrieved Partridge a good deal, who said sourly as she proffered two loin chops in an entrée dish:

"Miss Burton said especially as she was going to be *in*."

I ate both chops in an attempt to atone for Joanna's lapse. All the same, I wondered where my sister was. She had taken to being very mysterious about her doings of late.

It was half past three when Joanna burst into the drawing room. I had heard a car stop outside and I half expected to see Griffith, but the car drove on and Joanna came in alone.

Her face was very red and she seemed upset. I perceived that something had happened.

"What's the matter?" I asked.

Joanna opened her mouth, closed it again, sighed, plumped herself down in a chair and stared in front of her.

She said, "I've had the most awful day."

"What's happened"

"I've done the most incredible things. It was awful—"

"But what—"

"I just started out for a walk, an ordinary walk—I went up over the hill and on to the moor. I walked miles—I felt like it. Then I dropped down into a hollow. There's a farm there—a God-forsaken lonely sort of spot. I was thirsty and I wondered if they had any milk or something. So I wandered into the farmyard and then the door opened and Owen came out."

"Yes?"

"He thought it might be the district nurse. There was a woman in there having a baby. He was expecting the nurse and he'd sent word to her to get hold of another doctor. It—things were going wrong."

"Yes?"

"So he said—to *me*, 'Come on, you'll do—better than nobody.' I said

I couldn't, and he said what did I mean? I said I'd never done anything like that, that I didn't know anything—

"He asked me what the hell that mattered. And then he was *awful*. He turned on me. He said, 'You're a woman, aren't you? I suppose you can do your durnedest to help another woman?' And he went on at me—said I'd talked as though I was interested in doctoring and had said I wished I was a nurse. 'All pretty talk, I suppose! You didn't mean anything real by it, but this *is* real and you're going to behave like a decent human being and not a useless ornamental nitwit!"

"I've done the most indiscernible things, Jerry. Held instruments and boiled them and handed things. I'm so tired I can hardly stand up. It was dreadful. But he saved her—and the baby. It was born alive. He didn't think at one time he could save it. Oh, dear!"

Joanna covered her face with her hands.

I contemplated her with a certain amount of pleasure and mentally took my hat off to Owen Griffith. He'd brought Joanna slap up against reality for once.

I said, "There's a letter for you in the hall. From Paul, I think."

"Eh?" She paused for a minute and then said, "I'd no idea, Jerry, what doctors had to do. The nerve they've got to have!"

I went out into the hall and brought Joanna her letter. She opened it, glanced vaguely at its contents, and let it drop.

"He was—really—rather wonderful. The way he fought—the way he wouldn't be beaten! He was rude and horrible to *me*—but he *was* wonderful."

I observed Paul's disregarded letter with some pleasure. Plainly, Joanna was cured of Paul.

Things never come when they are expected.

I was full of Joanna's and my personal affairs and was quite taken aback the next morning when Nash's voice said over the telephone:

"*We've got her*, Mr. Burton!"

I was so startled I nearly dropped the receiver.

"You mean the—"

He interrupted: "Can you be overheard where you are?"

"No, I don't think so—well, perhaps—"

It seemed to me that the baize door to the kitchen had swung open a trifle.

"Perhaps you'd care to come down to the station?"

115

"I will. Right away."

I was at the police station in next to no time. In an inner room Nash and Sergeant Parkins were together. Nash was wreathed in smiles.

"It's been a long chase," he said. "But we're there at last."

He flicked a letter across the table. This time it was all typewritten. It was, of its kind, fairly mild:

"It's no use thinking you're going to step into a dead woman's shoes. The whole town is laughing at you. Get out now. Soon it will be too late. This is a warning. Remember what happened to that other girl. Get out and stay out."

It finished with some mildly obscene language.

"That reached Miss Holland this morning," said Nash.

"Thought it was funny she hadn't had one before," said Sergeant Parkins.

"Who wrote it?" I asked.

Some of the exultation faded out of Nash's face.

He looked tired and concerned. He said soberly:

"I'm sorry about it, because it will hit a decent man hard, but there it is. Perhaps he's had his suspicions already."

"Who wrote it?" I reiterated.

"Miss Aimée Griffith."

Nash and Parkins went to the Griffiths' house that afternoon with a warrant.

By Nash's invitation I went with them.

"The doctor," he said, "is very fond of you. He hasn't many friends in this place. I think if it is not too painful to you, Mr. Burton, that you might help him to bear up under the shock."

I said I would come. I didn't relish the job, but I thought I might be some good.

We rang the bell and asked for Miss Griffith and we were shown into the drawing room. Elsie Holland, Megan and Symmington were there having tea.

Nash behaved very circumspectly.

He asked Aimée if he might have a few words with her privately.

She got up and came toward us. I thought I saw just a faint hunted look in her eye. If so, it went again. She was perfectly normal and hearty.

"Want me? Not in trouble over my car lights again, I hope?"

She led the way out of the drawing room and across the hall into a small study.

As I closed the drawing-room door, I saw Symmington's head

jerk up sharply. I supposed his legal training had brought him in contact with police cases, and he had recognized something in Nash's manner. He half rose.

That is all I saw before I shut the door and followed the others.

Nash was saying his piece. He was very quiet and correct. He cautioned her and then told her that he must ask her to accompany him. He had a warrant for her arrest and he read out the charge.

I forget now the exact legal term. It was the letters, not murder yet.

Aimée Griffith flung up her head and bayed with laughter. She boomed out:

"What ridiculous nonsense! As though I'd write a packet of indecent stuff like that. You must be mad. I've never written a word of the kind."

Nash had produced the letter to Elsie Holland. He said, "Do you deny having written this, Miss Griffith?"

If she hesitated it was only for a split second.

"Of course I do. I've never seen it before."

Nash said quietly:

"I must tell you, Miss Griffith, that you were observed to type that letter on the machine at the Women's Institute between eleven and eleven-thirty P.M. on the night before last. Yesterday you entered the post office with a bunch of letters in your hand—"

"I never posted this."

"No, you did not. While waiting for stamps, you dropped it inconspicuously on the floor, so that somebody should come along unsuspectingly and pick it up and post it."

"I never—"

The door opened and Symmington came in. He said sharply, "What's going on? Aimée, if there is anything wrong, you ought to be legally represented. If you wish me—"

She broke then. Covered her face with her hands and staggered to a chair. She said, "Go away, Dick, go away. Not you! Not *you!*"

"You need a solicitor, my dear girl."

"Not you. I—I couldn't bear it. I don't want you to know—all this."

He understood then, perhaps. He said quietly, "I'll get hold of Mildmay, of Exhampton. Will that do?"

She nodded. She was sobbing now.

Symmington went out of the room. In the doorway he collided with Owen Griffith.

"What's this?" said Owen violently. "My sister—"

"I'm sorry, Dr. Griffith. Very sorry. But we have no alternative."

"You think she—was responsible for those letters?"

"I'm afraid there is no doubt of it, sir," said Nash—he turned to Aimée: "You must come with us now, please, Miss Griffith—you shall have every facility for seeing a solicitor, you know."

Owen cried, "Aimée?"

She brushed past him without looking at him.

She said, "Don't talk to me. Don't say anything. And for heaven's sake don't *look* at me!"

They went out. Owen stood like a man in a dream.

I waited a bit, then I came up to him.

"If there's anything I can do, Griffith, tell me."

He said like a man in a dream, "Aimée? I don't believe it."

"It may be a mistake," I suggested feebly.

He said slowly, "She wouldn't take it like that if it were. But I would never have believed it. I *can't* believe it."

He sank down on a chair. I made myself useful by finding a stiff drink and bringing it to him. He swallowed it down and it seemed to do him good.

He said, "I couldn't take it in at first. I'm all right now. Thanks, Burton, but there's nothing you can do. Nothing *anyone* can do."

The door opened and Joanna came in. She was very white.

She came over to Owen and looked at me.

She said, "Get out, Jerry. This is my business."

As I went out of the door, I saw her kneel down by his chair.

8

I can't tell you coherently the events of the next twenty-four hours. Various incidents stand out, unrelated to other incidents.

I remember Joanna coming home, very white and drawn, and how I tried to cheer her up, saying:

"Now who's being a ministering angel?"

And of how she smiled in a pitiful twisted way and said, "He says he won't have me, Jerry. He's very *very* proud and stiff!"

And I said, "My girl won't have me either. . . ."

We sat there for a while, Joanna saying at last, "The Burton family isn't exactly in demand at the moment!"

I said, "Never mind, my sweet, we still have each other," and Joanna said, "Somehow or other, Jerry, that doesn't comfort me much just now. . . ."

Owen came the next day and rhapsodized in the most fulsome way about Joanna. She was wonderful, marvelous! The way she'd come to him, the way she was willing to marry him—at once if he liked. But he wasn't going to let her do that. No, she was too good, too fine to be associated with the kind of muck that would start as soon as the papers got hold of the news.

I was fond of Joanna, and knew she was the kind who's all right when standing by in trouble, but I got rather bored with all this highfalutin stuff. I told Owen rather irritably not to be so damned noble.

I went down to the High Street and found everybody's tongue

wagging nineteen to the dozen. Emily Barton was saying that she had never really trusted Aimée Griffith. The grocer's wife was saying with gusto that she'd always thought Miss Griffith had a queer look in her eye—

They had completed the case against Aimée, so I learned from Nash. A search of the house had brought to light the cut pages of Emily Barton's book—in the cupboard under the stairs, of all places, wrapped up in an old roll of wallpaper.

"And a jolly good place too," said Nash appreciatively. "You never know when a prying servant won't tamper with a desk or a locked drawer—but those junk cupboards full of last year's tennis balls and old wallpaper are never opened except to shove something more in."

"The lady would seem to have had a penchant for that particular hiding place," I said.

"Yes. The criminal mind seldom has much variety. By the way, talking of the dead girl, we've got one fact to go upon: There's a large heavy pestle missing from the doctor's dispensary. I'll bet anything you like that's what she was stunned with."

"Rather an awkward thing to carry about," I objected.

"Not for Miss Griffith. She was going to the Guides that afternoon, but she was going to leave flowers and vegetables at the Red Cross stall on the way, so she'd got a whopping great basket with her."

"You haven't found the skewer?"

"No, and I shan't. The poor devil may be mad, but she wasn't mad enough to keep a bloodstained skewer just to make it easy for us, when all she'd got to do was to wash it and return it to a kitchen drawer."

"I suppose," I conceded, "that you can't have everything."

The vicarage had been one of the last places to hear the news. Old Miss Marple was very much distressed by it. She spoke to me very earnestly on the subject:

"It isn't *true*, Mr. Burton. I'm sure it isn't true."

"It's true enough, I'm afraid. They were lying in wait, you know. They actually *saw* her type that letter."

"Yes, yes—perhaps they did. Yes, I can understand *that*."

"And the printed pages from which the letters were cut were found where she'd hidden them in her house."

Miss Marple stared at me. Then she said, in a very low voice, "But that is horrible—really *wicked*."

Mrs. Dane Calthrop came up with a rush and joined us and said, "What's the matter, Jane?"

Miss Marple was murmuring helplessly, "Oh, dear, oh, dear, what can one *do*?"

"What's upset you, Jane?"

Miss Marple said, "There must be *something*. But I am so old and so ignorant and, I am afraid, so foolish."

I felt rather embarrassed and was glad when Mrs. Dane Calthrop took her friend away.

I was to see Miss Marple again that afternoon, however. Much later when I was on my way home.

She was standing near the little bridge at the end of the village, near Mrs. Cleat's cottage, and talking to Megan, of all people.

I wanted to see Megan. I had been wanting to see her all day. I quickened my pace. But as I came up to them, Megan turned on her heel and went off in the other direction.

It made me angry and I would have followed her, but Miss Marple blocked my way.

"I wanted to speak to you," she said. "No, don't go after Megan now. It wouldn't be wise."

I was just going to make a sharp rejoinder when she disarmed me by saying, "That girl has great courage—a very high order of courage."

I still wanted to go after Megan, but Miss Marple said, "Don't try and see her now. I do know what I am talking about. She must keep her courage intact."

There was something about the old lady's assertion that chilled me. It was as though she knew something that I didn't.

I was afraid and didn't know why I was afraid.

I didn't go home. I went back into the High Street and walked up and down aimlessly. I don't know what I was waiting for, nor what I was thinking about. . . .

I got caught by that awful old bore Colonel Appleby. He asked after my pretty sister as usual and then went on:

"What's all this about Griffith's sister being mad as a hatter? They say she's been at the bottom of this anonymous letter business that's been such a confounded nuisance to everybody? Couldn't believe it at first, but they say it's quite true."

I said it was true enough.

"Well, well—I must say our police force is pretty good on the whole. Give 'em time, that's all, give 'em time. Funny business this anonymous letter stunt—these desiccated old women are always the ones who go in for it—though the Griffith woman wasn't bad-looking even if she was a bit long in the tooth. But there aren't any decent-looking girls in this part of the world—except that governess girl of the Symmingtons. She's worth looking at. Pleasant girl, too. Grateful if one does any little thing for her.

"Came across her having a picnic or something with those kids not long ago. They were romping about in the heather and she was knitting—ever so vexed she'd run out of wool. 'Well,' I said, 'like me to run into Lymstock? I've got to call for a rod of mine there. I shan't be more than ten minutes getting it, then I'll run you back again.' She was a bit doubtful about leaving the boys. 'They'll be all right,' I said. 'Who's to harm them?' Wasn't going to have the boys along, no fear! So I ran her in, dropped her at the wool shop, picked her up again later and that was that. Thanked me very prettily. Grateful and all that. Nice girl."

I managed to get away from him.

It was after that, that I caught sight of Miss Marple for the third time. She was coming out of the police station.

Where do one's fears come from? Where do they shape themselves? Where do they hide before coming out into the open?

Just one short phrase. Heard and noted and never quite put aside: "Take me away— It's so awful being here—feeling so wicked . . ."

Why had Megan said that? What had she to feel wicked about?

There could be nothing in Mrs. Symmington's death to make Megan feel wicked.

Why had the child felt wicked? Why? Why?

Could it be because she felt responsible in any way?

Megan? Impossible! *Megan* couldn't have had anything to do with those letters—those foul obscene letters.

Owen Griffith had known a case up north—a schoolgirl . . .

What had Inspector Graves said?

Something about an *adolescent mind . . .*

Innocent middle-aged ladies on operating tables babbled words they hardly knew. Little boys chalking up things on walls.

No, no, not *Megan.*

Heredity? Bad blood? An unconscious inheritance of something abnormal? Her misfortune, not her fault, a curse laid upon her by a past generation?

"I'm not the wife for you. I'm better at hating than loving."

Oh, my Megan, my little child. Not *that!* Anything but that. And that old Tabby is after you, she suspects. She says you have courage. Courage to do *what*?

It was only a brainstorm. It passed. But I wanted to see Megan—I wanted to see her badly.

At half past nine that night I left the house and went down to the town and along to the Symmingtons'.

It was then that an entirely new idea came into my mind. The idea of a woman whom nobody had considered for a moment.

(Or had Nash considered her?)

Wildly unlikely, wildly improbable, and I would have said up to today impossible, too. But that was not so. No, not *impossible*.

I redoubled my pace. Because it was now even more imperative that I should see Megan straightaway.

I passed through the Symmingtons' gate and up to the house. It was a dark overcast night. A little rain was beginning to fall. The visibility was bad.

I saw a line of light from one of the windows. The little morning room?

I hesitated a moment or two, then instead of going up to the front door, I swerved and crept very quietly up to the window, skirting a big bush and keeping low.

The light came from a chink in the curtains, which were not quite drawn. It was easy to look through and see.

It was a strangely peaceful and domestic scene. Symmington in a big armchair, and Elsie Holland, her head bent, busily patching a boy's torn shirt.

I could hear as well as see, for the window was open at the top.

Elsie Holland was speaking:

"But I do think, really, Mr. Symmington, that the boys are quite old enough to go to boarding school. Not that I shan't hate leaving them because I shall. I'm ever so fond of them both."

Symmington said, "I think perhaps you're right about Brian, Miss Holland. I've decided that he shall start next term at Winhays—my old prep school. But Colin is a little young yet. I'd prefer him to wait another year."

"Well, of course I see what you mean. And Colin is perhaps a little young for his age—"

Quiet domestic talk—quiet domestic scene—and a golden head bent over needlework.

Then the door opened and Megan came in.

She stood very straight in the doorway, and I was aware at once of something tense and strung up about her. The skin of her face was tight and drawn and her eyes bright and resolute. There was no diffidence about her tonight and no childishness.

She said, addressing Symmington, but giving him no title (and I suddenly reflected that I never had heard her call him anything. Did she address him as father or as Dick or what?):

"I would like to speak to you, please. Alone."

Symmington looked surprised and, I fancied, not best pleased. He frowned, but Megan carried her point with a determination unusual in her.

She turned to Elsie Holland and said, "Do you mind, Elsie?"

"Oh, of course." Elsie Holland jumped up. She looked startled and a little flurried.

She went to the door and Megan came farther in so that Elsie passed her.

Just for a minute Elsie stood motionless in the doorway looking over her shoulder.

Her lips were closed, she stood quite still, one hand stretched out, the other clasping her needlework to her.

I caught my breath, overwhelmed suddenly by her beauty.

When I think of her now, I always think of her like that—in arrested motion, with that matchless deathless perfection that belonged to ancient Greece.

Then she went out shutting the door.

Symmington said rather fretfully, "Well, Megan, what is it? What do you want?"

Megan had come right up to the table. She stood there looking down at Symmington. I was struck anew by the resolute determination of her face and by something else—a hardness new to me.

Then she opened her lips and said something that startled me to the core.

"I want some money," she said.

The request didn't improve Symmington's temper. He said sharply, "Couldn't you have waited until tomorrow morning? What's the matter, do you think your allowance is inadequate?"

A fair man, I thought even then, open to reason, though not to emotional appeal.

Megan said, "I want a good deal of money."

Symmington sat up straight in his chair. He said coldly:

"You will come of age in a few months' time. Then the money left you by your grandmother will be turned over to you by the Public Trustee."

Megan said:

"You don't understand. I want money from *you*." She went on, speaking faster: "Nobody's ever talked much to me about my father. They've not wanted me to know about him. But I do know that he went to prison and I know why. It was for blackmail!"

She paused.

"Well, I'm his daughter. And perhaps I take after him. Anyway, I'm asking you to give me money because—if you don't—" She stopped and then went on very slowly and evenly—"if you don't—*I shall say what I saw you doing to the cachet that day in my mother's room.*"

There was a pause. Then Symmington said in a completely emotionless voice, "I don't know what you mean."

Megan said, "I think you do."

And she smiled. It was not a nice smile.

Symmington got up. He went over to the writing desk. He took out a checkbook from his pocket and wrote out a check. He blotted it carefully and then came back. He held it out to Megan.

"You're grown up now," he said. "I can understand that you may feel you want to buy something rather special in the way of clothes and all that. I don't know what you're talking about. I didn't pay attention. But here's a check."

Megan looked at it, then she said, "Thank you. That will do to go on with."

She turned and went out of the room. Symmington stared after her and at the closed door, then he turned around and as I saw his face I made a quick uncontrolled movement forward.

It was checked in the most extraordinary fashion. The big bush that I had noticed by the wall stopped being a bush. Superintendent Nash's arms went around me and Superintendent Nash's voice just breathed in my ear:

"Quiet, Burton. For God's sake."

Then, with infinite caution he beat a retreat, his arm impelling me to accompany him.

Around the side of the house he straightened himself and wiped his forehead.

"Of course," he said. "You *would* have to butt in!"

"That girl isn't safe," I said urgently. "You saw his face? We've got to get her out of here."

Nash took a firm grip of my arm.

"Now, look here, Mr. Burton, you've got to *listen*."

Well, I listened.

I didn't like it—but I gave in.

But I insisted on being on the spot and I swore to obey orders implicitly.

So that is how I came with Nash and Parkins into the house by the back door, which was already unlocked.

And I waited with Nash on the upstairs landing behind the velvet curtain masking the window alcove until the clocks in the house struck two, and Symmington's door opened and he went across the landing and into Megan's room.

I did not stir or make a move for I knew that Sergeant Parkins was inside masked by the opening door, and I knew that Parkins was a good man and knew his job, and I knew that I couldn't have trusted myself to keep quiet and not break out.

And waiting there, with my heart thudding, I saw Symmington come out with Megan in his arms and carry her downstairs, with Nash and myself a discreet distance behind him.

He carried her through to the kitchen and he had just arranged her comfortably with her head in the gas oven and had turned on the gas when Nash and I came through the kitchen door and switched on the light.

And that was the end of Richard Symmington. He collapsed. Even while I was hauling Megan out and turning off the gas I saw the collapse. He didn't even try to fight. He knew he'd played and lost.

Upstairs I sat by Megan's bed waiting for her to come around and occasionally cursing Nash.

"How do you know she's all right? It was too big a risk."

Nash was very soothing.

"Just a soporific in the milk she always had by her bed. Nothing more. It stands to reason, he couldn't risk her being poisoned. As far as he's concerned the whole business is closed with Miss Griffith's arrest. He can't afford to have any mysterious death. No violence, no poison. But if a rather unhappy type of girl broods over her mother's suicide, and finally goes and puts her head in the gas oven—well, people just say that she was never quite normal and the shock of her mother's death finished her."

I said, watching Megan, "She's a long time coming around."

"You heard what Dr. Griffith said? Heart and pulse quite all right—she'll just sleep and wake naturally. Stuff he gives a lot of his patients, he says."

Megan stirred. She murmured something.

Superintendent Nash unobtrusively left the room.

Presently Megan opened her eyes.

"Jerry."

"Hullo, sweet."

"Did I do it well?"

"You might have been blackmailing ever since your cradle!"

Megan closed her eyes again. Then she murmured:

"Last night—I was writing to you—in case anything went—went wrong. But I was too sleepy to finish. It's over there."

I went across to the writing table. In a shabby little blotter I found Megan's unfinished letter.

"My dear Jerry," it began primly:

"I was reading my school Shakespeare and the sonnet that begins:

> "'So are you to my thoughts as food to life
> Or as sweet-season'd showers are to the
> ground'

and I see that I am in love with you after all, because that is what I feel." . . .

"So you see," said Mrs. Dane Calthrop, "I was quite right to call in an expert."

I stared at her. We were all at the vicarage. The rain was pouring down outside and there was a pleasant log fire, and Mrs. Dane Calthrop had just wandered around, beat up a sofa cushion and put it for some reason of her own on the top of the grand piano.

"But did you?" I said, surprised. "Who was it? What did he do?"

"It wasn't a he," said Mrs. Dane Calthrop.

With a sweeping gesture she indicated Miss Marple. Miss Marple had finished the fleecy knitting and was now engaged with a crochet hook and a ball of cotton.

"That's my expert," said Mrs. Dane Calthrop. "Jane Marple. Look at her well. I tell you, that woman knows more about the different kinds of human wickedness than anyone I've ever known."

"I don't think you should put it quite like that, dear," murmured Miss Marple.

"But you do."

"One sees a good deal of human nature living in a village all the year around," said Miss Marple placidly.

Then, seeming to feel it was expected of her, she laid down her crochet, and delivered a gentle old-maidish dissertation on murder.

"The great thing in these cases is to keep an absolutely open mind. Most crimes, you see, are so absurdly simple. This one was. Quite sane and straightforward—and quite understandable—in an unpleasant way, of course."

"Very unpleasant!"

"The truth was really so very obvious. You saw it, you know, Mr. Burton."

"Indeed I did not."

"But you did. You indicated the whole thing to me. You saw perfectly the relationship of one thing to the other, but you just hadn't enough self-confidence to see what those feelings of yours meant. To begin with, that tiresome phrase 'No smoke without fire.' It irritated you, but you proceeded quite correctly to label it for what it was—a smoke screen. Misdirection, you see—everybody looking at the wrong thing—the anonymous letters, but the whole point was that there *weren't* any anonymous letters!"

"But, my dear Miss Marple, I can assure you that there *were*. I had one."

"Oh, yes, but they weren't real at all. Dear Maud here tumbled to that. Even in peaceful Lymstock there are plenty of scandals, and I can assure you any *woman* living in the place would have known about them and used them. But a man, you see, isn't interested in gossip in the same way—especially a detached logical man like Mr. Symmington. But a genuine woman writer of those letters would have made her letters much more to the point.

"So you see that if you disregard the smoke and come to the fire you know where you are. You just come down to the actual facts of what happened. And putting aside the letters, just one thing happened—Mrs. Symmington died.

"So then, naturally, one thinks of who might have wanted Mrs.

Symmington to die, and of course the very first person one thinks of in such a case is, I am afraid, the *husband*. And one asks oneself is there any *reason?*—any *motive?*—for instance, *any other woman?*

"And the very first thing I hear is that there is a very attractive young governess in the house. So clear, isn't it? Mr. Symmington, a rather dry repressed unemotional man, tied to a querulous and neurotic wife and then suddenly this radiant young creature comes along.

"I'm afraid, you know, that gentlemen, when they fall in love at a certain age, get the disease very badly. It's quite a madness. And Mr. Symmington, as far as I can make out, was never actually a *good* man—he wasn't very kind or very affectionate or very sympathetic—his qualities were all negative—so he hadn't really the strength to fight his madness. And in a place like this, only his wife's death would solve his problem. He wanted to marry the girl, you see. She's very respectable and so is he. And besides, he's devoted to his children and didn't want to give them up. He wanted everything, his home, his children, his respectability and Elsie. And the price he would have to pay for that was murder.

"He chose, I do think, a very clever way. He knew so well from his experience of criminal cases how soon suspicion falls on the husband if a wife dies unexpectedly—and the possibility of exhumation in the case of poison. So he created a death which seemed only incidental to something else. He created a nonexistent anonymous letter writer. And the clever thing was that the police were certain to suspect a *woman*—and they were quite right in a way. All the letters were a woman's letters; he cribbed them very cleverly from the letters in the case last year and from a case Dr. Griffith told him about. I don't mean that he was so crude as to reproduce any letter verbatim, but he took phrases and expressions from them and mixed them up, and the net result was that the letters definitely represented a woman's mind—a half-crazy repressed personality.

"He knew all the tricks that the police use, handwriting, typewriting tests, etc. He's been preparing his crime for some time. He typed all the envelopes before he gave away the typewriter to the Women's Institute, and he cut the pages from the book at Little Furze probably quite a long time ago when he was waiting in the drawing room one day. People don't open books of sermons much!

"And finally, having got his false Poison Pen well established, he staged the real thing. A fine afternoon when the governess and the boys and his stepdaughter would be out, and the servants having their regular day out. He couldn't foresee that the little maid Agnes would quarrel with her boy friend and come back to the house."

Joanna asked, "But what did she see? Do you know that?"

"I don't *know*. I can only guess. My guess would be that she didn't see anything."

"That it was all a mare's nest?"

"No, no, my dear, I mean that she stood at the pantry window all the afternoon waiting for the young man to come and make it up and that—quite literally she saw nothing. That is, *no one* came to the house at all, not the postman, nor anybody else."

"It would take her some time, being slow, to realize that that was very odd—because apparently Mrs. Symmington *had* received an anonymous letter that afternoon."

"Didn't she receive one?" I asked, puzzled.

"But of course not! As I say, this crime is so simple. Her husband just put the cyanide in the top cachet of the ones she took in the afternoon when her sciatica came on after lunch. All Symmington had to do was to get home before, or at the same time as Elsie Holland, call his wife, get no answer, go up to her room, drop a spot of cyanide in the plain glass of water she had used to swallow the cachet, toss the crumpled-up anonymous letter into the grate, and put by her hand the scrap of paper with '*I can't go on*' written on it."

Miss Marple turned to me.

"You were quite right about that, too, Mr. Burton. A 'scrap of paper' was all wrong. People don't leave suicide notes on small torn scraps of paper. They use a *sheet* of paper—and very often an envelope too. Yes, the scrap of paper was wrong and you knew it."

"You are rating me too high," I said. "I knew nothing."

"But you did, you really *did*, Mr. Burton. Otherwise why were you immediately impressed by the message your sister left scribbled on the telephone pad?"

I repeated slowly: " 'Say that I *can't go on Tuesday*'—I see! 'I can't go on'?"

Miss Marple beamed on me.

"Exactly. Mr. Symmington came across such a message and saw its possibilities. He tore off the words he wanted for when the time came—a message genuinely in his wife's handwriting."

"Was there any further brilliance on my part?" I asked.

Miss Marple twinkled at me.

"You put me on the track, you know. You assembled those facts together for me—in sequence—and on top of it you told me the most important thing of all—that Elsie Holland had never received any anonymous letters."

"Do you know," I said, "last night I thought that *she* was the letter writer and that that was why there had been no letters written to her?"

"Oh, dear me, no. . . . The person who writes anonymous letters practically always sends them to herself as well. That's part of the— well, the excitement, I suppose. No, no, the fact interested me for *quite* another reason. It was really, you see, Mr. Symmington's one weakness. He couldn't bring himself to write a foul letter to the girl he loved. It's a very interesting sidelight on human nature—and a credit to him, in a way—but it's where he gave himself away."

Joanna said, "And he killed Agnes? But surely that was quite unnecessary?"

"Perhaps it was, but what you don't realize, my dear (not having killed anyone), is that your judgment is distorted afterward and everything seems exaggerated. No doubt he heard the girl telephoning to Partridge, saying she'd been worried ever since Mrs. Symmington's death, that there was something she didn't understand. He can't take any chances—this stupid foolish girl has seen *something*, knows something."

"Yet apparently he was at his office all that afternoon?"

"I should imagine he killed her before he went. Miss Holland was in the dining room and kitchen. He just went out into the hall, opened and shut the front door as though he was going out, then slipped into the little cloakroom.

"When only Agnes was left in the house, he probably rang the front-door bell, slipped back into the cloakroom, came out behind her and hit her on the head as she was opening the front door, and then after thrusting the body into the cupboard, he hurried along to his office, arriving just a little late if anyone had happened to notice it, but they probably didn't. You see, no one was suspecting a *man*."

"Abominable brute," said Mrs. Dane Calthrop.

"You're not sorry for him, Mrs. Dane Calthrop?" I inquired.

"Not in the least. Why?"

"I'm glad to hear it, that's all."

Joanna said:

"But why Aimée Griffith? I know that the police have found the pestle taken from Owen's dispensary—and the skewer too. I suppose it's not so easy for a man to return things to kitchen drawers. And guess where they were? Superintendent Nash only told me just now when I met him on my way here. In one of those musty old deed boxes in his office. Estate of Sir Jasper Harrington-West, deceased."

"Poor Jasper," said Mrs. Dane Calthrop. "He was a cousin of mine. Such a correct old boy. He would have had a fit!"

"Wasn't it madness to keep them?" I asked.

"Probably madder to throw them away," said Mrs. Dane Calthrop. "No one had any suspicions about Symmington."

"He didn't strike her with the pestle," said Joanna. "There was a clock weight there too, with hair and blood on it. He pinched the pestle, they think, on the day Aimée was arrested, and hid the book pages in her house. And that brings me back to my original question. What about Aimée Griffith? The police actually *saw* her write that letter."

"Yes, of course," said Miss Marple. "She did write *that* letter."

"But why?"

"Oh, my dear, surely you have realized that Miss Griffith had been in love with Symmington all her life?"

"Poor thing!" said Mrs. Dane Calthrop mechanically.

"They'd always been good friends, and I daresay she thought, after Mrs. Symmington's death, that some day, perhaps—well—" Miss Marple coughed delicately. "And then the gossip began spreading about Elsie Holland and I expect that upset her badly. She thought of the girl as a designing minx worming her way into Symmington's affections and quite unworthy of him. And so, I think, she succumbed to temptation. Why not add one more anonymous letter, and frighten the girl out of the place? It must have seemed quite safe to her and she took, as she thought, every precaution."

"Well?" said Joanna. "Finish the story."

"I should imagine," said Miss Marple slowly, "that when Miss Holland showed that letter to Symmington he realized at once who had written it, and he saw a chance to finish the case once and for all, and make himself safe. Not very nice—no, not very nice, but he was frightened, you see. The police wouldn't be satisfied until they'd got the anonymous letter writer. When he took the letter down to the police and he found they'd actually seen Aimée writing it, he felt he'd got a chance in a thousand of finishing the whole thing.

"He took the family to tea there that afternoon and as he came from the office with his attaché case, he could easily bring the torn-out book pages to hide under the stairs and clinch the case. Hiding them under the stairs was a neat touch. It recalled the disposal of Agnes' body, and, from the practical point of view, it was very easy for him. When he followed Aimée and the police, just a minute or two in the hall passing through would be enough."

"All the same," I said, "there's one thing I can't forgive you for, Miss Marple—roping in Megan."

Miss Marple put down her crochet which she had resumed. She looked at me over her spectacles and her eyes were stern.

"My dear young man, *something* had to be done. There was no evidence against this very clever and unscrupulous man. I needed someone to help me, someone of high courage and good brains. I found the person I needed."

"It was very dangerous for her."

"Yes, it was dangerous, but we are not put into this world, Mr. Burton, to avoid danger when an innocent fellow creature's life is at stake. You understand me?"

I understood.

It was morning in the High Street.

Miss Emily Barton came out of the grocer's with her shopping bag. Her cheeks were pink and her eyes were excited.

"Oh, dear, Mr. Burton, I really am in such a flutter. To think I really am going on a cruise at last!"

"I hope you'll enjoy it."

"Oh, I'm sure I shall. I should never have dared to go by myself. It does seem so *providential* the way everything has turned out. For a long time I've felt that I ought to part with Little Furze, that my means were really too straitened, but I couldn't bear the idea of *strangers* there.

"But now that you have bought it and are going to live there with Megan—it is quite different. And then dear Aimée, after her terrible ordeal, not quite knowing what to do with herself, and her brother getting married (how nice to think you have *both* settled down with us!), and agreeing to come with me. We mean to be away quite a long time. We might even"—Miss Emily dropped her voice—"*go around the world!* And Aimée is so splendid and so practical. I really do think—don't you?—that everything turns out for the *best.*"

Just for a fleeting moment I thought of Mrs. Symmington and Agnes Woddell in their graves in the churchyard and wondered if they would agree, and then I remembered that Agnes' boy friend hadn't been very fond of her and that Mrs. Symmington hadn't been very nice to Megan, and, what the hell? We've all got to die some time! And I agreed with happy Miss Emily that everything was for the best in the best of possible worlds.

I went along the High Street and in at the Symmingtons' gate and Megan came out to meet me.

It was not a romantic meeting because an outsize old English sheep dog came out with Megan and nearly knocked me over with his ill-timed exuberance.

"Isn't he *adorable*?" said Megan.

"A little overwhelming. Is he ours?"

"Yes, he's a wedding present from Joanna. We *have* had nice wedding presents, haven't we? That fluffy woolly thing that we don't know what it's for from Miss Marple, and the lovely Crown Derby tea set from Mr. Pye, and Elsie has sent me a toast rack—"

"How typical!" I interjected.

"And she's got a post with a dentist and is very happy. And—where was I?"

"Enumerating wedding presents. Don't forget if you change your mind you'll have to send them all back."

"I shan't change my mind. What else have we got? Oh, yes, Mrs. Dane Calthrop has sent an Egyptian scarab."

"Original woman," I said.

"Oh! Oh! But you don't know the best. *Partridge* has actually sent me a present. It's the most hideous tea cloth you've ever seen. But I think she *must* like me now because she says she embroidered it all with her own hands."

"In a design of sour grapes and thistles, I suppose?"

"No; true lover's knots."

"Dear, dear," I said, "Partridge *is* coming on."

Megan dragged me into the house.

She said:

"There's just one thing I can't make out. Besides the dog's own collar and lead, Joanna has sent an extra collar and lead. What do you think that's for?"

"That," I said, "is Joanna's little joke."

Agatha Christie

—◆—

A Murder
Is
Announced

To Ralph and Anne Newman
at whose house I first tasted
"Delicious Death!"

Contents

CONTENTS

1

"A Murder Is Announced"

Between 7:30 and 8:30 every morning except Sundays, Johnnie Butt made the round of the village of Chipping Cleghorn on his bicycle, whistling vociferously through his teeth and alighting at each house or cottage to shove through the letter box such morning papers as had been ordered by the occupants of the house in question from Mr. Totman, stationer, of the High Street. Thus at Colonel and Mrs. Easterbrook's he delivered *The Times* and the *Daily Graphic*; at Mrs. Swettenham's he left *The Times* and the *Daily Worker*; at Miss Hinchliffe and Miss Murgatroyd's he left the *Daily Telegraph* and the *News Chronicle*; at Miss Blacklock's he left the *Telegraph*, *The Times* and the *Daily Mail*.

At all these houses, and indeed at practically every house in Chipping Cleghorn, he delivered every Friday a copy of the *North Benham News and Chipping Cleghorn Gazette*, known locally simply as the *Gazette*.

Thus, on Friday mornings, after a hurried glance at the headlines in the daily paper (INTERNATIONAL SITUATION CRITICAL! U.N.O. MEETS TODAY! BLOODHOUNDS SEEK BLOND TYPIST'S KILLER! THREE COLLIERIES IDLE. TWENTY-THREE DIE OF FOOD POISONING IN SEASIDE HOTEL, *etc.*), most of the inhabitants of Chipping Cleghorn eagerly opened the *Gazette* and plunged into the local news. After a cursory glance at CORRESPONDENCE (in which the passionate hates and feuds of rural life found full play), nine out of ten subscribers then turned to the PERSONAL column. Here were grouped together higgledy-piggledy articles for sale or wanted, frenzied appeals for domestic help, innumerable insertions regarding dogs, announcements concerning poultry and garden equipment; and various other items of an interesting nature to those living in the small community of Chipping Cleghorn.

This particular Friday, October 29th—was no exception to the rule. . . .

II

Mrs. Swettenham, pushing back the pretty little gray curls from her forehead, opened *The Times,* looked with a lackluster eye at the left-hand center page, decided that, as usual, if there *was* any exciting news, *The Times* had succeeded in camouflaging it in an impeccable manner; took a look at the BIRTHS, MARRIAGES and DEATHS, particularly the latter; then, her duty done, she put aside *The Times* and eagerly seized the Chipping Cleghorn *Gazette.*

When her son Edmund entered the room a moment later, she was already deep in the PERSONAL column.

"Good morning, dear," said Mrs. Swettenham. "The Smedleys are selling their Daimler. A 1935—that's rather a long time ago, isn't it?"

Her son grunted, poured himself a cup of coffee, helped himself to a couple of kippers, sat down at the table and opened the *Daily Worker* which he propped up against the toast rack.

"Bull mastiff puppies," read out Mrs. Swettenham. "I really don't know how people manage to feed big dogs nowadays—I really don't. . . . H'm, Selina Lawrence is advertising for a cook again. I could tell her it's just a waste of time advertising in these days. She hasn't put her address, only a box number—that's quite fatal—I could have told her so—servants simply insist on knowing where they are going. They like a good address. . . . False teeth—I can't think why false teeth are so popular. Best prices paid. . . . Beautiful bulbs. Our special selection. They sound rather cheap. . . . Here's a girl wants an Interesting post—would travel. I daresay! Who wouldn't? Dachshunds . . . I've never really cared for dachshunds myself—I don't mean because they're German, because we've got over all that—I just don't care for them, that's all. Yes, Mrs. Finch?"

The door had opened to admit the head and torso of a grim-looking female in an aged velvet beret.

"Good morning, mum," said Mrs. Finch. "Can I clear?"

"Not yet. We haven't finished," said Mrs. Swettenham. "Not quite finished," she added ingratiatingly.

Casting a look at Edmund and his paper, Mrs. Finch sniffed and withdrew.

"I've only just begun," said Edmund, just as his mother remarked:

"I do wish you wouldn't read that horrid paper, Edmund. Mrs. Finch doesn't like it at all."

"I don't see what my political views have to do with Mrs. Finch."

"And it isn't," pursued Mrs. Swettenham, "as though you were a worker. You don't do any work at all."

"That's not in the least true," said Edmund indignantly. "I'm writing a book."

"I meant real work," said Mrs. Swettenham. "And Mrs. Finch does matter. If she takes a dislike to us and won't come, who else could we get?"

"Advertise in the *Gazette*," said Edmund, grinning.

"I've just told you that's no use. Oh, dear me, nowadays unless one has an old Nannie in the family, who will go into the kitchen and do everything, one is simply sunk."

"Well, why haven't we an old Nannie? How remiss of you not to have provided me with one! What were you thinking about?"

"You had an *ayah*, dear."

"No foresight," murmured Edmund.

Mrs. Swettenham was once more deep in the PERSONAL column.

"Second-hand motor-mower for sale. Now I wonder—Goodness, what a price! . . . More dachshunds. . . . Do write or communicate, desperate, Woggles. What silly nicknames people have. . . . Cocker Spaniels . . . do you remember darling Susie, Edmund? She really was human. Understood every word you said to her. . . . Sheraton sideboard for sale. Genuine family antique. Mrs. Lucas, Dayas Hall. What a liar that woman is! Sheraton indeed!"

Mrs. Swettenham sniffed and then continued her reading:

"All a mistake, darling. Undying love. Friday as usual. J.—I suppose they've had a lovers' quarrel—or do you think it's a code for burglars? More dachshunds! Really, I do think people have gone a little crazy about breeding dachshunds. I mean, there are other dogs. Your uncle Simon used to breed Manchester terriers. Such graceful little things. I do like dogs with legs. . . . Lady going abroad will sell her navy two-piece suiting . . . no measurements or price given. A marriage is announced—no, *a murder . . . what?* Well, I never! Edmund,

Edmund, listen to this: *A murder is announced and will take place on Friday, October 29th, at Little Paddocks, at 6:30 P.M. Friends please accept this, the only intimation.* What an extraordinary thing! *Edmund!*"

"What's that?" Edmund looked up from his newspaper.

"Friday, October 29th—why, that's today."

"Let me see." Her son took the paper from her.

"But what does it mean?" Mrs. Swettenham asked with lively curiosity.

Edmund Swettenham rubbed his nose doubtfully.

"Some sort of party, I suppose. The Murder Game—that kind of thing."

"Oh," said Mrs. Swettenham doubtfully. "It seems a very odd way of doing it. Just sticking it in the advertisements like that. Not at all like Letitia Blacklock, who always seems to me such a sensible woman."

"Probably got up by the bright young things she has in the house."

"It's very short notice. Today. Do you think we're just supposed to go?"

"It says, 'Friends please accept this, the only intimation,'" her son pointed out.

"Well, I think these new-fangled ways of giving invitations are very tiresome," said Mrs. Swettenham decidedly.

"All right, Mother, you needn't go."

"No," agreed Mrs. Swettenham.

There was a pause.

"Do you really want that last piece of toast, Edmund?"

"I should have thought my being properly nourished mattered more than letting that old hag clear the table."

"Sh, dear, she'll hear you . . . Edmund, what happens at a Murder Game?"

"I don't know exactly. They pin pieces of paper upon you, or something—no, I think you draw them out of a hat. And somebody's the victim and somebody else is a detective—and then they turn the lights out and somebody taps you on the shoulder and then you scream and lie down and sham dead."

"It sounds quite exciting."

"Probably a beastly bore. I'm not going."

"Nonsense, Edmund," said Mrs. Swettenham resolutely. "I'm going and you're coming with me. That's settled!"

III

"Archie," said Mrs. Easterbrook to her husband, "listen to this."

Colonel Easterbrook paid no attention, because he was already snorting with impatience over an article in *The Times*.

"Trouble with these fellows is," he said, "that none of them know the first thing about India! Not the first thing!"

"I know, dear, I know."

"If they did, they wouldn't write such piffle."

"Yes, I know. Archie, do listen. *A murder is announced and will take place on Friday, October 29th* (that's today), *at Little Paddocks, at 6:30 P.M. Friends please accept this, the only intimation.*"

She paused triumphantly. Colonel Easterbrook looked at her indulgently but without much interest.

"Murder Game," he said.

"Oh."

"That's all it is. Mind you," he unbent a little, "it can be very good fun if it's well done. But it needs good organizing by someone who knows the ropes. You draw lots. One person's the murderer, nobody knows who. Lights out. Murderer chooses his victim. The victim has to county twenty before he screams. Then the person who's chosen to be the detective takes charge. Questions everybody. Where they were, what they were doing, tries to trip the real fellow up. Yes, it's a good game—if the detective—er—knows something about police work."

"Like you, Archie. You had all those interesting cases to try in your district."

Colonel Easterbrook smiled indulgently and gave his mustache a complacent twirl.

"Yes, Laura," he said. "I daresay I could give them a hint or two." And he straightened his shoulders.

"Miss Blacklock ought to have asked you to help her in getting the thing up."

The colonel snorted.

"Oh, well, she's got that young cub staying with her. Expect this is his idea. Nephew or something. Funny idea, though, sticking it in the paper."

"It was in the PERSONAL column. We might never have seen it. I suppose it is an invitation, Archie?"

"Funny kind of invitation. I can tell you one thing. They can count me out."

"Oh, Archie," Mrs. Easterbrook's voice rose in a shrill wail.

"Short notice. For all they know I might be busy."

"But you're not, are you, darling?" Mrs. Easterbrook lowered her voice persuasively. "And I do think, Archie, that you really ought to go—just to help poor Miss Blacklock out. I'm sure she's counting on you to make the thing a success. I mean, you know so much about police work and procedure. The whole thing will fall flat if you don't go and help to make it a success. After all, one must be neighborly."

Mrs. Easterbrook put her synthetic blond head on one side and opened her blue eyes very wide.

"Of course, if you put it like that, Laura . . ." Colonel Easterbrook twirled his gray mustache again importantly, and looked with indulgence on his fluffy little wife. Mrs. Easterbrook was at least thirty years younger than her husband.

"If you put it like that, Laura," he said.

"I really do think it's your duty, Archie," said Mrs. Easterbrook solemnly.

IV

The Chipping Cleghorn *Gazette* had also been delivered at Boulders, the picturesque three cottages knocked into one, inhabited by Miss Hinchliffe and Miss Murgatroyd.

"Hinch?"

"What is it, Murgatroyd?"

"Where are you?"

"Henhouse."

"Oh."

Paddling gingerly through the long wet grass, Miss Amy Murgatroyd approached her friend. The latter, attired in corduroy slacks and battle-dress tunic, was conscientiously stirring in handfuls of balancer meal to a repellently steaming basin full of cooked potato peelings and cabbage stumps.

She turned her head with its short manlike crop and weather-beaten countenance towards her friend.

Miss Murgatroyd, who was fat and amiable, wore a checked tweed skirt and a shapeless pullover of brilliant royal blue. Her curly

146

bird's-nest of gray hair was in a good deal of disorder and she was slightly out of breath.

"In the *Gazette*," she panted. "Just listen—what can it mean? *A murder is announced and will take place on Friday, October 29th, at Little Paddocks, at 6:30 P.M. Friends please accept this, the only intimation.*"

She paused, breathless, as she finished reading, and awaited some authoritative pronouncement.

"Daft," said Miss Hinchliffe.

"Yes, but what do you think it means?"

"Means a drink, anyway," said Miss Hinchliffe.

"You think it's a sort of invitation?"

"We'll find out what it means when we get there," said Miss Hinchliffe. "Bad sherry, I expect. You'd better get off the grass, Murgatroyd. You've got your bedroom slippers on still. They're soaked."

"Oh, dear." Miss Murgatroyd looked down ruefully at her feet. "How many eggs today?"

"Seven. That damned hen's still broody. I must get her into the coop."

"It's a funny way of putting it, don't you think?" Amy Murgatroyd asked, reverting to the notice in the *Gazette*. Her voice was slightly wistful.

But her friend was made of sterner and more single-minded stuff. She was intent on dealing with recalcitrant poultry and no announcement in a paper, however enigmatic, could deflect her.

She squelched heavily through the mud and pounced upon a speckled hen. There was a loud and indignant squawking.

"Give me ducks every time," said Miss Hinchliffe. "Far less trouble."

V

"Oo scrumptious!" said Mrs. Harmon across the breakfast table to her husband, the Rev. Julian Harmon. "There's going to be a murder at Miss Blacklock's."

"A murder?" said her husband, slightly surprised. "When?"

"This afternoon . . . at least this evening. Six-thirty. Oh, bad luck, darling; you've got your preparations for confirmation then. It is a shame. And you do so love murders!"

"I don't really know what you're talking about, Bunch."

Mrs. Harmon, the roundness of whose form and face had early

led to the sobriquet of "Bunch" being substituted for her baptismal name of Diana, handed the *Gazette* across the table.

"There. All among the second-hand pianos and the old teeth."

"What a very extraordinary announcement."

"Isn't it?" said Bunch happily. "You wouldn't think that Miss Black-lock cared about murders and games and things, would you? I suppose it's the young Simmonses put her up to it—though I should have thought Julia Simmons would find murders rather crude. Still, there it is, and I do think, darling, it's a shame you can't be there. Anyway, I'll go and tell you all about it, though it's rather wasted on me, because I don't really like games that happen in the dark. They frighten me, and I do hope I shan't have to be the one who's murdered. If someone suddenly puts a hand on my shoulder and whispers, 'You're dead,' I know my heart will give such a big bump that perhaps it really might kill me! Do you think that's likely?"

"No, Bunch. I think you're going to live to be an old, old woman—with me."

"And die on the same day and be buried in the same grave. That would be lovely."

Bunch beamed from ear to ear at this agreeable prospect.

"You see very happy, Bunch," said her husband, smiling.

"Who'd not be happy if they were me?" demanded Bunch rather confusedly. "With you and Susan and Edward, and all of you fond of me and not caring if I'm stupid—And the sun shining! And this lovely big house to live in!"

The Rev. Julian Harmon looked round the big bare dining room and assented doubtfully.

"Some people would think it was the last straw to have to live in this great rambling draughty place."

"Well, I like big rooms. All the nice smells from outside can get in and stay there. And you can be untidy and leave things about and they don't clutter you."

"No labor-saving devices or central heating? It means a lot of work for you, Bunch."

"Oh, Julian, it doesn't. I get up at half past six and light the boiler and rush round like a steam-engine, and by eight it's all done. And I keep it nice, don't I, with beeswax and polish and big jars of autumn leaves? It's not really harder to keep a big house clean than a small one. You go round with mops and things much quicker, because your behind isn't always bumping into things like it is in a small room.

And I like sleeping in a big cold room—it's so cozy to snuggle down with just the tip of your nose telling you what it's like up above. And whatever size house you live in, you peel the same amount of potatoes and wash up the same amount of plates and all that. Think how nice it is for Edward and Susan to have a big empty room to play in where they can have railways and dolls' tea parties all over the floor and never have to put them away. And then it's nice to have extra bits of the house that you can let people have to live in. Jimmy Symes and Johnnie Finch—they'd have had to live with their in-laws otherwise. And you know, Julian, it isn't nice living with your in-laws. You're devoted to mother, but you wouldn't really have liked to start our married life living with her and father. And I shouldn't have liked it either. I'd have gone on feeling like a little girl."

Julian smiled at her.

"You're rather like a little girl still, Bunch."

Julian Harmon himself had clearly been a model designed by nature for the age of sixty. He was still about twenty-five years short of achieving Nature's purpose.

"I know I'm stupid—"

"You're not stupid, Bunch. You're very clever."

"No, I'm not. I'm not a bit intellectual. Though I do try . . . and I really love it when you talk to me about books and history and things. I think perhaps it wasn't an awfully good idea to read Gibbon aloud to me in the evenings, because if it's been a cold wind out, and it's nice and hot by the fire, there's something about Gibbon that does rather make me go to sleep."

Julian laughed.

"But I do love listening to you, Julian. Tell me the story again about the old vicar who preached about Ahasuerus."

"You know that by heart, Bunch."

"Just tell it me again. Please."

Her husband complied.

"It was old Scrymgour. Somebody looked into his church one day. He was leaning out of the pulpit and preaching fervently to a couple of old charwomen. He was shaking his finger at them and saying, 'Aha! I know what you are thinking. You think that the Great Ahasuerus of the First Lesson was Artaxerxes the Second. But he wasn't!' And then with enormous triumph, 'He was Artaxerxes the Third!' "

It had never struck Julian Harmon as a particularly funny story, but it never failed to amuse Bunch.

Her clear laugh floated out.

"The old pet!" she exclaimed. "I think you'll be exactly like that some day, Julian."

Julian looked rather uneasy.

"I know," he said with humility. "I do feel very strongly that I can't always get the proper simple approach."

"I shouldn't worry," said Bunch, rising and beginning to pile the breakfast plates on a tray. "Mrs. Butt told me yesterday that Butt, who never went to church and used to be practically the local atheist, comes every Sunday now on purpose to hear you preach."

She went on, with a very fair imitation of Mrs. Butt's super refined voice:

"'And Butt was saying only the other day, Madam, to Mr. Timkins from Little Worsdale, that we'd got real culture here in Chipping Cleghorn. Not like Mr. Goss, at Little Worsdale, who talks to the congregation as though they were children who hadn't had any education. Real culture, Butt said, that's what we've got. Our vicar's a highly educated gentleman—Oxford, not Milchester—and he gives us the full benefit of his education. All about the Romans and the Greeks he knows, and the Babylonians and the Assyrians, too. And even the vicarage cat, Butt says, is called after an Assyrian king!' So there's glory for you," finished Bunch triumphantly. "Goodness, I must get on with things or I shall never get done. Come along, Tiglath-Pileser, you shall have the herring bones."

Opening the door and holding it dexterously ajar with her foot, she shot through with the loaded tray, singing in a loud and not particularly tuneful voice, her own version of a sporting song:

> "It's a fine murdering day" (sang Bunch),
> "And as balmy as May,
> And the sleuths from the village are gone,"

A rattle of crockery being dumped in the sink drowned the next lines, but as the Rev. Julian Harmon left the house, he heard the final triumphant assertion:

> "And we'll all go a'murdering today!"

2

Breakfast at Little Paddocks

At Little Paddocks also breakfast was in progress.

Miss Blacklock, a woman of sixty-odd, the owner of the house, sat at the head of the table. She wore country tweeds—and with them, rather incongruously, a choker necklace of large false pearls. She was reading Lane Norcott in the *Daily Mail*. Julia Simmons was languidly glancing through the *Telegraph*. Patrick Simmons was checking up on the crossword in *The Times*. Miss Dora Bunner was giving her attention wholeheartedly to the local weekly paper.

Miss Blacklock gave a subdued chuckle, Patrick muttered, "Adherent—not adhesive—that's where I went wrong."

Suddenly a loud cluck, like a startled hen, came from Miss Bunner.

"Letty—Letty—have you seen this? Whatever can it mean?"

"What's the matter, Dora?"

"The most extraordinary advertisement. It says Little Paddocks quite distinctly. But whatever can it mean?"

"If you'd let me see, Dora dear—"

Miss Bunner obediently surrendered the paper into Miss Blacklock's outstretched hand, pointing to the item with a tremulous forefinger.

"Just look, Letty."

Miss Blacklock looked. Her eyebrows went up. She threw a quick scrutinizing glance round the table. Then she read the advertisement out loud:

"A murder is announced and will take place on Friday, October 29th, at Little Paddocks, at 6:30 p.m. Friends please accept this, the only intimation."

Then she said sharply:

"Patrick, is this your idea?"

Her eyes rested searchingly on the handsome devil-may-care face of the young man at the other end of the table.

Patrick Simmons' disclaimer came quickly.

"No, indeed, Aunt Letty. Whatever put that idea into your head? Why should I know anything about it?"

"I wouldn't put it past you," said Miss Blacklock grimly. "I thought it might be your idea of a joke."

"A joke? Nothing of the kind."

"And you, Julia?"

Julia, looking bored, said: "Of course not."

Miss Bunner murmured: "Do you think Mrs. Haymes—" and looked at an empty place where someone had breakfasted earlier.

"Oh, I don't think our Phillipa would try and be funny," said Patrick. "She's a serious girl, she is."

"But what's the idea, anyway?" said Julia, yawning. "What does it mean?"

Miss Blacklock said slowly, "I suppose—it's some silly sort of hoax."

"But why?" Dora Bunner exclaimed. "What's the point of it? It seems a very stupid sort of joke. And in very bad taste."

Her flabby cheeks quivered indignantly, and her shortsighted eyes sparkled with indignation.

Miss Blacklock smiled at her.

"Don't work yourself up over it, Bunny," she said. "It's just somebody's idea of humor, but I wish I knew whose."

"It says today," pointed out Miss Bunner. "Today at 6:30 p.m. What do you think is going to happen?"

"Death!" said Patrick in sepulchral tones. "Delicious Death."

"Be quiet, Patrick," said Miss Blacklock as Miss Bunner gave a little yelp.

"I only meant the special cake that Mitzi makes," said Patrick apologetically. "You know we always call it Delicious Death."

Miss Blacklock smiled a little absent-mindedly.

Miss Bunner persisted, "But, Letty, what do you really think—"

Her friend cut across the words with reassuring cheerfulness.

"I know one thing that will happen at 6:30," she said dryly. "We'll have half the village up here, agog with curiosity. I'd better make sure we've got some sherry in the house."

II

"You are worried, aren't you, Letty?"

Miss Blacklock started. She had been sitting at her writing table, absent-mindedly drawing little fishes on the blotting paper. She looked up into the anxious face of her old friend.

She was not quite sure what to say to Dora Bunner. Bunny, she knew, mustn't be worried or upset. She was silent for a moment or two, thinking.

She and Dora Bunner had been at school together. Dora then had been a pretty, fair-haired, blue-eyed, rather stupid girl. Her being stupid hadn't mattered, because her gaiety and high spirits and her prettiness had made her an agreeable companion. She ought, her friend thought, to have married some nice Army officer, or a country solicitor. She had so many good qualities—affection, devotion, loyalty. But life had been unkind to Dora Bunner. She had had to earn her living. She had been painstaking but never competent at anything she undertook.

The two friends had lost sight of each other. But six months ago a letter had come to Miss Blacklock, a rambling, pathetic letter. Dora's health had given way. She was living in one room, trying to subsist on her old age pension. She endeavored to do needlework, but her fingers were stiff with rheumatism. She mentioned their schooldays—since then life had driven them apart—but could—possibly—her old friend help?

Miss Blacklock had responded impulsively. Poor Dora, poor, pretty, silly, fluffy Dora. She had swooped down upon Dora, had carried her off, had installed her at Little Paddocks with the comforting fiction that "the housework is getting too much for me. I need someone to help me run the house." It was not for long—the doctor had told her that—but sometimes she found poor old Dora a sad trial. She muddled everything, upset the temperamental foreign "help," miscounted the laundry, lost bills and letters—and sometimes reduced the competent Miss Blacklock to an agony of exasperation. Poor old muddle-headed Dora, so loyal, so anxious to help, so pleased and proud to think she was of assistance—and, alas, so completely unreliable.

Miss Blacklock said sharply:

"Don't, Dora. You know I asked you—"

"Oh." Miss Bunner looked guilty. "I know. I forgot. But—but you are, aren't you?"

"Worried? No. At least," she added truthfully, "not exactly. You mean about that silly notice in the *Gazette*?"

"Yes—even if it's a joke, it seems to me it's a—a spiteful sort of joke."

"Spiteful?"

"Yes. It seems to me there's spite there somewhere. I mean—it's not a nice kind of joke."

Miss Blacklock looked at her friend. The mild eyes, the long obstinate mouth, the slightly upturned nose. Poor Dora, so maddening, so muddle-headed, so devoted and such a problem. A dear fussy old idiot and yet, in a queer way, with an instinctive sense of values.

"I think you're right, Dora," said Miss Blacklock. "It's not a nice joke."

"I don't like it at all," said Dora Bunner with unsuspected vigor. "It frightens me." She added suddenly: "And it frightens you, Letitia."

"Nonsense," said Miss Blacklock with spirit.

"It's dangerous. I'm sure it is. Like those people who send you bombs done up in parcels."

"My dear, it's just some silly idiot trying to be funny."

"But it isn't funny."

It wasn't really very funny . . . Miss Blacklock's face betrayed her thoughts, and Dora cried triumphantly, "You see. You think so, too!"

"But, Dora, my dear—"

She broke off. Through the door there surged a tempestuous young woman with a well-developed bosom heaving under a tight jersey. She had on a dirndl skirt of a bright color and had greasy dark braids wound round and round her head. Her eyes were dark and flashing.

She said gustily:

"I can speak to you, yes, please, no?"

Miss Blacklock sighed.

"Of course, Mitzi, what is it?"

Sometimes she thought it would be preferable to do the entire work of the house as well as the cooking rather than be bothered with the eternal nerve storms of her refugee "lady help."

"I tell you at once—it is in order, I hope? I give you my notices and I go—I go at once!"

"For what reason? Has somebody upset you?"

"Yes, I am upset," said Mitzi dramatically. "I do not wish to die! Already in Europe I escape. My family they all die—they are all killed—my mother, my little brother, my so sweet little niece—all, all they are killed. But me I run away—I hide. I get to England. I work. I do work that never—never would I do in my own country—I—"

"I know all that," said Miss Blacklock crisply. It was, indeed, a constant refrain on Mitzi's lips. "But why do you want to leave now?"

"Because again they come to kill me!"

"Who do?"

"My enemies. The Nazis! Or perhaps this time it is the Bolsheviks. They find out I am here. They come to kill me. I have read it—yes—it is in the newspaper!"

"Oh, you mean in the *Gazette*?"

"Here, it is written here." Mitzi produced the *Gazette* from where she had been holding it behind her back. "See—here it says a murder. At Little Paddocks. That is here, is it not? This evening at six-thirty. Ah! I do not want to be murdered—no."

"But why should this apply to you? It's—we think it is a joke."

"A joke? It is not a joke to murder someone."

"No, of course not. But, my dear child, if anyone wanted to murder you, they wouldn't advertise the fact in the paper, would they?"

"You do not think they would?" Mitzi seemed a little shaken. "You think, perhaps, they do not mean to murder anyone at all? Perhaps it is you they mean to murder, Miss Blacklock."

"I certainly can't believe anyone wants to murder me," said Miss Blacklock lightly. "And, really, Mitzi, I don't see why anyone should want to murder you. After all, why should they?"

"Because they are bad peoples . . . very bad peoples. I tell you, my mother, my little brother, my so sweet niece . . ."

"Yes, yes." Miss Blacklock stemmed the flow adroitly. "But I cannot really believe anyone wants to murder you, Mitzi. Of course, if you want to go off like this at a moment's notice, I cannot possibly stop you. But I think you will be very silly if you do."

She added firmly, as Mitzi looked doubtful:

"We'll have that beef the butcher sent stewed for lunch. It looks very tough."

"I make you a goulash, a special goulash."

"If you prefer to call it that, certainly. And perhaps you could use up that rather hard bit of cheese in making some cheese straws. I think some people may come in this evening for drinks."

"This evening? What do you mean, this evening?"

"At half past six."

"But that is the time in the paper? Who should come then? Why should they come?"

"They're coming to the funeral," said Miss Blacklock with a twinkle. "That'll do now, Mitzi. I'm busy. Shut the door after you," she added firmly.

"And that's settled her for the moment," she said as the door closed behind a puzzled-looking Mitzi.

"You are so efficient, Letty," said Miss Bunner admiringly.

3

At 6:30 P.M.

"Well, here we are, all set," said Miss Blacklock. She looked round the double drawing-room with an appraising eye. The rose-patterned chintzes—the two bowls of bronze chrysanthemums, the small vase of violets and the silver cigarette box on a table by the wall, the tray of drinks on the center table.

Little Paddocks was a medium-sized house built in the early Victorian style. It had a long shallow veranda and green-shuttered windows. The long narrow drawing-room, which lost a good deal of light owing to the veranda roof, had originally had double doors at one end, leading into a small room with a bay window. A former generation had removed the double doors and replaced them with the portieres of velvet. Miss Blacklock had dispensed with the portieres so that the two rooms had become definitely one. There was a fireplace each end, but neither fire was lit, although a gentle warmth pervaded the room.

"You've had the central heating lit," said Patrick.

Miss Blacklock nodded.

"It's been so misty and damp lately. The whole house felt clammy. I got Evans to light it before he went."

"The precious, precious coke?" said Patrick, mockingly.

"As you say, the precious coke. But otherwise there would have been the even more precious coal. You know the Fuel Office won't even let us have the little bit that's due us each week—not unless we can say definitely that we haven't any other means of cooking."

"I suppose once there were heaps of coke and coal for everybody?" said Julia, with the interest of one hearing about an unknown country.

"Yes, and cheap, too."

"And anyone could go and buy as much as they wanted, without filling in anything, and there wasn't any shortage? There was lots of it then?"

"All kinds and qualities—and not all stones and slates like what we get nowadays."

"It must have been a wonderful world," said Julia with awe in her voice.

Miss Blacklock smiled. "Looking back on it, I certainly think so. But then I'm an old woman. It's natural for me to prefer my own times. But you young things oughtn't to think so."

"I needn't have had a job then," said Julia. "I could just have stayed at home and done the flowers, and written notes . . . why did one write notes and who were they to?"

"All the people that you now ring up on the telephone," said Miss Blacklock with a twinkle. "I don't believe you even know how to write, Julia."

"Not in the style of that delicious *Complete Letter Writer* I found the other day. Heavenly! It told you the correct way of refusing a proposal of marriage from a widower."

"I doubt if you would have enjoyed staying at home as much as you think," said Miss Blacklock. "There were duties, you know." Her voice was dry. "However, I don't really know much about it. Bunny and I," she smiled affectionately at Dora Bunner, "went into the labor market early."

"Oh, we did, we did indeed," agreed Miss Bunner. "Those naughty, naughty children. I'll never forget them. Of course Letty was clever. She was a business woman, secretary to a big financier."

The door opened and Phillipa Haymes came in. She was tall and fair and placid-looking. She looked round the room in surprise.

"Hullo," she said. "Is it a party? Nobody told me."

"Of course," cried Patrick. "Our Phillipa doesn't know. The only woman in Chipping Cleghorn who doesn't, I bet."

Phillipa looked at him inquiringly.

"Here you behold," said Patrick dramatically, waving a hand, "the scene of a murder!"

Phillipa Haymes looked faintly puzzled.

"Here," Patrick indicated the two big bowls of chrysanthemums, "are the funeral wreaths and these dishes of cheese straws and olives represent the funeral baked meats."

Phillipa looked inquiringly at Miss Blacklock.

"Is it a joke?" she asked. "I'm always terribly stupid at seeing jokes."

"It's a very nasty joke," said Dora Bunner with energy. "I don't like it at all."

"Show her the advertisement," said Miss Blacklock. "I must go and shut up the ducks. It's dark. They'll be in by now."

"Let me do it," said Phillipa.

"Certainly not, my dear. You've finished your day's work."

"I'll do it, Aunt Letty," offered Patrick.

"No, you won't," said Miss Blacklock with energy. "Last time you didn't latch the door properly."

"I'll do it, Letty dear," cried Miss Bunner. "Indeed, I should love to. I'll just slip on my galoshes—and now where did I put my cardigan?"

But Miss Blacklock, with a smile, had already left the room.

"It's no good, Bunny," said Patrick. "Aunt Letty's so efficient that she can never bear anybody else to do things for her. She really much prefers to do everything herself."

"She loves it," said Julia.

"I didn't notice you making any offers of assistance," said her brother.

Julia smiled lazily.

"You've just said Aunt Letty likes to do things herself," she pointed out. "Besides," she held out a well-shaped leg in a sheer stocking, "I've got my best stockings on."

"Death in silk stockings!" declaimed Patrick.

"Not silk; nylons, you idiot."

"That's not nearly such a good title."

"Won't somebody please tell me," cried Phillipa plaintively, "why there is all this insistence on death?"

Everybody tried to tell her at once—nobody could find the *Gazette* to show her because Mitzi had taken it into the kitchen.

Miss Blacklock returned a few minutes later.

"There," she said briskly, "that's done." She glanced at the clock. "Twenty past six. Somebody ought to be here soon—unless I'm entirely wrong in my estimate of my neighbors."

"I don't see why anybody should come," said Phillipa, looking bewildered.

"Don't you, dear? I daresay you wouldn't. But most people are rather more inquisitive than you are."

"Phillipa's attitude to life is that she just isn't interested," said Julia, rather nastily.

Phillipa did not reply.

Miss Blacklock was glancing round the room. Mitzi had put the sherry and three dishes containing olives, cheese straws and some little fancy pastries on the table in the middle of the room.

"You might move that tray—or the whole table if you like—round the corner into the bay window in the other room, Patrick, if you don't mind. After all, I am not giving a party! I haven't asked anyone. And I don't intend to make it obvious that I expect people to turn up."

"You wish, Aunt Letty, to disguise your intelligent anticipation?"

"Very nicely put, Patrick. Thank you, my dear boy."

"Now we can all give a lovely performance of a quiet evening at home," said Julia, "and be quite surprised when somebody drops in."

Miss Blacklock had picked up the sherry bottle. She stood holding it uncertainly in her hand.

Patrick reassured her.

"There's quite half a bottle there. It ought to be enough."

"Oh, yes—yes . . ." She hesitated. Then, with a slight flush, she said:

"Patrick, would you mind . . . there's a new bottle in the cupboard in the pantry . . . bring it and a corkscrew. I—we—might as well have a new bottle. This—this has been opened some time."

Patrick went on his errand without a word. He returned with the new bottle and drew the cork. He looked up curiously at Miss Blacklock as he placed it on the tray.

"Taking things seriously, aren't you, darling?" he asked gently.

"Oh," cried Dora Bunner, shocked. "Surely, Letty, you can't imagine—"

"Hush," said Miss Blacklock quickly. "That's the bell. You see, my intelligent anticipation is being justified."

II

Mitzi opened the door of the drawing-room and admitted Colonel and Mrs. Easterbrook. She had her own methods of announcing people.

"Here is Colonel and Mrs. Easterbrook to see you," she said conversationally.

Colonel Easterbrook was very bluff and breezy to cover some slight embarrassment.

"Hope you don't mind us dropping in," he said. (A subdued gurgle came from Julia.) "Happened to be passing this way—eh, what? Quite a mild evening. Notice you've got your central heating on. We haven't started ours yet."

"Aren't your chrysanthemums lovely?" gushed Mrs. Easterbrook. "Such beauties!"

"They're rather scraggy really," said Julia.

Mrs. Easterbrook greeted Phillipa Haymes with a little extra cordiality to show that she quite understood that Phillipa was not really an agricultural laborer.

"How is Mrs. Lucas's garden getting on?" she asked. "Do you think it will ever be straight again? Completely neglected all through the war—and then only that dreadful old man Ashe who simply did nothing but sweep up a few leaves and put in a few cabbage plants."

"It's yielding to treatment," said Phillipa. "But it will take a little time."

Mitzi opened the door again and said:

"Here are the ladies from Boulders."

"Evening," said Miss Hinchliffe, striding over and taking Miss Blacklock's hand in her formidable grip. "I said to Murgatroyd: 'Let's just drop in at Little Paddocks!' I wanted to ask you how your ducks are laying."

"The evenings do draw in so quickly now, don't they?" said Miss Murgatroyd to Patrick in a rather fluttery way. "What lovely chrysanthemums!"

"Scraggy!" said Julia.

"Why can't you be cooperative?" murmured Patrick to her in a reproachful aside.

"You've got your central heating on," said Miss Hinchliffe. She said it accusingly. "Very early."

"The house gets so damp this time of year," said Miss Blacklock.

Patrick signaled with his eyebrows: "Sherry yet?" and Miss Blacklock signaled back: "Not yet."

She said to Colonel Easterbrook:

"Are you getting any bulbs from Holland this year?"

The door again opened and Mrs. Swettenham came in rather guiltily, followed by a scowling and uncomfortable Edmund.

"Here we are!" said Mrs. Swettenham, gaily, gazing round her with frank curiosity. Then, feeling suddenly uncomfortable, she went on: "I just thought I'd pop in and ask you if by any chance you wanted a kitten, Miss Blacklock? Our cat is just—"

"About to be brought to bed of the progeny of a ginger tom," said Edmund. "The result will, I think, be frightful. Don't say you haven't been warned!"

"She's a very good mouser," said Mrs. Swettenham hastily. And added: "What lovely chrysanthemums!"

"You've got your central heating on, haven't you?" asked Edmund with an air of originality.

"Aren't people just like gramophone records?" murmured Julia.

"I don't like the news," said Colonel Easterbrook to Patrick, button-holing him fiercely. "I don't like it at all. If you ask me, war's inevitable—absolutely inevitable."

"I never pay any attention to news," said Patrick.

Once more the door opened and Mrs. Harmon came in.

Her battered felt hat was stuck on the back of her head in a vague attempt to be fashionable and she had put on a rather limp frilly blouse instead of her usual pullover.

"Hullo, Miss Blacklock," she exclaimed, beaming all over her round face. "I'm not too late, am I? When does the murder begin?"

III

There was an audible series of gasps. Julia gave an approving little giggle, Patrick crinkled up his face and Miss Blacklock smiled at her latest guest.

"Julian is just frantic with rage that he can't be here," said Mrs. Harmon. "He adores murders. That's really why he preached such a good sermon last Sunday—I suppose I oughtn't to say it was a good sermon as he's my husband—but it really was good, didn't you think? So much better than his usual sermons. But as I was saying it was all because of *Death Does the Hat Trick*. Have you read it? The girl at Boots kept it for me specially. It's simply baffling. You keep thinking you know—and then the whole thing switches round—and there are a lovely lot of murders, four or five of them. Well, I left it in the study when Julian was shutting himself up there to do his sermon, and he just picked it up and simply could not put it down! And consequently he had to write his sermon in a frightful hurry and had to just put down what he wanted to say very simply—without any scholarly twists and bits and learned references—

and naturally it was heaps better. Oh, dear, I'm talking too much. But do tell me, when is the murder going to begin?"

Miss Blacklock looked at the clock on the mantelpiece.

"If it's going to begin," she said cheerfully, "it ought to begin soon. It's just a minute to the half hour. In the meantime, have a glass of sherry."

Patrick moved with alacrity through the archway. Miss Blacklock went to the table by the archway where the cigarette box was.

"I'd love some sherry," said Mrs. Harmon. "But what do you mean by if?"

"Well," said Miss Blacklock. "I'm as much in the dark as you are. I don't know what—"

She stopped and turned her head as the little clock on the mantelpiece began to chime. It had a sweet, silvery, bell-like tone. Everybody was silent and nobody moved. They all stared at the clock.

It chimed a quarter—and then the half. As the last note died away all the lights went out.

IV

Delighted gasps and feminine squeaks of appreciation were heard in the darkness. "It's beginning," cried Mrs. Harmon in an ecstasy. Dora Bunner's voice cried out plaintively, "Oh, I don't like it!" Other voices said, "How terribly, terribly frightening!" "It gives me the creeps." "Archie, where are you?" "What do I have to do?" "Oh dear—did I step on your foot? I'm so sorry."

Then, with a crash, the door swung open. A powerful flashlight played rapidly round the room. A man's hoarse nasal voice, reminiscent to all of pleasant afternoons at the movies, directed the company crisply to:

"Stick 'em up! Stick 'em up, I tell you!" the voice barked.

Delightedly, hands were raised willingly above heads.

"Isn't it wonderful?" breathed a female voice. "I'm so thrilled."

And then, unexpectedly, a revolver spoke. It spoke twice. The ping of two bullets shattered the complacency of the room. Suddenly the game was no longer a game. Somebody screamed . . .

The figure in the doorway whirled suddenly around, it seemed to hesitate, a third shot rang out, it crumpled and then it crashed to the ground. The flashlight dropped and went out. There was darkness once again. And gently, with a little Victorian protesting moan, the drawing-room door, as was its habit when not propped open, swung gently to and latched with a click.

V

Inside the drawing-room there was pandemonium. Various voices spoke at once. "Lights!" "Can't you find the switch?" "Who's got a lighter?" "Oh, I don't like it, I don't like it." "But those shots were real!" "It was a real revolver he had." "Was it a burglar?" "Oh, Archie, I want to get out of here." "Please, has somebody got a lighter?"

And then, almost at the same moment, two lighters clicked and burned with small steady flames.

Everybody blinked and peered at each other. Startled face looked into startled face. Against the wall by the archway Miss Blacklock stood with her hand up to her face. The light was too dim to show more than that something dark was trickling over her fingers.

Colonel Easterbrook cleared his throat and rose to the occasion. "Try the switches, Swettenham," he ordered.

Edmund, near the door, obediently jerked the switch up and down.

"Off at the main, or a fuse," said the colonel. "Who's making that awful row?"

A female voice had been screaming steadily from somewhere beyond the closed door. It rose now in pitch and with it came the sound of fists hammering on a door.

Dora Bunner, who had been sobbing quietly, called out: "It's Mitzi. Somebody's murdering Mitzi . . ."

Patrick muttered: "No such luck."

Miss Blacklock said: "We must get candles. Patrick, will you—"

The colonel was already opening the door. He and Edmund, their lighters flickering, stepped into the hall. They almost stumbled over a recumbent figure there.

"Seems to have knocked him out," said the colonel. "Where's that woman making that hellish noise?"

"In the dining room," said Edmund.

The dining room was just across the hall. Someone was beating on the panels and howling and screaming.

"She's locked in," said Edmund, stooping down. He turned the key and Mitzi came out like a bounding tiger.

The dining room light was still on. Silhouetted against it, Mitzi presented a picture of insane terror and continued to scream. A touch of comedy was introduced by the fact that she had been engaged in cleaning silver and was still holding a chamois leather and a large fish slice.

"Be quiet, Mitzi," said Miss Blacklock.

"Stop it," said Edmund, and as Mitzi showed no disposition to stop screaming, he leaned forward and gave her a sharp slap on the cheek. Mitzi gasped and hiccuped into silence.

"Get some candles," said Miss Blacklock. "In the kitchen cupboard. Patrick, you know where the fusebox is?"

"The passage behind the scullery? Right, I'll see what I can do."

Miss Blacklock had moved forward into the light thrown from the dining room and Dora Bunner gave a sobbing gasp. Mitzi let out another full-blooded scream.

"The blood, the blood!" she gasped. "You are shot—Miss Blacklock, you bleed to death."

"Don't be so stupid," snapped Miss Blacklock. "I'm hardly hurt at all. It just grazed my ear."

"But, Aunt Letty," said Julia, "the blood."

And indeed Miss Blacklock's white blouse and pearls and her hand were a horrifyingly gory sight.

"Ears always bleed," said Miss Blacklock. "I remember fainting in the hairdresser's when I was a child. The man had only just snipped my ear. There seemed to be a basin of blood at once. But we must have some light."

"I get the candles," said Mitzi.

Julia went with her and they returned with several candles stuck into saucers.

"Now let's have a look at our malefactor," said the colonel. "Hold the candles down low, will you, Swettenham? As many as you can."

"I'll come the other side," said Phillipa.

With a steady hand she took a couple of saucers. Colonel Easterbrook knelt down.

The recumbent figure was draped in a roughly made black cloak with a hood on it. There was a black mask over the face and he wore black cotton gloves. The hood had slipped back disclosing a ruffled fair head.

Colonel Easterbrook turned him over, felt the pulse, the heart . . . then drew away his fingers with an exclamation of distaste, looking down on them. They were sticky and red.

"Shot himself," he said.

"Is he badly hurt?" asked Miss Blacklock.

"H'm. I'm afraid he's dead. May have been suicide—or he may have tripped himself up with that cloak thing and the revolver went off as he fell. If I could see better—"

At the moment, as though by magic, the lights came on again.

With a queer feeling of unreality those inhabitants of Chipping Cleghorn who stood in the hall of Little Paddocks realized that they stood in the presence of violent and sudden death. Colonel Easterbrook's hand was stained red. Blood was still trickling down Miss Blacklock's neck over her blouse and skirt, and the grotesquely sprawled figure of the intruder lay at her feet.

Patrick, coming from the dining room, said, "It seemed to be just one fuse gone . . ." He stopped.

Colonel Easterbrook tugged at the small black mask.

"Better see who the fellow is," he said. "Though I don't suppose it's anyone we know."

He detached the mask. Necks were craned forward. Mitzi hiccupped and gasped, but the others were very quiet.

"He's quite young," said Mrs. Harmon with a note of pity in her voice.

And suddenly Dora Bunner cried out excitedly:

"Letty, Letty, it's the young man from the Spa Hotel in Medenham Wells. The one who came out here and wanted you to give him money to get back to Switzerland and you refused. I suppose the whole thing was just a pretext—to spy out the house. . . . Oh, dear—he might easily have killed you."

Miss Blacklock, in command of the situation, said incisively:

"Phillipa, take Bunny into the dining room and give her a half glass of brandy. Julia dear, just run up to the bathroom and bring me the sticking plaster out of the bathroom cupboard—it's so messy bleeding like a pig. Patrick, will you ring up the police at once?"

4

The Royal Spa Hotel

George Rydesdale, Chief Constable of Middleshire, was a quiet man. Of medium height, with shrewd eyes under rather bushy brows, he was in the habit of listening rather than talking. Then, in his unemotional voice, he would give a brief order—and the order was obeyed.

He was listening now to Detective Inspector Dermot Craddock. Craddock was now officially in charge of the case. Rydesdale had recalled him last night from Liverpool where he had been sent to make certain inquiries in connection with another case. Rydesdale had a good opinion of Craddock. He not only had brains and imagination, he had also, which Rydesdale appreciated even more, the self-discipline to go slow, to check and examine each fact and to keep an open mind until the very end of a case.

"Constable Legg took the call, sir," Craddock was saying. "He seems to have acted very well, with promptitude and presence of mind. And it can't have been easy. About a dozen people all trying to talk at once, including one of those Mittel Europas who go off the deep end at the mere sight of a policeman. Made sure she was going to be locked up, and fairly screamed the place down."

"Deceased has been identified?"

"Yes, sir. Rudi Scherz. Swiss nationality. Employed at the Royal Spa Hotel, Mendenham Wells, as a receptionist. If you agree, sir, I thought I'd take the Royal Spa Hotel first, and go out to Chipping Cleghorn afterwards. Sergeant Fletcher is out there now. He'll see the bus people and then go on to the house."

Rydesdale nodded approval.

The door opened and the Chief Constable looked up.

"Come in, Henry," he said. "We've got something here that's a little out of the ordinary."

Sir Henry Clithering, ex-Commissioner of Scotland Yard, came in with slightly raised eyebrows. He was a tall, distinguished-looking, elderly man.

"It may appeal to even your blase palate," went on Rydesdale.

"I was never blase," said Sir Henry indignantly.

"The latest idea," said Rydesdale, "is to advertise one's murders beforehand. Show Sir Henry that advertisement, Craddock."

"The *North Benham News and Chipping Cleghorn Gazette,*" said Sir Henry. "Quite a mouthful." He read the half inch of print indicated by Craddock's finger. "Hm, yes, somewhat unusual."

"Any line on who inserted this advertisement?" asked Rydesdale.

"By the description, sir, it was handed in by Rudi Scherz himself—on Wednesday."

"Nobody questioned it? The person who accepted it didn't think it odd?"

"The adenoidal blonde who receives the advertisements is quite incapable of thinking, I should say, sir. She just counted the words and took the money."

"What was the idea?" asked Sir Henry.

"Get a lot of the locals curious," suggested Rydesdale. "Get them all together at a particular place at a particular time, then hold them up and relieve them of their spare cash and valuables. As an idea, it's not without originality."

"What sort of a place is Chipping Cleghorn?" asked Sir Henry.

"A large, sprawling, picturesque village. Butcher, baker, grocer, quite a good antique shop—two tea shops. Self-consciously a beauty spot. Caters to the motoring tourist. Also highly residential. Cottages formerly lived in by agricultural laborers now converted and lived in by elderly spinsters and retired couples. A certain amount of building done round about in Victorian times."

"I know," said Sir Henry. "Nice old pussies and retired colonels. Yes, if they noticed that advertisement they'd all come sniffing around at 6:30 to see what was up. Lord, I wish I had my own particular old pussy here. Wouldn't she like to get her nice ladylike teeth into this? Right up her street it would be."

"Who's your own particular pussy, Henry? An aunt?"

"No." Sir Henry sighed. "She's no relation." He said reverently:

"She's just the finest detective God ever made. Natural genius culti-vated in a suitable soil."

He turned upon Craddock.

"Don't you despise the old pussies in this village of yours, my boy," he said. "In case this turns out to be a high-powered mystery, which I don't suppose for a moment it will, remember that an elderly unmarried woman who knits and gardens is streets ahead of any de-tective sergeant. She can tell you what might have happened and what ought to have happened and even what actually did happen! And she can tell you why it happened!"

"I'll bear that in mind, sir," said Detective Inspector Craddock in his most formal manner, and nobody would have guessed that Der-mot Eric Craddock was actually Sir Henry's godson and was on easy and intimate terms with his godfather.

Rydesdale gave a quick outline of the case to his friend.

"They'd all turn up at 6:30, I grant you that," he said. "But would that Swiss fellow know they would? And another thing, would they be likely to have much loot on them to be worth the taking?"

"A couple of old-fashioned brooches, a string of seed pearls—a little loose change, perhaps a note or two—not more," said Sir Henry thought-fully. "Did this Miss Blacklock keep much money in the house?"

"She says not, sir. Five pounds odd, I understand."

"Mere chicken feed," said Rydesdale.

"What you're getting at," said Sir Henry, "is that this fellow liked to play-act—it wasn't the loot, it was the fun of playing and acting the holdup. Movie stuff, eh? It's quite possible. How did he manage to shoot himself?"

Rydesdale drew a paper towards him.

"Preliminary medical report. The revolver was discharged at close range—singeing . . . h'm . . . nothing to show whether accident or suicide. Could have been done deliberately, or he could have tripped and fallen and the revolver which he was holding close to him could have gone off. Probably the latter." He looked at Craddock. "You'll have to question the witnesses very carefully and make them say exactly what they saw."

Detective Inspector Craddock said sadly, "They'll all have seen something different."

"It's always interested me," said Sir Henry, "what people do see at a moment of intense excitement and nervous strain. What they do see and, even more interesting, what they don't see."

"Where's the report on the revolver?"

"Foreign make—fairly common on the Continent—Scherz did not hold a permit for it—and did not declare it on coming into England."

"Bad lad," said Sir Henry.

"Unsatisfactory character all round. Well, Craddock, go and see what you can find out about him at the Royal Spa Hotel."

II

At the Royal Spa Hotel Inspector Craddock was taken straight to the manager's office.

The manager, Mr. Rowlandson, a tall florid man with a hearty manner, greeted Inspector Craddock with expansive geniality.

"Glad to help you in any way we can, Inspector," he said. "Really, a most surprising business. I'd never have credited—never. Scherz seemed a very ordinary, pleasant young chap—not at all my idea of a holdup man."

"How long has he been with you, Mr. Rowlandson?"

"I was looking that up just before you came. A little over three months. Quite good credentials, the usual permits, etc."

"And you found him satisfactory?"

Without seeming to do so, Craddock marked the infinitesimal pause before Rowlandson replied,

"Quite satisfactory."

Craddock made use of a technique he had found efficacious before now.

"No, no, Mr. Rowlandson," he said, gently shaking his head. "That's not really quite the case, is it?"

"We-ll—" The manager seemed slightly taken aback.

"Come now, there was something wrong. What was it?"

"That's just it. I don't know."

"But you thought there was something wrong?"

"Well—yes—I did . . . but I've nothing really to go upon. I shouldn't like my conjectures to be written down and quoted against me."

Craddock smiled pleasantly.

"I know just what you mean. You needn't worry. But I've got to get some idea of what this fellow Scherz was like. You suspected him of—what?"

Rowlandson said, rather reluctantly:

"Well, there was trouble, once or twice, about the bills. Items charged that oughtn't to have been there."

"You mean you suspected that he charged up certain items which didn't appear in the hotel records, and that he pocketed the difference when the bill was paid?"

"Something like that. Put it at the best, there was gross carelessness on his part. Once or twice quite a big sum was involved. Frankly, I got our accountant to go over his books, suspecting that he was—well, a wrong 'un; but though there were various mistakes and a good deal of slipshod method, the actual cash was quite correct. So I came to the conclusion that I must be mistaken."

"Supposing you hadn't been wrong? Supposing Scherz had been helping himself to various small sums here and there, he could have covered himself, I suppose, by making good the money?"

"Yes, if he had the money. But people who help themselves to 'small sums' as you put it—are usually hard up for those sums and spend them offhand."

"So if he wanted money to replace missing sums, he would have had to get money—by a holdup or other means?"

"Yes. I wonder if this is his first attempt."

"Might be. It was certainly a very amateurish one. Is there anyone else he could have got money from? Any woman in his life?"

"One of the waitresses in the Grill. Her name's Myrna Harris."

"I'd better have a talk with her."

III

Myrna Harris was a pretty girl with a glorious head of red hair and a pert nose.

She was alarmed and wary, and deeply conscious of the indignity of being interviewed by the police.

"I don't know a thing about it, sir. Not a thing," she protested. "If I'd known what he was like I'd never have gone out with Rudi at all. Naturally, seeing as he worked as receptionist here, I thought he was all right. Naturally I did. What I say is, the hotel ought to be more careful when they employ people—especially foreigners. Because you never know where you are with foreigners. I suppose he might have been in with one of these gangs you read about."

"We think," said Craddock, "that he was working quite on his own."

"Fancy—and him so quiet and respectable. You'd never think.

171

Though there have been things missed—now I come to think of it. A diamond brooch—and a little gold locket, I believe. But I never dreamed that it could have been Rudi."

"I'm sure you didn't," said Craddock. "Anyone might have been taken in. You know him fairly well?"

"I don't know that I'd say well."

"But you were friendly?"

"Oh, we were friendly—that's all, just friendly. Nothing serious at all. I'm always on my guard with foreigners, anyway. They've often got a way with them, but you never know, do you? Some of those Poles during the war! And even some of the Americans! Never let on they're married men until it's too late. Rudi talked big and all that—but I always took it with a grain of salt."

Craddock seized on the phrase.

"Talked big, did he? That's very interesting, Miss Harris. I can see you're going to be a lot of help to us. In that way did he talk big?"

"Well, about how rich his people were in Switzerland—and how important. But that didn't go with his being as short of money as he was. He always said that because of the money regulation he couldn't get money from Switzerland over here. That might be, I suppose, but his things weren't expensive. His clothes, I mean. They weren't really class. I think, too, that a lot of the stories he used to tell me were so much hot air. About climbing in the Alps, and saving people's lives on the edge of a glacier. Why, he turned quite giddy just going along the edge of Boulter's Gorge. Alps, indeed!"

"You went out with him a good deal?"

"Yes—well—yes, I did. He had awfully good manners and he knew how to—to look after a girl. The best seats at the pictures, always. And even flowers he'd buy me sometimes. And he was just a lovely dancer—lovely."

"Did he mention this Miss Blacklock to you at all?"

"She comes in and lunches here sometimes, doesn't she? And she's stayed here once. No, I don't think Rudi ever mentioned her. I didn't know he knew her."

"Did he mention Chipping Cleghorn?"

He thought a faintly wary look came into Myrna Harris's eyes but he couldn't be sure.

"I don't think so . . . I think he did once ask about buses—what time they went—but I can't remember if that was Chipping Cleghorn or somewhere else. It wasn't just lately."

He couldn't get more out of her. Rudi Scherz had seemed just as usual. She hadn't seen him the evening before. She'd had no idea—no idea at all—she stressed the point, that Rudi Scherz was a crook.

And probably, Craddock thought, that was quite true.

5

Miss Blacklock and Miss Bunner

Little Paddocks was very much as Detective Inspector Craddock had imagined it to be. He noted ducks and chickens, and what had been until lately an attractive herbaceous border and in which a few late Michaelmas daisies showed a last dying splash of purple beauty. The lawn and the paths showed signs of neglect.

Summing up, Detective Inspector Craddock thought: Probably not much money to spend on gardeners—fond of flowers and a good eye for planning and massing a border. House needs painting. Most houses do nowadays. Pleasant little property.

As Craddock's car stopped before the front door, Sergeant Fletcher came round the side of the house. With an erect military bearing, Sergeant Fletcher looked like a guardsman, and was able to impart several different meanings to the one monosyllable: "Sir."

"So there you are, Fletcher."

"Sir," said Sergeant Fletcher.

"Anything to report?"

"We've finished going over the house, sir. Scherz doesn't seem to have left any fingerprints anywhere. He wore gloves, of course. No signs of any of the doors or windows being forced to effect an entrance. He seems to have come out from Medenham on the bus, arriving here at six o'clock. Side door of the house was locked at 5:30, I understand. Looks as though he must have walked in through the front door. Miss Blacklock states that the door isn't usually locked until the house is shut up for the night. The maid, on the other hand, states that the front door was locked all the afternoon—but she'd say anything. Very temperamental you'll find her. Mittel Europa refugee of some kind."

"Difficult, is she?"

"Sir!" said Sergeant Fletcher, with intense feeling.

Craddock smiled.

Fletcher resumed his report.

"Lighting system is quite in order everywhere. We haven't spotted yet how he operated the lights. It was just the one circuit went. Drawing-room and hall. Of course, nowadays, the wall brackets and lamps wouldn't all be on one fuse—but this is old-fashioned installation and wiring. Don't see how he could have tampered with the fuse box because it's out by the scullery and he'd have had to go through the kitchen, so the maid would have seen him."

"Unless she was in it with him?"

"That's very possible. Both foreigners—and I wouldn't trust her a yard—not a yard."

Craddock noticed two enormous frightened black eyes peering out of a window by the front door. The face, flattened against the pane, was hardly visible.

"That her there?"

"That's right, sir."

The face disappeared.

Craddock rang the front doorbell.

After a long wait the door was opened by a good-looking young woman with chestnut hair and a bored expression.

"Detective Inspector Craddock," said Craddock.

The young woman gave him a cool stare out of very attractive hazel eyes and said:

"Come in. Miss Blacklock is expecting you."

The hall, Craddock noted, was long and narrow and seemed almost incredibly full of doors.

The young woman threw open one on the left, and said: "Inspector Craddock, Aunt Letty. Mitzi wouldn't go to the door. She's shut herself up in the kitchen and she's making the most marvelous moaning noises. I shouldn't think we'd get any lunch."

She added in an explanatory manner to Craddock: "She doesn't like the police," and withdrew, shutting the door behind her.

Craddock advanced to meet the owner of Little Paddocks.

He saw a tall active-looking woman of about sixty. Her gray hair had a slight natural wave and made a distinguished setting for an intelligent resolute face. She had keen gray eyes and a square determined chin. There was a surgical dressing on her left ear. She wore no makeup and was plainly dressed in a well-cut tweed coat and skirt and pullover. Round the neck of the latter she wore, rather unexpectedly, a set of old-fashioned cameos—a Victorian touch which seemed to hint at a sentimental streak not otherwise apparent.

Close beside her, with an eager round face and untidy hair escaping from a hairnet, was a woman of about the same age whom Craddock had no difficulty in recognizing as the "Dora Bunner—companion" of Constable Legg's notes—to which the latter had added an off-the-record commentary of "Scatty!"

Miss Blacklock spoke in a pleasant well-bred voice.

"Good morning, Inspector Craddock. This is my friend, Miss Bunner, who helps me run the house. Won't you sit down? You won't smoke, I suppose?"

"Not on duty, I'm afraid, Miss Blacklock."

"What a shame!"

Craddock's eyes took in the room with a quick, practiced glance. Typical Victorian double drawing-room. Two long windows in this room, built-out bay window in the other . . . chairs . . . sofa . . . center table with a big bowl of chrysanthemums—another bowl in the window—all fresh and pleasant without much originality. The only incongruous note was a small silver vase with dead violets in it on a table near the archway into the further room. Since he could not imagine Miss Blacklock tolerating dead flowers in a room, he imagined it to be the only indication that something out of the way had occurred to distract the routine of a well-run household.

He said:

"I take it, Miss Blacklock, that this is the room in which the—incident occurred?"

"Yes."

"And you should have seen it last night," Miss Bunner exclaimed. "Such a mess. Two little tables knocked over, and the leg off one—people barging about in the dark—and someone put down a lighted cigarette and burnt one of the best bits of furniture. People—young people especially—are so careless about these things . . . Luckily none of the china got broken—"

Miss Blacklock interrupted gently but firmly:

"Dora, all these things, vexations as they may be, are only trifles.

It will be best, I think, if we just answer Inspector Craddock's questions."

"Thank you, Miss Blacklock. I shall come to what happened last night presently. First of all, I want you to tell me when you first saw the dead man—Rudi Scherz."

"Rudi Scherz?" Miss Blacklock looked slightly surprised. "Is that his name? Somehow, I thought— Oh, well, it doesn't matter. My first encounter with him was when I was in Medenham Spa for a day's shopping about—let me see—about three weeks ago. We—Miss Bunner and I—were having lunch at the Royal Spa Hotel. As we were just leaving after lunch, I heard my name spoken. It was this young man. He said: 'It is Miss Blacklock, is it not?' And went on to say that perhaps I did not remember him, but that he was the son of the proprietor of the Hotel des Alpes at Montreux, where my sister and I had stayed for nearly a year during the war."

"The Hotel des Alpes, Montreux," noted Craddock. "And did you remember him, Miss Blacklock?"

"No, I didn't. Actually, I had no recollection of ever having seen him before. These boys at hotel reception desks all look exactly alike. We had had a very pleasant time at Montreux and the proprietor there had been extremely obliging, so I tried to be as civil as possible and said I hoped he was enjoying being in England, and he said, yes, that his father had sent him over for six months to learn the hotel business. It all seemed quite natural."

"And your next encounter?"

"About—yes, it must have been ten days ago, he suddenly turned up here. I was very surprised to see him. He apologized for troubling me, but said I was the only person he knew in England. He told me that he urgently needed money to return to Switzerland as his mother was dangerously ill."

"But Letty didn't give it to him," Miss Bunner put in breathlessly.

"It was a thoroughly fishy story," said Miss Blacklock with vigor. "I made up my mind that he was definitely a wrong 'un. That story about wanting the money to return to Switzerland was nonsense. His father could easily have wired for arrangements to have been made in this country. These hotel people are all in with each other. I suspected that he'd been embezzling money or something of that kind." She paused and said dryly, "In case you think I'm hardhearted, I was secretary for many years to a big financier and one becomes wary about appeals for money. I know simply all the hard luck stories there are.

"The only thing that did surprise me," she added thoughtfully, "was that he gave in so easily. He went away at once without any more argument. It's as though he had never expected to get the money."

"Do you think now, looking back on it, that his coming was really by way of a pretext to spy out the land?"

Miss Blacklock nodded her head vigorously.

"That's exactly what I do think—now. He made certain remarks as I let him out—about the rooms. He said, 'You have a very nice dining room' (which, of course, it isn't—it's a horrid dark little room), just as an excuse to look inside. And then he sprang forward and unfastened the front door; he said, 'Let me.' I think now he wanted to have a look at the fastening. Actually, like most people round here, we never lock the front door until it gets dark. Anyone could walk in."

"And the side door? There is a side door to the garden, I understand?"

"Yes. I went out through it to shut up the ducks not long before the people arrived."

"Was it locked when you went out?"

Miss Blacklock frowned.

"I can't remember . . . I think so. I certainly locked it when I came in."

"That would be about quarter past six?"

"Somewhere about then."

"And the front door?"

"That's not usually locked until later."

"Then Scherz could have walked in quite easily that way. Or he could have slipped in whilst you were out shutting up the ducks. He'd already spied out the lay of the land and had probably noted various places of concealment—cupboards, etc. Yes, that all seems quite clear."

"I beg your pardon, it isn't at all clear," said Miss Blacklock. "Why on earth should anyone take all that elaborate trouble to come and burgle this house and stage that silly sort of holdup?"

"Do you keep much money in the house, Miss Blacklock?"

"About five pounds in that desk there, and perhaps a pound or two in my purse."

"Jewelry?"

"A couple of rings and brooches and the cameos I'm wearing. You must agree with me, Inspector, that the whole thing's absurd."

"It wasn't burglary at all," cried Miss Bunner. "I've told you so,

Letty, all along. It was revenge! Because you wouldn't give him that money! He deliberately shot at you—twice."

"Ah," said Craddock. "We'll come now to last night. What happened exactly, Miss Blacklock? Tell me in your own words as nearly as you can remember."

Miss Blacklock reflected a moment.

"The clock struck," she said. "The one on the mantelpiece. I remember saying that if anything were going to happen it would have to happen soon. And then the clock struck. We all listened to it without saying anything. It chimes, you know. It chimed the two quarters and then, quite suddenly, the lights went out."

"What lights were on?"

"The wall brackets in here and in the further room. The standard lamp and the two small reading lamps weren't on."

"Was there a flash first, or a noise when the lights went out?"

"I don't think so."

"I'm sure there was a flash," said Dora Bunner. "And a crackling noise. Dangerous!"

"And then, Miss Blacklock?"

"The door opened—"

"Which door? There are two in the room."

"Oh, this door in here. The one in the other room doesn't open. It's a dummy. The door opened and there he was, a masked man with a revolver. It just seemed too fantastic for words, but, of course, at the time I just thought it was a silly joke. He said something—I forget what—"

"Hands up or I shoot!" supplied Miss Bunner dramatically.

"Something like that," said Miss Blacklock, rather doubtfully.

"And you all put your hands up?"

"Oh yes," said Miss Bunner. "We all did. I mean, it was part of it."

"I didn't," said Miss Blacklock crisply. "It seemed so utterly silly. And I was annoyed by the whole thing."

"And then?"

"The flashlight was right in my eyes. It dazzled me. And then, quite incredibly, I heard a bullet whiz past me and hit the wall by my head. Somebody shrieked and then I felt a burning pain in my ear and heard the second report."

"It was terrifying," put in Miss Bunner.

"And what happened next, Miss Blacklock?"

"It's difficult to say—I was so staggered by the pain and the surprise. The—the figure turned away and seemed to stumble and then there was another shot and his flashlight went out and everybody began pushing and calling out. All banging into each other."

"Where were you standing, Miss Blacklock?"

"She was over by the table. She'd got the vase of violets in her hand," said Miss Bunner breathlessly.

"I was over here." Miss Blacklock went over to the small table by the archway. "Actually, it was the cigarette box I'd got in my hand."

Inspector Craddock examined the wall behind her. The two bullet holes showed plainly. The bullets themselves had been extracted and had been sent for comparison with the revolver.

He said quietly:

"You had a very near escape, Miss Blacklock."

"He did shoot at her," said Miss Bunner. "Deliberately at her! I saw him. He turned the flash round on everybody until he found her and then he held it right at her and just fired at her. He meant to kill you, Letty."

"Dora dear, you've just got that into your head from mulling the whole thing over and over."

"He shot at you," repeated Dora stubbornly. "He meant to shoot you and when he'd missed, he shot himself. I'm certain that's the way it was!"

"I don't think he meant to shoot himself for a minute," said Miss Blacklock. "He wasn't the kind of man who shoots himself."

"You tell me, Miss Blacklock, that until the revolver was fired you thought the whole business was a joke?"

"Naturally. What else could I think it was?"

"Who did you think was the author of this joke?"

"You thought Patrick had done it at first," Dora Bunner reminded her.

"Patrick?" asked the Inspector, sharply.

"My young cousin, Patrick Simmons," Miss Blacklock continued sharply, annoyed with her friend. "It did occur to me when I saw this advertisement that it might be some attempt at humor on his part, but he denied it absolutely."

"And then you were worried, Letty," said Miss Bunner. "You were worried, although you pretended not to be. And you were quite right to be worried. It said a murder is announced—and it was announced—your murder! And if the man hadn't missed, you would have been murdered. And then where should we all be?"

Dora Bunner was trembling as she spoke. Her face was puckered up and she looked as though she were going to cry.

Miss Blacklock patted her on the shoulder.

"It's all right, Dora dear—don't get excited. It's so bad for you. Everything's quite all right. We've had a nasty experience, but it's over now." She added, "You must pull yourself together for my sake, Dora. I rely on you, you know, to keep the house going. Isn't it the day for the laundry to come?"

"Oh, dear me, Letty, how fortunate you reminded me! I wonder if they'll return that missing pillowcase. I must make a note in the book about it. I'll go and see to it at once."

"And take these violets away," said Miss Blacklock. "There's nothing I hate more than dead flowers."

"What a pity. I picked them fresh yesterday. They haven't lasted at all—Oh, dear, I must have forgotten to put any water in the vase. Fancy that! I'm always forgetting things. Now I must go and see about the laundry. They might be here any moment."

She bustled away, looking quite happy again.

"She's not very strong," said Miss Blacklock, "and excitements are bad for her. Is there anything more you want to know, Inspector?"

"I just want to know exactly how many people make up your household here and something about them."

"Yes, well in addition to myself and Dora Bunner, I have two young cousins living here at present, Patrick and Julia Simmons."

"Cousins? Not a nephew and niece?"

"No, they call me Aunt Letty, but actually they are distant cousins. Their mother was my second cousin."

"Have they always made their home with you?"

"Oh, dear, no; only for the last two months. They lived in the South of France before the war. Patrick went into the Navy and Julia, I believe, was in one of the Ministries. She was at Llandudno. When the war was over their mother wrote and asked me if they could possibly come to me as paying guests—Julia is training as a dispenser in Milchester General Hospital, Patrick is studying for an engineering degree at Milchester University. Milchester, as you know, is only fifty minutes by bus, and I was very glad to have them here. This house is really too large for me. They pay a small sum for board and lodging and it all works out very well." She added with a smile, "I like having somebody young about the place."

"Then there is a Mrs. Haymes, I believe?"

"Yes. She works as an assistant gardener at Dayas Hall, Mrs. Lucas's place. The cottage there is occupied by the old gardener and his wife and Mrs. Lucas asked if I could billet her here. She's a very nice girl. Her husband was killed in Italy, and she has a boy of eight who is at a prep school and whom I have arranged to have here in the holidays."

"And by way of domestic help?"

"A Mrs. Huggins from the village comes up five mornings a week and I have a foreign refugee with a most unpronounceable name as a kind of lady cook help. You will find Mitzi rather difficult, I'm afraid. She has a kind of persecution mania."

Craddock nodded. He was conscious in his own mind of yet another of Constable Legg's invaluable commentaries. Having appended the word "Scatty" to Dora Bunner, and "All right" to Letitia Blacklock, he had embellished Mitzi's record with the one word, "Liar."

As though she had read his mind Miss Blacklock said:

"Please don't be too prejudiced against the poor thing because she's a liar. I do really believe that, like so many liars, there is a real substratum of truth behind her lies. I mean that though, to take an instance, her atrocity stories have grown and grown until every kind of unpleasant story that has ever appeared in print has happened to her or her relatives personally, she did have a bad shock initially and did see one, at least, of her relatives killed. I think a lot of these displaced persons feel, perhaps justly, that their claim to our notice and sympathy lies in their atrocity value and so they exaggerate and invent."

She added, "Quite frankly, Mitzi is a maddening person. She exasperates and infuriates us all, she is suspicious and sulky, is perpetually having 'feelings' and thinking herself insulted. But, in spite of it all, I really am sorry for her." She smiled. "And, also, when she wants to, she can cook very nicely."

"I'll try not to ruffle her more than I can help," said Craddock soothingly. "Was that Miss Julia Simmons who opened the door to me?"

"Yes. Would you like to see her now? Patrick has gone out. Phillipa Haymes you will find working at Dayas Hall."

"Thank you, Miss Blacklock. I'd like to see Miss Simmons now if I may."

6

Julia, Mitzi and Patrick

Julia, when she came into the room and sat down in the chair vacated by Letitia Blacklock, had an air of composure that Craddock, for some reason, found annoying. She fixed a limpid gaze on him and waited for his questions.

Miss Blacklock had tactfully left the room.

"Please tell me about last night, Miss Simmons?"

"Last night?" murmured Julia with a blank stare. "Oh, we all slept like logs. Reaction, I suppose."

"I mean last night from six o'clock onwards."

"Oh, I see. Well, a lot of tiresome people came—"

"They were?"

She gave him another limpid stare.

"Don't you know all this already?"

"I'm asking the questions, Miss Simmons," said Craddock pleasantly.

"My mistake. I always find repetitions so dreary. Apparently you don't . . . Well, there were Colonel and Mrs. Easterbrook, Miss Hinchliffe and Miss Murgatroyd, Mrs. Swettenham and Edmund Swettenham, and Mrs. Harmon, the vicar's wife. They arrived in that order. And if you want to know what they said—they all said the same things in turn. 'I see you've got your central heating on' and 'What lovely chrysanthemums!'"

Craddock bit his lip. The mimicry was good.

"The exception was Mrs. Harmon. She's rather a pet. She came in with her hat falling off and her shoelaces untied and she asked

183

straight out when the murder was going to happen? It embarrassed everybody because they'd all been pretending they'd dropped in by chance. Aunt Letty said in her dry way that it was due to happen quite soon. And then that clock chimed and just as it finished the lights went out, the door was flung open and a masked figure said, 'Stick 'em up, guys,' or something like that. It was exactly like a bad film. Really, quite ridiculous. And then he fired two shots at Aunt Letty and suddenly it wasn't ridiculous any more."

"Where was everybody when this happened?"

"When the lights went out? Well, just standing about, you know. Mrs. Harmon was sitting on the sofa—Hinch (that's Miss Hinchliffe) had taken up a manly stance in front of the fireplace."

"You were all in this room, or the far room?"

"Mostly, I think, in this room. Patrick had gone into the other to get the sherry. I think Colonel Easterbrook went after him, but I don't really know. We were—well—as I said, just standing about."

"Where were you yourself?"

"I think I was over by the window. Aunt Letty went to get the cigarettes."

"On that table by the archway?"

"Yes—and then the lights went out and the bad film started."

"The man had a powerful flashlight. What did he do with it?"

"Well, he shone it on us. Horribly dazzling. It just made you blink."

"I want you to answer this very carefully, Miss Simmons. Did he hold it steady or did he move it about?"

Julia considered. Her manner was definitely less weary.

"He moved it," she said slowly. "Like a spotlight in a dance hall. It was full in my eyes and then it went on round the room and then the shots came. Two shots."

"And then?"

"He whirled round—and Mitzi began to scream like a siren from somewhere and his flashlight went out and there was another shot. And then the door closed (it does, you know, slowly, with a whining noise—quite uncanny) and there we were all in the dark, not knowing what to do, and poor Bunny squealing like a pig and Mitzi going all out across the hall."

"Would it be your opinion that the man shot himself deliberately, or do you think he stumbled and the revolver went off accidentally?"

"I haven't the faintest idea. The whole thing was so stagy. Actually, I thought it was still some silly joke—until I saw the blood from Letty's ear. But even if you were actually going to fire a revolver to make the thing more real, you'd be careful to fire it well above someone's head, wouldn't you?"

"You would indeed. Do you think he could see clearly who he was firing at? I mean, was Miss Blacklock clearly outlined in the light of the torch?"

"I've no idea. I wasn't looking at her. I was looking at the man."

"What I'm getting at is—do you think the man was deliberately aiming at her—at her in particular, I mean?"

Julia seemed a little startled by the idea.

"You mean deliberately picking on Aunt Letty? Oh, I shouldn't think so . . . After all, if he wanted to take a pot shot at Aunt Letty, there would be heaps of more suitable opportunities. There would be no point in collecting all the friends and neighbors just to make it more difficult. He could have shot her from behind a hedge in the good old Irish fashion any day of the week, and probably got away with it."

And that, thought Craddock, was a very complete reply to Dora Bunner's suggestion of a deliberate attack on Letitia Blacklock.

He said, with a sigh, "Thank you, Miss Simmons, I'd better go and see Mitzi now."

"Mind her fingernails," warned Julia. "She's a tartar!"

II

Craddock, with Fletcher in attendance, found Mitzi in the kitchen. She was rolling pastry and looked up suspiciously as they entered.

Her black hair hung over her eyes; she looked sullen and the purple jumper and brilliant green skirt she wore were not becoming to her pasty complexion.

"What do you come in my kitchen for, Mr. Policemen? You are police, yes? Always, always there is persecution—ah! I should be used to it by now. They say it is different here in England, but no, it is just the same. You come to torture me, yes, to make me say things, but I shall say nothing. You will tear off my fingernails, and put lighted matches on my skin—oh, yes, and worse than that. But I will not speak, do you hear? I shall say nothing—nothing at all. And you will send me away to a concentration camp, and I shall not care."

Craddock looked at her thoughtfully, selecting what was likely to be the best method of attack. Finally he sighed and said:

"O.K. then; get your hat and coat."

"What is that you say?" Mitzi looked startled.

"Get your hat and coat and come along. I haven't got my nail-pulling apparatus and the rest of the bag of tricks with me. We keep all that down at the station. Got the handcuffs handy, Fletcher?"

"Sir!" said Sergeant Fletcher, with appreciation.

"But I do not want to come!" screeched Mitzi, backing away from him.

"Then you'll answer civil questions civilly. If you like, you can have a solicitor present."

"A lawyer? I do not like a lawyer. I do not want a lawyer."

She put the rolling-pin down, dusted her hands on a cloth and sat down.

"What do you want to know?" she asked sulkily.

"I want your account of what happened here last night."

"You know very well what happened."

"I want your account of it."

"I tried to go away. Did she tell you that? When I saw that in the paper saying about murder, I wanted to go away. She would not let me. She is very hard—not at all sympathetic. She made me stay. But I knew—I knew what would happen. I knew I should be murdered."

"Well, you weren't murdered, were you?"

"No," admitted Mitzi grudgingly.

"Come now, tell me what happened."

"I was nervous. Oh, I was nervous. All that evening. I hear things. People moving about. Once I think someone is in the hall moving stealthily—but it is only that Mrs. Haymes coming in through the side door so as not to dirty the front steps, she says. Much she cares! She is a Nazi herself, that one, with her fair hair and her blue eyes, so superior and looking at me and thinking that I—I am only dirt—"

"Never mind Mrs. Haymes."

"Who does she think she is? Has she had expensive university education like I have? Has she a degree in Economics? No, she is just a paid laborer. She digs and mows grass and is paid so much ever Saturday. Who is she to call herself a lady?"

"Never mind Mrs. Haymes, I said. Go on."

"I take the sherry and the glasses, and the little pastries that I have made so nice into the drawing-room. Then the bell rings and I answer the door. Again and again and again I answer the door. It is degrading—but I do it. And then I go back into the pantry and I start to polish the silver, and I think it will be very handy, that, because if someone comes to kill me, I have there close at hand the big carving knife, all sharp."

"Very foresighted of you."

"And then, suddenly—I hear shots. I think: It has come—it is happening. I run through the dining room (the other door—it will not open). I stand a moment to listen and then there comes another shot and a big thud, out there in the hall, and I turn the door handle, but it is locked outside. I am shut in there like a rat in a trap. And I go mad with fear. I scream and I scream and I beat upon the door. And at last—at last—they turn the key and let me out. And then I bring candles, many, many candles—and the lights go on, and I see blood—blood! Ah, *Gott in Himmel*, the blood! It is not the first time I have seen blood. My little brother—I see him killed before my eyes—I see blood in the street—people shot, dying—I—"

"Yes," said Inspector Craddock. "Thank you very much."

"And now," said Mitzi dramatically, "you can arrest me and take me to prison!"

"Not today," said Inspector Craddock.

III

As Craddock and Fletcher went through the hall to the front door it was flung open and a tall, handsome young man almost collided with them.

"Sleuths, as I live!" cried the young man.

"Mr. Patrick Simmons?"

"Quite right, Inspector. You're the Inspector, aren't you, and the other's the Sergeant?"

"You are quite right, Mr. Simmons. Can I have a word with you, please?"

"I am innocent, Inspector. I swear I am innocent."

"Now then, Mr. Simmons, don't play the fool. I've a good many other people to see and I don't want to waste time. What's this room? Can we go in here?"

"It's the so-called study—but nobody studies."

"I was told that you were studying?" said Craddock.

"I found I couldn't concentrate on mathematics, so I came home."

In a businesslike manner Inspector Craddock demanded full name, age, details of war service.

"And now, Mr. Simmons, will you describe what happened last night?"

"We killed the fatted calf, Inspector. That is, Mitzi set her hand to making savory pastries, Aunt Letty opened a new bottle of sherry—"

Craddock interrupted.

"A new bottle? Was there an old one?"

"Yes, half full. But Aunt Letty didn't seem to fancy it."

"Was she nervous then?"

"Oh, not really. She's extremely sensible. It was old Bunny, I think, who had put the wind up—prophesying disaster all day."

"Miss Bunner was definitely apprehensive then?"

"Oh, yes, she enjoyed herself thoroughly."

"She took the advertisement seriously?"

"It scared her into fits."

"Miss Blacklock seems to have thought, when she first read that advertisement, that you had had something to do with it. Why was that?"

"Ah, sure, I get blamed for everything round here!"

"You didn't have anything to do with it, did you, Mr. Simmons?"

"Me? Never in the world."

"Had you ever seen or spoken to this Rudi Scherz?"

"Never saw him in my life."

"It was the kind of joke you might have played, though?"

"Who's been telling you that? Just because I once made Bunny an apple pie bed—and sent Mitzi a postcard saying the Gestapo was on her track—"

"Just give me your account of what happened."

"I'd just gone into the small drawing-room to fetch the drinks when, hey, presto, the lights went out. I turned round and there's a fellow standing in the doorway saying, 'Stick your hands up,' and everybody gasping and squealing, and just when I'm wondering if I can rush him, he starts firing a revolver and then crash down he goes and his flashlight goes out and we're in the dark again, and Colonel Easterbrook starts shouting orders in his barrack-room voice. 'Lights!' he says, and will my lighter go on? No, it won't, as is the way of those cussed inventions."

"Did it seem to you that the intruder was definitely aiming at Miss Blacklock?"

"Ah, how could I tell? I should say he just loosed off his revolver for the fun of the thing—and then found, maybe, he'd gone too far."

"And shot himself?"

"It could be. When I saw the face of him, he looked like the kind of little pasty thief who might easily lose his nerve."

"And you're sure you had never seen him before?"

"Never."

"Thank you, Mr. Simmons. I shall want to interview the other people who were here last night. What would be the best order in which to take them?"

"Well, our Phillipa—Mrs. Haymes—works at Dayas Hall. The gates of it are nearly opposite this gate. After that, the Swettenhams are the nearest. Anyone will tell you."

7

Among Those Present

Dayas Hall had certainly suffered during the war years. Couch grass grew enthusiastically over what had once been an asparagus bed, as evidenced by a few waving tufts of asparagus foliage. Groundsel, bindweed and other garden pests showed every sign of vigorous growth.

A portion of the kitchen garden bore evidence of having been reduced to discipline and here Craddock found a sour-looking old man leaning pensively on a spade.

"It's Mrs. 'Aymes you want? I couldn't say where you'd find 'er. 'As 'er own ideas, she 'as, about what she'll do. Not one to take advice. I could show 'er—show 'er willing—but what's the good? Won't listen, these young ladies won't! Think they know everything because they've put on breeches and gone for a ride on a tractor. But it's gardening that's needed here. And that isn't learned in a day. Gardening, that's what this place needs."

"It looks as though it does," said Craddock.

The old man chose to take this remark as an aspersion.

"No, look here, mister, who do you suppose I can do with a place this size? Three men and a boy, that's what it used to 'ave. And that's what it wants. There's not many men could put in the work on it that I do. 'Ere sometimes, I am, till eight o'clock at night. Eight o'clock."

"What do you work by? An oil lamp?"

"Naterally I don't mean this time o' year. Naterally. Summer evenings I'm talking about."

"Oh," said Craddock. "I'd better go and look for Mrs. Haymes."

The rustic displayed some interest.

"What are you wanting 'er for? Police, aren't you? She been in trouble, or is it the do there was up to Little Paddocks? Masked men bursting in and holding up a roomful of people with a revolver. Ah! That sort of thing wouldn't 'ave 'appened afore the war. Deserters, that's what it is. Desperate men roaming the countryside. Why don't the military round 'em up?"

"I've no idea," said Craddock. "I suppose this holdup caused a lot of talk?"

"That it did. What's us coming to? That's what Ned Barker said. Comes of going to the pictures so much, he said. But Tom Riley, he says it comes of letting these furriners run about loose. And depend on it, he says, that girl as cooks up there for Miss Blacklock and 'as such a nasty temper—she's in it, he said. She's a Communist or worse, he says, and we don't like that sort 'ere. And Marlene, who's behind the bar, you understand, she will 'ave it that there must be something very valuable up at Miss Blacklock's. Not that you'd think it, she says, for I'm sure Miss Blacklock goes about as plain as plain, except for them great rows of false pearls she wears. And then she says—supposin' as them pearls is real; and Florrie (that's old Bellamy's daughter), she says, 'Nonsense,' she says—'noovo art—that's what they are—costume jewelry,' she says. Costume jewelry—that's a fine way of labeling a string of false pearls. Roman pearls, the gentry used to call 'em once—and Parisian diamonds—my wife was a lady's maid and I know. But what does it all mean—just glass! I suppose it's costume jewelry that young Miss Simmons wears—gold ivy leaves and dogs and such like. 'Tisn't often you see a real bit of gold nowadays—even wedding rings they make of this gray platting-hum stuff. Shabby, I call it—for all that it costs the earth."

Old Ashe paused for breath and then continued:

"'Miss Blacklock don't keep much money in the 'ouse, that I do know,' says Jim Huggins, speaking up. He should know, for it's his wife as goes up and does for 'em at Little Paddocks, and she's a woman as knows most of what's going on. Nosy, if you get me."

"Did he say what Mrs. Huggins's view was?"

"That Mitzi's mixed up in it, that's what she thinks. Awful temper she 'as, and the airs she gives herself! Called Mrs. Huggins a working woman to her face the other morning."

Craddock stood a moment, checking over in his orderly mind the substance of the old gardener's remarks. It gave him a good cross section of rural opinion in Chipping Cleghorn, but he didn't think there was anything to help him in his task. He turned away and the old man called after him grudgingly:

"Maybe you'd find her in the apple orchard. She's younger than I am for getting the apples down."

And sure enough, in the apple orchard Craddock found Phillipa Haymes. His first view was a pair of nice legs encased in breeches, sliding easily down the trunk of a tree. Then Phillipa, her face flushed, her fair hair ruffled by the branches, stood looking at him in a startled fashion.

Make a good Rosalind, Craddock thought automatically, for Detective Inspector Craddock was a Shakespeare enthusiast and had played the part of the melancholy Jacques with great success in a performance of *As You Like It* for the Police Orphanage.

A moment later he amended his view. Phillipa Haymes was too wooden for Rosalind, her fairness and her impassivity were intensely English, but English of the twentieth rather than of the sixteenth century. Well-bred, unemotional English, without a sparkle of mischief.

"Good morning, Mrs. Haymes. I'm sorry if I startled you. I'm Detective Inspector Craddock of the Middleshire Police. I wanted to have a word with you."

"About last night?"

"Yes."

"Will it take long? Shall we—"

She looked about her rather doubtfully.

Craddock indicated a fallen tree trunk.

"Rather informal," he said pleasantly, "but I don't want to interrupt your work longer than necessary."

"Thank you."

"It's just for the record. You came in from work at what time last night?"

"At about half past five. I'd stayed about twenty minutes later in order to finish some watering in the greenhouse."

"You came in by which door?"

"The side door. One cuts across by the ducks and the henhouse from the drive. It saves going round and, besides it avoids dirtying up the front porch. I'm in rather a mucky state sometimes."

"You always come in that way?"

"Yes."

"The door was unlocked?"

"Yes. During the summer it's usually wide open. This time of the year it's shut but not locked. We all go out and in that way a good deal. I locked it when I came in."

"Do you always do that?"

"I've been doing it for the last week. You see, it gets dark at six. Miss Blacklock goes out to shut up the ducks and the hens sometime in the evening, but she very often goes out through the kitchen door."

"And you are quite sure you did lock the side door this time?"

"I really am quite sure about that."

"Quite so, Mrs. Haymes. And what did you do when you came in?"

"Kicked off my muddy footwear and went upstairs, had a bath and changed. Then I came down and found that a kind of party was in progress. I hadn't known anything about this funny advertisement until then."

"Now please describe just what occurred when the holdup happened."

"Well, the lights went out suddenly—"

"Where were you?"

"By the mantelpiece. I was searching for my lighter which I thought I had put down there. The lights went out—and everybody giggled. Then the door was flung open and this man shone a flashlight on us and flourished a revolver and told us to put our hands up."

"Which you proceeded to do?"

"Well, I didn't, actually. I thought it was just fun, and I was tired and didn't think I really needed to put them up."

"In fact, you were bored by the whole thing?"

"I was, rather. And then the revolver went off. The shots sounded deafening and I was really frightened. The flashlight went whirling round and dropped and went out, and then Mitzi started screaming. It was just like a pig being killed."

"Did you find the flashlight very dazzling?"

"No, not particularly. It was quite a strong one, though. It lit up Miss Bunner for a moment and she looked quite like a turnip ghost—you know, all white and staring with her mouth open and her eyes starting out of her head."

"The man moved the flashlight?"

"Oh, yes, he played it all round the room."

"As though he were looking for someone?"

"Not particularly, I should say."

"And after that, Mrs. Haymes?"

Phillipa Haymes frowned.

193

"Oh, it was all a terrible muddle and confusion. Edmund Swetten-ham and Patrick Simmons switched on their lighters and they went out into the hall and we followed, and someone opened the dining room door—the lights hadn't gone out there—and Edmund Swetten-ham gave Mitzi a terrific slap on the cheek and brought her out of her screaming fit, and after that it wasn't so bad."

"You saw the body of the dead man?"

"Yes."

"Was he known to you? Had you ever seen him before?"

"Never."

"Have you any opinion as to whether his death was accidental, or do you think he shot himself deliberately?"

"I haven't the faintest idea."

"You didn't see him when he came to the house previously?"

"No. I believe it was in the middle of the morning and I wouldn't have been there."

"Thank you, Mrs. Haymes. One thing more. You haven't any valuable jewelry? Rings, bracelets, anything of that kind?"

Phillipa shook her head.

"My engagement ring—a couple of brooches."

"And, as far as you know, there was nothing of particular value in the house?"

"No. I mean there is some quite nice silver—but nothing out of the ordinary."

"Thank you, Mrs. Haymes."

II

As Craddock retraced his steps through the kitchen garden he came face to face with a large, red-faced lady, carefully corseted.

"Good morning," she said belligerently. "What do you want here?"

"Mrs. Lucas? I am Detective Inspector Craddock."

"Oh, that's who you are. I beg your pardon. I don't like strangers forcing their way into my garden, wasting the gardeners' time. But I quite understand you have to do your duty."

"Quite so."

"May I ask if we are to expect a repetition of that outrage last night at Miss Blacklock's? Is it a gang?"

"We are satisfied, Mrs. Lucas, that it was not the work of a gang."

"There are far too many robberies nowadays. The police are getting slack." Craddock did not reply. "I suppose you've been talking to Phillipa Haymes?"

"I wanted her account as an eye-witness."

"You couldn't have waited until one o'clock, I suppose? After all, it would be fairer to question her in her time, rather than in mine."

"I'm anxious to get back to headquarters."

"Not that one expects consideration nowadays. Or a decent day's work. On duty late, half an hour's pottering. A break for relief at ten o'clock. No work done at all the moment the rain starts. When you want the lawn mowed there's always something wrong with the mower. And off duty five or ten minutes before the proper time."

"I understand from Mrs. Haymes that she left here at twenty minutes past five yesterday instead of five o'clock."

"Oh, I daresay she did. Give her her due, Mrs. Haymes is quite keen on her work, though there have been days when I have come out here and not been able to find her anywhere. She is a lady by birth, of course, and one feels it one's duty to do something for these poor young war widows. Not that it isn't very inconvenient. Those long school holidays, and the arrangement is that she has extra time off then. I told her that there are really excellent camps nowadays where children can be sent and where they have a delightful time and enjoy it far more than wandering about with their parents. They need practically not come home at all in the summer holidays."

"But Mrs. Haymes didn't take kindly to that idea?"

"She's as obstinate as a mule, that girl. Just the time of year when I want the tennis court mowed and marked nearly every day. Old Ashe gets the lines crooked. But my convenience is never considered!"

"I presume Mrs. Haymes takes a smaller salary than is usual."

"Naturally. What else could she expect?"

"Nothing, I'm sure," said Craddock. "Good morning, Mrs. Lucas."

III

"It was dreadful," said Mrs. Swettenham happily. "Quite—quite—dreadful, and what I say is that they ought to be far more careful what advertisements they accept at the *Gazette* office. At the time, when I read it, I thought it was very, very odd. I said so, didn't I, Edmund?"

"Do you remember just what you were doing when the lights went out, Mrs. Swettenham?" asked the Inspector.

"How that reminds me of my old Nannie! *Where was Moses when the light went out?* The answer, of course, was 'In the dark.' Just like us yesterday evening. All standing about and wondering what was going to happen. And then, you know, the thrill when it suddenly went pitch black. And the door opening—just a dim figure standing there with a revolver and that blinding light and a menacing voice saying, 'Your money or your life!' Oh, I've never enjoyed anything so much. And then, a minute later, of course, it was all dreadful. Real bullets, just whistling past our ears! It must have been just like the commandos in the war."

"Whereabouts were you standing or sitting at the time, Mrs. Swettenham?"

"Now, let me see, where was I? Who was I talking to, Edmund?"

"I really haven't the least idea, Mother."

"Was it Miss Hinchliffe I was asking about giving the hens cod liver oil in the cold weather? Or was it Mrs. Harmon—no, she'd only just arrived. I think I was just saying to Colonel Easterbrook that I thought it was really very dangerous to have an atom research station in England. It ought to be on some lonely island in case the radio activity gets loose."

"You don't remember if you were sitting or standing?"

"Does it really matter, Inspector? I was somewhere over by the window or near the mantelpiece, because I know I was quite near the clock when it struck. Such a thrilling moment! Waiting to see if anything might be going to happen."

"You describe the light from the flashlight as blinding. Was it turned full on you?"

"It was right in my eyes. I couldn't see a thing."

"Did the man hold it still, or did he move it about, from person to person?"

"Oh, I don't really know. Which did he do, Edmund?"

"It moved rather slowly over us all, so as to see what we were all doing, I suppose, in case we should try to rush him."

"And where exactly in the room were you, Mr. Swettenham?"

"I'd been talking to Julia Simmons. We were both standing up in the middle of the room—the long room."

"Was everyone in that room, or was there someone in the far room?"

"Phillipa Haymes had moved in there, I think. She was over by that far mantelpiece. I think she was looking for something."

"Have you any idea as to whether the third shot was suicide or an accident?"

"I've no idea at all. The man seemed to swerve round very suddenly and then crumple up and fall—but it was all very confused. You must realize that you couldn't really see anything. And then that refugee girl started yelling the place down."

"I understand it was you who unlocked the dining room door and let her out?"

"Yes."

"The door was definitely locked on the outside?"

Edmund looked at him curiously.

"Certainly it was. Why, you don't imagine—"

"I just like to get my facts quite clear. Thank you, Mr. Swettenham."

IV

Inspector Craddock was forced to spend quite a long time with Colonel and Mrs. Easterbrook. He had to listen to a long disquisition on the psychological aspect of the case.

"The psychological approach—that's the only thing nowadays," the colonel told him. "You've got to understand your criminal. Now, the whole setup here is plain as plain to a man who's had the wide experience that I have. Why does this fellow put that ad in? Psychology. He wants to advertise himself—to focus attention on himself. He's been passed over, perhaps despised as a foreigner by the other employees at the Spa Hotel. A girl has turned him down, perhaps. He wants to rivet her attention on him. Who is the idol of the movies nowadays—the gangster—the tough guy? Very well, he will be a tough guy. Robbery with violence. A mask? A revolver? But he wants an audience—he must have an audience. So he arranges for an audience. And then, at the supreme moment, his part runs away with him—he's more than a burglar. He's a killer. He shoots—blindly—"

Inspector Craddock caught gladly at a word.

"You say 'blindly,' Colonel Easterbrook. You didn't think that he was firing deliberately at one particular person—at Miss Blacklock, that is to say?"

"No, no. He just loosed off, as I say, blindly. And that's what brought him to himself. The bullet hit someone—actually, it was only a graze, but he doesn't know that. He comes to himself with a bang. All this—this make-believe he's been indulging in—is real. He's shot at someone—perhaps killed someone. . . . It's all up with him. And so, in blind panic, he turns the revolver on himself."

Colonel Easterbrook paused, cleared his throat appreciatively and said, in a satisfied voice, "Plain as a pikestaff, that's what it is; plain as a pikestaff."

"It really is wonderful," said Mrs. Easterbrook, "the way you know exactly what happened, Archie."

Her voice was warm with admiration.

Inspector Craddock thought it was wonderful, too, but he was not quite so warmly appreciative.

"Exactly where were you in the room, Colonel Easterbrook, when the actual shooting business took place?"

"I was standing with my wife—near a center table with some flowers on it."

"I caught hold of your arm, didn't I, Archie, when it happened? I was simply scared to death. I just had to hold on to you."

"Poor little kitten," said the colonel playfully.

V

The Inspector ran Miss Hinchliffe to earth beside a pigsty.

"Nice creatures, pigs," said Miss Hinchliffe, scratching a wrinkled pink back. "Coming on well, isn't he? Good bacon round about Christmas time. Well, what do you want to see me about? I told your people last night I hadn't the least idea who the man was. Never saw him anywhere in the neighborhood snooping about or anything of that sort. Our Mrs. Mopp says he came from one of the big hotels in Medenham Wells. Why didn't he hold up someone there if he wanted to? Get a much better haul."

That was undeniable—Craddock proceeded with his inquiries.

"Where were you exactly when the incident took place?"

"Incident! Reminds me of my A.R.P. days. Saw some incidents then, I can tell you. Where was I when the shooting started? That what you want to know?"

"Yes."

"Leaning up against the mantelpiece, hoping to God someone would offer me a drink soon," replied Miss Hinchliffe promptly.

"Do you think that the shots were fired blindly, or aimed carefully at one particular person?"

"You mean aimed at Letty Blacklock? How the devil should I know? Damned hard to sort out what your impressions really were or what really happened, after it's all over. All I know is the lights went out, and that flashlight went whirling round, dazzling us all, and then the shots were fired and I thought to myself, If that damned young fool Patrick Simmons is playing his jokes with a loaded revolver, somebody will get hurt."

"You thought it was Patrick Simmons?"

"Well, it seemed likely. Edmund Swettenham is intellectual and writes books and doesn't care for horseplay, and old Colonel Easterbrook wouldn't think that sort of thing funny. But Patrick's a wild boy. However, I apologize to him for the idea."

"Did your friend think it might be Patrick Simmons?"

"Murgatroyd? You'd better talk to her yourself. Not that you'll get any sense out of her. She's down in the orchard. I'll yell for her if you like."

Miss Hinchliffe raised her stentorian voice in a powerful bellow: "Hi-youp, Murgatroyd!"

"Coming—" floated back a thin cry.

"Hurry up—poleece!" bellowed Miss Hinchliffe.

Miss Murgatroyd arrived at a brisk trot, very much out of breath. Her skirt was down at the hem and her hair was escaping from an inadequate hairnet. Her round good-natured face beamed.

"Is it Scotland Yard?" she asked breathlessly. "I'd no idea, or I wouldn't have left the house."

"We haven't called in Scotland Yard yet, Miss Murgatroyd. I'm Inspector Craddock from Milchester."

"Well, that's very nice, I'm sure," said Miss Murgatroyd vaguely. "Have you found any clues?"

"Where were you at the time of the crime, that's what he wants to know, Murgatroyd?" said Miss Hinchliffe. She winked at Craddock.

"Oh, dear," gasped Miss Murgatroyd. "Of course. I ought to have been prepared. Alibis, of course. Now, let me see, I was just with everybody else."

"You weren't with me," said Miss Hinchliffe.

"Oh, dear, Hinch, wasn't I? No, of course, I'd been admiring the chrysanthemums. Very poor specimens really. And then it all happened—only I didn't really know it had happened—I mean I didn't know that anything like that had happened. I didn't imagine for a moment it was a real revolver—and all so awkward in the dark, and that dreadful screaming. I got it all wrong, you know. I thought she was being murdered—I mean the refugee girl. I thought she was having her throat cut across the hall somewhere. I didn't know it was him—I mean I didn't even know there was a man. It was really just a voice, you know, saying, 'Put them up, please.'"

"'Stick 'em up!'" Miss Hinchliffe corrected. "And no suggestion of 'please' about it."

"It's so terrible to think that until that girl started screaming I was actually enjoying myself. Only being in the dark was very awkward and I got a knock on my corn. Agony, it was. Is there anything more you want to know, Inspector?"

"No," said Inspector Craddock, eyeing Miss Murgatroyd speculatively. "I don't really think there is."

Her friend gave a short bark of laughter.

"He's got you taped, Murgatroyd."

"I'm sure, Hinch," said Miss Murgatroyd, "that I'm only too willing to say anything I can."

"He doesn't want that," said Miss Hinchliffe.

She looked at the Inspector. "If your doing this geographically, I suppose you'll go to the vicarage next. You might get something there. Mrs. Harmon looks as vague as they make them—but I sometimes think she's got brains. Anyway, she's got something."

As they watched Inspector and Sergeant Fletcher stalk away, Amy Murgatroyd said breathlessly:

"Oh, Hinch, was I very awful? I do get so flustered!"

"Not at all," Miss Hinchliffe smiled. "On the whole, I should say you did very well."

VI

Inspector Craddock looked round the big shabby room with a sense of pleasure. It reminded him a little of his own Cumberland home. Faded chintz, big shabby chairs, flowers and books strewn about and a spaniel in a basket. Mrs. Harmon, too, with her distraught air, her general disarray and her eager face he found sympathetic.

But she said at once, frankly, "I shan't be any help to you, because I shut my eyes. I hate being dazzled. And then there were shots and I screwed them up tighter than ever. And I did wish, oh, I did wish, that it had been a quiet murder. I don't like bangs."

"So you didn't see anything." The Inspector smiled at her. "But you heard—"

"Oh, my goodness, yes, there was plenty to hear. Doors opening and shutting, and people saying silly things and gasping and old

Mitzi screaming like a steam-engine—and poor Bunny squealing like a trapped pig. And everyone pushing and falling over everyone else. However, when there really didn't seem to be any more bangs coming, I opened my eyes. Everyone was out in the hall then, with candles. And then the lights came on and suddenly it was all as usual—I don't mean really as usual, but we were ourselves again, not just—people in the dark. People in the dark are quite different, aren't they?"

"I think I know what you mean, Mrs. Harmon."

Mrs. Harmon smiled at him.

"And there he was," she said. "A rather weaselly looking foreigner—all pink and surprised-looking—lying there dead—with a revolver beside him. It didn't—oh, it didn't seem to make sense somehow."

It did not make sense to the Inspector either. . . .

The whole business worried him.

8

Enter Miss Marple

Craddock laid the typed transcript of the various interviews before the Chief Constable. The latter had just finished reading the wire received from the Swiss police.

"So he had a police record all right," said Rydesdale. "Hm—very much as one thought."

"Yes, sir."

"Jewelry . . . hm, yes . . . falsified entries . . . yes . . . check. Definitely a dishonest fellow."

"Yes, sir—in a small way."

"Quite so. And small things lead to large things."

"I wonder, sir."

The Chief Constable looked up.

"Worried, Craddock?"

"Yes, sir."

"Why? It's a straightforward story. Or isn't it? Let's see what all these people you've been talking to have to say."

He drew the report towards him and read it through rapidly.

"The usual thing—plenty of inconsistencies and contradictions. Different people's accounts of a few moments of stress never agree. But the main picture seems clear enough."

"I know, sir—but it's an unsatisfactory picture. If you know what I mean—it's the wrong picture."

"Well, let's take the facts. Rudi Scherz took the 5:20 bus from Medenham to Chipping Cleghorn, arriving there at six o'clock. Evidence of conductor and two passengers. From the bus stop he walked away in the direction of Little Paddocks. He got into the house with no particular difficulty—probably through the front door. He held up the company with a revolver, he fired two shots, one of which slightly wounded Miss Blacklock; he then killed himself with a third shot, whether accidentally or deliberately there is not sufficient evidence to show. The reasons why he did all this are profoundly unsatisfactory, I agree. But why isn't really a question we are called upon to answer. A coroner's jury may bring it in suicide—or accidental death. Whichever verdict it is, it's the same as far as we're concerned. We can write finis."

"You mean we can always fall back upon Colonel Easterbrook's psychology," said Craddock gloomily.

Rydesdale smiled.

"After all, the colonel's probably had a good deal of experience," he said. "I'm pretty sick of the psychological jargon that's used so glibly about everything nowadays—but we can't really rule it out."

"I still feel the picture's all wrong, sir."

"Any reason to believe that someone in the setup at Chipping Cleghorn is lying to you?"

Craddock hesitated.

"I think the foreign girl knows more than she lets on. But that may be just prejudice on my part."

"You think she might possibly have been in it with this fellow? Let him into the house? Put him up to it?"

"Something of the kind. I wouldn't put it past her. But that surely indicates that there really was something valuable, money or jewelry, in the house, and that doesn't seem to have been the case. Miss Blacklock negatived it quite decidedly. So did the others. That leaves us with the proposition that there was something valuable in the house that nobody knew about—"

"Quite a best-seller plot."

"I agree it's ridiculous, sir. The only other point is Miss Bunner's certainty that it was a definite attempt by Scherz to murder Miss Blacklock."

"Well, from what you say—and from her statement—this Miss Bunner—"

"Oh, I agree, sir," Craddock put in quickly, "she's an utterly unreliable witness. Highly suggestible. Anyone could put a thing into her head—but the interesting thing is that this is quite her own theory—no one has suggested it to her. Everybody else negatives it. For once she's not swimming with the tide. It definitely is her own impression."

"And why should Rudi Scherz want to kill Miss Blacklock?"

"There you are, sir. I don't know. Miss Blacklock doesn't know—unless she's a much better liar than I think she is. Nobody knows. So presumably it isn't true."

He sighed.

"Cheer up, Craddock," said the Chief Constable. "I'm taking you off to lunch with Sir Henry and myself. The best that the Royal Spa Hotel in Medenham Wells can provide."

"Thank you, sir." Craddock looked slightly surprised.

"You see, we received a letter—" He broke off as Sir Henry Clithering entered the room. "Ah, there you are, Henry."

Sir Henry, informal this time, said, "Morning, Dermot."

"I've got something for you, Henry," said the Chief Constable.

"What's that?"

"Authentic letter from an old pussy. Staying at the Royal Spa Hotel. Something she thinks we might like to know in connection with this Chipping Cleghorn business."

"The old pussies," said Sir Henry triumphantly. "What did I tell you? They hear everything. They see everything. And, unlike the famous adage, they speak all evil. What's this particular one got hold of?"

Rydesdale consulted the letter.

"Writes just like my old grandmother," he complained. "Spiky. Like a spider in the ink bottle, and all underlined. A good deal about how she hopes it won't be taking up our valuable time, but might possibly be of some slight assistance etc, etc. What's her name? Jane—something—Murple—no, Marple, Jane Marple."

"Ye gods and little fishes," said Sir Henry, "can it be? George, it's my own particular, one and only, four-starred pussy. The super pussy of all old pussies. And she has managed somehow to be at Medenham Wells, instead of peacefully at home in St. Mary Mead, just at the right time to be mixed up in a murder. Once more a murder is announced—for the benefit and enjoyment of Miss Marple."

"Well, Henry," said Rydesdale sardonically. "I'll be glad to see your paragon. Come on! We'll have lunch at the Royal Spa and we'll interview the lady. Craddock, here, is looking highly skeptical."

"Not at all, sir," said Craddock politely.

He thought to himself that sometimes his godfather carried things a bit far.

II

Miss Jane Marple was very nearly, if not quite, as Craddock had pictured her. She was far more benignant than he had imagined and a good deal older. Indeed she seemed very old. She had snow-white hair and a pink, crinkled face and very soft, innocent blue eyes, and she was heavily enmeshed in fleecy wool. Wool round her shoulders in the form of a lacy cape and wool that she was knitting and which turned out to be a baby's shawl.

She was all incoherent delight and pleasure at seeing Sir Henry, and became quite flustered when introduced to the Chief Constable and Detective Inspector Craddock.

"But really, Sir Henry, how fortunate . . . how very fortunate. So long since I have seen you . . . Yes, my rheumatism. Very bad of late. Of course, I couldn't have afforded this hotel (really fantastic what they charge nowadays), but Raymond—my nephew, Raymond West, you may remember him—"

"Everyone knows his name."

"Yes, the dear boy has been so successful with his clever books. The last one was the Book Society choice—quite the worst one he has written, actually, but I do think that is so often the case, don't you? The dear boy insisted on paying all my expenses. And his dear wife is making a name for herself, too, as an artist. Mostly jugs of dying flowers and broken combs on windowsills. I never dare tell her, but I still admire Blair Leighton and Alma-Tadema. Oh, but I'm chattering. And the Chief Constable himself—indeed I never expected—so afraid I shall be taking up his time—"

Completely ga-ga, thought the disgusted Detective Inspector Craddock.

"Come into the manager's private room," said Rydesdale. "We can talk better there."

When Miss Marple had been disentangled from her wool and her spare knitting-pins collected, she accompanied them, fluttering and protesting, to Mr. Rowlandson's comfortable sitting room.

"Now, Miss Marple, let's hear what you have to tell us," said the Chief Constable.

Miss Marple came to the point with unexpected brevity.

"It was a check," she said. "He altered it."

"He?"

"The young man at the desk here, the one who is supposed to have staged that holdup and shot himself."

"He altered a check, you say?"

Miss Marple nodded.

"Yes. I have it here." She extracted it from her bag and laid it on the table. "It came this morning with my others from the bank. You can see, it was for seven pounds, and he altered it to seventeen. A stroke in front of the seven, and *teen* added after the word seven with a nice artistic little blot just blurring the whole word. Really, very nicely done. A certain amount of practice, I should say. It's the same ink, because I wrote the check actually at the desk. I should think he'd done it quite often before, wouldn't you?"

"He picked the wrong person to do it to, this time," remarked Sir Henry.

Miss Marple nodded agreement.

"Yes. I'm afraid he would never have gone very far in crime. I was quite the wrong person. Some busy young married woman, or some girl having a love affair—that's the kind who write checks for all sorts of different sums and don't really look through their passbooks carefully. But an old woman who has to be careful of the pennies, and who has formed habits—that's quite the wrong person to choose. Seventeen pounds is a sum I never write a check for. Twenty pounds, a round sum, for the monthly wages and books. And for my personal expenditure I usually cash seven—it used to be five, but everything has gone up so."

"And perhaps he reminded you of someone?" prompted Sir Henry, mischief in his eye.

Miss Marple smiled and shook her head at him.

"You are very naughty, Sir Henry. As a matter of fact he did. Fred Tyler, at the fish shop. Always slipped an extra one in the shillings column. Eating so much fish as we do nowadays, it made a long bill, and lots of people never added it up. Just ten shillings in his pocket every time; not much but enough to get himself a few neckties and take Jessie Spragge (the girl in the draper's) to the pictures. Cut a splash, that's what these young fellows want to do. Well, the very first week I was here, there was a mistake in my bill. I pointed it out to the young man and he apologized very nicely and looked very much upset; but I thought to myself then, You've got a shifty eye, young man.

"What I mean by a shifty eye," continued Miss Marple, "is the kind that looks very straight at you and never looks away nor blinks."

Craddock gave a sudden movement of appreciation. He thought to himself, Jim Kelly to the life, remembering a notorious swindler he had helped to put behind bars not long ago.

"Rudi Scherz was a thoroughly unsatisfactory character," said Rydesdale. "He's got a police record in Switzerland, we find."

"Made the place too hot for him, I suppose, and came over here with forged papers?" said Miss Marple.

"Exactly," said Rydesdale.

"He was going about with the little red-haired waitress from the dining room," said Miss Marple. "Fortunately I don't think her heart's affected at all. She just liked to have someone a bit different, and he used to give her flowers and chocolates, which the English boys don't do much. Has she told you all she knows?" she asked, turning suddenly to Craddock. "Or not quite all yet?"

"I'm not absolutely sure," said Craddock cautiously.

"I think there's a little to come," said Miss Marple. "She's looking very worried. Brought me kippers instead of herrings this morning, and forgot the milk jug. Usually she's an excellent waitress. Yes, she's worried. Afraid she might have to give evidence or something like that. But I expect—" her candid blue eyes swept over the manly proportions and handsome face of Detective Inspector Craddock with truly feminine Victorian appreciation, "that you will be able to persuade her to tell you all she knows."

Detective Inspector Craddock blushed and Sir Henry chuckled.

"It might be important," said Miss Marple. "He may have told her who it was."

Rydesdale stared at her.

"Who what was?"

"I express myself so badly. Who it was who put him up to it, I mean."

"So you think someone put him up to it?"

Miss Marple's eyes widened in surprise.

"Oh, but surely—I mean— Here's a personable young man—who filches a little bit here and a little bit there—alters a small check, perhaps helps himself to a small piece of jewelry if it's left lying around or takes a little money from the till—all sorts of small, petty thefts. Keeps himself going in ready money so that he can dress well and take a girl about—all that sort of thing. And then, suddenly, he goes off with a revolver, holds up a roomful of people and shoots at someone. He'd never have done a thing like that—not for a moment! He wasn't that kind of person. It doesn't make sense."

Craddock drew in his breath sharply. That was what Letitia Blacklock had said. What the vicar's wife had said. What he himself felt with increasing force. *It didn't make sense.* And now Sir Henry's old pussy was saying it, too, with complete certainty in her fluting old lady's voice.

"Perhaps you'll tell us, Miss Marple," he said, and his voice was suddenly aggressive, "what did happen, then?"

She turned on him in surprise.

"But how should I know what happened? There was an account in the paper—but it says so little. One can make conjectures, of course, but one has no accurate information."

"George," said Sir Henry, "would it be very unorthodox if Miss Marple were allowed to read the notes of the interviews Craddock had with these people at Chipping Cleghorn?"

"It may be unorthodox," said Rydesdale, "but I've not got where I am by being orthodox. She can read them. I'd be curious to hear what she has to say."

Miss Marple was all embarrassment.

"I'm afraid you've been listening to Sir Henry. Sir Henry is always too kind. He thinks too much of any little observations I may have made in the past. Really, I have no gifts—no gifts at all—except perhaps a certain knowledge of human nature. People, I find, are apt to be far too trustful. I'm afraid that I have a tendency always to believe the worst. Not a nice trait, but so often justified by subsequent events."

"Read these," said Rydesdale, thrusting the typewritten sheets upon her. "They won't take you long. After all, these people are your kind—you must know a lot of people like them. You may be able to spot something that we haven't. The case is just going to be closed. Let's have an amateur's opinion on it before we shut up the files. I don't mind telling you that Craddock here isn't satisfied. He says, like you, that it doesn't make sense."

There was silence whilst Miss Marple read. She put the typewritten sheets down at last.

"It's very interesting," she said with a sigh. "All the different things that people say—and think. The things they see—or think that they see. And all so complex, nearly all so trivial and if one thing isn't trivial, it's so hard to spot which one—like a needle in a haystack."

Craddock felt a twinge of disappointment. Just for a moment or two, he had wondered if Sir Henry might be right about this funny old lady. She might have put her finger on something—old people were often very sharp. He'd never, for instance, been able to conceal anything from his own great-aunt Emma. She had finally told him that his nose twitched when he was about to tell a lie.

But just a few fluffy generalities, that was all that Sir Henry's famous Miss Marple could produce. He felt annoyed with her and said rather curtly:

"The truth of the matter is that the facts are indisputable. Whatever conflicting details these people give, they all saw one thing. They saw a masked man with a revolver and a flashlight open the door and hold them up, and whether they think he said, 'Stick 'em up,' or 'Your money or your life,' or whatever phrase is associated with a holdup in their minds, they saw him."

"But surely," said Miss Marple gently. "They couldn't—actually— have seen anything at all . . ."

Craddock caught his breath. She'd got it! She was sharp, after all. He was testing her by that speech of his, but she hadn't fallen for it. It didn't actually make any difference to the facts, or to what happened, but she'd realized, as he had, that those people who had seen a masked man holding them up couldn't really have seen him at all.

"If I understand rightly," Miss Marple had a pink flush on her cheeks, her eyes were bright and pleased as a child's, "there wasn't any light in the hall outside—and not on the landing upstairs either?"

"That's right," said Craddock.

"And so, if a man stood in the doorway and flashed a powerful light into the room, *nobody could see anything but that light*, could they?"

"No, they couldn't. I tried it out."

"And so when some of them say they saw a masked man, et cetera, they are really, though they don't realize it, recapitulating from what they saw afterwards—when the lights came on. So it all fits in very well, doesn't it, on the assumption that Rudi Scherz was the—I think 'fall guy' is the expression I mean?"

Rydesdale stared at her in such surprise that she grew pinker still.

"I may have got the term wrong," she murmured. "I am not very clever about Americanisms—and I understand they change very quickly. I got it from one of Mr. Dashiell Hammett's stories. (I understand from my nephew Raymond that he is considered at the top of the tree in what is called the tough style of literature.) A 'fall guy,' if I understand it rightly, means someone who will be blamed for a crime really committed by someone else. This Rudi Scherz seems to me exactly the right type for that. Rather stupid really, you know, but full of cupidity and probably extremely credulous."

Rydesdale said, smiling tolerantly:

"Are you suggesting that he was persuaded by someone to go out and take pot shots at a roomful of people? Rather a tall order."

"I think he was told that it was a joke," said Miss Marple. "He was paid for doing it, of course. Paid, that is, to put an advertisement in the newspaper, to go out and spy out the household premises and then, on the night in question, he was to go there, assume a mask and a black cloak and throw open a door, brandish a flashlight and cry, 'Hands up!'"

"And fire off a revolver?"

"No, no," said Miss Marple. "He never had a revolver."

"But everyone says—" began Rydesdale, and stopped.

"Exactly," said Miss Marple. "Nobody could possibly have seen a revolver even if he had one. And I don't think he had. I think that after he'd called 'Hands up' somebody came up quietly behind him in the darkness and fired those two shots over his shoulder. It frightened him to death. He swung round and as he did so, that other person shot him and then let the revolver drop beside him . . ."

The three men looked at her. Sir Henry said softly:

"It's a possible theory."

"But who is Mr. X who came up in the darkness?" asked the Chief Constable.

Miss Marple coughed.

"You'll have to find out from Miss Blacklock who wanted to kill her."

Good for old Dora Bunner, thought Craddock. Instinct against intelligence every time.

"So you think it was a deliberate attempt on Miss Blacklock's life?" asked Rydesdale.

"It certainly has that appearance," said Miss Marple. "Though there are one or two difficulties. But what I was really wondering about was whether there mightn't be a short cut. I've no doubt that whoever arranged this with Rudi Scherz took pains to tell him to keep his mouth shut about it, and perhaps he did keep his mouth shut; but if he talked to anybody it would probably be to that girl, Myrna Harris. And he may—he just may—have dropped some hint as to the kind of person who'd suggested the whole thing."

"I'll see her now," said Craddock, rising.

Miss Marple nodded.

"Yes, do, Inspector Craddock. I'll feel happier when you have. Because once she's told you anything she knows she'll be much safer."

"Safer? Yes, I see."

He left the room. The Chief Constable said doubtfully, but tactfully:

"Well, Miss Marple, you've certainly given us something to think about."

III

"I'm sorry about it, I am really," said Myrna Harris. "It's ever so nice of you not to be ratty about it. But you see Mum's the sort of person who fusses like anything. And it did look as though I'd—what's the phrase—been an accessory before the fact." (The words ran glibly off her tongue.) "I mean, I was afraid you'd never take my word for it that I only thought it was just a bit of fun."

Inspector Craddock repeated the reassuring phrases with which he had broken down Myrna's resistance.

"I will. I'll tell you all about it. But you will keep me out of it if you can because of Mum? It all started with Rudi breaking a date with me. We were going to the pictures that evening and then he said he wouldn't be able to come and I was a bit standoffish with him about it—because, after all, it had been his idea and I don't fancy being stood up by a foreigner. And he said it wasn't his fault, and I said that was a likely story, and then he said he'd got a bit of a lark on that night—and that he wasn't going to be out of pocket by it and how would I fancy a wristwatch? So I said what did he mean by a lark? And he said not to tell anyone, but there was to be a party somewhere and he was to stage a sham holdup. Then he showed me the advertisement he'd put in and I had to laugh. He was a bit scornful about it all. Said it was kids' stuff really—but that was just like the English. They never really grew up—and of course I said what did he mean by talking like that about us—and we had a bit of an argument, but we made it up. Only you can understand, can't you, sir, that when I read all about it, and it hadn't been a joke at all and Rudi had shot someone and then shot himself—why, I didn't know what to do. I thought if I said I knew about it beforehand, it would look as though I were in on the whole thing. But it really did seem like a joke when he told me about it. I'd have sworn he meant it that way. I didn't even know he'd got a revolver. He never said anything about taking a revolver with him."

Craddock comforted her and then asked the most important question.

"Who did he say it was who had arranged this party?"

But there he drew a blank.

"He never said who it was that was getting him to do it. I suppose nobody was, really, It was all his own doing."

"He didn't mention a name? Did he say he—or she?"

"He didn't say anything except that it was going to be a scream. 'I shall laugh to see all their faces.' That's what he said."

He hadn't had long to laugh, Craddock thought.

IV

"It's only a theory," said Rydesdale as they drove back to Medenham. "Nothing to support it, nothing at all. Put it down as old maid's vaporings and let it go, eh?"

"I'd rather not do that, sir."

"It's all very improbable. A mysterious X appearing suddenly in the darkness behind our Swiss friend. Where did he come from? Who was he? Where had he been?"

"He could have come in through the side door," said Craddock, "just as Scherz came. Or," he added slowly, "he could have come from the kitchen."

"She could have come from the kitchen, you mean?"

"Yes, sir, it's a possibility. I've not been satisfied about that girl all along. She strikes me as a nasty bit of goods. All that screaming and hysterics—it could have been put on. She could have worked on this young fellow, let him in at the right moment, rigged the whole thing, shot him, bolted back into the dining room, caught up her bit of silver and her chamois and started her screaming act."

"Against that we have the fact that—er—What's-his-name—oh, yes, Edmund Swettenham, definitely says the key was turned on the outside of the door, and that he turned it to release her. Any other door into that part of the house?"

"Yes, there's a door to the back stairs and kitchen just under the stairs, but it seems the handle came off three weeks ago and nobody's come to put it on yet. In the meantime, you can't open the door. I'm bound to say that story seems correct. The spindle and the two handles were on a shelf outside the door in the hall and they were thickly coated with dust, but, of course, a professional would have ways of opening that door all right."

"Better look up the girl's record. See if her papers are in order. But it seems to me the whole thing is very theoretical."

Again the Chief Constable looked inquiringly at his subordinate. Craddock replied quietly:

"I know, sir, and, of course, if you think the case ought to be closed, it must be. But I'd appreciate it if I could work on it for just a little longer."

Rather to his surprise the Chief Constable said quietly and approvingly:

"Good lad."

"There's the revolver to work on. If this theory is correct, it wasn't Scherz's revolver and certainly nobody so far has been able to say that Scherz ever had a revolver."

"It's a German make."

"I know, sir. But this country's absolutely full of continental makes of guns. All the Americans brought them back and so did our chaps. You can't go by that."

"True enough. Any other lines of inquiry?"

"There's got to be a motive. If there's anything in this theory at all, it means that last Friday's business wasn't a mere joke and wasn't an ordinary holdup; it was a cold-blooded attempt at murder. Somebody tried to murder Miss Blacklock. Now why? It seems to me that if anyone knows the answer to that, it must be Miss Blacklock herself."

"I understand she rather poured cold water on that idea?"

"She poured cold water on the idea that Rudi Scherz wanted to murder her. And she was quite right. And there's another thing, sir."

"Yes?"

"Somebody might try again."

"That would certainly prove the truth of the theory," said the Chief Constable dryly. "By the way, look after Miss Marple, won't you?"

"Miss Marple? Why?"

"I gather she is taking up residence at the vicarage in Chipping Cleghorn and coming into Medenham Wells twice a week for her treatments. It seems that Mrs. What's-her-name is the daughter of an old friend of Miss Marple's. Good sporting instincts, that old bean.

Oh, well, I suppose she hasn't much excitement in her life and sniffing round after possible murderers gives her a kick."

"I wish she wasn't coming," said Craddock seriously.

"Going to get under your feet?"

"Not that, sir, but she's a nice old thing. I shouldn't like anything to happen to her . . . always supposing, I mean, that there's anything in this theory."

9

Concerning a Door

"I'm sorry to bother you again, Miss Blacklock—"

"Oh, it doesn't matter. I suppose, as the inquest was adjourned for a week, you're hoping to get more evidence?"

Detective Inspector Craddock nodded.

"To begin with, Miss Blacklock, Rudi Scherz was not the son of the proprietor of the Hotel des Alpes at Montreux. He seems to have started his career as an orderly in a hospital at Berne. A good many of the patients missed small pieces of jewelry. Under another name he was a waiter at one of the small winter sports places. His specialty there was making out duplicate bills in the restaurant with items on one that didn't appear on the other. The difference, of course, went into his pocket. After that he was in a department store in Zurich. Their losses from shoplifting were rather above the average while he was with them. It seems likely that the shoplifting wasn't entirely due to customers."

"He was a picker-up of unconsidered trifles, in fact?" siad Miss Blacklock dryly. "Then I was right in thinking that I had not seen him before?"

"You were quite right. No doubt you were pointed out to him at the Royal Spa Hotel and he pretended to recognize you. The Swiss police had begun to make his own country rather too hot for him, and he came over here with a very nice set of forged papers and took a job at the Royal Spa."

"Quite a good hunting ground," said Miss Blacklock dryly. "It's

215

extremely expensive and very well off people who stay there. Some of them are careless about their bills, I expect."

"Yes," said Craddock. "There were prospects of a satisfactory harvest."

Miss Blacklock was frowning.

"I see all that," she said. "But why come to Chipping Cleghorn? What does he think we've got here that could possibly be better than the rich Royal Spa Hotel?"

"You stick to your statement that there's nothing of especial value in the house?"

"Of course there isn't. I should know. I can assure you, Inspector, we've not got an unrecognized Rembrandt or anything like that."

"Then it looks, doesn't it, as though your friend Miss Bunner were right? He came here to attack you."

("There, Letty, what did I tell you!" "Oh, nonsense, Bunny.")

"But is it nonsense?" said Craddock. "I think, you know, that it's true."

Miss Blacklock stared very hard at him.

"Now let's get this straight. You really believe that this young man came out here—having previously arranged by means of an advertisement that half the village would turn up agog—at that particular time—"

"But he mayn't have meant that to happen," interrupted Miss Bunner eagerly. "It may have been just a horrid sort of warning—to you, Letty—that's how I read it at the time. *'A murder is announced.'* I felt in my bones that it was sinister—if it had all gone as planned he would have shot you and got away—and how would anyone have ever known who it was?"

"That's true enough," said Miss Blacklock. "But—"

"I knew that advertisement wasn't a joke, Letty. I said so. And look at Mitzi—she was frightened, too!"

"Ah," said Craddock, "Mitzi. I'd like to know rather more about that young woman."

"Her permit and papers are quite in order."

"I don't doubt that," said Craddock dryly. "Scherz's papers appeared to be quite correct, too."

"But why should this Rudi Scherz want to murder me? That's what they don't attempt to explain, Inspector Craddock."

"There may have been someone behind Scherz," said Craddock slowly. "Have you thought of that?"

216

He used the words metaphorically though it flashed across his mind that if Miss Marple's theory was correct, the words would also be true in a literal sense. In any case, they made little impression on Miss Blacklock who still looked skeptical.

"The point remains the same," she said. "Why on earth should anyone want to murder me?"

"It's the answer to that that I want you to give me, Miss Blacklock."

"Well, I can't! That's flat. I've no enemies. As far as I'm aware I've always lived on perfectly good terms with my neighbors. I don't know any guilty secrets about anyone. The whole idea is ridiculous! And if what you're hinting is that Mitzi has something to do with this, that's absurd, too. As Miss Bunner has just told you, she was frightened to death when she saw that advertisement in the *Gazette.* She actually wanted to pack up and leave the house then and there."

"That may have been a clever move on her part. She may have known you'd press her to stay."

"Of course, if you've made up your mind about it, you'll find an answer to everything. But I can assure you that if Mitzi had taken an unreasoning dislike to me, she might conceivably poison my food, but I'm sure she wouldn't go in for all this elaborate rigmarole.

"The whole idea's absurd. I believe you police have got an anti-foreigner complex. Mitzi may be a liar but she's not a cold-blooded murderer. Go and bully her if you must. But when she's departed in a whirl of indignation, or shut herself up howling in her room, I've a good mind to make you cook the dinner. Mrs. Harmon is bringing some old lady who is staying with her to tea this afternoon and I wanted Mitzi to make some little cakes—but I suppose you'll upset her completely. Can't you possibly go and suspect somebody else?"

II

Craddock went out to the kitchen. He asked Mitzi questions that he had asked her before and received the same answers.

Yes, she had locked the front door soon after four o'clock. No, she did not always do so, but that afternoon she had been nervous because of "that dreadful advertisement." It was no good locking the side door because Miss Blacklock and Miss Bunner went out that way to shut up the ducks and feed the chickens and Mrs. Haymes usually came in that way from work.

"Mrs. Haymes says she locked the door when she came in at 5:30."

"Ah, and you believe her—oh, yes, you believe her—"

"Do you think we shouldn't believe her?"

"What does it matter what I think? You will not believe me."

"Supposing you give us a chance. You think Mrs. Haymes didn't lock that door?"

"I thinking she was very careful not to lock it."

"What do you mean by that?" asked Craddock.

"That young man, he does not work alone. No, he knows where to come, he knows that when he comes a door will be left open for him—oh, very conveniently open!"

"What are you trying to say?"

"What is the use of what I say? You will not listen. You say I am a poor refugee girl who tells lies. You say that a fair-haired English lady, oh, no, she does not tell lies—she is so British—so honest. So you believe her and not me. But I could tell you. Oh, yes, I could tell you!"

She banged down a saucepan on the stove.

Craddock was in two minds whether to take notice of what might be only a stream of spite.

"We note everything we are told," he said.

"I shall not tell you anything at all. Why should I? You are all alike. You persecute and despise poor refugees. If I say to you that when, a week before, that young man come to ask Miss Blacklock for money and she sends him away, as you say, with a flea in the ear—if I tell you that after that I hear him talking with Mrs. Haymes—yes, out there in the summer-house—all you say is that I make it up!"

And so you probably are making it up, thought Craddock. But he said aloud:

"You couldn't hear what was said out in the summer-house."

"There you are wrong," screamed Mitzi triumphantly. "I go out to get nettles—it makes very nice vegetables, nettles. They do not think so, but I cook it and not tell them. And I hear them talking in there. He say to her, 'But where can I hide?' And she say, 'I will show you'—and then she say, 'At a quarter past six,' and I think, *Ach*, so that is how you behave, my fine lady! After you come back from work, you go out to meet a man. You bring him into the house. Miss Blacklock, I think, she will not like that. She will turn you out. I will watch, I think, and listen and then I will tell Miss Blacklock. But I understand now I was wrong. It was not love she planned with him, it was to rob and to murder. But you will say I make all this up. Wicked Mitzi, you will say. I will take her to prison."

Craddock wondered. She might be making it up. But possibly she might not. He asked cautiously,

"You are sure it was this Rudi Scherz she was talking to?"

"Of course I am. He just leave and I see him go from the drive across to the summer-house. And presently," said Mitzi defiantly, "I go out to see if there are any nice young green nettles."

Would there, the Inspector wondered, be any nice young green nettles in October? But he appreciated that Mitzi had had to produce a hurried reason for what had undoubtedly been nothing more than plain snooping.

"You didn't hear any more than what you have told me?"

Mitzi looked aggrieved.

"That Miss Bunner, the one with the long nose, she call and call me. 'Mitzi! Mitzi!' So I have to go. Oh, she is irritating. Always interfering. Says she will teach me to cook. Her cooking! It tastes, yes, everything she does, of water, water, water!"

"Why didn't you tell me this the other day?" asked Craddock sternly.

"Because I did not remember—I did not think . . . Only afterwards do I say to myself, it was planned then—planned with her."

"You are quite sure it was Mrs. Haymes?"

"Oh, yes, I am sure. Oh, yes, I am very sure. She is a thief, that Mrs. Haymes. A thief and the associate of thieves. What she gets for working in the garden, it is not enough for such a fine lady, no. She had to rob Miss Blacklock who has been kind to her. Oh, she is bad, bad, bad, that one!"

"Supposing," said the Inspector, watching her closely, "that someone was to say that you had been talking to Rudi Scherz?"

The suggestion had less effect than he had hoped for. Mitzi merely snorted and tossed her head.

"If anyone they see me talking to him, that is lies, lies, lies, lies," she said contemptuously. "To tell lies about anyone, that is easy, but in England you have to prove them true. Miss Blacklock tell me that, and it is true, is it not? I do not speak with murderers and thieves. And no English policeman shall say I do. And how can I do cooking for lunch if you are here, talk, talk, talk? Go out of my kitchens, please. I want now to make a very careful sauce."

Craddock went obediently. He was a little shaken in his suspicions of Mitzi. Her story about Phillipa Haymes had been told with great conviction. Mitzi might be a liar (he thought she was), but he fancied that there might be some substratum of truth in this particular tale. He resolved to speak to Phillipa on the subject. She had seemed to him, when he questioned her, a quiet, well-bred young woman. He had had no suspicion of her.

Crossing the hall, in his abstraction he tried to open the wrong door. Miss Bunner, descending the staircase, hastily put him right.

"Not that door," she said. "It doesn't open. The next one to the left. Very confusing, isn't it? So many doors."

"There are a good many," said Craddock, looking up and down the narrow hall.

Miss Bunner amiably enumerated them for him.

"First, the door to the cloakroom, and then the cloaks cupboard door and then the dining room—that's on that side. And on this side, the dummy door that you were trying to get through and then there's the drawing-room door proper, and then the china cupboard door and the door of the little flower room and at the end the side door. Most confusing. Especially these two being so near together. I've often tried the wrong one by mistake. We used to have the hall table against it, as a matter of fact, but then we moved it along against the wall there."

Craddock had noted, almost mechanically, a thin line horizontally across the panels of the door he had been trying to open. He realized now it was the mark where the table had been. Something stirred vaguely in his mind as he asked, "Moved? How long ago?"

In questioning Dora Bunner there was fortunately no need to give a reason for any questions. Any query on any subject seemed perfectly natural to the garrulous Miss Bunner, who delighted in the giving of information however trivial.

"Now let me see, really quite recently—ten days or a fortnight ago."

"Why was it moved?"

"I really can't remember. Something to do with the flowers. I think Phillipa did a big vase—she arranges flowers quite beautifully—all autumn coloring and twigs and branches, and it was so big it caught your hair as you went past, and so Phillipa said, 'Why not move the table along and anyway the flowers would look much better against the bare wall than against the panels of the door.' Only we had to take down Wellington at Waterloo. Not a print I'm really very fond of. We put it under the stairs."

"It's not really a dummy, then?" Craddock asked, looking at the door.

"Oh, no, it's a real door, if that's what you mean. It's the door of the small drawing-room, but when the rooms were thrown into one, one didn't need two doors, so this one was fastened up."

"Fastened up?" Craddock tried it again gently. "You mean it's nailed up? Or just locked?"

"Oh, locked, I think, and bolted, too."

He saw the bolt at the top and tried it. The bolt slid back easily—too easily . . .

"When was it last open?" he asked Miss Bunner.

"Oh, years and years ago, I imagine. It's never been opened since I've been here, I know that."

"You don't know where the key is?"

"There are a lot of keys in the hall table drawer. It's probably among those."

Craddock followed her and looked at a rusty assortment of old keys pushed far back in the drawer. He scanned them and selected one that looked different from the rest and went back to the door. The key fitted and turned easily. He pushed and the door slid open noiselessly.

"Oh, do be careful," cried Miss Bunner. "There may be something resting against it inside. We never open it."

"Don't you?" said the Inspector.

His face was now grim. He said with emphasis:

"This door's been opened quite recently, Miss Bunner. The lock's been oiled and the hinges."

She stared at him, her foolish face agape.

"But who could have done that?" she asked.

"That's what I mean to find out," said Craddock grimly. He thought—X from outside? No—X was here—in this house—X was in the drawing-room that night.

10

Pip and Emma

Miss Blacklock listened to him this time with more attention. She was an intelligent woman, as he had known, and she grasped the implications of what he had to tell her.

"Yes," she said quietly, "that does alter things . . . No one had any right to meddle with that door. Nobody has meddled with it to my knowledge."

"You see what it means," the Inspector urged. "When the lights went out, anybody in this room the other night could have slipped out of that door, come up behind Rudi Scherz and fired at you."

"Without being seen or heard or noticed?"

"Without being seen or heard or noticed. Remember, when the lights went out people moved, exclaimed, bumped into each other. And after that all that could be seen was the blinding light of the flashlight."

Miss Blacklock said slowly, "And you believe that one of those people—one of my nice commonplace neighbors—slipped out and tried to murder me? Me? But why? For goodness' sake, why?"

"I've a feeling that you must know the answer to that question, Miss Blacklock."

"But I don't, Inspector. I can assure you I don't."

"Well, let's make a start. Who gets your money if you were to die?"

Miss Blacklock said rather reluctantly:

"Patrick and Julia. I've left the furniture in this house and a small annuity to Bunny. Really I've not much to leave. I had holdings in German and Italian securities which became worthless, and what with taxation and the lower percentages that are now paid on invested capital, I can assure you I'm not worth murdering—I put most of my money into an annuity about a year ago."

"Still you have some income, Miss Blacklock, and your nephew and niece would come into it."

"And so Patrick and Julia would plan to murder me? I simply don't believe it. They're not desperately hard up or anything like that."

"Do you know that for a fact?"

"No. I suppose I only know it from what they've told me . . . But I really refuse to suspect them. Some day I might be worth murdering, but not now."

"What do you mean by some day you might be worth murdering, Miss Blacklock?" Inspector Craddock pounced on the statement.

"Simply that one day—possibly quite soon—I may be a very rich woman."

"That sounds interesting. Will you explain?"

"Certainly. You may not know it, but for more than twenty years I was secretary to, and closely associated with, Randall Goedler."

Craddock was interested. Randall Goedler had been a big name in the world of finance. His daring speculations and the rather theatrical publicity with which he surrounded himself had made him a personality not quickly forgotten. He had died, if Craddock remembered rightly, in 1937 or 1938.

"He's rather before your time, I expect," said Miss Blacklock. "But you've probably heard of him."

"Oh, yes. He was a millionaire, wasn't he?"

"Oh, several times over—though his finances fluctuated. He always risked most of what he made on some new *coup*."

She spoke with a certain animating, her eyes brightened by memory.

"Anyway, he died a very rich man. He had no children. He left his fortune in trust for his wife during her lifetime and after her death to me absolutely."

A vague memory stirred in the Inspector's mind.

IMMENSE FORTUNE TO COME TO FAITHFUL SECRETARY—something of that kind.

"For the last twelve years or so," said Miss Blacklock with a slight twinkle, "I've had an excellent motive for murdering Mrs. Goedler—but that doesn't help you, does it?"

"Did—excuse me for asking this—did Mrs. Goedler resent her husband's disposition of his fortune?"

Miss Blacklock was now looking frankly amused.

"You needn't be so very discreet. What you really mean is, was I Randall Goedler's mistress? No, I wasn't. I don't think Randall ever gave me a sentimental thought, and I certainly didn't give him one. He was in love with Belle (his wife), and remained in love with her until he died. I think in all probability it was gratitude on his part that prompted his making his will. You see, Inspector, in the very early days, when Randall was still on an insecure footing, he came very near to disaster. It was a question of just a few thousand of actual cash. It was a big *coup*, and a very exciting one; daring, as all his schemes were; but he just hadn't got that little bit of cash to tide him over. I came to the rescue. I had a little money of my own. I believed in Randall. I sold out every penny I had and gave it to him. It did the trick. A week later he was an immensely wealthy man.

"After that, he treated me more or less as a junior partner. Oh, they were exciting days!" She sighed. "I enjoyed it all thoroughly. Then my father died, and my other sister was left a hopeless invalid. I had to give it all up and go and look after her. Randall died a couple of years later. I had made quite a lot of money during our association and I didn't really expect him to leave me anything, but I was very touched, yes, and very proud, to find that if Belle predeceased me (and she was one of those delicate creatures whom everyone always says won't live long), I was to inherit his entire fortune. I really think the poor man didn't know who to leave it to. Belle's a dear, and she was delighted about it. She's really a very sweet person. She lives up in Scotland. I haven't seen her for years—we just write at Christmas. I went with my sister to a sanatorium in Switzerland just before the war. She died of consumption out there."

She was silent for a moment or two, then said:

"I only came back to England just over a year ago."

"You said you might be a rich woman very soon. How soon?"

"I heard from the nurse attendant who looks after Belle Goedler that Belle is sinking rapidly. It may be—only a few weeks."

She added sadly,

"The money won't mean much to me now. I've got quite enough still for my rather simple needs. Once I should have enjoyed playing the markets again—but now . . . Oh, well, one grows old. Still, you do see, Inspector, don't you, that if Patrick and Julia wanted to kill me for a financial reason they'd be crazy not to wait for another few weeks."

"Yes, Miss Blacklock, but what happens if you should predecease Mrs. Goedler? Who does the money go to then?"

"Do you know, I've never really thought. Pip and Emma, I suppose . . ."

Craddock stared and Miss Blacklock smiled.

"Does that sound rather crazy? I believe, if I predecease Belle, the money would go to the legal offspring—or whatever the term is—of Randall's only sister, Sonia. Randall had quarreled with his sister. She married a man whom he considered a crook and worse."

"And was he a crook?"

"Oh, definitely, I should say. But I believe a very attractive person to women. He was a Greek or a Roumanian or something—what was his name now?—Stamfordis, Dmitri Stamfordis."

"Randall Goedler cut his sister out of his will when she married this man?"

"Oh, no! Sonia was a very wealthy woman in her own right. Randall had already settled packets of money on her, as far as possible in a way so that her husband couldn't touch it. But I believe that when the lawyers urged him to put in someone in case I predeceased Belle, he reluctantly put down Sonia's offspring, simply because he couldn't think of anyone else and he wasn't the sort of man to leave money to charities."

"And there were children of the marriage?"

"Well, there are Pip and Emma." She laughed. "I know it sounds ridiculous. All I know is that Sonia wrote once to Belle after her marriage, telling her to tell Randall that she was extremely happy and that she had just had twins and was calling them Pip and Emma. As far as I know she never wrote again. But Belle, of course, may be able to tell you more."

Miss Blacklock had been amused by her own recital. The Inspector did not look amused.

"It comes to this," he said. "If you had been killed the other night, there are presumably at least two people in the world who would have come into a very large fortune. You were wrong, Miss Blacklock, when you say that there is no one who had a motive for desiring your death. There are two people, at least, who are vitally interested. How old would this brother and sister be?"

Miss Blacklock frowned.

"Let me see . . . 1922 . . . no—it's difficult to remember . . . I suppose about twenty-five or twenty-six." Her face had sobered. "But you surely don't think—"

"I think somebody shot at you with the intent to kill you. I think it possible that the same person or persons might try again. I would like you, if you will, to be very, very careful, Miss Blacklock. One murder has been arranged and did not come off. I think it possible that another murder may be arranged very soon."

II

Phillipa Haymes straightened her back and pushed back a tendril of hair from her damp forehead. She was cleaning a flower border.

"Yes, Inspector?"

She looked at him inquiringly. In return he gave her a rather closer scrutiny than he had done before. Yes, a good-looking girl, a very English type with her pale ash-blond hair and her rather long face. An obstinate chin and mouth. Something of repression—of tautness about her. The eyes were blue, very steady in their glance, and told you nothing at all. The sort of girl, he thought, who would keep a secret well.

"I'm sorry always to bother you when you're at work, Mrs. Haymes," he said, "but I didn't want to wait until you came back for lunch. Besides, I thought it might be easier to talk to you here, away from Little Paddocks."

"Yes, Inspector?"

No emotion and little interest in the voice. But was there a note of wariness—or did he imagine it?

"A certain statement has been made to me this morning. This statement concerns you?"

Phillipa raised her eyebrows very slightly.

"You told me, Mrs. Haymes, that this man Rudi Scherz was quite unknown to you?"

"Yes."

"That when you saw him there, dead, it was the first time you had set eyes on him. Is that so?"

"Certainly. I had never seen him before."

"You did not, for instance, have a conversation with him in the summer-house of Little Paddocks?"

"In the summer-house?"

He was almost sure he caught a note of fear in her voice.

"Yes, Mrs. Haymes."

"Who says so?"

"I am told that you had a conversation with this man Rudi Scherz, and that he asked you where he could hide and you replied that you would show him, and that a time, a quarter past six, was definitely mentioned. It would be a quarter past six, roughly, when Scherz would get here from the bus stop on the evening of the holdup."

There was a moment's silence. Then Phillipa gave a short scornful laugh. She looked amused.

"I don't know who told you that," she said. "At least I can guess. It's a very silly clumsy story—spiteful, of course. For some reason Mitzi dislikes me even more than she dislikes the rest of us."

"You deny it?"

"Of course it's not true . . . I never met or saw Rudi Scherz in my life, and I was nowhere near the house that morning. I was over here working."

Inspector Craddock said very gently,

"Which morning?"

There was a momentary pause. Her eyelids flickered.

"Every morning. I'm here every morning. I don't get away until one o'clock."

She added scornfully:

"It's no good listening to what Mitzi tells you. She tells lies all the time."

"And that's that," said Craddock, when he was walking away with Sergeant Fletcher. "Two young women whose stories flatly contradict each other. Which one am I to believe?"

"Everyone seems to agree that this foreign girl tells whoppers," said Fletcher. "It's been my experience in dealing with aliens that lying comes more easy than truth-telling. Seems to be clear she's got a spite against this Mrs. Haymes."

"So if you were me, you'd believe Mrs. Haymes?"

"Unless you've got reason to think otherwise, sir."

And Craddock hadn't, not really—only the remembrance of a pair of over-steady blue eyes and the glib enunciation of the words "that morning." For to the best of his recollection he hadn't said whether the interview in the summer-house had taken place in the morning or the afternoon.

Still, Miss Blacklock, or if not Miss Blacklock, certainly Miss Bunner, might have mentioned the visit of the young foreigner who had come to cadge his fare back to Switzerland. And Phillipa Haymes might have therefore assumed that the conversation was supposed to have taken place on that particular morning.

But Craddock still thought that there had been a note of fear in her voice as she asked:

"In the summer-house?"

He decided to keep an open mind on the subject.

III

It was very pleasant in the vicarage garden. One of those sudden spells of autumn warmth had descended upon England. Inspector Craddock could never remember if it was St. Martin's or St. Luke's summer, but he knew that it was very pleasant—and also very enervating. He sat in a deck chair provided for him by an energetic Bunch, just on her way to a Mothers' Meeting, and, well protected with shawls and a large rug round her knees, Miss Marple sat knitting beside him. The sunshine, the peace, the steady click of Miss Marple's knitting-needles, all combined to produce a soporific feeling in the Inspector. And yet, at the same time, there was a nightmarish feeling at the back of his mind. It was like the familiar dream where an undertone of menace grows and finally turns ease into terror . . .

He said abruptly, "You oughtn't to be here."

Miss Marple's needles stopped clicking for a moment. Her placid china-blue eyes regarded him thoughtfully.

She said, "I know what you mean. You're a very conscientious boy. But it's perfectly all right. Bunch's father (he was rector of our parish, a very fine scholar) and her mother (who is a most remarkable woman—real spiritual power) are very old friends of mine. It's the most natural thing in the world that when I'm at Medenham I should come on here to stay with Bunch for a little."

"Oh, perhaps," said Craddock. "But—but don't snoop around . . . I've a feeling—I have really—that it isn't safe."

Miss Marple smiled a little.

"But I'm afraid," she said, "that we old women always do snoop. It would be very odd and much more noticeable if I didn't. Questions about mutual friends in different parts of the world and whether they remember so and so, and do they remember who it was that Lady Somebody's daughter married? All that helps, doesn't it?"

"Helps?" said the Inspector rather stupidly.

"Helps to find out if people are who they say they are," said Miss Marple.

She went on:

"Because that's what's worrying you, isn't it? And that's really the particular way the world has changed since the war. Take this place, Chipping Cleghorn, for instance. It's very much like St. Mary Mead where I live. Fifteen years ago one knew who everybody was. The Bantrys in the big house—and the Hartnells and the Price Ridleys and the Weatherbys . . . They were people whose fathers and mothers and grandfathers and grandmothers, or whose aunts and uncles, had lived there before them. If somebody new came to live there, they brought letters of introduction, or they'd been in the same regiment or served on the same ship as someone already there. If anybody new— really new—really a stranger—came, well, they stuck out—everybody wondered about them and didn't rest till they found out."

She nodded her head gently:

"But it's not like that any more. Every village and small country place is full of people who've just come and settled there without any ties to bring them. The big houses have been sold, and the cottages have been converted and changed. And people just come—and all you know about them is what they say of themselves. They've come, you see, from all over the world. People from India and Hong Kong and China, and people who used to live in France and Italy in little cheap places and odd islands. And people who've made a little money and can afford to retire. But nobody knows any more who anyone is. You can have Benares brassware in your house and talk about tiffin and *chota Hazri*—and you can have pictures of Taormina and talk about the English church and the library—like Miss Hinchliffe and Miss Murgatroyd. You can come from the South of France, or have spent your life in the East. People take you at your own valuation. They don't wait to call until they've had a letter from a friend saying that the So-and-So's are delightful people and she's known them all their lives."

And that, thought Craddock, was exactly what was oppressing him. He didn't know. There were just faces and personalities and they were backed up by ration books and identity cards—nice neat identity cards with numbers on them, without photographs or fingerprints. Anybody who took the trouble could have a suitable identity card— and partly because of that, the subtler links that had held English social rural life together had fallen apart. In a town nobody expected to know his neighbor. In the country now nobody knew his neighbor either, though possibly he still thought he did . . .

Because of the oiled door, Craddock knew that there had been somebody in Letitia Blacklock's drawing-room who was not the pleasant friendly country neighbor he or she pretended to be . . .

And because of that he was afraid for Miss Marple who was frail and old and who noticed things . . .

He said: "We can, to a certain extent, check up on these people . . ." But he knew that that wasn't so easy. India and China and Hong Kong and the South of France . . . It wasn't as easy as it would have been fifteen years ago. There were people, as he knew only too well, who were going about the country with borrowed identities—borrowed from people who had met sudden death by "incidents" in the cities. There were organizations who bought up identities, who faked identity cards and ration books—there were a hundred small rackets springing into being. You could check up—but it would take time—and time was what he hadn't got, because Randall Goedler's widow was very near death.

It was then that, worried and tired, lulled by the sunshine, he told Miss Marple about Randall Goedler and about Pip and Emma.

"Just a couple of names," he said. "Nicknames at that! They mayn't exist. They may be respectable citizens living in Europe somewhere. On the other hand, one, or both, of them may be here in Chipping Cleghorn . . ."

Twenty-five years old approximately—who filled that description? He said, thinking aloud:

"That nephew and niece of hers—or cousins, or whatever they are . . . I wonder when she saw them last—"

Miss Marple said gently, "I'll find out for you, shall I?"

"Now, please, Miss Marple, don't—"

"It will be quite simple, Inspector; you really need not worry. And it won't be noticeable if I do it, because, you see, it won't be official. If there is anything wrong you don't want to put them on their guard."

Pip and Emma, thought Craddock, Pip and Emma? He was getting obsessed by Pip and Emma. That attractive dare-devil young man, the good-looking girl with the cool stare . . .

He said: "I may find out more about them in the next forty-eight hours. I'm going up to Scotland. Mrs. Goedler, if she's able to talk, may know a good deal more about them."

"I think that's a very wise move." Miss Marple hesitated. "I hope," she murmured, "that you have warned Miss Blacklock to be careful?"

"I've warned her, yes. And I shall leave a man here to keep an unobtrusive eye on things."

He avoided Miss Marple's eye which said plainly enough that a policeman keeping an eye on things would be little good if the danger was in the family circle . . .

"And remember," said Craddock, looking squarely at her, "I've warned you."

"I assure you, Inspector," said Miss Marple, "that I can take care of myself."

11

Miss Marple Comes to Tea

If Letitia Blacklock seemed slightly absent-minded when Mrs. Harmon came to tea and brought a guest who was staying with her, Miss Marple, the guest in question, was hardly likely to notice the fact since it was the first time she had met her hostess.

The old lady was very charming in her gentle gossipy fashion. She revealed herself almost at once to be one of those old ladies who have a constant preoccupation with burglars.

"They can get in anywhere, my dear," she assured her hostess, "absolutely anywhere nowadays. So many new American methods. I myself pin my faith to a very old-fashioned device. A cabin hook and eye. They can pick locks and draw back bolts but a brass hook and eye defeats them. Have you ever tried that?"

"I'm afraid we're not very good at bolts and bars," said Miss Blacklock cheerfully. "There's really nothing much to burgle."

"A chain on the front door," Miss Marple advised. "Then the maid need only open it a crack and see who is there and they can't force their way in."

"I expect Mitzi, our Mittel European, would love that."

"The holdup you had must have been very, very frightening," said Miss Marple. "Bunch has been telling me all about it."

"I was scared stiff," said Bunch.

"It was an alarming experience," admitted Miss Blacklock.

"It really seems like Providence that the man tripped himself up and shot himself. These burglars are so violent nowadays. How did he get in?"

"Well, I'm afraid we don't lock our doors much."

"Oh, Lotty," exclaimed Miss Bunner. "I forgot to tell you the Inspector was most peculiar this morning. He insisted on opening the second door—you know, the one that's never been opened—the one over there. He hunted for the key and everything and said the door had been oiled. But I can't see why because—"

Too late she got Miss Blacklock's signal to be quiet, and paused open-mouthed.

"Oh, Letty, I'm so—sorry—I mean, oh, I do beg your pardon, Letty— Oh, dear, how stupid I am."

"It doesn't matter," said Miss Blacklock, but she was annoyed. "Only I don't think Inspector Craddock wants that talked about. I didn't know you had been there when he was experimenting, Dora. You do understand, don't you, Mrs. Harmon?"

"Oh, yes," said Bunch. "We won't breathe a word, will we, Aunt Jane. But I wonder why he—"

She relapsed into thought. Miss Bunner fidgeted and looked miserable, bursting out at last: "I always say the wrong thing— Oh, dear, I'm nothing but a trial to you, Letty."

Miss Blacklock said quickly, "You're my great comfort, Dora. And, anyway, in a small place like Chipping Cleghorn, there aren't really any secrets."

"Now that is very true," said Miss Marple. "I'm afraid, you know, that things do get round in the most extraordinary way. Servants, of course, and yet it can't only be that, because one has so few servants nowadays. Still, there are the daily women and perhaps they are worse, because they go to everybody in turn and pass the news round."

"Oh," said Bunch Harmon suddenly. "I've got it! Of course, if that door could open, too, someone might have gone out of here in the dark and done the holdup—only, of course, they didn't—because it was the man from the Royal Spa Hotel. Or wasn't it? . . . No, I don't see after all . . ." She frowned.

"Did it all happen in this room then?" asked Miss Marple, adding apologetically, "I'm afraid you must think me sadly curious, Miss Blacklock—but it really is so very exciting—just like something one reads about in the paper—and actually to have happened to someone one knows . . . I'm just longing to hear all about it and picture it all, if you know what I mean—"

Immediately Miss Marple received a confused and voluble

account from Bunch and Miss Bunner—with occasional emendations and corrections from Miss Blacklock.

In the middle of it Patrick came in and good-naturedly entered into the spirit of the recital—going so far as to enact himself the part of Rudi Scherz.

"And Aunt Letty was there—in the corner by the archway—Go and stand there, Aunt Letty."

Miss Blacklock obeyed, and then Miss Marple was shown the actual bullet holes.

"What a marvelous—what a providential escape," she gasped.

"I was just going to offer my guests cigarettes—" Miss Blacklock indicated the big silver box on the table.

"People are so careless when they smoke," said Miss Bunner disapprovingly. "Nobody really respects good furniture as they used to do. Look at the horrid burn somebody made on this beautiful table by putting a cigarette down on it. Disgraceful."

Miss Blacklock sighed.

"Sometimes, I'm afraid, one thinks too much of one's possessions."

"But it's such a lovely table, Letty."

Miss Bunner loved her friend's possessions with as much fervor as though they had been her own. Bunch Harmon had always thought it was a very endearing trait in her. She showed no sign of envy.

"It is a lovely table," said Miss Marple politely. "And what a very pretty china lamp on it."

Again it was Miss Bunner who accepted the compliment as though she and not Miss Blacklock was the owner of the lamp.

"Isn't it delightful? Dresden. There is a pair of them. The other's in the spare room, I think."

"You know where everything in this house is, Dora—or you think you do," said Miss Blacklock good-humoredly. "You care far more about my things than I do."

Miss Bunner flushed.

"I do like nice things," she said. Her voice was half defiant—half wistful.

"I must confess," said Miss Marple, "that my own few possessions are very dear to me, too—so many memories, you know. It's the same with photographs. People nowadays have so few photographs about. Now I like to keep all the pictures of my nephews and nieces as babies—and then as children—and so on."

"You've got a horrible one of me, aged three," said Bunch. "Holding a fox terrier and squinting."

"I expect your aunt has many photographs of you," said Miss Marple, turning to Patrick.

"Oh, we're only distant cousins," said Patrick.

"I believe Elinor did send me one of you as a baby, Pat," said Miss Blacklock. "But I'm afraid I didn't keep it. I'd really forgotten how many children she had or what their names were until she wrote me about you two being over here."

"Another sign of the times," said Miss Marple. "Nowadays one so often doesn't know one's younger relations at all. In the old days, with all the big family reunions, that would have been impossible."

"I last saw Pat's and Julia's mother at a wedding thirty years ago," said Miss Blacklock. "She was a very pretty girl."

"That's why she has such handsome children," said Patrick with a grin.

"You've got a marvelous old album," said Julia. "Do you remember, Aunt Letty, we looked through it the other day. The hats!"

"And how smart we thought ourselves," said Miss Blacklock with a sigh.

"Never mind, Aunt Letty," said Patrick. "Julia will come across a snapshot of herself in about thirty years' time—and won't she think she looks a guy!"

"Did you do that on purpose?" said Bunch, as she and Miss Marple were walking home. "Talk about photographs I mean?"

"Well, my dear, it is interesting to know that Miss Blacklock didn't know either of her two young relatives by sight. Yes—I think Inspector Craddock will be interested to hear that."

12

Morning Activities in Chipping Cleghorn

Edmund Swettenham sat down rather precariously on a garden roller.

"Good morning, Phillipa," he said.

"Hullo."

"Are you very busy?"

"Moderately."

"What are you doing?"

"Can't you see?"

"No. I'm not a gardener. You seem to be playing with earth in some fashion."

"I'm pricking out winter lettuce."

"Pricking out? What a curious term! Like pinking. Do you know what pinking is? I only learnt the other day. I always thought it was a term for professional dueling."

"Do you want anything particular?" asked Phillipa coldly.

"Yes. I want to see you."

Phillipa gave him a quick glance.

"I wish you wouldn't come here like this. Mrs. Lucas won't like it."

"Doesn't she allow you to have followers?"

"Don't be absurd."

"Followers. That's another nice word. It describes my attitude perfectly. Respectful—at a distance—but firmly pursuing."

"Please go away, Edmund. You've no business to come here."

"You're wrong," said Edmund triumphantly. "I have business here. Mrs. Lucas rang up my mama this morning and said she had a good many vegetable marrows."

"Masses of them."

"And would we like to exchange a pot of honey for a vegetable marrow or so?"

"That's not a fair exchange at all! Vegetable marrows are quite unsalable at the moment—everybody has such a lot."

"Naturally. That's why Mrs. Lucas rang up. Last time, if I remember rightly, the exchange suggested was some skim milk—skim milk, mark you—in exchange for some lettuces. It was then very early in the season for lettuces. They were about a shilling each."

Phillipa did not speak.

Edmund tugged at his pocket and extracted a pot of honey.

"So here," he said, "is my alibi. Used in a loose and quite indefensible meaning of the term. If Mrs. Lucas pops her bust round the door of the potting shed, I'm here in quest of vegetable marrows. There is absolutely no question of dalliance."

"I see."

"Do you ever read Tennyson?" enquired Edmund conversationally.

"Not very often."

"You should. Tennyson is shortly going to make a comeback in a big way. When you turn on your radio in the evening it will be the *Idylls of the King* you will hear and not interminable Trollope. I always thought the Trollope pose was the most unbearable affectation. Perhaps a little of Trollope, but not to drown in him. But speaking of Tennyson, have you read *Maud*?"

"Once, long ago."

"It's got some points about it." He quoted softly: " 'Faultily faultless, icily regular, splendidly null.' That's you, Phillipa."

"Hardly a compliment!"

"No, it wasn't meant to be. I gather Maud got under the poor fellow's skin just like you've got under mine."

"Don't be absurd, Edmund."

"Oh, hell, Phillipa, why are you like you are? What goes on behind your splendidly regular features? What do you think? What do you feel? Are you happy, or miserable, or frightened or what? There must be something."

Phillipa said quietly,

"What I feel is my own business."

"It's mine, too. I want to make you talk. I want to know what goes on in that quiet head of yours. I've a right to know. I have really. I didn't want to fall in love with you. I wanted to sit quietly and write my book. Such a nice book, all about how miserable the world is. It's frightfully easy to be clever about how miserable everybody is. And it's all a habit, really. Yes, I've suddenly become convinced of that. After reading a life of Burne-Jones."

Phillipa had stopped pricking out. She was staring at him with a puzzled frown.

"What has Burne-Jones got to do with it?"

"Everything. When you've read all about the Pre-Raphaelites you realize just what fashion is. They were all terrifically hearty and slangy and jolly, and laughed and joked, and everything was fine and wonderful. That was fashion, too. They weren't any happier or heartier than we are. And we're not any more miserable than they were. It's all fashion, I tell you. After the last war, we went in for sex. Now it's all frustration. None of it matters. Why are we talking about all this? I started out to talk about us. Only I got cold feet and shied off. Because you won't help me."

"What do you want me to do?"

"Talk! Tell me things. Is it your husband? Did you adore him and he's dead and so you've shut up like a clam? Is that it? All right, you adored him, and he's dead. Well, other girls' husbands are dead—lots of them—and some of the girls loved their husbands. They tell you so in bars, and cry a bit when they're drunk enough, and then want to go to bed with you so that they'll feel better. It's one way of getting over it, I suppose. You've got to get over it, Phillipa. You're young—and you're extremely lovely—and I love you like hell. Talk about your damned husband, tell me about him."

"There's nothing to tell. We met and got married."

"You must have been very young."

"Too young."

"Then you weren't happy with him? Go on, Phillipa."

"There's nothing to go on about. We were married. We were as happy as most people are, I suppose. Harry was born. Ronald went overseas. He—he was killed in Italy."

"And now there's Harry?"

"And now there's Harry."

"I like Harry. He's a really nice kid. He likes me. We'd get on. What about it, Phillipa? Shall we get married? You can go on gardening and I can go on writing my book and in the holidays we'll leave off working and enjoy ourselves. We can manage, with tact, not to have to live with mother. She can fork out a bit to support her adored son. I sponge, I write tripey books, I have defective eyesight and I talk too much. That's the worst. Will you try it?"

Phillipa looked at him. She saw a tall, rather solemn young man with an anxious face and large spectacles. His sandy head was rumpled and he was regarding her with a reassuring friendliness.

"No," said Phillipa.

"Definitely no?"

"Definitely no."

"Why?"

"You don't know anything about me."

"Is that all?"

"No, you don't know anything about anything."

Edmund considered.

"Perhaps not," he admitted. "But who does? Phillipa, my adored one—" He broke off.

A shrill and prolonged yapping was rapidly approaching.

> *"Pekes in the high hall garden,"* said Edmund,
> *"When twilight was falling* (only it's eleven A.M.);
> *Phil, Phil, Phil, Phil,*
> *They were crying and calling.*

"Your name doesn't lend itself to the rhythm, does it? Sounds like an Ode to a Fountain Pen. Have you got another name?"

"Joan. Please go away. That's Mrs. Lucas."

"*Joan, Joan, Joan, Joan.* Better, but still not good. *When greasy Joan the pot doth keel*—that's not a nice picture of married life, either."

"Mrs. Lucas is—"

"Oh, hell," said Edmund. "Get me a blasted vegetable marrow."

II

Sergeant Fletcher had the house at Little Paddocks to himself.

It was Mitzi's day off. She always went by the eleven o'clock bus into Medenham Wells. By arrangement with Miss Blacklock, Sergeant Fletcher had the run of the house. She and Dora Bunner had gone down to the village.

Fletcher worked fast. Someone in the house had oiled and prepared that door, and whoever had done it, had done it in order to be able to leave the drawing-room unnoticed as soon as the lights went out. That ruled out Mitzi who wouldn't have needed to use the door.

Who was left? The neighbors, Fletcher thought, might also be ruled out. He didn't see how they could have found an opportunity to oil and prepare the door. That left Patrick and Julia Simmons, Phillipa Haymes and possibly Dora Bunner. The young Simmonses were in Milchester. Phillipa Haymes was at work. Sergeant Fletcher was free to search out any secrets he could. But the house was disappointingly innocent. Fletcher, who was an expert on electricity, could find nothing suggestive in the wiring or appurtenances of the electric fixtures to show how the lights had been turned off. Making a rapid survey of the household bedrooms, he found an irritating normality. In Phillipa Haymes' room were photographs of a small boy with serious eyes, an earlier photo of the same child, a pile of schoolboy letters, a theater program or two. In Julia's room there was a drawer full of snapshots of the south of France. Bathing photos, a villa set amidst mimosa. Patrick's held some souvenirs of Naval days. Dora Bunner's held few personal possessions and they seemed innocent enough.

And yet, thought Fletcher, someone in the house must have oiled that door.

His thoughts broke off at a sound below stairs. He went quickly to the top of the staircase and looked down.

Mrs. Swettenham was crossing the hall. She had a basket on her arm. She looked into the drawing-room, crossed the hall and went into the dining room. She came out again without the basket.

Some faint sound that Fletcher made, a board that creaked unexpectedly under his feet, made her turn her head. She called up:

"Is that you, Miss Blacklock?"

"No, Mrs. Swettenham, it's me," said Fletcher.

Mrs. Swettenham gave a faint scream.

"Oh! How you startled me. I thought it might be another burglar."

Fletcher came down the stairs.

"This house doesn't seem very well protected against burglars," he said. "Can anybody always walk in and out just as they like?"

"I just brought up some of my quinces," explained Mrs. Swettenham. "Miss Blacklock wants to make quince jelly and she hasn't got a quince tree here. I left them in the dining room."

Then she smiled.

"Oh, I see, you mean how did I get in? Well, I just came in through the side door. We all walk in and out of each other's houses, Sergeant.

Nobody dreams of locking a door until it's dark. I mean it would be so awkward, wouldn't it, if you brought things and couldn't get in to leave them? It's not like the old days when you rang a bell and a servant always came to answer it." Mrs. Swettenham sighed. "In India, I remember," she said mournfully, "we had eighteen servants—eighteen. Not counting the ayah. Just as a matter of course. And at home, when I was a girl, we always had three—although mother always felt it was terribly poverty stricken not to be able to afford a kitchen maid. I must say that I find life very odd nowadays, Sergeant, though I know one mustn't complain. So much worse for the miners always getting psittacosis (or is that parrot disease?) and having to come out of the mines and try to be gardeners though they don't know weeds from spinach."

She added, as she tripped towards the door, "I mustn't keep you. I expect you're very busy. Nothing else is going to happen, is it?"

"Why should it, Mrs. Swettenham?"

"I just wondered, seeing you here. I thought it might be a gang. You'll tell Miss Blacklock about the quinces, won't you?"

Mrs. Swettenham departed. Fletcher felt like a man who has received an unexpected jolt. He had been assuming—erroneously, he now perceived—that it must have been someone in the house who had done the oiling of the door. He saw now that he was wrong. An outsider had only to wait until Mitzi had departed by bus and Letitia Blacklock and Dora Bunner were both out of the house. Such an opportunity must have been simplicity itself. That meant that he couldn't rule out anybody who had been in the drawing-room that night.

III

"Murgatroyd."

"Yes, Hinch?"

"I've been doing a bit of thinking."

"Have you, Hinch?"

"Yes, the great brain has been working. You know, Murgatroyd, the whole setup the other evening was decidedly fishy."

"Fishy?"

"Yes. Tuck your hair up, Murgatroyd, and take this trowel. Pretend it's a revolver."

"Oh," said Miss Murgatroyd nervously.

"All right. It won't bite you. Now come along to the kitchen door. You're going to be the burglar. You stand here. Now you're going into the kitchen to hold up a lot of nitwits. Take the flashlight. Switch it on."

"But it's broad daylight!"

"Use your imagination, Murgatroyd. Switch it on."

Miss Murgatroyd did so, rather clumsily, shifting the trowel under one arm while she did so.

"Now then," said Miss Hinchliffe, "off you go. Remember the time you played Hermia in *A Midsummer Night's Dream* at the Women's Institute? Act. Give it all you've got. 'Stick 'em up!' Those are your lines—and don't ruin them by saying 'Please.' "

Obediently, Miss Murgatroyd raised her flashlight, flourished the trowel and advanced on the kitchen door.

Transferring the torch to her right hand, she swiftly turned the handle and stepped forward, resuming the flashlight in her left hand.

"Stick 'em up!" she fluted, adding vexedly: "Dear me, this is very difficult, Hinch."

"Why?"

"The door. It's a swing door, it keeps coming back and I've got both hands full."

"Exactly," boomed Miss Hinchliffe. "And the drawing-room door at Little Paddocks always swings to. It isn't a swing-door like this, but it won't stay open. That's why Letty Blacklock bought that absolutely delectable heavy glass doorstop from Elliot's in the High Street. I don't mind saying I've never forgiven her for getting in ahead of me there. I was beating the old brute down most successfully. He'd come down from eight guineas to six pound ten, and then Blacklock comes along and buys the damned thing. I'd never seen as attractive a doorstop; you don't often get those glass bubbles in that big size."

"Perhaps the burglar put the doorstop against the door to keep it open," suggested Miss Murgatroyd.

"Use your common sense, Murgatroyd. What does he do? Throw the door open, say, 'Excuse me a moment,' stoop and put the stop into position and then resume business by saying, 'Hands up'? Try holding the door with your shoulder."

"It's still very awkward," complained Miss Murgatroyd.

"Exactly," said Miss Hinchliffe. "A revolver, a flashlight and a door to hold open—a bit too much, isn't it? So what's the answer?"

Miss Murgatroyd did not attempt to supply an answer. She looked inquiringly and admiringly at her masterful friend and waited to be enlightened.

"We know he'd got a revolver, because he fired it," said Miss Hinchliffe. "And we know he has a flashlight because we all saw it—that is, unless we're all the victims of mass hypnotism, like explanations of the Indian rope trick—(what a bore that old Easterbrook is with his Indian stories)—so the question is, did someone hold that door open for him?"

"But who could have done that?"

"Well, you could have for one, Murgatroyd. As far as I remember, you were standing directly behind it when the lights went out." Miss Hinchliffe laughed heartily. "Highly suspicious character, aren't you, Murgatroyd? But who'd think it to look at you? Here, give me that trowel—thank heavens it isn't really a revolver. You'd have shot yourself by now!"

IV

"It's a most extraordinary thing," muttered Colonel Easterbrook. "Most extraordinary. Laura."

"Yes, darling?"

"Come into my dressing room a moment."

"What is it, darling?"

Mrs. Easterbrook appeared through the open door.

"Remember my showing you that revolver of mine?"

"Oh, yes, Archie, a nasty horrid black thing."

"Yes. Hun souvenir. Was in this drawer, wasn't it?"

"Yes, it was."

"Well, it's not there now."

"Archie, how extraordinary!"

"You haven't moved it or anything?"

"Oh, no, I'd never dare to touch the horrid thing."

"Think old Mother What's-her-name did?"

"Oh, I shouldn't think so, for a minute. Mrs. Butt would never do a thing like that. Shall I ask her?"

"No—no, better not. Don't want to start a lot of talk. Tell me, do you remember when it was I showed it to you?"

"Oh, about a week ago. You were grumbling about your collars and the laundry and you opened this drawer wide and there it was at the back and I asked you what it was."

"Yes, that's right. About a week ago. You don't remember the date?"

Mrs. Easterbrook considered, eyelids down over her eyes, a shrewd brain working.

"Of course," she said. "It was Saturday. The day we were to have gone in to the pictures, but we didn't."

"Hm—sure it wasn't before that? Wednesday? Thursday, or even the week before that?"

"No, dear," said Mrs. Easterbrook. "I remember quite distinctly. It was Saturday, the 30th. It just seems a long time because of all the trouble there's been. And I can tell you how I remember. It's because it was the day after the holdup at Miss Blacklock's. Because when I saw your revolver it reminded me of the shooting the night before."

"Ah," said Colonel Easterbrook, "then that's a great load off my mind."

"Oh, Archie, why?"

"Just because if that revolver had disappeared before the shooting—well, it might possibly have been my revolver that was pinched by that Swiss fellow."

"But how would he have known you had one?"

"These gangs have a most extraordinary communication service. They get to know everything about a place and who lives there."

"What a lot you do know, Archie."

"Ha! Yes. Seen a thing or two in my time. Still, as you definitely remember seeing my revolver after the holdup—well, that settles it. The revolver that Swiss fellow used can't have been mine, can it?"

"Of course it can't."

"A great relief. I should have had to go to the police about it. And they ask a lot of awkward questions. Bound to. As a matter of fact, I never took out a license for it. Somehow, after a war, one forgets these peace-time regulations. I looked on it as a war souvenir, not as a firearm."

"Yes, I see. Of course."

"But all the same—where on earth can the damned thing be?"

"Perhaps Mrs. Butt took it. She's always seemed quite honest, but perhaps she felt nervous after the holdup and thought she'd like to—to have a revolver in the house. Of course, she'll never admit doing that. I shan't even ask her. She might get offended. And what should we do then? This is such a big house—I simply couldn't."

"Quite so," said Colonel Easterbrook. "Better not say anything."

13

Morning Activities in Chipping Cleghorn (Continued)

Miss Marple came out of the vicarage gate and walked down the little lane that led into the main street.

She walked fairly briskly with the aid of the Rev. Julian Harmon's stout ashplant stick.

She passed the Red Cow and the butcher's and stopped for a brief moment to look into the window of Mr. Elliot's antique shop. This was cunningly situated next door to the Bluebird Tea Room and Cafe so that rich motorists, after stopping for a nice cup of tea and the somewhat euphemistically named "Homemade Cakes" of a bright saffron color, could be tempted by Mr. Elliot's judiciously planned shop window.

In this antique bow frame, Mr. Elliot catered for all tastes. Two pieces of Waterford glass reposed on an impeccable wine cooler. A walnut bureau, made up of various bits and pieces, proclaimed itself a genuine bargain and on a table, in the window itself, was a nice assortment of cheap doorknockers and quaint pixies, a few chipped bits of Dresden, a couple of sad-looking bead necklaces, a mug with "A Present from Tunbridge Wells" on it and some tidbits of Victorian silver.

Miss Marple gave the window her rapt attention, and Mr. Elliot, an elderly obese spider, peeped out of his web to appraise the possibilities of this new fly.

But just as he decided that the charms of the "Present from Tunbridge Wells" were about to be too much for the lady who was staying at the vicarage (for, of course, Mr. Elliot, like everybody else, knew exactly who she was), Miss Marple saw out of the corner of her eye

Miss Dora Bunner entering the Bluebird Cafe, and immediately decided that what she needed to counteract the cold wind was a nice cup of morning coffee.

Four or five ladies were already engaged in sweetening their morning shopping by a pause for refreshment. Miss Marple, blinking a little in the gloom of the interior of the Bluebird, and hovering artistically, was greeted by the voice of Dora Bunner at her elbow.

"Oh, good morning, Miss Marple. Do sit down here. I'm all alone."

"Thank you."

Miss Marple subsided gratefully onto the rather angular little blue painted armchair which the Bluebird affected.

"Such a sharp wind," she complained. "And I can't walk very fast because of my rheumatic leg."

"Oh, I know. I had sciatica one year—and really most of the time I was in agony."

The two ladies talked rheumatism, sciatica and neuritis for some moments with avidity. A sulky-looking girl in a pink overall with a flight of bluebirds down the front of it took their order for coffee and cakes with a yawn and an air of weary patience.

"The cakes," Miss Bunner said in a conspiratorial whisper, "are really quite good here."

"I was so interested in that very pretty girl I met as we were coming away from Miss Blacklock's the other day," said Miss Marple. "I think she said she does gardening. Or is she on the land? Hynes—was that her name?"

"Oh, yes, Phillipa Haymes. Our Lodger, as we call her." Miss Bunner laughed at her own humor. "Such a nice quiet girl. A lady, if you know what I mean."

"I wonder now. I knew a Colonel Haymes—in the Indian cavalry. Her father perhaps?"

"She's Mrs. Haymes. A widow. Her husband was killed in Sicily or Italy. Of course it might have been his father."

"I wondered, perhaps, if there might be a little romance on the way," Miss Marple suggested roguishly. "With that tall young man?"

"With Patrick, do you mean? Oh, I don't—"

"No, I meant a young man with spectacles. I've seen him about."

"Oh, of course, Edmund Swettenham. Sh! That's his mother, Mrs. Swettenham, over in the corner. I don't know, I'm sure. You think he admires her? He's such an odd young man—says the most disturbing things sometimes. He's supposed to be clever, you know," said Miss Bunner with frank disapproval.

"Cleverness isn't everything," said Miss Marple, shaking her head. "Ah, here is our coffee."

The sulky girl deposited it with a clatter. Miss Marple and Miss Bunner pressed cakes on each other.

"I was so interested to hear you were at school with Miss Blacklock. Yours is indeed an old friendship."

"Yes, indeed," Miss Bunner sighed. "Very few people would be as loyal to their old friends as dear Miss Blacklock is. Oh, dear, those days seem a long time ago. Such a pretty girl and enjoyed life so much. It all seemed so sad."

Miss Marple, though with no idea of what had seemed so sad, sighed and shook her head.

"Life is indeed hard," she murmured.

"'And sad affliction bravely borne,'" murmured Miss Bunner, her eyes suffusing with tears. "I always think of that verse. True patience; true resignation. Such courage and patience ought to be rewarded, that is what I say. What I feel is that nothing is too good for dear Miss Blacklock, and whatever good things come to her, she truly deserves them."

"Money," said Miss Marple, "can do a lot to ease one's path in life."

She felt herself safe in this observation since she judged that it must be Miss Blacklock's prospects of future affluence to which her friend referred.

The remark, however, started Miss Bunner on another train of thought.

"Money!" she exclaimed with bitterness. "I don't believe, you know, that until one has really experienced it, one can know what money, or rather the lack of it, means."

Miss Marple nodded her white head sympathetically.

Miss Bunner went on rapidly, working herself up, and speaking with a flushed face.

"I've heard people say so often 'I'd rather have flowers on the table, than a meal without them.' But how many meals have those people ever missed? They don't know what it is—nobody knows who hasn't been through it—to be really hungry. Bread, you know, and a jar of meat paste, and a scrape of margarine. Day after day and how one longs for a good plate of meat and two vegetables. And the shabbiness. Darning one's clothes and hoping it won't show. And applying for jobs and always being told you're too old. And then perhaps getting a job and after all one isn't strong enough. One faints. And you're back again. It's the rent—always the rent—that's got to be paid—otherwise you're out in the street. And in these days it leaves so little over. One's old age pension doesn't go far—indeed it doesn't."

"I know," said Miss Marple gently. She looked with compassion at Miss Bunner's twitching face.

"I wrote to Letty. I just happened to see her name in the paper. It was a luncheon in aid of Milchester Hospital. There it was in black and white, Miss Letitia Blacklock. It brought the past back to me. I hadn't heard of her for years and years. She'd been secretary, you know, to that very rich man, Goedler. She was always a clever girl—the kind that gets on in the world. Not so much looks as character. I thought—well, I thought—perhaps she'll remember me—and she's one of the people I could ask for a little help. I mean someone you've known as a girl—been at school with—well, they do know about you—they know you're not just a—a begging letter writer—"

Tears came into Dora Bunner's eyes.

"And then Letty came and took me away—said she needed someone to help her. Of course, I was very surprised—very surprised—but then newspapers do get things wrong. How kind she was—and how sympathetic. And remembering all the old days so well . . . I'd do anything for her—I really would. And I try very hard, but I'm afraid sometimes I muddle things—my head's not what it was. I make mistakes. And I forget and say foolish things. She's very patient. What's so nice about her is that she always pretends that I am useful to her. That's real kindness, isn't it?"

Miss Marple said gently, "Yes, that's real kindness."

"I used to worry, you know, even after I came to Little Paddocks—about what would become of me if—if anything were to happen to Miss Blacklock. After all, there are so many accidents—these motors dashing about—one never knows, does one? But naturally I never said anything—but she must have guessed. Suddenly one day she told me that she'd left me a small annuity in her will—and—what I value far more—all her beautiful furniture. I was quite overcome— But she said nobody else would value it as I should—and that is quite true—I can't bear to see some lovely piece of china smashed—or wet glasses put down on a table and leaving a mark. I do really look after her things. Some people—some people especially, are so terribly careless—and sometimes worse than careless!

"I'm not really as stupid as I look," Miss Bunner continued with simplicity. "I can see, you know, when Letty's being imposed upon. Some people—I won't name names—but they take advantage. Dear Miss Blacklock is, perhaps, just a shade too trusting."

Miss Marple shook her head.

"That's a mistake."

"Yes, it is. You and I, Miss Marple, know the world. Dear Miss Blacklock—" She shook her head.

Miss Marple thought that as the secretary of a big financier Miss Blacklock might be presumed to know the world, too. But probably what Dora Bunner meant was that Letty Blacklock had always been comfortably off, and that the comfortably off do not know the deeper abysses of human nature.

"That Patrick!" said Miss Bunner with a suddenness and an asperity that made Miss Marple jump. "Twice, at least, to my knowledge, he's got money out of her. Pretending he's hard up. Run into debt. All that sort of thing. She's far too generous. All she said to me was when I remonstrated with her. 'The boy's young, Dora. Youth is the time to have your fling.'"

"Well, that's true enough," said Miss Marple. "Such a handsome young man, too."

"Handsome is as handsome does," said Dora Bunner. "Much too fond of poking fun at people. And a lot of going on with girls, I expect. I'm just a figure of fun to him—that's all. He doesn't seem to realize that people have their feelings."

"Young people are rather careless that way," said Miss Marple.

Miss Bunner leaned forward suddenly with a mysterious air.

"You won't breathe a word, will you, my dear?" she demanded. "But I can't help feeling that he was mixed up in this dreadful business. I think he knew that young man—or else Julia did. I daren't hint at such a thing to dear Miss Blacklock—at least I did, and she just snapped my head off. And, of course, it's awkward—because he's her nephew—or at any rate her cousin—and if the Swiss young man shot himself Patrick might be held morally responsible, mightn't he? If he'd put him up to it, I mean. I'm really terribly confused about the whole thing. Everyone making such a fuss about that other door into the drawing-room. That's another thing that worries me—the detective saying it had been oiled. Because you see, I saw—"

She came to an abrupt stop.

Miss Marple paused to select a phrase.

"Most difficult for you," she said sympathetically. "Naturally you wouldn't want anything to get round to the police."

"That's just it," Dora Bunner cried. "I lie awake at nights and worry . . . because, you see, I came upon Patrick in the shrubbery the other day. I was looking for eggs—one hen hides out—and there he was holding a feather and a cup—an oily cup. And he jumped most guiltily when he saw me and he said, 'I was just wondering what this was doing here.' Well, of course, he's a quick thinker. I should say he thought that up quickly when I startled him. And how did he come to find a thing like that in the shrubbery unless he was looking for it, knowing perfectly well it was there? Of course, I didn't say anything."

"No, no, of course not."

"But I gave him a look, if you know what I mean."

Dora Bunner stretched out her hand and bit abstractedly into a lurid salmon-colored cake.

"And then another day I happened to overhear him having a very curious conversation with Julia. They seemed to be having a kind of quarrel. He was saying, 'If I thought you had anything to do with a thing like that!' And Julia (she's always so calm, you know) said: 'Well, little brother, what would you do about it?' And then, most unfortunately, I trod on that board that always squeaks, and they saw me. So I said, quite gaily: 'You two having a quarrel?' and Patrick said, 'I'm warning Julia not to go in for these black market clothes coupons deals.' Oh, it was all very slick, but I don't believe they were talking about anything of the sort! And, if you ask me, I believe Patrick had tampered with that lamp in the drawing-room—to make the lights go out, because I remember distinctly that it was the shepherdess—not the shepherd. And the next day—"

She stopped and her face grew pink. Miss Marple turned her head to see Miss Blacklock standing beside them—she must just have come in.

"Coffee and gossip, Bunny?" said Miss Blacklock with quite a shade of reproach in her voice. "Good morning, Miss Marple. Cold, isn't it?"

"We were just talking about clothes coupons," said Miss Bunner hurriedly. "They really don't give us enough, do they? A little better now shoes have come off. But fifteen still for a winter coat is too much."

The doors flew open with a clang and Bunch Harmon came into the Bluebird with a rush.

"Hullo," she said, "am I too late for coffee?"

"No, dear," said Miss Marple. "Sit down and have a cup."

"We must get home," said Miss Blacklock. "Done your shopping, Bunny?"

Her tone was indulgent once more, but her eyes still held a slight reproach.

"Yes—yes, thank you, Letty. I must just pop into the chemist's in passing and get some aspirin and some corn plasters."

As the doors of the Bluebird swung to behind them, Bunch asked: "What were you talking about?"

Miss Marple did not reply at once. She waited whilst Bunch gave the order, then she said:

"Family solidarity is a very strong thing. Very strong. Do you remember some famous case—I really can't remember what it was. They said the husband poisoned his wife. In a glass of wine. Then, at the trial, the daughter said she'd drunk half her mother's glass—so that knocked the case against her father to pieces. They do say—but it may be just rumor—that she never spoke to her father or lived with him again. Of course, a father is one thing—and a nephew or a distant cousin is another. But, still, there it is—no one wants a member of their own family hanged, do they?"

"No," said Bunch considering. "I shouldn't think they would."

Miss Marple leaned back in her chair. She murmured under her breath, "People are really very alike, everywhere."

"Who am I like?"

"Well, really, dear, you are very much like yourself. I don't know that you remind me of anyone in particular. Except perhaps—"

"Here it comes," said Bunch.

"I was just thinking of a parlormaid of mine, dear."

"A parlormaid? I should make a terrible parlormaid."

"Yes, dear, so did she. She was no good at all at waiting at table. Put everything on the table crooked, mixed up the kitchen knives with the dining room ones and her cap (this was a long time ago, dear)—her cap was never straight."

Bunch adjusted her hat automatically.

"Anything else?" she demanded anxiously.

"I kept her because she was so pleasant to have about the house—and because she used to make me laugh. I liked the way she said things straight out. Came to me one day, 'Of course I don't know, ma'am,' she says, 'but Florrie, the way she sits down, it's just like a married woman.' And sure enough poor Florrie was in trouble—the gentlemanly assistant at the hairdresser's. Fortunately it was in good time, and I was able to have a little talk with him, and they had a very nice wedding and settled down quite happily. She was a good girl, Florrie, but inclined to be taken in by a gentlemanly appearance."

"She didn't do a murder, did she?" asked Bunch. "The parlormaid, I mean."

"No, indeed," said Miss Marple. "She married a Baptist Minister and they had a family of five."

"Just like me," said Bunch. "Though I've only got as far as Edward and Susan up to date."

She added, after a minute or two,

"Who are you thinking about now, Aunt Jane?"

"Quite a lot of people, dear, quite a lot of people," said Miss Marple vaguely.

"In St. Mary Mead?"

"Mostly . . . I was really thinking about Nurse Ellerton—really an excellent, kindly woman. Took care of an old lady, seemed really fond of her. Then the old lady died. And another came and she died. Morphia. It all came out. Done in the kindest way, and the shocking thing was that the woman herself really couldn't see that she'd done anything wrong. They hadn't long to live in any case, she said, and one of them had cancer and quite a lot of pain."

"You mean—it was a mercy killing?"

"No, no. They signed their money away to her. She liked money, you know . . .

"And then there was that young man on the liner—Mrs. Pusey at the paper shop, her nephew. Brought stuff home he'd stolen and got her to dispose of it. Said it was things that he'd bought abroad. She was quite taken in. And then when the police came round and started asking questions, he tried to bash her on the head, so that she shouldn't be able to give him away. . . . Not a nice young man—but very good-looking. Had two girls in love with him. He spent a lot of money on one of them."

"The nastiest one, I suppose," said Bunch.

"Yes, dear. And there was Mrs. Cray at the wool shop. Devoted to her son, spoilt him, of course. He got in with a very queer lot. Do you remember Joan Croft, Bunch?"

"N-no, I don't think so."

"I thought you might have seen her when you were with me on a visit. Used to stalk about smoking a cigar or a pipe. We had a bank holdup once, and Joan Croft was in the bank at the time. She knocked the man down and took his revolver away from him. She was congratulated on her courage by the Bench."

Bunch listened attentively. She seemed to be learning by heart.

"And—" she prompted.

"That girl at St. Jean des Collines that summer. Such a quiet girl—not so much quiet as silent. Everybody liked her, but they never got to know her much better. . . . We heard afterwards that her husband was a forger. It made her feel cut off from people. It made her, in the end, a little queer. Brooding does, you know."

"Any Anglo-Indian colonels in your reminiscences, darling?"

"Naturally, dear. There was Major Vaughan at The Larches and Colonel Wright at Simla Lodge. Nothing wrong with either of them. But I do remember Mr. Hodgson, the bank manager, went on a cruise and married a woman young enough to be his daughter. No idea of where she came from—except what she told him, of course."

"And that wasn't true?"

"No, dear, it definitely wasn't."

"Not bad," said Bunch nodding, and ticking people off on her fingers. "We've had devoted Dora, and handsome Patrick, and Mrs. Swettenham and Edmund, and Phillipa Haymes, and Colonel Easterbrook and Mrs. Easterbrook—and, if you ask me, I should say you're absolutely right about her. But there wouldn't be any reason for her murdering Letty Blacklock."

"Miss Blacklock, of course, might know something about her that she didn't want known."

"Oh, darling, that old Tanqueray stuff? Surely that's dead as the hills."

"It might not be. You see, Bunch, you are not the kind that minds much about what people think of you."

"I see what you mean," said Bunch suddenly. "If you'd been up against it, and then, rather like a shivering stray cat, you'd found a home and cream and a warm stroking hand and you were called Pretty Pussy and somebody thought the world of you . . . You'd do a lot to keep that . . . Well, I must say, you've presented me with a very complete gallery of people."

"You didn't get them all right, you know," said Miss Marple mildly.

"Didn't I? Where did I slip up? Julia? Julia, *pretty Juliar is peculiar*."

"Three and sixpence," said the sulky waitress, materializing out of the gloom.

"And," she added, her bosom heaving beneath the bluebirds, "I'd like to know, Mrs. Harmon, why you call me peculiar. I had an aunt who joined the Peculiar People, but I've always been good Church of England myself, as the late Rev. Hopkinson can tell you."

"I'm terribly sorry," said Bunch. "I was just quoting a song. I didn't mean you at all. I didn't know your name was Julia."

"Quite a coincidence," said the sulky waitress cheering up. "No offense, I'm sure, but hearing my name, as I thought—well, naturally, if you think someone's talking about you, it's only human nature to listen. Thank you."

She departed with her tip.

"Aunt Jane," said Bunch, "don't look so upset. What is it?"

"But surely," murmured Miss Marple. "That couldn't be so. There's no reason—"

"Aunt Jane!"

Miss Marple sighed and then smiled brightly.

"It's nothing, dear," she said.

"Did you think you knew who did the murder?" asked Bunch. "Who was it?"

"I don't know at all," said Miss Marple. "I got an idea for a moment—but it's gone. I wish I did know. Time's so short. So terribly short."

"What do you mean short?"

"That old lady up in Scotland may die any moment."

Bunch said staring:

"Then you really do believe in Pip and Emma. You think it was them—and that they'll try again?"

"Of course they'll try again," said Miss Marple almost absent-mindedly. "If they tried once, they'll try again. If you've made up your mind to murder someone, you don't stop because it didn't come off the first time. Especially if you're fairly sure you're not suspected."

"But if it's Pip and Emma," said Bunch, "there are only two people it could be. It must be Patrick and Julia. They're brother and sister and they're the only ones who are the right age."

"My dear, it isn't nearly as simple as that. There are all sorts of ramifications and combinations. There's Pip's wife if he's married, or Emma's husband. There's their mother—she's an interested party even if she doesn't inherit direct. If Letty Blacklock hasn't seen her for thirty years, she'd probably not recognize her now. One elderly woman is very like another. You remember Mrs. Wotherspoon drew her own and Mrs. Bartlett's old age pension although Mrs. Bartlett had been dead for years. Anyway, Miss Blacklock's shortsighted. Haven't you noticed how she peers at people? And then there's the father. Apparently he was a real bad lot."

"Yes, but he's a foreigner."

"By birth. But there's no reason to believe he speaks broken English and gesticulates with his hands. I daresay he could play the part of—of an Anglo-Indian colonel as well as anybody else."

"Is that what you think?"

"No, I don't. I don't indeed, dear. I just think that there's a great deal of money at stake, a great deal of money. And I'm afraid I know only too well the really terrible things that people will do to lay their hands on a lot of money."

"I suppose they will," said Bunch. "It doesn't really do them any good, does it? Not in the end?"

"No—but they don't usually know that."

"I can understand it." Bunch smiled suddenly, her sweet rather crooked smile. "One feels it would be different for oneself . . . Even I feel that." She considered, You pretend to yourself that you'd do a lot of good with all that money. Schemes. . . . Homes for unwanted children. . . . Tired mothers. . . . A lovely rest abroad somewhere for elderly women who have worked too hard. . . .

Her face grew somber. Her eyes were suddenly dark and tragic.

"I know what you're thinking," she said to Miss Marple. "You're thinking that I'd be the worst kind. Because I'd kid myself. If you just wanted the money for selfish reasons you'd at any rate see what you were like. But once you began to pretend about doing good with it, you'd be able to persuade yourself, perhaps, that it wouldn't very much matter killing someone."

Then her eyes cleared.

"But I shouldn't," she said. "I shouldn't really kill anyone. Not even if they were old, or ill or doing a lot of harm in the world. Not even if they were blackmailers or—or absolute beasts." She fished a fly carefully out of the dregs of the coffee and arranged it on the table to dry. "Because people like living, don't they? So do flies. Even if you're old and in pain and can just crawl out in the sun. Julian says those people like living even more than strong young people do. It's harder, he says, for them to die, the struggle's greater. I like living myself—not just being happy and enjoying myself and having a good time. I mean living—waking up and feeling, all over me, that I'm there—ticking over."

She blew on the fly gently; it waved its legs and flew rather drunkenly away.

"Cheer up, darling Aunt Jane," said Bunch. "I'd never kill anybody."

14

Excursion into the Past

After a night in the train Inspector Craddock alighted at a small station in the Highlands.

It struck him for a moment as strange that the wealthy Mrs. Goedler—an invalid—with a choice of a London house in a fashionable Square, an estate in Hampshire and a villa in the South of France, should have selected this remote Scottish home as her residence. Surely she was cut off here from many friends and distractions. It must be a lonely life—or was she too ill to notice or care about her surroundings?

A car was waiting to meet him. A big old-fashioned Daimler with an elderly chauffeur driving it. It was a sunny morning and the Inspector enjoyed the twenty-mile drive, though he marveled anew at this preference for isolation. A tentative remark to the chauffeur brought partial enlightenment.

"It's her own home as a girl. Ay, she's the last of the family. And she and Mr. Goedler were always happier here than anywhere, though it wasn't often he could get away from London. But when he did they enjoyed themselves like a couple of bairns."

When the gray walls of the old keep came in sight, Craddock felt that time was slipping backwards. An elderly butler received him, and after a wash and a shave he was shown into a room with a huge fire burning in the grate, and breakfast was served to him.

After breakfast, a tall middle-aged woman in nurse's dress, with a pleasant and competent manner, came in and introduced herself as Sister McClelland.

"I have my patient all ready for you, Mr. Craddock. She is, indeed, looking forward to seeing you."

"I'll do my best not to excite her," Craddock promised.

"I had better warn you of what will happen. You will find Mrs. Goedler apparently quite normal. She will talk and enjoy talking and then—quite suddenly—her powers will fail. Come away at once, then, and send for me. She is, you see, kept almost entirely under the influence of morphia. She drowses most of the time. In preparation for your visit, I have given her a strong stimulant. As soon as the effect of the stimulant wears off, she will relapse into semiconsciousness."

"I quite understand, Miss McClelland. Would it be in order for you to tell me exactly what the state of Mrs. Goedler's health is?"

"Well, Mr. Craddock, she is a dying woman. Her life cannot be prolonged for more than a few weeks. To say that she should have been dead years ago would strike you as odd, yet it is the truth. What has kept Mrs. Goedler alive is her intense enjoyment and love of being alive. That sounds, perhaps, an odd thing to say of someone who has lived the life of an invalid for many years and has not left her home here for fifteen years, but it is true. Mrs. Goedler has never been a strong woman—but she has retained to an astonishing degree the will to live." She added with a smile, "She is a very charming woman, too, as you will find."

Craddock was shown into a large bedroom where a fire was burning and where an old lady lay in a large canopied bed. Though she was only about seven or eight years older than Letitia Blacklock, her fragility made her seem older than her years.

Her white hair was carefully arranged, a froth of pale blue wool enveloped her neck and shoulders. There were lines of pain on the face, but lines of sweetness, too. And there was, strangely enough, what Craddock could only describe as a roguish twinkle in her faded blue eyes.

"Well, this is interesting," she said, "it's not often I receive a visit from the police. I hear Letitia Blacklock wasn't much hurt by this attempt on her? How is my dear Blackie?"

"She's very well, Mrs. Goedler. She sent you her love."

"It's a long time since I've seen her . . . For many years now, it's been just a card at Christmas. I asked her to come up here when she came back to England after Charlotte's death, but she said it would be painful after so long and perhaps she was right . . . Blackie always had a lot of sense. I had an old school friend to see me about a year ago and, Lor'—" she smiled, "we bored each other to death. After we'd finished all the 'Do you remembers?' there wasn't anything to say. Most embarrassing."

Craddock was content to let her talk before pressing his questions. He wanted, as it were, to get back into the past, to get the feel of the Goedler-Blacklock menage.

"I suppose," said Belle shrewdly, "that you want to ask about the money? Randall left it all to go to Blackie after my death. Really, of course, Randall never dreamed that I'd outlive him. He was a big strong man, never a day's illness, and I was always a mass of aches and pains and complaints and doctors coming and pulling long faces over me."

"I don't think complaints would be the right word, Mrs. Goedler."

The old lady chuckled.

"I didn't mean it in the complaining sense. I've never been too sorry for myself. But it was always taken for granted that I, being the weakly one, would go first. It didn't work out that way. No—it didn't work out that way . . ."

"Why, exactly, did your husband leave his money the way he did?"

"You mean, why did he leave it to Blackie? Not for the reason you've probably been thinking." The roguish twinkle was very apparent. "What minds you policemen have! Randall was never in the least in love with her and she wasn't with him. Letitia, you know, has really got a man's mind. She hasn't any feminine feelings or weaknesses. I don't believe she was ever in love with any man. She was never particularly pretty and she didn't care for clothes. She used a little make-up in deference to prevailing custom, but not to make herself look prettier." There was pity in the old voice as she went on: "She never knew any of the fun of being a woman."

Craddock looked with interest at the frail little figure in the big bed. Belle Goedler, he realized, had enjoyed—still enjoyed—being a woman. She twinkled at him.

"I've always thought," she said, "it must be terribly dull to be a man."

Then she said thoughtfully,

"I think Randall looked on Blackie very much as a kind of younger brother. He relied on her judgment which was always excellent. She kept him out of trouble more than once, you know."

"She told me that she came to his rescue once with money."

"That, yes, but I meant more than that. One can speak the truth after all these years. Randall couldn't really distinguish between what was crooked and what wasn't. His conscience wasn't sensitive. The poor dear really didn't know what was just smart—and what was dishonest. Blackie kept him straight. That's one thing about Letitia Blacklock, she's absolutely dead straight. She would never do anything that was dishonest. She's a very fine character, you know. I've always admired her. They had a terrible girlhood, those girls. The father was an old country doctor—terrifically pigheaded and narrowminded—the complete family tyrant. Letitia broke away, came to London and trained herself as a chartered accountant. The other sister was an invalid, there was a deformity of kinds and she never saw people or went out. That's why, when the old man died, Letitia gave up everything to go home and look after her sister. Randall was wild with her—but it made no difference. If Letitia thought a thing was her duty, she'd do it. And you couldn't move her."

"How long was that before your husband died?"

"A couple of years, I think. Randall made his will before she left the firm, and he didn't alter it. He said to me: 'We've no one of our own.' (Our little boy died, you know, when he was two years old). 'After you and I are gone, Blackie had better have the money. She'll play the markets and make 'em sit up.'

"You see," Belle went on, "Randall enjoyed the whole moneymaking game so much—it wasn't just the money—it was the adventure, the risks, the excitement of it all. And Blackie liked it, too. She had the same adventurous spirit and the same judgment. Poor darling, she'd never had any of the usual fun—being in love, and leading men on and teasing them—and having a home and children and all the real fun of life."

Craddock thought it was odd, the real pity and indulgent contempt felt by this woman, a woman whose life had been hampered by illness, whose only child had died, whose husband had died, leaving her to a lonely widowhood, and who had been a hopeless invalid for years.

She nodded her head at him.

"I know what you're thinking. But I've had all the things that make life worth while—they may have been taken from me—but I have had them. I was pretty and gay as a girl, I married the man I loved, and he never stopped loving me. My child died, but I had him for two precious years. I've had a lot of physical pain—but if you have pain, you know how to enjoy the exquisite pleasure of the times when pain stops. And everyone's been kind to me, always . . . I'm a lucky woman, really."

Craddock seized upon an opening in her former remarks.

"You said just now, Mrs. Goedler, that your husband left his fortune to Miss Blacklock because he had no one else to leave it to. But that's not strictly true, is it? He had a sister."

"Oh, Sonia. But they'd quarreled years ago and made a clean break of it."

"He disapproved of her marriage?"

"Yes, she married a man called—now what was his name—?"

"Stamfordis."

"That's it. Dmitri Stamfordis. Randall always said he was a crook. The two men didn't like each other from the first. But Sonia was wildly in love with him and quite determined to marry him. And I really never saw why she shouldn't. Men have such odd ideas about these things. Sonia wasn't a mere girl—she was twenty-five, and she knew exactly what she was doing. He was a crook, I daresay—I mean really a crook, I believe he had a criminal record—and Randall always suspected the name he was passing under wasn't his own. Sonia knew all that. The point was, which, of course, Randall couldn't appreciate, that Dmitri was really a wildly attractive person to women. And he was just as much in love with Sonia as she was with him. Randall insisted that he was just marrying her for her money—but that wasn't true. Sonia was very handsome, you know. And she had plenty of spirit. If the marriage had turned out badly, if Dmitri had been unkind to her or unfaithful to her, she would just have cut her losses and walked out on him. She was a rich woman and could do as she chose with her life."

"The quarrel was never made up?"

"No. Randall and Sonia never had got on very well. She resented his trying to prevent the marriage. She said, 'Very well. You're quite impossible! This is the last you hear of me!'"

"But it was not the last you heard of her?"

Belle smiled.

"No, I got a letter from her about eighteen months afterwards. She wrote from Budapest, I remember, but she didn't give an address. She told me to tell Randall that she was extremely happy and that she'd just had twins."

"And she told you their names?"

Again Belle smiled. "She said they were born just after midday—

and she intended to call them Pip and Emma. That may have been just a joke, of course."

"Didn't you hear from her again?"

"No. She said she and her husband and the babies were going to America on a short stay. I never heard any more. . . ."

"You don't happen, I suppose, to have kept that letter?"

"No, I'm afraid not . . . I read it to Randall and he just grunted: 'She'll regret marrying that fellow one of these days.' That's all he ever said about it. We really forgot about her. She went right out of our lives. . . ."

"Nevertheless, Mr. Goedler left his estate to her children in the event of Miss Blacklock predeceasing you?"

"Oh, that was my doing. I said to him, when he told me about the will: 'And suppose Blackie dies before I do?' He was quite surprised. I said, 'Oh, I know Blackie is as strong as a horse and I'm a delicate creature—but there's such a thing as accidents, you know, and there's such a thing as creaking gates . . .' And he said, 'There's no one—absolutely no one.' I said, 'There's Sonia.' And he said at once, 'And let that fellow get hold of my money? No—indeed!' I said, 'Well, her children then. Pip and Emma, and there may be lots more by now'—and so he grumbled, but he did put it in."

"And from that day to this," Craddock said slowly, "you've heard nothing of your sister-in-law or her children?"

"Nothing—They may be dead—they may be—anywhere."

They may be in Chipping Cleghorn, thought Craddock.

As though she read his thoughts, a look of alarm came into Belle Goedler's eyes. She said, "Don't let them hurt Blackie. Blackie's good—really good—you mustn't let harm come to—"

Her voice trailed off suddenly. Craddock saw the sudden gray shadows round her mouth and eyes.

"You're tired," he said. "I'll go."

She nodded.

"Send Mac to me," she whispered. "Yes, tired. . . ." She made a feeble motion of her hand. "Look after Blackie . . . nothing must happen to Blackie . . . look after her . . ."

"I'll do my very best, Mrs. Goedler." He rose and went to the door.

Her voice, a thin thread of sound, followed him . . .

"Not long now—until I'm dead—dangerous for her—take care . . ."

Sister McClelland passed him as he went out. He said uneasily,

"I hope I haven't done her harm."

"Oh, I don't think so, Mr. Craddock. I told you she would tire quite suddenly."

Later, he asked the nurse:

"The only thing I hadn't time to ask Mrs. Goedler was whether she had any old photographs? If so, I wonder—"

She interrupted him.

"I'm afraid there's nothing of that kind. All her personal papers and things were stored with her furniture from the London house at the beginning of the war. Mrs. Goedler was desperately ill at the time. Then the storage depository was blitzed. Mrs. Goedler was very upset at losing so many personal souvenirs and family papers. I'm afraid there's nothing of that kind."

So that was that, Craddock thought.

Yet he felt his journey had not been in vain. Pip and Emma, those twin wraiths, were not quite wraiths.

Craddock thought, Here's a brother and sister brought up somewhere in Europe. Sonia Goedler was a rich woman at the time of her marriage, but money in Europe hasn't remained money. Queer things have happened to money during these war years. And so there are two young people, the son and daughter of a man who had a criminal record. Suppose they came to England, more or less penniless? What would they do? Find out about any rich relatives. Their uncle, a man of vast fortune, is dead. Possibly the first thing they'd do would be to look up that uncle's will. See if by any chance money had been left to them or to their mother. So they go to Somerset House and learn the contents of his will, and then, perhaps, they learn of the existence of Miss Letitia Blacklock. Then they make inquiries about Randall Goedler's widow. She's an invalid, living up in Scotland, and they find out she hasn't long to live. If this Letitia Blacklock dies before her, they will come into a vast fortune. What then?

Craddock thought, They wouldn't go to Scotland. They'd find out where Letitia Blacklock is living now. And they'd go there—but not as themselves . . . They'd go together—or separately? Emma . . . I wonder . . . Pip and Emma. . . . I'll eat my hat if Pip, or Emma, or both of them, aren't in Chipping Cleghorn now.

15

Delicious Death

In the kitchen at Little Paddocks, Miss Blacklock was giving instructions to Mitzi.

"Sardine sandwiches as well as the tomato ones. And some of those little scones you make so nicely. And I'd like you to make that special cake of yours."

"It is a party, then, that you want all these things?"

"It's Miss Bunner's birthday, and some people will be coming to tea."

"At her age one does not have birthdays. It is better to forget."

"Well, she doesn't want to forget. Several people are bringing her presents—and it will be nice to make a little party of it."

"That is what you say last time—and see what happened!"

Miss Blacklock controlled her temper.

"Well, it won't happen this time."

"How do you know what may happen in this house? All day long I shiver and at night I lock my door and I look in the wardrobe to see no one is hidden there."

"That ought to keep you nice and safe," said Miss Blacklock coldly.

"The cake that you want me to make, it is the—" Mitzi uttered a sound that to Miss Blacklock's English ear sounded like *Schwitzebzr* or, alternatively, like cats spitting at each other.

"That's the one. The rich one."

"Yes. It is rich. For it I have nothing! Impossible to make such a cake. I need for it chocolate and much butter, and sugar and raisins."

"You can use this tin of butter that was sent to us from America.

And some of the raisins we were keeping for Christmas, and here is a slab of chocolate and a pound of sugar."

Mitzi's face suddenly burst into radiant smiles.

"So, I make him for you good—good!" she cried, in an ecstasy. "It will be rich, rich, of a melting richness! And on top I will put the icing—chocolate icing—I make him so nice—and write on it *Good Wishes*. These English people with their cakes that taste of sand, never, never will they have tasted such a cake. Delicious, they will say— delicious—"

Her face clouded again.

"Mr. Patrick. He called it Delicious Death. My cake! I will not have my cake called that!"

"It was a compliment really," said Miss Blacklock. "He meant it was worth dying to eat such a cake."

Mitzi looked at her doubtfully.

"Well, I do not like that word—death. They are not dying because they eat my cake, no, they feel much much better."

"I'm sure we all shall."

Miss Blacklock turned away and left the kitchen with a sigh of relief at the successful ending of the interview. With Mitzi one never knew.

She ran into Dora Bunner outside.

"Oh, Letty, shall I run in and tell Mitzi just how to cut the sandwiches?"

"No," said Miss Blacklock, steering her friend firmly into the hall. "She's not in a good mood now and I don't want her disturbed."

"But I could just show her—"

"Please don't show her anything, Dora. These central Europeans don't like being shown. They hate it."

Dora looked at her doubtfully. Then she suddenly broke into smiles.

"Edmund Swettenham just rang up. He wished me many happy returns of the day and said he was bringing me a pot of honey as a present this afternoon. Isn't he kind? I can't imagine how he knew it was my birthday."

"Everybody seems to know. You must have been talking about it, Dora."

"Well, I did just happen to mention that today I should be fifty-nine—"

"You're sixty-four," said Miss Blacklock with a twinkle.

"And Miss Hinchliffe said, 'You don't look it. What age do you think I am?' Which was rather awkward because Miss Hinchliffe always looks so peculiar that she might be any age. She said she was bringing me some eggs, by the way. I said our hens hadn't been laying very well lately."

"We're not doing so badly out of your birthday," said Miss Blacklock. "Honey, eggs—a magnificent box of chocolates from Julia—"

"I don't know where she gets such things."

"Better not ask. Her methods are probably strictly illegal."

"And your lovely brooch." Miss Bunner looked down proudly at her bosom on which was pinned a small diamond leaf.

"Do you like it? I'm glad. I never cared for jewelry."

"I love it."

"Good. Let's go and feed the ducks."

II

"Ha!" cried Patrick dramatically, as the party took their places round the dining room table. "What do I see before me? Delicious Death."

"Hush," said Miss Blacklock. "Don't let Mitzi hear you. She objects to your name for her cake very much."

"Nevertheless, Delicious Death it is! Is it Bunny's birthday cake?"

"Yes, it is," said Miss Bunner. "I really am having the most wonderful birthday."

Her cheeks were flushed with excitement and had been ever since Colonel Easterbrook had handed her a small box of sweets and declaimed with a bow, "Sweets to the Sweet!"

Julia had turned her head away hurriedly, and had been frowned at by Miss Blacklock.

Full justice was done to the good things on the tea table and they rose from their seats after a round of crackers.

"I feel slightly sick," said Julia. "It's that cake. I remember I felt just the same last time."

"It's worth it," said Patrick.

"These foreigners certainly understand confectionery," said Miss Hinchliffe. "What they can't make is a plain boiled pudding."

Everybody was respectfully silent, though it seemed to be hovering on Patrick's lips to ask if anyone really wanted a plain boiled pudding.

"Got a new gardener?" asked Miss Hinchliffe of Miss Blacklock as they returned to the drawing-room.

"No, why?"

"Saw a man snooping round the henhouse. Quite a decent looking Army type."

"Oh that," said Julia. "That's our detective."

Mrs. Easterbrook dropped her handbag.

"Detective?" she exclaimed. "But—but—why?"

"I don't know," said Julia. "He prowls about and keeps an eye on the house. He's protecting Aunt Letty, I suppose."

"Absolute nonsense," said Miss Blacklock. "I can protect myself, thank you."

"But surely it's all over now," cried Mrs. Easterbrook. "Though I meant to ask you, why did they adjourn the inquest?"

"Police aren't satisfied," said her husband. "That's what that means."

"But aren't satisfied of what?"

Colonel Easterbrook shook his head with the air of a man who could say a good deal more if he chose. Edmund Swettenham, who disliked the colonel, said, "The truth of it is, we're all under suspicion."

"But suspicion of what?" repeated Mrs. Easterbrook.

"Never mind, kitten," said her husband.

"Loitering with intent," said Edmund. "The intent being to commit murder upon the first opportunity."

"Oh, don't, please don't, Mr. Swettenham." Dora Bunner began to cry. "I'm sure nobody here could possibly want to kill dear, dear Letty."

There was a moment of horrible embarrassment. Edmund turned scarlet, murmured, "Just a joke." Phillipa suggested in a high clear voice that they might listen to the six o'clock news and the suggestion was received with enthusiastic assent.

Patrick murmured to Julia: "We need Mrs. Harmon here. She'd be sure to say in that high clear voice of hers, 'But I suppose somebody is still waiting for a good chance to murder you, Miss Blacklock?'"

"I'm glad she and the old Miss Marple couldn't come," said Julia. "That old woman is the prying kind. And a mind like a sink, I should think. Real Victorian type."

Listening to the news led easily into a pleasant discussion on the horrors of atomic warfare. Colonel Easterbrook said that the real menace to civilization was undoubtedly Russia, and Edmund said that he had several charming Russian friends—which announcement was coldly received.

The party broke up with renewed thanks to the hostess.

"Enjoy yourself, Bunny?" asked Miss Blacklock, as the last guest was sped.

"Oh, I did. But I've got a terrible headache. It's the excitement, I think."

"It's the cake," said Patrick. "I feel a bit livery myself. And you've been nibbling chocolates all the morning."

"I'll go and lie down, I think," said Miss Bunner. "I'll take a couple of aspirin and try and have a nice sleep."

"That would be a very good plan," said Miss Blacklock.

Miss Bunner departed upstairs.

"Shall I shut up the ducks for you, Aunt Letty?"

Miss Blacklock looked at Patrick severely.

"If you'll be sure to latch that door properly."

"I will. I swear I will."

"Have a glass of sherry, Aunt Letty," said Julia. "As my old nurse used to say, 'It will settle your stomach.' A revolting phrase—but curiously apposite at this moment."

"Well, I daresay it might be a good thing. The truth is, one isn't used to rich things. Oh, Bunny, how you made me jump. What is it?"

"I can't find my aspirin," said Miss Bunner disconsolately.

"Well, take some of mine, dear; they're by my bed."

"There's a bottle on my dressing table," said Phillipa.

"Thank you—thank you very much. If I can't find mine—but I know I've got it somewhere. A new bottle. Now where could I have put it?"

"There's heaps in the bathroom," said Julia impatiently. "This house is chock full of aspirin."

"It vexes me to be so careless and mislay things," replied Miss Bunner, retreating up the stairs again.

"Poor old Bunny," said Julia, holding up her glass. "Do you think we ought to have given her some sherry?"

"Better not, I think," said Miss Blacklock. "She's had a lot of excitement today, and it isn't really good for her. I'm afraid she'll be the worse for it tomorrow. Still, I really do think she has enjoyed herself!"

"She's loved it," said Phillipa.

"Let's give Mitzi a glass of sherry," suggested Julia. "Hi, Pat," she called as she heard him entering the side door, "fetch Mitzi."

So Mitzi was brought in and Julia poured her a glass of sherry.

"Here's to the best cook in the world," said Patrick raising his glass.

Mitzi was gratified—but felt nevertheless that a protest was due.

"That is not so. I am not really a cook. In my country I do intellectual work."

"Then you're wasted," said Patrick. "What's intellectual work compared to a chef-d'oeuvre like Delicious Death?"

"Oo—I say to you I do not like—"

"Never mind what you like, my girl," said Patrick. "That's my name for it and here's to it. Let's all drink to Delicious Death and to hell with the after effects."

III

"Phillipa, my dear, I want to talk to you."

"Yes, Miss Blacklock?"

Phillipa Haymes looked up in slight surprise.

"You're not worrying about anything, are you?"

"Worrying?"

"I've noticed that you've looked worried lately. There isn't anything wrong, is there?"

"Oh, no, Miss Blacklock. What should there be?"

"Well—I wondered. I thought, perhaps, that you and Patrick—"

"Patrick?" Phillipa looked really surprised.

"It's not so, then. Please forgive me if I've been impertinent. But you've been thrown together a lot—and although Patrick is a relation, I don't think he's the type to make a satisfactory husband. Not for some time to come, at all events."

Phillipa's face had frozen into a hard immobility.

"I shan't marry again," she said.

"Oh, yes, you will some day, my child. You're young. But we needn't discuss that. There's no other trouble? You're not worried about—money, for instance?"

"No, I'm quite all right."

"I know you get anxious sometimes about your boy's education. That's why I want to tell you something. I drove into Milchester this afternoon to see Mr. Beddingfeld, my lawyer. Things haven't been very settled lately and I thought I would like to make a new will—in view of certain eventualities. Apart from Bunny's legacy, everything goes to you, Phillipa."

"What?" Phillipa spun round. Her eyes stared. She looked dismayed, almost frightened.

"But I don't want it—really, I don't . . . Oh I'd rather not . . . And, anyway, why? Why to me?"

"Perhaps," said Miss Blacklock in a peculiar voice, "because there's no one else."

"But there's Patrick and Julia."

"Yes, there's Patrick and Julia." The odd note in Miss Blacklock's voice was still there.

"They are your relations."

"Very distant ones. They have no claim on me."

"But I—I haven't either—I don't know what you think—Oh, I don't want it."

Her gaze held more hostility than gratitude. There was something almost like fear in her manner.

"I know what I'm doing, Phillipa. I've become fond of you—and there's the boy . . . You won't get very much if I should die now—but in a few weeks' time it might be different."

Her eyes met Phillipa's steadily.

"But you're not going to die!" Phillipa protested.

"Not if I can avoid it by taking due precautions."

"Precautions?"

"Yes. Think it over . . . And don't worry any more."

She left the room abruptly. Phillipa heard her speaking to Julia in the hall.

Julia entered the drawing-room a few moments later.

There was a slightly steely glitter in her eyes.

"Played your cards rather well, haven't you, Phillipa? I see you're one of those quiet ones . . . a dark horse . . ."

"So you heard—"

"Yes, I heard. I rather think I was meant to hear."

"What do you mean?"

"Our Letty's no fool . . . Well, anyway, you're all right, Phillipa. Sitting pretty, aren't you?"

"Oh, Julia—I didn't mean—I never meant—"

"Didn't you? Of course you did. You're fairly up against things, aren't you? Hard up for money. But just remember this—if anyone bumps off Aunt Letty now, you'll be suspect Number 1."

"But I shan't be. It would be idiotic if I killed her now when—if I waited—"

"So you know about old Mrs. What's-her-name dying up in Scotland? I wondered . . . Phillipa, I'm beginning to believe you're a very dark horse indeed."

"I don't want to do you and Patrick out of anything."

"Don't you, my dear? I'm sorry—but I don't believe you."

16

Inspector Craddock Returns

Inspector Craddock had had a bad night on his journey home. His dreams had been less dreams than nightmares. Again and again he was racing through the gray corridors of an old-world castle in a desperate attempt to get somewhere, or to prevent something, in time. Finally, he dreamt that he awoke. An enormous relief surged over him. Then the door of his compartment slid slowly open, and Letitia Blacklock looked in at him with blood running down her face, and said reproachfully: "Why didn't you save me? You could have if you'd tried."

This time he really awoke.

Altogether, the Inspector was thankful finally to reach Milchester. He went straight away to make his report to Rydesdale who listened carefully.

"It doesn't take us much further," he said. "But it confirms what Miss Blacklock told you. Pip and Emma—hm, I wonder."

"Patrick and Julia Simmons are the right age, sir. If we could establish that Miss Blacklock hadn't seen them since they were children—"

With a very faint chuckle, Rydesdale said: "Our ally, Miss Marple, has established that for us. Actually, Miss Blacklock had never seen either of them at all until two months ago."

"Then surely, sir—"

"It's not so easy as all that, Craddock. We've been checking up. On what we've got, Patrick and Julia seem definitely to be out of it. His Naval record is genuine—quite a good record barring a tendency to 'insubordination.' We've checked with Cannes, and an indignant

Mrs. Simmons says of course her son and daughter are at Chipping Cleghorn with her cousin Letitia Blacklock. So that's that!"

"And Mrs. Simmons *is* Mrs. Simmons?"

"She's been Mrs. Simmons for a very long time, that's all I can say," said Rydesdale dryly.

"That seems clear enough. Only—those two fitted. Right age. Not known to Miss Blacklock personally. If we wanted a Pip and Emma—well, there they were."

The Chief Constable nodded thoughtfully, then he pushed a paper across to Craddock.

"Here's a little something we've dug up on Mrs. Easterbrook."

The Inspector read with lifted eyebrows.

"Very interesting," he remarked. "Hoodwinked that old ass pretty well, hasn't she? It doesn't tie in with this business though, as far as I can see."

"Apparently not."

"And here's an item that concerns Mrs. Haymes."

Again Craddock's eyebrows rose.

"I think I'll have to have another talk with the lady," he said.

"You think this information might be relevant?"

"I think it might be. It would be a long shot, of course . . ."

The two men were silent for a moment or two.

"How has Fletcher got on, sir?"

"Fletcher has been exceedingly active. He's made a routine search of the house by agreement with Miss Blacklock—but he didn't find anything significant. Then he's been checking up on who could have had the opportunity of oiling that door. Checking who was up at the house on the days that that foreign girl was out. A little more complicated than we thought, because it appears she goes for a walk most afternoons. Usually down to the village where she has a cup of coffee at the Bluebird. So that when Miss Blacklock and Miss Bunner are out—which is most afternoons—they go blackberrying—the coast is clear."

"And the doors are always left unlocked?"

"They used to be. I don't suppose they are now."

"What are Fletcher's results? Who's known to have been in the house when it was left empty?"

"Practically the whole lot of them."

Rydesdale consulted a page in front of him.

"Miss Murgatroyd was there with a hen to sit on some eggs. (Sounds complicated but that's what she says.) Very flustered about it all and contradicts herself, but Fletcher thinks that's temperamental and not a sign of guilt."

"Might be," Craddock admitted. "She flaps."

"Then Mrs. Swettenham came up to fetch some horse meat that Miss Blacklock had left for her on the kitchen table because Miss Blacklock had been in to Milchester in the car that day and always gets Mrs. Swettenham's horse meat for her. That make sense to you?"

Craddock considered.

"Why didn't Miss Blacklock leave the horse meat when she passed Mrs. Swettenham's house on her way back from Milchester?"

"I don't know, but she didn't. Mrs. Swettenham says she (Miss B.) always leaves it on the kitchen table, and she (Mrs. S.) likes to fetch it when Mitzi isn't there because Mitzi is sometimes so rude."

"Hangs together quite well. And the next?"

"Miss Hinchliffe. Says she wasn't there at all lately. But she was. Because Mitzi saw her coming out of the side door one day and so did a Mrs. Butt (she's one of the locals). Miss H. then admitted she might have been there but had forgotten. Can't remember what she went for. Says she probably just dropped in."

"That's rather odd."

"So was her manner, apparently. Then there's Mrs. Easterbrook. She was exercising the dear dogs out that way and she just popped in to see if Miss Blacklock would lend her a knitting pattern but Miss Blacklock wasn't in. She says she waited a little."

"Just so. Might be snooping round. Or might be oiling a door. And the colonel?"

"Went there one day with a book on India that Miss Blacklock had expressed a desire to read."

"Had she?"

"Her account is that she tried to get out of having to read it, but it was no use."

"And that's fair enough," sighed Craddock. "If anyone is really determined to lend you a book, you never can get out of it!"

"We don't know if Edmund Swettenham was up there. He's extremely vague. Said he did drop in occasionally on errands for his mother, but thinks not lately."

"In fact, it's all inconclusive."

"Yes."

Rydesdale said, with a slight grin:

"Miss Marple has also been active. Fletcher reports she had morning coffee at the Bluebird. She's been to sherry at Boulders and to tea at Little Paddocks. She's admired Mrs. Swettenham's garden—and dropped in to see Colonel Easterbrook's Indian curios."

"She may be able to tell us if Colonel Easterbrook's a pukka colonel or not."

"She'd know, I agree—he seems all right. We'd have to check with the Far East authorities to get certain identification."

"And in the meantime—" Craddock broke off. "Do you think Miss Blacklock would consent to go away?"

"Go away from Chipping Cleghorn?"

"Yes. Take the faithful Bunner with her, perhaps, and leave for an unknown destination. Why shouldn't she go up to Scotland and stay with Belle Goedler? It's a pretty unforgettable place."

"Stop there and wait for her to die? I don't think she'd do that. I don't think any nice-natured woman would like that suggestion."

"If it's a matter of saving her life—"

"Come now, Craddock, it isn't quite so easy to bump someone off as you seem to think."

"Isn't it, sir?"

"Well—in one way—it's easy enough, I agree. Plenty of methods. Weed-killer. A bash on the head when she's out shutting up the poultry, a pot shot from behind a hedge. All quite simple. But to bump someone off and not be suspected of bumping them off—that's not quite so easy. And they must realize by now that they're all under observation. The original carefully planned scheme failed. Our unknown murderer has got to think up something else."

"I know that, sir. But there's the time element to consider. Mrs. Goedler's a dying woman—she might pop off any minute. That means that our murderer can't afford to wait."

"True."

"And another thing, sir. He—or she—must know that we're checking up on everybody."

"And that takes time," said Rydesdale with a sigh. "It means checking with the East, with India. Yes, it's a long, tedious business."

"So that's another reason for—hurry. I'm sure, sir, that the danger is very real. It's a very large sum that's at stake. If Belle Goedler dies—"

He broke off as a constable entered.

"Constable Legg on the line from Chipping Cleghorn, sir."

"Put him through here."

Inspector Craddock, watching the Chief Constable, saw his features harden and stiffen.

"Very good," barked Rydesdale. "Detective Inspector Craddock will be coming out immediately."

He put the receiver down.

"Is it—" Craddock broke off.

Rydesdale shook his head.

"No," he said. "It's Dora Bunner. She wanted some aspirin. Apparently she took some from a bottle beside Letitia Blacklock's bed. There were only a few tablets left in the bottle. She took two and left one. The doctor's got that one and is sending it to be analyzed. He says it's definitely not aspirin."

"She's dead?"

"Yes, found dead in her bed this morning. Died in her sleep. Doctor says he doesn't think it was natural, though her health was in a bad state. Narcotic poisoning, that's his guess. Autopsy's fixed for to-night."

"Aspirin tablets by Letitia Blacklock's bed. The clever, clever devil. Patrick told me Miss Blacklock threw away a half bottle of sherry—opened a new one. I don't suppose she'd have thought of doing that with an open bottle of aspirin. Who had been in the house this time—within the last day or two? The tablets can't have been there long."

Rydesdale looked at him.

"All our lot were there yesterday," he said. "Birthday party for Miss Bunner. Any of them could have nipped upstairs and done a neat little substitution. Or, of course, anyone living in the house could have done it any time."

17

The Album

Standing by the vicarage gate, well wrapped up, Miss Marple took the note from Bunch's hand.

"Tell Miss Blacklock," said Bunch, "that Julian is terribly sorry he can't come up himself. He's got a parishioner dying out at Locke Hamlet. He'll come up after lunch if Miss Blacklock would like to see him. The note's about the arrangements for the funeral. He suggests Wednesday if the inquest's on Tuesday. Poor old Bunny. It's so typical of her, somehow, to get hold of poisoned aspirin meant for someone else. Good-by, darling. I hope the walk won't be too much for you. But I've simply got to get the child to hospital at once."

Miss Marple said the walk wouldn't be too much for her, and Bunch rushed off.

Whilst waiting for Miss Blacklock, Miss Marple looked round the drawing-room, and wondered just exactly what Dora Bunner had meant that morning in the Bluebird by saying that she believed Patrick had "tampered with the lamp" to "make the lights go out." What lamp? And how had he "tampered" with it?

She must, Miss Marple decided, have meant the small lamp that stood on the table by the archway. She had said something about a shepherdess or a shepherd—and this was actually a delicate piece of Dresden china, a shepherd in a blue coat and pink breeches, holding what had originally been a candlestick and had now been adapted to electricity. The shade was of plain vellum and a little too big so that it almost masked the figure. What else was it that Dora Bunner had said? "I remember distinctly that it was the shepherdess. And the next day—" Certainly it was a shepherd now.

Miss Marple remembered that when she and Bunch had come to tea, Dora Bunner had said something about the lamp being one of a pair. Of course—a shepherd and a shepherdess. And it had been the shepherdess on the day of the holdup—and the next morning it had been the other lamp—the lamp that was here now, the shepherd. The lamps had been changed over during the night. And Dora Bunner had had reason to believe (or had believed without reason) that it was Patrick who had changed them.

Why? Because, if the original lamp were examined, it would show just how Patrick had managed to "make the lights go out." How had he managed? Miss Marple looked earnestly at the lamp in front of her. The cord ran along the table over the edge and was plugged into the wall. There was a small pear-shaped switch halfway along the cord. None of it suggested anything to Miss Marple because she knew very little about electricity.

Where was the shepherdess lamp, she wondered. In the "spare room" or thrown away, or—where was it Dora Bunner had come upon Patrick Simmons with a feather and an oily cup? In the shrubbery? Miss Marple made up her mind to put all these points to Inspector Craddock.

At the very beginning Miss Blacklock had leaped to the conclusion that her nephew Patrick had been behind the insertion of that advertisement. That kind of instinctive belief was often justified, or so Miss Marple believed. Because, if you knew people fairly well, you knew the kind of things they thought of . . .

Patrick Simmons . . .

A handsome young man. An engaging young man. A young man whom women liked, both young women and old women. The kind of man, perhaps, that Randall Goedler's sister had married. Could Patrick Simmons be Pip? But he'd been in the Navy during the war. The police could soon check up on that.

Only—sometimes—the most amazing impersonations did happen. You could get away with a great deal if you had enough audacity . . .

The door opened and Miss Blacklock came in. She looked, Miss Marple thought, many years older. All the life and energy had gone out of her.

"I'm very sorry, disturbing you like this," said Miss Marple. "But the vicar had a dying parishioner and Bunch had to rush a sick child to hospital. The vicar wrote you a note."

She held it out and Miss Blacklock took it and opened it.

"Do sit down, Miss Marple," she said. "It's very kind of you to have brought this."

She read the note through.

"The vicar's a very understanding man," she said quietly. "He doesn't offer one fatuous consolations . . . Tell him that these arrangements will do very well. Her—her favorite hymn was *Lead, Kindly Light*."

Her voice broke suddenly.

Miss Marple said gently:

"I am only a stranger, but I am so very, very sorry."

And suddenly, uncontrollably, Letitia Blacklock wept. It was a piteous, overmastering grief, with a kind of hopelessness about it. Miss Marple sat quite still.

Miss Blacklock sat up at last. Her face was swollen and blotched with tears.

"I'm sorry," she said. "It—it just came over me. What I've lost. She—she was the only link with the past, you see. The only one who—who remembered. Now that she's gone I'm quite alone."

"I know what you mean," said Miss Marple. "One is alone when the last one who remembers is gone. I have nephews and nieces and kind friends—but there's no one who knew me as a young girl—no one who belongs to the old days. I've been alone for quite a long time now."

Both women sat silent for some moments.

"You understand very well," said Letitia Blacklock. She rose and went over to her desk. "I must write a few words to the vicar." She held the pen rather awkwardly and wrote slowly.

"Arthritic," she explained. "Sometimes I can hardly write at all."

She sealed up the envelope and addressed it.

"If you wouldn't mind taking it, it would be very kind."

Hearing a man's voice in the hall, she said quickly:

"That's Inspector Craddock."

She went to the mirror over the fireplace and applied a small powder puff to her face.

Craddock came in with a grim angry face.

He looked at Miss Marple with disapprobation.

"Oh," he said. "So you're here."

Miss Blacklock turned from the mantelpiece.

"Miss Marple kindly came up with a note from the vicar."

Miss Marple said in a flurried manner:

"I am going at once—at once. Please don't let me hamper you in any way."

"Were you at the tea party here yesterday afternoon?"

Miss Marple said, nervously:

"No—no, I wasn't. Bunch drove me over to call on some friends."

"Then there's nothing you can tell me." Craddock held the door open in a pointed manner, and Miss Marple scuttled out in a somewhat abashed fashion.

"Nosy Parkers, these old women," said Craddock.

"I think you're being unfair to her," said Miss Blacklock. "She really did come with a note from the vicar."

"I bet she did."

"I don't think it was idle curiosity."

"Well, perhaps you're right, Miss Blacklock, but my own diagnosis would be a severe attack of Nosy Parkeritis . . ."

"She's a very harmless old creature," said Miss Blacklock.

Dangerous as a rattlesnake if you only knew, the Inspector thought grimly. But he had no intention of taking anyone into his confidence unnecessarily. Now that he knew definitely there was a killer at large, he felt that the less said the better. He didn't want the next person bumped off to be Jane Marple.

Somewhere—a killer . . . Where?

"I won't waste time offering sympathy, Miss Blacklock," he said. "As a matter of fact, I feel pretty bad about Miss Bunner's death. We ought to have been able to prevent it."

"I don't see what you could have done."

"No—well, it wouldn't have been easy. But now we've got to work fast. Who's doing this, Miss Blacklock? Who's had two shots at killing you, and will probably, if we don't work fast enough, soon have another?"

Letitia Blacklock shivered. "I don't know, Inspector—I don't know at all!"

"I've checked up with Mrs. Goedler. She's given me all the help she can. It wasn't very much. There are just a few people who would definitely profit by your death. First: Pip and Emma. Patrick and Julia Simmons are the right age, but their background seems clear enough.

Anyway, we can't concentrate on those two alone. Tell me, Miss Black-lock, would you recognize Sonia Goedler if you saw her?"

"Recognize Sonia? Why, of course—" She stopped suddenly. "No," she said slowly, "I don't know that I would. It's a long time. Thirty years . . . She'd be an elderly woman now."

"What was she like as you remember her?"

"Sonia?" Miss Blacklock considered for some moments. "She was rather small, dark . . ."

"Any special peculiarities? Mannerisms?"

"No—no, I don't think so. She was gay—very gay."

"She mayn't be so gay now," said the Inspector. "Have you got a photograph of her?"

"Of Sonia? Let me see—not a proper photograph. I've got some old snapshots—in an album somewhere—at least I think there's one of her."

"Ah. Can I have a look at it?"

"Yes, of course. Now where did I put that album?"

"Tell me, Miss Blacklock, do you consider it remotely possible that Mrs. Swettenham might be Sonia Goedler?"

"Mrs. Swettenham?" Miss Blacklock looked at him in lively astonishment. "But her husband was in the Government Service—in India first, I think, and then in Hong Kong."

"What you mean is, that that's the story she's told you. You don't, as we say in the Courts, know it of your own knowledge, do you?"

"No," said Miss Blacklock slowly. "When you put it like that, I don't . . . But Mrs. Swettenham? Oh, it's absurd!"

"Did Sonia Goedler ever do any acting? Amateur theatricals?"

"Oh, yes. She was good."

"There you are! Another thing, Mrs. Swettenham wears a wig. At least," the Inspector corrected himself, "Mrs. Harmon says she does."

"Yes—yes, I suppose it might be a wig. All those little gray curls. But I still think it's absurd. She's really very nice and exceedingly funny sometimes."

"Then there's Miss Hinchliffe and Miss Murgatroyd. Could either of them be Sonia Goedler?"

"Miss Hinchliffe is too tall. She's as tall as a man."

"Miss Murgatroyd then?"

"Oh, but—oh, no, I'm sure Miss Murgatroyd couldn't be Sonia."

"You don't see very well, do you, Miss Blacklock?"

"I'm nearsighted; is that what you mean?"

"Yes. What I'd like to see is a snapshot of this Sonia Goedler, even if it's a long time ago and not a good likeness. We're trained, you know, to pick out resemblances, in a way no amateur can ever do."

"I'll try and find it for you."

"Now?"

"What, at once?"

"I'd prefer it."

"Very well. Now, let me see. I saw that album when we were tidying a lot of books out of the cupboard. Julia was helping me. She laughed, I remember, at the clothes we used to wear in those days . . . The books we put in the shelf in the drawing-room. Where did we put the albums and the big bound volumes of the *Art Journal*? What a wretched memory I have! Perhaps Julia will remember. She's at home today."

"I'll find her."

The Inspector departed on his quest. He did not find Julia in any of the downstairs rooms. Mitzi, asked where Miss Simmons was, said crossly that it was not her affair.

"Me! I stay in my kitchen and concern myself with the lunch. And nothing do I eat that I have not cooked myself. Nothing, do you hear?"

The Inspector called up the stairs "Miss Simmons," and getting no response, went up.

He met Julia face to face just as he turned the corner of the landing. She had just emerged from a door that showed behind it a small twisty staircase.

"I was up in the attic," she explained. "What is it?"

Inspector Craddock explained.

"Those old photograph albums? Yes, I remember them quite well. We put them in the big cupboard in the study, I think. I'll find them for you."

She led the way downstairs and pushed open the study door. Near the window there was a large cupboard. Julia pulled it open and disclosed a heterogeneous mass of objects.

"Junk," said Julia. "All junk. But elderly people simply will not throw things away."

The Inspector knelt down and took a couple of old-fashioned albums from the bottom shelf.

"Are these they?"

"Yes."

Miss Blacklock came in and joined them.

"Oh, so that's where we put them. I couldn't remember."

Craddock had the books on the table and was turning the pages.

Women in large cartwheel hats, women with dresses tapering down to their feet so that they could hardly walk. The photos had captions neatly printed underneath them, but the ink was old and faded.

"It would be in this one," said Miss Blacklock. "On about the second or third page. The other book is after Sonia had married and gone away." She turned a page. "It ought to be here." She stopped.

There were several empty spaces on the page. Craddock bent down and deciphered the faded writing: "Sonia . . . Self . . . R.G." A little further along, "Sonia and Belle on beach." And again on the opposite page, "Picnic at Skeyne." He turned over another page: "Charlotte, Self, Sonia. R.G."

Craddock stood up. His lips were grim.

"Somebody has removed these photographs—not long ago, I should say."

"There weren't any blank spaces when we looked at them the other day. Were there, Julia?"

"I didn't look very closely—only at some of the dresses. But no, you're right, Aunty Letty, there weren't any blank spaces."

Craddock looked grimmer still.

"Somebody," he said, "has removed every photo of Sonia Goedler from this album."

18

The Letters

"Sorry to worry you again, Mrs. Haymes."

"It doesn't matter," said Phillipa coldly.

"Shall we go into this room here?"

"The study? Yes, if you like, Inspector. It's very cold. There's no fire."

"It doesn't matter. It's not for long. And we're not so likely to be overheard here."

"Does that matter?"

"Not to me, Mrs. Haymes. It might to you."

"What do you mean?"

"I think you told me, Mrs. Haymes, that your husband was killed fighting in Italy?"

"Well?"

"Wouldn't it have been simpler to have told me the truth—that he was a deserter from his regiment."

He saw her face grow white, and her hands close and unclose themselves.

She said bitterly:

"Do you have to rake up everything?"

Craddock said dryly:

"We expect people to tell us the truth about themselves."

She was silent. Then she said:

"Well?"

"What do you mean by 'Well,' Mrs. Haymes?"

"I mean, what are you going to do about it? Tell everybody? Is that necessary—or fair—or kind?"

284

"Does nobody know?"

"Nobody here. Harry—" Her voice changed. "My son, he doesn't know. I don't want him to know. I don't want him to know—ever."

"Then let me tell you that you're taking a very big risk, Mrs. Haymes. When the boy is old enough to understand, tell him the truth. If he finds out by himself some day—it won't be good for him. If you go on stuffing him up with tales of his father dying like a hero—"

"I don't do that. I'm not completely dishonest. I just don't talk about it. His father was—killed in the war. After all, that's what it amounts to—for us."

"But your husband is still alive?"

"Perhaps. How should I know?"

"When did you see him last, Mrs. Haymes?"

Phillipa said quickly:

"I haven't seen him for years."

"Are you quite sure that's true? You didn't, for instance, see him about a fortnight ago?"

"What are you suggesting?"

"It never seemed to me very likely that you met Rudi Scherz in the summer-house here. But Mitzi's story was very emphatic. I suggest, Mrs. Haymes, that the man you came back from work to meet that morning was your husband."

"I didn't meet anybody in the summer-house."

"He was hard up for money, perhaps, and you supplied him with some?"

"I've not seen him, I tell you. I didn't meet anybody in the summer-house."

"Deserters are often rather desperate men. They often take part in robberies, you know. Holdups. Things of that kind. And they have foreign revolvers very often that they've brought back from abroad."

"I don't know where my husband is. I haven't seen him for years."

"Is that your last word, Mrs. Haymes?"

"I've nothing else to say."

II

Craddock came away from his interview with Phillipa Haymes feeling angry and baffled.

"Obstinate as a mule," he said to himself angrily.

He was fairly sure that Phillipa was lying, but he hadn't succeeded in breaking down her obstinate denials.

He wished he knew a little more about ex-Captain Haymes. His information was meager. An unsatisfactory Army record, but nothing to suggest that Haymes was likely to turn criminal.

And, anyway, Haymes didn't fit in with the oiled door.

Someone in the house had done that, or someone with easy access to it.

He stood looking up the staircase, and suddenly he wondered what Julia had been doing up in the attic. An attic, he thought, was an unlikely place for the fastidious Julia to visit.

What had she been doing up there?

He ran lightly up to the first floor. There was no one about. He opened the door out of which Julia had come and went up the narrow stairs to the attic.

There were trunks there, old suitcases, various broken articles of furniture, a chair with a leg off, a broken china lamp, part of an old dinner service.

He turned to the trunks and opened the lid of one.

Clothes. Old-fashioned, quite good quality women's clothes. Clothes belonging, he supposed, to Miss Blacklock, or to her sister who had died.

He opened another trunk.

Curtains.

He passed to a small attache case. It had papers in it and letters. Very old letters, yellowed with time.

He looked at the outside of the case which had the initials CLB on it. He deduced correctly that it had belonged to Letitia's sister Charlotte. He unfolded one of the letters. It began, *Dearest Charlotte: Yesterday Belle felt well enough to go for a picnic. R.G. also took a day off. The Asvogel flotation has gone splendidly; R.G. is terribly pleased about it. The preference shares are at a premium.*

He skipped the rest and looked at the signature:

Your loving sister Letitia.

He picked up another.

Darling Charlotte: I wish you would sometimes make up your mind to see people. You do exaggerate, you know. It isn't nearly as bad as you think. And people really don't mind things like that. It's not the disfigurement you think it is.

He nodded his head. He remembered Belle Goedler saying that

Charlotte Blacklock had a disfigurement or deformity of some kind. Letitia had, in the end, resigned her job to go and look after her sister. These letters all breathed the anxious spirit of her affection and love for an invalid. She had written her sister, apparently, long accounts of everyday happenings, of any little detail that she thought might interest the sick girl. And Charlotte had kept these letters. Occasionally odd snapshots had been enclosed.

Excitement suddenly flooded Craddock's mind. Here, it might be, he would find a clue. In these letters there would be written down things that Letitia Blacklock herself had long forgotten. Here was a faithful picture of the past and somewhere amongst it there might be a clue that would help him to identify the unknown. Photographs, too. There might, just possibly, be a photograph of Sonia Goedler here that the person who had taken the other photos out of the album did not know about.

Inspector Craddock packed the letters up again carefully, closed the case and started down the stairs.

Letitia Blacklock, standing on the landing below, looked at him in amazement.

"Was that you up in the attic? I heard footsteps. I couldn't imagine who—"

"Miss Blacklock, I have found some letters here, written by you to your sister Charlotte many years ago. Will you allow me to take them away and read them?"

She flushed angrily.

"Must you do a thing like that? Why? What good can they be to you?"

"They might give me a picture of Sonia Goedler, of her character—there may be some allusion—some incident—that will help."

"They are private letters, Inspector."

"I know."

"I suppose you will take them anyway . . . You have the power to do so, I suppose, or you can easily get it. Take them—take them! But you'll find very little about Sonia. She married and went away only a year or two after I began to work for Randall Goedler."

Craddock said obstinately:

"There may be something." He added, "We've got to try everything. I assure you the danger is very real."

She said, biting her lips:

"I know. Bunny is dead—from taking an aspirin tablet that was meant for me. It may be Patrick, or Julia, or Phillipa or Mitzi next—somebody young with their life in front of them. Somebody who drinks a glass of wine that is poured out for me, or eats a chocolate that is sent to me. Oh, take the letters—take them away. And afterwards burn them. They don't mean anything to anyone but me and Charlotte. It's all over—gone—past. Nobody remembers now. . . ."

Her hand went up to the choker of false pearls she was wearing. Craddock thought how incongruous it looked with her tweed coat and skirt.

She said again:

"Take the letters."

III

It was the following afternoon that the Inspector called at the vicarage.

It was a dark gusty day.

Miss Marple had her chair pulled close to the fire and was knitting. Bunch was on hands and knees, crawling about the floor, cutting out material to a pattern.

She sat back and pushed a mop of hair out of her eyes, looking up expectantly at Craddock.

"I don't know if it's a breach of confidence," said the Inspector, addressing himself to Miss Marple, "but I'd like you to look at this letter."

He explained the circumstances of his discovery in the attic.

"It's rather a touching collection of letters," he said. "Miss Blacklock poured out everything in the hopes of sustaining her sister's interest in life and keeping her health good. There's a very clear picture of an old father in the background—old Dr. Blacklock. A real old pigheaded bully, absolutely set in his ways, and convinced that everything he thought and said was right. Probably killed thousands of patients through obstinacy. He wouldn't stand for any new ideas or methods."

"I don't really know that I blame him there," said Miss Marple. "I always feel that the young doctors are only too anxious to experiment. After they've whipped out all our teeth, and administered quantities of very peculiar glands, and removed bits of our insides, they then confess that nothing can be done for us. I really prefer the old-fashioned remedy of big black bottles of medicine. After all, one can always pour those down the sink."

She took the letter that Craddock handed her.

He said:

"I want you to read it because I think that that generation is more easily understood by you than by me. I don't know really quite how these people's minds worked."

Miss Marple unfolded the fragile paper.

Dearest Charlotte,

I've not written for two days because we've been having the most terrible domestic complications. Randall's sister Sonia—(you remember her? She came to take you out in the car that day? How I wish you would go out more)—Sonia has declared her intention of marrying one Dmitri Stamfordis. I've only seen him once. Very attractive—not to be trusted, I should say. R.G. raves against him and says he is a crook and a swindler. Belle, bless her, just smiles and lies on her sofa. Sonia, who though she looks so impassive has really a terrific temper, is simply wild with R.G. I really thought yesterday she was going to murder him!

I've done my best. I've talked to Sonia and I've talked to R.G. and I've got them both into a more reasonable frame of mind and then they come together and it all starts over again! You've no idea how *tiring* it is. R.G. has been making enquiries—and it does really seem as though this Stamfordis man is thoroughly undesirable.

In the meantime, business is being neglected. I carry on at the office and in a way it's rather fun because R.G. gives me a free hand. He said to me yesterday: "Thank heaven, there's one sane person in the world. You're never likely to fall in love with a crook, Blackie, are you?" I said I didn't think I was likely to fall in love with anybody. R.G. said: "Let's start a few new hares in the city." He's really rather a mischievous devil sometimes and he sails terribly near the wind. "You're quite determined to keep me on the straight and narrow path, aren't you, Blackie?" he said the other day. And I shall, too! I can't understand how people can't *see* when a thing's dishonest—but R.G. really and truly *doesn't*. He only knows what is actually against the law.

Belle only laughs at all this. She thinks the fuss about Sonia is all nonsense. "Sonia has her own money," she said. "Why shouldn't she marry this man if she wants to?" I said it might turn out to be a terrible mistake and Belle said, "It's never a mistake to marry a man you want to marry—even if you regret it." And then she said, "I suppose Sonia doesn't want to break with Randall because of money. Sonia's very fond of money."

No more now. How is Father? I won't say give him my love. But you can if you think it's better to do so. Have you seen more people? You really must not be morbid, darling.

Sonia asks to be remembered to you. She has just come in and is closing and unclosing her hands like an angry cat sharpening its claws. I think she and R.G. have had another row. Of course Sonia can be very irritating. She stares you down with that cool stare of hers.

Lots of love, darling, and buck up. This iodine treatment may make a lot of difference. I've been enquiring about it and it really does seem to have good results.

Your loving sister,
Letitia

Miss Marple folded the letter and handed it back. She looked abstracted.

"Well, what you think about her?" Craddock urged. "What picture do you get of her?"

"Of Sonia? It's difficult, you know, to see anyone through another person's mind . . . Determined to get her own way—that, definitely, I think. And wanting the best of two worlds . . ."

"Closing and unclosing her hands like an angry cat," murmured Craddock. "You know, that reminds me of someone . . ."

He frowned.

"Making enquiries . . ." murmured Miss Marple.

"If we could get hold of the result of those enquiries—" said Craddock.

"Does that letter remind you of anything in St. Mary Mead?" asked Bunch, rather indistinctly since her mouth was full of pins.

"I really can't say it does, dear . . . Dr. Blacklock was, perhaps, a little like Mr. Curtiss the Wesleyan minister. He wouldn't let his child wear a plate on her teeth. Said it was the Lord's will if her teeth stuck out. 'After all,' I said to him, 'you do trim your beard and cut your hair. It might be the Lord's will that your hair should grow out.' He said that was quite different. So like a man. But that doesn't help us with our present problem."

"We've never traced that revolver, you know. It wasn't Rudi Scherz's. If I knew who had had a revolver in Chipping Cleghorn."

"Colonel Easterbrook has one," said Bunch. "He keeps it in his collar drawer."

"How do you know, Mrs. Harmon?"

"Mrs. Butt told me. She's my daily. Or rather, my twice weekly. Being a military gentleman, she said, he'd naturally have a revolver and very handy it would be if burglars were to come along."

"When did she tell you this?"

"Ages ago. About six months ago, I should think."

"Colonel Easterbrook?" murmured Craddock.

"It's like those pointer things at fairs, isn't it?" said Bunch, still speaking through a mouthful of pins. "Go round and round and stop at something different every time."

"You're telling me!" said Craddock and groaned.

"Colonel Easterbrook was up at Little Paddocks to leave a book there one day. He could have oiled that door then. He was quite straightforward about being there, though. Not like Miss Hinchliffe."

Miss Marple coughed gently.

"You must make allowances for the times we live in, Inspector," she said. Craddock looked at her uncomprehendingly.

"After all," said Miss Marple, "you *are* the police, aren't you? People can't say everything they'd like to say to the police, can they?"

"I don't see why not," said Craddock. "Unless they've got some criminal matter to conceal."

"She means butter," said Bunch, crawling actively round a table leg to anchor a floating bit of paper. "Butter and corn for hens and sometimes cream—and sometimes even a side of bacon."

"Show him that note from Miss Blacklock," said Miss Marple. "It's some time ago now, but it reads like a first-class mystery story."

"What have I done with it? Is this the one you mean, Aunt Jane?"

Miss Marple took it and looked at it.

"Yes," she said with satisfaction. "That's the one."

She handed it to the Inspector.

I have made inquiries—Thursday is the day, Miss Blacklock had written. *Any time after three. If there is any for me leave it in the usual place.*

Bunch spat out her pins and laughed. Miss Marple was watching the Inspector's face.

The vicar's wife took upon herself to explain.

"Thursday is the day one of the farms round here makes butter. They let anybody they like have a bit. It's usually Miss Hinchliffe who collects it. She's very much in with all the farmers—because of her pigs, I think. But it's all a bit hush-hush, you know; a kind of local scheme of barter. One person gets butter and sends along cucumbers, or something like that—and a little something when a pig's killed. And now and then an animal has an 'accident' and has to be destroyed. Oh, you know the sort of thing. Only one can't very well say it right out to the police. Because I suppose quite a lot of this barter is illegal—only nobody really knows because it's all so complicated. But I expect Hinch had slipped into Little Paddocks with a pound of butter or something and had put it in the 'usual place.' That's a flour bin under the cupboard, by the way. It doesn't have flour in it."

Craddock sighed.

"I'm glad I came here to you ladies," he said.

"There are clothing coupons, too," said Bunch. "Not usually bought—that's not considered honest. No money passes. But people like Mrs. Butt or Mrs. Finch or Mrs. Huggins like a nice woolen dress or a winter coat that hasn't seen too much wear and they pay for it with coupons instead of money."

"You'd better not tell me any more," said Craddock. "It's all against the law."

"Then there oughtn't to be such silly laws," said Bunch, filling her mouth up with pins again. "I don't do it, of course, because Julian doesn't like me to, so I don't. But I know what's going on, of course."

A kind of despair was coming over the Inspector.

"It all sounds so pleasant and ordinary," he said. "Funny and petty and simple. And yet one woman and a man have been killed, and another woman may be killed before I can get anything definite to go on. I've left off worrying about Pip and Emma for the moment. I'm concentrating on Sonia. I wish I knew what she looked like. There was a snapshot or two in with these letters, but not one that could have been her."

"How do you know it couldn't have been her? Do you know what she looked like?"

"She was small and dark, Miss Blacklock said."

"Really," said Miss Marple, "that's very interesting."

"There was one snap that reminded me vaguely of someone. A

tall fair girl with her hair all done up on top of her head. I don't know who she could have been. Anyway, it can't have been Sonia. Do you think Mrs. Swettenham could have been dark when she was a girl?"

"Not very dark," said Bunch. "She's got blue eyes."

"I hoped there might be a photo of Dmitri Stamfordis—but I suppose that was too much to hope for—Well"—he took up the letter— "I'm sorry this doesn't suggest anything to you, Miss Marple."

"Oh, but it does," said Miss Marple. "It suggests a good deal—Just read it through again, Inspector—especially where it says that Randall Goedler was making inquiries about Dmitri Stamfordis."

Craddock stared at her.

The telephone rang.

Bunch got up from the floor and went out into the hall where, in accordance with the best Victorian traditions, the telephone had originally been placed and where it still was.

She re-entered the room to say to Craddock:

"It's for you."

Slightly surprised, the Inspector went out to the instrument— carefully shutting the door of the living room behind him.

"Craddock? Rydesdale here."

"Yes, sir."

"I've been looking through your report. In the interview you had with Phillipa Haymes I see she states positively that she hasn't seen her husband since his desertion from the Army."

"That's right, sir—she was most emphatic. But in my opinion she wasn't speaking the truth."

"I agree with you. Do you remember a case about ten days ago— man run over by a lorry—taken to Milchester General with concussion and a fractured pelvis?"

"The fellow who snatched a child practically from under the wheels of a lorry, and got run down himself?"

"That's the one. No papers of any kind on him and nobody came forward to identify him. Looked as though he might be on the run. He died last night without regaining consciousness. But he's been identified—deserter from the Army—Ronald Haymes, ex-Captain in the South Loamshires."

"Phillipa Haymes' husband?"

"Yes. He had an old Chipping Cleghorn bus ticket on him, by the way—and quite a reasonable amount of money."

"So he did get money from his wife? I always thought he was the man Mitzi overheard talking to her in the summerhouse. She denied it flatly, of course. But surely, sir, that lorry accident was before—"

Rydesdale took the words out of his mouth.

"Yes, he was taken to Milchester General on the 28th. The holdup at Little Paddocks was on the 29th. That lets him out of any possible connection with it. But his wife, of course, knew nothing about the accident. She may have been thinking all along that he was concerned in it. She'd hold her tongue—naturally—after all he was her husband."

"It was a fairly gallant bit of work, wasn't it, sir?" said Craddock slowly.

"Rescuing that child from the lorry? Yes. Plucky. Don't suppose it was cowardice that made Haymes desert. Well, all that's past history. For a man who'd blotted his copybook, it was a good death."

"I'm glad for her sake," said the Inspector. "And for that boy of theirs."

"Yes, he needn't be too ashamed of his father. And the young woman will be able to marry again now."

Craddock said slowly:

"I was thinking of that, sir . . . It opens up—possibilities."

"You'd better break the news to her since you're on the spot."

"I will, sir. I'll push along there now. Or perhaps I'd better wait until she's back at Little Paddocks. It may be rather a shock—and there's someone else I rather want to have a word with first."

19

Reconstruction of the Crime

"I'll put on a lamp by you before I go," said Bunch. "It's so dark in here. There's going to be a storm, I think."

She lifted the small reading lamp to the other side of the table where it would throw light on Miss Marple's knitting as she sat in a wide high-backed chair.

As the cord pulled across the table, Tiglath-Pileser, the cat, leapt upon it and bit and clawed it violently.

"No, Tiglath-Pileser, you mustn't. He really is awful. Look, he's nearly bitten it through—it's all frayed. Don't you understand, you idiotic puss, that you may get a nasty electric shock if you do that?"

"Thank you, dear," said Miss Marple, and put out a hand to turn on the lamp.

"It doesn't turn on there. You have to press that silly little switch halfway along the cord. Wait a minute. I'll take these flowers out of the way."

She lifted a bowl of Christmas roses across the table. Tiglath-Pileser, his tail switching, put out a mischievous paw and clawed Bunch's arm. She spilled some of the water out of the vase. It fell on the frayed area of cord and on Tiglath-Pileser himself, who leapt to the floor with an indignant hiss.

Miss Marple pressed the small pear-shaped switch. Where the water had soaked the frayed cord there was a flash and a crackle.

"Oh, dear," said Bunch. "It's blown out. Now I suppose all the lights in here are off." She tried them. "Yes, they are. So stupid being all on the same thingamabob. And it's made a burn on the table, too.

295

Naughty Tiglath-Pileser—it's all his fault. Aunt Jane—what's the matter? Did it startle you?"

"It's nothing, dear. Just something I saw quite suddenly which I ought to have seen before. . . ."

"I'll go and fix the fuse and get the lamp from Julian's study."

"No, dear, don't bother. You'll miss your bus. I don't want any more light. I just want to sit quietly and—think about something. Hurry, dear, or you won't catch your bus."

When Bunch had gone, Miss Marple sat quite still for about two minutes. The air of the room was heavy and menacing with the gathering storm outside.

Miss Marple drew a sheet of paper towards her.

She wrote first: *Lamp?* and underlined it heavily.

After a moment or two, she wrote another word.

Her pencil traveled down the paper, making brief monosyllabic notes. . . .

II

In the rather dark living room of Boulders with its low ceiling and latticed windowpanes, Miss Hinchliffe and Miss Murgatroyd were having an argument.

"The trouble with you, Murgatroyd," said Miss Hinchliffe, "is that you won't try."

"But I tell you, Hinch, I can't remember a thing."

"Now look here, Amy Murgatroyd, we're going to do some constructive thinking. So far we haven't shone on the detective angle. I was quite wrong over that door business. You didn't hold the door open for the murderer after all. You're cleared, Murgatroyd!"

Miss Murgatroyd gave a rather watery smile.

"It's just our luck to have the only silent cleaning woman in Chipping Cleghorn," continued Miss Hinchliffe. "Usually I'm thankful for it, but this time it means we've got off to a bad start. Everybody else in the place knows about that second door in the drawing-room being used—and we only heard about it yesterday—"

"I still don't quite understand how—"

"It's perfectly simple. Our original premises were quite right. You can't hold open a door, wave a flashlight and shoot with a revolver all at the same time. We kept in the revolver and the flashlight and cut out the door. Well, we were wrong. It was the revolver we ought to have cut out."

"But he did have a revolver," said Miss Murgatroyd. "I saw it. It was there on the floor beside him."

"When he was dead, yes. It's all quite clear. He didn't fire that revolver—"

"Then who did?"

"That's what we're going to find out. But whoever did it, the same person put a couple of poisoned aspirin tablets by Letty Blacklock's bed—and thereby bumped off poor Dora Bunner. And that couldn't have been Rudi Scherz, because he's as dead as a doornail. It was someone who was in the room that night of the holdup and probably someone who was at the birthday party, too. And the only person that lets out is Mrs. Harmon."

"You think someone put those aspirins there the day of the birthday party?"

"Why not?"

"But how could they?"

"Well, we all went to the lou, didn't we?" said Miss Hinchliffe coarsely. "And I washed my hands in the bathroom because of that sticky cake. And little Sweetie Easterbrook powdered her grubby little face in Blacklock's bathroom, didn't she?"

"Hinch! Do you think she—"

"I don't know yet. Rather obvious, if she did. I don't think, if you were going to plant some tablets, that you'd want to be seen in the bedroom at all. Oh, yes, there were plenty of opportunities."

"The men didn't go upstairs."

"There are back stairs. After all, if a man leaves the room, you don't follow him to see if he really is going where you think he is going. It wouldn't be delicate! Anyway, don't argue, Murgatroyd. I want to get back to the original attempt on Letty Blacklock. Now, to begin with, get the facts firmly into your head, because it's all going to depend upon you."

Miss Murgatroyd looked alarmed.

"Oh, dear, Hinch, you know what a muddle I get into!"

"It's not a question of your brains, or the gray fluff that passes for brains with you. It's a question of eyes. It's a question of what you saw."

"But I didn't see anything."

"The trouble with you is, Murgatroyd, as I said just now, that you

won't try. Now pay attention. This is what happened: Whoever it is
that's got it in for Letty Blacklock was there in that room that evening.
He (I say he because it's easier, but there's no reason why it should be
a man more than a woman except, of course, that men are dirty dogs),
well, he has previously oiled that second door that leads out of the
drawing-room and which is supposed to be nailed up or something.
Don't ask me when he did it, because that confuses things. Actually,
by choosing my time, I could walk into any house in Chipping Cleghorn and do anything I liked there for half an hour or so with no one
being the wiser. It's just a question of working out where the daily
women are and when the occupiers are out and exactly where they've
gone and how long they'll be. Just good staff work. Now to continue:
He's oiled that second door. It will open without a sound. Here's the
setup: Lights go out, door A (the front door) opens with a flourish.
Business with flashlight and holdup lines. In the meantime, while
we're all goggling, X (that's the best terms to use) slips quietly out by
door B into the dark hall, comes up behind that Swiss idiot, takes a
couple of shots at Letty Blacklock and then shoots the Swiss. Drops the
revolver, where lazy thinkers like you will assume it's evidence that
the Swiss did the shooting, and nips back into the room again by the
time that someone gets a lighter going. Got it?"

"Yes—ye-es, but who was it?"

"Well, if you don't know, Murgatroyd, nobody does!"

"Me?" Miss Murgatroyd fairly twittered in alarm. "But I don't
know anything at all. I don't really, Hinch!"

"Use that fluff of yours you call a brain. To begin with, where was
everybody when the lights went out?"

"I don't know."

"Yes, you do. You're maddening, Murgatroyd. You know where
you were, don't you? You were behind the door."

"Yes—yes, I was. It knocked against my corn when it flew open."

"Why don't you go to a proper chiropodist instead of messing
about yourself with your feet? You'll give yourself blood poisoning
one of these days. Come on now—you're behind the door. I'm standing against the mantelpiece with my tongue hanging out for a drink.
Letty Blacklock is by the table near the archway, getting the cigarettes. Patrick Simmons has gone through the archway into the small
room where Letty Blacklock has had the drinks put. Agreed?"

"Yes, yes, I remember all that."

"Good; now somebody else followed Patrick into that room or

was just starting to follow him. One of the men. The annoying thing is that I can't remember whether it was Easterbrook or Edmund Swettenham. Do you remember?"

"No, I don't."

"You wouldn't! And there was someone else who went through to the small room; Phillipa Haymes. I remember that distinctly because I remember noticing what a nice flat back she has, and I thought to myself that girl would look well on a horse. I was watching her and thinking just that. She went over to the mantelpiece in the other room. I don't know what it was she wanted there, because at that moment the lights went out.

"So that's the position. In the far drawing-room are Patrick Simmons, Phillipa Haymes and either Colonel Easterbrook or Edmund Swettenham—we don't know which. Now, Murgatroyd, pay attention. The most probable thing is that it was one of those three who did it. If anyone wanted to get out of that far door, they'd naturally take care to put themselves in a convenient place when the lights went out. So, as I say, in all probability, it's one of those three. And in that case, Murgatroyd, there's not a thing you can do about it!"

Miss Murgatroyd brightened perceptibly.

"On the other hand," continued Miss Hinchliffe, "there's the possibility that it wasn't one of those three. And that's where you come in, Murgatroyd."

"But how should I know anything about it?"

"As I said before, if you don't nobody does."

"But I don't! I really don't! I couldn't see, anything at all!"

"Oh, yes, you could. You're the only person who could see. You were standing behind the door. You couldn't look at the flashlight—because the door was between you and it. You were facing the other way, the same way as the flashlight was pointing. The rest of us were just dazzled. But you weren't dazzled."

"No—no, perhaps not, but I didn't see anything, the flashlight went round and round—"

"Showing you what? It rested on faces, didn't it? And on tables? And on chairs?"

"Yes—yes, it did . . . Miss Bunner, her mouth wide open and her eyes popping out of her head, staring and blinking."

"That's the stuff!" Miss Hinchliffe gave a sigh of relief. "The difficulty there is in making you use that gray fluff of yours! Now then, keep it up."

"But I didn't see any more, I didn't really."

"You mean you saw an empty room? Nobody standing about? Nobody sitting down?"

"No, of course not that. Mrs. Harmon was sitting on the arm of a chair. She had her eyes tight shut and her knuckles all doubled up to her face—like a child."

"Good, that's Mrs. Harmon and Miss Bunner. Don't you see yet what I'm getting at? The difficulty is that I don't want to put ideas into your head. But when we've eliminated who you did see—we can get on to the important point which is, was there anyone you didn't see. Got it? Besides the tables and the chairs and the chrysanthemums and the rest of it, there were certain people: Julia Simmons, Mrs. Swettenham, Mrs. Easterbrook—either Colonel Easterbrook or Edmund Swettenham—Dora Bunner and Bunch Harmon. All right, you saw Bunch Harmon and Dora Bunner. Cross them off. Now think, Murgatroyd, *think*, was there one of those people who definitely *wasn't* there?"

Miss Murgatroyd jumped slightly as a branch knocked against the open window. She shut her eyes. She murmured to herself . . .

"The flowers . . . on the table . . . the big armchair . . . the flashlight didn't come round as far as you, Hinch—Mrs. Harmon, yes. . . ."

The telephone rang sharply. Miss Hinchliffe went to it.

"Hullo, yes? The station?"

The obedient Miss Murgatroyd, her eyes closed, was reliving the night of the 29th. The flashlight sweeping slowly round . . . a group of people . . . the windows . . . the sofa . . . Dora Bunner . . . the wall . . . the table with the lamp . . . the archway . . . the sudden spat of the revolver . . .

". . . but that's extraordinary!" said Miss Murgatroyd.

"What?" Miss Hinchliffe was barking angrily into the telephone. "Been there since this morning? What time? Damn and blast you, and you only ring me up now? I'll set the S.P.C.A. after you. An oversight? Is that all you've got to say?"

She banged down the receiver.

"It's that dog," she said. "The red setter. Been at the station since this morning—since this morning at eight o'clock! Without a drop of water! And the idiots only ring me up now. I'm going to get her right away."

She plunged out of the room, Miss Murgatroyd squeaking shrilly in her wake.

"But listen, Hinch, a most extraordinary thing . . . I don't understand it . . ."

Miss Hinchliffe had dashed out of the door and across to the shed which served as a garage.

"We'll go on with it when I come back," she called. "I can't wait for you to come with me. You've got your bedroom slippers on as usual."

She pressed the starter of the car and backed out of the garage with a jerk. Miss Murgatroyd skipped nimbly sideways.

"But listen, Hinch, I must tell you—"

"When I come back . . ."

The car jerked and shot forwards. Miss Murgatroyd's voice came faintly after it on a high excited note:

"But, Hinch, she wasn't there . . ."

III

Overhead, the clouds had been gathering thick and dark. As Miss Murgatroyd stood looking after the retreating car, the first big drops began to fall.

In an agitated fashion, Miss Murgatroyd plunged across to a line of string on which she had, some hours previously, hung out a couple of jumpers and a pair of woolen combinations to dry.

She was murmuring under her breath:

"Really most extraordinary . . . Oh, dear, I shall never get these down in time . . . and they were nearly dry. . . ."

She struggled with a recalcitrant clothespeg, then turned her head, as she heard someone approaching.

Then she smiled a pleased welcome.

"Hullo—do go inside; you'll get wet."

"Let me help you."

"Oh, if you don't mind . . . so annoying if they all get soaked again. I really ought to let down the line, but I think I can just reach."

"Here's your scarf. Shall I put it round your neck?"

"Oh, thank you . . . Yes, perhaps . . . If I could just reach this peg. . . ."

The woolen scarf was slipped round her neck, and then, suddenly, pulled tight . . .

Miss Murgatroyd's mouth opened, but no sound came except a small choking gurgle.

And the scarf was pulled tighter still . . .

IV

On her way back from the station, Miss Hinchliffe stopped the car to pick up Miss Marple who was hurrying along the street.

"Hullo," she shouted. "You'll get very wet. Come and have tea with us. I saw Bunch waiting for the bus. You'll be all alone at the vicarage. Come and join us. Murgatroyd and I are doing a bit of reconstruction of the crime. I rather think we're just getting somewhere. Mind the dog. She's rather nervous."

"What a beauty."

"Yes, lovely bitch, isn't she? Those fools kept her at the station since this morning without letting me know. I told them off, the lazy devils. Oh! Excuse my language. I was brought up by grooms at home in Ireland."

The little car turned with a jerk into the small back yard of Boulders.

A crowd of eager ducks and fowls encircled the two ladies as they descended.

"Curse Murgatroyd," said Miss Hinchliffe, "she hasn't given 'em their corn."

"Is it difficult to get corn?" Miss Marple inquired.

Miss Hinchliffe winked.

"I'm in with most of the farmers," she said.

Shooing away the hens, she escorted Miss Marple towards the cottage.

"Hope you're not too wet?"

"No, this is a very good mackintosh."

"I'll light the fire if Murgatroyd hasn't lit it. Hiyah, Murgatroyd? Where is the woman? Murgatroyd! Where's that dog? She's disappeared now."

A slow dismal howl came from outside.

"Curse the silly bitch." Miss Hinchliffe tramped to the door and called:

"Hyoup, Cutie—Cutie! Damn silly name but that's what they called her apparently. We must find her another name. Hiyah, Cutie!"

The red setter was sniffing at something lying below the taut line where a row of garments swirled in the wind.

"Murgatroyd's not even had the sense to bring the washing in. Where is she?"

Again the red setter nosed at what seemed to be a pile of clothes, and raised her nose high in the air and howled again.

"What's the matter with the dog?"

Miss Hinchliffe strode across the grass.

And quickly, apprehensively, Miss Marple ran after her. They stood there, side by side, the rain beating down on them and the older woman's arm went round the younger one's shoulders.

She felt the muscles go stiff and taut as Miss Hinchliffe stood looking down on the thing lying there, with the blue congested face and the protruding tongue.

"I'll kill whoever did this," said Miss Hinchliffe in a low quiet voice, "if I once get my hands on her. . . ."

Miss Marple said questioningly:

"Her?"

Miss Hinchliffe turned a ravaged face towards her.

"Yes. I know who it is—near enough . . . that is, it's one of three possibles."

She stood for another moment, looking down at her dead friend, and then turned towards the house. Her voice was dry and hard.

"We must ring up the police," she said. "And while we're waiting for them, I'll tell you. My fault, in a way, that Murgatroyd's lying out there. I made a game of it . . . Murder isn't a game . . ."

"No," said Miss Marple. "Murder isn't a game."

"You know something about it, don't you?" said Miss Hinchliffe as she lifted the receiver and dialed.

She made a brief report and hung up.

"They'll be here in a few minutes . . . Yes, I heard that you'd been mixed up in this sort of business before . . . I think it was Edmund Swettenham told me so . . . Do you want to hear what we were doing, Murgatroyd and I?"

Succinctly she described the conversation held before her departure for the station.

"She called after me, you know, just as I was leaving . . . That's how I know it's a woman and not a man . . . If I'd waited—if I'd only listened! God dammit, the dog could have stopped where she was for another quarter of an hour."

"Don't blame yourself, my dear. That does no good. One can't foresee."

"No, one can't. . . . Something tapped against the window, I remember. Perhaps she was outside there then—yes, of course, she must have been . . . coming to the house . . . and there were Murgatroyd and I shouting at each other. Top of our voices . . . She heard . . . She heard it all . . ."

"You haven't told me yet what your friend said."

"Just one sentence! *'She wasn't there.'* "

She paused. "You see? There were three women we hadn't eliminated. Mrs. Swettenham, Mrs. Easterbrook, Julia Simmons. And one of those three—*wasn't there* . . . She wasn't there in the drawing-room because she had slipped out through the other door and was out in the hall."

"Yes," said Miss Marple, "I see."

"It's one of those three women. I don't know which. But I'll find out!"

"Excuse me," said Miss Marple. "But did she—did Miss Murgatroyd, I mean—say it exactly as you said it?"

"How d'you mean—as I said it?"

"Oh, dear, how can I explain? You said it like this. *She wasn't there.* An equal emphasis on every word. You see, there are three ways you could say it. You could say, *'She* wasn't there.' Very personal. Or again. *'She wasn't* there.' Confirming some suspicion already held. Or else you could say (and this is nearer to the way you said it just now), 'She wasn't *there.'* Quite blankly—with the emphasis, if there was emphasis—on the *there.*"

"I don't know." Miss Hinchliffe shook her head. "I can't remember . . . How the hell can I remember? I think, yes, surely she'd say, *'She* wasn't there.' That would be the natural way, I should think. But I simply don't know. Does it make any difference?"

"Yes," said Miss Marple thoughtfully. "I think so. It's a very *slight* indication, of course, but I think it *is* an indication. Yes, I should think it makes a lot of difference."

20

Miss Marple Is Missing

The postman, rather to his disgust, had lately been given orders to make an afternoon delivery of letters in Chipping Cleghorn as well as a morning one.

On this particular afternoon he left three letters at Little Paddocks at exactly ten minutes to five.

One was addressed to Phillipa Haymes in a schoolboy's hand; the other two were for Miss Blacklock. She opened them as she and Phillipa sat down at the tea table. The torrential rain had enabled Phillipa to leave Dayas Hall early today, since once she had shut up the greenhouses there was nothing more to do.

Miss Blacklock tore open her first letter which was a bill for repairing the kitchen boiler. She snorted angrily.

"Dymond's prices are preposterous—quite preposterous. Still, I suppose all the other people are just as bad."

She opened the second letter which was in a handwriting quite unknown to her.

Dear Cousin Letty (it said),

I hope it will be all right for me to come to you on Tuesday?
I wrote to Patrick two days ago but he hasn't answered. So I
presume it's all right. Mother is coming to England next month
and hopes to see you then.

My train arrives at Chipping Cleghorn at 6:15 if that's convenient?

Yours affectionately,
Julia Simmons

Miss Blacklock read the letter once with astonishment pure and simple, and then again with a certain grimness. She looked up at Phillipa who was smiling over her son's letter.

"Are Julia and Patrick back, do you know?"

Phillipa looked up.

"Yes, they came in just after I did. They went upstairs to change. They were wet."

"Perhaps you'd not mind going and calling them."

"Of course I will."

"Wait a moment—I'd like you to read this."

She handed Phillipa the letter she had received.

Phillipa read it and frowned. "I don't understand . . ."

"Nor do I, quite . . . I think it's about time I did. Call Patrick and Julia, Phillipa."

Phillipa called from the bottom of the stairs:

"Patrick! Julia! Miss Blacklock wants you."

Patrick came running down the stairs and entered the room.

"Don't go, Phillipa," said Miss Blacklock.

"Hullo, Aunt Letty," said Patrick cheerfully. "Want me?"

"Yes, I do. Perhaps you'll give me an explanation of this?"

Patrick's face showed an almost comical dismay as he read.

"I meant to telegraph her! What an ass I am!"

"This letter, I presume, is from your sister Julia?"

"Yes— Yes, it is."

Miss Blacklock said grimly:

"*Then who, may I ask, is the young woman whom you brought here as Julia Simmons*, and whom I was given to understand was your sister and my cousin?"

"Well—you see—Aunt Letty—the fact of the matter is—I can explain it all—I know I oughtn't to have done it—but it really seemed more of a lark than anything else. If you'll just let me explain—"

"I am waiting for you to explain. *Who is this young woman?*"

"Well, I met her at a cocktail party soon after I got demobbed. We got talking and I said I was coming here and then—well, we thought it might be rather a good wheeze if I brought her along . . . You see Julia, the real Julia, was mad to go on the stage and mother had seven fits at the idea—however, Julia got a chance to join a jolly good repertory company up in Perth or somewhere and she thought she'd give it a try—but she thought she'd keep Mum calm by letting Mum think

306

that she was here with me, studying to be a dispenser like a good little girl."

"I still want to know who this other young woman is?"

Patrick turned with relief as Julia, cool and aloof, came into the room.

"The balloon's gone up," he said.

Julia raised her eyebrows. Then, still cool, she came forward and sat down.

"O.K.," she said. "That's that. I suppose you're very angry?" She studied Miss Blacklock's face with almost dispassionate interest. "I should be if I were you."

"Who are you?"

Julia sighed.

"I think the moment's come when I make a clean breast of things. Here we go. I'm one-half of the Pip and Emma combination. To be exact, my christened name is Emma Jocelyn Stamfordis—only father soon dropped the Stamfordis. I think he called himself De Courcy next.

"My father and mother, let me tell you, split up about three years after Pip and I were born. Each of them went their own way. And they split us up. I was father's part of the loot. He was a bad parent on the whole, though quite a charming one. I had various desert spells of being educated in convents—when father hadn't any money, or was preparing to engage in some particularly nefarious deal. He used to pay the first term with every sign of affluence and then depart and leave me on the nuns' hands for a year or two. In the intervals, he and I had some very good times together, moving in cosmopolitan society. However, the war separated us completely. I've no idea of what's happened to him. I had a few adventures myself. I was with the French Resistance for a time. Quite exciting. To cut a long story short, I landed up in London and began to think about my future. I knew that mother's brother, with whom she'd had a frightful row, had died a very rich man. I looked up his will to see if there was anything for me. There wasn't—not directly, that is to say. I made a few inquiries about his widow—it seemed she was quite gaga and kept under drugs and was dying by inches. Frankly, it looked as though *you* were my best bet. You were going to come into a hell of a lot of money and from all I could find out, you didn't seem to have anyone much to spend it on. I'll be quite frank. It occurred to me that if I could get to know you in a friendly kind of way, and if you took a fancy to me—well, after all, conditions have changed a bit, haven't they, since Uncle Randall died? I mean, any money we ever had has been swept away in the cataclysm of Europe. I thought you might pity a poor orphan girl, all alone in the world, and make her, perhaps, a small allowance."

"Oh, you did, did you?" said Miss Blacklock grimly.

"Yes. Of course, I hadn't seen you then . . . I visualized a kind of sob stuff approach. . . . Then, by a marvelous stroke of luck, I met Patrick here—and he turned out to be your nephew or your cousin, or something. Well, that struck me as a marvelous chance. I went bullheaded for Patrick and he fell for me in a most gratifying way. The real Julia was all wet about this acting stuff and I soon persuaded her it was her duty to Art to go and fix herself up in some uncomfortable lodgings in Perth and train to be the new Sarah Bernhardt.

"You mustn't blame Patrick too much. He felt awfully sorry for me, all alone in the world—and he soon thought it would be a really marvelous idea for me to come here as his sister and do my stuff."

"And he also approved of your continuing to tell a tissue of lies to the police?"

"Have a heart, Letty. Don't you see that when that ridiculous holdup business happened—or rather after it happened—I began to feel I was in a bit of a spot. Let's face it; I've got a perfectly good motive for putting you out of the way. You've only got my word for it now that I wasn't the one who tried to do it. You can't expect me deliberately to go and incriminate myself. Even Patrick got nasty ideas about me from time to time, and if even *he* could think things like that, what on earth would the police think? That Detective Inspector struck me as a man of singularly skeptical mind. No. I figured out the only thing for me to do was to sit tight as Julia and just fade away when term came to an end.

"How was I to know that fool Julia, the real Julia, would go and have a row with the producer, and fling the whole thing up in a fit of temperament? She writes to Patrick and asks if she can come here, and instead of wiring to her 'Keep away,' he goes and forgets to do anything at all!" She cast an angry glance at Patrick. "Of all the utter idiots!"

She sighed.

"You don't know the straits I've been put to in Milchester! Of course, I haven't been to the hospital at all. But I had to go somewhere.

Hours and hours I've spent in the pictures, seeing the most frightful films over and over again."

"*Pip and Emma*," murmured Miss Blacklock. "I never believed, somehow, in spite of what the Inspector said, that they were real—"

She looked searchingly at Julia.

"You're Emma," she said. "Where's Pip?"

Julia's eyes, limpid and innocent, met hers.

"I don't know," she said. "I haven't the least idea."

"I think you're lying, Julia. When did you see him last?"

Was there a momentary hesitation before Julia spoke?

She said clearly and deliberately:

"I haven't seen him since we were both three years old—when my mother took him away. I haven't seen either him or my mother. I don't know where they are."

"And that's all you have to say?"

Julia sighed.

"I could say I was sorry. But it wouldn't really be true; because actually I'd do the same thing again—though not if I'd known about this murder business, of course."

"Julia," said Miss Blacklock, "I call you that because I'm used to it. You were with the French Resistance, you say?"

"Yes. For eighteen months."

"Then I suppose you learned to shoot?"

Again those cool blue eyes met hers.

"I can shoot all right. I'm a first-class shot. I didn't shoot at you, Letitia Blacklock, though you've only got my word for that. But I can tell you this, that if *I* had shot at you, I wouldn't have been likely to miss."

II

The sound of a car driving up to the door broke through the tenseness of the moment.

"Who can that be?" asked Miss Blacklock.

Mitzi put a tousled head in. She was showing the whites of her eyes.

"It is the police come again," she said. "This, it is persecution! Why will they not leave us alone? I will not bear it. I will write to the Prime Minister. I will write to your King."

Craddock's hand put her firmly and not too kindly aside. He came in with such a grim set to his lips that they all looked at him apprehensively. This was a new Inspector Craddock.

He said sternly:

"Miss Murgatroyd has been murdered. She was strangled— not more than an hour ago." His eye singled out Julia. "You—Miss Simmons—where have you been all day?"

Julia said warily:

"In Milchester. I've just got in."

"And you?" The eye went on to Patrick.

"Yes."

"Did you both come back here together?"

"Yes—yes, we did," said Patrick.

"No," said Julia. "It's no good, Patrick. That's the kind of lie that will be found out at once. The bus people know us well. I came back on the earlier bus, Inspector—the one that gets here at four o'clock."

"And what did you do then?"

"I went for a walk."

"In the direction of Boulders?"

"No, I went across the fields."

He stared at her. Julia, her face pale, her lips tense, stared back.

Before anyone could speak, the telephone rang.

Miss Blacklock, with an inquiring glance at Craddock, picked up the receiver.

"Yes. Who? Oh, Bunch. What? No. No, she hasn't. I've no idea . . . Yes, he's here now."

She lowered the instrument and said:

"Mrs. Harmon would like to speak to you, Inspector. Miss Marple has not come back to the vicarage and Mrs. Harmon is worried about her."

Craddock took two strides forward and gripped the telephone.

"Craddock speaking."

"I'm worried, Inspector." Bunch's voice came through with a childish tremor in it. "Aunt Jane's out somewhere—and I don't know where. And they say that Miss Murgatroyd's been killed. Is it true?"

"Yes, it's true, Mrs. Harmon. Miss Marple was there, with Miss Hinchliffe, when they found the body."

"Oh, so that's where she is." Bunch sounded relieved.

"No—no, I'm afraid she isn't. Not now. She left there about—let me see—half an hour ago. She hasn't got home?"

"No—she hasn't. It's only ten minutes' walk. Where can she be?"

"Perhaps she's called in on one of your neighbors?"

"I've rung them up—all of them. She's not there. I'm frightened, Inspector."

So am I, thought Craddock.

He said quickly:

"I'll come round to you—at once."

"Oh, do—there's a piece of paper. She was writing on it before she went out. I don't know if it means anything . . . It just seems gibberish to me."

Craddock replaced the receiver.

Miss Blacklock said anxiously:

"Has something happened to Miss Marple? Oh, I hope not."

"I hope not, too." His mouth was grim.

"She's so old—and frail."

"I know."

Miss Blacklock, standing with her hand pulling at the choker of pearls round her neck, said in a hoarse voice:

"It's getting worse and worse. Whoever's doing these things must be mad, Inspector—quite mad . . ."

"I wonder."

The choker of pearls round Miss Blacklock's neck broke under the clutch of her nervous fingers. The smooth white globules rolled all over the room.

Letitia cried out in an anguished tone:

"My pearls—my *pearls*—" The agony in her voice was so acute that they all looked at her in astonishment. She turned, her hand to her throat, and rushed sobbing out of the room.

Phillipa began picking up the pearls.

"I've never seen her so upset over anything," she said. "Of course—she always wears them. Do you think, perhaps, that someone special gave them to her? Randall Goedler, perhaps?"

"It's possible," said the Inspector slowly.

"They're not—they couldn't be—real by any chance?" Phillipa asked from where, on her knees, she was still collecting the shining white globes.

Taking one in his hand, Craddock was just about to reply contemptuously, "Real? Of course not!" when he suddenly stifled the words.

After all, *could* the pearls be real?

They were so large, so even, so white that their falseness seemed palpable, but Craddock remembered suddenly a police case where a string of real pearls had been bought for a few shilling in a pawn-broker's shop.

Letitia Blacklock had assured him that there was no jewelry of value in the house. If these pearls were, by any chance, genuine, they must be worth a fabulous sum. And if Randall Goedler had given them to her—then they might be worth any sum you cared to name.

They looked false—they *must* be false, but—if they were real?

Why not? She might herself be unaware of their value. Or she might choose to protect her treasure by treating it as though it were a cheap ornament worth a couple of guineas at most. What would they be worth if real? A fabulous sum . . . Worth doing murder for—*if anybody knew about them* . . .

With a start, the Inspector wrenched himself away form his speculations. Miss Marple was missing. He must go to the vicarage.

III

He found Bunch and her husband waiting for him, their faces anxious and drawn.

"She hasn't come back," said Bunch.

"Did she say she was coming back here when she left Boulders?" asked Julian.

"She didn't actually say so," said Craddock slowly, throwing his mind back to the last time he had seen Jane Marple.

He remembered the grimness of her lips and the severe frosty light in those usually gentle blue eyes.

Grimness, an inexorable determination . . . to do what? To go where?

"She was talking to Sergeant Fletcher when I last saw her," he said. "Just by the gate. And then she went through it and out. I took it she was going straight home to the vicarage. I would have sent her in the car—but there was so much to attend to, and she slipped away very quietly. Fletcher may know something! Where's Fletcher?"

But Sergeant Fletcher, it seemed, as Craddock learned when he rang up Boulders, was neither to be found there nor had he left any message where he had gone. There was some idea that he had returned to Milchester for some reason.

The Inspector rang up headquarters in Milchester, but no news of Fletcher was to be found there.

Then Craddock turned to Bunch as he remembered what she had told him over the telephone.

"Where's that paper? You said she'd been writing something on a bit of paper."

Bunch brought it to him. He spread it out on the table and looked down on it. Bunch leant over his shoulder and spelled it out as he read. The writing was shaky and not easy to read:

Lamp.

Then came the word *Violets.*

Then, after a space:

Where is bottle of aspirin?

The next item in this curious list was more difficult to make out. "Delicious Death," Bunch read. "That's Mitzi's cake."

"Making enquiries," read Craddock.

"Inquiries? What about, I wonder? What's this? *Severe affliction bravely borne* . . . What on earth—!"

"Iodine," read the Inspector. "Pearls. Ah, pearls."

"And then *Lotty*—no, *Letty.* Her *e*'s look like *o*'s. And then *Berne.* And what's this? *Old Age Pension* . . ."

They looked at each other in bewilderment.

Craddock recapitulated swiftly:

"Lamp. Violets. Where is bottle of aspirin? Delicious Death. Making enquiries. Severe affliction bravely borne. Iodine. Pearls. Letty. Berne. Old Age Pension."

Bunch asked: "Does it mean anything? Anything at all? I can't see any connection."

Craddock said slowly: "I've just a glimmer—but I don't see. It's odd that she should have put that down about pearls."

"What about pearls? What does it mean?"

"Does Miss Blacklock always wear that three-tier choker of pearls?"

"Yes, she does. We laugh about it sometimes. They're so dreadfully false-looking, aren't they? But I suppose she thinks it's fashionable."

"There might be another reason," said Craddock slowly.

"You don't mean that they're *real*? Oh, they *couldn't* be!"

"How often have you had an opportunity of seeing real pearls of that size, Mrs. Harmon?"

"But they're so glassy."

Craddock shrugged his shoulders.

"Anyway, they don't matter now. It's Miss Marple that matters. We've got to find her."

They'd got to find her before it was too late—but perhaps it was already too late? Those penciled words showed that she was on the track . . . But that was dangerous—horribly dangerous. And where the hell was Fletcher?

Craddock strode out of the vicarage to where he'd left his car. Search—that was all he could so—search.

A voice spoke to him out of the dripping laurels:

"Sir!" said Sergeant Fletcher urgently. *"Sir . . ."*

21

Three Women

Dinner was over at Little Paddocks. It had been a silent and uncomfortable meal.

Patrick, uneasily aware of having fallen from grace, only made spasmodic attempts at conversation—and such as he did make were not well received. Phillipa Haymes was sunk in abstraction. Miss Blacklock herself had abandoned the effort to behave with her normal cheerfulness. She had changed for dinner and had come down wearing her necklace of cameos but for the first time fear showed from her darkly circled eyes, and betrayed itself by her twitching hands.

Julia alone had maintained her air of cynical detachment throughout the evening.

"I'm sorry, Letty," she said, "that I can't pack my bag and go. But I presume the police wouldn't allow it. I don't suppose I'll darken your roof—or whatever the expression is—for long. I should imagine that Inspector Craddock will be round with a warrant and the handcuffs any moment. In fact, I can't imagine why something of the kind hasn't happened already."

"He's looking for the old lady—for Miss Marple," said Miss Blacklock.

"Do you think she's been murdered, too?" Patrick asked with scientific curiosity. "But why? What could she know?"

"I don't know," said Miss Blacklock dully. "Perhaps Miss Murgatroyd told her something."

"If she's been murdered, too," said Patrick, "there seems to be logically only one person who could have done it."

"Who?"

"Hinchliffe, of course," said Patrick triumphantly. "That's where she was last seen alive—at Boulders. My solution would be that she never left Boulders."

"My head aches," said Miss Blacklock in a dull voice. She pressed her fingers to her forehead. "Why should Hinch murder Miss Marple? It doesn't make sense."

"It would if Hinch had really murdered Murgatroyd," said Patrick triumphantly.

Phillipa came out of her apathy to say:

"Hinch wouldn't murder Murgatroyd."

Patrick was in an argumentative mood.

"She might have if Murgatroyd had blundered on something to show that she—Hinch—was the criminal."

"Anyway, Hinch was at the station when Murgatroyd was killed."

"She could have murdered Murgatroyd before she left."

Startling them all, Letitia Blacklock suddenly screamed out:

"Murder, murder, *murder*—! Can't you talk *anything* else? I'm frightened, don't you understand? I'm frightened. I wasn't before. I thought I could take care of myself . . . But what can you do against a murderer who's waiting—and watching—and biding his time! Oh, God!"

She dropped her head forward on her hands. A moment later she looked up and apologized stiffly.

"I'm sorry. I—I lost control."

"That's all right, Aunt Letty," said Patrick affectionately. "I'll look after you."

"You?" was all Letitia Blacklock said, but the disillusionment behind the word was almost an accusation.

That had been shortly before dinner, and Mitzi had then created a diversion by coming and declaring that she was not going to cook the dinner.

"I do not do anything more in this house. I go to my room. I lock myself in. I stay there until it is daylight. I am afraid—people are being killed—that Miss Murgatroyd with her stupid English face—who would want to kill her? Only a maniac! Then it is a maniac that is about! And a maniac does not care who he kills. But me, I do not want to be killed! There are shadows in that kitchen—and I hear noises—I think there is someone out in the yard and then I think I see a shadow by the larder door and then it is footsteps I hear. So I go now to my room and I lock the door and perhaps even I put the chest of drawers against it. And in the morning I tell that cruel hard policeman that I go away from here. And if he will not let me, I say: 'I scream and I scream and I scream until you have to let me go!' "

Everybody, with a vivid recollection of what Mitzi could do in the screaming line, shuddered at the threat.

"So I go to my room," said Mitzi, repeating the statement once more to make her intentions quite clear. With a symbolic action, she cast off the cretonne apron she had been wearing. "Good night, Miss Blacklock. Perhaps, in the morning, you may not be alive. So, in case that is so, I say good-by."

She departed abruptly and the door, with its usual gentle little whine, closed softly after her.

Julia got up.

"I'll see to dinner," she said in a matter-of-fact way. "Rather a good arrangement—less embarrassing for you all than having me sit down at table with you. Patrick (since he's constituted himself your protector, Aunt Letty) had better taste every dish first. I don't want to be accused of poisoning you on top of everything else."

So Julia had cooked and served a really excellent meal.

Phillipa had come out to the kitchen with an offer of assistance but Julia had said firmly that she didn't want any help.

"Julia, there's something I want to say—"

"This is no time for girlish confidences," said Julia firmly. "Go on back in the dining room, Phillipa."

Now dinner was over and they were in the drawing-room with coffee on the small table by the fire—and nobody seemed to have anything to say. They were waiting—that was all.

At 8:30 Inspector Craddock rang up.

"I shall be with you in about a quarter of an hour's time," he announced. "I'm bringing Colonel and Mrs. Easterbrook and Mrs. Swettenham and her son with me."

"But, really, Inspector . . . I can't cope with people tonight—"

Miss Blacklock's voice sounded as though she were at the end of her tether.

"I know how you feel, Miss Blacklock. I'm sorry. But this is urgent."

"Have you—found Miss Marple?"

"No," said the Inspector and rang off.

Julia took the coffee tray out to the kitchen where, to her surprise, she found Mitzi contemplating the piled up dishes and plates by the sink.

Mitzi burst into a torrent of words:

"See what you do in my so nice kitchen! That frying pan—only, *only* for omelettes do I use it! And you, what have you used it for?"

"Frying onions."

"Ruined—*ruined*! It will have now to be *washed* and never—*never*—do I wash my omelette pan. I rub it carefully over with a greasy newspaper, that is all. And this saucepan here that you have used—that one, I use him only for milk—"

"Well, I don't know what pans you use for what," said Julia crossly. "You chose to go to bed and why on earth you've chosen to get up again, I can't imagine. Go away again and leave me to wash up in peace."

"No, I will not let you use my kitchen."

"Oh, Mitzi, you *are* impossible!"

Julia stalked angrily out of the kitchen and at that moment the doorbell rang.

"I do not go to the door," Mitzi called from the kitchen. Julia muttered an impolite Continental expression under her breath and stalked to the front door.

It was Miss Hinchliffe.

"Evening," she said in her gruff voice. "Sorry to barge in. Inspector's rung up, I expect?"

"He didn't tell us you were coming," said Julia, leading the way to the drawing-room.

"He said I needn't come unless I liked," said Miss Hinchliffe. "But I do like."

Nobody offered Miss Hinchliffe sympathy or mentioned Miss Murgatroyd's death. The ravaged face of the tall vigorous woman told its own tale, and would have made any expression of sympathy an impertinence.

"Turn all the lights on," said Miss Blacklock. "And put more coal on the fire. I'm cold—horribly cold. Come and sit here by the fire, Miss Hinchliffe. The Inspector said he would be here in a quarter of an hour. It must be nearly that now."

"Mitzi's come down again," said Julia.

"Has she? Sometimes I think that girl's mad—quite mad. But then perhaps we're all mad."

"I've no patience with this saying that all people who commit crimes are mad," barked Miss Hinchliffe. "Horribly and intelligently sane—that's what I think a criminal is!"

The sound of a car was heard outside and presently Craddock came in with Colonel and Mrs. Easterbrook and Edmund and Mrs. Swettenham.

They were all curiously subdued.

Colonel Easterbrook said in a voice that was like an echo of his usual tones:

"Ha! A good fire."

Mrs. Easterbrook wouldn't take off her fur coat and sat down close to her husband. Her face, usually pretty and rather vapid, was like a little pinched weasel face. Edmund was in one of his furious moods and scowled at everybody. Mrs. Swettenham made what was evidently a great effort, and which resulted in a kind of parody of herself.

"It's awful—isn't it?" she said conversationally. "Everything, I mean. And, really, the less one says, the better. Because one doesn't know *who next*—like the plague. Dear Miss Blacklock, don't you think you ought to have a little brandy? Just half a wineglass even? I always think there's nothing like brandy—such a wonderful stimulant. I—it seems so terrible of us—forcing our way in here like this, but Inspector Craddock made us come. And it seems so terrible—she hasn't been found, you know. That poor old thing from the vicarage, I mean. Bunch Harmon is nearly frantic. Nobody knows where she went instead of going home. She didn't come to us. I've not even seen her today. And I should know if she had come to the house because I was in the drawing-room—at the back, you know, and Edmund was in his study writing—and that's at the front—so if she'd come either way we should have seen. And, oh, I do hope and pray that nothing has happened to that dear sweet old thing—all her faculties still and *everything.*"

"Mother," said Edmund in a voice of acute suffering, "can't you shut up?"

"I'm sure, dear, I don't want to say a *word,*" said Mrs. Swettenham, and sat down on the sofa by Julia.

Inspector Craddock stood near the door. Facing him, almost in a row, were the three women. Julia and Mrs. Swettenham on the sofa. Mrs. Easterbrook on the arm of her husband's chair. He had not brought about this arrangement, but it suited him very well.

Miss Blacklock and Miss Hinchliffe were crouching over the fire. Edmund stood near them. Phillipa was far back in the shadows.

Craddock began without preamble.

"You all know that Miss Murgatroyd's been killed," he began.

"We've reason to believe that the person who killed her was a woman. And for certain other reasons we can narrow it down still more. I'm about to ask certain ladies here to account for what they were doing between the hours of 4:00 and 4:20 this afternoon. I have already had an account of her movements from—from the young lady who has been calling herself Miss Simmons. I will ask her to repeat that statement. At the same time, Miss Simmons, I must caution you that you need not answer if you think your answers may incriminate you, and anything you say will be taken down by Constable Edwards and may be used as evidence in court."

"You have to say that, don't you?" said Julia. She was rather pale, but still composed. "I repeat that between 4:00 and 4:20 I was walking along the field leading down to the brook by Compton Farm. I came back to the road by that field with three poplars in it. I didn't meet anyone as far as I can remember. I did not go near Boulders."

"Mrs. Swettenham?"

Edmund said, "Are you cautioning all of us?"

The Inspector turned to him.

"No. At the moment only Miss Simmons. I have no reason to believe that any other statement made will be incriminating, but anyone, of course, is entitled to have a solicitor present and to refuse to answer questions unless one *is* present."

"Oh, but that would be very silly and a complete waste of time," cried Mrs. Swettenham. "I'm sure I can tell you at once exactly what I was doing. That's what you want, isn't it? Shall I begin now?"

"Yes, please, Mrs. Swettenham."

"Now let me see." Mrs. Swettenham closed her eyes, opened them again. "Of course, I had nothing *at all* to do with killing Miss Murgatroyd. I'm sure *everybody* here knows *that*. But I'm a woman of the world, I know quite well that the police have to ask all the most unnecessary questions and write the answers down very carefully, because it's all for what they call 'the record.' That's it, isn't it?" Mrs. Swettenham flashed the question at the diligent Constable Edwards and added graciously, "I'm not going too fast for you, I hope?"

Constable Edwards, a good shorthand writer, but with little social *savoir faire*, turned red to the ears and replied:

"It's quite all right, madam. Well, perhaps a *little* slower would be better."

Mrs. Swettenham resumed her discourse with emphatic pauses where she considered a comma or a full stop might be appropriate.

"Well, of course, it's difficult to say—exactly—because I've not got, really, a very good sense of time. And ever since the war quite half our clocks haven't gone at all, and the ones that do go are often either fast or slow or stop because we haven't wound them up." Mrs. Swettenham paused to let this picture of confused time sink in and then went on earnestly, "What I *think* I was doing at four o'clock was turning the heel of my sock (and for some extraordinary reason I was going round the wrong way—in purl, you know, not plain), but if I *wasn't* doing that, I must have been outside, snipping off the dead chrysanthemums—no, that was earlier—before the rain."

"The rain," said the Inspector, "started at 4:10 exactly."

"Did it now? That helps a lot. Of course, I was upstairs putting a wash basin in the passage where the rain always comes through. And it was coming through so fast that I guessed at once that the gutter was stopped up again. So I came down and got my mackintosh and rubber boots. I called Edmund, but he didn't answer, so I thought perhaps he'd got to a very important place in his novel and I wouldn't disturb him, and I've done it quite often myself before. With the broom handle, you know, tied onto that long thing you push up windows with."

"You mean," said Craddock, noting bewilderment on his subordinate's face, "that you were cleaning out the gutter?"

"Yes, it was all choked up with leaves. It took a long time and I got rather wet, but I got it clear at last. And then I went in and got changed and washed—so *smelly*, dead leaves— And then I went into the kitchen and put the kettle on. It was 6:15 by the kitchen clock."

Constable Edwards blinked.

"Which means," finished Mrs. Swettenham triumphantly, "that it was exactly twenty minutes to five. Or near enough," she added.

"Did anybody see what you were doing whilst you were out cleaning the gutter?"

"No, indeed," said Mrs. Swettenham, "I'd soon have roped them in to help if they had! It's a most difficult thing to do single-handed."

"So, by your own statement, you were outside, in a mackintosh and boots, at the time when the rain was coming down, and, according to you, you were employed during that time in cleaning out a gutter, but you have no one who can substantiate that statement?"

"You can look at the gutter," said Mrs. Swettenham. "It's beautifully clear."

"Did you hear your mother call to you, Mr. Swettenham?"

"No," said Edmund. "I was fast asleep."

"Edmund," said his mother reproachfully, "I thought you were writing."

Inspector Craddock turned to Mrs. Easterbrook.

"Now, Mrs. Easterbrook?"

"I was sitting with Archie in his study," said Mrs. Easterbrook, fixing wide innocent eyes on him. "We were listening to the radio together, weren't we, Archie?"

There was a pause. Colonel Easterbrook was very red in the face. He took his wife's hand in his.

"You don't understand these things, kitten," he said. "I—well, I must say, Inspector, you've rather sprung this business on us. My wife, you know, has been terribly upset by all this. She's nervous and highly strung and doesn't appreciate the importance of—of taking due consideration before she makes a statement."

"Archie," cried Mrs. Easterbrook reproachfully, "are you going to say you weren't with me?"

"Well, I wasn't, was I, my dear? I mean, one's got to stick to the facts. Very important in this sort of inquiry. I was talking to Lampson, the farmer at Croft End, about some chicken netting. That was about a quarter to four. I didn't get home until after the rain had stopped. Just before tea. A quarter to five. Laura was toasting the scones."

"And had *you* been out also, Mrs. Easterbrook?"

The pretty face looked more like a weasel's than ever. Her eyes had a trapped look.

"No—no, I just sat listening to the radio. I didn't go out. Not then. I'd been out earlier. About—about half past three. Just for a little walk. Not far."

She looked as though she expected more questions, but Craddock said quietly:

"That's all, Mrs. Easterbrook."

He went on: "These statements will be typed out. You can read them and sign them if they are substantially correct."

Mrs. Easterbrook looked at him with sudden venom.

"Why don't you ask the others where they were? That Haymes woman? And Edmund Swettenham? How do you know he *was* asleep indoors? Nobody saw him."

Inspector Craddock said quietly,

"Miss Murgatroyd, before she died, made a certain statement. On the night of the holdup here, *someone* was absent from this room.

Someone who was supposed to have been in the room all the time. Miss Murgatroyd told her friend the names of the people she *did* see. By a process of elimination, she made the discovery that there was someone she did *not* see."

"Nobody could see anything," said Julia.

"Murgatroyd could," said Miss Hinchliffe, speaking suddenly in her deep voice. "She was over there behind the door, where Inspector Craddock is now. She was the only person who could see anything of what was happening."

"Aha! That is what you think, is it?" demanded Mitzi.

She had made one of her dramatic entrances, flinging open the door and almost knocking Craddock sideways. She was in a frenzy of excitement.

"Ah, you do not ask Mitzi to come in here with the others, do you, you stiff policeman? I am only Mitzi! Mitzi in the kitchen! Let her stay in the kitchen where she belongs! But I tell you that Mitzi, as well as anyone else, and perhaps better, yes, better, can see things. Yes, I see things. I see something the night of the burglary. I see something and I do not quite believe it, and I hold my tongue till now. I think to myself I will not tell what it is I have seen, not yet. I will wait."

"And when everything had calmed down, you meant to ask for a little money from a certain person, eh?" said Craddock.

Mitzi turned on him like an angry cat.

"And why not? Why look down your nose? Why should I not be paid for it if I have been so generous as to keep silence? Especially if some day there will be money—much, *much* money. Oh! I have heard things—I know what goes on. I know this Pippemmer—this secret society of which *she*"—she flung a dramatic finger towards Julia—"is an agent. Yes, I would have waited and asked for money—but now I am afraid. I would rather be *safe*. For soon, perhaps, someone will kill *me*. So I will tell what I know."

"All right then," said the Inspector skeptically. "What *do* you know?"

"I tell you." Mitzi spoke solemnly. "On that night I am *not* in the pantry cleaning silver as I say—I am already in the dining room when I hear the gun go off. I look through the keyhole. The hall it is black, but the gun go off again and the flashlight it falls—and it swings round as it falls—and I see *her*. I see *her* there close to him, with the gun in her hand. I see Miss Blacklock."

"Me?" Miss Blacklock sat up in astonishment. "You must be mad!"

"But that's impossible!" cried Edmund. "Mitzi couldn't have seen Miss Blacklock—"

Craddock cut in and his voice had the corrosive quality of a deadly acid.

"*Couldn't she, Mr. Swettenham? And why not?* Because it *wasn't* Miss Blacklock who was standing there with the gun? It was *you*, wasn't it?"

"I? Of course not—what the *hell*!"

"*You* took Colonel Easterbrook's revolver. *You* fixed up the business with Rudi Scherz—as a good joke. You had followed Patrick Simmons into the far room and when the lights went out, you slipped out through the carefully oiled door. You shot at Miss Blacklock and then you killed Rudi Scherz. A few seconds later you were back in the drawing-room, clicking your lighter."

For a moment Edmund seemed at a loss for words, then he spluttered out:

"The whole idea is *monstrous*. Why *me*? What earthly motive have *I* got?"

"If Miss Blacklock dies before Mrs. Goedler, two people inherit—remember? The two we know of as Pip and Emma. Julia Simmons has turned out to be Emma—"

"And you think I'm Pip?" Edmund laughed. "Fantastic—absolutely *fantastic*! I'm about the right age—nothing else. And I can prove to you, you damned fool, that I *am* Edmund Swettenham. Birth certificate, schools, university—everything."

"He isn't Pip." The voice came from the shadows in the corner. Phillipa Haymes came forward, her face pale. "*I'm Pip*, Inspector."

"*You*, Mrs. Haymes?"

"Yes. Everybody seems to have assumed that Pip was a boy—Julia knew, of course, that her twin was another girl—I don't know why she didn't say so this afternoon—"

"Family solidarity," said Julia. "I suddenly realized who you were. I'd had no idea till that moment."

"I'd had the same idea as Julia did," said Phillipa, her voice trembling a little. "After I—lost my husband and the war was over, I wondered what I was going to do. My mother died many years ago. I found out about my Goedler relations. Mrs. Goedler was dying and at her death the money would go to a Miss Blacklock. I found out where Miss Blacklock lived and I—I came here. I took a job with Mrs. Lucas. I hoped that, since this Miss Blacklock was an elderly woman without relatives, she might, perhaps, be willing to help. Not me, because I could work, but help with Harry's education. After all, it *was* Goedler money and she'd no one particular of her own to spend it on.

"And then," Phillipa spoke faster; it was as though now her long reserve had broken down, she couldn't get the words out fast enough, "that holdup happened and I began to be frightened. Because it seemed to me that the only possible person with a motive for killing Miss Blacklock was *me*. I hadn't the least idea who Julia was—we weren't identical twins and we're not much alike to look at. No, it seemed as though I was the only one bound to be suspected."

She stopped and pushed her fair hair back from her face, and Craddock suddenly realized that a faded snapshot in the box of letters must have been a photograph of Phillipa's mother. The likeness was undeniable. He knew too why that mention of closing and unclosing hands had seemed familiar—Phillipa was doing it now.

"Miss Blacklock has been very good to me. Very, *very* good to me—I didn't try to kill her. I never thought of killing her. But all the same, I'm Pip." She added, "You see, you needn't suspect Edmund any more."

"Needn't I?" said Craddock. Again there was that acid biting tone in his voice. "Edmund Swettenham's a young man who's fond of money. A young man, perhaps, who would like to marry a rich wife. But she wouldn't be a rich wife *unless Miss Blacklock died before Mrs. Goedler*. And since it seemed almost certain that Mrs. Goedler would die before Miss Blacklock, well—he had to do something about it— *didn't you, Mr. Swettenham?*"

"It's a damned lie!" Edmund shouted.

And then, suddenly, a sound rose on the air. It came from the kitchen—a long unearthly shriek of terror.

"That isn't Mitzi!" cried Julia.

"No," said Inspector Craddock, "it's someone who's murdered three people . . ."

22

The Truth

When the Inspector turned on Edmund Swettenham, Mitzi had crept quietly out of the room and back to the kitchen. She was running water into the sink when Miss Blacklock entered.

Mitzi gave her a shame-faced sideways look.

"What a liar you are, Mitzi," said Miss Blacklock pleasantly. "Here—that isn't the way to wash up. The silver first, and fill the sink right up. You can't wash up in about two inches of water."

Mitzi turned the taps on obediently.

"You are not angry at what I say, Miss Blacklock?" she asked.

"If I were to be angry at all the lies you tell, I should never be out of a temper," said Miss Blacklock.

"I will go and say to the Inspector that I make it all up, shall I?" asked Mitzi.

"He knows that already," said Miss Blacklock pleasantly.

Mitzi turned off the taps and as she did so two hands came up behind her head and with one swift movement forced it down into the water-filled sink.

"Only *I* know that you're telling the truth for once," said Miss Blacklock viciously.

Mitzi thrashed and struggled but Miss Blacklock was strong and her hands held the girl's head firmly under water.

Then, from somewhere quite close behind her, Dora Bunner's voice rose piteously on the air:

"Oh, Lotty—Lotty—don't do it . . . Lotty!"

Miss Blacklock screamed. Her hands flew up in the air, and Mitzi, released, came up choking and spluttering.

Miss Blacklock screamed again and again. For there was no one there in the kitchen with her—

"Dora, Dora, forgive me. I had to . . . I had to—"

She rushed distractedly towards the scullery door—and the bulk of Sergeant Fletcher barred her way, just as Miss Marple stepped, flushed and triumphant, out of the broom cupboard.

"I could always mimic people's voices," said Miss Marple.

"You'll have to come with me, madam," said Sergeant Fletcher. "I was a witness of your attempt to drown this girl. And there will be other charges. I must warn you, Letitia Blacklock—"

"Charlotte Blacklock," corrected Miss Marple. "That's who she is, you know. Under that choker of pearls she always wears you'll find the scar of the operation."

"Operation?"

"Operation for goiter."

Miss Blacklock, quite calm now, looked at Miss Marple.

"So you know all about it?" she said.

"Yes, I've known for some time."

Charlotte Blacklock sat down by the table and began to cry.

"You shouldn't have done that," she said. "Not made Dora's voice come. I loved Dora. I really loved Dora."

Inspector Craddock and the others had crowded in the doorway.

Constable Edwards, who added a knowledge of first aid and artificial respiration to his other accomplishments, was busy with Mitzi. As soon as Mitzi could speak she was lyrical with self-praise.

"I do that good, do I not? I am clever! And I am brave! Oh, I am brave! Very, very nearly was *I* murdered, too. But I am so brave I risk *everything.*"

With a rush Miss Hinchliffe thrust aside the others and leapt upon the weeping figure of Charlotte Blacklock by the table.

It took all Sergeant Fletcher's strength to hold her off.

"Now then—" he said. "Now then— No, no, Miss Hinchliffe—"

Between clenched teeth Miss Hinchliffe was muttering:

"Let me get at her. Just let me get at her. It was she who killed Amy Murgatroyd."

Charlotte Blacklock looked up and sniffed.

"I didn't want to kill her. I didn't want to kill anybody—I had to—But it's Dora I mind about—after Dora was dead, I was all alone—ever since she died—I've been alone—oh, Dora—Dora—"

And once again she dropped her head on her hands and wept.

23

Evening at the Vicarage

Miss Marple sat in the tall armchair. Bunch was on the floor in front of the fire with her arms round her knees.

The Reverend Julian Harmon was leaning forward and was for once looking more like a schoolboy than a man foreshadowing his own maturity. And Inspector Craddock was smoking his pipe and drinking a whiskey and soda and was clearly very much off duty. An outer circle was composed of Julia, Patrick, Edmund and Phillipa.

"I think it's your story, Miss Marple," said Craddock.

"Oh, no, my dear boy. I only just helped a little, here and there. *You* were in charge of the whole thing, and conducted it all, and you know so much that I don't."

"Well, tell it together," said Bunch impatiently. "Bits each. Only let Aunt Jane start because I like the muddly way her mind works. When did you first think that the whole thing was a put-up job by the Blacklock?"

"Well, my dear Bunch, it's hard to say. Of course, right at the very beginning, it did seem as though the ideal person—or rather the *obvious* person, I should say—to have arranged the holdup *was* Miss Blacklock herself. She was the only person who was known to have been in contact with Rudi Scherz, and how much easier to arrange something like that when it's your own house. The central heating, for instance. No fires—because that would have meant light in the room. But the only person who could have arranged *not* to have a fire was the mistress of the house herself.

"Not that I thought of all that at the time—it just seemed to me that it was a pity it *couldn't* be as simple as that! Oh no, I was taken in like everyone else, I thought that someone really did want to kill Letitia Blacklock."

"I think I'd like to get clear first on what really happened," said Bunch. "Did this Swiss boy recognize her?"

"Yes. He'd worked in—"

She hesitated and looked at Craddock.

"In Dr. Adolf Koch's clinic in Berne," said Craddock. "Koch was a world famous specialist on operations for goiter. Charlotte Blacklock went there to have her goiter removed and Rudi Scherz was one of the orderlies. When he came to England he recognized in the hotel a lady who had been a patient and on the spur of the moment he spoke to her. I daresay he mightn't have done that if he'd paused to think, because he left the place under a cloud, but that was sometime after Charlotte had been there, so she wouldn't know anything about it."

"So he never said anything to her about Montreux and his father being a hotel proprietor?"

"Oh, no, she made that up to account for his having spoken to her."

"It must have been a great shock to her," said Miss Marple thoughtfully. "She felt reasonably safe—and then—the almost impossible mischance of somebody turning up who had known her—not as one of the two Miss Blacklocks—she was prepared for *that*—but definitely as *Charlotte* Blacklock, a patient who'd been operated on for goiter.

"But you wanted to go through it all from the beginning. Well, the beginning, I think—if Inspector Craddock agrees with me—was when Charlotte Blacklock, a pretty, light-hearted, affectionate girl, developed that enlargement of the thyroid gland that's called a goiter. It ruined her life, because she was a very sensitive girl. A girl, too, who had always set a lot of stress on her personal appearance. And girls just at that age in their teens are particularly sensitive about themselves. If she'd had a mother, or a reasonable father, I don't think she would have got into the morbid state she undoubtedly did get into. She had no one, you see, to take her out of herself and force her to see people and lead a normal life and not think too much about her infirmity. And, of course, in a different household, she might have been sent for an operation many years earlier.

"But Mr. Blacklock, I think, was an old-fashioned, narrowminded, tyrannical and obstinate man. He didn't believe in these operations. Charlotte must take it from him that nothing could be done—apart from dosage with iodine and other drugs. Charlotte *did* take it from him, and I think her sister also placed more faith in Dr. Blacklock's powers as a physician than he deserved.

"Charlotte was devoted to her father in a rather weak and soppy way. She thought, definitely, that her father knew best. But she shut herself up more and more as the goiter became larger and more unsightly, and refused to see people. She was actually a kindly affectionate creature."

"That's an odd description of a murderess," said Edmund.

"I don't know that it is," said Miss Marple. "Weak and kindly people are often very treacherous. And if they've got a grudge against life it saps the little moral strength that they may possess.

"*Letitia* Blacklock, of course, had quite a different personality. Inspector Craddock told me that Belle Goedler described her as really *good*—and I think Letitia *was* good. She was a woman of great integrity who found—as she put it herself—a great difficulty in understanding how people couldn't see what was dishonest. Letitia Blacklock, however tempted, would never have contemplated any kind of fraud for a moment.

"Letitia was devoted to her sister. She wrote her long accounts of everything that happened in an effort to keep her sister in touch with life. She was worried by the morbid state Charlotte was getting into.

"Finally, Dr. Blacklock died. Letitia, without hesitation, threw up her position with Randall Goedler and devoted herself to Charlotte. She took her to Switzerland to consult authorities there on the possibility of operating. It had been left until very late—but, as we know, the operation was successful. The deformity was gone—and the scar this operation had left was easily hidden by a choker of pearls or beads.

"The war had broken out. A return to England was difficult and the two sisters stayed in Switzerland, doing various Red Cross and other work. That's right, isn't it, Inspector?"

"Yes, Miss Marple."

"They got occasional news from England—amongst other things, I expect, they heard that Belle Goedler could not live long. I'm sure it would be only human nature for them both to have planned and talked together of the days ahead when a big fortune would be theirs to spend. One has got to realize, I think, that this prospect meant much more to *Charlotte* than it did to Letitia. For the first time in her life, Charlotte could go about feeling herself a normal woman, a woman at whom no one looked with either repulsion or pity. She was free at last to enjoy life—and she had a whole lifetime, as it were, to crowd into her remaining years. To travel, to have a house and beautiful grounds—to have clothes and jewels, and go to plays and concerts, to gratify every whim—it was all a kind of fairy tale come true to Charlotte.

"And then Letitia, the strong healthy Letitia, got flu which turned to pneumonia and she died within the space of a week! Not only had Charlotte lost her sister, but the whole dream existence she had planned for herself was canceled. I think, you know, that she may have felt almost resentful towards Letitia. Why need Letitia have died, just then, when they had just had a letter saying Belle Goedler could not last long? Just one more month, perhaps, and the money would have been Letitia's—and hers when Letitia died . . .

"Now this is where I think the difference between the two came in. Charlotte didn't really feel that what she suddenly thought of doing was wrong—not really wrong. The money was meant to come to Letitia—it *would* have come to Letitia in the course of a few months—and she regarded herself and Letitia as one.

"Perhaps the idea didn't occur to her until the doctor or someone asked her sister's Christian name—and then she realized how to nearly everyone they had appeared as the two Miss Blacklocks—elderly, well-bred Englishwomen, dressed much the same, with a strong family resemblance—(and, as I pointed out to Bunch, one elderly woman is *so* like another). Why shouldn't it be *Charlotte* who had died and *Letitia* who was alive?

"It was an impulse, perhaps, more than a plan. Letitia was buried under Charlotte's name. 'Charlotte' was dead, 'Letitia' came to England. All the natural initiative and energy, dormant for so many years, were now in the ascendant. As Charlotte, she had played second fiddle. She now assumed the airs of command, the feeling of command that had been Letitia's. They were not really so unlike in mentality—though there was, I think, a big difference *morally*.

"Charlotte had, of course, to take one or two obvious precautions. She bought a house in a part of England quite unknown to her. The only people she had to avoid were a few people in her own native town in Cumberland (where, in any case, she'd lived as a recluse) and, of course, Belle Goedler, who had known Letitia so well that any impersonation would have been out of the question. Handwriting difficulties were got over by the arthritic condition of her hands. It was really very easy because so few people had ever really known Charlotte."

"But supposing she'd met people who'd known Letitia?" asked Bunch. "There must have been plenty of those."

"They wouldn't matter in the same way. Someone might say: 'I came across Letitia Blacklock the other day. She's changed so much I really wouldn't have known her.' But there still wouldn't have been any suspicion in their minds that she wasn't Letitia. People *do* change in the course of ten years. *Her* failure to recognize *them* could always be put down to her nearsightedness: and you must remember that she knew every detail of Letitia's life in London—the people she met—the places she went. She'd got Letitia's letters to refer to, and she could quickly have disarmed any suspicion by mention of some incident, or an inquiry after a mutual friend. No, it was recognition as *Charlotte* that was the only thing she had to fear.

"She settled down at Little Paddocks, got to know her neighbors and, when she got a letter asking dear Letitia to be kind, she accepted with pleasure the visit of two young cousins she had never seen. Their acceptance of her as Aunt Letty increased her security.

"The whole thing was going splendidly. And then—she made her big mistake. It was a mistake that arose solely from her kindness of heart and her naturally affectionate nature. She got a letter from an old school friend who had fallen on evil days, and she hurried to the rescue. Perhaps it may have been partly because she was, in spite of everything, lonely. Her secret kept her in a way apart from people. And she had been genuinely fond of Dora Bunner and remembered her as a symbol of her own gay carefree days at school. Anyway, on an impulse, she answered Dora's letter in person. And very surprised Dora must have been! She'd written to *Letitia* and the sister who turned up in answer to her letter was *Charlotte*. There was never any question of pretending to be Letitia to Dora. Dora was one of the few old friends who had been admitted to see Charlotte in her lonely and unhappy days.

"And because she knew that Dora would look at the matter in exactly the same way as she did herself, she told Dora what she had done. Dora approved wholeheartedly. In her confused muddle-headed mind it seemed only right that dear Lotty should not be done out of her inheritance by Letty's untimely death. Lotty *deserved* a reward for all the patient suffering she had borne so bravely. It would have been most unfair if all that money should have gone to someone nobody had ever heard of.

"She quite understood that nothing must be allowed to get out. It was like an extra pound of butter. You couldn't talk about it but there was nothing wrong about having it. So Dora came to Little Paddocks—and very soon Charlotte began to understand that she had made a terrible mistake. It was not merely the fact that Dora Bunner, with her muddles and her mistakes and her bungling, was quite maddening to live with. Charlotte could have put up with that—because she really cared for Dora, and, anyway, knew from the doctor that Dora hadn't a very long time to live. But Dora very soon became a real danger. Though Charlotte and Letitia had called each other by their full names, Dora was the kind of person who always uses abbreviations. To her the sisters had always been Letty and Lotty. And though she schooled her tongue resolutely to call her friend Letty—the old name often slipped out. Memories of the past, too, were rather apt to come to her tongue—and Charlotte had constantly to be on the watch to check these forgetful allusions. It began to get on her nerves.

"Still, nobody was likely to pay much attention to Dora's inconsistencies. The real blow to Charlotte's security came, as I say, when she was recognized and spoken to by Rudi Scherz at the Royal Spa Hotel.

"I think that the money Rudi Scherz used to replace his earlier defalcations at the hotel may have come from Charlotte Blacklock. Inspector Craddock doesn't believe—and I don't either—that Rudi Scherz applied to her for money with any idea of blackmail in his head."

"He hadn't the faintest idea he knew anything to blackmail her about," said Inspector Craddock. "He knew that he was quite a personable young man—and he was aware by experience that personable young men sometimes can get money out of elderly ladies if they tell a hard luck story convincingly enough.

"But she may have seen it differently. She may have thought that it *was* a form of insidious blackmail, that perhaps he suspected something—and that later, if there was publicity in the papers, as there might be after Belle Goedler's death, he would realize that in her he had found a gold mine.

"And she was committed to the fraud now. She'd established herself as Letitia Blacklock. With the bank. With Mrs. Goedler. The only snag was this rather dubious Swiss hotel clerk, an unreliable character and possibly a blackmailer. If only he were out of the way—she'd be safe.

"Perhaps she made it all up as a kind of fantasy first. She'd been starved of emotion and drama in her life. She pleased herself by working out the details. How would she go about getting rid of him?

"She made her plan. And at last she decided to act on it. She told her story of a sham holdup at a party to Rudi Scherz, explained that she wanted a stranger to act the part of the 'gangster' and offered him a generous sum for his cooperation.

"And the fact that he agreed without any suspicion is what makes me quite certain that Scherz had no idea that he had any kind of hold over her. To him she was just a rather foolish old woman, very ready to part with money.

"She gave him the advertisement to insert, arranged for him to pay a visit to Little Paddocks to study the geography of the house and showed him the spot where she would meet him and let him into the house on the night in question. Dora Bunner, of course, knew nothing about all this.

"The day came—" He paused.

Miss Marple took up the tale in her gentle voice.

"She must have spent a very miserable day. You see, it still wasn't too late to draw back. . . . Dora Bunner told us that Letty was frightened that day and she must have been frightened. Frightened of what she was going to do, frightened of the plan going wrong—but not frightened enough to draw back.

"It had been fun, perhaps, getting the revolver out of Colonel Easterbrook's collar drawer. Taking along eggs, or jam—slipping upstairs in the empty house. It had been fun getting the second door in the drawing-room oiled, so that it would open and shut noiselessly. Fun suggesting the moving of the table outside the door so that Phillipa's flower arrangements would show to better advantage. It may have all seemed like a game. But what was going to happen next definitely wasn't a game any longer. Oh, yes, she was frightened . . . Dora Bunner was right about that."

"All the same, she went through with it," said Craddock. "And it all went according to plan. She went out just after six to 'shut up the ducks,' and she let Scherz in then and gave him the mask and the cloak and gloves and the flashlight. Then, at 6:30, when the clock begins to strike, she's ready by that table near the archway with her hand on the cigarette box. It's all so natural. Patrick, acting as host, has gone for the drinks. She, the hostess, is fetching the cigarettes. She's judged, quite correctly, that when the clock begins to strike, everyone will look at the clock. They did. Only one person, the devoted Dora, kept her eyes fixed on her friend. And she told us, in her very first statement, exactly what Miss Blacklock did. She said that Miss Blacklock had picked up the vase of violets.

"She'd previously frayed the cord of the lamp so that the wires were nearly bare. The whole thing only took a second. The cigarette box, the vase and the little switch were all close together. She picked up the violets, spilt the water on the frayed place and switched on the lamp. Water's a good conductor of electricity. The wires burned out."

"Just like the other afternoon at the vicarage," said Bunch. "That's what startled you so, wasn't it, Aunt Jane?"

"Yes, my dear. I'd been puzzling about those lights. I'd realized that there were two lamps, a pair, and that one had been changed for the other—probably during the night."

"That's right," said Craddock. "When Fletcher examined that lamp the next morning it was, like all the others, perfectly in order, no frayed cord or burned out wires."

"I'd understood what Dora Bunner meant by saying it had been the *shepherdess* the night before," said Miss Marple, "but I fell into the error of thinking, as she thought, that *Patrick* had been responsible. The interesting thing about Dora Bunner was that she was quite unreliable in repeating things she had heard—she always used her imagination to exaggerate or distort them, and she was usually wrong in what she *thought*—but she was quite accurate about the things she *saw*. She saw Letitia pick up the violets—"

"And she saw what she described as a flash and a crackle," put in Craddock.

"And, of course, when dear Bunch spilt the water from the Christmas roses onto the lamp wire—I realized at once that only Miss Blacklock herself could have put out the lights because only she was near that table."

"I could kick myself," said Craddock. "Dora Bunner even prattled about a burn on the table where someone had 'put their cigarette down'—but nobody had even lit a cigarette . . . And the violets were dead because there was no water in the vase—a slip on Letitia's part—she ought to have filled it up again. But I suppose she thought nobody would notice and, as a matter of fact, Miss Bunner was quite ready to believe that she herself had put no water in the vase to begin with."

He went on:

"She was highly suggestible, of course. And Miss Blacklock took advantage of that more than once. Bunny's suspicions of Patrick were, I think, induced by her."

"Why pick on me?" demanded Patrick in an aggrieved tone.

"It was not, I think, a serious suggestion—but it would keep

Bunny distracted from any suspicion that Miss Blacklock might be stage managing the business. Well, we know what happened next. As soon as the lights went and everyone was exclaiming, she slipped out through the previously oiled door and up behind Rudi Scherz who was turning his flashlight round the room and playing his part with gusto. I don't suppose he realized for a moment she was there behind him with her gardening gloves pulled on and the revolver in her hand. She waits till the light reaches the spot she must aim for—the wall near which she is supposed to be standing. Then she fires rapidly twice and as he swings round startled, she holds the revolver close to his body and fires again. She lets the revolver fall by his body, throws her gloves carelessly on the hall table, then back through the other door and across to where she had been standing when the light went out. She nicked her ear—I don't quite know how—"

"Nail scissors, I expect," said Miss Marple. "Just a snip on the lobe of the ear lets out a lot of blood. That was very good psychology, of course. The actual blood running down over her white blouse made it seem certain that she *had* been shot at, and that it had been a near miss."

"It ought to have gone off quite all right," said Craddock. "Dora Bunner's insistence that Scherz had definitely aimed at Miss Blacklock had its uses. Without meaning it, Dora Bunner conveyed the impression that she'd actually seen her friend wounded. It might have been brought in suicide or accidental death. And the case would have been closed. That it was kept open is due to Miss Marple here."

"Oh, no, no." Miss Marple shook her head energetically. "Any little efforts on my part were quite incidental. It was you who weren't satisfied, Mr. Craddock. It was *you* who wouldn't let the case be closed."

"I wasn't happy about it," said Craddock. "I knew it was all wrong somewhere. But I didn't see *where* it was wrong, till you showed me. And after that Miss Blacklock had a real piece of bad luck. I discovered that that second door had been tampered with. Until that moment, whatever we agreed *might* have happened—we'd nothing to go upon but a pretty theory. But the oiled door was *evidence*. And I hit upon it by pure chance—by catching hold of a handle by mistake."

"I think you were *led* to it, Inspector," said Miss Marple. "But then I'm old-fashioned."

"So the hunt was up again," said Craddock. "But this time with a difference. We were looking now for someone with a motive to kill Letitia Blacklock."

"And there *was* someone with a motive, and Miss Blacklock knew it," said Miss Marple. "I think she recognized Phillipa almost at once. Because Sonia Goedler seems to have been one of the very few people who had been admitted to Charlotte's privacy. And when one is old (you wouldn't know this yet, Mr. Craddock) one has a much better memory for a face you've seen when you were young than you have for anyone you've only met a year or two ago. Phillipa must have been just about the same age as her mother was as Charlotte remembered her, and she was very like her mother. The odd thing is that I think Charlotte was very pleased to recognize Phillipa. She became very fond of Phillipa and I think, unconsciously, it helped to stifle any qualms of conscience she may have had. She told herself that when she inherited the money, she was going to look after Phillipa. She would treat her as a daughter. Phillipa and Harry should live with her. She felt quite happy and beneficent about it. But once the Inspector began asking questions and finding out about 'Pip and Emma,' Charlotte became very uneasy. She didn't want to make a scapegoat of Phillipa. Her whole idea had been to make the business look like a holdup by a young criminal and his accidental death. But now, with the discovery of the oiled door, the whole viewpoint was changed. And, except for Phillipa, there wasn't (as far as *she* knew, for she had absolutely no idea of Julia's identity) anyone with the least possible motive for wishing to kill her. She did her best to shield Phillipa's identity. She was quick-witted enough to tell you, when you asked her, that Sonia was small and dark and she took the old snapshots out of the album so that you shouldn't notice any resemblance at the same time that she removed snapshots of Letitia herself."

"And to think I suspected Mrs. Swettenham of being Sonia Goedler," said Craddock disgustedly.

"My poor mama," murmured Edmund. "A woman of blameless life—or so I have always believed."

"But, of course," Miss Marple went on, "it was Dora Bunner who was the real danger. Every day Dora got more forgetful and more talkative. I remember the way Miss Blacklock looked at her the day we went to tea there. Do you know why? Dora had just called her Lotty again. It seemed to us a mere harmless slip of the tongue. But it frightened Charlotte. And so it went on. Poor Dora could not stop herself talking. That day we had coffee together in the Bluebird, I had the oddest impression that Dora was talking about *two* people, not one—and so, of course, she was. At one moment she spoke of her friend as not pretty but having so much character—but almost at the same mo-

338

ment she described her as a pretty, light-hearted girl. She'd talk of Letty as so clever and so successful—and then say what a sad life she'd had, and then there was that quotation about stern affliction bravely borne—which really didn't seem to fit Letitia's life at all. Charlotte must, I think, have overheard a good deal that morning she came into the cafe. She certainly must have heard Dora mention about the lamp having been changed—about its being the shepherd and not the shepherdess. And she realized then what a very real danger to her security poor devoted Dora Bunner was.

"I'm afraid that that conversation with me in the cafe really sealed Dora's fate—if you'll excuse such a melodramatic expression. But I think it would have come to the same in the end . . . Because life couldn't be safe for Charlotte while Dora Bunner was alive. She loved Dora—she didn't want to kill Dora—but she couldn't see any other way. And, I expect (like Nurse Ellerton that I was telling you about, Bunch) she persuaded herself that it was really almost a *kindness*. Poor Bunny—not long to live anyway and perhaps a painful end. The queer thing is that she did her best to make Bunny's last day a happy day. The birthday party—and the special cake . . ."

"Delicious Death," said Phillipa with a shudder.

"Yes—yes, it was rather like that . . . she tried to give her friend a delicious death . . . The party, and all the things she liked to eat, and trying to stop people saying things to upset her. And then the tablets, whatever they were, in the aspirin bottle by her own bed so that Bunny, when she couldn't find the new bottle of aspirin she'd just bought, would go there to get some. And it would look, as it did look, that the tablets had been meant for *Letitia* . . .

"And so Bunny died in her sleep, quite happily, and Charlotte felt safe again. But she missed Dora Bunner—she missed her affection and her loyalty, she missed being able to talk to her about the old days . . . She cried bitterly the day I came up with that note from Julian—and her grief was quite genuine. She'd killed her own dear friend . . ."

"That's horrible," said Bunch. "Horrible."

"But it's very human," said Julian Harmon. "One forgets how human murderers are."

"I know," said Miss Marple. "Human. And often very much to be pitied. But very dangerous, too. Especially a weak, kindly murderer like Charlotte Blacklock. Because, once a weak person gets *really* frightened, they get quite savage with terror and they've no self-control at all."

"Murgatroyd?" said Julian.

"Yes, poor Miss Murgatroyd. Charlotte must have come up to the cottage and heard them rehearsing the murder. The window was open and she listened. It had never occurred to her until that moment that there was anyone else who could be a danger to her. Miss Hinchliffe was urging her friend to remember what she'd seen and until that moment Charlotte hadn't realized that anyone could have seen anything at all. She'd assumed that everybody would automatically be looking at Rudi Scherz. She must have held her breath outside the window and listened. Was it going to be all right? And then, just as Miss Hinchliffe rushed off to the station, Miss Murgatroyd got to a point which showed that she had stumbled on the truth. She called after Miss Hinchliffe: 'She wasn't *there* . . .'

"I asked Miss Hinchliffe, you know, if that was the way she said it . . . Because if she'd said '*She* wasn't there,' it wouldn't have meant the same thing."

"Now that's too subtle a point for me," said Craddock.

Miss Marple turned her eager pink and white face to him.

"Just think what's going on in Miss Murgatroyd's mind . . . One does see things, you know, and not know one sees them. In a railway accident once, I remember noticing a large blister of paint at the side of the carriage. I could have *drawn* it for you afterward. And once, when there was a fly bomb in London—splinters of glass everywhere—and the shock—but what I remember best is a woman standing in front of me who had a big hole halfway up the leg of her stocking and the stockings didn't match. So when Miss Murgatroyd stopped thinking and just tried to remember what she *saw,* she remembered a good deal

"She started, I think, near the mantelpiece, where the torch must have hit first—then it went along the two windows and there were people in between the windows and her. Mrs. Harmon with her knuckles screwed into her eyes for instance. She went on in her mind, following the torch past Miss Bunner with her mouth open and her eyes staring—past a blank wall and a table with a lamp and a cigarette box. And then came the shots—and quite suddenly she remembered a most incredible thing. She'd seen the wall where, later, there were the two bullet holes, the wall where Letitia Blacklock had been standing when she was shot, and at the moment when the revolver went off and Letty was shot, *Letty hadn't been there* . . .

"You see what I mean now? She'd been thinking of the three

women Miss Hinchliffe had told her to think about. If one of them hadn't been there, it would have been the *personality* she'd have fastened upon. She'd have said—in effect—'*That's* the one! *She* wasn't there!' But it was a *place* that was in her mind—a place where someone should have been—but the place wasn't filled—there wasn't anybody there. The place was there—but the person wasn't. And she couldn't take it in all at once. 'How extraordinary, Hinch,' she said. 'She wasn't *there*' . . . So that could only mean Letitia Blacklock . . ."

"But you knew before that, didn't you?" said Bunch. "When the lamp went out. When you wrote down those things on the paper."

"Yes, my dear. It all came together then, you see—all the various isolated bits—and made a coherent pattern."

Bunch quoted softly:

"*Lamp?* Yes. *Violets?* Yes. *Bottle of aspirin.* You meant that Bunny had been going to buy a new bottle that day, and so she ought not to have needed to take Letitia's?"

"Not unless her own bottle had been taken or hidden. It had to appear as though Letitia Blacklock was the one meant to be killed."

"Yes, I see. And then 'Delicious Death.' The cake—but more than the cake. The whole party setup. A happy day for Bunny before she died. Treating her rather like a dog you were going to destroy. That's what I find the most horrible thing of all—the sort of—of spurious kindness."

"She *was* quite a kindly woman. What she said at the last in the kitchen was quite true. 'I didn't want to kill anybody.' What she wanted was a great deal of money that didn't belong to her! And before that desire—(and it had become a kind of obsession—the money was to pay her back for all the suffering life had inflicted on her)—everything else went to the wall. People with a grudge against the world are always dangerous. They seem to think life owes them something. I've known many an invalid who has suffered far worse and been cut off from life much more than Charlotte Blacklock—and they've managed to lead happy contented lives. It's what's in *yourself* that makes you happy or unhappy. But, oh, dear, I'm afraid I'm straying away from what we were talking about. Where were we?"

"Going over your list," said Bunch. "What did you mean by "Making enquiries'? Inquiries about what?"

Miss Marple shook her head playfully at Inspector Craddock.

"You ought to have seen that, Inspector Craddock. You showed me that letter from Letitia Blacklock to her sister. It had the word 'enquiries' in it twice—each time spelt with an *e*. But in the note I asked Bunch to show you, Miss Blacklock had written 'inquiries' with an *i*. People don't usually alter their spelling as they get older. It seemed to me very significant."

"Yes," Craddock agreed. "I ought to have spotted that."

Bunch was continuing: *"Severe affliction bravely borne.* That's what Bunny said to you in the cafe and, of course, Letitia hadn't had any affliction. *Iodine.* That put you on the track of goiter?"

"Yes, dear. Switzerland, you know, and Miss Blacklock giving the impression that her sister had died of consumption. But I remembered then that the greatest authorities on goiter and the most skillful surgeons operating on it are Swiss. And it linked up with those really rather preposterous pearls that Letitia Blacklock always wore. Not really her *style*—but just right for concealing the scar."

"I understand now her agitation the night the string broke," said Craddock. "It seemed at the time quite disproportionate."

"And after that, it was Lotty you wrote, not Letty as we thought," said Bunch.

"Yes, I remembered that the sister's name was Charlotte, and that Dora Bunner had called Miss Blacklock Lotty once or twice—and that each time she did so, she had been very upset afterwards."

"And what about Berne and Old Age Pension?"

"Rudi Scherz had been an orderly in a hospital in Berne."

"And Old Age Pension."

"Oh, my dear Bunch, I mentioned that to you in the Bluebird though I didn't really see the application then. How Mrs. Wotherspoon drew Mrs. Bartlett's Old Age Pension as well as her own—though Mrs. Bartlett had been dead for years—simply because one old woman is so like another old woman—Yes, it all made a pattern and I felt so worked up I went out to cool my head a little and think what could be done about proving all this. Then Miss Hinchliffe picked me up and we found Miss Murgatroyd . . ."

Miss Marple's voice dropped. It was no longer excited and pleased. It was quiet and remorseless.

"I knew then something had *got* to be done. Quickly! But there still wasn't any *proof.* I thought out a possible plan and I talked to Sergeant Fletcher."

"And have I had Fletcher on the carpet for it!" said Craddock. "He'd no business to go agreeing to your plans without reporting first to me."

"He didn't like it, but I talked him into it," said Miss Marple. "We went up to Little Paddocks and I got hold of Mitzi."

Julia drew a deep breath and said, "I can't imagine how you ever got her to do it."

"I worked on her, my dear," said Miss Marple. "She thinks far too much about herself anyway, and it will be good for her to have done something for others. I flattered her up, of course, and said I was sure if she'd been in her own country she'd have been in the Resistance movement, and she said, 'Yes, indeed.' And I said I could see she had got just the temperament for that sort of work. She was brave, didn't mind taking risks and could act a part. I told her stories of deeds done by girls in the Resistance movements, some of them true, and some of them, I'm afraid, invented. She got tremendously worked up!"

"Marvelous," said Patrick.

"And then I got her to agree to do her part. I rehearsed her till she was word perfect. Then I told her to go upstairs to her room and not come down until Inspector Craddock came. The worst of these excitable people is that they're apt to go off half-cocked and start the whole thing before the time."

"She did it very well," said Julia.

"I don't quite see the point," said Bunch. "Of course, I wasn't there—" she added apologetically.

"The point? It was a little complicated—and rather touch and go. The idea was that Mitzi, whilst admitting, as though casually, that blackmail *had* been in her mind, was now so worked up and terrified that she was willing to come out with the truth. She'd seen, through the keyhole of the dining room, Miss Blacklock in the hall with a revolver behind Rudi Scherz. She'd seen, that is, *what had actually taken place.* Now the only danger was that Charlotte Blacklock might have realized that, as the key was in the keyhole, Mitzi couldn't possibly have seen anything at all. But I banked on the fact that you don't think of things like that when you've just had a bad shock. All she could take in was that Mitzi had seen her."

Craddock took over the story.

"But—and this was essential—I pretended to receive this with skepticism, and I made an immediate attack, as though unmasking my batteries at last, upon someone who had not been previously suspected. I accused Edmund—"

"And very nicely *I* played *my* part," said Edmund. "Hot denial. All according to plan. What wasn't according to plan, Phillipa, my love, was you throwing in your little chirp and coming out into the open as 'Pip.' Neither the Inspector nor I had any idea you were Pip. *I* was going to be Pip! It threw us off our stride for the moment, but the Inspector made a masterly comeback and made some perfectly filthy insinuations about my wanting a rich wife which will probably stick in your subconscious and make irreparable trouble between us one day."

"I don't see why that was necessary."

"Don't you? It meant that, *from Charlotte Blacklock's point of view,* the only person who suspected or knew the truth, was *Mitzi.* The suspicions of the police were elsewhere. They had treated Mitzi for the moment as a liar. But if Mitzi were to persist, they might listen to her and take her seriously. So Mitzi had got to be silenced."

"Mitzi went straight out of the room and back to the kitchen—just like I had told her," said Miss Marple. "Miss Blacklock came out after her almost immediately. Mitzi was apparently alone in the kitchen. Sergeant Fletcher was behind the scullery door. And I was in the broom cupboard in the kitchen. Luckily I'm very thin."

Bunch looked at Miss Marple.

"What did you expect to happen, Aunt Jane?"

"One of two things. Either Charlotte would offer Mitzi money to hold her tongue—and Sergeant Fletcher would be a witness to that offer, or else—or else I thought she'd try to kill Mitzi."

"But she couldn't hope to get away with *that*? She'd have been suspected at once."

"Oh, my dear, she was past reasoning. She was just a snapping, terrified, cornered rat. Think what had happened that day. The scene between Miss Hinchliffe and Miss Murgatroyd. Miss Hinchliffe driving off to the station. As soon as she comes back Miss Murgatroyd will explain that Letitia Blacklock wasn't in the room that night. There's just a few minutes in which to make sure Miss Murgatroyd can't tell anything. No time to make a plan or set a stage. Just crude murder. She greets the poor woman and strangles her. Then a quick rush home, to change, to be sitting by the fire when the others come in, as though she'd never been out.

"And then came the revelation of Julia's identity. She breaks her pearls and is terrified they may notice her scar. Later, the Inspector telephones that he's bringing everyone there. No time to think, to rest. Up to her neck in murder now, no mercy killing—or undesirable young man to be put out of the way. Crude plain murder. Is she safe?

Yes, so far. And then comes Mitzi—yet *another* danger. Kill Mitzi, stop her tongue! She's beside herself with fear. Not human any longer. Just a dangerous animal."

"But why were you in the broom cupboard, Aunt Jane?" asked Bunch. "Couldn't you have left it to Sergeant Fletcher?"

"It was safer with two of us, my dear. And, besides, I knew I could mimic Dora Bunner's voice. If anything could break Charlotte Blacklock down that would."

"And it did . . . !"

"Yes . . . she went to pieces."

There was a long silence as memory laid hold of them and then, speaking with determined lightness, to ease the strain, Julia said:

"It's made a wonderful difference to Mitzi. She told me yesterday that she was taking a post near Southampton. And she said (Julia produced a very good imitation of Mitzi's accent):

"'I got there and if they say to me you have to register with the police—you are an alien, I say to them, "Yes, I will register! The police, they know me well. I assist the police! Without me the police never would they have made the arrest of a very dangerous criminal. I risked my life because I am brave—brave like a lion—I do not care about risks" "Mitzi," they say to me, "you are a *heroine*, you are superb." "Ach! it is nothing, I say."'"

Julia stopped.

"And a great deal more," she added.

"I think," said Edmund thoughtfully, "that soon Mitzi will have assisted the police in not one but hundreds of cases!"

"She's softened toward me," said Phillipa. "She actually presented me with the recipe for Delicious Death as a kind of wedding present. She added that I was on no account to divulge the secret to Julia, because Julia had ruined her omelette pan."

"Mrs. Lucas," said Edmund, "is all over Phillipa now that since Belle Goedler's death, Phillipa and Julia have inherited the Goedler millions. She sent us some silver asparagus tongs as a wedding present. I shall have enormous pleasure in *not* asking her to the wedding!"

"And so they lived happily ever after," said Patrick. "Edmund and Phillipa—And Julia and Patrick?" he added tentatively.

"Not with me, you won't live happily ever after," said Julia. "The remarks that Inspector Craddock improvised to address to Edmund apply far more aptly to you. You *are* the sort of soft young man who would like a rich wife. Nothing doing!"

"There's gratitude for you," said Patrick. "After all I did for that girl."

"Nearly landed me in prison on a murder charge—that's what your forgetfulness nearly did for me," said Julia. "I shall never forget that evening when your sister's letter came. I really thought I was in for it. I couldn't see any way out. As it is," she added musingly, "I think I shall go on the stage."

"What? You, too?" groaned Patrick.

"Yes. I might go to Perth. See if I can get your Julia's place in the Rep there. Then, when I've learnt my job, I shall go into theater management—and put on Edmund's plays, perhaps."

"I thought you wrote novels," said Julian Harmon.

"Well, so did I," said Edmund. "I began writing a novel. Rather good it was. Pages about an unshaven man getting out of bed and what he smelt like, and the gray streets, and a horrible old woman with dropsy and a vicious young tart who dribbled down her chin— and they all talked interminably about the state of the world and wondered what they were alive for. And suddenly I began to wonder, too . . . And then a rather comic idea occurred to me . . . and I jotted it down—and then I worked up rather a good little scene . . . All very obvious stuff. But, somehow, I got interested . . . and before I knew what I was doing I'd finished a roaring farce in three acts."

"What's it called?" asked Patrick. *"What the Butler Saw?"*

"Well, it easily might be . . . As a matter of fact I've called it *Elephants Do Forget.* What's more, it's been accepted and it's going to be produced!"

"Elephants Do Forget," murmured Bunch. "I thought they didn't?"

The Rev. Julian Harmon gave a guilty start.

"My goodness! I've been so interested. My *sermon* . . ."

"Detective stories again," said Bunch. "Real life ones this time."

"You might preach on *Thou Shalt Do No Murder,*" suggested Patrick.

"No," said Julian Harmon quietly, "I shan't take that as my text."

"No," said Bunch. "You're quite right, Julian. I know a much nicer text, a happy text." She quoted in her fresh voice, " 'For lo, the Spring is here and the Voice of the Turtle is heard in the Land'—I haven't got it quite right—but you know the one I mean. Though why a *turtle* I can't think. I shouldn't think turtles have got nice voices at all."

"The word turtle," explained the Rev. Julian Harmon, "is not very happily translated. It doesn't mean a reptile but the turtle dove. The Hebrew word in the original is—"

Bunch interrupted him by giving him a hug and saying:

"I know one thing— *You* think that the Ahasuerus of the Bible is Artaxerxes the Second, but between you and me it was Artaxerxes the Third."

As always, Julian Harmon wondered why his wife should think that story so particularly funny. . . .

"Tiglath-Pileser wants to go and help you," said Bunch. "He ought to be a very proud cat. *He* showed us how the lights went out."

Epilogue

"We ought to order some papers," said Edmund to Phillipa upon the day of their return to Chipping Cleghorn after the honeymoon. "Let's go along to Totman's."

Mr. Totman, a heavy-breathing, slow-moving man, received them with affability.

"Glad to see you back, sir. *And* madam."

"We want to order some papers."

"Certainly, sir. And your mother is keeping well, I hope? Quite settled down at Bournemouth?"

"She loves it," said Edmund who had not the faintest idea whether this was so or not, but like most sons, preferred to believe that all was well with those loved, but frequently irritating beings, parents.

"Yes, sir. Very agreeable place. Went there for my holiday last year. Mrs. Totman enjoyed it very much."

"I'm glad. About papers, we'd like—"

"And I hear you have a play on in London, sir. Very amusing, so they tell me."

"Yes, it's doing very well."

"Called *Elephants Do Forget,* so I hear. You'll excuse me, sir, asking you, but I always thought that they *didn't*—forget, I mean."

"Yes—yes, exactly—I've begun to think it was a mistake calling it that. So many people have said just what you say."

"A kind of natural history fact, I've always understood."

"Yes—yes. Like earwigs making good mothers."

"Do they indeed, sir? Now that's a fact I *didn't* know."

"About the papers—"

"*The Times,* sir, I think it was?" Mr. Totman paused with pencil uplifted.

"The *Daily Worker,*" said Edmund firmly. "And the *Daily Telegraph,*" said Phillipa. "And the *New Statesman,*" said Edmund. "The *Radio Times,*" said Phillipa. "The *Spectator,*" said Edmund. "The *Gardener's Chronicle,*" said Phillipa.

They both paused to take breath.

"Thank you, sir," said Mr. Totman. *"And* the *Gazette,* I suppose?"

"No," said Edmund.

"No," said Phillipa.

"Excuse me, you *do* want the *Gazette*?"

"No."

"No."

"You mean—" Mr. Totman liked to get things perfectly clear. "You *don't* want the *Gazette!*"

"No, we don't."

"Certainly not."

"You don't want the *North Benham News and Chipping Cleghorn Gazette*?"

"No."

"You don't want me to send it along to you every week?"

"No." Edmund added: "Is that quite clear now?"

"Oh, yes, sir—yes."

Edmund and Phillipa went out, and Mr. Totman padded into his back parlor.

"Got a pencil, Mother?" he said. "My pen's run out."

"Here you are," said Mrs. Totman, seizing the order book. "I'll do it. What do they want?"

"*Daily Worker, Daily Telegraph—Radio Times, New Statesman, Spectator*—let me see—*Gardener's Chronicle.*"

"*Gardener's Chronicle,*" repeated Mrs. Totman, writing busily. "And the *Gazette.*"

"They don't want the *Gazette.*"

"What?"

"They don't want the *Gazette.* They said so."

"Nonsense," said Mrs. Totman. "You don't hear properly. Of course they want the *Gazette*! Everybody has the *Gazette.* How else would they know what's going on round here?"

Agatha Christie

—

4:50 From Paddington

Previously titled *What Mrs. McGillicuddy Saw!*

1

Mrs. McGillicuddy panted along the platform in the wake of the porter carrying her suitcase. Mrs. McGillicuddy was short and stout, the porter was tall and free-striding. In addition, Mrs. McGillicuddy was burdened with a large quantity of parcels; the result of a day's Christmas shopping. The race was, therefore, an uneven one, and the porter turned the corner at the end of the platform while Mrs. McGillicuddy was still coming up the straight.

No. 1 platform was not at the moment unduly crowded, since a train had just gone out; but, in the no man's land beyond, a milling crowd was rushing in several directions at once, to and from undergrounds, left-luggage offices, tea rooms, inquiry offices, indicator boards and the two outlets, Arrival and Departure, to the outside world.

Mrs. McGillicuddy and her parcels were buffeted to and fro, but she arrived eventually at the entrance to No. 3 platform, and deposited one parcel at her feet while she searched her bag for the ticket that would enable her to pass the stern, uniformed guardian at the gate.

At that moment, a voice, raucous yet refined, burst into speech over her head.

"The train standing at Platform 3," the voice told her, "is the 4:54 for Brackhampton, Milchester, Waverton, Carvil Junction, Roxeter and stations to Chadmouth. Passengers for Brackhampton and Milchester travel at the rear of the train. Passengers for Vanequay change at Roxeter." The voice shut itself off with a click, and then re-opened conversation by announcing the arrival at Platform 9 of the 4:35 from Birmingham and Wolverhampton.

Mrs. McGillicuddy found her ticket and presented it. The man clipped it, murmured: "On the right—rear portion."

Mrs. McGillicuddy padded up the platform and found her porter, looking bored and staring into space, outside the door of a third-class carriage.

"Here you are, lady."

"I'm traveling first class," said Mrs. McGillicuddy.

"You didn't say so." grumbled the porter. His eye swept her masculine-looking pepper-and-salt tweed coat disparagingly.

Mrs. McGillicuddy who had said so, did not argue the point. She was sadly out of breath.

The porter retrieved the suitcase and marched with it to the adjoining coach where Mrs. McGillicuddy was installed in solitary splendor. The 4:54 was not much patronized, the first-class clientele preferring either the faster morning express or the 6:40 with dining cars. Mrs. McGillicuddy handed the porter his tip which he received with disappointment, clearly considering it more applicable to third-class than to first-class travel. Mrs. McGillicuddy, though prepared to spend money on comfortable travel after a night journey from the North and a day's feverish shopping, was at no time an extravagant tipper.

She settled herself back on the plush cushions with a sigh and opened a magazine. Five minutes later, whistles blew and the train started. The magazine slipped from Mrs. McGillicuddy's hand, her head dropped sideways, three minutes later she was asleep. She slept for thirty-five minutes and awoke refreshed. Resettling her hat which had slipped askew, she sat up and looked out of the window at what she could see of the flying countryside. It was quite dark now, a dreary, misty December day—Christmas was only five days ahead. London had been dark and dreary; the country was no less so, though occasionally rendered cheerful with its constant clusters of lights as the train flashed through towns and stations.

"Serving last tea now," said an attendant, whisking open the corridor door like a jinni. Mrs. McGillicuddy had already partaken of tea at a large department store. She was for the moment amply nourished. The attendant went on down the corridor uttering his monotonous cry. With a pleased expression, Mrs. McGillicuddy looked up at the rack where her various parcels reposed. The face towels had been excellent value and just what Margaret wanted, the space gun for Robby and the rabbit for Jean were highly satisfactory, and that evening coatee was just the thing she herself wanted, warm but dressy. The pullover for Hector, too . . . her mind dwelt with approval on the soundness of her purchases.

Her satisfied gaze returned to the window, a train traveling in the opposite direction rushed by with a screech, making the windows rattle and causing her to start. The train clattered over points and passed through a station.

Then it began suddenly to slow down, presumably in obedience to a signal. For some minutes it crawled along, then stopped, presently it began to move forward again. Another up train passed them, though with less vehemence than the first one. The train gathered speed again. At that moment another train, also on a down line, swerved inward toward them, for a moment with almost alarming effect. For a time the two trains ran parallel, now one gaining a little, now the other. Mrs. McGillicuddy looked from her window through the windows of the parallel carriages. Most of the blinds were down, but occasionally the occupants of the carriages were visible. The other train was not very full and there were many empty carriages.

At the moment when the two trains gave the illusion of being stationary, a blind in one of the carriages flew up with a snap. Mrs. McGillicuddy looked into the lighted first-class carriage that was only a few feet away.

Then she drew her breath with a gasp and half rose to her feet.

Standing with his back to the window and to her was a man. His hands were round the throat of a woman who faced him, and he was slowly, remorselessly, strangling her. Her eyes were starting from their sockets, her face was purple and congested. As Mrs. McGillicuddy watched, fascinated, the end came, the body went limp and crumpled in the man's hands.

At the same moment, Mrs. McGillicuddy's train slowed down again and the other began to gain speed. It passed forward and a moment or two later it had vanished from sight.

Almost automatically Mrs. McGillicuddy's hand went up to the communication cord, then paused, irresolute. After all, what use would it be ringing the cord of the train in which she was traveling? The horror of what she had seen at such close quarters and the unusual circumstances made her feel paralyzed. Some immediate action was necessary—but what?

The door of her compartment was drawn back and a ticket collector said, "Ticket, please."

Mrs. McGillicuddy turned to him with vehemence.

"A woman has been strangled," she said. "In a train that has just passed. I saw it."

The ticket collector looked at her doubtfully.

"I beg your pardon, Madam?"

"A man strangled a woman! In a train. I saw it—through there." She pointed to the window.

The ticket collector looked extremely doubtful.

"Strangled?" he said disbelievingly.

"Yes, strangled! I saw it, I tell you. You must do something at once!"

The ticket collector coughed apologetically.

"You don't think, Madam, that you may have had a little nap and—er—" he broke off tactfully.

"I have had a nap, but if you think this was a dream, you're quite wrong. I saw it, I tell you."

The ticket collector's eyes dropped to the open magazine lying on the seat. On the exposed page was a girl being strangled while a man with a revolver threatened the pair from an open doorway.

He said persuasively: "Now don't you think, Madam, that you'd been reading an exciting story, and that you just dropped off, and awaking a little confused—"

Mrs. McGillicuddy interrupted him.

"I saw it," she said. "I was as wide awake as you are. And I looked out of the window into the window of the train alongside, and a man was strangling a woman. And what I want to know, is what are you going to do about it?"

"Well—Madam—"

"You're going to do something, I suppose?"

The ticket collector sighed reluctantly and glanced at his watch.

"We shall be in Brackhampton in exactly seven minutes. I'll report what you've told me. In what direction was the train you mention going?"

"This direction, of course. You don't suppose I'd have been able to see all this if a train had flashed past going in the other direction?"

The ticket collector looked as though he thought Mrs. McGillicuddy was quite capable of seeing anything anywhere as the fancy took her. But he remained polite.

"You can rely on me, Madam," he said. "I will report your statement. Perhaps I might have your name and address—just in case—"

Mrs. McGillicuddy gave him the address where she would be staying for the next few days and her permanent address in Scotland, and he wrote them down. Then he withdrew with the air of a man who has done his duty and dealt successfully with a tiresome member of the traveling public.

Mrs. McGillicuddy remained frowning and vaguely unsatisfied. Would the ticket collector really report her statement? Or had he just been soothing her down? There were, she supposed vaguely, a lot of elderly women traveling around, fully convinced that they had unmasked Communist plots, were in danger of being murdered, saw flying saucers and secret spaceships, and reported murders that had never taken place. If the man dismissed her as one of those . . .

The train was slowing down, now, passing over points, and running through the bright lights of a large town.

Mrs. McGillicuddy opened her handbag, pulled out a receipted bill which was all she could find, wrote a rapid note on the back of it with her ballpoint pen, put it into a spare envelope that she fortunately happened to have, stuck the envelope down and wrote on it.

The train drew slowly into a crowded platform. The usual ubiquitous voice was intoning:

"The train now arriving at Platform 1 is the 5:38 for Milchester, Waverton, Roxeter and stations to Chadmouth. Passengers for Market Basing take the train now waiting at No. 3 platform. No. 1 Bay for stopping train to Carbury."

Mrs. McGillicuddy looked anxiously along the platform. So many passengers and so few porters. Ah, there was one! She hailed him authoritatively.

"Porter! Please take this at once to the stationmaster's office."

She handed him the envelope and with it a shilling.

Then, with a sigh, she leaned back. Well, she had done what she could. Her mind lingered with an instant's regret on the shilling. Sixpence would really have been enough . . .

Her mind went back to the scene she had witnessed. Horrible, quite horrible. She was a strong-nerved woman, but she shivered. What a strange—what a fantastic thing to happen to her, Elspeth McGillicuddy. If the blind of the carriage had not happened to fly up . . . But that, of course, was Providence.

357

Providence had willed that she, Elspeth McGillicuddy, should be a witness of the crime. Her lips set grimly.

Voices shouted, whistles blew, doors were banged shut. The 5:38 drew slowly out of Brackhampton Station. An hour and five minutes later it stopped at Milchester.

Mrs. McGillicuddy collected her parcels and her suitcase and got out. She peered up and down the platform. Her mind reiterated its former judgment: not enough porters. Such porters as there were seemed to be engaged with mailbags and luggage vans. Passengers nowadays seemed always expected to carry their own cases. Well, she couldn't carry her suitcase and her umbrella and all her parcels. She would have to wait. In due course she secured a porter.

"Taxi?"

"There will be something to meet me, I expect."

Outside Milchester Station, a taxi driver who had been watching the exit came forward. He spoke in a soft local voice.

"Is it Mrs. McGillicuddy? For St. Mary Mead?"

Mrs. McGillicuddy acknowledged her identity. The porter was recompensed, adequately if not handsomely. The car, with Mrs. McGillicuddy, her suitcase and her parcels, drove off into the night. It was a nine-mile drive. Sitting bolt upright in the car, Mrs. McGillicuddy was unable to relax. Her feelings yearned for expression. At last the taxi drove along the familiar village street and finally drew up at its destination; Mrs. McGillicuddy got out and walked up the brick path to the door. The driver deposited the cases inside as the door was opened by an elderly maid. Mrs. McGillicuddy passed straight through the hall to where, at the open sitting-room door, her hostess awaited her: an elderly, frail old lady.

"Elspeth!"

"Jane!"

They kissed, and without preamble or circumlocution, Mrs. McGillicuddy burst into speech.

"Oh, Jane!" she wailed. "I've just seen a murder!"

2

True to the precepts handed down to her by her mother and grand-mother—to wit: that a true lady can neither be shocked nor surprised—Miss Marple merely raised her eyebrows and shook her head, as she said:

"Most distressing for you, Elspeth, and surely most unusual. I think you had better tell me about it at once."

That was exactly what Mrs. McGillicuddy wanted to do. Allowing her hostess to draw her nearer to the fire, she sat down, pulled off her gloves and plunged into a vivid narrative.

Miss Marple listened with close attention. When Mrs. McGillicuddy at last paused for breath, Miss Marple spoke with decision.

"The best thing, I think, my dear, is for you to go upstairs and take off your hat and have a wash. Then we will have supper—during which we will not discuss this at all. After supper we can go into the matter thoroughly and discuss it from every aspect."

Mrs. McGillicuddy concurred with this suggestion. The two ladies had supper, discussing as they ate various aspects of life as lived in the village of St. Mary Mead. Miss Marple commented on the general distrust of the new organist, related the recent scandal about the chemist's wife, and touched on the hostility between the schoolmistress and the Village Institute. They then discussed Miss Marple's and Mrs. McGillicuddy's gardens.

"Peonies," said Miss Marple as she rose from table, "are most unaccountable. Either they do—or they don't do. But if they do establish themselves, they are with you for life, so to speak, and really most beautiful varieties nowadays."

They settled themselves by the fire again, and Miss Marple brought out two old Waterford glasses from a corner cupboard, and from another cupboard produced a bottle.

"No coffee tonight for you, Elspeth," she said. "You are already overexcited—and no wonder!—and probably would not sleep. I prescribe a glass of my cowslip wine, and later, perhaps, a cup of camomile tea."

Mrs. McGillicuddy acquiescing in these arrangements, Miss Marple poured out the wine.

"Jane," said Mrs. McGillicuddy, as she took an appreciative sip, "you don't think, do you, that I dreamed it, or imagined it?"

"Certainly not," said Miss Marple with warmth.

Mrs. McGillicuddy heaved a sigh of relief.

"That ticket collector," she said, "he thought so. Quite polite, but all the same—"

"I think, Elspeth, that that was quite natural under the circumstances. It sounded—and indeed was—a most unlikely story. And you were a complete stranger to him. No, I have no doubt at all that you saw what you've told me you saw. It's very extraordinary—but not at all impossible. I recollect myself being interested, when a train ran parallel to one in which I was traveling, to notice what a vivid and intimate picture one got of what was going on in one or two of the carriages. A little girl, I remember once, was playing with a Teddy Bear and suddenly she threw it deliberately at a fat man who was asleep in the corner, and he bounced up and looked most indignant, and the other passengers looked so amused. I saw them all quite vividly. I could have described afterward exactly what they looked like and what they had on."

Mrs. McGillicuddy nodded gratefully.

"That's just how it was."

"The man had his back to you, you say. So you didn't see his face?"

"No."

"And the woman, you can describe her? Young? Old?"

"Youngish. Between thirty and thirty-five, I should think. I couldn't say closer than that."

"Good-looking?"

"That again, I couldn't say. Her face, you see, was all contorted and—"

360

Miss Marple said quickly:

"Yes, yes, I quite understand. How was she dressed?"

"She had on a fur coat of some kind, a palish fur. No hat. Her hair was blonde."

"And there was nothing distinctive that you can remember about the man?"

Mrs. McGillicuddy took a little time to think carefully before she replied.

"He was tallish—and dark, I think. He had a heavy coat on so that I couldn't judge his build very well." She added despondently, "It's not really very much to go on."

"It's something," said Miss Marple. She paused before saying: "You feel quite sure, in your own mind, that the girl was—dead?"

"She was dead, I'm sure of it. Her tongue came out and—I'd rather not talk about it. . . ."

"Of course not. Of course not," said Miss Marple quickly. "We shall know more, I expect, in the morning."

"In the morning?"

"I should imagine it will be in the morning papers. After this man had attacked and killed her, he would have a body on his hands. What would he do? Presumably he would leave the train quickly at the first station—by the way, can you remember if it was a corridor carriage?"

"No, it was not."

"That seems to point to a train that was not going far afield. It would almost certainly stop at Brackhampton. Let us say he leaves the train at Brackhampton, perhaps arranging the body in a corner seat, with the face hidden by the fur collar to delay discovery. Yes—I think that that is what he would do. But of course it will be discovered before very long—and I should imagine that the news of a murdered woman discovered on a train would be almost certain to be in the morning papers. We shall see."

II

But it was not in the morning papers.

Miss Marple and Mrs. McGillicuddy, after making sure of this, finished their breakfast in silence. Both were reflecting.

After breakfast, they took a turn round the garden. But this, usually an absorbing pastime, was today somewhat halfhearted. Miss

Marple did indeed call attention to some new and rare species she had acquired for her rock garden but did so in an almost absentminded manner. And Mrs. McGillicuddy did not, as was customary, counter-attack with a list of her own recent acquisitions.

"The garden is not looking at all as it should," said Miss Marple, but still speaking absentmindedly. "Doctor Haydock has absolutely forbidden me to do any stooping or kneeling—and really, what can you do if you don't stoop or kneel? There's old Edwards, of course—but so opinionated. And all this jobbing gets them into bad habits, lots of cups of tea and so much pottering—not any real work."

"Oh I know," said Mrs. McGillicuddy. "Of course there's no question of my being forbidden to stoop, but really, especially after meals—and having put on weight"—she looked down at her ample proportions—"it does bring on heartburn."

There was a silence and then Mrs. McGillicuddy planted her feet sturdily, stood still, and turned on her friend.

"Well?" she said.

It was a small, insignificant word but it acquired full significance from Mrs. McGillicuddy's tone, and Miss Marple understood its meaning perfectly.

"I know," she said.

The two ladies looked at each other.

"I think," said Miss Marple, "we might walk down to the police station and talk to Sergeant Cornish. He's intelligent and patient, and I know him very well and he knows me. I think he'll listen—and pass the information on to the proper quarter."

Accordingly some three quarters of an hour later, Miss Marple and Mrs. McGillicuddy were talking to a fresh-faced, grave man between thirty and forty who listened attentively to what they had to say.

Frank Cornish received Miss Marple with cordiality and even deference. He set chairs for the two ladies and said: "Now, what can we do for you, Miss Marple?"

Miss Marple said: "I would like you, please, to listen to my friend Mrs. McGillicuddy's story."

And Sergeant Cornish had listened. At the close of the recital he remained silent for a moment or two.

Then he said:

"That's a very extraordinary story." His eyes, without seeming to do so, had sized Mrs. McGillicuddy up while she was telling it.

On the whole, he was favorably impressed. A sensible woman,

able to tell a story clearly; not, so far as he could judge, an over-imaginative or hysterical woman. Moreover, Miss Marple, so it seemed, believed in the accuracy of her friend's story and he knew all about Miss Marple. Everybody in St. Mary Mead knew Miss Marple; fluffy and dithery in appearance, but inwardly as sharp and as shrewd as they make them.

He cleared his throat and spoke.

"Of course," he said, "you may have been mistaken—I'm not saying you were, mind—but you may have been. There's a lot of horseplay goes on. It mayn't have been serious or fatal."

"I know what I saw," said Mrs. McGillicuddy grimly.

"And you won't budge from it," thought Frank Cornish, "and I'd say that likely or unlikely, you may be right."

Aloud he said: "You reported it to the railway officials, and you've come and reported it to me. That's the proper procedure and you may rely on me to have inquiries instituted."

He stopped. Miss Marple nodded her head gently, satisfied. Mrs. McGillicuddy was not quite so satisfied, but she did not say anything. Sergeant Cornish addressed Miss Marple, not so much because he wanted her ideas, as because he wanted to hear what she would say.

"Granted the facts are as reported," he said. "What do you think has happened to the body?"

"There seem to be only two possibilities," said Miss Marple without hesitation. "The more likely one, of course, is that the body was left in the train, but that seems improbable now, for it would have been found sometime last night by another traveler or by the railway staff at the train's ultimate destination."

Frank Cornish nodded.

"The only other course open to the murderer would be to push the body out of the train on to the line. It must, I suppose, be still on the track somewhere as yet undiscovered—though that does seem a little unlikely. But there would be, as far as I can see, no other way of dealing with it."

"You read about bodies being put in trunks," said Mrs. McGillicuddy, "but no one travels with trunks nowadays, only suitcases, and you couldn't get a body into a suitcase."

"Yes," said Cornish. "I agree with you both. The body, if there is a body, ought to have been discovered by now, or will be very soon. I'll let you know any developments there are—though I daresay you'll read about them in the papers. There's the possibility, of course, that the woman, though savagely attacked, was not actually dead. She may have been able to leave the train on her own feet."

"Hardly without assistance," said Miss Marple. "And if so, it will have been noticed. A man, supporting a woman whom he says is ill."

"Yes, it will have been noticed," said Cornish. "Or if a woman was found unconscious or ill in a carriage and was removed to a hospital, that, too, will be on record. I think you may rest assured that you'll hear about it all in a very short time."

But that day passed and the next day. On that evening Miss Marple received a note from Sergeant Cornish.

In regard to the matter on which you consulted me, full inquiries have been made, with no result. No woman's body has been found. No hospital has administered treatment to a woman such as you describe, and no case of a woman suffering from shock or taken ill, or leaving a station supported by a man has been observed. You may take it that the fullest inquiries have been made. I suggest that your friend may have witnessed a scene such as she described but that it was much less serious than she supposed.

3

"Less serious? Fiddlesticks!" said Mrs. McGillicuddy. "It was murder!"

She looked defiantly at Miss Marple and Miss Marple looked back at her.

"Go on, Jane," said Mrs. McGillicuddy. "Say it was all a mistake! Say I imagined the whole thing! That's what you think now, isn't it?"

"Anyone can be mistaken," Miss Marple pointed out gently. "Anybody, Elspeth, even you. I think we must bear that in mind. But I still think, you know, that you were most probably not mistaken. You use glasses for reading, but you've got very good far sight—and what you saw impressed you very powerfully. You were definitely suffering from shock when you arrived here."

"It's a thing I shall never forget," said Mrs. McGillicuddy with a shudder. "The trouble is, I don't see what I can do about it!"

"I don't think," said Miss Marple thoughtfully, "that there's anything more you can do about it." (If Mrs. McGillicuddy had been alert to the tones of her friend's voice, she might have noticed a very faint stress laid on the *you*.) "You've reported what you saw—to the railway people and to the police. No, there's nothing more you can do."

"That's a relief, in a way," said Mrs. McGillicuddy, "because, as you know, I'm going out to Ceylon immediately after Christmas to stay with Roderick and I certainly do not want to put that visit off—I've been looking forward to it so much. Though of course I would put it off if I thought it was my duty," she added conscientiously.

"I'm sure you would, Elspeth, but as I say, I consider you've done everything you possibly could do."

"It's up to the police," said Mrs. McGillicuddy. "And if the police choose to be stupid—"

Miss Marple shook her head decisively.

"Oh no," she said, "the police aren't stupid. And that makes it interesting, doesn't it?"

Mrs. McGillicuddy looked at her without comprehension and Miss Marple reaffirmed her judgment of her friend as a woman of excellent principles and no imagination.

"One wants to know," said Miss Marple, "what really happened."

"She was killed."

"Yes, but who killed her, and why, and what happened to her body? Where is it now?"

"That's the business of the police to find out."

"Exactly! And they haven't found out. That means, doesn't it, that the man was clever—very clever. I can't imagine, you know," said Miss Marple knitting her brows, "how he disposed of it. You kill a woman in a fit of passion—it must have been unpremeditated; you'd never choose to kill a woman in such circumstances just a few minutes before running into a big station. No, it must have been a quarrel—jealousy—something of that kind. You strangle her—and there you are, as I say, with a dead body on your hands and on the point of running into a station. What could you do except as I said at first, prop the body up in a corner as though asleep, hiding the face, and then yourself leave the train as quickly as possible. And yet there must have been one. . . ."

Miss Marple lost herself in thought.

Mrs. McGillicuddy spoke to her twice before Miss Marple answered.

"You're getting deaf, Jane."

"Just a little, perhaps. People do not seem to me to enunciate their words as clearly as they used to do. But it wasn't that I didn't hear you. I'm afraid I wasn't paying attention."

"I just asked about the trains to London tomorrow. Would the afternoon be all right? I'm going to Margaret's and she isn't expecting me before teatime."

"I wonder, Elspeth, if you would mind going up by the 12:15? We could have an early lunch."

"Of course and—"

Miss Marple went on, drowning out her friend's words:

"And I wonder, too, if Margaret would mind if you didn't arrive for tea—if you arrived about seven, perhaps?"

Mrs. McGillicuddy looked at her friend curiously.

"What's on your mind, Jane?"

"I suggest, Elspeth, that I should travel up to London with you, and that we should travel down again as far as Brackhampton in the train you traveled by the other day. You would then return to London from Brackhampton and I would come on here as you did. I, of course, would pay the fares," Miss Marple stressed this point firmly.

Mrs. McGillicuddy ignored the financial aspect.

"What on earth do you expect, Jane?" she asked. "Another murder?"

"Certainly not," said Miss Marple shocked. "But I confess I should like to see for myself, under your guidance, the—the—really it is most difficult to find the correct term—the terrain of the crime."

So accordingly on the following day Miss Marple and Mrs. McGillicuddy found themselves in two opposite corners of a first-class carriage speeding out of London by the 4:54 from Paddington. Paddington had been even more crowded than on the preceding Friday, as there were now only two days to go before Christmas, but the 4:54 was comparatively peaceful—at any rate in the rear portion.

On this occasion no train drew level with them, or they with another train. At intervals trains flashed past them toward London. On two occasions trains flashed past them the other way going at high speed. At intervals Mrs. McGillicuddy consulted her watch doubtfully.

"It's hard to tell just when—We'd passed through a station I know . . ." But they were continually passing through stations.

"We're due in Brackhampton in five minutes," said Miss Marple.

A ticket collector appeared in the doorway. Miss Marple raised her eyes interrogatively. Mrs. McGillicuddy shook her head. It was not the same ticket collector. He clipped their tickets and passed on, staggering just a little as the train swung round a long curve. It slackened speed as it did so.

"I expect we're coming into Brackhampton," said Mrs. McGillicuddy.

"We're getting into the outskirts, I think," said Miss Marple.

There were lights flashing past outside, buildings, an occasional glimpse of streets and trams. Their speed slackened further. They began crossing points.

"We'll be there in a minute," said Mrs. McGillicuddy, "and I can't really see this journey has been any good at all. Has it suggested anything to you, Jane?"

"I'm afraid not," said Miss Marple in a rather doubtful voice.

"A sad waste of good money," said Mrs. McGillicuddy but with less disapproval than she would have used had she been paying for herself. Miss Marple had been quite adamant on that point.

"All the same," said Miss Marple, "one likes to see with one's own eyes where a thing happened. This train's just a few minutes late. Was yours on time on Friday?"

"I think so. I didn't really notice."

The train drew slowly into the busy length of Brackhampton Station. The loudspeaker announced hoarsely, doors opened and shut, people got in and out, milled up and down the platform. It was a busy, crowded scene.

Easy, thought Miss Marple, for a murderer to merge into that crowd, to leave the station in the midst of that pressing mass of people, or even to select another carriage and go on in the train to wherever its ultimate destination might be. Easy to be one male passenger among many. But not so easy to make a body vanish into thin air. That body must be somewhere.

Mrs. McGillicuddy had descended. She spoke now from the platform, through the open window.

"Now take care of yourself, Jane," she said. "Don't catch a chill. It's a nasty treacherous time of year, and you're not so young as you were."

"I know," said Miss Marple.

"And don't let's worry ourselves any more over all this. We've done what we could."

Miss Marple nodded and said:

"Don't stand about in the cold, Elspeth. Or you'll be the one to catch a chill. Go and get yourself a good hot cup of tea in the refreshment room. You've got time, twelve minutes before your train back to town."

"I think perhaps I will. Good-by, Jane."

"Good-by, Elspeth. A happy Christmas to you. I hope you find Margaret well. Enjoy yourself in Ceylon, and give my love to dear Roderick—if he remembers me at all which I doubt."

"Of course he remembers you—very well. You helped him in some way when he was at school—something to do with money that was disappearing from a locker. He's never forgotten it."

"Oh, that!" said Miss Marple.

Mrs. McGillicuddy turned away, a whistle blew, the train began to move. Miss Marple watched the sturdy thick-set body of her friend recede. Elspeth could go to Ceylon with a clear conscience—she had done her duty and was freed from further obligation.

Miss Marple did not lean back as the train gathered speed. Instead she sat upright and devoted herself seriously to thought. Though in speech Miss Marple was woolly and diffuse, in mind she was clear and sharp. She had a problem to solve, the problem of her own future conduct; and, perhaps strangely, it presented itself to her as it had to Mrs. McGillicuddy, as a question of duty.

Mrs. McGillicuddy had said that they had both done all that they could do. It was true of Mrs. McGillicuddy, but about herself Miss Marple did not feel so sure.

It was a question, sometimes, of using one's special gifts. But perhaps that was conceited. After all, what could she do? Her friend's words came back to her, "You're not so young as you were . . ."

Dispassionately, like a general planning a campaign, or an accountant assessing a business, Miss Marple weighed up and set down in her mind the facts for and against further enterprise. On the credit side were the following:

1) *My long experience of life and human nature.*
2) *Sir Henry Clithering and his nephew (now at Scotland Yard, I believe), who were so very nice in the Little Paddocks case.*
3) *My nephew Raymond's second boy, David, who is, I am almost sure, in British Railways.*
4) *Griselda's boy Leonard who is so very knowledgeable about maps.*

Miss Marple reviewed these assets and approved them. They were all very necessary to reinforce the weaknesses on the debit side—in particular her own bodily weakness.

"It's not," thought Miss Marple, "as though I could go here, there and everywhere, making inquiries and finding out things."

Yes, that was the chief objection, her own age and weakness. Although, for her age, her health was good, yet she was old. And if Doctor Haydock had strictly forbidden her to do practical gardening he would hardly approve of her starting out to track down a murderer. For that, in effect, was what she was planning to do—and it was there that her loophole lay. For if heretofore murder had, so to speak, been forced upon her, in this case it would be that she herself set out deliberately to seek it. And she was not sure that she wanted to do so. She was old—old and tired. She felt at this moment, at the end of a tiring day, a great reluctance to enter upon any project at all. She wanted nothing at all but to reach home and sit by the fire with a nice tray of supper, and go to bed, and potter about the next day just snipping off a few things in the garden, tidying up in a very mild way, without stooping, without exerting herself.

"I'm too old for any more adventures," said Miss Marple to herself, watching absently out of the window the curving line of an embankment.

A curve.

Very faintly something stirred in her mind. Just after the ticket collector had clipped their tickets . . .

It suggested an idea. Only an idea. An entirely different idea . . .

A little pink flush came into Miss Marple's face. Suddenly she did not feel tired at all!

"I'll write to David tomorrow morning," she said to herself.

And at the same time another valuable asset flashed through her mind.

"Of course. My faithful Florence!"

II

Miss Marple set about her plan of campaign methodically and making due allowance for the Christmas season which was a definitely retarding factor.

She wrote to her great-nephew, David West, combining Christmas wishes with an urgent request for information.

Fortunately she was invited, as on previous years, to the vicarage for Christmas dinner, and here she was able to tackle young Leonard, home for the Christmas season, about maps.

Maps of all kinds were Leonard's passion. The reason for the old lady's inquiry about a large-scale map of a particular area did not rouse his curiosity. He discoursed on maps generally with fluency, and wrote down for her exactly what would suit her purpose best. In fact, he did better. He actually found that he had such a map among his collection and he lent it to her, Miss Marple promising to take great care of it and return it in due course.

III

"Maps," said his mother Griselda who still, although she had a grown-up son, looked strangely young and blooming to be inhabiting the shabby old vicarage. "What does she want with maps? I mean, what does she want them for?"

"I don't know," said young Leonard, "I don't think she said exactly."

"I wonder now . . ." said Griselda. "It seems very fishy to me. At her age the old pet ought to give up that sort of thing."

Leonard asked what sort of thing, and Griselda said elusively:

"Oh, poking her nose into things. Why maps, I wonder?"

In due course Miss Marple received a letter from her great-nephew David West. It ran affectionately:

> "Dear Aunt Jane. Now what are you up to? I've got the information you wanted. There are only two trains that can possibly apply—the 4:33 and the 5 o'clock. The former is a slow train and stops at Haling Broadway, Barwell Heath, Brackhampton and then stations to Market Basing. The 5 o'clock is the Welsh express for Cardiff, Newport and Swansea. The former might be overtaken somewhere by the 4:54, although it is due in Brackhampton five minutes earlier and the latter passes the 4:54 just before Brackhampton.
>
> In all this do I smell some village scandal of a fruity character? Did you, returning from a shopping spree in town by the 4:54, observe in a passing train the mayor's wife being embraced by the sanitary inspector? But why does it matter which train it was? A weekend at Porthcawl, perhaps? Thank you for the pullover. Just what I wanted.
>
> How's the garden? Not very active this time of year, I should imagine.
>
> Yours ever,
> David."

Miss Marple smiled a little, then considered the information thus presented to her. Mrs. McGillicuddy had said definitely that the carriage had not been a corridor one. Therefore—not the Swansea express. The 4:33 was indicated.

Also some more traveling seemed unavoidable. Miss Marple sighed, but made her plans.

She went up to London as before on the 12:15, but this time returned not by the 4:54, but by the 4:33 as far as Brackhampton. The journey was uneventful, but she registered certain details. The train was not crowded—4:33 was before the evening rush hour. Of the first-class carriages only one had an occupant—a very old gentleman reading the *New Statesman*. Miss Marple traveled in an empty compartment and at the two stops, Haling Broadway and Barwell Heath, leaned out of the window to observe passengers entering and leaving the train. A small number of third-class passengers got in at Haling Broadway. At Barwell Heath several third-class passengers got out. Nobody entered or left a first-class carriage except the old gentleman carrying his *New Statesman.*

As the train neared Brackhampton, sweeping around a curve of line, Miss Marple rose to her feet and stood experimentally with her back to the window over which she had drawn down the blind.

Yes, she decided, the impetus of the sudden curving of the line and the slackening of speed did throw one off one's balance back against the window and the blind might, in consequence, very easily fly up. She peered out into the night. It was lighter than it had been when Mrs. McGillicuddy had made the same journey—only just dark, but there was little to see. For observation she must make a daylight journey.

On the next day she went up by the early-morning train, purchased four linen pillowcases (tut-tutting at the price!) so as to combine investigation with the provision of household necessities, and returned by a train leaving Paddington at 12:15. Again she was alone in a first-class carriage. "This taxation," thought Miss Marple, "that's what it is. No one can afford to travel first class except businessmen in the rush hours. I suppose because they can charge it to expenses."

About a quarter of an hour before the train was due at Brackhampton, Miss Marple got out the map with which Leonard had supplied her and began to observe the countryside. She had studied the map very carefully beforehand, and after noting the name of a station they passed through, she was soon able to identify where she was just as the train began to slacken for a curve. It was a very considerable curve, indeed. Miss Marple, her nose glued to the window, studied the ground beneath her (the train was running on a fairly high embankment) with close attention. She divided her attention between the country outside and her map until the train finally ran into Brackhampton.

That night she wrote and posted a letter addressed to Miss Florence Hill, 4 Madison Road, Brackhampton. On the following morning, going to the county library, she studied a *Brackhampton Directory and Gazeteer,* and a county history.

Nothing so far had contradicted the very faint and sketchy idea that had come to her. What she had imagined was possible. She would go no farther than that.

But the next step involved action—a good deal of action—the kind of action for which she, herself, was physically unfit. If her theory were to be definitely proved or disproved, she must at this point have help from some other person. The question was—who? Miss Marple reviewed various names and possibilities, rejecting them all with a vexed shake of the head. The intelligent people, on whose intelligence she could rely, were all far too busy. Not only had they all got jobs of varying importance, their leisure hours were usually apportioned long beforehand. The unintelligent who had time on their hands, were simply, Miss Marple decided, no good.

She pondered in growing vexation and perplexity.

Then suddenly her forehead cleared. She ejaculated aloud a name. "Of course!" said Miss Marple. "Lucy Eyelesbarrow!"

4

The name of Lucy Eyelesbarrow had already made itself felt in certain circles.

Lucy Eyelesbarrow was thirty-two. She had taken a First in mathematics at Oxford, was acknowledged to have a brilliant mind and was confidently expected to take up a distinguished academic career.

But Lucy Eyelesbarrow, in addition to scholarly brilliance, had a core of good, sound common sense. She could not fail to observe that a life of academic distinction was singularly ill rewarded. She had no desire whatever to teach and she took pleasure in contacts with minds much less brilliant than her own. In short, she had a taste for people, all sorts of people—and not the same people the whole time. She also, quite frankly, liked money. To gain money one must exploit shortage.

Lucy Eyelesbarrow hit at once upon a very serious shortage—the shortage of any kind of skilled domestic labor. To the amazement of her friends and fellow scholars, Lucy Eyelesbarrow entered the field of domestic labor.

Her success was immediate and assured. By now, after a lapse of some years, she was known all over the British Isles. It was quite customary for wives to say joyfully to husbands, "It will be all right. I can go with you to the States. *I've got Lucy Eyelesbarrow!*" The point of Lucy Eyelesbarrow was that once she came into a house, all worry, anxiety and hard work went out of it. Lucy Eyelesbarrow did everything. She was unbelievably competent in every conceivable sphere. She looked after elderly parents, accepted the care of young children, nursed the sickly, cooked divinely, got on well with any old crusted servants there might happen to be (there usually weren't), was tactful with impossible people, soothed habitual drunkards, was wonderful with dogs. Best of all she never minded what she did. She scrubbed the kitchen floor, dug in the garden, cleaned up dog messes and carried coals!

One of her rules was never to accept an engagement for any long length of time. A fortnight was her usual period—a month at most under exceptional circumstances. For that fortnight you had to pay the earth! But, during that fortnight, your life was heaven. You could relax completely, go abroad, stay at home, do as you pleased, secure that all was going well on the home front in Lucy Eyelesbarrow's capable hands.

Naturally the demand for her services was enormous. She could have booked herself up if she chose for about three years ahead. She had been offered enormous sums to go as a permanency. But Lucy had no intention of being a permanency, nor would she book herself for more than six months ahead. And within that period, unknown to her clamoring clients, she always kept certain free periods which enabled her either to take a short luxurious holiday (since she spent nothing otherwise and was handsomely paid and kept) or to accept any position at short notice that happened to take her fancy, either by reason of its character, or because she "liked the people." Since she was at liberty to pick and choose among the vociferous claimants for her services, she went very largely by personal liking. Mere riches would not buy you the services of Lucy Eyelesbarrow. She could pick and choose and she did pick and choose. She enjoyed her life very much and found in it a continual source of entertainment.

Lucy Eyelesbarrow read and reread the letter from Miss Marple. She had made Miss Marple's acquaintance two years ago when her services had been retained by Raymond West, the novelist, to go and look after his old aunt who was recovering from pneumonia. Lucy had accepted the job and had gone down to St. Mary Mead. She had liked Miss Marple very much. As for Miss Marple, once she had caught a glimpse out of her bedroom window of Lucy Eyelesbarrow really trenching for sweet peas in the proper way, she had leaned back on her pillows with a sigh of relief, eaten the tempting little meals that Lucy Eyelesbarrow brought to her, and listened, agreeably surprised, to the tales told by her elderly irascible maidservant of how "I taught that Miss Eyelesbarrow a crochet pattern what she'd never heard of! Proper grateful she was." And had surprised her doctor by the rapidity of her convalescence.

Miss Marple wrote asking if Miss Eyelesbarrow could undertake a certain task for her—rather an unusual one. Perhaps Miss Eyelesbarrow could arrange a meeting at which they could discuss the matter.

Lucy Eyelesbarrow frowned for a moment or two as she considered. She was in reality fully booked up. But the word *unusual*, and her recollection of Miss Marple's personality, carried the day and she rang up Miss Marple straightaway explaining that she could not come down to St. Mary Mead as she was at the moment working, but that she was free from two to four on the following afternoon and could meet Miss Marple anywhere in London. She suggested her own club, a rather nondescript establishment which had the advantage of having several small dark writing rooms which were usually empty.

Miss Marple accepted the suggestion and on the following day the meeting took place.

Greetings were exchanged: Lucy Eyelesbarrow led her guest to the gloomiest of the writing rooms, and said: "I'm afraid I'm rather booked up just at present, but perhaps you'll tell me what it is you want me to undertake?"

"It's very simple, really," said Miss Marple. "Unusual, but simple. I want you to find a body."

For a moment the suspicion crossed Lucy's mind that Miss Marple was mentally unhinged, but she rejected the idea. Miss Marple was eminently sane. She meant exactly what she had said.

"What kind of a body?" asked Lucy Eyelesbarrow with admirable composure.

"A woman's body," said Miss Marple. "The body of a woman who was murdered—strangled actually—in a train."

Lucy's eyebrows rose slightly.

"Well, that's certainly unusual. Tell me about it."

Miss Marple told her. Lucy Eyelesbarrow listened attentively, without interrupting. At the end she said:

"It all depends on what your friend saw—or thought she saw—?"

She left the sentence unfinished with a question in it.

"Elspeth McGillicuddy doesn't imagine things," said Miss Marple. "That's why I'm relying on what she said. If it had been Dorothy Cartwright, now, it would have been quite a different matter. Dorothy always has a good story and quite often believes it herself, and there is usually a kind of basis of truth but certainly no more. But Elspeth is the kind of woman who finds it very hard to make herself believe that anything at all extraordinary or out of the way could happen. She's most unsuggestible, rather like granite."

"I see," said Lucy thoughtfully. "Well, let's accept it all. Where do I come in?"

"I was very much impressed by you," said Miss Marple, "and you see I haven't got the physical strength nowadays to get about and do things."

"You want me to make inquiries? That sort of thing? But won't the police have done all that? Or do you think they have been just slack?"

"Oh no," said Miss Marple. "They haven't been slack. It's just that I've got a theory about the woman's body. It's got to be somewhere. If it wasn't found in the train, then it must have been pushed or thrown out of the train—but it hasn't been discovered anywhere on the line. So I traveled down the same way to see if there was anywhere where the body could have been thrown off the train and yet wouldn't have been found on the line—and there was. The railway line makes a big curve before getting into Brackhampton, on the edge of a high embankment. If a body were thrown out there, when the train was leaning at an angle, I think it would pitch right down the embankment."

"But surely it would still be found—even there?"

"Oh yes. It would have to be taken away. But we'll come to that presently. Here's the place—on this map."

Lucy bent to study where Miss Marple's finger pointed.

"It is right in the outskirts of Brackhampton now," said Miss Marple, "but originally it was a country house with extensive park and grounds and it's still there, untouched—ringed round now with building estates and small suburban houses. It's called Rutherford Hall. It was built by a man called Crackenthorpe, a very rich manufacturer, in 1884. The original Crackenthorpe's son, an elderly man, is living there still with, I understand, a daughter. The railway encircles quite half of the property."

"And you want me to do—what?"

Miss Marple replied promptly.

"I want you to get a post there. Everyone is crying out for efficient domestic help. I should not imagine it would be difficult."

"No, I don't suppose it would be difficult."

"I understand that Mr. Crackenthorpe is said locally to be somewhat of a miser. If you accept a low salary, I will make it up to the proper figure which should, I think, be rather more than the current rate."

"Because of the difficulty?"

"Not the difficulty so much as the danger. It might, you know, be dangerous. It's only right to warn you of that."

"I don't know," said Lucy pensively, "that the idea of danger would deter me."

"I didn't think it would," said Miss Marple. "You're not that kind of person."

"I dare say you thought it might even attract me? I've encountered very little danger in my life. But do you really believe it might be dangerous?"

"Somebody," Miss Marple pointed out, "has committed a very successful crime. There has been no hue and cry, no real suspicion. Two elderly ladies have told a rather improbable story, the police have investigated it and found nothing in it. So everything is nice and quiet. I don't think that this somebody, whoever he may be, will care about the matter being raked up—especially if you are successful."

"What do I look for exactly?"

"Any signs along the embankment, a scrap of clothing, broken bushes—that kind of thing."

Lucy nodded.

"And then?"

"I shall be quite close at hand," said Miss Marple. "An old maid-servant of mine, my faithful Florence, lives in Brackhampton. She has looked after her old parents for years. They are now both dead, and she takes in lodgers—all most respectable people. She has arranged for me to have rooms with her. She will look after me most devotedly, and I feel I should like to be close at hand. I would suggest that you mention you have an elderly aunt living in the neighborhood, and that you want a post within easy distance of her, and also that you stipulate for a reasonable amount of spare time so that you can go and see her often."

Again Lucy nodded.

"I was going to Taomina the day after tomorrow," she said. "The holiday can wait. But I can only promise three weeks. After that, I am booked up."

"Three weeks should be ample," said Miss Marple. "If we can't find out anything in three weeks, we might as well give up the whole thing as a mare's nest."

Miss Marple departed, and Lucy, after a moment's reflection, rang up a registry office in Brackhampton, the manageress of which she knew very well. She explained her desire for a post in the neighborhood so as to be near her "aunt." After turning down, with a little difficulty and a good deal of ingenuity, several more desirable places, Rutherford Hall was mentioned.

"That sounds exactly what I want," said Lucy firmly.

The registry office rang up Miss Crackenthorpe, Miss Crackenthorpe rang up Lucy.

Two days later Lucy left London en route for Rutherford Hall.

II

Driving her own small car, Lucy Eyelesbarrow turned through an imposing pair of vast iron gates. Just inside them was what had originally been a small lodge which now seemed completely derelict, whether through war damage or merely through neglect, it was difficult to be sure. A long, winding drive led through large gloomy clumps of rhododendrons up to the house. Lucy caught her breath in a slight gasp when she saw the house which was a kind of miniature Windsor Castle. The stone steps in front of the door could have done with attention and the gravel sweep was green with neglected weeds.

She pulled an old-fashioned wrought-iron bell, and its clamor sounded, echoing away inside. A slatternly woman, wiping her hands on her apron, opened the door and looked at her suspiciously.

"Expected, aren't you?" she said. "Miss Somethingbarrow, she told me."

"Quite right," said Lucy.

The house was desperately cold inside. Her guide led her along a dak hall and opened a door on the right. Rather to Lucy's surprise, it was quite a pleasant sitting room, with books and chintz-covered chairs.

"I'll tell her," said the woman, and went away shutting the door after having given Lucy a look of profound disfavor.

After a few minutes the door opened again. From the first moment Lucy decided that she liked Emma Crackenthorpe.

She was a middle-aged woman with no very outstanding characteristics, neither good looking nor plain, sensibly dressed in tweeds and pullover, with dark hair swept back from her forehead, steady hazel eyes and a very pleasant voice.

She said: "Miss Eyelesbarrow?" and held out her hand.

Then she looked doubtful.

"I wonder," she said, "if this post is really what you're looking for? I don't want a housekeeper, you know, to supervise things. I want someone to do the work."

Lucy said that that was what most people needed.

Emma Crackenthorpe said apologetically:

"So many people, you know, seem to think that just a little light dusting will answer the case, but I can do all the light dusting myself."

"I quite understand," said Lucy. "You want cooking and washing up, and housework and stoking the boiler. That's all right. That's what I do. I'm not at all afraid of work."

"It's a big house, I'm afraid, and inconvenient. Of course we only live in a portion of it—my father and myself, that is. He is rather an invalid. We live quite quietly, and there is an Aga stove. I have several brothers, but they are not here very often. Two women come in, a Mrs. Kidder in the morning and Mrs. Hart three days a week, to do brasses and things like that. You have your own car?"

"Yes. It can stand out in the open if there's nowhere to put it. It's used to it."

"Oh, there are any amount of old stables. There's no trouble about that." She frowned a moment, then said "Eyelesbarrow—rather an unusual name. Some friends of mine were telling me about a Lucy Eyelesbarrow—the Kennedys?"

"Yes. I was with them in North Devon when Mrs. Kennedy was having a baby."

Emma Crackenthorpe smiled.

"I know they said they'd never had such a wonderful time as when you were there seeing to everything. But I had the idea that you were terribly expensive. The sum I mentioned—"

"That's quite all right," said Lucy. "I want particularly, you see, to be near Brackhampton. I have an elderly aunt in a critical state of health and I want to be within easy distance of her. That's why the salary is a secondary consideration. I can't afford to do nothing. If I could be sure of having some time off most days?"

"Oh, of course. Every afternoon, till six, if you like?"

"That seems perfect."

Miss Crackenthorpe hesitated a moment before saying: "My father is elderly and a little—difficult—sometimes. He is very keen on economy, and he says things sometimes that upset people. I wouldn't like—"

Lucy broke in quickly.

"I'm quite used to elderly people of all kinds," she said. "I always manage to get on well with them."

Emma Crackenthorpe looked relieved.

"Trouble with father!" diagnosed Lucy. "I bet he's an old tartar."

She was apportioned a large, gloomy bedroom which a small electric heater did its inadequate best to warm, and was shown round the house, a vast uncomfortable mansion. As they passed a door in the hall a voice roared out:

"That you, Emma? Got the new girl there? Bring her in. I want to look at her."

Emma flushed, glanced at Lucy apologetically.

The two women entered the room. It was richly upholstered in dark velvet, the narrow windows let in very little light, and it was full of heavy mahogany Victorian furniture.

Old Mr. Crackenthorpe was stretched out in an invalid's chair, a silverheaded stick by his side.

He was a big gaunt man, his flesh hanging in loose folds. He had a face rather like a bulldog, with a pugnacious chin. He had thick, dark hair flecked with gray, and small suspicious eyes.

"Let's have a look at you, young lady."

Lucy advanced, composed and smiling.

"There's just one thing you'd better understand straight away. Just because we live in a big house doesn't mean we're rich. We're not rich. We live simply—do you hear?—simply! No good coming here with a lot of highfalutin ideas. Cod's as good a fish as turbot any day and don't you forget it. I don't stand for waste. I live here because my father built the house and I like it. After I'm dead they can sell it up if they want to—and I expect they will want to. No sense of family. This house is well built—it's solid, and we've got our own land round us. Keeps us private. It would bring in a lot for building land but not while I'm alive. You won't get me out of here until you take me out feet first."

He glared at Lucy.

"Your house is your castle," said Lucy.

"Laughing at me?"

"Of course not. I think it's very exciting to have a real country place all surrounded by town."

"Quite so. Can't see another house from here, can you? Fields with cows in them—right in the middle of Brackhampton. You hear the traffic a bit when the wind's that way, but otherwise it's still country."

He added, without pause or change of tone, to his daughter:

"Ring up that damnfool of a doctor. Tell him that last medicine's no good at all."

Lucy and Emma retired. He shouted after them:

"And don't let that damned woman who sniffs dust in here. She's disarranged all my books."

Lucy asked:

"Has Mr. Crackenthorpe been an invalid long?"

Emma said, rather evasively:

"Oh, for years now . . . this is the kitchen."

The kitchen was enormous. A vast kitchen range stood cold and neglected. An Aga stood demurely beside it.

Lucy asked times of meals and inspected the larder. Then she said cheerfully to Emma Crackenthorpe:

"I know everything now. Don't bother. Leave it all to me."

Emma Crackenthorpe heaved a sigh of relief as she went up to bed that night.

"The Kennedys were quite right," she said. "She's wonderful."

Lucy rose at six the next morning. She did the house, prepared vegetables, assembled, cooked and served breakfast. With Mrs. Kidder she made the beds and at eleven o'clock they sat down to strong tea and biscuits in the kitchen. Mollified by the fact that Lucy "had no airs about her" and also by the strength and sweetness of the tea, Mrs. Kidder relaxed into gossip. She was a small, spare woman with a sharp eye and tight lips.

"Regular old skinflint he is. What she has to put up with! All the same, she's not what I call downtrodden. Can hold her own all right when she has to. When the gentlemen come down she sees to it there's something decent to eat."

"The gentlemen?"

"Yes. Big family it was. The eldest, Mr. Edmund, he was killed in the war. Then there's Mr. Cedric, he lives abroad somewhere. He's not married. Paints pictures in foreign parts. Mr. Harold's in the City, lives in London—married an earl's daughter. Then there's Mr. Alfred, he's got a nice way with him, but he's a bit of a black sheep, been in trouble once or twice—and there's Miss Edith's husband, Mr. Bryan, ever so nice he is. She died some years ago, but he's always stayed one of the family. And there's Master Alexander, Miss Edith's little boy. He's at school, comes here for part of the holidays always; Miss Emma's terribly set on him."

Lucy digested all this information, continuing to press tea on her informant. Finally, reluctantly, Mrs. Kidder rose to her feet.

"Seem to have got along a treat we do, this morning," she said wonderingly. "Want me to give you a hand with the potatoes, dear?"

"They're already done."

"Well, you are a one for getting on with things! I might as well be getting along myself as there doesn't seem anything else to do."

Mrs. Kidder departed and Lucy, with time on her hands, scrubbed the kitchen table which she had been longing to do, but which she had put off so as not to offend Mrs. Kidder whose job it properly was. Then she cleaned the silver till it shone radiantly. She cooked lunch, cleared it away, washed up, and at two-thirty was ready to start exploration. She had set out the tea things ready on a tray, with sandwiches and bread and butter covered over with a damp napkin to keep them moist.

She strolled first round the gardens which would be the normal thing to do. The kitchen garden was sketchily cultivated with a few vegetables. The hothouses were in ruins. The paths everywhere were overgrown with weeds. A herbaceous border near the house was the only thing that showed free of weeds and in good condition and Lucy suspected that that had been Emma's hand. The gardener was a very old man, somewhat deaf, who was only making a show of working. Lucy spoke to him pleasantly. He lived in a cottage adjacent to the big stable yard.

Extending out from the stable yard, a back drive led through the park, which was fenced on either side of it, and under a railway arch into a small back lane.

Every few minutes a train thundered along the main line over the railway arch. Lucy watched the trains as they slackened speed going round the sharp curve that encircled the Crackenthorpe property. She passed under the railway arch and out into the lane. It seemed a little-used track. On the one side was the railway embankment, on the other was a high wall which enclosed some tall factory buildings. Lucy followed the lane until it came out into a street of small houses. She could hear a short distance away the busy hum of main-road traffic. She glanced at her watch. A woman came out of a house nearby and Lucy stopped her.

"Excuse me, can you tell me if there is a public telephone near here?"

"Post office just at the corner of the road."

Lucy thanked her and walked along until she came to the post office, which was a combination shop and post office. There was a telephone box at one side. Lucy went into it and made a call. She asked to speak to Miss Marple. A woman's voice spoke in a sharp bark.

"She's resting. And I'm not going to disturb her! She needs her rest—she's an old lady. Who shall I say called?"

"Miss Eyelesbarrow. There's no need to disturb her. Just tell her that I've arrived and everything is going on well and that I'll let her know when I've any news."

She replaced the receiver and made her way back to Rutherford Hall.

5

"I suppose it will be all right if I just practice a few iron shots in the park?" asked Lucy.

"Oh yes, certainly. Are you fond of golf?"

"I'm not much good, but I like to keep in practice. It's a more agreeable form of exercise than just going for a walk."

"Nowhere to walk outside this place," growled Mr. Crackenthorpe. "Nothing but pavements and miserable little bandboxes of houses. Like to get hold of my land and build more of them. But they won't until I'm dead. And I'm not going to die to oblige anybody. I can tell you that! Not to oblige anybody!"

Emma Crackenthorpe said mildly:

"Now, Father."

"I know what they think—and what they're waiting for. All of 'em. Cedric, and that sly fox Harold with his smug face. As for Alfred I wonder he hasn't had a shot at bumping me off himself. Not for sure he didn't, at Christmastime. That was a very odd turn I had. Puzzled old Quimper. He asked me a lot of discreet questions."

"Everyone gets these digestive upsets now and again, Father."

"All right, all right, say straight out that I ate too much! That's what you mean. And why did I eat too much? Because there was too much food on the table, far too much. Wasteful and extravagant. And that reminds me—you, young woman. Five potatoes you sent in for lunch—good-sized ones, too. Two potatoes are enough for anybody. So don't send in more than four in future. The extra one was wasted today."

"It wasn't wasted, Mr. Crackenthorpe. I've planned to use it in a Spanish omelet tonight."

"Urgh!" As Lucy went out of the room carrying the coffee tray she heard him say, "Slick young woman, that, always got all the answers. Cooks well, though—and she's a handsome kind of girl."

Lucy Eyelesbarrow took a light iron out of the set of golf clubs she had had the forethought to bring with her and strolled out into the park, climbing over the fencing.

She began playing a series of shots. After five minutes or so, a ball, apparently sliced, pitched on the side of the railway embankment. Lucy went up and began to hunt about for it. She looked back toward the house. It was a long way off and nobody was in the least interested in what she was doing. She continued to hunt for the ball. Now and then she played shots from the embankment down into the grass. During the afternoon she searched about a third of the embankment. Nothing. She played her ball back toward the house.

Then, on the next day, she came upon something. A thornbush growing about halfway up the bank had been snapped off. Bits of it lay scattered about. Lucy examined the tree itself. Impaled on one of the thorns was a torn scrap of fur. It was almost the same color as the wood, a pale brownish color. Lucy looked at it for a moment, then she took a pair of scissors out of her pocket and snipped it carefully in half. The half she had snipped off she put in an envelope which she had in her pocket. She came down the steep slope searching about for anything else. She looked carefully at the rough grass of the field. She thought she could distinguish a kind of track which someone had made walking through the long grass. But it was very faint—not nearly so clear as her own tracks were. It must have been made some time ago and it was too sketchy for her to be sure that it was not merely imagination on her part.

She began to hunt carefully down in the grass at the foot of the embankment just below the broken thornbush. Presently her search was rewarded. She found a powder compact, a small cheap enameled affair. She wrapped it in her handkerchief and put it in her pocket. She searched on but did not find anything more.

On the following afternoon, she got into her car and went to see her invalid aunt. Emma Crackenthorpe said kindly, "Don't hurry back. We shan't want you until dinnertime."

"Thank you, but I shall be back at six by the latest."

No. 4, Madison Road was a small drab house in a small drab street. It had very clean Nottingham lace curtains, a shining white doorstep and a well-polished brass door-handle. The door was opened by a tall, grim-looking woman, dressed in black with a large knob of iron-gray hair.

She eyed Lucy in suspicious appraisal as she showed her in to Miss Marple.

Miss Marple was occupying the back sitting room which looked out on to a small, tidy square of garden. It was aggressively clean with a lot of mats and doilies, a great many china ornaments, a rather big Jacobean suite and two ferns in pots. Miss Marple was sitting in a big chair by the fire busily engaged in crocheting.

Lucy came in and shut the door. She sat down in the chair facing Miss Marple.

"Well!" she said, "it looks as though you were right."

She produced her findings and gave the details of their discovery.

A faint flush of achievement came into Miss Marple's cheeks.

"Perhaps one ought not to feel so," she said, "but it is rather gratifying to form a theory and get proof that it is correct!"

She fingered the small tuft of fur. "Elspeth said the woman was wearing a light-colored fur coat. I suppose the compact was in the pocket of the coat and fell out as the body rolled down the slope. It doesn't seem distinctive in any way, but it may help. You didn't take all the fur?"

"No, I left half of it on the thornbush."

Miss Marple nodded approval.

"Quite right. You are very intelligent, my dear. The police will want to check exactly."

"You are going to the police—with these things?"

"Well—not quite yet. . . ." Miss Marple considered. "It would be better, I think, to find the body first. Don't you?"

"Yes, but isn't that rather a tall order? I mean, granting that your estimate is correct. The murderer pushed the body out of the train, then presumably got out himself at Brackhampton and at some time— probably that same night—came along and removed the body. But what happened after that? He may have taken it anywhere."

"Not anywhere," said Miss Marple. "I don't think you've followed the thing to its logical conclusion, my dear Miss Eyelesbarrow."

"Do call me Lucy. Why not anywhere?"

"Because, if so, he might much more easily have killed the girl in some lonely spot and driven the body away from there. You haven't appreciated—"

Lucy interrupted.

"Are you saying—do you mean—that this was a premeditated crime?"

"I didn't think so at first," said Miss Marple. "One wouldn't—naturally. It seemed like a quarrel and a man losing control and strangling the girl and then being faced with the problem of disposing of his victim—a problem which he had to solve within a very few minutes. But it really is too much of a coincidence that he should kill the girl in a fit of passion, and then look out of the window and find the train was going round a curve exactly at a spot where he could tip the body out, and where he could be sure of finding his way later and removing it! If he'd just thrown her out there by chance, he'd have done no more about it, and the body would, long before now, have been found."

She paused. Lucy stared at her.

"You know," said Miss Marple thoughtfully, "it's really quite a clever way to have planned a crime—and I think it was very carefully planned. There's something so anonymous about a train. If he'd killed her in the place where she lived or was staying, somebody might have noticed him come or go. Or if he'd driven her out into the country somewhere, someone might have noticed the car and its number and make. But a train is full of strangers coming and going. In a non-corridor carriage, alone with her, it was quite easy—especially if you realize that he knew exactly what he was going to do next. He knew—he must have known—all about Rutherford Hall—its geographical position, I mean, its queer isolation: an island bounded by railway lines."

"It was exactly like that," said Lucy. "It's an anachronism out of the past. Bustling urban life goes on all around it, but doesn't touch it. The tradespeople deliver in the mornings and that's all."

"So we assume, as you said, that the murderer comes to Rutherford Hall that night. It is already dark when the body falls and no one is likely to discover it before the next day."

"No, indeed."

"The murderer would come—how? In a car? Which way?"

Lucy considered.

"There's a rough lane, alongside a factory wall. He'd probably come that way, turn in under the railway arch and along the back drive. Then he could climb the fence, go along at the foot of the embankment, find the body, and carry it back to the car."

"And then," continued Miss Marple, "he took it to some place he had already chosen beforehand. This was all thought out, you know. And I don't think, as I say, that he would take it away from Rutherford Hall, or if so, not very far. The obvious thing, I suppose, would be to bury it somewhere?" She looked inquiringly at Lucy.

"I suppose so," said Lucy considering. "But it wouldn't be quite as easy as it sounds."

Miss Marple agreed.

"He couldn't bury it in the park. Too hard work and very noticeable. Somewhere where the earth was turned already?"

"The kitchen garden, perhaps, but that's very close to the gardener's cottage. He's old and deaf—but still it might be risky."

"Is there a dog?"

"No."

"Then in a shed, perhaps, or an outhouse?"

"That would be simpler and quicker. There are a lot of unused old buildings: broken down pigsties, harness rooms, workshops that nobody ever goes near. Or he might perhaps have thrust it into a clump of rhododendrons or shrubs somewhere."

Miss Marple nodded.

"Yes, I think that's much more probable."

There was a knock on the door and the grim Florence came in with a tray.

"Nice for you to have a visitor," she said to Miss Marple, "I've made you my special scones you used to like."

"Florence always made the most delicious teacakes," said Miss Marple.

Florence, gratified, creased her features into a totally unexpected smile and left the room.

"I think, my dear," said Miss Marple, "we won't talk any more about murder during tea. Such an unpleasant subject!"

II

After tea Lucy rose.

"I'll be getting back," she said. "As I've already told you, there's no one actually living at Rutherford Hall who could be the man we're looking for. There's only an old man and a middle-aged woman, and an old, deaf gardener."

"I didn't say he was actually living there," said Miss Marple. "All I mean is that he's someone who knows Rutherford Hall very well. But we can go into that after you've found the body."

"You seem to assume quite confidently that I shall find it," said Lucy. "I don't feel nearly so optimistic."

"I'm sure you will succeed, my dear Lucy. You are such an efficient person."

"In some ways, but I haven't had any experience in looking for bodies."

"I'm sure all it needs is a little common sense," said Miss Marple encouragingly.

Lucy looked at her, then laughed. Miss Marple smiled back at her.

Lucy set to work systematically the next afternoon.

She poked round outhouses, prodded the briars which wreathed the old pigsties, and was peering into the boiler room under the greenhouse when she heard a dry cough and turned to find old Hillman, the gardener, looking at her disapprovingly.

"You be careful you don't get a nasty fall, Miss," he warned her. "Them steps isn't safe, and you was up in the loft just now and the floor there ain't safe neither."

Lucy was careful to display no embarrassment.

"I expect you think I'm very nosy," she said cheerfully. "I was just wondering if something couldn't be made out of this place—growing mushrooms for the market, that sort of thing. Everything seems to have been let go terribly."

"That's the master, that is. Won't spend a penny. Ought to have two men and a boy here, I ought, to keep the place proper, but won't hear of it, he won't. Had all I could do to make him get a motor mower. Wanted me to mow all that front grass by hand, he did."

"But if the place could be made to pay—with some repairs?"

"Won't get a place like this to pay—too far gone. And he wouldn't care about that, anyway. Only cares about saving. Knows well enough what'll happen after he's gone—the young gentlemen'll sell up as fast as they can. Only waiting for him to pop off, they are. Going to come into a tidy lot of money when he dies, so I've heard."

"I suppose he's a very rich man?" said Lucy.

"Crackenthorpe's Fancies, that's what they are. The old gentleman started it, Mr. Crackenthorpe's father. A sharp one he was, by all accounts. Made his fortune and built this place. Hard as nails, they say, and never forgot an injury. But with all that, he was openhanded. Nothing of the miser about him. Disappointed in both his sons, so the story goes. Give 'em an education and brought 'em up to be gentlemen—Oxford and all. But they were too much of gentlemen to want to go into the business. The younger one married an actress and then smashed himself up in a car accident when he'd been drinking. The elder one, our one here, his father never fancied so much. Abroad a lot, he was, bought a lot of heathen statues and had them sent home. Wasn't so close with his money when he was young—come on him more in middle age, it did. No, they never did hit it off, him and his father, so I've heard."

Lucy digested this information with an air of polite interest. The old man leaned against the wall and prepared to go on with his saga. He much preferred talking to doing any work.

"Died afore the war, the old gentleman did. Terrible temper he had. Didn't do to give him any sauce, he wouldn't stand for it."

"And after he died, this Mr. Crackenthorpe came and lived here?"

"Him and his family, yes. Nigh to grown up they was by then."

"But surely—Oh, I see, you mean the 1914 war."

"No, I don't. Died in 1928, that's what I mean."

Lucy supposed that 1928 qualified as "before the war" though it was not the way she would have described it herself.

She said: "Well, I expect you'll be wanting to go on with your work. You mustn't let me keep you."

"Ar," said old Hillman without enthusiasm, "not much you can do this time of day. Light's too bad."

Lucy went back to the house, pausing to investigate a likely looking copse of birch and azalea on her way.

She found Emma Crackenthorpe standing in the hall reading a letter. The afternoon post had just been delivered.

"My nephew will be here tomorrow—with a school friend. Alexander's room is the one over the porch. The one next to it will do for James Stoddart-West. They'll use the bathroom just opposite."

"Yes, Miss Crackenthorpe. I'll see the rooms are prepared."

"They'll arrive in the morning before lunch." She hesitated. "I expect they'll be hungry."

"I bet they will," said Lucy. "Roast beef, do you think? And perhaps treacle tart?"

"Alexander's very fond of treacle tart."

The two boys arrived on the following morning. They both had well-brushed hair, suspiciously angelic faces, and perfect manners. Alexander Eastley had fair hair and blue eyes, Stoddart-West was dark and spectacled.

They discoursed gravely during lunch on events in the sporting world, with occasional references to the latest space fiction. Their manner was that of elderly professors discussing paleolithic implements. In comparison with them, Lucy felt quite young.

The sirloin of beef vanished in no time and every crumb of the treacle tart was consumed.

Mr. Crackenthorpe grumbled: "You two will eat me out of house and home."

Alexander gave him a blue-eyed reproving glance.

"We'll have bread and cheese if you can't afford meat, Grandfather."

"Afford it? I can afford it. I don't like waste."

"We haven't wasted any, sir," said Stoddart-West, looking down at his plate which bore clear testimony of that fact.

"You boys both eat twice as much as I do."

"We're at the body-building stage," Alexander explained. "We need a big intake of proteins."

The old man grunted.

As the two boys left the table, Lucy heard Alexander say apologetically to his friend:

"You mustn't pay any attention to my grandfather. He's on a diet or something and that makes him rather peculiar. He's terribly mean, too. I think it must be a complex of some kind."

Stoddart-West said comprehendingly:

"I had an aunt who kept thinking she was going bankrupt. Really, she had oodles of money. Pathological, the doctor said. Have you got that football, Alex?"

After she had cleared away and washed up lunch, Lucy went out. She could hear the boys calling out in the distance on the lawn. She herself went in the opposite direction, down the front drive, and from there she struck across to some clumped masses of rhododendron bushes. She began to hunt carefully, holding back the leaves and peering inside. She moved from clump to clump systematically, and was raking inside with a golf club when the polite voice of Alexander Eastley made her start.

"Are you looking for something, Miss Eyelesbarrow?"

"A golf ball," said Lucy promptly. "Several golf balls, in fact. I've been practicing golf shots most afternoons and I've lost quite a lot of balls. I thought that today I really must find some of them."

"We'll help you," said Alexander obligingly.

"That's very kind of you. I thought you were playing football."

"One can't go on playing footer," explained Stoddart-West. "One gets too hot. Do you play a lot of golf?"

"I'm quite fond of it. I don't get much opportunity."

"I suppose you don't. You do the cooking here, don't you?"

"Yes."

"Did you cook the lunch today?"

"Yes. Was it all right?"

"Simply wizard," said Alexander. "We get awful meat at school, all dried up. I love beef that's pink and juicy inside. That treacle tart was pretty smashing, too."

"You must tell me what things you like best."

"Could we have apple meringue one day? It's my favorite thing."

"Of course."

Alexander sighed happily.

"There's a clock golf set under the stairs," he said. "We could fix it up on the lawn and do some putting. What about it, Stodders?"

"Good oh!" said Stoddart-West.

"He isn't really Australian," explained Alexander courteously. "But he's practicing talking that way in case his people take him out to see the Test Match next year."

Encouraged by Lucy, they went off to get the clock golf set. Later, as she returned to the house, she found them setting it out on the lawn and arguing about the position of the numbers.

"We don't want it like a clock," said Stoddart-West. "That's kid stuff. We want to make a course of it. Long holes and short ones. It's a pity the numbers are so rusty. You can hardly see them."

"They need a lick of white paint," said Lucy. "You might get some tomorrow and paint them."

"Good idea." Alexander's face lighted up. "I say, I believe there are some old pots of paint in the Long Barn—left there by the painters. Shall we see?"

"What's the Long Barn?" asked Lucy.

Alexander pointed to a long, stone building a little way from the house near the back drive.

"It's quite old," he said. "Grandfather calls it a Leak Barn and says it's Elizabethan, but that's just swank. It belonged to the farm that was here originally. My great-grandfather pulled it down and built this awful house instead."

He added: "A lot of grandfather's collection is in the barn. Things he had sent home from abroad when he was a young man. Most of them are pretty frightful, too. The Long Barn is used sometimes for whist drives and things like that. Women's Institute stuff. And Conservative Sales of Work. Come and see it."

Lucy accompanied them willingly.

There was a big oak, nail-studded door to the barn.

Alexander raised his hand and detached a key on a nail just under some ivy to the right hand of the top of the door. He turned it in the lock, pushed the door open and they went in.

At a first glance Lucy felt that she was in a singularly bad museum. The heads of two Roman emperors in marble glared at her out of bulging eyeballs, there was a huge sarcophagus of a decadent Greco-Roman period, a simpering Venus stood on a pedestal clutching her falling draperies. Besides these works of art, there were a couple of trestle tables, some stacked-up chairs, and sundry oddments such as a rusted hand mower, two buckets, a couple of moth-eaten car seats, and a green-painted, iron garden seat that had lost a leg.

"I think I saw the paint over here," said Alexander vaguely. He went to a corner and pulled aside a tattered curtain that shut it off.

They found a couple of paint pots and brushes; the latter dry and stiff.

"You really need some turpentine," said Lucy.

They could not, however, find any. The boys suggested bicycling off to get some, and Lucy urged them to do so. Painting the clock golf numbers would keep them amused for some time, she thought.

The boys went off, leaving her in the barn.

"This really could do with a clear up," she had murmured.

"I shouldn't bother," Alexander advised her. "It gets cleaned up if it's going to be used for anything, but it's practically never used this time of year."

"Do I hang the key up outside the door again? Is that where it's kept?"

"Yes. There's nothing to pinch here, you see. Nobody would want those awful marble things and anyway they weigh a ton."

Lucy agreed with him. She could hardly admire old Mr. Crackenthorpe's taste in art. He seemed to have an unerring instinct for selecting the worst specimen of any period.

She stood looking round her after the boys had gone. Her eyes came to rest on the sarcophagus and stayed there.

That sarcophagus. . . .

The air in the barn was faintly musty as though unaired for a long time. She went over to the sarcophagus. It had a heavy, close-fitting lid. Lucy looked at it speculatively.

Then she left the barn, went to the kitchen, found a heavy crowbar, and returned.

It was not an easy task but Lucy toiled doggedly.

Slowly the lid began to rise, pried up by the crowbar.

It rose sufficiently for Lucy to see what was inside.

6

A few minutes later Lucy, rather pale, left the barn, locked the door and put the key back on the nail.

She went rapidly to the stables, got out her car and drove down the back drive. She stopped at the post office at the end of the road. She went to the telephone box, put in the money and dialed.

"I want to speak to Miss Marple."

"She's resting, Miss. It's Miss Eyelesbarrow, isn't it?"

"Yes."

"I'm not going to disturb her and that's flat, Miss. She's an old lady and she needs her rest."

"You must disturb her. It's urgent."

"I'm not—"

"Please do what I say at once."

When she chose, Lucy's voice could be as incisive as steel. Florence knew authority when she heard it.

Presently Miss Marple's voice spoke.

"Yes, Lucy?"

Lucy drew a deep breath.

"You were quite right," she said. "I've found it."

"A woman's body?"

"Yes. A woman in a fur coat. It's in a stone sarcophagus in a kind of Barn-*cum*-Museum near the house. What do you want me to do? I ought to inform the police, I think."

"Yes. You must inform the police. At once."

"But what about the rest of it? About you? The first thing they'll

396

want to know is why I was prying up a lid that weighs tons for apparently no reason. Do you want me to invent a reason? I can."

"No. I think, you know," said Miss Marple in her gentle serious voice, "that the only thing to do is to tell the exact truth."

"About you?"

"About everything."

A sudden grin split the whiteness of Lucy's face.

"That will be quite simple for me," she said. "But I imagine they'll find it quite hard to believe!"

She rang off, waited a moment, and then rang and got the police station.

"I have just discovered a dead body in a sarcophagus in the Long Barn at Rutherford Hall."

"What's that?"

Lucy repeated her statement and anticipating the next question gave her name.

She drove back, put the car away and entered the house.

She paused in the hall for a moment, thinking.

Then she gave a brief sharp nod of the head and went to the library where Miss Crackenthorpe was sitting helping her father to do the *Times* crossword.

"Can I speak to you a moment, Miss Crackenthorpe?"

Emma looked up, a shade of apprehension on her face. The apprehension was, Lucy thought, purely domestic. In such words do useful household staff announce their imminent departure.

"Well, speak up, girl, speak up," said old Mr. Crackenthorpe irritably.

Lucy said to Emma, "I'd like to speak to you alone, please."

"Nonsense," said Mr. Crackenthorpe. "You say straight out here what you've got to say."

"Just a moment, Father." Emma rose and went toward the door.

"All nonsense. It can wait," said the old man angrily.

"I'm afraid it can't wait," said Lucy.

Mr. Crackenthorpe said, "What impertinence!"

Emma came out into the hall. Lucy followed her and shut the door behind them.

"Yes?" said Emma, "what is it? If you think there's too much to do with the boys here, I can help you and —"

"It's not that at all," said Lucy. "I didn't want to speak before your father because I understand he is an invalid and it might give him a shock. You see, I've just discovered the body of a murdered woman in that big sarcophagus in the Long Barn."

Emma Crackenthorpe stared at her.

"In the sarcophagus? A murdered woman? It's impossible!"

"I'm afraid it's quite true. I've rung up the police. They will be here at any minute."

A slight flush came into Emma's cheek.

"You should have told me first—before notifying the police."

"I'm sorry," said Lucy.

"I didn't hear you ring up—" Emma's glance went to the telephone on the hall table.

"I rang up from the post office just down the road."

"But how extraordinary—why not from here?"

Lucy thought quickly.

"I was afraid the boys might be about—might hear—if I rang up from the hall here."

"I see . . . yes—I see. They are coming—the police, I mean?"

"They're here now," said Lucy, as with a squeal of brakes a car drew up at the front door and the bell pealed through the house.

II

"I'm sorry, very sorry—to have asked this of you," said Inspector Bacon.

His hand under her arm, he led Emma Crackenthorpe out of the barn. Emma's face was very pale; she looked sick, but she walked firmly erect.

"I'm quite sure that I've never seen the woman before in my life."

"We're very grateful to you, Miss Crackenthorpe. That's all I wanted to know. Perhaps you'd like to lie down?"

"I must go to my father. I telephoned to Doctor Quimper as soon as I heard about this and he is with him now."

Doctor Quimper came out of the library as they crossed the hall. He was a tall, genial man, with a casual, offhand, cynical manner that his patients found very stimulating.

He and the Inspector nodded to each other.

"Miss Crackenthorpe has performed an unpleasant task very bravely," said Bacon.

"Well done, Emma," said the doctor, patting her on the shoulder. "You can take things. I've always known that. Your father's all right.

Just go in and have a word with him, and then go into the dining room and get yourself a glass of brandy. That's a prescription."

Emma smiled at him gratefully and went into the library.

"That woman's the salt of the earth," said the doctor looking after her. "A thousand pities she's never married. The penalty of being the only female in a family of men. The other sister got clear, married at seventeen, I believe. This one's quite a handsome woman, really. She'd have been a success as a wife and mother."

"Too devoted to her father, I suppose," said Inspector Bacon.

"She's not really as devoted as all that—but she's got the instinct some women have to make their menfolk happy. She sees that her father likes being an invalid, so she lets him be an invalid. She's the same with her brothers. Cedric feels he's a good painter, what's-his-name, Harold, knows how much she relies on his sound judgment—she lets Alfred shock her with his stories of his clever deals. Oh yes, she's a clever woman—no fool. Well, do you want me for anything? Want me to have a look at our corpse now Johnstone has done with it" (Johnstone was the police surgeon) "and see if it happens to be one of my medical mistakes?"

"I'd like you to have a look, yes, Doctor. We want to get her identified. I suppose it's impossible for old Mr. Crackenthorpe? Too much of a strain?"

"Strain? Fiddlesticks. He'd never forgive you or me if you didn't let him have a peep. He's all agog. Most exciting thing that's happened to him for fifteen years or so—and it won't cost him anything!"

"There's nothing really much wrong with him, then?"

"He's seventy-two," said the doctor. "That's all, really, that's the matter with him. He has odd rheumatic twinges—who doesn't? So he calls it arthritis. He has palpitations after meals—as well he may—he puts them down to 'heart.' But he can always do anything he wants to do! I've plenty of patients like that. The ones who are really ill usually insist desperately that they're perfectly well. Come on, let's go and see this body of yours. Unpleasant, I suppose?"

"Johnstone estimates she's been dead between a fortnight and three weeks."

"Quite unpleasant, then."

The doctor stood by the sarcophagus and looked down with frank curiosity, professionally unmoved by what he had named the "unpleasantness."

"Never seen her before. No patient of mine. I don't remember ever seeing her about in Brackhampton. She must have been quite good-looking once—hm—somebody had it in for her all right."

They went out again into the air. Doctor Quimper glanced up at the building.

"Found in the—what do they call it?—the Long Barn—in a sar-cophagus! Fantastic! Who found her?"

"Miss Lucy Eyelesbarrow."

"Oh, the latest lady help? What was she doing, poking about in sarcophagi?"

"That," said Inspector Bacon grimly, "is just what I am going to ask her. Now, about Mr. Crackenthorpe. Will you—?"

"I'll bring him along."

Mr. Crackenthorpe, muffled in scarves, came walking at a brisk pace, the doctor beside him.

"Disgraceful," he said. "Absolutely disgraceful! I brought back that sarcophagus from Florence in—let me see—it must have been in 1908—or was it 1909?"

"Steady now," the doctor warned him. "This isn't going to be nice, you know."

"No matter how ill I am, I've got to do my duty, haven't I?"

A very brief visit inside the Long Barn was, however, quite long enough. Mr. Crackenthorpe shuffled out into the air again with remarkable speed.

"Never saw her before in my life!" he said. "What's it mean? Absolutely disgraceful. It wasn't Florence—I remember now—it was Naples. A very fine specimen. And some fool of a woman has to come and get herself killed in it!"

He clutched at the folds of his overcoat on the left side.

"Too much for me . . . my heart . . . where's Emma? Doctor. . . ."

Doctor Quimper took his arm.

"You'll be all right," he said. "I prescribe a little stimulant Brandy."

They went back together toward the house.

"Sir. Please, sir."

Inspector Bacon turned. Two boys had arrived, breathless, on bicycles. Their faces were full of eager pleading.

"Please, sir, can we see the body?"

"No, you can't," said Inspector Bacon.

"Oh sir, please, sir. You never know. We might know who she was. Oh please, sir, do be a sport. It's not fair. Here's a murder, right in our own barn. It's the sort of chance that might never happen again. Do be a sport, sir."

"Who are you two?"

"I'm Alexander Eastley and this is my friend James Stoddart-West."

"Have you ever seen a blonde woman wearing a light-colored, dyed squirrel coat anywhere about the place?"

"Well—I can't remember exactly," said Alexander astutely. "If I were to have a look—"

"Take 'em in, Sanders," said Inspector Bacon to the constable who was standing by the barn door. "One's only young once!"

"Oh, sir, thank you, sir." Both boys were vociferous. "It's very kind of you, sir."

Bacon turned away toward the house.

"And now," he said to himself grimly, "for Miss Lucy Eyelesbarrow!"

III

After leading the police to the Long Barn and giving a brief account of her actions, Lucy had retired into the background, but she was under no illusion that the police had finished with her.

She was preparing potatoes for chips that evening when word was brought to her that Inspector Bacon required her presence. Putting aside the large bowl of cold water and salt in which the chips were reposing, Lucy followed the policeman to where the Inspector awaited her. She sat down and awaited his questions composedly.

She gave her name, her address in London, and added of her own accord:

"I will give you some names and addresses of reference if you want to know all about me."

The names were very good ones. An Admiral of the Fleet, the provost of an Oxford college and a Dame of the British Empire. In spite of himself Inspector Bacon was impressed.

"Now, Miss Eyelesbarrow, you went into the Long Barn to find some paint—is that right? And after having found the paint you got a crowbar, forced up the lid of this sarcophagus and found the body. What were you looking for in the sarcophagus?"

"I was looking for a body," said Lucy.

"You were looking for a body—and you found one! Doesn't that seem to you a very extraordinary story?"

"Oh yes, it is an extraordinary story. Perhaps you will let me explain it to you."

"I certainly think you had better do so."

Lucy gave him a precise recital of the events which had led up to her sensational discovery.

The Inspector summed it up in an outraged voice.

"You were engaged by an elderly lady to obtain a post here and to search the house and grounds for a dead body? Is that right?"

"Yes."

"Who is this elderly lady?"

"Miss Jane Marple. She is at present living at 4 Madison Road."

The Inspector wrote it down.

"You expect me to believe this story?"

Lucy said gently:

"Not, perhaps, until after you have interviewed Miss Marple and got her confirmation of it."

"I shall interview her all right. She must be cracked."

Lucy forbore to point out that to be proved right is not really a proof of mental incapacity. Instead she said:

"What are you proposing to tell Miss Crackenthorpe? About me, I mean?"

"Why do you ask?"

"Well as far as Miss Marple is concerned I've done my job. I've found the body she wanted found. But I'm still engaged by Miss Crackenthorpe, and there are two hungry boys in the house and probably some more of the family will soon be coming down after all this upset. She needs domestic help. If you go and tell her that I only took this post in order to hunt for dead bodies she'll probably throw me out. Otherwise I can get on with my job and be useful."

The Inspector looked hard at her.

"I'm not saying anything to anyone at the present," he said. "I haven't verified your statement yet. For all I know you may be making the whole thing up."

Lucy rose.

"Thank you. Then I'll go back to the kitchen and get on with things."

7

"We'd better have the Yard in on it; is that what you think, Bacon?"

The Chief Constable looked inquiringly at Inspector Bacon. The Inspector was a big solid man—his expression was that of one utterly disgusted with humanity.

"The woman wasn't a local, sir," he said. "There's some reason to believe—from her underclothing—that she might have been a foreigner. Of course," added Inspector Bacon hastily, "I'm not letting on about that yet awhile. We're keeping it up our sleeves until after the inquest."

The Chief Constable nodded.

"The inquest will be purely formal, I suppose?"

"Yes, sir. I've seen the coroner."

"And it's fixed for—when?"

"Tomorrow. I understand the other members of the Crackenthorpe family will be here for it. There's just a chance one of them might be able to identify her. They'll all be here."

He consulted a list he held in his hand.

"Harold Crackenthorpe, he's something in the City—quite an important figure, I understand. Alfred—don't quite know what he does. Cedric—that's the one who lives abroad. Paints!" The Inspector invested the word with its full quota of sinister significance. The Chief Constable smiled into his mustache.

"No reason, is there, to believe the Crackenthorpe family are connected with the crime in any way?" he asked.

"Not apart from the fact that the body was found on the premises," said Inspector Bacon. "And of course it's just possible that this artist member of the family might be able to identify her. What beats me is this extraordinary rigmarole about the train."

"Ah yes. You've been to see this old lady, this—er"—he glanced at the memorandum lying on his desk—"Miss Marple?"

"Yes, sir. And she's quite set and definite about the whole thing. Whether she's barmy or not, I don't know, but she sticks to her story— about what her friend saw and all the rest of it. As far as all that goes, I dare say it's just make believe—sort of thing old ladies do make up, like seeing flying saucers at the bottom of the garden, and Russian agents in the lending library. But it seems quite clear that she did engage this young woman, the lady help, and told her to look for a body—which the girl did."

"And found one," observed the Chief Constable. "Well, it's all a very remarkable story. Marple, Miss Jane Marple—the name seems familiar somehow . . . Anyway, I'll get on to the Yard. I think you're right about its not being a local case—though we won't advertize the fact just yet. For the moment we'll tell the press as little as possible."

II

The inquest was a purely formal affair. No one came forward to identify the dead woman. Lucy was called to give evidence of finding the body and medical evidence was given as to the cause of death—strangulation. The proceedings were then adjourned.

It was a cold, blustery day when the Crackenthorpe family came out of the hall where the inquest had been held. There were five of them all told: Emma, Cedric, Harold, Alfred and Bryan Eastley, the husband of the dead daughter Edith. There was also Mr. Wimborne, the senior partner of the firm of solicitors who dealt with the Crackenthorpes' legal affairs. He had come down specially from London at great inconvenience to attend the inquest. They all stood for a moment on the pavement, shivering. Quite a crowd had assembled; the piquant details of the "Body in the Sarcophagus" had been fully reported in both the London and the local press.

A murmur went round: "That's them . . ."

Emma said sharply: "Let's get away."

The big hired Daimler drew up to the curb. Emma got in and motioned to Lucy. Mr. Wimborne, Cedric and Harold followed. Bryan

Eastley said: "I'll take Alfred with me in my little bus." The chauffeur shut the door and the Daimler prepared to roll away.

"Oh, stop!" cried Emma. "There are the boys!"

The boys, in spite of aggrieved protests, had been left behind at Rutherford Hall, but they now appeared grinning from ear to ear.

"We came on our bicycles," said Stoddart-West. "The policeman was very kind and let us in at the back of the hall. I hope you don't mind, Miss Crackenthorpe," he added politely.

"She doesn't mind," said Cedric, answering for his sister. "You're only young once. Your first inquest, I expect?"

"It was rather disappointing," said Alexander. "All over so soon."

"We can't stay here talking," said Harold irritably. "There's quite a crowd. And all those men with cameras."

At a sign from him, the chauffeur pulled away from the curb. The boys waved cheerfully.

"All over so soon!" said Cedric. "That's what they think, the young innocents! It's just beginning."

"It's all very unfortunate. Most unfortunate," said Harold. "I suppose—"

He looked at Mr. Wimborne who compressed his thin lips and shook his head with distaste.

"I hope," he said sententiously, "that the whole matter will soon be cleared up satisfactorily. The police are very efficient. However, the whole thing, as Harold says, has been most unfortunate."

He looked, as he spoke, at Lucy, and there was distinct disapproval in his glance. "If it had not been for this young woman," his eyes seemed to say, "poking about where she had no business to be, none of this would have happened."

This sentiment, or one closely resembling it, was voiced by Harold Crackenthorpe.

"By the way—er—Miss er—er Eyelesbarrow, just what made you go looking in that sarcophagus?"

Lucy had already wondered just when this thought would occur to one of the family. She had known that the police would ask it first thing: what surprised her was that it seemed to have occurred to no one else until this moment.

Cedric, Emma, Harold and Mr. Wimborne all looked at her.

Her reply, for what it was worth, had naturally been prepared for some time.

"Really," she said in a hesitating voice, "I hardly know. . . . I did feel that the whole place needed a thorough clearing out and cleaning. And there was"—she hesitated—"a very peculiar and disagreeable smell—"

She had counted accurately on the immediate shrinking of everyone from the unpleasantness of this idea.

Mr. Wimborne murmured: "Yes, yes, of course . . . about three weeks the police surgeon said. I think, you know, we must all try and not let our minds dwell on this thing." He smiled encouragingly at Emma who had turned very pale. "Remember," he said, "this wretched young woman was nothing to do with any of us."

"Ah, but you can't be so sure of that, can you?" said Cedric.

Lucy Eyelesbarrow looked at him with some interest. She had already been intrigued by the rather startling differences between the three brothers. Cedric was a big man with a weather-beaten, rugged face, unkempt dark hair and a jocund manner. He had arrived from the airport unshaven, and though he had shaved in preparation for the inquest, he was still wearing the clothes in which he had arrived and which seemed to be the only ones he had: old gray-flannel trousers and a patched and rather threadbare baggy jacket. He looked the stage Bohemian to the life and proud of it.

His brother Harold, on the contrary, was the perfect picture of a city gentleman and a director of important companies. He was tall with a neat, erect carriage, had dark hair going slightly bald on the temples, a small black mustache, and was impeccably dressed in a dark, well-cut suit and a pearl-gray tie. He looked what he was, a shrewd and successful businessman.

He now said stiffly:

"Really, Cedric, that seems a most uncalled-for remark."

"Don't see why. She was in our barn after all. What did she come there for?"

Mr. Wimborne coughed and said:

"Possibly some—er—assignation. I understand that it was a matter of local knowledge that the key was kept outside on a nail."

His tone indicated outrage at the carelessness of such procedure. So clearly marked was this that Emma spoke apologetically.

"It started during the war. For the air-raid wardens. There was a little spirit stove and they made themselves hot cocoa. And afterward, since there was really nothing there anybody could have wanted to take, we went on leaving the key hanging up. It was convenient for the Women's Institute people. If we'd kept it in the house it might have been awkward—when there was no one at home to give it them when they wanted it to get the place ready. With only daily women and no resident servants . . ."

Her voice tailed away. She had spoken mechanically, giving a wordy explanation without interest, as though her mind was elsewhere.

Cedric gave her a quick, puzzled glance.

"You're worried, Sis. What's up?"

Harold spoke with exasperation:

"Really, Cedric, can you ask?"

"Yes, I do ask. Granted a strange young woman has got herself killed in the barn at Rutherford Hall (sounds like a Victorian melodrama) and granted it gave Emma a shock at the time—but Emma's always been a sensible girl—I don't see why she goes on being worried now. Dash it, one gets used to everything."

"Murder takes a little more getting used to by some people than it may in your case," said Harold acidly. "I dare say murders are two a penny in Majorca and—"

"Iviza, not Majorca."

"It's the same thing."

"Not at all—it's quite a different island."

Harold went on talking:

"My point is that though murder may be an everyday commonplace to you, living among hot-blooded Latin people, nevertheless in England we take such things seriously." He added with increasing irritation, "And really, Cedric, to appear at a public inquest in those clothes—"

"What's wrong with my clothes? They're comfortable."

"They're unsuitable."

"Well, anyway, they're the only clothes I've got with me. I didn't pack my wardrobe trunk when I came rushing home to stand in with the family over this business. I'm a painter and painters like to be comfortable in their clothes."

"So you're still trying to paint?"

"Look here, Harold, when you say trying to paint—"

Mr. Wimborne cleared his throat in an authoritative manner.

"This discussion is unprofitable," he said reprovingly. "I hope, my dear Emma, that you will tell me if there is any further way in which I can be of service to you before I return to town?"

The reproof had its effect. Emma Crackenthorpe said quickly:

"It was most kind of you to come down."

"Not at all. It was advisable that someone should be at the inquest to watch the proceedings on behalf of the family. I have arranged for an interview with the Inspector at the house. I have no doubt that, distressing as all this has been, the situation will soon be clarified. In my own mind, there seems little doubt as to what occurred. As Emma has told us, the key of the Long Barn was known locally to hang outside the door. It seems highly probable that the place was used in the winter months as a place of assignation by local couples. No doubt there was a quarrel and some young man lost control of himself. Horrified at what he had done, his eye lit on the sarcophagus and he realized that it would make an excellent place of concealment."

Lucy thought to herself, "Yes, it sounds most plausible. That's just what one might think."

Cedric said, "You say a local couple—but nobody's been able to identify the girl locally."

"It's early days yet. No doubt we shall get an identification before long. And it is possible, of course, that the man in question was a local resident, but that the girl came from elsewhere, perhaps from some other part of Brackhampton. Brackhampton's a big place—it's grown enormously in the last twenty years."

"If I were a girl coming to meet my young man, I'd not stand for being taken to a freezing-cold barn miles from anywhere," Cedric objected. "I'd stand to for a nice bit of cuddle in the cinema, wouldn't you, Miss Eyelesbarrow?"

"Do we need to go into all this?" Harold demanded plaintively.

And with the voicing of the question the car drew up before the front door of Rutherford Hall and they all got out.

8

On entering the library Mr. Wimborne blinked a little as his shrewd old eyes went past Inspector Bacon whom he had already met, to the fair-haired, good-looking man beyond him.

Inspector Bacon performed introductions.

"This is Detective Inspector Craddock of New Scotland Yard," he said.

"New Scotland Yard—hm." Mr. Wimborne's eyebrows rose.

Dermot Craddock, who had a pleasant manner, went easily into speech.

"We have been called in on the case, Mr. Wimborne," he said. "As you are representing the Crackenthorpe family, I feel it is only fair that we should give you a little confidential information."

Nobody could make a better show of presenting a very small portion of the truth and implying that it was the whole truth than young Inspector Craddock.

"Inspector Bacon will agree, I am sure," he added, glancing at his colleague.

Inspector Bacon agreed with all due solemnity and not at all as though the whole matter had been prearranged.

"It's like this," said Craddock. "We have reason to believe, from information that has come into our possession, that the dead woman is not a native of these parts, that she actually traveled down here from London and that she had recently come from abroad. Probably—though we are not sure of that—from France."

Mr. Wimborne again raised his eyebrows.

"Indeed," he said. "Indeed?"

"That being the case," explained Inspector Bacon, "the Chief Constable felt that the Yard was better fitted to investigate the matter."

"I can only hope," said Mr. Wimborne, "that the case will be solved quickly. As you can no doubt appreciate, the whole business has been a source of much distress to the family. Although not personally concerned in any way, they are—"

He paused for a bare second, but Inspector Craddock filled the gap quickly.

"It's not a pleasant thing to find a murdered woman on your property. I couldn't agree with you more. Now I should like to have a brief interview with the various members of the family—"

"I really cannot see—"

"What they can tell me? Probably nothing of interest—but one never knows. I dare say I can get most of the information I want from you, sir. Information about this house and the family."

"And what can that possibly have to do with an unknown young woman coming from abroad and getting herself killed here?"

"Well, that's rather the point," said Craddock. "Why did she come here? Had she once had some connection with this house? Had she been, for instance, a servant here at one time? A lady's maid, for instance. Or did she come here to meet a former occupant of Rutherford Hall—"

Mr. Wimborne said coldly that Rutherford Hall had been occupied by the Crackenthorpes ever since Josiah Crackenthorpe built it in 1884.

"That's interesting in itself," said Craddock. "If you'd just give me a brief outline of the family history—"

Mr. Wimborne shrugged his shoulders.

"There is very little to tell. Josiah Crackenthorpe was a manufacturer of sweet and savory biscuits, relishes, pickles, etc. He accumulated a vast fortune. He built this house. Luther Crackenthorpe, his eldest son, lives here now."

"Any other sons?"

"One other son, Henry, who was killed in a motor accident in 1911."

"And the present Mr. Crackenthorpe has never thought of selling the house?"

"He is unable to do so," said the lawyer dryly. "By the terms of his father's will."

"Perhaps you'll tell me about the will?"

"Why should I?"

Inspector Craddock smiled.

"Because I can look it up myself if I want to at Somerset House."

Against his will, Mr. Wimborne gave a crabbed little smile.

"Quite right, Inspector. I was merely protesting that the information you ask for is quite irrelevant. As to Josiah Crackenthorpe's will, there is no mystery about it. He left his very considerable fortune in trust, the income from it to be paid to his son Luther for life, and after Luther's death the capital to be divided equally among Luther's children, Edmund, Cedric, Harold, Alfred, Emma and Edith. Edmund was killed in the war and Edith died four years ago, so that on Luther Crackenthorpe's decease the money will be divided among Cedric, Harold, Alfred, Emma and Edith's son Alexander Eastley."

"And the house?"

"That will go to Luther Crackenthorpe's eldest surviving son or his issue."

"Was Edmund Crackenthorpe married?"

"No."

"So the property will actually go—?"

"To the next son—Cedric."

"Mr. Luther Crackenthorpe himself cannot dispose of it?"

"No."

"And he has no control of the capital."

"No."

"Isn't that rather unusual? I suppose," said Inspector Craddock shrewdly, "that his father didn't like him."

"You suppose correctly," said Mr. Wimborne. "Old Josiah was disappointed that his eldest son showed no interest in the family business—or indeed in business of any kind. Luther spent his time traveling abroad and collecting *objets d'art*. Old Josiah was very unsympathetic to that kind of thing. So he left his money in trust for the next generation."

"But in the meantime the next generation have no income except what they make or what their father allows them, and their father has considerable capital but no power of disposal of it."

"Exactly. And what all this has to do with the murder of an unknown young woman of foreign origin I cannot imagine!"

"It doesn't seem to have anything to do with it," Inspector Craddock agreed promptly. "I just wanted to ascertain all the facts."

Mr. Wimborne looked at him sharply; then, seemingly satisfied with the result of his scrutiny, rose to his feet.

"I am proposing now to return to London," he said. "Unless there is anything further you wish to know?"

He looked from one man to the other.

"No, thank you, sir."

The sound of the gong rose fortissimo from the hall outside.

"Dear me," said Mr. Wimborne. "One of the boys, I think, must be performing."

Inspector Craddock raised his voice to be heard above the clamor, as he said:

"We'll leave the family to have lunch in peace, but Inspector Bacon and I would like to return after it—say at 2:15—and have a short interview with every member of the family."

"You think that is necessary?"

"Well—" Craddock shrugged his shoulders. "It's just an off chance. Somebody might remember something that would give us a clue to the woman's identity."

"I doubt it, Inspector. I doubt it very much. But I wish you good luck. As I said just now, the sooner this distasteful business is cleared up, the better for everybody."

Shaking his head, he went slowly out of the room.

II

Lucy had gone straight to the kitchen on getting back from the inquest, and was busy with preparations for lunch when Bryan Eastley put his head in.

"Can I give you a hand in any way?" he asked. "I'm handy about the house."

Lucy gave him a quick, slightly preoccupied glance. Bryan had arrived at the inquest direct in his small M.G. car and she had not as yet had much time to size him up.

What she saw was likeable enough. Eastley was an amicable-looking young man of thirty-odd with brown hair, rather plaintive blue eyes and an enormous fair mustache.

"The boys aren't back yet," he said, coming in and sitting on the end of the kitchen table. "It will take 'em another twenty minutes on their bikes."

Lucy smiled.

"They were certainly determined not to miss anything."

"Can't blame them. I mean to say—first inquest in their young lives and right in the family, so to speak."

"Do you mind getting off the table, Mr. Eastley? I want to put the baking dish down there."

Bryan obeyed.

"I say, that fat's corking hot. What are you going to put in it?"

"Yorkshire pudding."

"Good old Yorkshire. Roast beef of old England, is that the menu for today?"

"Yes."

"The funeral baked meats, in fact. Smells good," he sniffed appreciatively. "Do you mind my gassing away?"

"If you came in to help I'd rather you helped." She drew another pan from the oven. "Here—turn all these potatoes over so that they brown on the other side."

Bryan obeyed with alacrity.

"Have all these things been fizzling away in here while we've been at the inquest? Supposing they'd been all burned up."

"Most improbable. There's a regulating number on the oven."

"Kind of electric brain, eh what? Is that right?"

Lucy threw a swift look in his direction.

"Quite right. Now put the pan in the oven. Here, take the cloth. On the second shelf—I want the top one for the Yorkshire pudding."

Bryan obeyed, but not without uttering a shrill yelp.

"Burn yourself?"

"Just a bit. It doesn't matter. What a dangerous game cooking is!"

"I suppose you never do your own cooking?"

"As a matter of fact I do—quite often. But not this sort of thing. I can boil an egg, if I don't forget to look at the clock. And I can do eggs and bacon. And I can put a steak under the grill or open a tin of soup. I've got one of those little electric whatnots in my flat."

"You live in London?"

"If you call it living—yes."

His tone was despondent. He watched Lucy shoot in the dish with the Yorkshire pudding mixture.

"This is awfully jolly," he said, and sighed.

Her immediate preoccupations over, Lucy looked at him with more attention.

"What is—this kitchen?"

"Yes—reminds me of our kitchen at home—when I was a boy."

It struck Lucy that there was something strangely forlorn about Bryan Eastley. Looking closely at him, she realized that he was older than she had at first thought. He must be close on forty. It seemed difficult to think of him as Alexander's father. He reminded her of innumerable young pilots she had known during the war when she had been at the impressionable age of fourteen. She had gone on and grown up into a postwar world—but she felt as though Bryan had not gone on but had been overtaken in the passage of years. His next words confirmed this. He had subsided onto the kitchen table again.

"It's a difficult sort of world," he said, "isn't it? To get your bearings in, I mean. You see, one hasn't been trained for it."

Lucy recalled what she had heard from Emma.

"You were a fighter pilot, weren't you?" she said. "You've got a D.F.C."

"That's the sort of thing that puts you wrong. You've got a decoration and so people try to make it easy for you. Give you a job and all that. Very decent of them. But they're all white-collar jobs, and one simply isn't any good at that sort of thing. Sitting at a desk getting tangled up in figures. I've had ideas of my own, you know, tried out a wheeze or two. But you can't get the backing. Can't get the chaps to come in and put down the money. If I had a bit of capital—"

He brooded.

"You didn't know Edie, did you? My wife. No, of course you didn't. She was quite different from all this lot. Younger, for one thing. She was in the Air Force. She always said her old man was an Ebenezer Scrooge. He is, you know. Mean as hell over money. And it's not as though he could take it with him. It's got to be divided up when he dies. Edie's share will go to Alexander, of course. He won't be able to touch the capital until he's twenty-one, though."

"I'm sorry, but will you get off the table again. I want to dish up and make gravy."

At that moment Alexander and Stoddart-West arrived with rosy faces and very much out of breath.

"Hello, Bryan," said Alexander kindly to his father. "So this is where you've got to. I say, what a smashing piece of beef. Is there Yorkshire pudding?"

"Yes, there is."

"We have awful Yorkshire pudding at school—all damp and limp."

"Get out of my way," said Lucy. "I want to make the gravy."

414

"Make lots of gravy. Can we have two sauceboats full?"

"Yes."

"Good oh!" said Stoddart-West, pronouncing the words carefully.

"I don't like it pale," said Alexander anxiously.

"It won't be pale."

"She's a smashing cook," said Alexander to his father.

Lucy had a momentary impression that their roles were reversed. Alexander spoke like a kindly father to his son.

"Can we help you, Miss Eyelesbarrow?" asked Stoddart-West politely.

"Yes, you can. Alexander, go and sound the gong. James, will you carry this tray into the dining room? And will you take the joint in, Mr. Eastley? I'll bring the potatoes and the Yorkshire pudding."

"There's a Scotland Yard man here," said Alexander. "Do you think he will have lunch with us?"

"That depends on what your aunt arranges."

"I don't suppose Aunt Emma would mind. She's very hospitable. But I suppose Uncle Harold wouldn't like it. He's being very sticky over this murder." Alexander went out through the door with the tray, adding a little additional information over his shoulder. "Mr. Wimborne's in the library with the Scotland Yard men now. But he isn't staying to lunch. He said he had to get back to London. Come on, Stodders. Oh, he's gone to do the gong."

At that moment the gong took charge. Stoddart-West was an artist; he gave it everything he had and all further conversation was inhibited.

Bryan carried in the joint, Lucy followed with the vegetables—returned to the kitchen to get the two brimming sauceboats of gravy.

Mr. Wimborne was standing in the hall putting on his gloves as Emma came quickly down the stairs.

"Are you really sure you won't stop for lunch, Mr. Wimborne? It's all ready."

"No. I've an important appointment in London. There is a restaurant car on the train."

"It was very good of you to come down," said Emma gratefully.

The two police officers emerged from the library.

Mr. Wimborne took Emma's hand in his.

"There's nothing to worry about, my dear," he said. "This is Detective Inspector Craddock from New Scotland Yard who has come down to take charge of the case. He is coming back at 2:15 to ask you for any facts that may assist him in his inquiry. But as I say, you have nothing to worry about." He looked toward Craddock. "I may repeat to Miss Crackenthorpe what you have told me?"

"Certainly, sir."

"Inspector Craddock has just told me that this almost certainly was not a local crime. The murdered woman is thought to have come from London and was probably a foreigner."

Emma Crackenthorpe said sharply, "A foreigner. Was she French?"

Mr. Wimborne had clearly meant his statement to be consoling. He looked slightly taken aback. Dermot Craddock's glance went quickly from him to Emma's face.

He wondered why she had leaped to the conclusion that the murdered woman was French, and why that thought disturbed her so much?

9

The only people who really did justice to Lucy's excellent lunch were the two boys and Cedric Crackenthorpe, who appeared completely unaffected by the circumstances which had caused him to return to England. He seemed, indeed, to regard the whole thing as a rather good joke of a macabre nature.

This attitude, Lucy noted, was most unpalatable to his brother Harold. Harold seemed to take the murder as a kind of personal insult to the Crackenthorpe family and so great was his sense of outrage that he ate hardly any lunch. Emma looked worried and unhappy and also ate very little. Alfred seemed lost in a train of thought of his own and spoke very little. He was a good-looking man with a thin, dark face and eyes set rather too close together.

After lunch the police officers returned and politely asked if they could have a few words with Mr. Cedric Crackenthorpe.

Inspector Craddock was very pleasant and friendly.

"Sit down, Mr. Crackenthorpe. I understand you have just come back from the Balearics? You live out there?"

"Have done for the last six years. In Iviza. Suits me better than this dreary country."

"You get a good deal more sunshine than we do, I expect," said Inspector Craddock agreeably. "You were home not so very long ago, I understand—for Christmas, to be exact. What made it necessary for you to come back again so soon?"

Cedric grinned.

"Got a wire from Emma—my sister. We've never had a murder on the premises before. Didn't want to miss anything—so along I came."

"You are interested in criminology?"

"Oh, we needn't put it in such highbrow terms! I just like murders. Whodunnits and all that! With a whodunnit parked right on the family doorstep, it seemed the chance of a lifetime. Besides I thought poor old Em might need a spot of help—managing the old man and the police and all the rest of it."

"I see. It appealed to your sporting instincts and also to your family feelings. I've no doubt your sister will be very grateful to you—although her two other brothers have also come to be with her."

"But not to cheer and comfort," Cedric told him. "Harold is terrifically put out. It's not at all the thing for a city magnate to be mixed up with the murder of a questionable female."

Craddock's eyebrows rose gently.

"Was she—a questionable female?"

"Well, you're the authority on that point. Going by the facts, it seemed to me likely."

"I thought perhaps you might have been able to make a guess at who she was?"

"Come now, Inspector, you already know—or your colleagues will tell you—that I haven't been able to identify her."

"I said a guess, Mr. Crackenthorpe. You might never have seen the woman before, but you might have been able to make a guess at who she was—or who she might have been?"

Cedric shook his head.

"You're barking up the wrong tree. I've absolutely no idea. You're suggesting, I suppose, that she may have come to the Long Barn to keep an assignation with one of us? But we none of us live here—the only people in the house were a woman and an old man. You don't seriously believe that she came here to keep a date with my revered Pop?"

"Our point is—Inspector Bacon agrees with me—that the woman may once have had some association with this house. It may have been a considerable number of years ago. Cast your mind back, Mr. Crackenthorpe—"

Cedric thought a moment or two, then shook his head.

"We've had foreign help from time to time, like most people, but I can't think of any likely possibility. Better ask the others. They'd know more than I would."

"We shall do that, of course."

Craddock leaned back in his chair and went on:

"As you have heard at the inquest, the medical evidence cannot fix the time of death very accurately. Longer than two weeks, less than four—which brings it somewhere around Christmastime. You have told me you came home for Christmas. When did you arrive in England and when did you leave?"

Cedric reflected.

"Let me see . . . I flew. Got here on the Saturday before Christmas—that would be the twenty-first."

"You flew straight from Majorca?"

"Yes. Left at five in the morning and got here midday."

"And you left?"

"I flew back on the following Friday, the twenty-seventh."

"Thank you."

Cedric grinned.

"Leaves me well within the limit, unfortunately. But really, Inspector, strangling young women is not my favorite form of Christmas fun."

"I hope not, Mr. Crackenthorpe."

Inspector Bacon merely looked disapproving.

"There would be a remarkable absence of peace and good will about such an action, don't you agree?"

Cedric addressed this question to Inspector Bacon who merely grunted. Inspector Craddock said politely:

"Well, thank you, Mr. Crackenthorpe. That will be all."

"And what do you think of him?" Craddock asked as Cedric shut the door behind him.

Bacon grunted again.

"Cocky enough for anything," he said. "I don't care for the type, myself. A loose living lot, these artists, and very likely to be mixed up with a disreputable class of women."

Craddock smiled.

"I don't like the way he dresses, either," went on Bacon. "No respect—going to an inquest like that. Dirtiest pair of trousers I've seen in a long while. And did you see his tie? Looked as though it was made of colored string. If you ask me, he's the kind that would easily strangle a woman and make no bones about it."

"Well, he didn't strangle this one—if he didn't leave Majorca until the twenty-first. And that's a thing we can verify easily enough."

Bacon threw him a sharp glance.

"I notice that you're not tipping your hand yet about the actual date of the crime."

"No, we'll keep that dark for the present. I always like to have something up my sleeve in the early stages."

Bacon nodded in full agreement.

"Spring it on 'em when the time comes," he said. "That's the best plan."

"And now," said Craddock, "we'll see what our correct City gentleman has to say about it all."

Harold Crackenthorpe, thin-lipped, had very little to say about it. It was most distasteful—a very unfortunate incident. The newspapers, he was afraid—Reporters, he understood, had already been asking for interviews. All that sort of thing . . . most regrettable . . .

Harold's staccato unfinished sentences ended. He leaned back in his chair with the expression of a man confronted with a very bad smell.

The Inspector's probing produced no result. No, he had no idea who the woman was or could be. Yes, he had been at Rutherford Hall for Christmas. He had been unable to come down until Christmas Eve, but had stayed on over the following weekend.

"That's that, then," said Inspector Craddock, without pressing his questions further. He had already made up his mind that Harold Crackenthorpe was not going to be helpful.

He passed on to Alfred, who came into the room with a nonchalance that seemed just a trifle overdone.

Craddock looked at Alfred Crackenthorpe with a faint feeling of recognition. Surely he had seen this particular member of the family somewhere before. Or had it been his picture in the paper? There was something discreditable attached to the memory. He asked Alfred his occupation and Alfred's answer was vague.

"I'm in insurance at the moment. Until recently I've been interested in putting a new type of talking machine on the market. Quite revolutionary. I did very well out of that, as a matter of fact."

Inspector Craddock looked appreciative, and no one could have had the least idea that he was noticing the superficially smart appearance of Alfred's suit and gauging correctly the low price it had cost. Cedric's clothes had been disreputable, almost threadbare, but they had been originally of good cut and excellent material. Here there was a cheap smartness that told its own tale. Craddock passed pleasantly on to his routine questions. Alfred seemed interested, even slightly amused.

"It's quite an idea, that the woman might once have had a job here.

Not as a lady's maid; I doubt if my sister has ever had such a thing. I don't think anyone has nowadays. But of course, there is a good deal of foreign domestic labor floating about. We've had Poles, and a temperamental German or two. As Emma definitely didn't recognize the woman, I think that washes your idea out, Inspector. Emma's got a very good memory for a face. No, if the woman came from London . . . what gives you the idea she came from London, by the way?"

He slipped the question in quite casually, but his eyes were sharp and interested.

Inspector Craddock smiled and shook his head.

Alfred looked at him keenly.

"Not telling, eh? Return ticket in her coat pocket, perhaps, is that it?"

"It could be, Mr. Crackenthorpe."

"Well, granting she came from London, perhaps the chap she came to meet had the idea that the Long Barn would be a nice place to do a quiet murder. He knows the setup here, evidently. I should go looking for him if I were you, Inspector."

"We are," said Inspector Craddock, and made the two little words sound quiet and confident.

He thanked Alfred and dismissed him.

"You know," he said to Bacon, "I've seen that chap somewhere before. . . ."

Inspector Bacon gave his verdict.

"Sharp customer," he said. "So sharp that he cuts himself sometimes."

II

"I don't suppose you want to see me," said Bryan Eastley apologetically, coming into the room and hesitating by the door. "I don't exactly belong to the family."

"Let me see, you are Mr. Bryan Eastley, the husband of Miss Edith Crackenthorpe, who died four years ago?"

"That's right."

"Well, it's very kind of you, Mr. Eastley, especially if you know something that you think could assist us in some way?"

"But I don't. Wish I did. Whole thing seems so ruddy peculiar, doesn't it? Coming along and meeting some fellow in that drafty old barn in the middle of winter. Wouldn't be my cup of tea!"

"It is certainly very perplexing," Inspector Craddock agreed.

"Is it true that she was a foreigner? Word seems to have got round to that effect."

"Does that fact suggest anything to you?" The Inspector looked at him sharply, but Bryan seemed amiably vacuous.

"No, it doesn't, as a matter of fact."

"Maybe she was French," said Inspector Bacon, with dark suspicion.

Bryan was roused to slight animation. A look of interest came into his blue eyes, and he tugged at his big, fair mustache.

"Really? Gay Paree?" He shook his head. "On the whole, it seems to make it even more unlikely, doesn't it? Messing about in the barn, I mean. You haven't had any other sarcophagus murders, have you? One of these fellows with an urge—or a complex? Thinks he's Caligula or someone like that?"

Inspector Craddock did not even trouble to reject this speculation. Instead, he asked in a casual manner:

"Nobody in the family got any French connections, or—or—relationships that you know of?"

Bryan said that the Crackenthorpes weren't a very gay lot.

"Harold's respectably married," he said. "Fish-faced woman, some impoverished peer's daughter. Don't think Alfred cares about women much—spends his life going in for shady deals which usually go wrong in the end. I dare say Cedric's got a few Spanish señoritas jumping through hoops for him in Iviza. Women rather fall for Cedric. Doesn't always shave and looks as though he never washes. Don't see why that should be attractive to women, but apparently it is—I say, I'm not being very helpful, am I?"

He grinned at them.

"Better get young Alexander on the job. He and James Stoddart-West are out hunting for clues in a big way. Bet you they turn up something."

Inspector Craddock said he hoped they would. Then he thanked Bryan Eastley and said he would like to speak to Miss Emma Crackenthorpe.

III

Inspector Craddock looked with more attention at Emma Crackenthorpe than he had done previously. He was still wondering about the expression that he had surprised on her face before lunch.

A quiet woman. Not stupid. Not brilliant, either. One of those comfortable, pleasant women whom men were inclined to take for granted, and who had the art of making a house into a home, giving it an atmosphere of restfulness and quiet harmony. Such, he thought, was Emma Crackenthorpe.

Women such as this were often underrated. Behind their quiet exterior they had force of character, they were to be reckoned with. Perhaps, Craddock thought, the clue to the mystery of the dead woman in the sarcophagus was hidden away in the recesses of Emma's mind.

While these thoughts were passing through his head, Craddock was asking various unimportant questions.

"I don't suppose there is much that you haven't already told Inspector Bacon," he said. "So I needn't worry you with many questions."

"Please ask me anything you like."

"As Mr. Wimborne told you, we have reached the conclusion that the dead woman was not a native of these parts. That may be a relief to you—Mr. Wimborne seemed to think it would be—but it makes it really more difficult for us. She's less easily identified."

"But didn't she have anything? A handbag? Papers?"

Craddock shook his head.

"No handbag, nothing in her pockets."

"You've no idea of her name—where she came from—anything at all?"

Craddock thought to himself: She wants to know—she's very anxious to know—who the woman is. Has she felt like that all along, I wonder? Bacon didn't give me that impression—and he's a shrewd man. . . .

"We know nothing about her," he said. "That's why we hoped one of you could help us. Are you sure you can't? Even if you didn't recognize her, can you think of anyone she might be?"

He thought, but perhaps he imagined it, that there was a very slight pause before she answered.

"I've absolutely no idea," she said.

Imperceptibly, Inspector Craddock's manner changed. It was hardly noticeable except as a slight hardness in his voice.

"When Mr. Wimborne told you that the woman was a foreigner, why did you assume that she was French?"

Emma was not disconcerted. Her eyebrows rose slightly.

"Did I? Yes, I believe I did. I don't really know why, except that one always tends to think foreigners are French until one finds out what nationality they really are. Most foreigners in this country are French, aren't they?"

"Oh, I really wouldn't say that was so, Miss Crackenthorpe. Not nowadays. We have so many nationalities over here. Italians, Germans, Austrians, all the Scandinavian countries."

"Yes, I suppose you're right."

"You didn't have some special reason for thinking that this woman was likely to be French?"

She didn't hurry to deny it. She just thought a moment and then shook her head almost regretfully.

"No," she said. "I really don't think so."

Her glance met his placidly, without flinching.

Craddock looked toward Inspector Bacon. The latter leaned forward and presented a small, enamel powder compact.

"Do you recognize this, Miss Crackenthorpe?"

She took it and examined it.

"No. It's certainly not mine."

"You've no idea to whom it belonged?"

"No."

"Then I don't think we need worry you any more—for the present."

"Thank you."

She smiled briefly at them, got up, and left the room. Again he may have imagined it, but Craddock thought she moved rather quickly, as though a certain relief hurried her.

"Think she knows anything?" asked Bacon.

Inspector Craddock said ruefully:

"At a certain stage one is inclined to think everyone knows a little more than they are willing to tell you."

"They usually do, too," said Bacon out of the depth of his experience. "Only," he added, "it quite often isn't anything to do with the business in hand. It's some family peccadillo or some silly scrape that people are afraid is going to be dragged into the open."

"Yes, I know. Well, at least—"

But whatever Inspector Craddock had been about to say never got said, for the door was flung open and old Mr. Crackenthorpe shuffled in, in a high state of indignation.

"A pretty pass," he said. "Things have come to a pretty pass when Scotland Yard comes down and doesn't have the courtesy to talk to the head of the family first! Who's the master of this house, I'd like to know? Answer me that? Who's master here?"

"You are, of course, Mr. Crackenthorpe," said Craddock soothingly and rising as he spoke. "But we understood that you had already told Inspector Bacon all you knew, and that your health not being good, we must not make too many demands upon it. Doctor Quimper said—"

"I dare say. I dare say. I'm not a strong man. As for Doctor Quimper, he's a regular old woman—perfectly good doctor, understands my case—but inclined to wrap me up in cotton wool. Got a bee in his bonnet about food. Went on at me Christmastime when I had a bit of a turn. What did I eat? When? Who cooked it? Who served it? Fuss, fuss, fuss! But though I may have indifferent health, I'm well enough to give you all the help that's in my power. Murder in my own house, or at any rate in my own barn! Interesting building, that Elizabethan. Local architect says not—but the fellow doesn't know what he's talking about. Not a day later than 1580—but that's not what we're talking about. What do you want to know? What's your present theory?"

"It's a little too early for theories, Mr. Crackenthorpe. We are still trying to find out who the woman was."

"Foreigner, you say?"

"We think so."

"Enemy agent?"

"Unlikely, I should say."

"You'd say! You'd say! They're everywhere, these people. Infiltrating! Why the Home Office lets them in beats me. Spying on industrial secrets, I'd bet. That's what she was doing."

"In Brackhampton?"

"Factories everywhere. One outside my own back gate."

Craddock shot an inquiring glance at Bacon who responded.

"Metal Boxes."

"How do you know that's what they're really making? Can't swallow all these fellows tell you. All right, if she wasn't a spy, who do you think she was? Think she was mixed up with one of my precious sons? It would be Alfred, if so. Not Harold, he's too careful. And Cedric doesn't condescend to live in this country. All right, then, she was Alfred's bit of skirt. And some violent fellow followed her down here, thinking she was coming to meet him, and did her in. How's that?"

Inspector Craddock said diplomatically that it was certainly a theory. But Mr. Alfred Crackenthorpe, he said, had not recognized her.

"Pah! Afraid, that's all! Alfred always was a coward. But he's a liar, remember, always was! Lie himself black in the face. None of my sons are any good. Crowd of vultures, waiting for me to die, that's their real occupation in life." He chuckled. "And they can wait. I won't die to oblige them! Well, if that's all I can do for you . . . I'm tired. Got to rest."

He shuffled out again.

"Alfred's bit of skirt?" said Bacon questioningly. "In my opinion the old man just made that up." He paused, hesitated. "I think, personally, Alfred's quite all right—perhaps a shifty customer in some ways, but not our present cup of tea. Mind you, I did just wonder about that Air Force chap."

"Bryan Eastley?"

"Yes. I've run into one or two of his type. They're what you might call adrift in the world—had danger and death and excitement too early in life. Now they find it tame. Tame and unsatisfactory. In a way, we've given them a raw deal. Though I don't really know what we could do about it. But there they are, all past and no future, so to speak. And they're the kind that don't mind taking chances. The ordinary fellow plays safe by instinct, it's not so much morality as prudence. But these fellows aren't afraid—playing safe isn't really in their vocabulary. If Eastley were mixed up with a woman and wanted to kill her—" He stopped, threw out a hand hopelessly. "But why should he want to kill her? And if you do kill a woman, why plant her in your father-in-law's sarcophagus? No, if you ask me, none of this lot had anything to do with the murder. If they had, they wouldn't have gone to all the trouble of planting the body on their own back doorstep, so to speak."

Craddock agreed that that hardly made sense.

"Anything more you want to do here?"

Craddock said there wasn't.

Bacon suggested coming back to Brackhampton and having a cup of tea, but Inspector Craddock said that he was going to call on an old acquaintance.

10

Miss Marple, sitting erect against a background of china dogs and presents from Margate, smiled approvingly at Inspector Dermot Craddock.

"I'm so glad," she said, "that you have been assigned to the case. I hoped you would be."

"When I got your letter," said Craddock, "I took it straight to the Assistant Commissioner. As it happened he had just heard from the Brackhampton people calling us in. They seemed to think it wasn't a local crime. The A.C. was very interested in what I had to tell him about you. He'd heard about you, I gather, from my uncle."

"Dear Sir Henry," murmured Miss Marple affectionately.

"He got me to tell him all about the Little Paddocks business. Do you want to hear what he said next?"

"Please tell me if it is not a breach of confidence."

"He said, 'Well, as this seems a completely cockeyed business, all thought up by a couple of old ladies who've turned out, against all probability, to be right, and since you already know one of these old ladies, I'm sending you down on the case.' So here I am! And now, my dear Miss Marple, where do we go from here? This is not, as you probably appreciate, an official visit. I haven't got my henchmen with me. I thought you and I might take down our back hair together first."

Miss Marple smiled at him.

"I'm sure," she said, "that no one who only knows you officially would ever guess that you could be so human, and better-looking than ever—don't blush. Now what, exactly, have you been told so far?"

427

"I've got everything, I think. Your friend Mrs. McGillicuddy's original statement to the police at St. Mary Mead, confirmation of her statement by the ticket collector and also the note to the stationmaster at Brackhampton. I may say that all the proper inquiries were made by the people concerned—the railway people and the police. But there's no doubt that you outsmarted them all by a most fantastic process of guesswork."

"Not guesswork," said Miss Marple. "And I had a great advantage. I knew Elspeth McGillicuddy. Nobody else did. There was no obvious confirmation of her story, and if there was no question of any woman being reported missing, then quite naturally they would think it was just an elderly lady imagining things—as elderly ladies often do, but not Elspeth McGillicuddy."

"Not Elspeth McGillicuddy," agreed the Inspector. "I'm looking forward to meeting her, you know. I wish she hadn't gone to Ceylon. We're arranging for her to be interviewed there, by the way."

"My own process of reasoning was not really original," said Miss Marple. "It's all in Mark Twain. The boy who found the horse. I just imagined where I would go if I were a horse and I went there and there was the horse."

"You imagined what you'd do if you were a cruel and cold-blooded murderer?" said Craddock, looking thoughtfully at Miss Marple's pink and white elderly fragility. "Really, your mind—"

"Like a sink, my nephew Raymond used to say," Miss Marple agreed, nodding her head briskly. "But as I always told him, sinks are necessary domestic equipment and actually very hygienic."

"Can you go a little further still, put yourself in the murderer's place, and tell me just where he is now?"

Miss Marple sighed.

"I wish I could. I've no idea—no idea at all. But he must be someone who has lived in, or knows all about, Rutherford Hall."

"I agree. But that opens up a very wide field. Quite a succession of daily women have worked there. There's the Women's Institute, and the air-raid wardens before them. They all know the Long Barn and the sarcophagus and where the key was kept. The whole setup there is widely known locally. Anybody living roundabout might hit on it as a good spot for his purpose."

"Yes, indeed. I quite understand your difficulties."

Craddock said: "We'll never get anywhere until we identify the body."

"And that, too, may be difficult?"

"Oh, we'll get there—in the end. We're checking up on all the reported disappearances of a woman of that age and appearance. There's no one outstanding who fits the bill. The Medical Officer puts her down as about thirty-five, healthy, probably a married woman, has had at least one child. Her fur coat is a cheap one, purchased at a London store. Hundreds of such coats were sold in the last three months, about sixty percent of them to blonde women. No salesgirl can recognize the photograph of the dead woman, or is likely to if the purchase were made just before Christmas. Her other clothes seem mainly of foreign manufacture, mostly purchased in Paris. There are no English laundry marks. We've communicated with Paris and they are checking up there for us. Sooner or later, of course, someone will come forward with a missing relative or lodger. It's just a matter of time."

"The compact wasn't any help?"

"Unfortunately, no. It's a type sold by the hundred in the rue de Rivoli, quite cheap. By the way, you ought to have turned that over to the police at once, you know, or rather Miss Eyelesbarrow should have done so."

Miss Marple shook her head.

"But at that moment there wasn't any question of a crime having been committed," she pointed out. "If a young lady, practicing golf shots, picks up an old compact of no particular value in the long grass, surely she doesn't rush straight off to the police with it?" Miss Marple paused, and then added firmly: "I thought it much wiser to find the body first."

Inspector Craddock was tickled.

"You don't seem to have ever had any doubts but that it would be found?"

"I was sure it would. Lucy Eyelesbarrow is a most efficient and intelligent person."

"I'll say she is! She scares the life out of me, she's so devastatingly efficient. No man will ever dare marry that girl."

"Now you know, I wouldn't say that. It would have to be a special type of man, of course." Miss Marple brooded on this thought a moment. "How is she getting on at Rutherford Hall?"

"They're completely dependent upon her as far as I can see. Eating out of her hand—literally as you might say. By the way, they know nothing about her connection with you. We've kept that dark."

"She has no connection now with me. She has done what I asked her to do."

"So she could hand in her notice and go if she wanted to?"

"Yes."

"But she stays on. Why?"

"She has not mentioned her reasons to me. She is a very intelligent girl. I suspect that she has become interested."

"In the problem? Or in the family?"

"It may be," said Miss Marple, "that it is rather difficult to separate the two."

Craddock looked hard at her.

"Have you got anything particular in mind?"

"Oh no—oh, dear me, no."

"I think you have."

Miss Marple shook her head.

Dermot Craddock sighed. "So all I can do is to 'prosecute my inquiries'—to put it in jargon. A policeman's life is a dull one!"

"You'll get results, I'm sure."

"Any ideas for me? More inspired guesswork?"

"I was thinking of things like theatrical companies," said Miss Marple rather vaguely. "Touring from place to place and perhaps not many home ties. One of those young women would be much less likely to be missed."

"Yes. Perhaps you've got something there. We'll pay special attention to that angle." He added, "What are you smiling about?"

"I was just thinking," said Miss Marple, "of Elspeth McGillicuddy's face when she hears we've found a body!"

II

"Well!" said Mrs. McGillicuddy. "Well!"

Words failed her. She looked across at the nicely spoken, pleasant young man who had called upon her with official credentials and then down at the photographs that he had handed her.

"That's her all right," she said. "Yes, that's her. Poor soul. Well, I must say I'm glad you've found her body. Nobody believed a word I said! The police or the railway people or anyone else. It's very galling not to be believed. At any rate, nobody could say I didn't do all I possibly could."

The nice young man made sympathetic and appreciative noises.

"Where did you say the body was found?"

"In a barn at a house called Rutherford Hall, just outside Brackhampton."

"Never heard of it. How did it get there, I wonder?"

The young man did not reply.

"Jane Marple found it, I suppose. Trust Jane."

"The body," said the young man, referring to some notes, "was found by a Miss Lucy Eyelesbarrow."

"Never heard of her either," said Mrs. McGillicuddy. "I still think Jane Marple had something to do with it."

"Anyway, Mrs. McGillicuddy, you definitely identify this picture as that of the woman whom you saw in a train?"

"Being strangled by a man. Yes, I do."

"Now, can you describe this man?"

"He was a tall man," said Mrs. McGillicuddy.

"Yes?"

"And dark."

"Yes?"

"That's all I can tell you," said Mrs. McGillicuddy. "He had his back to me. I didn't see his face."

"Would you be able to recognize him if you saw him?"

"Of course I shouldn't! He had his back to me. I never saw his face."

"You've no idea at all as to his age?"

Mrs. McGillicuddy considered.

"No—not really—I mean, I don't know. He wasn't, I'm almost sure, very young. His shoulders looked—well set, if you know what I mean." The young man nodded. "Thirty and upward, I can't get closer than that. I wasn't really looking at him, you see. It was her—with those hands round her throat and her face—all blue. . . . You know, sometimes I dream of it even now."

"It must have been a very distressing experience," said the young man sympathetically.

He closed his notebook and said, "When are you returning to England?"

"Not for another three weeks. It isn't necessary, is it, for me?"

He quickly reassured her.

"Oh no. There's nothing you could do at present. Of course, if we make an arrest . . ."

It was left like that.

The mail brought a letter from Miss Marple to her friend. The writing was spiky and spidery and heavily underlined. Long practice made it easy for Mrs. McGillicuddy to decipher. Miss Marple wrote a very full account to her friend who devoured every word with great satisfaction.

She and Jane had shown them all right!

11

"I simply can't make you out," said Cedric Crackenthorpe.

He eased himself down on the decaying wall of a long-derelict pigsty and stared at Lucy Eyelesbarrow.

"What can't you make out?"

"What you're doing here."

"I'm earning my living."

"As a skivvy?" He spoke disparagingly.

"You're out of date," said Lucy. "Skivvy, indeed! I'm a household help, a professional domestician, or an answer to prayer, mainly the latter."

"You can't like all the things you have to do—cooking and making beds and whirring about with a Hoover cleaner and sinking your arms up to the elbows in greasy water."

Lucy laughed.

"Not the details, perhaps, but cooking satisfies my creative instincts, and there's something in me that really revels in clearing up mess."

"I live in a permanent mess," said Cedric. "I like it," he added defiantly.

"You look as though you did."

"My cottage in Iviza is run on simple straightforward lines. Three plates, two cups and saucers, a bed, a table and a couple of chairs. There's dust everywhere and smears of paint and chips of stone—I sculpt as well as paint—and nobody's allowed to touch a thing. I won't have a woman near the place."

"Not in any capacity?"

"Just what do you mean by that?"

"I was assuming that a man of such artistic tastes presumably had some kind of love life."

"My love life, as you call it, is my own business," said Cedric with dignity. "What I won't have is a woman in her tidying-up, interfering, bossing capacity!"

"How I'd love to have a go at your cottage," said Lucy. "It would be a challenge!"

"You won't get the opportunity."

"I suppose not."

Some bricks fell out of the pigsty. Cedric turned his head and looked into its nettle-ridden depths.

"Dear old Madge," he said. "I remember her well. A sow of most endearing disposition and a prolific mother. Seventeen in the last litter, I remember. We used to come here on fine afternoons and scratch Madge's back with a stick. She loved it."

"Why has this whole place been allowed to get into the state it's in? It can't only be the war?"

"You'd like to tidy this up, too, I suppose? What an interfering female you are. I quite see now why you would be the person to discover a body! You couldn't even leave a Greco-Roman sarcophagus alone." He paused and then went on. "No, it's not only the war. It's my father. What do you think of him, by the way?"

"I haven't had much time for thinking."

"Don't evade the issue. He's as mean as hell and in my opinion a bit crazy as well. Of course he hates all of us, except perhaps Emma. That's because of my grandfather's will."

Lucy looked inquiring.

"My grandfather was the man who mada-da-monitch. With the Crunchies and the Cracker Jacks and the Cozy Crisps. All the afternoon-tea delicacies, and then, being farsighted, he switched on very early to cheesies and canapés so that now we cash in on cocktail parties in a big way. Well, the time came when father intimated that he had a soul above Crunchies. He traveled in Italy and the Balkans and Greece and dabbled in art. My grandfather was peeved. He decided my father was no man of business and a rather poor judge of art (quite right in both cases), so left all his money in trust for his grandchildren. Father had the income for life, but he couldn't touch the capital. Do you know what he did? He stopped spending money. He came here and began to save. I'd say that by now he's accumulated nearly as big a fortune as my grandfather left. And in the meantime all of us, Harold, myself, Alfred and Emma haven't got a penny of grandfather's money. I'm a stony-broke painter. Harold went into business and is now a prominent man in the City—he's the one with the money-making touch, though I've heard rumors that he's in Queer Street lately. Alfred. Well, Alfred is usually known in the privacy of the family as Flash Alf."

"Why?"

"What a lot of things you want to know! The answer is that Alf is the black sheep of the family. He's not actually been to prison yet, but he's been very near it. He was in the Ministry of Supply during the war, but left it rather abruptly under questionable circumstances. And after that there were some dubious deals in tinned fruits, and trouble over eggs. Nothing in a big way—just a few doubtful deals on the side."

"Isn't it rather unwise to tell strangers all these things?"

"Why? Are you a police spy?"

"I might be."

"I don't think so. You were here slaving away before the police began to take an interest in us. I should say—"

He broke off as his sister Emma came through the door of the kitchen garden.

"Hullo, Em? You're looking very perturbed about something."

"I am. I want to talk to you, Cedric."

"I must get back to the house," said Lucy, tactfully.

"Don't go," said Cedric. "Murder has made you practically one of the family."

"I've got a lot to do," said Lucy. "I only came out to get some parsley."

She beat a rapid retreat to the kitchen garden. Cedric's eyes followed her.

"Good-looking girl," he said. "Who is she really?"

"Oh, she's quite well known," said Emma. "She's made a specialty of this kind of thing. But never mind Lucy Eyelesbarrow, Cedric. I'm terribly worried. Apparently the police think that this girl was a foreigner, perhaps French. Cedric, you don't think she could possibly be—Martine?"

II

For a moment or two Cedric stared at her as though uncomprehending.

"Martine? But who on earth—oh, you mean Martine?"

"Yes. Do you think—"

"Why on earth should it be Martine?"

"Well, her sending that telegram was odd when you come to think of it. It must have been roughly about the same time. Do you think that she may, after all, have come down here and . . ."

"Nonsense. Why should Martine come down here and find her way into the Long Barn? What for? It seems wildly unlikely to me."

"You don't think, perhaps, that I ought to tell Inspector Bacon, or the other one?"

"Tell him what?"

"Well—about Martine. About her letter."

"Now don't you go complicating things, Sis, by bringing up a lot of irrelevant stuff that has nothing to do with all this. I was never very convinced about that letter from Martine, anyway."

"I was."

"You've always been good at believing impossible things before breakfast, old girl. My advice to you is, sit tight and keep your mouth shut. It's up to the police to identify their precious corpse. And I bet Harold would say the same."

"Oh, I know Harold would. And Alfred, also. But I'm worried, Cedric, I really am worried. I don't know what I ought to do."

"Nothing," said Cedric promptly. "You keep your mouth shut, Emma. Never go halfway to meet trouble, that's my motto."

Emma Crackenthorpe sighed. She went slowly back to the house, uneasy in her mind.

As she came into the drive, Doctor Quimper emerged from the house and opened the door of his battered Austin car. He paused when he saw her; then, leaving the car, he came toward her.

"Well, Emma," he said. "Your father's in splendid shape. Murder suits him. It's given him an interest in life. I must recommend it for more of my patients."

Emma smiled mechanically. Doctor Quimper was always quick to notice reactions.

"Anything particular the matter?" he asked.

Emma looked up at him. She had come to rely a lot on the kindliness and sympathy of the doctor. He had become a friend on whom to lean, not only a medical attendant. His calculated brusqueness did not deceive her; she knew the kindness that lay behind it.

"I am worried, yes," she admitted.

"Care to tell me? Don't, if you don't want to."

"I'd like to tell you. Some of it you know already. The point is I don't know what to do."

"I should say your judgment was usually most reliable. What's the trouble?"

"You remember—or perhaps you don't—what I once told you about my brother—the one who was killed in the war?"

"You mean about his having married, or wanting to marry, a French girl? Something of that kind?"

"Yes. Almost immediately after I got that letter, he was killed. We never heard anything of or about the girl. All we knew, actually, was her Christian name. We always expected her to write or to turn up, but she didn't. We never heard anything—until about a month ago, just before Christmas."

"I remember. You got a letter, didn't you?"

"Yes. Saying she was in England and would like to come and see us. It was all arranged and then, at the last minute, she sent a wire that she had to return unexpectedly to France."

"Well?"

"The police think that this woman who was killed—was French."

"They do, do they? She looked more of an English type to me, but one can't really judge. What's worrying you, then, is that just possibly the dead woman might be your brother's girl?"

"Yes."

"I think it's most unlikely," said Doctor Quimper, adding: "But all the same, I understand what you feel."

"I'm wondering if I ought not to tell the police about—about it all. Cedric and the others say it's quite unnecessary. What do you think?"

"Hm." Doctor Quimper pursed up his lips. He was silent for a moment or two, deep in thought. Then he said, almost unwillingly, "It's much simpler, of course, if you say nothing. I can understand what your brothers feel about it. All the same—"

"Yes?"

Quimper looked at her. His eyes had an affectionate twinkle in them.

"I'd go ahead and tell 'em," he said. "You'll go on worrying if you don't. I know you."

Emma flushed a little.

"Perhaps I'm foolish."

"You do what you want to do, my dear, and let the rest of the family go hang! I'd back your judgment against the lot of them any day."

12

"Girl! You, girl! Come in here."

Lucy turned her head, surprised. Old Mr. Crackenthorpe was beckoning to her fiercely from just inside a door.

"You want me, Mr. Crackenthorpe?"

"Don't talk so much. Come in here."

Lucy obeyed the imperative finger. Old Mr. Crackenthorpe took hold of her arm and pulled her inside the door and shut it.

"Want to show you something," he said.

Lucy looked round her. They were in a small room evidently designed to be used as a study, but equally evidently not used as such for a very long time. There were piles of dusty papers on the desk and cobwebs festooned from the corners of the ceiling. The air smelled damp and musty.

"Do you want me to clean this room?" she asked.

Old Mr. Crackenthorpe shook his head fiercely.

"No, you don't! I keep this room locked up. Emma would like to fiddle about in here, but I don't let her. It's my room. See these stones? They're geological specimens."

Lucy looked at a collection of twelve or fourteen lumps of rock, some polished and some rough.

"Lovely," she said kindly. "Most interesting."

"You're quite right. They are interesting. You're an intelligent girl. I don't show them to everybody. I'll show you some more things."

"It's very kind of you, but I ought really to get on with what I was doing. With six people in the house—"

"Eating me out of house and home. That's all they do when they come down here! Eat. They don't offer to pay for what they eat, either. Leeches! All waiting for me to die. Well, I'm not going to die just yet— I'm not going to die to please them. I'm a lot stronger than even Emma knows."

"I'm sure you are."

"I'm not so old, either. She makes out I'm an old man, treats me as an old man. You don't think I'm old, do you?"

"Of course not," said Lucy.

"Sensible girl. Take a look at this."

He indicated a large, faded chart which hung on the wall. It was, Lucy saw, a genealogical tree; some of it done so finely that one would have had to have a magnifying glass to read the names. The remote forebears, however, were written in large, proud capitals with crowns over the names.

"Descended from kings," said Mr. Crackenthorpe. "My mother's family tree, that is, not my father's. He was a vulgarian! Common old man! Didn't like me. I was a cut above him always. Took after my mother's side. Had a natural feeling for art and classical sculpture—he couldn't see anything in it, silly old fool. Don't remember my mother—died when I was two. Last of her family. They were sold up and she married my father. But you look there—Edward the Confessor—Ethelred the Unready—whole lot of them. And that was before the Normans came. Before the Normans—that's something, isn't it?"

"It is indeed."

"Now I'll show you something else." He guided her across the room to an enormous piece of dark oak furniture. Lucy was rather uneasily conscious of the strength of the fingers clutching her arm. There certainly seemed nothing feeble about old Mr. Crackenthorpe today. "See this? Came out of Lushington—that was my mother's people's place. Elizabethan, this is. Takes four men to move it. You don't know what I keep inside it, do you? Like me to show you?"

"Do show me," said Lucy politely.

"Curious, aren't you? All women are curious." He took a key from his pocket and unlocked the door of the lower cupboard. From this he took out a surprisingly new-looking cash box. This, again, he unlocked.

"Take a look here, my dear. Know what these are?"

He lifted out a small, paper-wrapped cylinder and pulled away the paper from one end. Gold coins trickled out into his palm.

"Look at these, young lady. Look at 'em, hold 'em, touch 'em. Know what they are? Bet you don't! You're too young. Sovereigns—that's what they are. Good, golden sovereigns. What we used before all these dirty bits of paper came into fashion. Worth a lot more than silly pieces of paper. Collected them a long time back. I've got other things in this box, too. Lots of things put away in here. All ready for the future. Emma doesn't know. Nobody knows. It's our secret, see, girl? D'you know why I'm telling you and showing you?"

"Why?"

"Because I don't want you to think I'm a played-out, sick old man. Lots of life in the old dog yet. My wife's been dead a long time. Always objecting to everything, she was. Didn't like the names I gave the children—good Saxon names. No interest in that family tree. I never paid any attention to what she said, though, and she was a poor-spirited creature—always gave in. Now you're a spirited filly—a very nice filly, indeed. I'll give you some advice. Don't throw yourself away on a young man. Young men are fools! You want to take care of your future. You wait—" His fingers pressed into Lucy's arm. He leaned to her ear. "I don't say more than that. Wait. Those silly fools think I'm going to die soon. I'm not. Shouldn't be surprised if I outlived the lot of them. And then we'll see! Oh yes, then we'll see. Harold's got no children. Cedric and Alfred aren't married. Emma—Emma will never marry now. She's a bit sweet on Quimper, but Quimper will never think of marrying Emma. There's Alexander, of course. Yes, there's Alexander. But, you know, I'm fond of Alexander. Yes, that's awkward. I'm fond of Alexander."

He paused for a moment, frowning, then said:

"Well, girl, what about it? What about it, eh?"

"Miss Eyelesbarrow . . ."

Emma's voice came faintly through the closed study door. Lucy seized gratefully at the opportunity.

"Miss Crackenthorpe's calling me. I must go. Thank you so much for all you have shown me."

"Don't forget . . . our secret . . ."

"I won't forget," said Lucy and hurried out into the hall, not quite certain as to whether she had or had not just received a conditional proposal of marriage.

II

Dermot Craddock sat at his desk in his room at New Scotland Yard. He was slumped sideways in an easy attitude and was talking into the telephone receiver which he held with one elbow propped up on the table. He was speaking in French, a language in which he was tolerably proficient.

"It was only an idea, you understand," he said.

"But decidedly it is an idea," said the voice at the other end, from the Prefecture in Paris. "Already I have set inquiries in motion in those circles. My agent reports that he has two or three promising lines of inquiry. Unless there is some family life or a lover, these women drop out of circulation very easily and no one troubles about them. They have gone on tour, or there is some new man—it is no one's business to ask. It is a pity that the photograph you sent me is so difficult for anyone to recognize. Strangulation, it does not improve the appearance. Still, that cannot be helped. I go now to study the latest reports of my agents on this matter. There will be, perhaps, something. *Au revoir, mon cher.*"

As Craddock reiterated the farewell politely, a slip of paper was placed before him on the desk. It read:

> Miss Emma Crackenthorpe
> To see Detective Inspector Craddock.
> Rutherford Hall case.

He replaced the receiver and said to the police constable:

"Bring Miss Crackenthorpe up."

As he waited, he leaned back in his chair, thinking.

So he had not been mistaken; there was something that Emma Crackenthorpe knew—not much, perhaps, but something. And she had decided to tell him.

He rose to his feet as she was shown in, shook hands, settled her in a chair and offered her a cigarette which she refused. Then there was a momentary pause. She was trying, he decided, to find just the words she wanted. He leaned forward.

"You have come to tell me something, Miss Crackenthorpe? Can I help you? You've been worried about something, haven't you? Some little thing, perhaps, that you feel probably has nothing to do with the case, but on the other hand just might be related to it. You've come here to tell me about it, haven't you? It's to do, perhaps, with the identity of the dead woman. You think you know who she was?"

"No, no, not quite that. I think really it's most unlikely. But—"

"But there is some possibility that worries you. You'd better tell me about it, because we may be able to set your mind at rest."

Emma took a moment or two before speaking. Then she said:

"You have seen three of my brothers. I had another brother, Edmund, who was killed in the war. Shortly before he was killed, he wrote to me from France."

She opened her handbag and took out a worn and faded letter. She read from it:

"I hope this won't be a shock to you, Emmie, but I'm getting married—to a French girl. It's all been very sudden, but I know you'll be fond of Martine and look after her if anything happens to me. Will write you all the details in my next, by which time I shall be a married man! Break it gently to the old man, won't you? He'll probably go up in smoke."

Inspector Craddock held out a hand. Emma hesitated, then put the letter into it. She went on, speaking rapidly.

"Two days after receiving this letter, we had a telegram saying Edmund was missing, believed killed. Later he was definitely reported killed. It was just before Dunkirk and a time of great confusion. There was no Army record, as far as I could find out, of his having been married, but as I say, it was a confused time. I never heard anything from the girl. I tried, after the war, to make some inquiries, but I only knew her Christian name and that part of France had been occupied by the Germans and it was difficult to find out anything, without knowing the girl's surname and more about her. In the end I assumed that the marriage had never taken place and that the girl had probably married someone else before the end of the war, or might possibly herself have been killed."

Inspector Craddock nodded. Emma went on.

"Imagine my surprise to receive a letter, just about a month ago, signed *Martine Crackenthorpe*."

"You have it?"

Emma took it from her bag and handed it to him. Craddock read it with interest. It was written in a slanting French hand, an educated hand.

Dear Mademoiselle,

I hope it will not be a shock to you to get this letter. I do not even know if your brother Edmund told you that we were married. He said he was going to do so. He was killed only a few days after our marriage, and at the same time the Germans occupied our village. After the war ended, I decided that I would not write to you or approach you, though Edmund had told me to do so. But by then I had made a new life for myself, and it was not necessary. But now things have changed. For my son's sake I write this letter. He is your brother's son, you see, and I can no longer give him the advantages he ought to have. I am coming to England early next week. Will you let me know if I can come and see you? My address for letters is 126 Elvers Crescent, N. 10. I hope again this will not be the great shock to you.

I remain with assurance of my excellent sentiments,

Martine Crackenthorpe.

Craddock was silent for a moment or two. He reread the letter carefully before handing it back.

"What did you do on receipt of this letter, Miss Crackenthorpe?"

"My bother-in-law, Bryan Eastley, happened to be staying with me at the time and I talked to him about it. Then I rang up my brother Harold in London and consulted him about it. Harold was rather skeptical about the whole thing and advised extreme caution. We must, he said, go carefully into this woman's credentials."

Emma paused and then went on:

"That, of course, was only common sense and I quite agreed. But if this girl—woman—was really the Martine about whom Edmund had written to me, I felt that we must make her welcome. I wrote to the address she gave in the letter, inviting her to come down to Rutherford Hall and meet us. A few days later I received a telegram from London—*Very sorry forced to return to France unexpectedly. Martine.* There was no further letter or news of any kind."

"All this took place, when?"

Emma frowned.

"It was shortly before Christmas. I know, because I wanted to suggest her spending Christmas with us. But my father would not hear of it, so I suggested she should come down the weekend after

Christmas while the family would still be there. I think the wire saying she was returning to France came actually a few days before Christmas."

"And you believe that this woman whose body was found in the sarcophagus might be this Martine?"

"No, of course I don't. But when you said she was probably a foreigner, well, I couldn't help wondering . . . if perhaps—"

Her voice died away.

Craddock spoke quickly and reassuringly.

"You did quite right to tell me about this. We'll look into it. I should say there is probably little doubt that the woman who wrote to you actually did go back to France and is there now, alive and well. On the other hand, there is a certain coincidence of dates, as you yourself have been clever enough to realize. As you heard at the inquest, the woman's death, according to the police surgeon's evidence, must have occurred about three to four weeks ago. Now don't worry, Miss Crackenthorpe, just leave it to us." He added casually, "You consulted Mr. Harold Crackenthorpe. What about your father and your other brothers?"

"I had to tell my father, of course. He got very worked up." She smiled faintly. "He was convinced it was a put-up thing to get money out of us. My father gets very excited about money. He believes, or pretends to believe, that he is a very poor man and that he must save every penny he can. I believe elderly people do get obsessions of that kind sometimes. It's not true, of course; he has a very large income and doesn't actually spend a quarter of it, or used not to until these days of high income tax. Certainly he has a large amount of savings put by." She paused and then went on. "I told my other two brothers also. Alfred seemed to consider it rather a joke, though he, too, thought it was almost certainly an imposture. Cedric just wasn't interested. He's inclined to be self-centered. Our idea was that the family would receive Martine, and that our lawyer, Mr. Wimborne, should also be asked to be present."

"What did Mr. Wimborne think about the matter?"

"We hadn't got as far as discussing the matter with him. We were on the point of doing so when Martine's telegram arrived."

"You have taken no further steps?"

"Yes. I wrote to the address in London with *Please forward* on the envelope, but I have had no reply of any kind."

"Rather a curious business. Hm . . ."

He looked at her sharply.

"What do you yourself think about it?"

"I don't know what to think."

"What were your reactions at the time? Did you think the letter was genuine, or did you agree with your father and brothers? What about your brother-in-law, by the way, what did he think?"

"Oh, Bryan thought that the letter was genuine."

"And you?"

"I wasn't sure."

"And what were your feelings about it, supposing that this girl really was your brother Edmund's widow?"

Emma's face softened.

"I was very fond of Edmund. He was my favorite brother. The letter seemed to me exactly the sort of letter that a girl like Martine would write under the circumstances. The course of events she described were entirely natural. I assumed that by the time the war ended she had either married again or was with some man who was protecting her and the child. Then, perhaps, this man had died or left her, and it then seemed right to her to apply to Edmund's family, as he himself had wanted her to do. The letter seemed genuine and natural to me, but of course, Harold pointed out that if it was written by an impostor, it would be written by some woman who had known Martine and who was in possession of all the facts, and so could write a thoroughly plausible letter. I had to admit the justice of that, but all the same—"

She stopped.

"You wanted it to be true?" said Craddock gently.

She looked at him gratefully.

"Yes, I wanted it to be true. I would be so glad if Edmund had left a son."

Craddock nodded.

"As you say, the letter, on the face of it, sounds genuine enough. What is surprising is the sequel; Martine Crackenthorpe's abrupt departure for Paris and the fact that you have never heard from her since. You had replied kindly to her, were prepared to welcome her. Why, even if she had to return to France, did she not write again? That is, presuming her to be the genuine article. If she were an impostor, of course, it's easier to explain. I thought perhaps that you might have consulted Mr. Wimborne, and that he might have instituted inquiries which alarmed the woman. That, you tell me, is not so. But it's still possible that one or other of your brothers may have done something of the kind. It's possible that this Martine may have had a background that would not stand investigation. She may have assumed that she would be dealing only with Edmund's affectionate sister, not with hardheaded, suspicious businessmen. She may have hoped to get sums of money out of you for the child—hardly a child now, a boy presumably of fifteen or sixteen—without many questions being asked. But instead she found she was going to run up against something quite different. After all, I should imagine that serious legal aspects would arise. If Edmund Crackenthorpe left a son, born in wedlock, he would be one of the heirs to your grandfather's estate?"

Emma nodded.

"Moreover, from what I have been told, he would in due course inherit Rutherford Hall and the land round it, very valuable building land, probably, by now."

Emma looked slightly startled.

"Yes, I hadn't thought of that."

"Well, I shouldn't worry," said Inspector Craddock. "You did quite right to come and tell me. I shall make inquiries, but it seems to me highly probable that there is no connection between the woman who wrote the letter—and who was probably trying to cash in on a swindle—and the woman whose body was found in the sarcophagus."

Emma rose with a sigh of relief.

"I'm so glad I've told you. You've been very kind."

Craddock accompanied her to the door.

Then he rang for Detective Sergeant Wetherall.

"Bob, I've got a job for you. Go to 126 Elvers Crescent, N. 10. Take photographs of the Rutherford Hall woman with you. See what you can find out about a woman calling herself Mrs. Crackenthorpe—Mrs. Martine Crackenthorpe—who was either living there or calling for letters there, between the dates of, say the fifteenth to the end of December."

"Right, sir."

Craddock busied himself with various other matters that were waiting attention on his desk. In the afternoon he went to see a theatrical agent who was a friend of his. His inquiries were not fruitful.

Later in the day when he returned to his office he found a wire from Paris on his desk.

PARTICULARS GIVEN BY YOU MIGHT APPLY TO ANNA STRAVIN-
SKA OF BALLET MARITSKI. SUGGEST YOU COME OVER. DESSIN,
PREFECTURE.

Craddock heaved a big sigh of relief and his brow cleared.

At last! So much, he thought, for the Martine Crackenthorpe hare.
He decided to take the night ferry to Paris.

13

"It's so very kind of you to have asked me to take tea with you," said Miss Marple to Emma Crackenthorpe.

Miss Marple was looking particularly woolly and fluffy, a picture of a sweet old lady. She beamed as she looked round her: at Harold Crackenthorpe in his well-cut dark suit, at Alfred handing her sandwiches with a charming smile, at Cedric standing by the mantelpiece in a ragged tweed jacket, scowling at the rest of his family.

"We are very pleased that you could come," said Emma politely.

There was no hint of the scene which had taken place after lunch that day when Emma had exclaimed: "Dear me, I quite forgot. I told Miss Eyelesbarrow that she could bring her old aunt to tea today."

"Put her off," said Harold brusquely. "We've still got a lot to talk about. We don't want strangers here."

"Let her have tea in the kitchen or somewhere with the girl," said Alfred.

"Oh no, I couldn't do that," said Emma firmly. "That would be very rude."

"Oh, let her come," said Cedric. "We can draw her out a little about the wonderful Lucy. I should like to know more about that girl, I must say. I'm not sure that I trust her. Too smart by half."

"She's very well connected and quite genuine," said Harold. "I've made it my business to find out. One wanted to be sure. Poking about and finding the body the way she did . . ."

"If we only knew who this damned woman was," said Alfred.

Harold added angrily, "I must say, Emma, that I think you were out of your senses, going and suggesting to the police that the dead woman might be Edmund's French girlfriend. It will make them convinced that she came here, and that probably one or other of us killed her."

"Oh no, Harold. Don't exaggerate."

"Harold's quite right," said Alfred. "Whatever possessed you, I don't know. I've a feeling I'm being followed everywhere I go by plainclothes men."

"I told her not to do it," said Cedric. "Then Quimper backed her up."

"It's no business of his," said Harold angrily. "Let him stick to pills and powders and national health."

"Oh, do stop quarreling," said Emma wearily. "I'm really glad this old Miss What's-her-name is coming to tea. It will do us all good to have a stranger here and be prevented from going over and over the same things again and again. I must go and tidy myself up a little."

She left the room.

"This Lucy Eyelesbarrow," said Harold and stopped. "As Cedric says, it is odd that she should nose about in the barn and go opening up a sarcophagus—really a Herculean task. Perhaps we ought to take steps. Her attitude, I thought, was rather antagonistic at lunch."

"Leave her to me," said Alfred. "I'll soon find out if she's up to anything."

"I mean, why open up that sarcophagus?"

"Perhaps she isn't really Lucy Eyelesbarrow at all," suggested Cedric.

"But what would be the point—" Harold looked thoroughly upset. "Oh, damn!"

They looked at each other with worried faces.

"And here's this pestilential old woman coming to tea. Just when we want to think."

"We'll talk things over this evening," said Alfred. "In the meantime, we'll pump the old aunt about Lucy."

So Miss Marple had duly been fetched by Lucy and installed by the fire, and she was now smiling up at Alfred as he handed her sandwiches with the approval she always showed toward a good-looking man.

"Thank you so much. May I ask—? Oh, egg and sardine, yes that will be very nice. I'm afraid I'm always rather greedy over my tea. As one gets on, you know—and of course, at night only a very light meal—I have to be careful. I shall be ninety next year. Yes, indeed."

"Eighty-seven," said Lucy.

"No, dear, ninety. You young people don't know best about every-thing." Miss Marple spoke with a faint acidity. Then she turned to her hostess once more. "What a beautiful house you have. And so many beautiful things in it. Those bronzes, now, they remind me of some my father bought at the Paris Exhibition. Really, your grandfather did? In the classical style, aren't they? Very handsome. How delight-ful for you having your brothers with you. So often families are scattered—India, though I suppose that is all done with now, and Africa—the West Coast such a bad climate."

"Two of my brothers live in London."

"That is very nice for you."

"But my brother Cedric is a painter and lives in Iviza, one of the Balearic Islands."

"Painters are so fond of islands, are they not?" said Miss Marple. "Chopin—that was Majorca, was it not? but he was a musician. It is Gauguin I am thinking of. A sad life; misspent, one feels. I myself never really cared for paintings of native women, and although I know he is very much admired, I have never cared for that lurid mustard color. One really feels quite bilious looking at his pictures."

She eyed Cedric with a slightly disapproving air.

"Tell us about Lucy as a child, Miss Marple," said Cedric.

She smiled up at him delightedly.

"Lucy was always so clever," she said. "Yes, you were dear. Now don't interrupt. Quite remarkable at arithmetic. Why I remember when the butcher overcharged me for topside of beef—"

Miss Marple launched full steam ahead into reminiscences of Lucy's childhood and from there to experiences of her own in village life.

The stream of reminiscence was interrupted by the entry of Bryan and the boys, rather wet and dirty as a result of an enthusiastic search for clues. Tea was brought in and with it came Doctor Quimper who raised his eyebrows slightly as he looked round after acknowledging his introduction to the old lady.

"Hope your father's not under the weather, Emma?"

"Oh no—that is, he was just a little tired this afternoon."

"Avoiding visitors, I expect," said Miss Marple with a roguish smile. "How well I remember my own dear father. 'Got a lot of old pussies coming?' he would say to my mother. 'Send my tea into the study.' Very naughty about it, he was."

"Please don't think—" began Emma, but Cedric cut in:

"It's always tea in the study when his dear sons come down. Psychologically to be expected, eh, doctor?"

Doctor Quimper, who was devouring sandwiches and coffee cake with the frank appreciation of a man who has usually too little time to spend on his meals, said:

"Psychology's all right if it's left to the psychologists. Trouble is, everyone is an amateur psychologist nowadays. My patients tell me exactly what complexes and neuroses they're suffering from, without giving me a chance to tell them. Thanks, Emma. I will have another cup. No time for lunch today."

"A doctor's life, I always think, is so noble and self-sacrificing," said Miss Marple.

"You can't know many doctors," said Doctor Quimper. "Leeches they used to be called and leeches they often are! At any rate we do get paid nowadays, the state sees to that. No sending in of bills that you know won't ever be met. Trouble is that all one's patients are determined to get everything they can 'out of the government,' and as a result if little Jenny coughs twice in the night, or little Tommy eats a couple of green apples, out the poor doctor has to come in the middle of the night. Oh well! Glorious cake, Emma. What a cook you are!"

"Not mine. Miss Eyelesbarrow's."

"You make 'em just as good," said Quimper loyally.

"Will you come and see Father?"

She rose and the doctor followed her. Miss Marple watched them leave the room.

"Miss Crackenthorpe is a very devoted daughter, I see," she said.

"Can't imagine how she sticks the old man, myself," said the outspoken Cedric.

"She has a very comfortable home here, and Father is very much attached to her," said Harold quickly.

"Em's all right," said Cedric. "Born to be an old maid." There was a faint twinkle in Miss Marple's eye as she said:

"Oh, do you think so?"

Harold said quickly:

"My brother didn't use the term old maid in any derogatory sense, Miss Marple."

"Oh, I wasn't offended," said Miss Marple. "I just wondered if he was right. I shouldn't say myself that Miss Crackenthorpe would be an old maid. She's the type, I think, that's quite likely to marry late in life, and make a success of it."

"Not very likely living here," said Cedric. "Never sees anybody she could marry."

Miss Marple's twinkle became more pronounced than ever.

"There are always clergymen and doctors."

Her eyes, gentle and mischievous, went from one to another.

It was clear that she had suggested to them something that they had never thought of and which they did not find over-pleasing.

Miss Marple rose to her feet, dropping as she did so several little wooly scarves and her bag.

The three brothers were most attentive picking things up.

"So kind of you," fluted Miss Marple. "Oh yes, and my little blue muffler. Yes, as I say, so kind to ask me here. I've been picturing, you know, just what your home was like, so that I can visualize dear Lucy working here."

"Perfect home conditions, with murder thrown in," said Cedric.

"Cedric!" Harold's voice was angry.

Miss Marple smiled up at Cedric.

"Do you know who you remind me of? Young Thomas Eade, our bank manager's son. Always out to shock people. It didn't do in banking circles, of course, so he went to the West Indies. He came home when his father died and inherited quite a lot of money. So nice for him. He was always better at spending money than making it."

II

Lucy took Miss Marple home. On her way back a figure stepped out of the darkness and stood in the glare of the headlights just as she was about to turn into the back lane. He held up his hand and Lucy recognized Alfred Crackenthorpe.

"That's better," he observed, as he got in. "Brr, it's cold! I fancied I'd like a nice bracing walk. I didn't. Taken the old lady home all right?"

"Yes. She enjoyed herself very much."

"One could see that. Funny what a taste old ladies have for any kind of society, however dull. And really, nothing could be duller than Rutherford Hall. Two days here is about as much as I can stand. How do you manage to stick it out, Lucy? Don't mind if I call you Lucy, do you?"

"Not at all. I don't find it dull. Of course with me it's not a permanency."

"I've been watching you. You're a smart girl, Lucy. Too smart to
waste yourself cooking and cleaning."

"Thank you, but I prefer cooking and cleaning to the office desk."

"So would I. But there are other ways of living. You could be a
free lance."

"I am."

"Not this way. I mean, working for yourself, pitting your wits
against—"

"Against what?"

"The powers that be! All the silly pettifogging rules and regulations that hamper us all nowadays. The interesting thing is there's always a way round them if you're smart enough to find it. And you're
smart. Come now, does the idea appeal to you?"

"Possibly."

Lucy maneuvered the car into the stable yard.

"Not going to commit yourself?"

"I'd have to hear more."

"Frankly, my dear girl, I could use you. You've got the sort of
manner that's invaluable, creates confidence."

"Do you want me to help you sell gold bricks?"

"Nothing so risky. Just a little bypassing of the law—no more."
His hand slipped up her arm. "You're a damned attractive girl, Lucy.
I'd like you as a partner."

"I'm flattered."

"Meaning, nothing doing? Think about it. Think of the fun, the
pleasure you'd get out of outwitting all the sobersides. The trouble is,
one needs capital."

"I'm afraid I haven't got any."

"Oh, it wasn't a touch! I'll be laying my hands on some before
long. My revered Papa can't live forever, mean old brute. When he
pops off, I lay my hands on some real money. What about it, Lucy?"

"What are the terms?"

"Marriage if you fancy it. Women seem to, no matter how advanced
and self-supporting they are. Besides, married women can't be made to
give evidence against their husbands."

"Not so flattering!"

"Come off it, Lucy. Don't you realize I've fallen for you?"

Rather to her surprise Lucy was aware of a queer fascination.

There was a quality of charm about Alfred, perhaps due to sheer animal magnetism. She laughed and slipped from his encircling arm.

"This is no time for dalliance. There's dinner to think about."

"So there is, Lucy, and you're a lovely cook. What's for dinner?"

"Wait and see! You're as bad as the boys!"

They entered the house and Lucy hurried to the kitchen. She was surprised to be interrupted in her preparations by Harold Crackenthorpe.

"Miss Eyelesbarrow, can I speak to you about something?"

"Would later do, Mr. Crackenthorpe? I'm rather behindhand."

"Certainly. Certainly. After dinner?"

"Yes, that will do."

Dinner was duly served and appreciated. Lucy finished washing up and came out into the hall to find Harold Crackenthorpe waiting for her.

"Yes, Mr. Crackenthorpe?"

"Shall we come in here?" He opened the door of the drawing room and led the way. He shut the door behind her.

"I shall be leaving early in the morning," he explained, "but I want to tell you how struck I have been by your ability."

"Thank you," said Lucy feeling a little surprised.

"I feel that your talents are wasted here—definitely wasted."

"Do you? I don't."

At any rate, he can't ask me to marry him, thought Lucy. He's got a wife already.

"I suggest that having very kindly seen us through this lamentable crisis, you call upon me in London. If you will ring up and make an appointment, I will leave instructions with my secretary. The truth is that we could use someone of your outstanding ability in the firm. We could discuss fully in what field your talents would be most ably employed. I can offer you, Miss Eyelesbarrow, a very good salary indeed with brilliant prospects. I think you will be agreeably surprised."

His smile was magnanimous.

Lucy said demurely, "Thank you, Mr. Crackenthorpe, I'll think about it."

"Don't wait too long. These opportunities should not be missed by a young woman anxious to make her way in the world."

Again his teeth flashed.

"Good night, Miss Eyelesbarrow, sleep well."

"Well," said Lucy to herself, "well. . . . This is all very interesting."

On her way up to bed, Lucy encountered Cedric on the stairs.

"Look here, Lucy, there's something I want to say to you."

"Do you want me to marry you and come to Iviza and look after you?"

Cedric looked very much taken aback and slightly alarmed.

"I never thought of such a thing."

"Sorry. My mistake."

"I just wanted to know if you've a timetable in the house?"

"Is that all? There's one on the hall table."

"You know," said Cedric, reprovingly, "you shouldn't go about thinking everyone wants to marry you. You're quite a good-looking girl but not as good-looking as all that. There's a name for that sort of thing. It grows on you and you get worse. Actually you're the last girl in the world I should care to marry. The last girl."

"Indeed?" said Lucy. "You needn't rub it in. Perhaps you'd prefer me as a stepmother?"

"What's that?" Cedric stared at her, stupefied.

"You heard me," said Lucy, and went into her room and shut the door.

14

Dermot Craddock was fraternizing with Armand Dessin of the Paris Prefecture. The two men had met on one or two occasions and got on well together. Since Craddock spoke French fluently, most of their conversation was conducted in that language.

"It is an idea only," Dessin warned him. "I have a picture here of the corps de ballet. That is she, the fourth from the left. It says anything to you, yes?"

Inspector Craddock said that actually it didn't. A strangled young woman is not easy to recognize, and in this picture all the young women concerned were heavily made up and were wearing extravagant bird headdresses.

"It could be," he said. "I can't go further than that. Who was she? What do you know about her?"

"Almost less than nothing," said the other cheerfully. "She was not important, you see. And the Ballet Maritski—it is not important, either. It plays in suburban theaters and goes on tour. It has no real names, no stars, no famous ballerinas. But I will take you to see Madame Joliet who runs it."

Madame Joliet was a brisk businesslike Frenchwoman with a shrewd eye, a small mustache, and a good deal of adipose tissue.

"Me, I do not like the police!" She scowled at them, without camouflaging her dislike of the visit. "Always, if they can, they make me embarrassments."

"No, no, Madame, you must not say that," said Dessin who was a tall, thin, melancholy looking man. "When have I ever caused you embarrassments?"

"Over that little fool who drank the carbolic acid," said Madame Joliet promptly. "And all because she has fallen in love with the *chef d'orchestre*, who does not care for women and has other tastes. Over that you made the big brou ha ha! Which is not good for my beautiful ballet."

"On the contrary, big box-office business," said Dessin. "And that was three years ago. You should not bear malice. Now about this girl, Anna Stravinska."

"Well, what about her?"

"Is she Russian?" asked Inspector Craddock.

"No, indeed. You mean, because of her name? But they all call themselves names like that, these girls. She was not important, she did not dance well, she was not particularly good-looking. *Elle etait assez bien, c'est tout.* She danced well enough for the corps de ballet, but no solos."

"Was she French?"

"Perhaps. She had a French passport. But she told me once that she had an English husband."

"She told you that she had an English husband? Alive or dead?"

Madame Joliet shrugged her shoulders.

"Dead, or he had left her. How should I know which? These girls—there is always some trouble with men."

"When did you last see her?"

"I take my company to London for six weeks. We play at Torquay, at Bournemouth, at Eastbourne, at somewhere else I forget and at Hammersmith. Then we come back to France, but Anna, she does not come. She sends a message only that she leaves the company, that she goes to live with her husband's family, some nonsense of that kind. I did not think it is true, myself. I think it more likely that she has met a man, you understand."

Inspector Craddock nodded. He perceived that that was what Madame Joliet would invariably think.

"And it is no loss to me. I do not care. I can get girls just as good and better to come and dance, so I shrug the shoulders and do not think of it any more. Why should I? They are all the same, these girls, mad about men."

"What date was this?"

"When we return to France? It was—yes—the Sunday before Christmas. And Anna she leaves two, or is it three, days before that? I cannot remember exactly. But the end of the week at Hammersmith we have to dance without her, and it means rearranging things. It was very naughty of her, but these girls—the moment they meet a man they are all the same. Only I say to everybody, 'Zut, I do not take her back, that one!'"

"Very annoying for you."

"Ah! me—I do not care. No doubt she passes the Christmas holiday with some man she has picked up. It is not my affair. I can find other girls—girls who will leap at the chance of dancing in the Ballet Maritski and who can dance as well or better than Anna."

Madame Joliet paused and then asked with a sudden gleam of interest. "Why do you want to find her? Has she come into money?"

"On the contrary," said Inspector Craddock politely. "We think she may have been murdered."

Madame Joliet relapsed into indifference.

"*Ça se peut!* It happens. Ah well! She was a good Catholic. She went to Mass on Sundays, and no doubt to confession."

"Did she ever speak to you, Madame, of a son?"

"A son? Do you mean she had a child? That, now, I should consider most unlikely. These girls, all—all of them—know a useful address to which to go. M. Dessin knows that as well as I do."

"She may have had a child before she adopted a stage life," said Craddock. "During the war, for instance."

"*Ah! dans la guerre.* That is always possible. But if so, I know nothing about it."

"Who among the other girls were her closest friends?"

"I can give you two or three names, but she was not very intimate with anyone."

They could get nothing else useful from Madame Joliet.

Shown the compact, she said Anna had one of that kind, but so had most of the other girls. Anna had perhaps bought a fur coat in London, she did not know. "Me, I occupy myself with the rehearsals, with the stage lighting, with all the difficulties of my business. I have not time to notice what my artists wear."

After Madame Joliet, they interviewed the girls whose names she had given them. One or two of them had known Anna fairly well, but they all said that she had not been one to talk much about herself, and that when she did, it was, so one girl said, mostly lies.

"She liked to pretend things—stories about having been the mistress of a grand duke or of a great English financier or how she worked for the Resistance in the war, even a story about being a film star in Hollywood."

Another girl said:

"I think that really she had had a very tame bourgeoise existence. She liked to be in ballet because she thought it was romantic, but she was not a good dancer. You understand that if she were to say, 'My father was a draper in Amiens,' that would not be romantic! So instead she made up things."

"Even in London," said the first girl, "she threw out hints about a very rich man who was going to take her on a cruise round the world, because she reminded him of his dead daughter who had died in a car accident. *Quelle blague!*"

"She told me she was going to stay with a rich lord in Scotland," said the second girl. "She said she would shoot the deer there."

None of this was helpful. All that seemed to emerge from it was that Anna Stravinska was a proficient liar. She was certainly not shooting deer with a peer in Scotland, and it seemed equally unlikely that she was on the sundeck of a liner cruising round the world. But neither was there any real reason to believe that her body had been found in a sarcophagus at Rutherford Hall. The identification by the girls and Madame Joliet was very uncertain and hesitating. It looked something like Anna, they all agreed. But really! All swollen up—it might be anybody!

The only fact that was established was that, on December 19, Anna Stravinska had decided not to return to France, and that on the twentieth of December a woman resembling her in appearance had traveled to Brackhampton by the 4:54 train and had been strangled.

If the woman in the sarcophagus was not Anna Stravinska, where was Anna now?

To that, Madame Joliet's answer was simple and inevitable:

"With a man!"

And it was probably the correct answer, Craddock reflected ruefully.

One other possibility had to be considered, raised by the casual remark that Anna had once referred to having an English husband.

Had that husband been Edmund Crackenthorpe?

It seemed unlikely, considering the word picture of Anna that had been given him by those who knew her. What was much more probable was that Anna had at one time known the girl Martine sufficiently intimately to be acquainted with the necessary details. It might have been Anna who wrote that letter to Emma Crackenthorpe and, if so, Anna would have been quite likely to have taken fright at any question of an investigation. Perhaps she had even thought it prudent to sever her connection with the Ballet Maritski. Again, where was she now?

And again, inevitably, Madame Joliet's answer seemed the most likely.

With a man.

II

Before leaving Paris, Craddock discussed with Dessin the question of the woman named Martine. Dessin was inclined to agree with his English colleague that the matter had probably no connection with the woman found in the sarcophagus. All the same, he agreed, the matter ought to be investigated.

He assured Craddock that the Sûreté would do their best to discover if there actually was any record of a marriage between Lieutenant Edmund Crackenthorpe of the 4th Southshire Regiment and a French girl whose Christian name was Martine. Time: just prior to the fall of Dunkirk.

He warned Craddock, however, that a definite answer was doubtful. The area in question had not only been occupied by the Germans at almost exactly that time, but subsequently that part of France had suffered severe war damage at the time of the invasion. Many buildings and records had been destroyed.

"But rest assured, my dear colleague, we shall do our best."

With this, he and Craddock took leave of each other.

III

On Craddock's return Sergeant Wetherall was waiting to report with gloomy relish:

"Accommodation address, sir—that's what 126 Elvers Crescent is. Quite respectable and all that."

"Any identifications?"

"No. Nobody could recognize the photograph as that of a woman who had called for letters, but I don't think they would anyway. It's a month ago, very near, and a good many people use the place. It's actually a boardinghouse for students."

"She might have stayed there under another name."

"If so, they didn't recognize her as the original of the photograph." He added:

"We circularized the hotels—nobody registering as Martine Crackenthorpe anywhere. On receipt of your call from Paris, we checked up on Anna Stravinska. She was registered with other members of the company in a cheap hotel off Brook Green—mostly theatricals there. She cleared out on the night of Thursday the nineteenth after the show. No further record."

Craddock nodded. He suggested a line of further inquiries, though he had little hope of success from them.

After some thought, he rang up Wimborne, Henderson and Carstairs and asked for an appointment with Mr. Wimborne.

In due course, he was ushered into a particularly airless room where Mr. Wimborne was sitting behind a large old-fashioned desk covered with bundles of dusty-looking papers. Various deed boxes labeled *Sir John ffouldes, dec. Lady Derrin, George Rowbotham, Esq.*, ornamented the walls; whether as relics of a bygone era or as part of present-day legal affairs, the Inspector did not know.

Mr. Wimborne eyed his visitor with the polite wariness characteristic of a family lawyer toward the police.

"What can I do for you, Inspector?"

"This letter." Craddock pushed Martine's letter across the table. Mr. Wimborne touched it with a distasteful finger but did not pick it up. His color rose very slightly and his lips tightened.

"Quite so," he said, "quite so! I received a letter from Miss Emma Crackenthorpe yesterday morning, informing me of her visit to Scotland Yard and of—ah—all the circumstances. I may say that I am at a loss to understand—quite at a loss—why I was not consulted about this letter at the time of its arrival! Most extraordinary! I should have been informed immediately."

Inspector Craddock repeated soothingly such platitudes as seemed best calculated to reduce Mr. Wimborne to an amenable frame of mind.

"I'd no idea that there was ever any question of Edmund's having married," said Mr. Wimborne in an injured voice.

Inspector Craddock said that he supposed, in wartime . . . and left it to trail away vaguely.

"Wartime!" snapped Mr. Wimborne with waspish acerbity. "Yes, indeed, we were in Lincoln's Inn Fields at the outbreak of war and there was a direct hit on the house next door, and a great number of our records were destroyed. Not the really important documents, of course; they had been removed to the country for safety. But it caused a great deal of confusion. Of course, the Crackenthorpe business was in my father's hands at that time. He died six years ago. I dare say he may have been told about this so-called marriage of Edmund's, but on the face of it, it looks as though that marriage, even if contemplated, never, took place, and so, no doubt my father did not consider the story of any importance. I must say, all this sounds very fishy to me. This coming forward, after all these years, and claiming a marriage and a legitimate son. Very fishy, indeed. What proofs had she got, I'd like to know?"

"Just so," said Craddock. "What would her position or her son's position be?"

"The idea was, I suppose, that she would get the Crackenthorpes to provide for her and for the boy."

"Yes, but I meant, what would she and the son be entitled to, legally speaking, if she could prove her claim?"

"Oh, I see." Mr. Wimborne picked up his spectacles which he had laid aside in his irritation, and put them on, staring through them at Inspector Craddock with shrewd attention. "Well, at the moment, nothing. But if she could prove that the boy was the son of Edmund Crackenthorpe, born in lawful wedlock, then the boy would be entitled to his share of Josiah Crackenthorpe's trust, on the death of Luther Crackenthorpe. More than that, he'd inherit Rutherford Hall, since he's the son of the eldest son."

"Would anyone want to inherit the house?"

"To live in? I should say, certainly not. But that estate, my dear Inspector, is worth a considerable amount of money. Very considerable. Land for industrial and building purposes. Land which is now in the heart of Brackhampton. Oh yes, a very considerable inheritance."

"If Luther Crackenthorpe dies, I believe you told me that Cedric gets it?"

"He inherits the real estate, yes, as the eldest surviving son."

"Cedric Crackenthorpe, I have been given to understand, is not interested in money?"

Mr. Wimborne gave Craddock a cold stare.

"Indeed? I am inclined, myself, to take statements of such a nature with what I might term a grain of salt. There are doubtless certain unworldly people who are indifferent to money. I myself have never met one."

Mr. Wimborne obviously derived a certain satisfaction from this remark.

Inspector Craddock hastened to take advantage of this ray of sunshine.

"Harold and Alfred Crackenthorpe," he ventured, "seem to have been a good deal upset by the arrival of this letter?"

"Well they might be," said Mr. Wimborne. "Well they might be."

"It would reduce their eventual inheritance?"

"Certainly. Edmund Crackenthorpe's son—always presuming there is a son—would be entitled to a fifth share of the trust money."

"That doesn't really seem a very serious loss?"

Mr. Wimborne gave him a shrewd glance.

"It is a totally inadequate motive for murder, if that is what you mean."

"But I suppose they're both pretty hard up," Craddock murmured.

He sustained Mr. Wimborne's sharp glance with perfect impassivity.

"Oh! So the police have been making inquiries? Yes, Alfred is almost incessantly in low water. Occasionally he is very flush of money for a short time, but it soon goes. Harold, as you seem to have discovered, is at present somewhat precariously situated."

"In spite of his appearance of financial prosperity?"

"Façade. All façade! Half these City concerns don't even know if they're solvent or not. Balance sheets can be made to look all right to the inexpert eye. But when the assets that are listed aren't really assets— when those assets are trembling on the brink of a crash—where are you?"

"Where, presumably, Harold Crackenthorpe is, in bad need of money."

"Well, he wouldn't have got it by strangling his late brother's widow," said Mr. Wimborne. "And nobody's murdered Luther Crackenthorpe which is the only murder that would do the family any good. So really, Inspector, I don't quite see where your ideas are leading you."

The worst of it was, Inspector Craddock thought, that he wasn't very sure himself.

15

Inspector Craddock had made an appointment with Harold Crackenthorpe at his office, and he and Sergeant Wetherall arrived there
punctually. The office was on the fourth floor of a big block of City
offices. Inside everything showed prosperity and the acme of modern
business taste.

A neat young woman took his name, spoke in a discreet murmur
through a telephone, and then rising, showed them into Harold
Crackenthorpe's own private office.

Harold was sitting behind a large leather-topped desk and was
looking as impeccable and self-confident as ever. If, as the Inspector's
private knowledge led him to surmise, he was close upon Queer
Street, no trace of it showed.

He looked up with a frank, welcoming interest.

"Good morning, Inspector Craddock. I hope this means that you
have some definite news for us at last."

"Hardly that, I am afraid, Mr. Crackenthorpe. It's just a few more
questions I'd like to ask."

"More questions? Surely by now we have answered everything
imaginable."

"I dare say it feels like that to you, Mr. Crackenthorpe, but it's just
a question of our regular routine."

"Well, what is it this time?" He spoke impatiently.

"I should be glad if you could tell me exactly what you were doing on the afternoon and evening of December the twentieth last, say
between the hours of three p.m. and midnight."

Harold Crackenthorpe went an angry shade of plum red.

"That seems to be a most extraordinary question to ask me. What does it mean, I should like to know?"

Craddock smiled gently.

"It just means that I should like to know where you were between the hours of three p.m. and midnight on Friday, December the twentieth."

"Why?"

"It would help to narrow things down."

"Narrow them down? You have extra information, then?"

"We hope that we're getting a little closer, sir."

"I'm not at all sure that I ought to answer your question. Not, that is, without having my solicitor present."

"That, of course, is entirely up to you," said Craddock. "You are not bound to answer any questions and you have a perfect right to have a solicitor present before you do so."

"You are not—let me be quite clear—er—warning me in anyway?"

"Oh no, sir." Inspector Craddock looked properly shocked. "Nothing of that kind. The questions I am asking you I am asking of several other people as well. There's nothing directly personal about this. It's just a matter of necessary eliminations."

"Well, of course, I'm anxious to assist in any way I can. Let me see now. Such a thing isn't easy to answer offhand, but we're very systematic here. Miss Ellis, I expect, can help."

He spoke briefly into one of the telephones of his desk and almost immediately a streamlined young woman in a well-cut black suit entered with a notebook.

"My secretary, Miss Ellis, Inspector Craddock. Now, Miss Ellis, the Inspector would like to know what I was doing on the afternoon and evening of—what was the date?"

"Friday, December the twentieth."

"Friday, December the twentieth. I expect you will have some record."

"Oh yes." Miss Ellis left the room, returned with an office memorandum calendar and turned the pages.

"You were in the office in the morning of December the twentieth. You had a conference with Mr. Goldie about the Cromartie merger, you lunched with Lord Forthville at the Berkeley—"

"Ah, it was that day, yes."

"You returned to the office at about three o'clock and dictated half a dozen letters. You then left to attend Sotheby's sale rooms where you were interested in some rare manuscripts which were coming up for sale that day. You did not return to the office again, but I have a note to remind you that you were attending the Catering Club dinner that evening." She looked up interrogatively.

"Thank you, Miss Ellis."

Miss Ellis glided from the room.

"That is all quite clear in my mind," said Harold. "I went to Sotheby's that afternoon but the items I wanted there went for far too high a price. I had tea in a small place in Jermyn Street—Russell's, I think it is called. I dropped into a News Theatre for about half an hour or so, then went home. I live at 43 Cardigan Gardens. The Catering Club dinner took place at seven-thirty at Caterers' Hall, and after it I returned home to bed. I think that should answer your questions?"

"That's all very clear, Mr. Crackenthorpe. What time was it when you returned home to dress?"

"I don't think I can remember exactly. Soon after six, I should think."

"And after the dinner?"

"It was, I think, half-past eleven when I got home."

"Did your manservant let you in? Or perhaps Lady Alice Crackenthorpe?"

"My wife, Lady Alice, is abroad in the South of France and has been since early in December. I let myself in with my latchkey."

"So there is no one who can vouch for your returning home when you say you did?"

Harold gave him a cold stare.

"I dare say the servants heard me come in. I have a man and wife. But really, Inspector—"

"Please, Mr. Crackenthorpe, I know these questions are annoying, but I have nearly finished. Do you own a car?"

"Yes, a Humber Hawk."

"You drive it yourself?"

"Yes. I don't use it much except at weekends. Driving in London is quite impossible nowadays."

"I presume you use it when you go down to see your father and sister at Brackhampton?"

"Not unless I am going to stay there for some length of time. If I just go down for the night, as, for instance, to the inquest the other day, I always go by train. There is an excellent train service and it is far quicker than going by car. The car my sister hires meets me at the station."

"Where do you keep your car?'"

"I rent a garage in the mews behind Cardigan Gardens. Any more questions?"

"I think that's all for now," said Inspector Craddock smiling and rising. "I'm very sorry for having to bother you."

When they were outside, Sergeant Wetherall, a man who lived in a state of dark suspicion of all and sundry, remarked meaningly:

"He didn't like those questions—didn't like them at all. Put out, he was."

"If you have not committed a murder, it naturally annoys you if it seems someone thinks that you have," said Inspector Craddock mildly. "It would particularly annoy an ultrarespectable man like Harold Crackenthorpe. There's nothing in that. What we've got to find out now is if anyone actually saw Harold Crackenthorpe at the sale that afternoon, and the same applies to the teashop place. He could easily have traveled by the 4:54, pushed the woman out of the train and caught a train back to London in time to appear at the dinner. In the same way he could have driven his car down that night, moved the body to the sarcophagus and driven back again. Make inquiries in the mews."

"Yes, sir. Do you think that's what he did do?"

"How do I know?" asked Inspector Craddock. "He's a tall, dark man. He could have been on that train and he's got a connection with Rutherford Hall. He's a possible suspect in this case. Now for brother Alfred."

II

Alfred Crackenthorpe had a flat in West Hampstead, in a big modern building of slightly jerry-built type with a large courtyard in which the owners of flats parked their cars with a certain lack of consideration for others.

The flat was of the modern built-in type, evidently rented furnished. It had a long plywood table that let down from the wall, a divan bed, and various chairs of improbable proportions.

Alfred Crackenthorpe met them with engaging friendliness but was, the Inspector thought, nervous.

"I'm intrigued," he said. "Can I offer you a drink, Inspector Crad-dock?" He held up various bottles invitingly.

"No, thank you, Mister Crackenthorpe."

"As bad as that?" He laughed at his own little joke, then asked what it was all about.

Inspector Craddock said his little piece.

"What was I doing on the afternoon and evening of December the twentieth? How should I know? Why, that's—what?—over three weeks ago."

"Your brother Harold has been able to tell us very exactly."

"Brother Harold, perhaps. Not brother Alfred." He added with a touch of something, envious malice possibly: "Harold is the success-ful member of the family—busy, useful, fully employed, a time for everything and everything at that time. Even if he were to commit a murder, shall we say? it would be carefully timed and exact."

"Any particular reason for using that example?"

"Oh no—it just came into my mind as a supreme absurdity."

"Now about yourself."

Alfred spread out his hands.

"It's as I tell you, I've no memory for times or places. If you were to say Christmas Day now, then I should be able to answer you—there's a peg to hang it on. I know where I was Christmas Day We spend that with my father at Brackhampton. I really don't know why. He grumbles at the expense of having us, and would grumble that we never came near him if we didn't come. We really do it to please my sister."

"And you did it this year?"

"Yes."

"But unfortunately your father was taken ill, was he not?"

Craddock was pursuing a side line deliberately, led by the kind of instinct that often came to him in his profession.

"He was taken ill. Living like a sparrow in the glorious cause of economy, sudden full eating and drinking had its effect."

"That was all it was, was it?"

"Of course. What else?"

"I gathered that his doctor was—worried."

"Oh, that old fool Quimper," Alfred spoke quickly and scornfully. "It's no use listening to him, Inspector. He's an alarmist of the worst kind."

"Indeed? He seemed a rather sensible kind of man to me."

"He's a complete fool. Father's not really an invalid, there's nothing wrong with his heart, but he takes in Quimper completely. Naturally, when father really felt ill, he made a terrific fuss, and had Quimper going and coming, asking questions, going into everything he'd eaten and drunk. The whole thing was ridiculous!" Alfred spoke with unusual heat.

Craddock was silent for a moment or two, rather effectively. Alfred fidgeted, shot him a quick glance, and then said petulantly:

"Well, what is all this? Why do you want to know where I was on a particular Friday, three or four weeks ago?"

"So you do remember that it was a Friday?"

"I thought you said so."

"Perhaps I did," said Inspector Craddock. "At any rate, Friday the twentieth is the day I am asking about."

"Why?"

"A routine inquiry."

"That's nonsense. Have you found out something more about this woman? About where she came from?"

"Our information is not yet complete."

Alfred gave him a sharp glance.

"I hope you're not being led aside by this wild theory of Emma's that she might have been my brother Edmund's widow. That's complete nonsense."

"This Martine did not at any time apply to you?"

"To me? Good Lord, no. That would have been a laugh."

"She would be more likely, you think, to go to your brother Harold?"

"Much more likely. His name's frequently in the papers. He's well off. Trying a touch there wouldn't surprise me. Not that she'd have got anything. Harold's as tight-fisted as the old man himself. Emma, of course, is the softhearted one of the family, and she was Edmund's favorite sister. All the same, Emma isn't credulous. She was quite alive to the possibility of this woman being phony. She had it all laid on for the entire family to be there—and a hardheaded solicitor as well."

"Very wise," said Craddock. "Was there a definite date fixed for this meeting?"

"It was to be soon after Christmas. The weekend of the twenty-seventh—" He stopped.

"Ah," said Craddock pleasantly. "So I see some dates have a meaning to you."

"I've told you no definite date was fixed."

"But you talked about it—when?"

"I really can't remember."

"And you can't tell me what yourself were doing on Friday, December the twentieth?"

"Sorry, my mind's an absolute blank."

"You don't keep an engagement book?"

"Can't stand the things."

"The Friday before Christmas—it shouldn't be too difficult."

"I played golf one day with a likely prospect." Alfred shook his head. "No, that was the week before. I probably just mooched around. I spend a lot of my time doing that. I find one's business gets done in bars more than anywhere else."

"Perhaps the people here, or some of your friends, may be able to help?"

"Maybe. I'll ask them. Do what I can."

Alfred seemed more sure of himself now.

"I can't tell you what I was doing that day," he said, "but I can tell you what I wasn't doing. I wasn't murdering anyone in the Long Barn."

"Why should you say that, Mr. Crackenthorpe?"

"Come now, my dear Inspector. You're investigating this murder, aren't you? And when you begin to ask 'Where were you on such and such a day at such and such a time?' you're narrowing down things. I'd very much like to know why you've hit on Friday the twentieth between—what?—lunchtime and midnight? It couldn't be medical evidence, not after all this time. Did somebody see the deceased sneaking into the barn that afternoon? She went in and she never came out, etc.? Is that it?"

The sharp, black eyes were watching him narrowly, but Inspector Craddock was far too old a hand to react to that sort of thing.

"I'm afraid we'll have to let you guess about that," he said pleasantly.

"The police are so secretive."

"Not only the police. I think, Mr. Crackenthorpe, you could remember what you were doing on that Friday if you tried. Of course, you may have reasons for not wishing to remember—"

"You won't catch me that way, Inspector. It's very suspicious, of course, very suspicious, indeed, that I can't remember, but there it is!

Wait a minute now! I went to Leeds that week, stayed at a hotel close to the town hall—can't remember its name, but you'd find it easily enough. That might have been on the Friday."

"We'll check up," said the Inspector unemotionally.

He rose: "I'm sorry you couldn't have been more cooperative, Mr. Crackenthorpe."

"Most unfortunate for me! There's Cedric with a safe alibi in Iviza, and Harold, no doubt, checked with business appointments and public dinners every hour, and here am I with no alibi at all. Very sad. And all so silly. I've already told you I don't murder people. And why should I murder an unknown woman anyway? What for? Even if the corpse is the corpse of Edmund's widow, why should any of us wish to do away with her? Now if she'd been married to Harold in the war and had suddenly reappeared, then it might have been awkward for the respectable Harold—bigamy and all that. But Edmund! Why, we'd all have enjoyed making Father stump up a bit to give her an allowance and send the boy to a decent school. Father would have been wild, but he couldn't in decency refuse to do something. Won't you have a drink before you go, Inspector? Sure? Too bad I haven't been able to help you."

III

"Sir, listen, do you know what?"

Inspector Craddock looked at his excited sergeant.

"Yes, Wetherall, what is it?"

"I've placed him, sir. That chap. All the time I was trying to fix it and suddenly it came. He was mixed up in that tinned-food business with Dicky Rogers. Never got anything on him—too cagey for that. And he's been in with one or more of the Soho lot. Watches and that Italian sovereign business."

Of course! Craddock realized now why Alfred's face had seemed vaguely familiar from the first. It had all been small-time stuff, never anything that could be proved. Alfred had always been on the outskirts of the racket with a plausible, innocent reason for having been mixed up in it at all. But the police had been quite sure that a small, steady profit came his way.

"That throws rather a light on things," Craddock said.

"Think he done it?"

"I shouldn't have said he was the type to do murder. But it explains other things—the reason why he couldn't come up with an alibi."

"Yes, that looks bad for him."

"Not really," said Craddock. "It's quite a clever line, just to say firmly you can't remember. Lots of people can't remember what they did and where they were even a week ago. It's especially useful if you don't particularly want to call attention to the way you spend your time—interesting rendezvous at lorry pull ups with the Dicky Rogers crowd, for instance."

"So you think he's all right?"

"I'm not prepared to think anyone's all right just yet," said Inspector Craddock. "You've got to work on it, Wetherall."

Back at his desk, Craddock sat frowning, and making little notes on the pad in front of him.

Murderer (he wrote). . . . A tall, dark man!!!

Victim?. . . . . Could have been Martine, Edmund Crackenthorpe's
      girlfriend or widow.

      or

      Could have been Anna Stravinska. Went out of circu-
      lation at appropriate time, right age and appearance,
      clothing, etc. No connection with Rutherford Hall as
      far as is known. Could be Harold's first wife! Bigamy!
            "   "   "   mistress.

      Blackmail?!

      If connection with Alfred, might be blackmail had
      knowledge that could have sent him to jail? If Cedric—
      might have had connection with him abroad—Paris?
      Balearics?

      or

      Victim could be Anna S. posing as Martine

      or

      Victim is unknown woman killed by unknown mur-
      derer!

"And most probably the latter," said Craddock aloud.

He reflected gloomily on the situation. You couldn't get far with a case until you had the motive. All the motives suggested so far seemed either inadequate or farfetched.

Now if only it had been the murder of old Mr. Crackenthorpe. Plenty of motive there.

Something stirred in his memory.

He made further notes on his pad.

> Ask Dr. Q. about Christmas illness.
> Cedric—alibi.
> Consult Miss M. for latest gossip.

16

When Craddock got to 4 Madison Road he found Lucy Eyelesbarrow with Miss Marple.

He hesitated for a moment on his plan of campaign and then decided that Lucy Eyelesbarrow might prove a valuable ally.

After greetings, he solemnly drew out his notecase, extracted three pound notes, added three shillings and pushed them across the table to Miss Marple.

"What's this, Inspector?"

"Consultation fee. You're a consultant—on murder! Pulse, temperature, local reactions, possible deep-seated cause of said murder. I'm just the poor harassed local G.P."

Miss Marple looked at him and twinkled. He grinned at her. Lucy Eyelesbarrow gave a faint gasp and then laughed.

"Why, Inspector Craddock, you're human after all."

"Oh well, I'm not strictly on duty this afternoon."

"I told you we had met before," said Miss Marple to Lucy. "Sir Henry Clithering is his godfather, a very old friend of mine."

"Would you like to hear, Miss Eyelesbarrow, what my godfather said about her, the first time we met? He described her as just the finest detective God ever made—natural genius cultivated in a suitable soil. He told me never to despise the"—Dermot Craddock paused for a moment to seek for a synonym for 'old pussies'—"er—elderly ladies. He said they could usually tell you what might have happened, what ought to have happened and even what actually did happen! And," he said, "they can tell you why it happened!" He added "that this particular—er—elderly lady was at the top of the class."

"Well!" said Lucy, "that seems to be a testimonial all right."

Miss Marple was pink and confused and looked unusually dithery.

"Dear Sir Henry," she murmured. "Always so kind. Really I'm not at all clever, just, perhaps, a slight knowledge of human nature—living, you know, in a village."

She added, with more composure:

"Of course, I am somewhat handicapped, by not actually being on the spot. It is so helpful, I always feel, when people remind you of other people, because types are alike everywhere and that is such a valuable guide."

Lucy looked a little puzzled, but Craddock nodded comprehendingly.

"But you've been to tea there, haven't you?" he said.

"Yes, indeed. Most pleasant. I was a little disappointed that I didn't see old Mr. Crackenthorpe, but one can't have everything."

"Do you feel that if you saw the person who had done the murder, you'd know?" asked Lucy.

"Oh, I wouldn't say that, dear. One is always inclined to guess, and guessing would be very wrong when it is a question of anything as serious as murder. All one can do is to observe the people concerned, or who might have been concerned, and see of whom they remind you."

"Like Cedric and the bank manager?"

Miss Marple corrected her.

"The bank manager's son, dear. Mr. Eade himself was far more like Mr. Harold, a very conservative man, but perhaps a little too fond of money—the sort of man, too, who would go a long way to avoid scandal."

Craddock smiled and said:

"And Alfred?"

"Jenkins at the garage," Miss Marple replied promptly. "He didn't exactly appropriate tools, but he used to exchange a broken or inferior jack for a good one. And I believe he wasn't very honest over batteries, though I don't understand these things very well. I know Raymond left off dealing with him and went to the garage on the Milchester road. As for Emma," continued Miss Marple thoughtfully, "she reminds me very much of Geraldine Webb—always very quiet, almost dowdy—and bullied a good deal by her elderly mother. Quite a surprise to everybody when the mother died unexpectedly and Geraldine came into a nice sum of money and went and had her hair cut and permed and went off on a cruise and came back married to a very nice barrister. They had two children."

The parallel was clear enough. Lucy said, rather uneasily: "Do you think you ought to have said what you did about Emma marrying? It seemed to upset the brothers."

Miss Marple nodded.

"Yes," she said. "So like men, quite unable to see what's going on under their eyes. I don't believe you noticed yourself."

"No," admitted Lucy. "I never thought of anything of that kind. They both seemed to me—"

"So old?" said Miss Marple smiling a little. "But Doctor Quimper isn't much over forty, I should say, though he's going gray on the temples, and it's obvious that he's longing for some kind of home life; and Emma Crackenthorpe is under forty, not too old to marry and have a family. The doctor's wife died quite young having a baby, so I have heard."

"I believe she did. Emma said something about it one day."

"He must be lonely," said Miss Marple. "A busy hardworking doctor needs a wife, someone sympathetic, not too young."

"Listen, darling," said Lucy. "Are we investigating crime, or are we matchmaking?"

Miss Marple twinkled.

"I'm afraid I am rather romantic. Because I am an old maid, perhaps. You know, dear Lucy, that as far as I am concerned, you have fulfilled your contract. If you really want a holiday abroad before taking up your next engagement, you would have time still for a short trip."

"And leave Rutherford Hall? Never! I'm the complete sleuth by now. Almost as bad as the boys. They spend their entire time looking for clues. They looked all through the dustbins yesterday. Most unsavory, and they hadn't really the faintest idea what they were looking for. If they come to you in triumph, Inspector Craddock, bearing a torn scrap of paper with *Martine—if you value your life keep away from the Long Barn!* on it, you'll know that I've taken pity on them and concealed it in the pigsty!"

"Why the pigsty, dear?" asked Miss Marple with interest. "Do they keep pigs?"

"Oh no, not nowadays. It's just that I go there sometimes."

For some reason Lucy blushed. Miss Marple looked at her with increased interest.

"Who's at the house now?" asked Craddock.

"Cedric's there, and Bryan's down for the weekend. Harold and Alfred are coming down tomorrow. They rang up this morning. I somehow got the impression that you had been putting the cat among the pigeons, Inspector Craddock."

Craddock smiled.

"I shook them up a little. Asked them to account for their movements on Friday, December the twentieth."

"And could they?"

"Harold could. Alfred couldn't or wouldn't."

"I think alibis must be terribly difficult," said Lucy. "Times and places and dates. They must be hard to check up on, too."

"It takes time and patience, but we manage." He glanced at his watch. "I'll be coming along to Rutherford Hall presently to have a word with Cedric, but I want to get hold of Doctor Quimper first."

"You'll be just about right. He has his surgery at six and he's usually finished about half-past. I must get back and deal with dinner."

"I'd like your opinion on one thing, Miss Eyelesbarrow. What's the family view about this Martine business, among themselves?"

Lucy replied promptly.

"They're all furious with Emma for going to you about it, and with Doctor Quimper who, it seemed, encouraged her to do so. Harold and Alfred think it was a try on and not genuine. Emma isn't sure. Cedric thinks it was phony, too, but he doesn't take it as seriously as the other two. Bryan, on the other hand, seems quite sure that it's genuine."

"Why I wonder?"

"Well, Bryan's rather like that. Just accepts things at their face value. He thinks it was Edmund's wife, or rather widow, and that she had suddenly to go back to France, but that they'll hear from her again sometime. The fact that she hasn't written or anything up to now, seems to him to be quite natural because he never writes letters himself. Bryan's rather sweet. Just like a dog that wants to be taken for a walk."

"And do you take him for a walk dear?" asked Miss Marple. "To the pigsties, perhaps?"

Lucy shot a keen glance at her.

"So many gentlemen in the house, coming and going," mused Miss Marple.

When Miss Marple uttered the word "gentlemen" she always gave it its full Victorian flavor—an echo from an era actually before her own time. You were conscious at once of dashing, full-blooded (and probably whiskered) males, sometimes wicked, but always gallant.

"You're such a handsome girl," pursued Miss Marple appraising Lucy. "I expect they pay you a good deal of attention, don't they?"

Lucy flushed slightly. Scrappy remembrances passed across her mind. Cedric leaning against the pigsty wall. Bryan sitting disconsolately on the kitchen table. Alfred's fingers touching hers as he helped her collect the coffee cups.

"Gentlemen," said Miss Marple, in the tone of one speaking of some alien and dangerous species, "are all very much alike in some ways— even if they are quite old . . ."

"Darling," cried Lucy. "A hundred years ago you would certainly have been burned as a witch!"

And she told her story of old Mr. Crackenthorpe's conditional proposal of marriage.

"In fact," said Lucy, "they've all made what you might call advances to me, in a way. Harold's was very correct; an advantageous financial position in the City. I don't think it's my attractive appearance; they must think I know something."

She laughed.

But Inspector Craddock did not laugh.

"Be careful," he said. "They might murder you instead of making advances to you."

"I suppose it might be simpler," Lucy agreed.

Then she gave a slight shiver.

"One forgets," she said. "The boys have been having such fun that one almost thought of it all as a game. But it's not a game."

"No," said Miss Marple. "Murder isn't a game."

She was silent for a moment or two before she said:

"Don't the boys go back to school soon?"

"Yes, next week. They go tomorrow to James Stoddart-West's home for the last few days of the holidays."

"I'm glad of that," said Miss Marple gravely. "I shouldn't like anything to happen while they're there."

"You mean to old Mr. Crackenthorpe. Do you think he's going to be murdered next?"

"Oh no!" said Miss Marple. "He'll be all right. I meant to the boys."

"To the boys?"

"Well, to Alexander."

"But surely—"

"Hunting about, you know, looking for clues. Boys love that sort of thing, but it might be very dangerous."

Craddock looked at her thoughtfully.

"You're not prepared to believe, are you, Miss Marple, that it's a case of an unknown woman murdered by an unknown man? You tie it up definitely with Rutherford Hall?"

"I think there's a definite connection, yes."

"All we know about the murderer is that he's a tall, dark man. That's what your friend says and all she can say. There are three tall, dark men at Rutherford Hall. On the day of the inquest, you know, I came out to see the three brothers standing waiting on the pavement for the car to drive up. They had their backs to me and it was astonishing how, in their heavy overcoats, they looked all alike. *Three tall, dark men.* And yet, actually, they're all three quite different types." He sighed. "It makes it very difficult."

"I wonder," murmured Miss Marple. "I have been wondering whether it might perhaps be all much simpler than we suppose. Murders so often are quite simple, with an obvious rather sordid motive . . ."

"Do you believe in the mysterious Martine, Miss Marple?"

"I'm quite ready to believe that Edmund Crackenthorpe either married, or meant to marry, a girl called Martine. Emma Crackenthorpe showed you his letter, I understand, and from what I've seen of her and from what Lucy tells me, I should say Emma Crackenthorpe is quite incapable of making up a thing of that kind. Indeed, why should she?"

"So granted Martine," said Craddock thoughtfully, "there is a motive of a kind. Martine's reappearance with a son would diminish the Crackenthorpe inheritance, though hardly to a point, one would think, to activate murder. They're all very hard up."

"Even Harold?" Lucy demanded incredulously.

"Even the prosperous-looking Harold Crackenthorpe is not the sober and conservative financier he appears to be. He's been plunging heavily and mixing himself up in some rather undesirable ventures. A large sum of money, soon, might avoid a crash."

"But if so—" said Lucy and stopped.

"Yes, Miss Eyelesbarrow—"

"I know, dear," said Miss Marple. "The wrong murder, that's what you mean."

"Yes, Martine's death wouldn't do Harold, or any of the others, any good. Not until—"

"Not until Luther Crackenthorpe died. Exactly. That occurred to me. And Mr. Crackenthorpe, senior, I gather from his doctor, is in much better life than any outsider would imagine."

"He'll last for years," said Lucy. Then she frowned.

"Yes?" Craddock spoke encouragingly.

"He was rather ill at Christmastime," said Lucy. "He said the doctor made a lot of fuss about it. 'Anyone would have thought I'd been poisoned by the fuss he made.' That's what he said."

She looked inquiringly at Craddock.

"Yes," said Craddock. "That's really what I want to ask Doctor Quimper about."

"Well, I must go," said Lucy. "Heavens, it's late."

Miss Marple put down her knitting and picked up the *Times* with a half-done crossword puzzle.

"I wish I had a dictionary here," she murmured. "Tontine and Tokay—I always mix those two words up. One, I believe, is a Hungarian wine."

"That's Tokay," said Lucy looking back from the door. "But one's a five-letter word and one's a seven. What's the clue?"

"Oh, it wasn't in the crossword," said Miss Marple vaguely. "It was in my head."

Inspector Craddock looked at her very hard. Then he said good-by and went.

17

Craddock had to wait a few minutes while Quimper finished his evening surgery, and then the doctor came to him. He looked tired and depressed.

He offered Craddock a drink and when the latter accepted he mixed one for himself as well.

"Poor devils," he said as he sank down in a worn easy chair. "So scared and so stupid—no sense. Had a painful case this evening. Woman who ought to have come to me a year ago. If she'd come then, she might have been operated on successfully. Now it's too late. Makes me mad. The truth is people are an extraordinary mixture of heroism and cowardice. She's been suffering agony and borne it without a word, just because she was too scared to come and find out that what she feared might be true. At the other end of the scale are the people who come and waste my time because they've got a dangerous swelling causing them agony on their little finger which they think may be cancer and which turns out to be a common or garden chilblain! Well, don't mind me. I've blown off steam now. What did you want to see me about?"

"First, I've got you to thank, I believe, for advising Miss Crackenthorpe to come to me with the letter that purported to be from her brother's widow."

"Oh, that? Anything in it? I didn't exactly advise her to come. She wanted to. She was worried. All the dear little brothers were trying to hold her back, of course."

482

"Why should they?"

The doctor shrugged his shoulders.

"Afraid the lady might be proved genuine, I suppose."

"Do you think the letter was genuine?"

"No idea. Never actually saw it. I should say it was someone who knew the facts, just trying to make a touch. Hoping to work on Emma's feelings. They were dead wrong, there. Emma's no fool. She wouldn't take an unknown sister-in-law to her bosom without asking a few practical questions first."

He added with some curiosity, "But why ask my views? I've got nothing to do with it?"

"I really came to ask you something quite different, but I don't quite know how to put it."

Doctor Quimper looked interested.

"I understand that not long ago—at Christmastime I think it was—Mr. Crackenthorpe had rather a bad turn of illness."

He saw a change at once in the doctor's face. It hardened.

"Yes."

"I gather a gastric disturbance of some kind?"

"Yes."

"This is difficult. Mr. Crackenthorpe was boasting of his health, saying he intended to outlive most of his family. He referred to you—you'll excuse me, Doctor—"

"Oh, don't mind me. I'm not sensitive as to what my patients say about me!"

"He spoke of you as an old fuss pot." Quimper smiled. "He said you had asked him all sorts of questions, not only as to what he had eaten, but as to who prepared it and served it."

The doctor was not smiling now. His face was hard again.

"Go on."

"He used some such phrase as 'talked as though he believed someone had poisoned me.'"

There was a pause.

"Had you any suspicion of that kind?"

Quimper did not answer at once. He got up and walked up and down. Finally he wheeled round on Craddock.

"What the devil do you expect me to say? Do you think a doctor can go about flinging accusations of poisoning here and there without any real evidence?"

"I'd just like to know, off the record, if that idea did enter your head?"

Doctor Quimper said evasively, "Old Crackenthorpe leads a fairly frugal life. When the family comes down, Emma steps up the food. Result—a nasty attack of gastroenteritis. The symptoms were consistent with that diagnosis."

Craddock persisted.

"I see. You were quite satisfied? You were not at all—shall we say—puzzled?"

"All right. All right. Yes, I was Yours Truly Puzzled! Does that please you?"

"It interests me," said Craddock. "What actually did you suspect, or fear?"

"Gastric cases vary, of course, but there were certain indications that would have been, shall we say, more consistent with arsenical poisoning than with plain gastroenteritis. Mind you, the two things are very much alike. Better men than myself have failed to recognize arsenical poisoning and have given a certificate in all good faith."

"And what was the result of your inquiries?"

"It seemed that what I suspected could not possibly be true. Mr. Crackenthorpe assured me that he had similar attacks before I attended him, and from the same cause, he said. They had always taken place when there was too much rich food about."

"Which was when the house was full? With the family? Or guests?"

"Yes. That seemed reasonable enough. But frankly, Craddock, I wasn't happy. I went so far as to write to old Doctor Morris. He was my senior partner and retired soon after I joined him. Crackenthorpe was his patient originally. I asked about these earlier attacks that the old man had had."

"And what response did you get?"

Quimper grinned.

"I got a flea in the ear. I was more or less told not to be a damned fool. Well—" He shrugged his shoulders. "Presumably I was a damned fool."

"I wonder." Craddock was thoughtful.

Then he decided to speak frankly.

"Throwing discretion aside, Doctor, there are people who stand to benefit pretty considerably from Luther Crackenthorpe's death." The doctor nodded. "He's an old man and a hale and hearty one. He may live to be ninety-odd?"

"Easily. He spends his life taking care of himself, and his constitution is sound."

"And his sons and daughter are all getting on, and they are all feeling the pinch?"

"You leave Emma out of it. She's no poisoner. These attacks only happen when the others are there, not when she and he are alone."

"An elementary precaution if she's the one," the Inspector thought, but was careful not to say so aloud.

He paused, choosing his words carefully.

"Surely—I'm ignorant in these matters—but supposing just as a hypothesis that arsenic was administered, hasn't Crackenthorpe been very lucky not to succumb?"

"Now there," said the doctor, "you have got something odd. It is exactly that fact that leads me to believe that I have been, as old Morris puts it, a damned fool. You see, it's obviously not a case of small doses of arsenic administered regularly, which is what you might call the classic method of arsenic poisoning. Crackenthorpe has never had any chronic gastric trouble. In a way, that's what makes these sudden violent attacks seem unlikely. So, assuming they are not due to natural causes, it looks as though the poisoner is muffing it every time, which hardly makes sense."

"Giving an inadequate dose, you mean?"

"Yes. On the other hand, Crackenthorpe's got a strong constitution and what might do in another man doesn't do him in. There's always personal idiosyncrasy to be reckoned with. But you'd think that by now, the poisoner—unless he's unusually timid—would have stepped up the dose. Why hasn't he?"

"That is," he added, "if there is a poisoner which there probably isn't! Probably all my ruddy imagination from start to finish."

"It's an odd problem," the Inspector agreed. "It doesn't seem to make sense."

II

"Inspector Craddock!"

The eager whisper made the Inspector jump.

He had been just on the point of ringing the front doorbell.

Alexander and his friend Stoddart-West emerged cautiously from the shadows.

"We heard your car and we wanted to get hold of you."

"Well, let's come inside." Craddock's hand went out to the doorbell again, but Alexander pulled at his coat with the eagerness of a pawing dog.

"We've found a clue," he breathed.

"Yes, we've found a clue," Stoddart-West echoed.

"Damn that girl," thought Craddock unamiably.

"Splendid," he said in perfunctory manner. "Let's go inside the house and look at it."

"No." Alexander was insistent. "Someone's sure to interrupt. Come to the harness room. We'll guide you."

Somewhat unwillingly, Craddock allowed himself to be guided round the corner of the house and along to the stable yard. Stoddart-West pushed open a heavy door, stretched up, and turned on a rather feeble electric light. The harness room, once the acme of Victorian spit and polish, was now the sad repository of everything that no one wanted. Broken garden chairs, rusted old garden implements, a vast decrepit mowing machine, rusted spring mattresses, hammocks and disintegrated tennis nets.

"We come here a good deal," said Alexander. "One can really be private here."

There were certain tokens of occupancy about. The decayed mattresses had been piled up to make a kind of divan, there was an old rusted table on which reposed a large tin of chocolate biscuits, there was a hoard of apples, a tin of coffee and a jigsaw puzzle.

"It really is a clue, sir," said Stoddart-West eagerly, his eyes gleaming behind his spectacles. "We found it this afternoon."

"We've been hunting for days. In the bushes—"

"And inside hollow trees."

"And we went all through the ashbins."

"There were some jolly interesting things there, as a matter of fact."

"And then we went into the boiler house—"

"Old Hillman keeps a great galvanized tub there full of waste paper."

"For when the boiler goes out and he wants to start it again."

"Any odd paper that's blowing about. He picks it up and shoves it in there."

"And that's where we found it."

"Found *what*?" Craddock interrupted the duet.

"The clue. Careful, Stodders, get your gloves on."

Importantly, Stoddart-West, in the best detective-story tradition, drew on a pair of rather dirty gloves and took from his pocket a Kodak photographic folder. From this he extracted in his gloved fingers with the utmost care a soiled and crumpled envelope which he handed importantly to the Inspector.

Both boys held their breath in excitement.

Craddock took it with due solemnity. He liked the boys and he was ready to enter into the spirit of the thing.

The letter had been through the post; there was no enclosure inside, it was just a torn envelope addressed to Mrs. Martine Crackenthorpe, 126 Elvers Crescent, N. 10.

"You see?" said Alexander breathlessly. "It shows she was here—Uncle Edmund's French wife, I mean—the one there's all the fuss about. She must have actually been here and dropped it somewhere. So it looks, doesn't it?"

Stoddart-West broke in, "It looks as though she was the one who got murdered—I mean, don't you think, sir, that it simply must have been her in the sarcophagus?"

They waited anxiously.

Craddock played up. "Possible, very possible," he said.

"This is important, isn't it?"

"You'll test it for fingerprints, won't you, sir?"

"Of course," said Craddock.

Stoddart-West gave a deep sigh.

"Smashing luck for us, wasn't it?" he said. "On our last day, too."

"Last day?"

"Yes," said Alexander. "I'm going to Stodders' place tomorrow for the last few days of the holidays. Stodders' people have got a smashing house—Queen Anne, isn't it?"

"William and Mary," said Stoddart-West.

"I thought your mother said—"

"Mum's French. She doesn't really know about English architecture."

"But your father said it was built—"

Craddock was examining the envelope.

Clever of Lucy Eyelesbarrow. How had she managed to fake the postmark? He peered closely, but the light was too feeble. Great fun for the boys, of course, but rather awkward for him. Lucy, drat her, hadn't considered that angle. If this were genuine, it would enforce a course of action. There—

Beside him a learned architectural argument was being hotly pursued. He was deaf to it.

"Come on boys," he said, "we'll go into the house. You've been very helpful."

18

Craddock was escorted by the boys through the back door into the house. This was, it seemed, their common mode of entrance. The kitchen was bright and cheerful. Lucy, in a large, white apron was rolling out pastry. Leaning against the dresser, watching her with a kind of doglike attention, was Bryan Eastley. With one hand he tugged at his large fair mustache.

"Hello, Dad," said Alexander kindly. "You out here again?"

"I like it out here," said Bryan, and added: "Miss Eyelesbarrow doesn't mind."

"Oh, I don't mind," said Lucy. "Good evening, Inspector Craddock."

"Coming to detect in the kitchen?" asked Bryan with interest.

"Not exactly. Mr. Cedric Crackenthorpe is still here, isn't he?"

"Oh yes, Cedric's here. Do you want him?"

"I'd like a word with him, yes, please."

"I'll go and see if he's in," said Bryan. "He may have gone round to the local pub."

He unpropped himself from the dresser.

"Thank you so much," said Lucy to him. "My hands are all over flour or I'd go."

"What are you making?" asked Stoddart-West anxiously.

"Peach flan."

"Good oh," said Stoddart-West.

"Is it nearly suppertime?" asked Alexander.

"No."

"Gosh! I'm terribly hungry."

"There's the end of the ginger cake in the larder."

The boys made a concerted rush and collided in the door.

"They're just like locusts," said Lucy.

"My congratulations to you," said Craddock.

"What on, exactly?"

"Your ingenuity, over this!"

"Over what?"

Craddock indicated the folder containing the letter.

"Very nicely done," he said.

"What are you talking about?"

"This, my dear girl, this." He half drew it out.

She stared at him uncomprehendingly.

Craddock felt suddenly dizzy.

"Didn't you fake this clue and put it in the boiler room for the boys to find? Quick—tell me."

"I haven't the faintest idea what you're talking about," said Lucy. "Do you mean that—"

Craddock slipped the folder quickly back in his pocket as Bryan returned.

"Cedric's in the library," he said. "Go on in."

He resumed his place on the dresser. Inspector Craddock went to the library.

II

Cedric Crackenthorpe seemed delighted to see the Inspector.

"Doing a spot more sleuthing down here?" he asked. "Got any farther?"

"I think I can say we are a little farther on, Mr. Crackenthorpe."

"Found out who the corpse was?"

"We've not got a definite identification, but we have a fairly shrewd idea."

"Good for you."

"Arising out of our latest information, we want to get a few statements. I'm starting with you, Mr. Crackenthorpe, as you're on the spot."

"I shan't be much longer. I'm going back to Iviza in a day or two."

"Then I seem to be just in time."

"Go ahead."

"I should like a detailed account, please, of exactly where you were and what you were doing on Friday, December the twentieth."

Cedric shot a quick glance at him. Then he leaned back, yawned, assumed an air of great nonchalance, and appeared to be lost in the effort of remembrance.

"Well, as I've already told you, I was in Iviza. Trouble is, one day there is so like another. Painting in the morning, siesta from three p.m. to five. Perhaps a spot of sketching if the light's suitable. Then an *apéritif*, sometimes with the mayor, sometimes with the doctor, at the café in the plaza. After that some kind of a scratch meal. Most of the evening in Scotty's Bar with some of my lower-class friends. Will that do you?"

"I'd rather have the truth, Mr. Crackenthorpe."

Cedric sat up.

"That's a most offensive remark, Inspector."

"Do you think so? You told me, Mr. Crackenthorpe, that you left Iviza on December the twenty-first and arrived in England that same day?"

"So I did. Em! Hi, Em!"

Emma Crackenthorpe came through the adjoining door from the small morning room. She looked inquiringly from Cedric to the Inspector.

"Look here, Em. I arrived here for Christmas on the Saturday before, didn't I? Came straight from the airport?"

"Yes," said Emma wonderingly. "You got here about lunchtime."

"There you are," said Cedric to the Inspector.

"You must think us very foolish, Mr. Crackenthorpe," said Craddock pleasantly. "We can check on these things, you know. I think, if you'll show me your passport—"

He paused expectantly.

"Can't find the damned thing," said Cedric. "Was looking for it this morning. Wanted to send it to Cook's."

"I think you could find it, Mr. Crackenthorpe. But it's not actually necessary. The records show that you actually entered this country on the evening of December the nineteenth. Perhaps you will now account to me for your movements between that time until lunchtime on December the twenty-first when you arrived here."

Cedric looked very cross indeed.

"That's the hell of life nowadays," he said angrily. "All this red tape and form filling. That's what comes of a bureaucratic state. Can't go where you like and do as you please any more! Somebody's always asking questions. What's all this fuss about the twentieth, anyway? What's special about the twentieth?"

"It happens to be the day we believe the murder was committed. You can refuse to answer, of course, but—"

"Who says I refuse to answer? Give a chap time. And you were vague enough about the date of the murder at the inquest. What's turned up new since then?"

Craddock did not reply.

Cedric said, with a sidelong glance at Emma, "Shall we go into the other room?"

Emma said quickly: "I'll leave you." At the door, she paused and turned.

"This is serious, you know, Cedric. If the twentieth was the day of the murder, then you must tell Inspector Craddock exactly what you were doing."

She went through into the next room and closed the door behind her.

"Good old Em," said Cedric. "Well, here goes! Yes, I left Iviza on the nineteenth all right. Planned to break the journey in Paris and spend a couple of days routing up some old friends on the Left Bank. But as a matter of fact, there was a very attractive woman on the plane. Quite a dish. To put it plainly, she and I got off together. She was on her way to the States, had to spend a couple of nights in London to see about some business or other. We got to London on the nineteenth. We stayed at the Kingsway Palace in case your spies haven't found that out yet! Called myself John Brown—never does to use your own name on these occasions."

"And on the twentieth?"

Cedric made a grimace.

"Morning pretty well occupied by a terrific hangover."

"And the afternoon. From three o'clock onward?"

"Let me see. Well, I mooned about, as you might say. Went into the National Gallery—that's respectable enough. Saw a film. *Rowenna of the Range.* I've always had a passion for Westerns. This was a corker. . . . Then a drink or two in the bar and a bit of sleep in my room, and out about ten o'clock with the girlfriend and a round of various hot spots. Can't even remember most of their names—Jumping Frog was one, I think. She knew 'em all. Got pretty well plastered and, to tell you the truth, don't remember much more till I woke up the next morning with an even worse hangover. Girlfriend hopped off to catch her plane and I poured cold water over my head, got a chemist to give me a devil's brew, and then started off for this place, pretending I'd just arrived at Heathrow. No need to upset Emma, I thought. You know what women are, always hurt if you don't come straight home. I had to borrow money from her to pay the taxi. I was completely cleaned out. No use asking the old man. He'd never cough up. Mean old brute. Well, Inspector, satisfied?"

"Can any of this be substantiated, Mr. Crackenthorpe? Say, between three p.m. and seven p.m."

"Most unlikely, I should think," said Cedric cheerfully. "National Gallery where the attendants look at you with lackluster eyes and a crowded picture house. No, not likely."

Emma reentered. She held a small engagement book in her hand.

"You want to know what everyone was doing on December the twentieth, is that right, Inspector Craddock?"

"Well—er—yes, Miss Crackenthorpe."

"I have just been looking in my engagement book. On the twentieth I went into Brackhampton to attend a meeting of the Church Restoration Fund. That finished about a quarter to one and I lunched with Lady Adington and Miss Bartlett, who was also on the committee, at the Cadena Café. After lunch I did some shopping, stores for Christmas and also Christmas presents. I went to Greenford's and Lyall and Swift's, Boot's, and probably several other shops. I had tea about a quarter to five in the Shamrock Tea Rooms and then went to the station to meet Bryan who was coming by train. I got home about six o'clock and found my father in a very bad temper. I had left lunch ready for him, but Mrs. Hart who was to come in in the afternoon and give him his tea had not arrived. He was so angry that he had shut himself in his room and would not let me in or speak to me. He does not like my going out in the afternoon, but I make a point of doing so now and then."

"You're probably wise. Thank you, Miss Crackenthorpe."

He could hardly tell her that as she was a woman, height five-foot seven, her movements that afternoon were of no great importance. Instead he said: "Your other two brothers came down later, I understand?"

"Alfred came down late on Saturday evening. He tells me he tried to ring me on the telephone the afternoon I was out, but my father, if he is upset, will never answer the telephone. My brother Harold did not come down until Christmas Eve."

"Thank you, Miss Crackenthorpe."

"I suppose I mustn't ask"—she hesitated—"what has come up new that prompts these inquiries?"

Craddock took the folder from his pocket. Using the tips of his fingers, he extracted the envelope.

"Don't touch it, please, but do you recognize this?"

"But—" Emma stared at him, bewildered. "That's my handwriting. That's the letter I wrote to Martine."

"I thought it might be."

"But how did you get it? Did she—? Have you found her—?"

"It would seem possible that we have—found her. This empty envelope was found here."

"In the house?"

"In the grounds."

"Then, she did come here! She—You mean, it was Martine, there in the sarcophagus?"

"It would seem very likely, Miss Crackenthorpe," said Craddock gently.

It seemed even more likely when he got back to town. A message was awaiting him from Armand Dessin.

"One of the girl friends has had a postcard from Anna Stravinska. Apparently the cruise story was true! She has reached Jamaica and is having, in your phrase, a wonderful time!"

Craddock crumpled up the message and threw it into the wastepaper basket.

III

"I must say," said Alexander, sitting up in bed, thoughtfully consuming a chocolate bar, "that this has been the most smashing day ever. Actually finding a real clue!"

His voice was awed.

"In fact the whole holidays have been smashing," he added happily. "I don't suppose such a thing will ever happen again."

"I hope it won't happen again to me," said Lucy who was on her knees packing Alexander's clothes into a suitcase. "Do you want all this space fiction with you?"

"Not those two top ones. I've read them. The football and my football boots and the gum boots can go separately."

"What difficult things you boys do travel with."

"It won't matter. They're sending the Rolls for us. They've got a smashing Rolls. They've got one of the new Mercedes Benz, too."

"They must be rich."

"Rolling! Jolly nice, too. All the same, I rather wish we weren't leaving here. Another body might turn up."

"I sincerely hope not."

"Well, it often does in books. I mean somebody who's seen something or heard something gets done in, too. It might be you," he added, unrolling a second chocolate bar.

"Thank you!"

"I don't want it to be you," Alexander assured her. "I like you very much and so does Stodders. We think you're out of this world as a cook. Absolutely lovely grub. You're very sensible, too."

This last was clearly an expression of high approval. Lucy took it as such and said: "Thank you. But I don't intend to get killed just to please you."

"Well, you'd better be careful, then," Alexander told her.

He paused to consume more nourishment and then said in a slightly offhand voice.

"If Dad turns up from time to time, you'll look after him, won't you?"

"Yes, of course," said Lucy, a little surprised.

"The trouble with Dad is," Alexander informed her, "that London life doesn't suit him. He gets in, you know, with quite the wrong type of women." He shook his head in a worried manner.

"I'm very fond of him," he added, "but he needs someone to look after him. He drifts about and gets in with the wrong people. It's a great pity Mum died when she did. Bryan needs a proper home life."

He looked solemnly at Lucy and reached out for another chocolate bar.

"Not a fourth one, Alexander," Lucy pleaded. "You'll be sick."

"Oh, I don't think so. I ate six running once and I wasn't I'm not the bilious type." He paused and then said, "Bryan likes you, you know."

"That's very nice of him."

"He's a bit of an ass in some ways," said Bryan's son, "but he was a jolly good fighter pilot. He's awfully brave. And he's awfully good-natured."

He paused. Then, averting his eyes to the ceiling, he said rather self-consciously:

"I think really, you know, it would be a good thing if he married again. Somebody decent. I shouldn't, myself, mind at all having a stepmother—not, I mean, if she was a decent sort. . . ."

With a sense of shock Lucy realized that there was a definite point in Alexander's conversation.

"All this stepmother bosh," went on Alexander, still addressing the ceiling, "is really quite out of date. Lots of chaps Stodders and I know have stepmothers—divorce and all that—and they get on quite well together. Depends on the stepmother, of course. And, of course, it does make a bit of confusion taking you out and on Sports Day and all that—I mean if there are two sets of parents, though again it helps if you want to cash in!" He paused, confronted with the problems of modern life. "It's nicest to have your own home and your own parents, but if your mother's dead—well, you see what I mean? If she's a decent sort," said Alexander for the third time.

Lucy felt touched.

"I think you're very sensible, Alexander," she said. "We must try and find a nice wife for your father."

"Yes," said Alexander noncommittally.

He added in an offhand manner, "I thought I'd just mention it. Bryan likes you very much. He told me so."

"Really," thought Lucy to herself. "There's too much matchmaking round here. First Miss Marple and now Alexander!"

For some reason or other, pigsties came into her mind. . . .

She stood up.

"Good night, Alexander. There will be only your washing things and pajamas to put in in the morning. Good night."

"Good night," said Alexander. He slid down in bed, laid his head on the pillow, closed his eyes, giving a perfect picture of a sleeping angel, and was immediately asleep.

19

"Not what you'd call conclusive," said Sergeant Wetherall with his usual gloom.

Craddock was reading through the report on Harold Crackenthorpe's alibi for December 20th.

He had been noticed at Sotheby's about 3:30, but was thought to have left shortly after that. His photograph had not been recognized at Russell's teashop, but as they did a busy trade there at teatime and he was not a habitué, that was hardly surprising. His manservant confirmed that he had returned to Cardigan Gardens to dress for his dinner party at a quarter to seven—rather late, since the dinner was at 7:30, and Mr. Crackenthorpe had been somewhat irritable in consequence. Did not remember hearing him come in that evening, but as it was some time ago could not remember accurately and, in any case, he frequently did not hear Mr. Crackenthorpe come in. He and his wife liked to retire early whenever they could. The garage in the mews where Harold kept his car was a private lockup that he rented and there was no one to notice who came or went or any reason to remember one evening in particular.

"All negative," said Craddock, with a sigh.

"He was at the Caterers' dinner all right, but left rather early before the end of the speeches."

"What about the railway stations?"

But there was nothing there, either at Brackhampton or at Paddington. It was nearly four weeks ago, and it was highly unlikely that anything would have been remembered.

Craddock sighed and stretched out his hand for the data on Cedric. That again was negative, though a taxi driver had made a doubtful recognition of having taken a fare to Paddington that day some time in the afternoon "what looked something like that bloke. Dirty trousers and a shock of hair. Cussed and swore a bit because fares had gone up since he was last in England." He identified the day because a horse called Crawler had won the 2:30 and he'd had a tidy bit on. Just after dropping the gent, he'd heard it on the radio in his cab and had gone home forthwith to celebrate.

"Thank God for racing," said Craddock, and put the report aside.

"And here's Alfred," said Sergeant Wetherall.

Some nuance in his voice made Craddock look up sharply. Wetherall had the pleased appearance of a man who has kept a tidbit until the end.

In the main the check was unsatisfactory. Alfred lived alone in his flat and came and went at unspecified times. His neighbors were not the inquisitive kind and were in any case office workers who were out all day. But toward the end of the report, Wetherall's large finger indicated the final paragraph.

Sergeant Leakie, assigned to a case of thefts from lorries, had been at the Load of Bricks, a lorry pullup on the Waddington-Brackhampton Road, keeping certain lorry drivers under observation. He had noticed, at an adjoining table, Chick Evans, one of the Dicky Rogers mob. With him had been Alfred Crackenthorpe whom he knew by sight, having seen him give evidence in the Dicky Rogers case. He'd wondered what they were cooking up together. Time: 9:30 P.M., Friday, December 20th. Alfred Crackenthorpe had boarded a bus a few minutes later, going in the direction of Brackhampton. William Baker, ticket collector at Brackhampton Station, had clipped ticket of gentleman whom he recognized by sight as one of Miss Crackenthorpe's brothers, just before departure of 11:55 train for Paddington. Remembers day as there had been story of some batty old lady who swore she had seen somebody murdered in a train that afternoon.

"Alfred?" said Craddock as he laid the report down. "Alfred? I wonder."

"Puts him right on the spot, there," Wetherall pointed out.

Craddock nodded. Yes, Alfred could have traveled down by the 4:33 to Brackhampton, committing murder on the way. Then he could have gone out by bus to the Load of Bricks. He could have left there at 9:30 and would have had plenty of time to go to Rutherford Hall, move the body from the embankment to the sarcophagus and get into Brackhampton in time to catch the 11:55 back to London. One of the Dicky Rogers gang might even have helped him move the body, though Craddock doubted this. An unpleasant lot, but not killers.

"Alfred?" he repeated speculatively.

II

At Rutherford Hall there had been a gathering of the Crackenthorpe family. Harold and Alfred had come down from London and very soon voices were raised and tempers were running high.

On her own initiative, Lucy mixed cocktails in a jug with ice and took them toward the library. The voices sounded clearly in the hall, and indicated that a good deal of acrimony was being directed toward Emma.

"Entirely your fault, Emma." Harold's deep-bass voice rang out angrily. "How you could be so shortsighted and foolish beats me. If you hadn't taken that letter to Scotland Yard and started all this—"

Alfred's higher-pitched voice said: "You must have been out of your senses!"

"Now don't bully her," said Cedric. "What's done is done. Much more fishy if they'd identified the woman as the missing Martine and we'd all kept mum about having heard from her."

"It's all very well for you, Cedric," said Harold angrily. "You were out of the country on the twentieth which seems to be the day they are inquiring about. But it's very embarrassing for Alfred and myself. Fortunately I can remember where I was that afternoon and what I was doing."

"I bet you can," said Alfred. "If you'd arranged a murder, Harold, you'd arrange your alibi very carefully, I'm sure."

"I gather you are not so fortunate," said Harold coldly.

"That depends," said Alfred. "Anything's better than presenting a cast-iron alibi to the police if it isn't really cast iron. They're so clever at breaking these things down."

"If you are insinuating that I killed the woman—"

"Oh, do stop, all of you," cried Emma. "Of course none of you killed the woman."

"And just for your information, I wasn't out of England on the twentieth," said Cedric. "And the police are wise to it! So we're all under suspicion."

"If it hadn't been for Emma—"

"Oh, don't begin again, Harold," cried Emma.

Doctor Quimper came out of the study where he had been closeted with old Mr. Crackenthorpe. His eye fell on the jug in Lucy's hand.

"What's this? A celebration?"

"More in the nature of oil on troubled waters. They're at it hammer and tongs in there."

"Recriminations?"

"Mostly abusing Emma."

Doctor Quimper's eyebrows rose.

"Indeed?" He took the jug from Lucy's hand, opened the library door and went in.

"Good evening."

"Ah, Doctor Quimper, I should like a word with you." It was Harold's voice, raised and irritable. "I should like to know what you meant by interfering in a private and family matter, and telling my sister to go to Scotland Yard about it."

Doctor Quimper said calmly, "Miss Crackenthorpe asked my advice. I gave it to her. In my opinion she did perfectly right."

"You dare to say—"

"Girl!"

It was old Mr. Crackenthorpe's familiar salutation. He was peering out of the study door just behind Lucy.

Lucy turned rather reluctantly.

"Yes, Mr. Crackenthorpe?"

"What are you giving us for dinner tonight? I want curry. You make a very good curry. It's ages since we've had curry."

"The boys don't care much for curry, you see."

"The boys, the boys—what do the boys matter? I'm the one who matters. And anyway, the boys have gone—good riddance. I want a nice hot curry, do you hear?"

"All right, Mr. Crackenthorpe, you shall have it."

"That's right. You're a good girl, Lucy. You look after me, and I'll look after you."

Lucy went back to the kitchen. Abandoning the fricassee of chicken which she had planned, she began to assemble the preparations for curry. The front door banged and from the window she saw Doctor Quimper stride angrily from the house to his car and drive away.

Lucy sighed. She missed the boys. And in a way she missed Bryan, too.

Oh well! She sat down and began to peel mushrooms.
At any rate she'd give the family a rattling good dinner.
Feed the brutes!

III

It was 3:00 A.M. when Doctor Quimper drove his car into the garage, closed the doors and came in pulling the front door behind him rather wearily. Well, Mrs. Josh Simpkins had a fine, healthy pair of twins to add to her present family of eight. Mr. Simpkins had expressed no elation over the arrival. "Twins," he had said gloomily. "What's the good of them? Quads now, they're good for something. All sorts of things you get sent, and the press comes round and there's pictures in the paper, and they do say as Her Majesty sends you a telegram. But what's twins except two mouths to feed instead of one? Never been twins in our family, nor in the missus's either. Don't seem fair, somehow."

Doctor Quimper walked upstairs to his bedroom and started throwing off his clothes. He glanced at his watch. Five minutes past three. It had proved an unexpectedly tricky business bringing those twins into the world, but all had gone well. He yawned. He was tired, very tired. He looked appreciatively at his bed.

Then the telephone rang.

Doctor Quimper swore and picked up the receiver.

"Doctor Quimper?"

"Speaking."

"This is Lucy Eyelesbarrow from Rutherford Hall. I think you'd better come over. Everybody seems to have been taken ill."

"Taken ill? How? What symptoms?"

Lucy detailed them.

"I'll be over straightaway. In the meantime—" He gave her short, sharp instructions.

Then he quickly resumed his clothes, flung a few extra things into his emergency bag, and hurried down to his car.

IV

It was some three hours later when the doctor and Lucy, both of them somewhat exhausted, sat down by the kitchen table to drink large cups of black coffee.

"Ha." Doctor Quimper drained his cup, set it down with a clatter

501

on the saucer. "I needed that. Now, Miss Eyelesbarrow, let's get down to brass tacks."

Lucy looked at him. The lines of fatigue showed clearly on his face, making him look older than his forty-four years; the dark hair on his temples was flecked with gray; and there were lines under his eyes.

"As far as I can judge," said the doctor, "they'll be all right now. But how come? That's what I want to know. Who cooked the dinner?"

"I did," said Lucy.

"And what was it? In detail."

"Mushroom soup. Curried chicken and rice. Sillabubs. A savory of chicken livers in bacon."

"*Canapés Diane,*" said Doctor Quimper unexpectedly.

Lucy smiled faintly.

"Yes, *Canapés Diane.*"

"All right, let's go through it. Mushroom soup, out of a tin, I suppose?"

"Certainly not. I made it."

"You made it. Out of what?"

"Half a pound of mushrooms, chicken stock, milk, a *roux* of butter and flour, and lemon juice."

"Ah. And one's supposed to say 'It must have been the mushrooms.'"

"It wasn't the mushrooms. I had some of the soup myself and I'm quite all right."

"Yes, you're quite all right. I hadn't forgotten that."

Lucy flushed.

"If you mean—"

"I don't mean. You're a highly intelligent girl. You'd be groaning upstairs, too, if I'd meant what you thought I meant. Anyway, I know all about you. I've taken the trouble to find out."

"Why on earth did you do that?"

Doctor Quimper's lips were set in a grim line.

"Because I'm making it my business to find out about the people who come here and settle themselves in. You're a bona fide young woman who does this particular job for a livelihood, and you seem never to have had any contact with the Crackenthorpe family previous to coming here. So you're not a girlfriend of either Cedric, Harold or Alfred, helping them to do a bit of dirty work."

"Do you really think?"

"I think quite a lot of things," said Quimper. "But I have to be careful. That's the worst of being a doctor. Now, let's get on. Curried chicken. Did you have some of that?"

"No. When you've cooked a curry, you've dined off the smell, I find. I tasted it, of course. I had soup and some sillabub."

"How did you serve the sillabub?"

"In individual glasses."

"Now then, how much of all this is cleared up?"

"If you mean washing up, everything was washed up and put away."

Doctor Quimper groaned.

"There's such a thing as being overzealous," he said.

"Yes, I can see that as things have turned out, but there it is, I'm afraid."

"What do you have still?"

"There's some of the curry left in a bowl in the larder. I was planning to use it as a basis for mulligatawny soup this evening. There's some mushroom soup left, too. No sillabub and none of the savory."

"I'll take the curry and the soup. What about chutney? Did they have chutney with it?"

"Yes. In one of those stone jars."

"I'll have some of that, too."

He rose: "I'll go up and have a look at them again. After that, can you hold the fort until morning? Keep an eye on them all? I can have a nurse round, with full instructions, by eight o'clock."

"I wish you'd tell me straight out. Do you think it's food poisoning—or—or, well, poisoning."

"I've told you already. Doctors can't think, they have to be sure. If there's a positive result from these food specimens I can go ahead. Otherwise—"

"Otherwise?" Lucy repeated.

Doctor Quimper laid a hand on her shoulder.

"Look after two people in particular," he said. "Look after Emma. I'm not going to have anything happen to Emma . . ."

There was emotion in his voice that could not be disguised. "She's not even begun to live yet," he said. "And you know, people like Emma Crackenthorpe are the salt of the earth. Emma—well, Emma means a lot to me. I've never told her so but I shall. Look after Emma."

"You bet I will," said Lucy.

"And look after the old man. I can't say that he's ever been my favorite patient but he is my patient and I'm damned if I'm going to let him be hustled out of the world because one or other of his unpleasant sons—or all three of them, maybe—want him out of the way so that they can handle his money."

He threw her a sudden quizzical glance.

"There," he said. "I've opened my mouth too wide. But keep your eyes skinned, there's a good girl and, incidentally, keep your mouth shut."

V

Inspector Bacon was looking upset.

"Arsenic?" he said. "Arsenic?"

"Yes. It was in the curry. Here's the rest of the curry, for your fellow to have a go at. I've only done a very rough test on a little of it, but the result was quite definite."

"So there's a poisoner at work?"

"It would seem so," said Doctor Quimper dryly.

"And they're all affected, you say, except that Miss Eyelesbarrow."

"Except Miss Eyelesbarrow."

"Looks a bit fishy for her."

"What motive could she possibly have?"

"Might be barmy," suggested Bacon. "Seem all right, they do, sometimes, and yet all the time they're right off their rocker, so to speak."

"Miss Eyelesbarrow isn't off her rocker. Speaking as a medical man, Miss Eyelesbarrow is as sane as you or I. If Miss Eyelesbarrow is feeding the family arsenic in their curry, she's doing it for a reason. Moreover, being a highly intelligent young woman, she'd be careful not to be the only one unaffected. What she'd do, what any intelligent poisoner would do, would be to eat a very little of the poisoned curry, and then exaggerate the symptoms."

"And then you wouldn't be able to tell?"

"That she'd had less than the others? Probably not. People don't all react alike to poisons anyway; the same amount will upset some people more than others. Of course," added Doctor Quimper cheerfully, "once the patient's dead, you can estimate fairly closely how much was taken."

"Then it might be—" Inspector Bacon paused to consolidate his ideas. "It might be that there's one of the family now who's making more fuss than he need, someone who you might say is mucking in with the rest so as to avoid arousing suspicion? How's that?"

"The idea has already occurred to me. That's why I'm reporting to you. It's in your hands now. I've got a nurse on the job that I can trust, but she can't be everywhere at once. In my opinion, nobody's had enough to cause death."

"Made a mistake, the poisoner did?"

"No. It seems to me more likely that the idea was to put enough in the curry to cause signs of food poisoning, for which probably the mushrooms would be blamed. People are always obsessed with the idea of mushroom poisoning. Then one person would probably take a turn for the worse and die."

"Because he'd been given a second dose?"

The doctor nodded.

"That's why I'm reporting to you at once, and why I've put a special nurse on the job."

"She knows about the arsenic?"

"Of course. She knows and so does Miss Eyelesbarrow. You know your own job best, of course, but if I were you, I'd get out there and make it quite clear to them all that they're suffering from arsenic poisoning. That will probably put the fear of the Lord into our murderer and he won't dare to carry out his plan. He's probably been banking on the food-poisoning theory."

The telephone rang on the Inspector's desk. He picked it up and said:

"O.K. Put her through." He said to Quimper. "It's your nurse on the phone. Yes, hullo—speaking . . . what's that? Serious relapse . . . yes . . . Doctor Quimper's with me now . . . if you'd like a word with him—"

He handed the receiver to the doctor.

"Quimper speaking . . . I see . . . yes . . . quite right . . . yes, carry on with that. We'll be along."

He put the receiver down and turned to Bacon.

"Who is it?"

"It's Alfred," said Doctor Quimper. "And he's dead."

20

Over the telephone, Craddock's voice came in sharp disbelief.

"Alfred?" he said. "Alfred?"

Inspector Bacon, shifting the telephone receiver a little, said: "You didn't expect that?"

"No, indeed. As a matter of fact, I'd just got him taped for the murderer!"

"I heard about him being spotted by the ticket collector. Looked bad for him all right. Yes, looked as though we'd got our man."

"Well," said Craddock flatly, "we were wrong."

There was a moment's silence. Then Craddock asked:

"There was a nurse in charge. How did she come to slip up?"

"Can't blame her. Miss Eyelesbarrow was all in and went to get a bit of sleep. The nurse had got five patients on her hands: the old man, Emma, Cedric, Harold and Alfred. She couldn't be everywhere at once. It seems old Mr. Crackenthorpe started creating in a big way. Said he was dying. She went in, got him soothed down, came back again and took Alfred in some tea with glucose. He drank it and that was that."

"Arsenic again?"

"Seems so. Of course it could have been a relapse, but Quimper doesn't think so and Johnson agrees."

"I suppose," said Craddock, doubtfully, "that Alfred was meant to be the victim?"

Bacon sounded interested. "You mean that whereas Alfred's death wouldn't do anyone a penn'orth of good, the old man's death would benefit the lot of them? I suppose it might have been a mistake; some-body *might* have thought the tea was intended for the old man."

"Are they sure that that's the way the stuff was administered?"

"No, of course they aren't sure. The nurse, like a good nurse, washed up the whole contraption. Cups, spoons, teapot—everything. But it seems the only feasible method."

"Meaning?" said Craddock thoughtfully, "that one of the patients wasn't as ill as the others. Saw his chance and doped the cup."

"Well, there won't be any more funny business," said Inspector Bacon grimly. "We've got two nurses on the job now, to say nothing of Miss Eyelesbarrow, and I've got a couple of men there, too. You coming down?"

"As fast as I can make it!"

II

Lucy Eyelesbarrow came across the hall to meet Inspector Craddock. She looked pale and drawn.

"You've been having a bad time of it," said Craddock.

"It's been like one long ghastly nightmare," said Lucy. "I really thought last night that they were all dying."

"About this curry—"

"It was the curry?"

"Yes, very nicely laced with arsenic. Quite the Borgia touch."

"If that's true," said Lucy. "It must—it's got to be—one of the family."

"No other possibility?"

"No, you see I only started making that damned curry quite late, after six o'clock, because Mr. Crackenthorpe specially asked for curry. And I had to open a new tin of curry powder, so that couldn't have been tampered with. I suppose curry would disguise the taste?"

"Arsenic hasn't any taste," said Craddock absently. "Now—opportunity. Which of them had the chance to tamper with the curry while it was cooking?"

Lucy considered.

"Actually," she said, "anyone could have sneaked into the kitchen while I was laying the table in the dining room."

"I see. Now who was there in the house? Old Mr. Crackenthorpe, Emma, Cedric—"

"Harold and Alfred. They'd come down from London in the

afternoon. Oh, and Bryan, Bryan Eastley. But he left just before dinner. He had to meet a man in Brackhampton."

Craddock said thoughtfully, "It ties up with the old man's illness at Christmas. Quimper suspected that that was arsenic. Did they all seem equally ill last night?"

Lucy considered. "I think old Mr. Crackenthorpe seemed the worst. Doctor Quimper had to work like a maniac on him. He's a jolly good doctor, I will say. Cedric made far the most fuss. Of course, strong, healthy people always do."

"What about Emma?"

"She has been pretty bad."

"Why Alfred I wonder?" said Craddock.

"I know," said Lucy. "I suppose it was meant to be Alfred?"

"Funny, I asked that too!"

"It seems, somehow, so pointless."

"If I could only get at the motive for all this business," said Craddock. "It doesn't seem to tie up. The strangled woman in the sarcophagus was Edmund Crackenthorpe's widow, Martine. Let's assume that. It's pretty well proved by now. There must be a connection between that and the deliberate poisoning of Alfred. It's all here, in the family somewhere. Even saying one of them's mad doesn't help."

"Not really," Lucy agreed.

"Well, look after yourself," said Craddock warningly. "There's a poisoner in this house, remember, and one of your patients upstairs probably isn't as ill as he pretends to be."

Lucy went upstairs again slowly after Craddock's departure. An imperious voice, somewhat weakened by illness, called to her as she passed old Mr. Crackenthorpe's room.

"Girl, girl, is that you? Come here."

Lucy entered the room. Mr. Crackenthorpe was lying in bed well propped up with pillows. For a sick man he was looking, Lucy thought, remarkably cheerful.

"The house is full of damned hospital nurses," complained Mr. Crackenthorpe. "Rustling about, making themselves important, taking my temperature, not giving me what I want to eat—a pretty penny all that must be costing. Tell Emma to send 'em away. You could look after me quite well."

"Everybody's been taken ill, Mr. Crackenthorpe," said Lucy. "I can't look after everybody, you know."

"Mushrooms," said Mr. Crackenthorpe. "Damned dangerous

things, mushrooms. It was that soup we had last night. You made it," he added accusingly.

"The mushrooms were quite all right, Mr. Crackenthorpe."

"I'm not blaming you, girl, I'm not blaming you. It's happened before. One blasted fungus slips in and does it. Nobody can tell. I know you're a good girl. You wouldn't do it on purpose. How's Emma?"

"Feeling rather better this afternoon."

"Ah. And Harold?"

"He's better too."

"What's this about Alfred having kicked the bucket?"

"Nobody's supposed to have told you that, Mr. Crackenthorpe."

Mr. Crackenthorpe laughed, a high, whinnying laugh of intense amusement. "I hear things," he said. "Can't keep things from the old man. They try to. So Alfred's dead, is he? He won't sponge on me any more, and he won't get any of the money either. They've all been waiting for me to die, you know; Alfred in particular. Now he's dead. I call that rather a good joke."

"That's not very kind of you, Mr. Crackenthorpe," said Lucy severely.

Mr. Crackenthorpe laughed again. "I'll outlive them all," he crowed. "You see if I don't, my girl. You see if I don't."

Lucy went to her room, took out her dictionary and looked up the word *tontine*. She closed the book thoughtfully and stared ahead of her.

III

"Don't see why you want to come to me," said Doctor Morris, irritably.

"You've known the Crackenthorpe family a long time," said Inspector Craddock.

"Yes, yes, I knew all the Crackenthorpes. I remember old Josiah Crackenthorpe. He was a hard nut—shrewd man, though. Made a lot of money." He shifted his aged form in his chair and peered under bushy eyebrows at Inspector Craddock. "So you've been listening to that young fool, Quimper," he said. "These zealous young doctors! Always getting ideas in their heads. Got it into his head that somebody was trying to poison Luther Crackenthorpe. Nonsense! Melodrama! Of course, he had gastric attacks. I treated him for them. Didn't happen very often, nothing peculiar about them."

"Doctor Quimper," said Craddock, "seemed to think there was."

"Doesn't do for a doctor to go thinking. After all, I should hope I could recognize arsenical poisoning when I saw it."

"Quite a lot of well-known doctors haven't noticed it," Craddock pointed out. "There was"—he drew upon his memory—"the Green-barrow case, Mrs. Reney, Charles Leeds, three people in the Westbury family, all buried nicely and tidily without the doctors who attended them having the least suspicion. Those doctors were all good, reputable men."

"All right, all right," said Doctor Morris, "you're saying that I could have made a mistake. Well, I don't think I did." He paused a minute and then said, "Who did Quimper think was doing it, if it was being done?"

"He didn't know," said Craddock. "He was worried. After all, you know," he added, "there's a great deal of money there."

"Yes, yes, I know, which they'll get when Luther Crackenthorpe dies. And they want it pretty badly. That is true enough, but it doesn't follow that they'd kill the old man to get it."

"Not necessarily," agreed Inspector Craddock.

"Anyway," said Doctor Morris, "my principle is not to go about suspecting things without due cause. Due cause," he repeated. "I'll admit that what you've just told me has shaken me up a bit. Arsenic on a big scale, apparently, but I still don't see why you come to me. All I can tell you is that I didn't suspect it. Maybe I should have. Maybe I should have taken those gastric attacks of Luther Crackenthorpe's much more seriously. But you've got a long way beyond that now."

Craddock agreed. "What I really need," he said, "is to know a little more about the Crackenthorpe family. Is there any queer mental strain in them, a kink of any kind?"

The eyes under the bushy eyebrows looked at him sharply. "Yes, I can see your thoughts might run that way. Well, old Josiah was sane enough. Hard as nails, very much all there. His wife was neurotic, had a tendency to melancholia. Came of an inbred family. She died soon after Luther was born. I'd say, you know, that Luther inherited a certain—well—instability from her. He was commonplace enough as a young man, but he was always at loggerheads with his father. His father was disappointed in him and I think he resented that and brooded on it, and in the end got a kind of obsession about it. He carried that on into his own married life. You'll notice, if you talk to him at all, that he's got a hearty dislike for all his own sons. His daughters he was fond of. Both Emma and Edie, the one who died."

"Why does he dislike the sons so much?" asked Craddock.

"You'll have to go to one of these new-fashioned psychiatrists to find that out. I'd just say that Luther has never felt very adequate as a man himself, and that he bitterly resents his financial position. He has possession of an income but no power of appointment of capital. If he had the power to disinherit his sons he probably wouldn't dislike them as much. Being powerless in that respect gives him a feeling of humiliation."

"That's why he's so pleased at the idea of outliving them all?" said Inspector Craddock.

"Possibly. It is the root, too, of his parsimony, I think. I should say that he's managed to save a considerable sum out of his large income, mostly, of course, before taxation rose to its present giddy heights."

A new idea struck Inspector Craddock. "I suppose he's left his savings by will to someone? That he can do."

"Oh, yes, though God knows who he has left it to. Maybe to Emma, but I should rather doubt it. She'll get her share of the old man's money. Maybe to Alexander, the grandson."

"He's fond of him, is he?" said Craddock.

"Used to be. Of course he was his daughter's child, not a son's child. That may have made a difference. And he had quite an affection for Bryan Eastley, Edie's husband. Of course I don't know Bryan well; it's some years since I've seen any of the family. But it struck me that he was going to be very much at a loose end after the war. He's got those qualities that you need in wartime: courage, dash and a tendency to let the future take care of itself. But I don't think he's got any stability. He'll probably turn into a drifter."

"As far as you know there's no peculiar kink in any of the younger generation?"

"Cedric's an eccentric type, one of those natural rebels. I wouldn't say he was perfectly normal, but you might say, who is? Harold's fairly orthodox, not what I call a very pleasant character, coldhearted, eye to the main chance. Alfred's got a touch of the delinquent about him. He's a wrong 'un, always was. Saw him taking money out of a missionary box once that they used to keep in the hall. That type of thing. Ah well, the poor fellow's dead, I suppose I shouldn't be talking against him."

"What about—" Craddock hesitated. "Emma Crackenthorpe?"

"Nice girl, quiet, one doesn't always know what she's thinking. Has her own plans and her own ideas but she keeps them to herself.

She's more character than you might think from her general manner and appearance."

"You knew Edmund, I suppose, the son who was killed in France?"

"Yes. He was the best of the bunch, I'd say. Goodhearted, gay, a nice boy."

"Did you ever hear that he was going to marry or had married a French girl just before he was killed?"

Doctor Morris frowned. "It seems as though I remember something about it," he said, "but it's a long time ago."

"Quite early on in the war, wasn't it?"

"Yes. Ah well, I daresay he'd have lived to regret it if he had married a foreign wife."

"There's some reason to believe that he did do just that," said Craddock.

In a few brief sentences he gave an account of recent happenings.

"I remember seeing something in the papers about a woman found in a sarcophagus. So it was at Rutherford Hall."

"And there's reason to believe that the woman was Edmund Crackenthorpe's widow."

"Well, well, that seems extraordinary. More like a novel than real life. But who'd want to kill the poor thing—I mean, how does it tie up with arsenical poisoning in the Crackenthorpe family?"

"In one of two ways," said Craddock, "but they are both very far-fetched. Somebody perhaps is greedy and wants the whole of Josiah Crackenthorpe's fortune."

"Damn fool if he does," said Doctor Morris. "He'll only have to pay the most stupendous taxes on the income from it."

21

"Nasty things, mushrooms," said Mrs. Kidder.

Mrs. Kidder had made the same remark about ten times in the last few days. Lucy did not reply.

"Never touch 'em myself," said Mrs. Kidder, "much too dangerous. It's a merciful Providence as there's only been one death. The whole lot might have gone and you too, Miss. A wonderful escape you've had."

"It wasn't the mushrooms," said Lucy. "They were perfectly all right."

"Don't you believe it," said Mrs. Kidder. "Dangerous they are, mushrooms. One toadstool in among the lot and you've had it.

"Funny," went on Mrs. Kidder, among the rattle of plates and dishes in the sink, "how things seem to come all together, as it were. My sister's eldest had measles and our Ernie fell down and broke 'is arm, and my 'usband came out all over with boils. All in the same week! You'd hardly believe it, would you. It's been the same thing here," went on Mrs. Kidder. "First that nasty murder and now Mr. Alfred dead with mushroom poisoning. Who'll be the next, I'd like to know?"

Lucy felt rather uncomfortably that she would like to know, too.

"My husband, he doesn't like me coming here now," said Mrs. Kidder, "thinks it's unlucky, but what I say is I've known Miss Crackenthorpe a long time now and she's a nice lady and she depends on me. And I couldn't leave poor Miss Eyelesbarrow, I said, not to do everything herself in the house. Pretty hard it is on you, Miss, all these trays."

Lucy was forced to agree that life did seem to consist very largely of trays at the moment. She was at the moment arranging trays to take to the various invalids.

"As for them nurses, they never do a hand's turn," said Mrs. Kidder. "All they want is pots and pots of tea made strong. And meals prepared. Wore out, that's what I am." She spoke in a tone of great satisfaction, though actually she had done very little more than her normal morning's work.

Lucy said solemnly, "You never spare yourself, Mrs. Kidder."

Mrs. Kidder looked pleased. Lucy picked up the first of the trays and started off up the stairs.

"What's this?" said Mr. Crackenthorpe disapprovingly.

"Beef tea and baked custard," said Lucy.

"Take it away," said Mr. Crackenthorpe. "I won't touch that sort of stuff. I told that nurse I wanted a beefsteak."

"Doctor Quimper thinks you ought not to have beefsteak just yet," said Lucy.

Mr. Crackenthorpe snorted. "I'm practically well again. I'm getting up tomorrow. How are the others?"

"Mr. Harold's much better," said Lucy. "He's going back to London tomorrow."

"Good riddance," said Mr. Crackenthorpe. "What about Cedric? Any hope that he's going back to his island tomorrow?"

"He won't be going just yet."

"Pity. What's Emma doing? Why doesn't she come and see me?"

"She's still in bed, Mr. Crackenthorpe."

"Women always coddle themselves," said Mr. Crackenthorpe, "but you're a good, strong girl," he added approvingly. "Run about all day, don't you?"

"I get plenty of exercise," said Lucy.

Old Mr. Crackenthorpe nodded his head approvingly. "You're a good strong girl," he said, "and don't think I've forgotten what I talked to you about before. One of these days you'll see what you'll see. Emma isn't always going to have things her own way. And don't listen to the others when they tell you I'm a mean old man. I'm careful of my money. I've got a nice little packet put by and I know who I'm going to spend it on when the time comes." He leered at her affectionately.

Lucy went rather quickly out of the room, avoiding his clutching hand.

The next tray was taken into Emma.

"Oh, thank you, Lucy. I'm really feeling quite myself again by now. I'm hungry, and that's a good sign, isn't it? My dear," went on Emma as Lucy settled the tray on her knees, "I'm really feeling very upset about your aunt. You haven't had any time to go and see her, I suppose?"

"No, I haven't, as a matter of fact."

"I'm afraid she must be missing you."

"Oh, don't worry. Miss Crackenthorpe. She understands what a terrible time we've been through."

"Have you rung her up?"

"No, I haven't just lately."

"Well, do. Ring her up every day. It makes such a difference to old people to get news."

"You're very kind," said Lucy. Her conscience smote her a little as she went down to fetch the next tray. The complications of illness in the house had kept her thoroughly absorbed and she had had no time to think of anything else. She decided that she would ring Miss Marple up as soon as she had taken Cedric his meal.

There was only one nurse in the house now and she passed Lucy on the landing, exchanging greetings.

Cedric, looking incredibly tidied up and neat, was sitting up in bed writing busily on sheets of paper.

"Hullo, Lucy," he said, "what hell brew have you got for me today? I wish you'd get rid of that god-awful nurse, she's simply too arch for words. Calls me 'we' for some reason. 'And how are we this morning? Have we slept well? Oh dear, we're very naughty, throwing off the bedclothes like that.'" He imitated the refined accents of the nurse in a high falsetto voice.

"You seem very cheerful," said Lucy. "What are you busy with?"

"Plans," said Cedric. "Plans for what to do with this place when the old man pops off. It's a jolly good bit of land here, you know. I can't make up my mind whether I'd like to develop some of it myself, or whether I'll sell it in lots all in one go. Very valuable for industrial purposes. The house will do for a nursing home or a school. I'm not sure I shan't sell half the land and use the money to do something rather outrageous with the other half. What do you think?"

"You haven't got it yet," said Lucy, dryly.

"I shall have it, though," said Cedric. "It's not divided up like the other stuff. I get it outright. And if I sell it for a good fat price the money will be capital, not income, so I shan't have to pay taxes on it. Money to burn. Think of it."

"I always understood you rather despised money," said Lucy.

"Of course I despise money when I haven't got any," said Cedric. "It's the only dignified thing to do. What a lovely girl you are, Lucy, or do I just think so because I haven't seen any good-looking women for a long time?"

"I expect that's it," said Lucy.

"Still busy tidying everyone and everything up?"

"Somebody seems to have been tidying you up," said Lucy, looking at him.

"That's that damned nurse," said Cedric with feeling. "Have they had the inquest on Alfred yet? What happened?"

"It was adjourned," said Lucy.

"Police being cagey. This mass poisoning does give one a bit of a turn, doesn't it? Mentally, I mean. I'm not referring to more obvious aspects," he added. "Better look after yourself, my girl."

"I do," said Lucy.

"Has young Alexander gone back to school yet?"

"I think he's still with the Stoddart-Wests. I think it's the day after tomorrow that school begins."

Before getting her own lunch Lucy went to the telephone and rang up Miss Marple.

"I'm so terribly sorry I haven't been able to come over, but I've really been very busy."

"Of course, my dear, of course. Besides there's nothing that can be done just now. We just have to wait."

"Yes, but what are we waiting for?"

"Elspeth McGillicuddy ought to be home very soon now," said Miss Marple. "I wrote to her to fly home at once. I said it was her duty. So don't worry too much, my dear." Her voice was kindly and reassuring.

"You don't think—" Lucy began, but stopped.

"That there will be any more deaths? Oh, I hope not, my dear. But one never knows, does one? When anyone is really wicked, I mean. And I think there is great wickedness here."

"Or madness," said Lucy.

"Of course I know that is the modern way of looking at things. I don't agree myself."

Lucy rang off, went into the kitchen and picked up her tray of lunch. Mrs. Kidder had divested herself of her apron and was about to leave.

"You'll be all right, Miss, I hope?" she asked solicitously.

"Of course I shall be all right," snapped Lucy.

She took her tray not into the big, gloomy dining room but into the small study. She was just finishing the meal when the door opened and Bryan Eastley came in.

"Hello," said Lucy, "this is very unexpected."

"I suppose it is," said Bryan. "How is everybody?"

"Oh, much better. Harold's going back to London tomorrow."

"What do you think about it all? Was it really arsenic?"

"It was arsenic all right," said Lucy.

"It hasn't been in the papers yet."

"No, I think the police are keeping it up their sleeves for the moment."

"Somebody must have a pretty good down on the family," said Bryan. "Who's likely to have sneaked in and tampered with the food?"

"I suppose I'm the most likely person, really," said Lucy.

Bryan looked at her anxiously. "But you didn't, did you?" he asked. He sounded slightly shocked.

"No. I didn't," said Lucy.

Nobody could have tampered with the curry. She had made it alone in the kitchen and brought it to table, and the only person who could have tampered with it was one of the five people who sat down to the meal.

"I mean, why should you?" said Bryan. "They're nothing to you, are they? I say," he added, "I hope you don't mind my coming back here like this?"

"No, no, of course I don't. Have you come to stay?"

"Well, I'd like to, if it wouldn't be an awful bore to you."

"No. No, we can manage."

"You see, I'm out of a job at the moment and I—well, I get rather fed up. Are you really sure you don't mind?"

"Oh, I'm not the person to mind, anyway. It's Emma."

"Oh, Emma's all right," said Bryan. "Emma's always been very nice to me. In her own way, you know. She keeps things to herself a lot, in fact she's rather a dark horse, old Emma. This living here and looking after the old man would get most people down. Pity she never married. Too late now, I suppose."

"I don't think it's too late at all," said Lucy.

"Well—" Bryan considered. "A clergyman perhaps," he said hopefully. "She'd be useful in the parish and tactful with the Mothers' Union. I do mean the Mothers' Union, don't I? Not that I know what it really is, but you come across it sometimes in books. And she'd wear a hat in church on Sundays," he added.

"Doesn't sound much of a prospect to me," said Lucy, rising and picking up the tray.

"I'll do that," said Bryan, taking the tray from her. They went into the kitchen together. "Shall I help you wash up? I do like this kitchen," he added. "In fact, I know it isn't the sort of thing that people do like nowadays, but I like this whole house. Shocking taste, I suppose, but there it is. You could land a plane quite easily in the park," he added with enthusiasm.

He picked up a glass cloth and began to wipe the spoons and forks.

"Seems a waste, it coming to Cedric," he remarked. "First thing he'll do is to sell the whole thing and go breaking off abroad again. Can't see, myself, why England isn't good enough for anybody. Harold wouldn't want this house either, and of course it's much too big for Emma. Now if only it came to Alexander, he and I would be as happy together here as a couple of sandboys. Of course it would be nice to have a woman about the house." He looked thoughtfully at Lucy. "Oh, well, what's the good of talking? If Alexander were to get this place it would mean a whole lot of them would have to die first, and that's not really likely, is it? Though from what I've seen of the old boy he might easily live to be a hundred, just to annoy them all. I don't suppose he was much cut up by Alfred's death, was he?"

Lucy said shortly, "No, he wasn't."

"Cantankerous old devil," said Bryan Eastley cheerfully.

22

"Dreadful, the things people go about saying," said Mrs. Kidder. "I don't listen, mind you, more than I can help. But you'd hardly believe it." She waited hopefully.

"Yes, I suppose so," said Lucy.

"About that body that was found in the Long Barn," went on Mrs. Kidder, moving crablike backward on her hands and knees, as she scrubbed the kitchen floor, "saying as how she'd been Mr. Edmund's fancy piece during the war, and how she come over here and a jealous husband followed her and did her in. It is a likely thing as a foreign would do, but it wouldn't be likely after all these years, would it?"

"It sounds most unlikely to me."

"But there's worse things than that, they say," said Mrs. Kidder. "Say anything, people will. You'd be surprised. There's those that say Mr. Harold married somewhere abroad and that she come over and found out he'd committed bigamy with that Lady Alice, and that she was going to bring 'im to court and that he met her down here and did her in and hid her body in the sarcoffus. Did you ever!"

"Shocking," said Lucy vaguely, her mind elsewhere.

"Of course I don't listen," said Mrs. Kidder virtuously, "I wouldn't put no stock in such tales myself. It beats me how people think up such things, let alone say them. All I hope is none of it gets to Miss Emma's ears. It might upset her and I shouldn't like that. She's a very nice lady, Miss Emma is, and I've not heard a word against her, not a word. And of course Mr. Alfred being dead nobody says anything

519

against him now. Not even that it's a judgment, which they well might do. But it's awful, Miss, isn't it, the wicked talk there is."

Mrs. Kidder spoke with immense enjoyment.

"It must be quite painful for you to listen to it," said Lucy.

"Oh, it is," said Mrs. Kidder. "It is, indeed. I says to my husband, I says, 'However can they?'"

The bell rang.

"There's the doctor, Miss. Will you let 'im in, or shall I?"

"I'll go," said Lucy.

But it was not the doctor. On the doorstep stood a tall, elegant woman in a mink coat. Drawn up to the gravel sweep was a purring Rolls with a chauffeur at the wheel.

"Can I see Miss Emma Crackenthorpe, please?"

It was an attractive voice, the R's slightly blurred. The woman was attractive, too. About thirty-five, with dark hair and expensively and beautifully made up.

"I'm sorry," said Lucy, "Miss Crackenthorpe is ill in bed and can't see anyone."

"I know she has been ill, yes, but it is very important that I should see her."

"I'm afraid," Lucy began.

The visitor interrupted her. "I think you are Miss Eyelesbarrow, are you not?" She smiled, an attractive smile. "My son has spoken of you, so I know. I am Lady Stoddart-West and Alexander is staying with me now."

"Oh, I see," said Lucy.

"And it is really important that I should see Miss Crackenthorpe," continued the other. "I know all about her illness and I assure you this is not just a social call. It is because of something that the boys have said to me—that my son has said to me. It is, I think, a matter of grave importance and I would like to speak to Miss Crackenthorpe about it. Please, will you ask her?"

"Come in." Lucy ushered her visitor into the hall and into the drawing room. Then she said, "I'll go up and ask Miss Crackenthorpe."

She went upstairs, knocked on Emma's door and entered.

"Lady Stoddart-West is here," she said. "She wants to see you very particularly."

"Lady Stoddart-West?" Emma looked surprised. A look of alarm came into her face. "There's nothing wrong, is there, with the boys—with Alexander?"

"No, no," Lucy reassured her. "I'm sure the boys are all right. It seems to be something the boys have told her or said to her."

"Oh. Well—" Emma hesitated. "Perhaps I ought to see her. Do I look all right, Lucy?"

"You look very nice," said Lucy.

Emma was sitting up in bed, a soft, pink shawl was round her shoulders and brought out the faint rose-pink of her cheeks. Her dark hair had been neatly brushed and combed by the nurse. Lucy had placed a bowl of autumn leaves on the dressing table the day before. Her room looked attractive and quite unlike a sickroom.

"I'm really quite well enough to get up," said Emma. "Doctor Quimper said I could tomorrow."

"You look really quite yourself again," said Lucy. "Shall I bring Lady Stoddart-West up?"

"Yes, do."

Lucy went downstairs again. "Will you come up to Miss Crackenthorpe's room?"

She escorted the visitor upstairs, opened the door for her to pass in and then shut it. Lady Stoddart-West approached the bed with outstretched hand.

"Miss Crackenthorpe? I really do apologize for breaking in on you like this. I have seen you, I think, at the sports at the school."

"Yes," said Emma, "I remember you quite well. Do sit down."

In the chair conveniently placed by the bed, Lady Stoddart-West sat down. She said in a quiet low voice, "You must think it very strange of me coming here like this, but I have a reason. I think it is an important reason. You see, the boys have been telling me things. You can understand that they were very excited about the murder that happened here. I confess I did not like it at the time. I was nervous. I wanted to bring James home at once. But my husband laughed. He said that obviously it was a murder that had nothing to do with the house and the family and he said that from what he remembered from his boyhood, and from James's letters, both he and Alexander were enjoying themselves so wildly that it would be sheer cruelty to bring them back. So I gave in and agreed that they should stay on until the time arranged for James to bring Alexander back with him."

Emma said: "You think we ought to have sent your son home earlier?"

"No, no, that is not what I mean at all. Oh, it is difficult for me, this! But what I have to say must be said. You see, they have picked up a good deal, the boys. They told me that this woman—the murdered woman—that the police have an idea that she may be a French girl whom your eldest brother, who was killed in the war, knew in France. That is so?"

"It is a possibility," said Emma, her voice breaking slightly, "that we are forced to consider. It may have been so."

"There is some reason for believing that the body is that of this girl, this Martine?"

"I have told you, it is a possibility."

"But why—why should they think that she was this Martine? Did she have letters on her—papers?"

"No. Nothing of that kind. But you see I had had a letter from this Martine."

"You had had a letter from *Martine*?"

"Yes. A letter telling me she was in England and would like to come and see me. I invited her down here, but got a telegram saying she was going back to France. Perhaps she did go back to France. We do not know. But since then an envelope was found here addressed to her. That seems to show that she had come down here. But I really don't see—" She broke off.

Lady Stoddart-West broke in quickly, "You really do not see what concern it is of mine? That is very true. I should not, in your place. But when I heard this, or rather, a garbled account of this, I had to come to make sure it was really so, because, if it is—"

"Yes?" said Emma.

"Then I must tell you something that I had never intended to tell you. You see, *I am Martine*."

Emma stared at her guest as though she could hardly take in the sense of her words.

"You!" she said. "You are Martine?"

The other nodded vigorously. "But yes. It surprises you, I am sure, but it is true. I met your brother Edmund in the first days of the war. He was indeed billeted at our house. Well, you know the rest. We fell in love. We intended to be married, and then there was the retreat to Dunkirk, Edmund was reported missing. Later he was reported killed. I will not speak to you of that time. It was long ago and it is over. But I will say to you that I loved your brother very much.

"Then came the grim realities of war. The Germans occupied France. I became a worker for the Resistance. I was one of those who was assigned to pass Englishmen through France to England. It was in that way that I met my present husband. He was an Air Force officer, parachuted into France to do special work. When the war ended we were married. I considered once or twice whether I should write to you or come and see you but I decided against it. It could do no good, I thought, to rake up old memories. I had a new life and I had no wish to recall the old." She paused and then said, "But it gave me, I will tell you, a strange pleasure when I found that my son James's greatest friend at his school was a boy whom I found to be Edmund's nephew. Alexander, I may say, is very like Edmund, as I dare say you yourself appreciate. It seemed to me a very happy state of affairs that James and Alexander should be such friends."

She leaned forward and placed her hand on Emma's arm. "But you see, dear Emma, do you not, that when I heard this story about the murder, about this dead woman being suspected to be the Martine that Edmund had known, that I had to come and tell you the truth. Either you or I must inform the police of the fact. Whoever the dead woman is, she is not Martine."

"I can hardly take it in," said Emma, "that you, you should be the Martine that dear Edmund wrote to me about." She sighed, shaking her head, then she frowned perplexedly. "But I don't understand. Was it you, then, who wrote to me?"

Lady Stoddart-West shook a vigorous head. "No, no, of course I did not write to you."

"Then—" Emma stopped.

"Then there was someone pretending to be Martine who wanted perhaps to get money out of you? That is what it must have been. But who can it be?"

Emma said slowly: "I suppose there were people at the time who knew?"

The other shrugged her shoulders. "Probably, yes. But there was no one intimate with me, no one very close to me. I have never spoken of it since I came to England. And why wait all this time? It is curious, very curious."

Emma said, "I don't understand it. We will have to see what Inspector Craddock has to say." She looked with suddenly softened eyes at her visitor. "I'm so glad to know you at last, my dear."

"And I you. Edmund spoke of you very often. He was very fond of you. I am happy in my new life, but all the same, I do not quite forget."

Emma leaned back and heaved a deep sigh. "It's a terrible relief," she said. "As long as we feared that the dead woman might be Martine, it seemed to be tied up with the family. But now, oh, it's an absolute load off my back. I don't know who the poor soul was but she can't have had anything to do with us!"

23

The streamlined secretary brought Harold Crackenthorpe his usual afternoon cup of tea.

"Thanks, Miss Ellis, I shall be going home early today."

"I'm sure you ought really not to have come at all, Mr. Crackenthorpe," said Miss Ellis. "You look quite pulled down still."

"I'm all right," said Harold Crackenthorpe, but he did feel pulled down. No doubt about it, he'd had a very nasty turn. Ah well, that was over.

Extraordinary, he thought broodingly, that Alfred should have succumbed and the old man should have come through. After all, what was he?—seventy-three, seventy-four? Been an invalid for years. If there was one person you'd have thought would have been taken off, it would have been the old man. But no. It had to be Alfred. Alfred who, as far as Harold knew, was a healthy, wiry sort of chap. Nothing much the matter with him.

He leaned back in his chair sighing. That girl was right. He didn't feel up to things yet, but he had wanted to come down to the office. Wanted to get the hang of how affairs were going. Touch and go, that's what it was! Touch and go. All this—he looked round him—the richly appointed office, the pale gleaming wood, the expensive modern chairs, it all looked prosperous enough, and a good thing, too! That's where Alfred had always gone wrong. If you looked prosperous, people thought you were prosperous. There were no rumors going around as yet about his financial stability. All the same, the crash couldn't be delayed very long. Now if only his father had passed out instead of

525

Alfred, as surely, surely he ought to have done. Practically seemed to thrive on arsenic! Yes, if his father had succumbed: well, there wouldn't have been anything to worry about.

Still, the great thing was not to seem worried. A prosperous appearance. Not like poor old Alfred who always looked seedy and shiftless, who looked in fact exactly what he was. One of those small-time speculators, never going all out boldly for the big money. In with a shady crowd here, doing a doubtful deal there, never quite rendering himself liable to prosecution but going very near the edge. And where had it got him? Short periods of affluence and then back to seediness and shabbiness once more. No broad outlook about Alfred. Taken all in all, you couldn't say Alfred was much loss. He'd never been particularly fond of Alfred and with Alfred out of the way the money that was coming to him from that old curmudgeon, his grandfather, would be sensibly increased, divided not into five shares but into four shares. Very much better.

Harold's face brightened a little. He rose, took his hat and coat and left the office. Better take it easy for a day or two. He wasn't feeling too strong yet. His car was waiting below and very soon he was weaving through the London traffic to his house.

Darwin, his manservant, opened the door.

"Her Ladyship has just arrived, sir," he said.

For a moment Harold stared at him. Alice! Good Heavens, was it today that Alice was coming home? He'd forgotten all about it. Good thing Darwin had warned him. It wouldn't have looked so good if he'd gone upstairs and looked too astonished at seeing her. Not that it really mattered, he supposed. Neither Alice nor he had many illusions about the feeling they had for each other. Perhaps Alice was fond of him; he didn't know.

All in all Alice was a great disappointment to him. He hadn't been in love with her, of course, but though a plain woman she was quite a pleasant one. And her family and connections had undoubtedly been useful. Not perhaps as useful as they might have been, because in marrying Alice he had been considering the position of hypothetical children. Nice relations for his boys to have. But there hadn't been any boys, or girls either, and all that had remained had been him and Alice growing older together without much to say to each other and with no particular pleasure in each other's company.

She stayed away a good deal with relations and usually went to the Riviera in the winter. It suited her and it didn't worry him.

He went upstairs now into the drawing room and greeted her punctiliously.

"So you're back, my dear. Sorry I couldn't meet you, but I was held up in the City. I got back as early as I could. How was San Raphael?"

Alice told him how San Raphael was. She was a thin woman with sandy-colored hair, a well-arched nose and vague, hazel eyes. She talked in a well-bred, monotonous and rather depressing voice. It had been a good journey back, the Channel a little rough. The customs, as usual, very trying at Dover.

"You should come by air," said Harold, as he always did. "So much simpler."

"I dare say, but I don't really like air travel. I never have. Makes me nervous."

"Saves a lot of time," said Harold.

Lady Alice Crackenthorpe did not answer. It was possible that her problem in life was not to save time but to occupy it. She inquired politely after her husband's health.

"Emma's telegram quite alarmed me," she said. "You were all taken ill, I understand."

"Yes, yes," said Harold.

"I read in the paper the other day," said Alice, "of forty people in a hotel going down with food poisoning at the same time. All this refrigeration is dangerous, I think. People keep things too long in them."

"Possibly," said Harold. Should he, or should he not mention arsenic? Somehow, looking at Alice, he felt himself quite unable to do so. In Alice's world, he felt, there was no place for poisoning by arsenic. It was a thing you read about in the papers. It didn't happen to you or your own family. But it had happened in the Crackenthorpe family. . . .

He went up to his room and lay down for an hour or two before dressing for dinner. At dinner, tête-à-tête with his wife, the conversation ran on much the same lines. Desultory, polite. The mention of acquaintances and friends at San Raphael.

"There's a parcel for you on the hall table, a small one," Alice said.

"Is there? I didn't notice it."

"It's an extraordinary thing but somebody was telling me about a murdered woman having been found in a barn or something like that. She said it was at Rutherford Hall. I suppose it must be some other Rutherford Hall."

"No," said Harold, "no, it isn't. It was in our barn, as a matter of fact."

"Really, Harold! A murdered woman in the barn at Rutherford Hall, and you never told me anything about it."

"Well, there hasn't been much time, really," said Harold, "and it was all rather unpleasant. Nothing to do with us, of course. The press milled round a good deal. Of course we had to deal with the police and all that sort of thing."

"Very unpleasant," said Alice. "Did they find out who did it?" she added, with rather perfunctory interest.

"Not yet," said Harold.

"What sort of a woman was she?"

"Nobody knows. French apparently."

"Oh, French," said Alice, and allowing for the difference in class, her tone was not unlike that of Inspector Bacon. "Very annoying for you all," she agreed.

They went out from the dining room and crossed into the small study where they usually sat when they were alone. Harold was feeling quite exhausted by now. I'll go up to bed early, he thought.

He picked up the small parcel from the hall table, about which his wife had spoken to him. It was a small neatly waxed parcel, done up with meticulous exactness. Harold ripped it open as he came to sit down in his usual chair by the fire.

Inside was a small tablet box bearing the label, *"Two to be taken nightly."* With it was a small piece of paper with the chemist's heading in Brackhampton. *"Sent by request of Doctor Quimper"* was written on it.

Harold Crackenthorpe frowned. He opened the box and looked at the tablets. Yes, they seemed to be the same tablets he had been having. But surely, surely Quimper had said that he needn't take any more? "You won't want them now." That's what Quimper had said.

"What is it, dear?" said Alice. "You look worried."

"Oh, it's just some tablets. I've been taking them at night. But I rather thought the doctor said don't take any more."

His wife said placidly, "He probably said don't forget to take them."

"He may have done, I suppose," said Harold doubtfully.

He looked across at her. She was watching him. Just for a moment or two he wondered—he didn't often wonder about Alice—exactly what she was thinking. That mild gaze of hers told him nothing. Her eyes were like windows in an empty house. What did Alice think about him, feel about him? Had she been in love with him once? He supposed she had. Or did she marry him because she thought he was doing well in the City and she was tired of her own impecunious existence? Well, on the whole, she'd done quite well out of it. She'd got a car and a house in London, she could travel abroad when she felt like it and get herself expensive clothes, though goodness knows they never looked like anything on Alice. Yes, on the whole, she'd done pretty well. He wondered if she thought so. She wasn't really fond of him, of course, but then he wasn't really fond of her. They had nothing in common, nothing to talk about, no memories to share. If there had been children, but there hadn't been any children. Odd that there were no children in the family except young Edie's boy. Young Edie. She'd been a silly girl, making that foolish, hasty wartime marriage. Well, he'd given her good advice.

He'd said, "It's all very well, these dashing young pilots, glamor, courage, all that, but he'll be no good in peacetime, you know. Probably be barely able to support you."

And Edie had said, what did it matter? She loved Bryan and Bryan loved her, and he'd probably be killed quite soon. Why shouldn't they have some happiness? What was the good of looking to the future when they might all be bombed any minute. And after all, Edie had said, the future doesn't really matter because some day there'll be all grandfather's money.

Harold squirmed uneasily in his chair. Really, that will of his grandfather's had been iniquitous! Keeping them all dangling on a string. The will hadn't pleased anybody. It didn't please the grandchildren and it made their father quite livid. The old boy was absolutely determined not to die. That's what made him take so much care of himself. But he'd have to die soon. Surely, surely he'd have to die soon. Otherwise—All Harold's worries swept over him once more, making him feel sick and tired and giddy.

Alice was still watching him, he noticed. Those pale, thoughtful eyes, they made him uneasy somehow.

"I think I shall go to bed," he said. "It's been my first day out in the City."

"Yes," said Alice, "I think that's a good idea. I'm sure the doctor told you to take things easily at first."

"Doctors always tell you that," said Harold.

"And don't forget to take your tablets, dear," said Alice. She picked up the box and handed it to him.

He said good night and went upstairs. Yes, he needed the tablets. It would have been a mistake to leave them off too soon. He took two of them and swallowed them with a glass of water.

24

"Nobody could have made more of a muck of it than I seem to have done," said Dermot Craddock gloomily.

He sat, his long legs stretched out, looking somehow incongruous in faithful Florence's somewhat overfurnished parlor. He was thoroughly tired, upset and dispirited.

Miss Marple made soft, soothing noises of dissent. "No, no, you've done very good work, my dear boy. Very good work, indeed."

"I've done very good work, have I? I've let a whole family be poisoned, Alfred Crackenthorpe's dead and now Harold's dead, too. What the hell's going on there? That's what I should like to know."

"Poisoned tablets," said Miss Marple thoughtfully.

"Yes. Devilishly cunning, really. They looked just like the tablets that he'd been having. There was a printed slip sent in with them *'by Doctor Quimper's instructions.'* Well, Quimper never ordered them. There were chemist's labels used. The chemist knew nothing about it, either. No. That box of tablets came from Rutherford Hall."

"Do you actually know it came from Rutherford Hall?"

"Yes. We've had a thorough checkup. Actually it's the box that held the sedative tablets prescribed for Emma."

"Oh, I see. For Emma . . ."

"Yes. It's got her fingerprints on it and the fingerprints of both the nurses and the fingerprint of the chemist who made it up. Nobody else's, naturally. The person who sent them was careful."

"And the sedative tablets were removed and something else substituted?"

"Yes. That of course is the devil with tablets. One tablet looks exactly like another."

"You are so right," agreed Miss Marple. "I remember so very well in my young days, the black mixture and the brown mixture—the cough mixture that was—and the white mixture, and Doctor So-and-So's pink mixture. People didn't mix those up nearly as much. In fact, you know, in my village in St. Mary Mead we still like that kind of medicine. It's a bottle they always want, not tablets. What were the tablets?" she asked.

"Aconite. They were the kind of tablets that are usually kept in a poison bottle, diluted one in a hundred for outside application."

"And so Harold took them and died," Miss Marple said thoughtfully. Dermot Craddock uttered something like a groan.

"You mustn't mind my letting off steam to you," he said. "Tell it all to Aunt Jane; that's how I feel!"

"That's very, very nice of you," said Miss Marple, "and I do appreciate it. As Sir Henry's godson I feel toward you quite differently from the way I should feel to any ordinary detective inspector."

Dermot Craddock gave her a fleeting grin. "But the fact remains that I've made the most ghastly mess of things all along the line," he said. "The Chief Constable down here calls in Scotland Yard, and what do they get? They get me making a prize ass of myself!"

"No, no," said Miss Marple.

"Yes, yes. I don't know who poisoned Alfred, I don't know who poisoned Harold, and to cap it all I haven't the least idea now who the original murdered woman was! This Martine business seemed a perfectly safe bet. The whole thing seemed to tie up. And now what happens? The real Martine shows up and turns out, most improbably, to be the wife of Sir Robert Stoddart-West. So who's the woman in the barn now? Goodness knows. First I go all out on the idea she's Anna Stravinska, and then she's out of it."

He was arrested by Miss Marple giving one of her small, peculiarly significant coughs.

"But is she?" she murmured.

Craddock stared at her. "Well, that postcard from Jamaica."

"Yes," said Miss Marple, "but that isn't really evidence, is it? I mean, anyone can get a postcard sent from almost anywhere, I suppose. I remember Mrs. Brierly, such a very bad nervous breakdown. Finally they said she ought to go to the mental hospital for observation, and she was so worried about the children knowing about it and so she wrote about fourteen postcards and arranged that they should be posted from different places abroad, and told them that Mummie was going abroad on a holiday." She added, looking at Dermot Craddock, "You see what I mean."

"Yes, of course," said Craddock, staring at her. "Naturally we'd have checked that postcard if it hadn't been for the Martine business fitting the bill so well."

"So convenient," murmured Miss Marple.

"It tied up," said Craddock. "After all there's the letter Emma received signed Martine Crackenthorpe. Lady Stoddart-West didn't send that, but somebody did. Somebody who was going to pretend to be Martine, and who was going to cash in, if possible, on being Martine. You can't deny that."

"No, no."

"And then, the envelope of the letter Emma wrote to her with the London address on it. Found at Rutherford Hall, showing she'd actually been there."

"But the murdered woman hadn't been there!" Miss Marple pointed out. "Not in the sense you mean. She only came to Rutherford Hall after she was dead. Pushed out of a train on to the railway embankment."

"Oh—yes."

"What the envelope really proves is that the murderer was there. Presumably he took that envelope off her with her other papers and things, and then dropped it by mistake—or—I wonder now, was it a mistake? Surely Inspector Bacon, and your men too, made a thorough search of the place, didn't they, and didn't find it. It only turned up later in the boiler house."

"That's understandable," said Craddock. "The old gardener chap used to spear up any odd stuff that was blowing about and shove it in there."

"Where it was very convenient for the boys to find," said Miss Marple thoughtfully.

"You think we were meant to find it?"

"Well, I just wonder. After all it would be fairly easy to know where the boys were going to look next, or even to suggest to them . . . yes, I do wonder. It stopped you thinking about Anna Stravinska any more, didn't it?"

Craddock said, "And you think it really may be her all the time?"

"I think someone may have got alarmed when you started making inquiries about her, that's all. I think somebody didn't want those inquiries made."

"Let's hold on to the basic fact that someone was going to impersonate Martine," said Craddock. "And then for some reason didn't. Why?"

"That's a very interesting question," said Miss Marple.

"Somebody sent a wire saying Martine was going back to France, then arranged to travel down with the girl and kill her on the way. You agree so far?"

"Not exactly," said Miss Marple. "I don't think, really, you're making it simple enough."

"Simple!" exclaimed Craddock. "You're mixing me up," he complained.

Miss Marple said in a distressed voice that she wouldn't think of doing anything like that.

"Come, tell me," said Craddock, "do you or do you not think you know who the murdered woman was?"

Miss Marple sighed. "It's so difficult," she said, "to put it the right way. I mean, I don't know *who* she was, but at the same time I'm fairly sure who she *was*, if you know what I mean."

Craddock threw up his head. "Know what you mean? I haven't the faintest idea." He looked out through the window. "There's your Lucy Eyelesbarrow coming to see you," he said. "Well, I'll be off. My *amour propre* is very low this afternoon and having a young woman coming in, radiant with efficiency and success, is more than I can bear."

25

"I looked up tontine in the dictionary," said Lucy.

The first greetings were over and now Lucy was wandering rather aimlessly round the room, touching a china dog here, an antimacassar there, the plastic work box in the window.

"I thought you probably would," said Miss Marple equably.

Lucy spoke slowly, quoting the words. "Lorenzo Tonti, Italian banker, originator, 1653, of a form of annuity in which the shares of subscribers who die are added to the profit shares of the survivors." She paused. "That's it, isn't it? That fits well enough, and you were thinking of it even then before the last two deaths."

She took up once more her restless, almost aimless prowl round the room. Miss Marple sat watching her. This was a very different Lucy Eyelesbarrow from the one she knew.

"I suppose it was asking for it really," said Lucy. "A will of that kind, ending so that if there was only one survivor left he'd get the lot. And yet, there was quite a lot of money, wasn't there? You'd think it would be enough shared out—" She paused, the words tailing off.

"The trouble is," said Miss Marple, "that people are greedy. Some people. That's so often, you know, how things start. You don't start with murder, with wanting to do murder or even thinking of it. You just start by being greedy, by wanting more than you're going to have." She laid her knitting down on her knee and stared ahead of her into space. "That's how I came across Inspector Craddock first, you know. A case in the country. Near Medenham Spa. That began the same way, just a weak amiable character who wanted a great deal of

535

money. Money that that person wasn't entitled to, but there seemed an easy way to get it. Not murder then. Just something so easy and simple that it hardly seemed wrong. That's how things begin. But it ended with three murders."

"Just like this," said Lucy. "We've had three murders now. The woman who impersonated Martine and who would have been able to claim a share for her son, and then Alfred, and then Harold. And now it only leaves two, doesn't it?"

"You mean," said Miss Marple, "there are only Cedric and Emma left?"

"Not Emma. Emma isn't a tall, dark man. No, I mean Cedric and Bryan Eastley. I never thought of Bryan because he's fair. He's got a great, fair mustache and blue eyes, but you see—the other day—" She paused.

"Yes, go on," said Miss Marple. "Tell me. Something has upset you very badly, hasn't it?"

"It was when Lady Stoddart-West was going away. She had said good-by and then suddenly turned to me just as she was getting into the car and asked: 'Who was that tall, dark man who was standing on the terrace as I came in?'

"I couldn't imagine who she meant at first, because Cedric was still laid up. So I said, rather puzzled, 'You don't mean Bryan Eastley?' and she said, 'Of course, that's who it was, Squadron Leader Eastley. He was hidden in our loft once in France during the Resistance. I remembered the way he stood, and the set of his shoulders,' and she said, 'I should like to meet him again,' and we couldn't find him."

Miss Marple said nothing, just waited.

"And then," said Lucy, "later I looked at him . . . he was standing with his back to me and I saw what I ought to have seen before. That even when a man's fair, his hair looks dark because he plasters it down with stuff. Bryan's hair is a sort of medium brown, I suppose, but it can look dark. So, you see, it might have been Bryan that your friend saw in the train. It might. . . ."

"Yes," said Miss Marple. "I had thought of that."

"I suppose you think of everything!" said Lucy bitterly.

"Well, dear, one has to really."

"But I can't see what Bryan would get out of it. I mean, the money would come to Alexander, not to him. I suppose it would make an easier life, they could have a bit more luxury, but he wouldn't be able to tap the capital for his schemes, or anything like that."

"But if anything happened to Alexander before he was twenty-one, then Bryan would get the money as his father and next of kin," Miss Marple pointed out.

Lucy cast a look of horror at her.

"He'd never do that. No father would ever do that just—just to get the money."

Miss Marple sighed: "People do, my dear. It's very sad and very terrible, but they do.

"People do very terrible things," Miss Marple continued. "I know a woman who poisoned three of her children just for a little bit of insurance money. And then there was an old woman, quite a nice old woman apparently, who poisoned her son when he came home on leave. Then there was that old Mrs. Stanwich. That case was in the paper. I dare say you read about it. Her daughter died and her son, and then she said she was poisoned herself. There was poison in some gruel, but it came out, you know, that she'd put it there herself. She was just planning to poison the last daughter. That wasn't exactly for money. She was jealous of them for being younger than she was and alive, and she was afraid—it's a terrible thing to say but it's true—they would enjoy themselves after she was gone. She'd always kept a very tight hold on the purse strings. Yes, of course she was a little peculiar, as they say, but I never see myself that that's any real excuse. I mean you can be a little peculiar in so many different ways. Sometimes you just go about giving all your possessions away and writing checks on bank accounts that don't exist, just so as to benefit people. It shows, you see, that behind being peculiar you have quite a nice disposition. But of course if you're peculiar and behind it you have a bad disposition, well, there you are. Now, does that help you at all, my dear Lucy?"

"Does what help me?" asked Lucy bewildered.

"What I've been telling you," said Miss Marple. She added gently, "You mustn't worry, you know. You really mustn't worry. Elspeth McGillicuddy will be here any day now."

"I don't see what that has to do with it."

"No, dear, perhaps not. But I think it's important myself."

"I can't help worrying," said Lucy. "You see I've got interested in the family."

"I know, dear, it's very difficult for you because you are quite strongly attracted to both of them, aren't you, in very different ways."

"What do you mean?" said Lucy. Her tone was sharp.

"I was talking about the two sons of the house," said Miss Marple. "Or rather the son and the son-in-law. It's fortunate that the two more unpleasant members of the family have died and the two more attractive ones are left. I can see that Cedric Crackenthorpe is very attractive. He is inclined to make himself out worse than he is and has a provocative way with him."

"He makes me fighting mad sometimes," said Lucy.

"Yes," said Miss Marple, "and you enjoy that, don't you? You're a girl with a lot of spirit and you enjoy a battle. Yes, I can see where that attraction lies. And then Mr. Eastley is a rather plaintive type, rather like an unhappy little boy. That of course is attractive, too."

"And one of them's a murderer," said Lucy bitterly, "and it may be either of them. There's nothing to choose between them really. There's Cedric, not caring a bit about his brother Alfred's death or about Harold's. He just sits back looking thoroughly pleased making plans for what he'll do with Rutherford Hall, and he keeps saying that it'll need a lot of money to develop it in the way he wants to do. Of course I know he's the sort of person who exaggerates his own callousness and all that. But that could be a cover, too. I mean everyone says that you're more callous than you really are. But you mightn't be. You might be even more callous than you seem!"

"Dear, dear Lucy, I'm sorry about all this."

"And then Bryan," went on Lucy. "It's extraordinary, but Bryan really seems to want to live there. He thinks he and Alexander would find it awfully jolly and he's full of schemes."

"He's always full of schemes of one kind or another, isn't he?"

"Yes, I think he is. They all sound rather wonderful, but I've got an uneasy feeling that they'd never really work. I mean, they're not practical. The idea sounds all right, but I don't think he ever considers the actual working difficulties."

"They are up in the air, so to speak?"

"Yes, in more ways than one. I mean they are usually literally up in the air. They are all air schemes. Perhaps a really good fighter pilot never does quite come down to earth again. . . ."

She added: "And he likes Rutherford Hall so much because it reminds him of the big rambling Victorian house he lived in when he was a child."

"I see," said Miss Marple thoughtfully. "Yes, I see."

Then, with a quick sideways glance at Lucy, she said with a kind of verbal pounce, "But that isn't all of it, is it, dear? There's something else."

"Oh yes, there's something else. Just something that I didn't realize until just a couple of days ago. Bryan was actually on that train."

"On the 4:33 from Paddington?"

"Yes. You see Emma thought she was required to account for her movements on December the twentieth and she went over it all very carefully—a committee meeting in the morning and then shopping in the afternoon and tea at the Green Shamrock, and then, she said, she went to meet Bryan at the station. I worked out when she'd had tea and the time, and the train she met must have been the 4:33. So I asked Bryan, quite casually, and he said, yes, it was, and added that his car had had a bump and was being repaired and so he had to come down by train—an awful bore, he said, he hates trains. He seemed quite natural about it all. It may be quite all right, but I wish, somehow, he hadn't been on that train. . . ."

"Actually on the train," said Miss Marple thoughtfully.

"It doesn't really prove anything. The awful thing is all this suspicion. Not to know. And perhaps we never shall know!"

"Of course we shall know, dear," said Miss Marple briskly. "I mean, all this isn't going to stop just at this point. The one thing I do know about murderers is that they can never let well alone. Or perhaps one should say, ill alone. At any rate," said Miss Marple with finality, "they can't once they've done a second murder. Now don't get too upset, Lucy. The police are doing all they can, and looking for everybody, and the great thing is that Elspeth McGillicuddy will be here very soon now!"

26

"Now, Elspeth, you're quite clear as to what I want you to do?"

"I'm clear enough," said Mrs. McGillicuddy, "but what I say to you is, Jane, that it seems very odd."

"It's not odd at all," said Miss Marple.

"Well, I think so. To arrive at the house and to ask almost immediately whether I can—er—go upstairs."

"It's very cold weather," Miss Marple pointed out, "and after all, you might have eaten something that disagreed with you and—er—have to ask to go upstairs. I mean, these things happen. I remember poor Louisa Felby came to see me once and she had to ask to go upstairs five times during one little half hour. That," added Miss Marple parenthetically, "was a bad Cornish pasty."

"If you'd just tell me what you're driving at, Jane," said Mrs. McGillicuddy.

"That's just what I don't want to do," said Miss Marple.

"How irritating you are, Jane. First you make me come all the way back to England before I need—"

"I'm sorry about that," said Miss Marple, "but I couldn't do anything else. Someone, you see, may be killed at any moment. Oh, I know they're all on their guard and the police are taking all the precautions they can, but there's always the outside chance that the murderer might be too clever for them. So you see, Elspeth, it was your duty to come back. After all, you and I were brought up to do our duty, weren't we?"

"We certainly were," said Mrs. McGillicuddy, "no laxness in our young days."

"So that's quite all right," said Miss Marple. "And that's the taxi now," she added, as a faint hoot was heard outside the house.

Mrs. McGillicuddy donned her heavy pepper-and-salt coat and Miss Marple wrapped herself up with a good many shawls and scarves. Then the two ladies got into the taxi and were driven to Rutherford Hall.

II

"Who can this be driving up?" Emma asked, looking out of the window, as the taxi swept past it. "I do believe it's Lucy's old aunt."

"What a bore," said Cedric.

He was lying back in a long chair looking at *Country Life* with his feet reposing on the side of the mantelpiece.

"Tell her you're not at home."

"When you say tell her I'm not at home, do you mean that I should go out and say so? Or that I should tell Lucy to tell her aunt so?"

"Hadn't thought of that," said Cedric. "I suppose I was thinking of our butler-and-footman days, if we ever had them. I seem to remember a footman before the war. He had an affair with the kitchen maid and there was a terrible rumpus about it. Isn't there one of those old hags about the place cleaning?"

But at that moment the door was opened by Mrs. Hart, whose afternoon it was for cleaning the brasses, and Miss Marple came in, very fluttery, in a whirl of shawls and scarves, with a tall, uncompromising figure behind her.

"I do hope," said Miss Marple, taking Emma's hand, "that we are not intruding. But you see, I'm going home the day after tomorrow, and I couldn't bear not to come over and see you and say goodby and thank you again for your goodness to Lucy. Oh, I forgot. May I introduce my friend, Mrs. McGillicuddy, who is staying with me?"

"How d'you do," said Mrs. McGillicuddy, looking at Emma with complete attention and then shifting her gaze to Cedric, who had now risen to his feet. Lucy entered the room at this moment.

"Aunt Jane, I had no idea . . ."

"I had to come and say good-by to Miss Crackenthorpe," said

Miss Marple, turning to her, "who has been so very, very kind to you, Lucy."

"It's Lucy who's been very kind to us," said Emma.

"Yes, indeed," said Cedric. "We've worked her like a galley slave. Waiting on the sick room, running up and down the stairs, cooking little invalid messes . . ."

Miss Marple broke in. "I was so very, very sorry to hear of your illness. I do hope you're quite recovered now, Miss Crackenthorpe?"

"Oh, we're quite well again now," said Emma.

"Lucy told me you were all very ill. So dangerous, isn't it, food poisoning? Mushrooms, I understand."

"The cause remains rather mysterious," said Emma.

"Don't you believe it," said Cedric. "I bet you've heard the rumors that are flying round, Miss—er—"

"Marple," said Miss Marple.

"Well, as I say, I bet you've heard the rumors that are flying around. Nothing like arsenic for raising a little flutter in the neighborhood."

"Cedric," said Emma, "I wish you wouldn't. You know Inspector Craddock said . . ."

"Bah," said Cedric, "everybody knows. Even you've heard something, haven't you?" He turned to Miss Marple and Mrs. McGillicuddy.

"I myself," said Mrs. McGillicuddy, "have only just returned from abroad. The day before yesterday," she added.

"Ah, well, you're not up in our local scandal then," said Cedric. "Arsenic in the curry, that's what it was. Lucy's aunt knows all about it, I bet."

"Well," said Miss Marple, "I did just hear—I mean, it was just a hint, but of course I didn't want to embarrass you in any way, Miss Crackenthorpe."

"You must pay no attention to my brother," said Emma. "He just likes making people uncomfortable." She gave him an affectionate smile as she spoke.

The door opened and Mr. Crackenthorpe came in, tapping angrily with his stick.

"Where's tea?" he said. "Why isn't tea ready? You! Girl!" he addressed Lucy, "why haven't you brought tea in?"

"It's just ready, Mr. Crackenthorpe. I'm bringing it in now. I was just setting the table ready."

Lucy went out of the room again and Mr. Crackenthorpe was introduced to Miss Marple and Mrs. McGillicuddy.

"Like my meals on time," said Mr. Crackenthorpe. "Punctuality and economy. Those are my watchwords."

"Very necessary, I'm sure," said Miss Marple, "especially in these times with taxation and everything."

Mr. Crackenthorpe snorted. "Taxation! Don't talk to me of those robbers. A miserable pauper, that's what I am. And it's going to get worse, not better. You wait, my boy," he addressed Cedric, "when you get this place ten to one the Socialists will have it off you and turn it into a Welfare Center or something. And take all your income to keep it up with!"

Lucy reappeared with a tea tray, Bryan Eastley following her carrying a tray of sandwiches, bread and butter and cake.

"What's this? What's this?" Mr. Crackenthorpe inspected the tray. "Frosted cake? We having a party today? Nobody told me about it."

A faint flush came into Emma's face.

"Doctor Quimper's coming to tea, Father. It's his birthday today and—"

"Birthday?" snorted the old man, "what's he doing with a birthday? Birthdays are only for children. I never count my birthdays, and I won't let anyone else celebrate them either."

"Much cheaper," agreed Cedric. "You save the price of candles on your cake."

"That's enough from you, boy," said Mr. Crackenthorpe.

Miss Marple was shaking hands with Bryan Eastley. "I've heard about you, of course," she said, "from Lucy. Dear me, you remind me so much of someone I used to know at St. Mary Mead. That's the village where I've lived for so many years, you know. Ronnie Wells, the solicitor's son. Couldn't seem to settle somehow when he went into his father's business. He went out to East Africa and started a series of cargo boats on the lakes out there. Victoria Nyanza, or is it Albert I mean? Anyway, I'm sorry to say that it wasn't a success, and he lost all his capital. Most unfortunate! Not any relation of yours, I suppose? The likeness is so great."

"No," said Bryan, "I don't think I've any relations called Wells."

"He was engaged to a very nice girl," said Miss Marple. "Very sensible. She tried to dissuade him, but he wouldn't listen to her. He was wrong of course. Women have a lot of sense, you know, when it comes to money matters. Not high finance, of course. No woman can hope to understand that, my dear father said. But everyday matters. . . . What a delightful view you have from this window," she added, making her way across and looking out.

Emma joined her.

"Such an expanse of parkland! How picturesque the cattle look against the trees. One would never dream that one was in the middle of a town."

"We're rather an anachronism, I think," said Emma. "If the windows were open now you'd hear far off the noise of the traffic."

"Oh, of course," said Miss Marple, "there's noise everywhere, isn't there? Even in St. Mary Mead. We're now quite close to an airfield, you know, and really the way those jet planes fly over. Most frightening. Two panes in my little greenhouse broken the other day. Going through the sound barrier, or so I understand, though what it means I never have known."

"It's quite simple, really," said Bryan, approaching amiably. "You see, it's like this."

Miss Marple dropped her handbag and Bryan politely picked it up. At the same moment Mrs. McGillicuddy approached Emma and murmured, in an anguished voice, and the anguish was quite genuine, since Mrs. McGillicuddy deeply disliked the task which she was now performing:

"I wonder, could I go upstairs for a moment?"

"Of course," said Emma.

"I'll take you," said Lucy.

Lucy and Mrs. McGillicuddy left the room together.

"Very cold, driving today," said Miss Marple in a vaguely explanatory manner.

"About the sound barrier," said Bryan, "you see, it's like this—Oh, hello, there's Quimper."

The doctor drove up in his car. He came in rubbing his hands and looking very cold.

"Going to snow," he said, "that's my guess. Hello, Emma, how are you? Good lord, what's all this?"

"We made you a birthday cake," said Emma. "D'you remember? You told me today was your birthday."

"I didn't expect all this," said Quimper. "You know it's years—why, it must be, yes, sixteen years—since anyone's remembered my birthday." He looked almost uncomfortably touched.

"Do you know Miss Marple?" Emma introduced him.

"Oh yes," said Miss Marple, "I met Doctor Quimper here before and he came and saw me when I had a very nasty chill the other day and he was most kind."

"All right again now, I hope?" said the doctor.

Miss Marple assured him that she was quite all right now.

"You haven't been to see me lately, Quimper," said Mr. Crackenthorpe. "I might be dying for all the notice you take of me!"

"I don't see you dying yet awhile," said Doctor Quimper.

"I don't mean to," said Mr. Crackenthorpe. "Come on, let's have tea. What're we waiting for?"

"Oh, please," said Miss Marple, "don't wait for my friend. She would be most upset if you did."

They sat down and started tea. Miss Marple accepted a piece of bread and butter first, and then went on to a sandwich.

"Are they—?" She hesitated.

"Fish," said Bryan. "I helped make 'em."

Mr. Crackenthorpe gave a cackle of laughter.

"Poisoned fishpaste," he said. "That's what they are. Eat 'em at your peril."

"Please, Father!"

"You've got to be careful what you eat in this house," said Mr. Crackenthorpe to Miss Marple. "Two of my sons have been murdered like flies. Who's doing it—that's what I want to know."

"Don't let him put you off," said Cedric, handing the plate once more to Miss Marple. "A touch of arsenic improves the complexion, they say, so long as you don't have too much."

"Eat one yourself, boy," said old Mr. Crackenthorpe.

"Want me to be official taster?" said Cedric. "Here goes."

He took a sandwich and put it whole into his mouth. Miss Marple gave a gentle, ladylike little laugh and took a sandwich. She took a bite and said:

"I do think it's so brave of you all to make these jokes. Yes, really, I think it's very brave indeed. I do admire bravery so much."

She gave a sudden gasp and began to choke. "A fish bone," she gasped out, "in my throat."

Quimper rose quickly. He went across to her, moved her backwards toward the window and told her to open her mouth. He pulled out a case from his pocket, selecting some forceps from it. With quick professional skill he peered down the old lady's throat. At that moment the door opened and Mrs. McGillicuddy, followed by Lucy, came in. Mrs. McGillicuddy gave a sudden gasp as her eyes fell on the tableau in front of her: Miss Marple leaning back and the doctor holding her throat and tilting up her head.

"But that's him," cried Mrs. McGillicuddy. "That's the man in the train. . . ."

With incredible swiftness Miss Marple slipped from the doctor's grasp and came toward her friend.

"I thought you'd recognize him, Elspeth!" she said. "No. Don't say another word." She turned triumphantly round to Doctor Quimper. "You didn't know, did you, Doctor, when you strangled that woman in the train, that somebody actually saw you do it? It was my friend here. Mrs. McGillicuddy. She saw you. Do you understand? *Saw you with her own eyes.* She was in another train that was running parallel with yours."

"What the hell—" Doctor Quimper made a quick step toward Mrs. McGillicuddy but again, swiftly, Miss Marple was between him and her.

"Yes," said Miss Marple. "She saw you, and she recognizes you, and she'll swear to it in court. It's not often, I believe," went on Miss Marple in her gentle plaintive voice, "that anyone actually sees a murder committed. It's usually circumstantial evidence of course. But in this case the conditions were very unusual. There was actually an eyewitness to murder."

"You devilish old hag," said Doctor Quimper. He lunged forward at Miss Marple but this time it was Cedric who caught him by the shoulder.

"So you're the murdering devil, are you?" said Cedric as he swung him round. "I never liked you and I always thought you were a wrong 'un, but Lord knows, I never suspected you."

Bryan Eastley came quickly to Cedric's assistance. Inspector Craddock and Inspector Bacon entered the room from the farther door.

"Doctor Quimper," said Bacon, "I must caution you that . . ."

"You can take your caution to hell," said Doctor Quimper. "Do you think anyone's going to believe what a couple of batty old women say? Who's ever heard of all this rigmarole about a train!"

Miss Marple said, "Elspeth McGillicuddy reported the murder to the police at once on the twentieth of December and gave a description of the man."

Doctor Quimper gave a sudden heave of the shoulders. "If ever a man had the devil's own luck," said Doctor Quimper.

"But—" said Mrs. McGillicuddy.

"Be quiet, Elspeth," said Miss Marple.

"Why should I want to murder a perfectly strange woman?" said Doctor Quimper.

"She wasn't a strange woman," said Inspector Craddock. "She was your wife."

27

"So you see," said Miss Marple, "it really turned out to be, as I began to suspect, very, very simple. The simplest kind of crime. So many men seem to murder their wives."

Mrs. McGillicuddy looked at Miss Marple and Inspector Craddock. "I'd be obliged," she said, "if you'd put me a little more up to date."

"He saw a chance, you see," said Miss Marple, "of marrying a rich wife, Emma Crackenthorpe. Only he couldn't marry her because he had a wife already. They'd been separated for years but she wouldn't divorce him. That fitted in very well with what Inspector Craddock told me of this girl who called herself Anna Stravinska. She had an English husband, so she told one of her friends, and it was also said she was a very devout Catholic. Doctor Quimper couldn't risk marrying Emma bigamously, so he decided, being a very ruthless and cold-blooded man, that he would get rid of his wife. The idea of murdering her in the train and later putting her body in the sarcophagus in the barn was really rather a clever one. He meant it to tie up, you see, with the Crackenthorpe family. Before that he'd written a letter to Emma which purported to be from the girl Martine whom Edmund Crackenthorpe had talked of marrying. Emma had told Doctor Quimper all about her brother, you see. Then, when the moment arose he encouraged her to go to the police with the story. He wanted the dead woman identified as Martine. I think he may have heard that inquiries were being made by the Paris police about Anna Stravinska, and so he arranged to have a postcard come from her from Jamaica.

"It was easy for him to arrange to meet his wife in London, to tell her that he hoped to be reconciled with her and that he would like her to come down and 'meet his family.' We won't talk about the next part of it, which is very unpleasant to think about. Of course he was a greedy man. When he thought about taxation, and how much it cuts into income, he began thinking that it would be nice to have a good deal more capital. Perhaps he'd already thought of that before he decided to murder his wife. Anyway he started spreading rumors that someone was trying to poison old Mr. Crackenthorpe so as to get the ground prepared, and then he ended by administering arsenic to the family. Not too much, of course, for he didn't want old Mr. Crackenthorpe to die."

"But I still don't see how he managed," said Craddock. "He wasn't in the house when the curry was being prepared."

"Oh, but there wasn't any arsenic in the curry then," said Miss Marple. "He added it to the curry afterward when he took it away to be tested. He probably put the arsenic in the cocktail jug earlier. Then of course it was quite easy for him in his role of medical attendant, to poison off Alfred Crackenthorpe and also to send the tablets to Harold in London, having safeguarded himself by telling Harold that he wouldn't need any more tablets. Everything he did was bold and audacious and cruel and greedy, and I am really very, very glad," finished Miss Marple, looking as fierce as a fluffy old lady can look, "that they haven't abolished capital punishment yet because I do feel that if there is anyone who ought to hang, it's Doctor Quimper."

"Hear, hear," said Inspector Craddock.

"It occurred to me, you know," continued Miss Marple, "that even if you only see anybody from the back view, so to speak, nevertheless a back view is characteristic. I thought that if Elspeth were to see Doctor Quimper in exactly the same position as she'd seen the man in the train, that is, with his back to her bent over a woman whom he was holding by the throat, then I was almost sure she would recognize him, or would make some kind of startled exclamation. That is why I had to lay my little plan with Lucy's kind assistance."

"I must say," said Mrs. McGillicuddy, "it gave me quite a turn. I said 'That's him' before I could stop myself. And yet, you know, I hadn't actually seen the man's face and . . ."

"I was terribly afraid that you were going to say so, Elspeth," said Miss Marple.

"I was," said Mrs. McGillicuddy. "I was going to say that of course I hadn't seen his face."

"That," said Miss Marple, "would have been quite fatal! You see, dear, he thought you really did recognize him. I mean, he couldn't know that you hadn't seen his face."

"A good thing I held my tongue then," said Mrs. McGillicuddy.

"I wasn't going to let you say another word," said Miss Marple.

Craddock laughed suddenly. "You two!" he said. "You're a marvelous pair. What next, Miss Marple? What's the happy ending? What happens to poor Emma Crackenthorpe, for instance?"

"She'll get over the doctor, of course," said Miss Marple, "and I dare say if her father were to die—and I don't think he's quite so robust as he thinks he is—that she'd go on a cruise or perhaps stay abroad like Geraldine Webb, and I dare say something might come of it. A nicer man than Doctor Quimper, I hope."

"What about Lucy Eyelesbarrow? Wedding bells there, too?"

"Perhaps," said Miss Marple. "I shouldn't wonder."

"Which of 'em is she going to choose?" said Dermot Craddock.

"Don't you know?" said Miss Marple.

"No, I don't," said Craddock. "Do you?"

"Oh yes, I think so," said Miss Marple.

And she twinkled at him.

DAME AGATHA CHRISTIE is the most widely published author of all time. In a career that spanned more than fifty years, Christie wrote eighty novels and short-story collections, nineteen plays—one of which, *The Mousetrap*, is the longest-running play in history—and five nonfiction books, including her autobiography. In addition she wrote six romantic novels under the pseudonym Mary Westmacott. Two of the characters she created, the ingenious Belgian Hercule Poirot and the irrepressible and relentless Miss Jane Marple, became world-famous detectives, immortalized on television by David Suchet and Joan Hickson.

Agatha Christie achieved Britain's highest honor when she was made a Dame of the British Empire. She died in 1976.